Martians and Madness

The Complete SF Novels of Fredric Brown

Edited by Ben Yalow

The NESFA Press
Post Office Box 809
Framingham, MA 01701

FIRST EDITION, September 2002

International Standard Book Number 1-886778-17-5

Original Appearances

Introduction (by Phil Klass)
Originally appeared in 1978 Bantam edition of *What Mad Universe*

What Mad Universe
First publication: Dutton, 1949
First paperback publication: Bantam, 1950
A short version appeared in *Startling Stories,* September 1948

The Lights in the Sky Are Stars
First publication: Dutton, 1953
First paperback publication: Bantam, 1955

Martians, Go Home
First publication: Dutton, 1955
First paperback publication: Bantam, 1956
A short version appeared in *Astounding Science Fiction,* October 1954

Rogue in Space
First publication: Dutton, 1957
First paperback publication: Bantam, 1957
Two novelettes, "Gateway to Darkness" (*Super Science Stories,* November 1949),
and "Gateway to Glory" (*Amazing Stories,* October 1950), were rewritten and
incorporated into this novel. Both of these novelettes appear in this volume.

The Mind Thing
Paperback original: Bantam, 1961
A serialization of this novel started in *Fantastic Universe,* March 1960.
The magazine folded after this issue, and the serialization was never completed.

Dedicated to Bruce Pelz
for too many reasons to list

Table of Contents

Martians and Madness

The Complete SF Novels of Fredric Brown

Introduction
by Philip Klass (William Tenn)

When you're a young writer, you dream of certain things peculiar to young writers. You dream—in a major key, let us say—of being offered the Nobel Prize in Literature, and of turning it down: "No, thank you. Not yet. Wait till next year when I'll have completed the trilogy." Or, in a minor key, of somehow discovering the name that Achilles used when he was one of the girls, and of making that name part of the rhyme scheme of a thoroughly dirty and beautifully intricate limerick. If you dream this way, you are inevitably going to dream of being allowed to write an introduction to Fred Brown's *What Mad Universe*.

And, at long last, here I go. I finally made it. I was a shade too young for Rabelais or Lewis Carroll, but now, thirty years later, I've managed to make it for Fred Brown.

I was crazy about the book from the moment I read it and deeply fond of its author from the first time I met him. It wasn't only that his wit was so dry that the merest twinkle from the guy would explode a guffaw in your mind for days and days—or that God, in His infinite love for the human race, had seen to it that Fred practically never spoke above that twinkle—it was most of all, and I'm not ashamed to admit it, that Fred Brown was the only man who ever made me feel huge.

One of Fred's editors, H. L. Gold, said of him, most conclusively, "He was much shorter and slighter than anybody." I've always been very short myself and in those days, before prosperity and a cream-filled ulcer diet, I was positively wispy—but beside Fred Brown? I clattered and I clunked. I felt as Jane Russell must have felt when she found herself playing opposite Marilyn Monroe in *Gentlemen Prefer Blondes:* now you know from "delicate."

If you add to all this the fact that Fred was the kind of person who thought best while playing a flute to the empty air, you will understand why, on those long night walks of ours, from one end of New York City to the other, I felt like an ogre shambling beside an elf. All of this happened as the forties turned into the fifties: he lived in New York for part of this time; later, when he and Beth had moved to Taos, New Mexico, and he'd come in for a few days with an

9

editor, he'd either meet me at the Hydra Club (an organization of science-fiction professionals who, when they were not expelling each other, devoted themselves to modernizing the orgy) or show up on my doorstep. And off we'd go for a night of walking and talking and drinking.

Not that Fred was elfin in any other way. He could always outwalk me: it was I who would suggest as we came back down Broadway that it was time to settle for the steak house on 72nd Street. He could definitely out-drink me, but then, so could most people; Fred, like the girls I had steadfastly tried to seduce since the age of seventeen by plying them with liquor, would reel me in (I tend to float majestically over fire plugs when unsober) and take me home and put me to bed. I had to give up drinking for lack of talent, but Fred of course went on to the Olympics.

And, most astonishing of all, he could outtalk me. I am considered voluble by everyone who knows me—I was born, after all, in the middle of a subordinate clause—and Fred Brown was thought to be a shade reticent by most stammerers, but when we were alone together he did the talking and I did the listening. Hard talking and respectful listening.

What did he talk about? Shop, mostly. Word rates and editors' crotchets, all kinds of narrative problems and—inevitably—how to get over writer's block. And he talked about his bad back and his boyhood in Cincinnati, Ohio, and his special friendship with his agent, Harry Altshuler, who had sold his first mystery novel, *The Fabulous Clipjoint,* to Nicholas Wreden at Dutton only after an even dozen publishers had bounced it as a poor novel and an inferior mystery (it won an Edgar, the Mystery Writers of America award, that year). He talked about what it had been like up to then to have lived and loved as a proofreader on a Milwaukee newspaper, a proofreader who supported his heavy poker habit with the sale of a science-fiction story here, a mystery there, and, thank God, a regular column on proofreaders' problems for a trade magazine, the *American Printer.* The poker group he belonged to in Milwaukee was composed of free-lance writers like himself, and when a man ran out of money he was allowed to bet a plot. The plot had to be reasonably original, and sometimes it showed up in game after game before a winner was able to make a salable story out of it.

Why did I listen so respectfully? Not because he was an older, more experienced, more successful writer, and I was brand-new and had just begun to scratch: almost everyone I knew at the time was older and more successful, but I was working out my own version of hell and looking for my own particular handbasket to go to it in. Nor did I listen to him because he voiced my carefully submerged fears about the area of writing in which I had begun my professional career: "Remember, Phil, you're a *writer,* not just a science-fiction writer. This is an exciting field, but it's also a weird one; you won't find anything like the science-fiction fans—the *organized* science-fiction fans—anywhere else in publishing. They're already dominating the magazines through the letter columns and they're about to move in as writers and critics and editors."

Ray Bradbury was then the only fan of whom our corner of the field was fully aware; the flood from the Futurians and points south was just materializing. A change was being registered as the Blishes, the Knights, and the Merrils rose out of the amateur publications and into the paying markets, but the change would be greater yet when the likes of the Gerrolds, the Certers, and the Panshins had served out their apprenticeships on the fan magazines. It was of these fan magazines that Richard Gehman, writing in the *New Republic* early in the fifties, was to comment that they were the damndest combination of *Screen Romances* and *Partisan Review.*

And it was of the fans themselves, the fans behind the fan magazines and the fan-letter columns, the untalented, unpublishable ones, the wistful, dreamy, and peculiarly arrogant ones, that Fred Brown had written in what I and many others considered the publishing event of the year, the original, pulp-magazine version of *What Mad Universe* as it appeared in *Startling Stories* for September 1948.

While Fred's company was delightful and his professional experience and advice frequently very helpful, what I wanted to study could only be called the special artistic component of *What Mad Universe,* the humor, the parody, the satire peculiar to magazine science fiction. I was trying to write it, and there were only a few men I recognized as masters of it: Henry Kuttner often, L. Sprague de Camp occasionally, and Fred Brown, in many of his short stories and most of all in that wacky, almost unprecedented, and weirdly straightfaced novel.

The novel was indeed special. It said something quite large and complicated both to me and to the fan for whom it was specifically written.

Let me begin by showing you that fan. *And* his world.

I have before me a tattered, Scotch-taped copy of the September 1948 *Startling Stories* ("Scientifiction at Its Best"), one of the three then-surviving pulp magazines that encouraged and printed a kind of razzmatazz correspondence from its readership, the organized fans as well as what Fred Brown called "the random fandom." The cover, by Bergey, gives us a frantic strawberry blonde wearing the regulation crotch-tight shorts and metal brassiere who, in the course of fleeing from a bug-eyed monster with very grabby, grabby hands, is at this moment poised between Saturn and Earth's moon and is about to make her last leap for safety out of the picture and into the reader's lap.

There are two stories mentioned on the cover, "Tetrahedra of Space" by P. Schuyler Miller, a reprint of a piece originally published by Hugo Gernsback in 1931, and the featured novel, *What Mad Universe* by Fredric Brown. The Saturnian rings and Lunar craters, referred to in the last few chapters of the novel, identify the cover as relating vaguely to *What Mad Universe;* the leaping girl in shorts also comes from the novel, although there she appears as a parody of such covers: but the bluish, sex-mad entity with the protruding hands, teeth, and eyes comes from nowhere but the cover artist's own warehouse.

Entities like this were a kind of spontaneous generation: they sprang into existence and lunges as soon as they detected the cuddlesome back of a frightened space heroine. They were particular pets of pulp-magazine publishers and had little to do with the interests of readers, writers, or editors of science fiction; their close relatives were the unshaven criminals on detective-story covers, and snarling rustlers or Indians on the westerns, and their continued survival on the covers of science-fiction periodicals attested to the confusion about that field felt by most of the chain-magazine publishers—after all, hadn't Campbell's *Astounding* proved years before that machines and swarms of meteors were sexy enough for this group of readers?

The other stories in the issue were "Rat Race" by Dorothy and John de Courcy, "Sanatoris Short-Cut," a Magnus Ridolph story by Jack Vance, and a piece illustrated with a beautiful, bubbly Virgil Finlay, John D. MacDonald's "Shenadun" (Travis McGee's adventures with the spectrum still lay ahead). There was an article by R. L. Farnsworth, president of the United States Rocket Society, pleading for government funds to develop a rocket to the moon. (That was vocabulary, then—"rocket to the moon"—some nine years before the Russians sent up Sputnik, to Eisenhower's utter bewilderment: "Nobody ever told me about this sort of thing.")

Advertised for the next issue were Arthur C. Clarke's *Against the Fall of Night* and A. E. Van Vogt's "Dormant." And an editorial note boasted of the "regulars" to be found in the magazine—"such regulars include names like Hamilton, Leinster, Kuttner, Bradbury, St. Clair, Loomis and Tenn among others." I grinned when I came to the last name. The only reason it's there, mentioned as a "regular," is that Sam Merwin, the editor, had just bought a story from me, the first I'd ever sold to that house. Anybody to whom his boss, Leo Margulies, paid out good money[1] just had to be both a "regular" and famous.

Startling Stories ("20¢—Published every other month by Better Publications, Inc.") was one of the very few games in town for science-fiction writers like Fredric Brown and fans like his novel's Joe Doppelberg. For hardbound book publication you usually had to go to small specialty houses, Prime Press or Arkham House or Shasta or Gnome, whose print orders were so small that today collectors might pay more for a single, rare copy of those editions than the author got as his entire advance. The major publishers, for the most part, stayed away from science fiction; an occasional, big bumpy anthology in time for the Christmas trade was all they would touch. A Nick Wreden at Dutton might bring out a book version of *What Mad Universe* a year after its magazine appearance, but that was more than anything else a favor to a successful mystery novelist who happened to have a strange writing hobby on the side: the awfulness of the jacket cover and the perfunctory quality of the advertising and promotion made clear that book and magazine publishers were equally uncomfortable with science fiction. The writers and the stories were strange enough, but the *fans!* The scribbling, feuding, underaged, overintellectualized fans!

---

[1] A cent a word for most stories, a cent-and-a-half if you turned out a masterpiece and had an agent with *good* connections in the underworld.

If a professional like Fred Brown who, by 1948, had been writing the stuff for over seven years found the fans too exotic to be entirely digestible, what was a good-guy editor like Sam Merwin, with his traditional literary background, to make of them as he was suddenly plunked down to reply in print to their letters and to run a reviewing column on their incredible fan publications?

"We were getting just about our usual quota of fanzines," he muses in the September 1948 *Startling*, "and stashing them in the bottom desk drawer (the double one)..." A little later, he reports on a recently received issue of *Fantasy Commentator* (Editor, A. Langley Searles): "Livened(?) by pictures of the late H. P. Lovecraft's maternal grandparents and of the author as a little boy (unlike Raymond Knight, he apparently failed to pose as a little girl as well), this is the usual scholarly, erudite and occasionally heavyweight fanzine entry. Sam Moskowitz' colossal history of stfandom carries on its installment way..."

The history referred to was eventually published as a book, *The Immortal Storm,* and Harry Warner, Jr., said of it, "If read immediately after a history of World War II, it does not seem like an anticlimax."

But the *What Mad Universe* paraphrase of Sam Merwin, Keith Winton, had to deal with the daydreams of Joe Doppelberg,[2] a fan much younger and much less monumental than even the thirty-years-ago Sam Moskowitz. A sampling, then, of letters from *The Ether Vibrates*(!) and self-portraits of the Joe Doppelbergs in September, 1948:

```
From Con Pederson (the complete letter)—
   Dear Editor:
   PLEASE DON'T print the letter I sent you re-
cently!!!! I just read Ray Bradbury's AND THE MOON
BE STILL AS BRIGHT—Don't print it don't print it
don't print it.

From Bob Tucker—
   ...I thought that the cover artist followed
Sneary's plot very well indeed and captured on
canvas the pictorial essence of the drama underly-
ing Sneary's magnificent tale.

From Chad Oliver—
   Perhaps we should turn Mr. Kuttner loose on
Winnie the Pooh. I can see it all now. The bear is
really a robot from Neptune, and Robin a psychia-
trist...
```

---

[2]There had been letters from a fan, Walt Dunkelberger, whose name fascinated Fred. He combined it with another word he liked and, in Chapter 16, played with them both: "You're Joe Doppelberg—or Doppelberg's Doppelgänger."

From William E. Stolze—

Shall we say that stf is like a strong shot of heroin? That once consumed, it creates such a living ache in one's heart that one cannot justifiably do without it? Or is that too strong?...At any rate, curiosity can kill even a Jovian were-cat...

From Marion "Astra" Zimmer—

After that long eulogy of Kuttner...one very minor gripe. Misprint or error? Jason's tutor was not "Charon"; Charon was the ferryman of the Styx. The centaur who tutored Jason was C-h-i-r-o-n. Remember? Kuttner, shame on you.

From Frank Evans Clark—

I've been wondering just to what extent is STF reading material primarily for escapists and frustrates... STF is divorced from reality to a greater extent than any other kind of fiction and is thus ideal for anyone who is pained by reality...

From Linda Bowles—

Bergey's cover was awful again—but then it usually is. I just looove the way his colors clash. That eye and that sickly yellow! Yipe! Well, Berg, ole man, try again next ish...

I think Fred Brown would have called this sampling a fair one. The letter-column slang is there, and the self-consciousness, the casual, substantial literacy as well as the equally casual, embarrassing illiteracy, the drive to scrutinize everything in detail, from the stories' premises to their illustrations. No other popular fiction form has ever had an audience this articulate, this voluble, this demanding; few workers in any art form ever had the experience of so much of their audience looking over their shoulders as they worked and making so many intense—and silly—and provocative—comments about the final product.

In this respect, *What Mad Universe* is a story whose audience is one of its chief characters: the audience is up there on the stage, participating in the action. Its Joe Doppelberg is not merely a science-fiction fan raised to be an exponential power as "Dopelle, master of a universe...Dopelle, superscientist, creator of Mekky, the only man who'd been to Arcturus and returned alive"— he is the reader, too, watching the author pulled down from professional status and sent sprawling through the letter columns of the magazine. Fred Brown worked as an editor at this publishing house in 1948 (he only worked a couple of days, long enough to discover that Leo Margulies's offer of "seventy-five" had meant seventy-five dollars a week and not seventy-five hundred a year!) so that the novel's protagonist uses the author's perceptions (Fred Brown's) as well as those of the editor for whom the novel was written (Sam Merwin's). Inevitably, therefore, the novel has to have a *double* conceptual spin: Keith Winton is not simply in the universe that Joe Doppelberg has dreamed up—he is in the universe that *he* thinks Joe Doppelberg *would* dream up. We are in an enormously complicated comic dialogue here, a dialogue between author and reader that occurs rarely outside of science fiction, a dialogue that Fred Brown sensed more acutely than most writers in the field and one that he told me many times that he was very much afraid of. He certainly kept warning me against it.

This is not to deny the point that Sam J. Lundwall, among many others, has made about *What Mad Universe:* "a parody on the clichés of science fiction." It is certainly that, but the parodies are part of this complicated dialogue. Take the "space-girl's" costume, for instance ("Yes, there were green trunks to go with the green bra. They were very brief trunks, very well shaped. Green leather boots came halfway up shapely calves. Between the boots and the trunks, the bare golden flesh of dimpled knees and rounded thighs."). The costume, of course, comes from the bug-eyed monster covers of magazines in which Fred Brown's stories appeared. But the language describing the costume? It's certainly not Fred Brown's own rather spare idiom, and it's not someone else's language being parodied. It's the language he needs to enter the dialogue between a fan character he's created and the writer-editor who has to live in that fan's psyche.

The novel is certainly rich in parodies of science fiction, from the total innocent flung into a new and dangerous situation—complete with new kinds of secret police hunting down intriguing new crimes—to the one wonderful heroic figure who can and will save the world from the monsters and who'll do it with that ultimate invention, the disembodied brain machine. But the brain machine itself, while a parody if there ever was one (just consider its name, Mekky—*Mekky? After all!*), circles right out of parody and becomes the thoughtful explainer as well as the deus ex machina (deus *in* machina, perhaps?). For Brown was pursuing yet another point.

"He liked to stand logic on its head," says Harry Altshuler, his agent of that time.

Any writer must deal with logic: it's the invisible cement that holds a narrative together, that binds a given character to his actions within a story. But there are ways to tamper with logic. One of them is a version of the parallel-time story, the "Wheel of If," as L. Sprague de Camp titled it, where you might have a present full of historical effects similar to the ones we now know but deriving from causes totally different from those in our records (Graf von Zeppelin, not the Wright brothers, invents the airplane instead of the dirigible in 1903; he has to emigrate to America because of the Kaiser's animosity; today the world is the one we are familiar with, except for a small change in nomenclature). Robert Silverberg traces the idea back to a story by Edward Everett

Hale in 1898. My own favorite ancestor of this form, however, is the last stanza of a 1916 poem by Robert Frost, "The Road Not Taken":

> *I shall be telling this with a sigh*
> *Somewhere ages and ages hence:*
> *Two roads diverged in a wood, and I—*
> *I took the one less traveled by,*
> *And that has made all the difference.*

A writer can alter logic much more noticeably by experimenting with an alternate universe. One of the earliest of these is H. G. Wells's *Men Like Gods,* a novel about a trip to an Earth much like the one we know but which at our point in history has developed a utopian civilization. Most alternate universes, however, function according to natural laws unlike ours and thus have to be described as fantasies. The Harold Shea stories (Fletcher Pratt and L. Sprague de Camp) in the old *Unknown* are examples of such fantasies—the hero by a kind of semantic spell projecting himself into Norse myth or the world of Spenser's *The Faerie Queene.* Fred Brown paid his respects to the father of all these fantasies when he referred in a novel to "Charles Lutwidge Dodgson, known in Wonderland as Lewis Carroll."

In *What Mad Universe,* however, a fusion occurs between the parallel-time story (science fiction) and the alternate universe story (fantasy). The space warp is invented early in the twentieth century, instead of the airplane, by a professor fooling around with his wife's sewing machine. That is science fiction. But it is invented because the professor lives in a universe created by a science fiction fan's daydreams about space travel. That is pure fantasy—about science fiction. Brown has developed a science fiction story with no limits at all. The late John W. Campbell's distinction between science fiction and fantasy—that the first should be logical and possible and good, and that the second need only be logical and good—blurs completely here.

There are certain notes that Fred Brown struck again and again in his stories—the aliens he depicts are almost always utterly vicious; his characters drink constantly and will drink anything at the flick of a bartender's thumb; size, as between one creature and another, is almost always an issue; the story will pause at any time, in the midst of any action, for a pun or a word game—but the one *large* theme to which he kept returning was the question of reality, how we really know what we know, how much of it is, as he put it in "Come and Go Mad," "truth under guise of falsehood."

This, the theme of *What Mad Universe,* was for Fred Brown the ultimate comic question, the investigation of the belief he voiced in "It Didn't Happen," that "the entire universe is the product of one's imagination—in my case, *my* imagination." He carried it about as far as his master, Lewis Carroll, had done, when Alice said of the Red King, "He was part of my dream, of course—but then I was part of his dream, too!"

I was talking about this recently with my wife, Fruma, who never met Fred Brown, but who has read his stories and who loves the word games he plays in them. "Ontology," I told her, "that was his preoccupation. Ontology: the science of being or reality."

"Ontology?" she repeated slowly. "Didn't he know that ontology recapitulates philology?"

Fred Brown died in 1972. I wish I could believe that he heard what Fruma said and that God now rests him on waves of laughter.

PHILIP KLASS

State College, PA
March 3, 1978

What Mad Universe

What Mad Universe

FLASH

The first attempt to send a rocket to the moon, in 1954, was a failure. Probably because of a structural defect in the operating mechanism, it fell back to Earth, causing a dozen casualties. Although not equipped with an explosive warhead, the rocket— in order that its landing on the moon might be observed from Earth—contained a Burton potentiomotor set to operate throughout the journey through space to build up a tremendous electrical potential which, when released on contact with the moon, would cause a flash several thousand times brighter than lightning—and several thousand times more disruptive.

Fortunately, the rocket fell in a thinly populated area in the Catskill foothills, landing upon the estate of a wealthy publisher of a chain of magazines. The publisher and his wife, two guests and eight servants were killed by the electrical discharge, which completely demolished the house and felled trees for a quarter of a mile around. Only eleven bodies were found. It is presumed that one of the guests, an editor, was so near the center of the flash that his body was completely disintegrated.

The next—and first successful—rocket was sent a year later in 1955.

Keith Winton was pretty well winded when the set of tennis was over, but he tried his darnedest not to show it. He hadn't played in years, and tennis—as he was just realizing—is definitely a young man's game. Not that he was old, by any means—but at thirty-one you get winded unless you've kept in condition. Keith hadn't; and he'd really had to extend himself to win that set.

Now he extended himself a bit more, enough to leap across the net to join the girl on the other side. He was panting a bit, but he managed to grin at her.

"Another set? Got time?"

Betty Hadley shook her blond head. "'Fraid not, Keith, I'm going to be late now. I couldn't have stayed this long except that Mr. Borden promised to have his chauffeur drive me to the airport at Greeneville and have me flown back to New York from there. Isn't he a wonderful man to work for?"

"Uh-huh," said Keith, not thinking about Mr. Borden at all. "You've *got* to get back?"

"Absolutely. It's an alumnae dinner. My own alma mater. And not only that but I've got to speak; to tell them how a love story magazine is edited."

"I could come along," Keith suggested, "and tell them how a science-fiction mag is edited. Or a horror mag, for that matter—I had *Bloodcurdling Tales* before Borden put me on *Surprising Stories.* That job used to give me nightmares. Maybe your fellow alumnae would like to hear about them, huh?"

Betty Hadley laughed. "They probably would. But it's strictly a hen party, Keith. And don't look so downhearted. I'll be seeing you at the office tomorrow. This isn't the end of the world, you know."

"Well, no," Keith admitted. He was wrong, in a way, but he didn't know that.

He fell into stride beside Betty as she started up the walk from the tennis court to the big house that was the summer estate of L. A. Borden, publisher of the Borden chain of magazines.

He said, "You really ought to stay around to see the fireworks, though."

"Fireworks? Oh, you mean the moon rocket. *Will* there be anything to see, Keith?"

"They're hoping so. Have you read much about it?"

"Not a lot. I know the rocket is supposed to make a flash like a flash of lightning when it hits the moon, if it does. And they're hoping it will be visible to the naked eye so everybody's going to be watching for it. And it's supposed to hit at a quarter after nine, isn't it?"

"Sixteen minutes after. I know *I'm* going to be watching for it. And if you get a chance, watch the moon dead center, between the horns of the crescent. It's a new moon, in case you haven't been looking, and it'll hit the dark area. If you're looking without a telescope, it'll be a faint small flash, like somebody striking a match a block away. You'll have to be watching closely."

"They say it doesn't contain explosives, Keith. What is it that will make the flash?"

"Electrical discharge, on a scale nobody's ever tried before. There's a new-fangled outfit in it—worked out by a Professor Burton—that uses the kickback of the acceleration and converts it into potential electrical energy—static electricity. The rocket itself will be something on the order of a monster Leyden jar. And it's traveling through a vacuum in space, so the charge can't flash over or leak off until it hits, and when it does—well, lightning won't be in it. It'll make the granddaddy of all short circuits."

"Wouldn't an explosive charge have been simpler?"

"Oh, sure, but we'll get a lot brighter flash from this—weight for weight—than even from an atomic warhead. And what they're interested in is a bright flash, not an explosion as such. Of course it *will* tear up a little landscape—not as much as an A-bomb, maybe, but more than a blockbuster—but that's incidental. And they expect to learn a lot about the exact composition of the surface of the moon by training spectroscopes on the flash through every big telescope on the night side of earth. And they—"

The side door of the house was ahead and Betty Hadley interrupted by putting her hand on his arm. "Sorry to interrupt you, Keith, but I *must* hurry. Honestly, or I'll miss the plane. 'Bye."

She put out her hand for him to take but Keith Winton put his hands on her shoulders instead and pulled her to him. He kissed her and, for a breathless second, her lips yielded under his. Then she broke away.

But her eyes were shining—and just a bit misty. She said, "'Bye, Keith. See you in New York."

"Tomorrow night? It's a date."

She nodded and ran on into the house. Keith stood there, a fatuous smile on his face, leaning against the doorpost.

In love again, only this time it was different from anything that had ever happened to him before.

He'd known Betty Hadley only three days; had, in fact, seen her only once before this marvelous weekend. That had been on Thursday when she'd first come to Borden Publications, Inc. The magazine which she edited, *Perfect Love Stories,* had just been bought by Borden from a lesser chain. And Borden had been smart enough to take over the editor along with the magazine. Betty Hadley had done very well with it in the three years she'd run the magazine; the only reason the Whaley Publishing Company had been willing to sell was the fact that they had been changing to the exclusive publication of digest magazines; *Perfect Love* had been their only surviving fiction publication.

So Keith had met Betty Hadley on Thursday and now, to Keith Winton, Thursday seemed just about the most important day in his life.

Friday he'd had to go to Philadelphia to see one of his writers, a guy who could really write but who'd been paid in advance for a lead novel and didn't seem to be doing anything about writing it. Keith had tried to get the writer started on a plot, and thought he'd succeeded.

Anyway, he'd missed seeing Joe Doppelberg, his prize fan, who'd picked Friday to happen to be in New York and to call at the Borden offices. Judging from Joe Doppelberg's letters, missing a chance to meet him in person had been a definite gain.

Then yesterday, Saturday, afternoon he'd come out here at L. A. Borden's invitation. This was Keith's third time here, but just another weekend at the boss's estate had turned into sheer magic when Betty Hadley turned out to be one of two other guests from the office,

Betty Hadley—tall and lithe and golden blond, with soft sun-tanned skin, with a face and figure that belonged on the television screen rather than in an editorial office—

Keith sighed and went on into the house.

In the big walnut-paneled living room, L. A. Borden and Walter Callahan, head accountant for Borden, were playing gin rummy.

Borden looked up and nodded. "Hi, Keith. Want to take over after this game? We're nearly finished. I've got some letters to write and Walter would probably as soon take your money as mine."

Keith shook his head. "Got to do some work myself, Mr. Borden. I'm smack against deadline on the Rocketalk Department; I brought along my portable and fan letter file."

"Oh, come now; I didn't bring you out here to *work*. Can't you do it at the office tomorrow?"

"Wish I could, Mr. Borden," Keith said. "But it's my own fault for getting behind, and the stuff has to go to the printer tomorrow morning at ten sharp. They're closing the forms at noon so there isn't any leeway. But it's only a couple of hours' work and I'd rather get it done now and be free this evening."

He went on through the living room and up the stairs. In his room he took his typewriter out of its case and put it on the desk. From his brief case he took the file folder that held the incoming correspondence addressed to the Rocketalk Department or, in the less inhibited cases, to The Rocketeer.

Joe Doppelberg's letter was on top of the stack. He'd put it there because it had said Joe Doppelberg might be coming to call in person and Keith wanted to have the letter handy.

He worked paper into the typewriter, put down *Rocketalk* as a heading, and dived in.

> *Well, fellow space pilots, tonight—the night I'm writing this, not the night you're reading it—is the big night, the big night, and the Ole Rocketeer was out there to see it. And see it he did, that flash of light on the dark of the moon that marked the landing of the first successful missile ever launched through space by man.*

He looked at it critically, then yanked the paper out of the machine and put in a fresh sheet. It was too formal, too stilted, for his fans. He lighted a cigarette and wrote it again, and it came out better—or worse.

In the pause while he read it over he heard a door open and close and the sound of high heels clicking down the stairs. That would be Betty, leaving. He got up to go to the door and then sat down again. No, it would be anti-climactic to say good-bye again, now, with the Bordens and Callahan around. Much better to leave it on the note of that quick but breathless kiss and the promise that she would see him tomorrow evening.

He sighed and picked up the top letter. Joe Doppelberg's. It said:

> *Dear Rocky-Tear: I shouldn't ought to write you atall, because your last ish stinks to high Arcturus, except for the Wheeler yarn. Who ever told that mug Gormley he could write? And his space navigation? The big bohunk couldn't peelot a rowboat across Mud Creek on a sunny day.*
>
> *And that Hooper cover—the gal was okay, more than okay, tho what gals aren't on covers? But that thing chasing her—is it supposed to be one of the Mercurian devils in the Wheeler story? Well, tell Hooper I can think of scarier Bems than them, cold sober, without even a slug of Venusian sappy-sap.*
>
> *Why don't she just turn around and chase it?*
>
> *Keep Hooper on the inside—his black and white stuff is okay—and get somebody else for covers. How about Rockwell Kent or Dali? I'll bet Dali could make a dilly of a BEM. Get it, Rocky? Dali-dilly.*

Lookit, Rocky, get the Uranian bug-juice ready and iced because I'm going to beard the lyin' in his den, some day this week. Not coming to Spaceport N'Yawk just to see you, Rocky, don't flatter yourself on that. But because I got to see a Martian about a dog-star anyway, I'll be in town, so I'm going to see if you're as ugly as they say you are.

One recent idea of yours, Rocky, is tops. That's running half-col pix of your best and regularest correspondents with their letters. So I got a sur-prise for you. I'm sending mine. I was going to bring it, but this letter'll get there before I do and I might miss an ish going to press in between.

Ennahoo, Rocky, kill the fatted moon-calf, because I'll be seeing you soon, if not sooner.

JOE DOPPELBERG

Keith Winton sighed again and picked up his blue pencil. He marked out the parts about the trip to New York; that wouldn't interest his other readers, and anyway he didn't want to give too many of them the idea of dropping in at the office; he could waste too much time that way.

He penciled out a few of the cornier phrases in the other parts of the letter, then picked up the snapshot that had come with the letter and glanced at it again.

Joe Doppelberg didn't look like his letter sounded. He was a not unhand-some, rather intelligent-looking kid of sixteen or seventeen. He had a nice grin. Probably, in person, he'd be as shy as his letter was brash.

Sure, he might as well run the picture. Should have sent it to the photoen-graver before but there was still time. He marked the copy to be set with a half-column runaround for a cut and wrote "½-col. Doppelberg" on the back of the photograph.

He put the second page of Joe's letter into the typewriter, thought a mo-ment, and then typed at the bottom:

So okay, Doppelberg, we'll get Rockwell Kent to do our next cover. You pay him. But as for having the glamour-gals chasing the bug-eyed monsters (Bems to you), it can't be done. In our stories the gals are always chaste. Get it, Doppelberg? Chaste-chased. And that ain't half as bad as your Dali-dilly, either.

He took the page out of the typewriter, sighed, and picked up the next letter.

He finished at six, which left him an hour before dinner. He took a quick shower and dressed and there was still half an hour left. He wandered down-stairs and out the French doors that led to the garden.

It was just turning dusk and the new moon was already visible in the clear sky. The seeing would be good, he thought. And, dammit, that rocket flash had *better* be visible to the naked eye or he'd have to write a new opening paragraph for the Rocketalk Department. Well, there'd be time for that after nine-sixteen.

He sat down on a wicker bench beside the main path through the garden and sniffed deeply of the fresh country air and the scent of flowers all about him.

He thought about Betty Hadley, and just what he thought about her need not be recorded here.

But thinking it kept him happy—or perhaps happily miserable would be a more apt phrase—until his mind wandered to the writer in Philadelphia and he wondered if the so-and-so was actually working on that story or was out getting plastered.

Then he thought about Betty Hadley again and wished that it was twenty-four hours later, Monday evening in New York instead of Sunday evening in the Catskills.

He glanced at his wrist watch and saw that they'd be ringing the dinner bell in a few minutes. That was good news because, in love or not in love, he was hungry.

And being hungry made him think, for no reason at all, of Claude Hooper, who did most of the covers for *Surprising Stories*. He wondered if he could keep on getting covers from Hooper. Hooper was a swell guy and a fairly good artist, and he could draw women who made your mouth water, but he just couldn't draw sufficiently horrible-looking monsters to pursue them. Maybe he just didn't have enough nightmares or had too happy a home life, or something. And most of the fans were kicking. Like Joe Doppelberg. What did Doppelberg—

The moon rocket, falling back to Earth, was traveling faster than sound and Keith neither saw nor heard it, although it struck only two yards away from him.

There was a flash.

THE PURPLE MONSTER

There was no sense of transition, of change or of movement, no lapse of time. It was merely as though, simultaneously with a bright flash, someone had pulled the wicker bench out from under him. He grunted from impact with the ground and, because he had been leaning against the back of the bench, went over backward full length. There he was lying flat on his back, staring up at the evening sky.

And it was seeing the sky that was the most amazing thing; it couldn't have been merely that the wicker bench had collapsed under him—or even merely vanished from under him—because the bench had been under a tree and there was now no tree between him and the dull blue dusk.

He raised his head first and then sat up, for the moment too shaken—not physically but mentally—to stand up. Somehow he wanted his bearings before he quite trusted his knees.

He was sitting on grass, smoothly mowed grass, in the middle of a yard. Behind him, when he turned his head around, he saw a house. A quite ordinary-looking house, not nearly so large or well designed as Mr. Borden's house. And it had the look, somehow, of a vacant house. At least there was no sign of life, no light at any window.

He stared at what should have been Mr. Borden's house, but wasn't, for several seconds, and then turned to look the other way. A hundred feet in that direction, at the edge of the lawn on which he sat, was a hedge; at the other side of the hedge were trees—two orderly rows of them, as though on either side of a road. They were tall and very beautiful poplars.

There was no maple tree—it had been a maple under which he had been sitting—anywhere in sight. Nor was there even a splinter of a wicker bench.

He shook his head to clear it and stood up cautiously. There was a momentary touch of dizziness but, outside of that, he was all right. Whatever had happened to him, he wasn't hurt. He stood still until the dizziness passed and then started walking toward a gate in the hedge.

He looked at his wrist watch. It was three minutes of seven and that was impossible, he thought. It had been three minutes of seven, just about, when he'd been sitting on the bench in Mr. Borden's garden. And wherever he was now he couldn't have got there in nothing flat.

He held the wrist watch to his ear; it was still ticking. But that didn't prove anything; maybe it stopped from—from whatever had happened, and had started again when he had stood up and started walking.

He looked up again at the sky to judge the time lapse; he could detect none. It had been dusk then and it was dusk now. The silver crescent moon was in the same place; at least it was the same distance from the zenith. He couldn't be sure here—wherever *here* was—about his bearings and directions.

The gateway through the hedge led to an asphalt-paved three-lane highway. There were no cars in sight.

As he closed the gate he looked again at the house behind him and saw something he had not previously noticed; there was a sign on one of the porch pillars that read: *For Sale. R. Blaisdell, Greeneville, N.Y.*

Then he must still be near Borden's estate, for Greeneville was the nearest town to Borden's. But that was obvious anyway; he *couldn't* have gone far. The real question was how he could be anywhere at all out of sight of where he'd been sitting only minutes ago.

He shook his head again to clear it, although it felt all right. Could he have suffered sudden amnesia? Had he walked here without knowing it? It didn't seem possible, particularly in a matter of minutes or less.

He stood looking uncertainly up and down the wide asphalt roadway between the tall poplars, wondering which way to walk. The road ran straight; he could see almost a quarter of a mile, to the next rise, in either direction, but there was no sign of human habitation. Yet there had to be a farmhouse somewhere near, as cultivated fields lay just beyond the far row of poplars. Probably the trees themselves blocked his view of the farmhouse that must be near by. If he walked to the fence that bounded the field across the road, he'd be able to see it.

He was halfway across the road when he heard the sound of an approaching car, still out of sight beyond the rise to his left. It was a very noisy car to make itself heard at that distance. He went the rest of the way across the road and by the time he turned, the car was in sight. Information from the driver of the car would be as valuable as information from a farmhouse; better, for perhaps he could persuade the driver to give him a lift to Borden's, at least if he was going in that direction anyway.

The car was a Model T of ancient vintage. A good omen, Keith knew. He'd done quite a bit of hitchhiking in his college days and he knew that the likelihood of getting a lift in a car was in direct proportion to its age and condition of decrepitude.

And there was no doubt about the decrepitude of this vehicle. It seemed barely to have made the rise it had just climbed; it chugged and labored to gather speed.

Keith waited until it was near enough and then stepped out into the road and waved his hand. The Ford slowed down and stopped beside him.

The man at the wheel leaned over and lowered the window on Keith's side— for no reason that Keith could see, for there wasn't any glass in the window anyway. "Want a lift, mister?" he asked.

He looked, Keith thought, almost too much like a farmer to be one. He was even chewing a long yellow straw, just the color of his hair, and his faded blue overalls matched his faded blue eyes.

Keith put a foot on the running board and leaned his head into the car through the open window, so he could make his voice heard above the chugging of the engine and the tinny rattle that came from all parts of the body even when the car was not in motion.

He said, "I'm afraid I'm lost. Do you know where L. A. Borden's place is?"

The farmer rolled the straw to the opposite corner of his mouth. He thought deeply, frowning with the effort.

"Nope," he said, finally. "Never heard of him. Don't have a farm on this road. Mebbe over on the pike; I don't know all the farms over there."

"It isn't a farm," Keith told him. "It's a big country estate. He's a publisher. Where does this road go? Into Greeneville?"

"Yep. It's ahead, the way I'm going, ten miles or so. Back t'other way it hits the Albany Highway at Carteret. Want a lift to Greeneville? Guess you can find out there where this Borden lives."

"Sure," Keith said. "Thanks." He got into the car.

The farmer gravely reached across him and turned a crank that raised the window that hadn't any glass in it. "Rattles," he explained, "if I leave it open."

He stepped on the clutch pedal and the gear pedal and the car groaned and started. The body rattle of the car sounded like hail on a tin roof. It reached its top speed and Keith estimated that it would take at least half an hour to reach a ten mile distant destination, if the car got there at all.

Well, if he got to Greeneville, he'd at least know where he was. He'd be plenty late for dinner, so maybe, he thought, he'd better phone Borden to reassure him, eat in town, and then hire a taxi, or some sort of vehicle, to drive him to the estate. He could be there by nine at the latest, plenty of time to be ready to watch the fireworks on the moon at sixteen minutes after. *That* was something he wasn't going to miss.

How was he going to explain to Mr. Borden? About the only thing he *could* say was that he'd taken a walk and had got lost; that he'd had to get a lift into Greeneville to get his bearings. It was going to sound rather silly, but not so silly as the truth. And he didn't want his employer to think he was subject to spells of insanity or amnesia.

The old car chugged along the long, straight road. His benefactor didn't seem to want to talk and Keith was glad of that. They'd have had to yell at each other anyway. And he'd much rather think and try to figure out what had happened.

Borden's estate was a big one and certainly must be well known in its immediate neighborhood. If the driver of the ancient jalopy knew everyone along the road, he couldn't possibly not have heard of Borden's if it were close. Yet it couldn't possibly be more than twenty miles away, because Borden lived ten miles from Greeneville—although Keith couldn't remember what direction it was from that town—and the spot where he'd been picked up along the road had also been about ten miles from Greeneville. Even if those two ten-mile distances were in diametrically opposite directions, he couldn't have gone over twenty miles—and even that far was silly, considering the short lapse of time.

They were coming to the outskirts of a town now and he looked at his watch again; it was seven thirty-five. He looked out of the window of the car at buildings they were passing until he saw a clock in the window of a store. His watch was right; it hadn't stopped and started again.

A few minutes later they were in the main business district of Greeneville. The driver swung into the curb and stopped. He said, "This is about the middle of town, mister. Guess you can look up your party in a phone book and you'll be all right. And there's a taxi stand right across the street to get you wherever you're going. Charge you a hell of a price, but they'll get you there."

"Thanks a lot," Keith told him. "Can I buy you a drink before I phone?"

"Nope, thanks. Got to get back quick. Mare's about to foal; I come in to pick up my brother. He's a vet and I want him there."

Keith thanked him again, and went into the drugstore on the corner just beyond where the farmer had let him out of the car. He went to the phone booth at the back and took up the slender Greeneville phone book hanging by a chain from one side of the booth. He leafed through it to the B's, and to—

There wasn't any Borden listed.

Keith frowned. Borden's phone was on the Greeneville exchange. He was sure of that because he'd phoned Borden several times on business from the office in New York. It had been a Greeneville number.

But of course it could be an unlisted number. Could he remember it? Of course he could—it had been three numbers all alike—ones. That was it: Greeneville 111. He remembered wondering if Borden had used pull with the phone company to get a number as easy to remember as that.

He pulled the door of the booth shut and fumbled a nickel out of the change in his pocket. But the phone was a type he hadn't seen before. There didn't seem to be any slot for a coin to go into. He looked all over and around it before he decided that maybe they didn't have coin phones in these little upstate towns and that he was probably supposed to pay the druggist for the call.

He picked up the receiver and when an operator's voice asked "Number please?" he gave it. There was a minute's pause and then the operator's voice came back on the line. "There is no such number listed, sir."

For a second, Keith wondered if he was really going insane; it didn't seem possible that he could be wrong on that number. Greeneville one-one-one; you couldn't forget a number like that, or remember it wrong.

He asked, "Will you please, then, find out the number of L. A. Borden's phone? I thought that was the number. I can't find him listed in the phone book, but I know he's got a phone. I've called him."

"One minute, sir... No, there is no such name on our records."

Keith said "Thanks," and put the receiver back on the hook.

He still didn't believe it. He stepped out of the booth so the light would be better, taking the phone book with him as far as its chain would let it go. He looked under B, and there still wasn't any Borden listed. He remembered that Borden called his estate Fouroaks, and he looked under that. There was no listing for Fouroaks.

Suddenly he snapped the book shut and looked at the cover, it read *Greeneville, N.Y.* A momentary suspicion that he was in the wrong Greeneville died a-borning; there could be only one Greeneville in New York State. Another and fainter suspicion died almost before he realized its existence when he read the smaller type under the name of the town: *Spring, 1954.*

He still didn't believe that L. A. Borden wasn't in that book; he had to fight the impulse to look through it page by page to see if the name was *not* there but out of alphabetical order.

Instead, he walked forward to the soda counter and sat down on one of the old-fashioned wide-legged stools. Behind the counter the druggist—a little gray-haired man with thick spectacles—was polishing glasses. He looked up. "Yes, sir?"

"A Coke, please," Keith said. He wanted to ask questions, but for the moment he couldn't think what questions to ask. He watched while the druggist mixed the coke and put it on the counter in front of him.

"Beautiful night out," the druggist said.

Keith nodded. That reminded him he'd have to remember to watch for the flash of the moon rocket, no matter where he was at the time. He glanced at his watch. It was almost eight o'clock; another hour and a quarter and he'd have to be in a clear space outdoors where he could watch the moon. It didn't look, now, as though he'd be back at Borden's by that time.

He drank the coke almost at a gulp. It was cool and tasted good, but it made him realize that he was getting hungry. And no wonder, if it was eight o'clock; dinner was over by now at the Bordens' place. Besides, he'd eaten a light lunch and played quite a bit of tennis since then.

He looked around back of the soda fountain for signs indicating that the druggist served sandwiches or other food. Apparently he didn't.

Keith took a quarter out of his pocket and put it on the marble top of the soda fountain.

It rang metallically and the druggist dropped the glass he had been polishing. Behind the thick spectacles the druggist's eyes got wide and scared; he stood there with his body rigid while his head turned back and forth as he looked from one end of the store to the other. He didn't seem to notice or to realize that he had dropped and broken a glass. The towel, too, fell from his fingers.

Then his hand went forward gingerly, covered the coin and picked it up. Again he looked both ways as though making sure that he and Keith were the only people in the store.

Then and only then did he look at the coin. Shielding it deep in cupped hands he stared at it, moving it close to his eyes. He turned it over and studied the other side.

His eyes, frightened and yet ecstatic, went back to Keith's face.

"Beautiful!" he said. "Hardly worn at all. And a nineteen twenty-eight." His voice dropped to a whisper. "But—who sent you?"

Keith closed his eyes and opened them again. Either he or the druggist must be crazy. He wouldn't have doubted which had it not been for the other things that had happened—his sudden teleportation from one place to another—the absence of L. A. Borden from the phone book and the records of the phone company.

"Who sent you?" the druggist asked again.

"Nobody," Keith said.

The little druggist smiled slowly. "You don't want to tell. It must have been K. Well, never mind that, in case it wasn't. I'll take a chance. I'll give you a thousand credits for it."

Keith didn't say anything.

"Fifteen hundred," the druggist said. His eyes, Keith thought, looked like a spaniel's eyes—the eyes of a hungry spaniel seeing a bone just beyond his reach.

The druggist took a deep breath. He said, "Two thousand, then. I know it's worth more, but that's all I can give you. If my wife—"

"All right," Keith said.

The hand that had been holding the coin concealed dived into the druggist's pocket like a prairie dog popping into its hole. Unnoticed glass crunched under the druggist's shoes as he walked down to the cash register at the end of the counter and punched a key. *No Sale* came up behind the glass window. The druggist came back, crunching glass again, his attention on the bills he was counting. He put a pile of them in front of Keith Winton.

"Two thousand," he said. "Means I'll have to give up part of the vacation I'd planned this year, but I guess it's worth it. I must be a little crazy."

Keith picked up the bills and looked long and hard at the top one. There was a familiar picture of George Washington in the center of it. The figure in the corners was *100* and under the oval portrait of Washington was spelled out *One Hundred Credits.*

And that was silly, too, Keith thought. Washington's picture belonged only on *one* dollar bills—unless things were different here.

Here? What did he mean by *here?* This was Greeneville, New York, U.S.A., in the year 1954. The phone book said so. George Washington's picture said so.

He looked again and read more of the printing. *United States of America,* he read. *Federal Reserve Note.*

And it wasn't a new bill. It looked worn and circulated and genuine. There were the familiar little silk threads. A serial number in blue ink. To the right of the portrait, *Series of 1945,* and a reproduced signature, *Fred M. Vinson,* over fine type that read *Secretary of the Treasury.*

Slowly, Keith folded the little stack of bills and put them into his coat pocket.

He looked up and his eyes met those of the druggist, looking out at him through the thick spectacles, looking anxiously.

The druggist's voice was just as anxious as his eyes. He said, "It's—it's all right, isn't it? You're not an agent? I mean, if you are, you've *got* me now for collecting. So you might as well arrest me and get it over with. I mean, I took a chance and, if I lose, there's no use keeping me in suspense, is there?"

"No," Keith said. "It's all right. I guess it's all right. Can I have another coke, please?"

This time some of the coke slopped out as the druggist put the glass down on the marble counter. And, as glass crunched again under the druggist's shoes, he smiled nervously and apologetically at Keith, got a broom from the corner and began to sweep behind the counter.

Keith sipped his second coke and thought. That is, he thought if one could call the whirl of things inside his head thinking. It was more nearly like riding on a pinwheel.

He watched until the druggist had finished with the broom.

"Look," he said, "I'd like to ask you a few questions that may seem—uh—crazy to you. But I've got a reason for asking them. Will you answer them, no matter how goofy they sound to you?"

The druggist eyed him cautiously. "What kind of questions?" he wanted to know.

"Well—what is the exact date?"

"June tenth, nineteen fifty-four."

"A.D.?"

The druggist's eyes got wide but he said, "Sure. A.D."

"And this is Greeneville, New York?"

"Yes. You mean you don't know—"

Keith said, "Let me ask the questions. There aren't two Greenevilles in the state, are there?"

"Not that I know of."

"Do you know a man—or know of a man—named L. A. Borden who has a big estate near here? A magazine publisher?"

"No. Of course I don't know everybody around here."

"You've heard of the Borden chain of magazines that he runs?"

"Oh, sure. We sell them. New issues just came in today of some of them. The July issues, over on the stands, there."

"And the moon ship— This is the night it lands?"

The druggist's brow furrowed with perplexity. "I don't understand what you mean. 'This is the night it lands.' It lands every night. It's in by now. We'll be getting customers any minute. Some of them drop in on their way to the hotel."

The answers hadn't been too bad up to that one. Keith closed his eyes and kept them closed for several seconds. When he opened them, the little druggist was still there, peering at him anxiously.

"Are you all right?" the druggist asked. "I mean, are you sick or something?"

"I'm all right," Keith said, and hoped he was telling the truth. He wanted to ask more questions, but he was afraid to. He wanted something familiar to reassure him and he thought he knew what it would be.

He got off the stool and walked over to the rack of magazines. He saw *Perfect Love Stories* first, and picked it up. The cover girl reminded him a little of the editor, Betty Hadley—only she wasn't as beautiful as Betty. How many magazines, he wondered, had editors more beautiful than their cover girls? Probably exactly one.

But he couldn't let himself daydream about Betty now; he shoved her resolutely out of his mind and looked for *Surprising Stories,* his own magazine. He saw it and picked it up.

The familiar cover of the July issue. The same as—

Was it? The cover pictured the same scene, but there was a subtle difference in the art work. It was better, more vivid. It was Hooper's technique, but it looked as though Hooper had been *taking lessons.*

The gal on the cover, in the transparent space suit, was much more beautiful—and much more sexy, too—than he remembered her to be from the cover proofs. And the monster pursuing her—

Keith shuddered.

In general outline it was the same monster and yet there was a subtle difference, a horrible difference, that he couldn't put his finger on—and that he felt he wouldn't *want* to put his finger on. Not even wearing asbestos gloves.

But Hooper's signature was there, he noticed when he was able to tear his eyes away from the monster. A tiny crooked characteristic H that was Hooper's way of signing all his pics.

And then, in the logo at the bottom right corner, he saw the price. It wasn't 20¢.

It was 2 cr.

Two credits?

What else could it be?

Very slowly and carefully he folded the two magazines, the two incredible magazines—for he saw now that *Perfect Love Stories* was also priced at 2 cr.— and put them into his pocket.

He wanted to get off somewhere by himself, far from the madding crowd, and study those two books, read and digest every word of them.

But first he'd have to pay for them and get out of here. Two credits each meant four credits. But how much was four credits? The druggist had given him two thousand credits for a quarter, but in such a manner that he didn't feel that constituted a true criterion. That quarter, for some reason he'd have to learn, had been a rare and precious object to the man who had bought it from him.

Yes, the magazines were a better clue. If their value was even approximately the same in credits that it was in dollars, then two credits must be at least roughly equivalent to twenty cents. And if that were true, the druggist had given him the equivalent of—let's see—two hundred dollars for a quarter coin. Why?

Change rattled in his pocket as he walked back to the soda counter. His hand fumbled among the coins and found a half dollar. How would the druggist react to that?

He shouldn't have done it; he should have been more careful. But the shock of seeing that almost-but-not-quite cover for the July issue of his own magazine made him a bit slap-happy for the moment.

Casually he tossed the half dollar down on the marble. "I'll take the two magazines," he said. "And take out for the cokes while you're at it."

The druggist reached out a hand for the coin, and the hand trembled so badly that he couldn't grip the edges of it.

Suddenly, Keith felt ashamed of himself. He shouldn't have done it. And besides, it would lead to conversation that would keep him from getting off by himself to read those magazines, and that was what he was in a hurry to do.

He said gruffly. "Keep it. You can have them both—the quarter and the half—for what you gave me." He turned quickly and started out of the store.

He started; that was all.

He took one step and froze. Something was coming in the open doorway of the drugstore. Something that wasn't human, that was a long, long way from being human.

Something that was well over seven feet tall—so tall that it had to stoop slightly to get through the doorway—and that was covered with bright purple fur except for its hands, feet and face. Those parts of its body were purple too, but they were covered with scales instead of fur. Its eyes were flat white disks, devoid of pupils. It had no nose, but it had teeth. It had no lack of teeth.

While Keith stood frozen, a hand grabbed his arm from behind. The druggist's voice, suddenly fierce and shrill, was shouting: "A nineteen forty-three coin! He gave me a nineteen forty-three coin! He's a *spy*, an *Arcturian!* Get him, Lunan. Kill him!"

The purple thing had paused just inside the doorway. Now it made a shrieking noise that was almost supersonic in pitch. It spread its thick purple arms so the hands were eight feet apart and came toward Keith looking like something out of a nightmare that Gargantua might have. Its purple lips bared two-inch fangs and its mouth opened, a green cavern.

And the druggist, yelling *"Kill him! Kill him, Lunan!"* was climbing up Keith's back. His hands closed around Keith's throat and tried to strangle him.

But in view of what was coming at him from the front, Keith hardly noticed that. He turned and ran the other way, to the back of the store, losing the druggist en route. He hadn't noticed a door at the back of the store, but there must be one. There'd *better* be one.

SHOOT ON SIGHT

There *was* a door.

Something clawed at his back as he went through it. He pulled free, hearing his coat rip. He slammed the door and heard a yelp of pain—not a human one—behind him. But he didn't turn around to apologize. He ran.

He didn't turn until, half a block away, he heard the sound of a pistol report behind him and felt a sudden pain as though a red-hot poker had just been drawn across his upper arm.

He looked back then, just for a second. The purple monster was still coming toward him. It was about halfway between the door he'd just left at the back of the store, and Keith. But despite its long legs it seemed to run slowly and awkwardly. Apparently he could easily outdistance it.

The purple creature carried no weapon. The shot that had seared Keith's shoulder, he saw, had come from the little druggist, who, a big old-fashioned revolver in his hand, was standing just outside the door. He was aiming the pistol for a second shot.

Keith heard the shot as he dived into the areaway between two buildings, but the bullet must have gone past him harmlessly for he didn't feel it.

Then he was between the buildings and for a terrifying moment he thought he had trapped himself in a cul-de-sac. There was only a blank brick wall at the end of the areaway, and it was too high for him to climb. But when he reached the back he saw that there were doors to the buildings on either side and that one of the doors was standing ajar. He didn't bother trying the closed door; he hurried through the open one and closed and locked it behind him.

He stood there in the dimness of a hallway, panting, and looked about him. In the direction toward the street, stairs led upward. In the other direction there was another door; undoubtedly it would lead to an alley.

Sudden hammering sounded on the door through which he had just entered—hammering and the babble of excited voices.

Keith ran to the back door, went through it and found himself in the alley. He ran between two buildings that fronted on the next street. He slowed down his pace as he neared the sidewalk and emerged walking at a normal pace.

He turned in the direction that would take him to the main street, half a block away, and then hesitated. It was a fairly crowded, busy street. But was there safety or danger in crowds? He stood in the shadow of a tree a dozen paces short of the corner and watched.

What he saw looked like normal traffic on a normal small city's main street—for a moment. Then, walking arm in arm, two of the purple-furred monsters went by. Both of them were slightly bigger than the one that had attacked him in the drugstore.

The monsters were strange enough, but there was something that was stranger: the fact that the people before and after them paid no attention to them. Whatever they were, they were—accepted. They were normal. They belonged here.

Here?

That word again. Where, what, when was *here?*

What mad universe was this that took for granted an alien race more horrible looking than the worst Bem that had ever leered from a science-fiction magazine cover?

What mad universe was this that gave him two hundred dollars for a quarter and tried to kill him when he offered a half dollar *free?* Yet whose credit-currency bore a picture of George Washington and current dates and which had provided—fortunately still folded and in his pocket—current and only subtly different issues of *Surprising Stories* and *Perfect Love Stories?*

A world with asthmatic Model T Fords—and space travel?

There must be space travel. Those purple things had never evolved on Earth—if this were Earth. And when he'd asked the druggist about the moon ship, he'd said, "It lands every night."

And then—what was it the druggist had shouted just before the purple thing had attacked him? *"Arcturian spy!"*? But that was absurd. Arcturus was light-years away. A technology that still used Model T Fords might possibly have perfected travel to the moon, but *Arcturus?* Could he have misunderstood that word?

And the druggist had called the monster *Lunan.* A proper name, or the designation of an inhabitant of Luna, the moon?

"It lands every night," the druggist had said. "It's in by now. We'll be getting customers any minute."

Bright purple customers seven feet tall?

Suddenly Keith was aware that his shoulder hurt him and that there was a wet, sticky feeling on his upper arm. He looked down and saw that the sleeve of his sport jacket was soaked with blood; blood that looked black rather than red in the dim light. And there was a deep gouge in the cloth where the bullet had creased it.

He needed attention for that wound, to stop the bleeding.

Why not walk out there, look for a policeman (Were there policemen here?) and give himself up, tell the truth?

But what was the truth?

Could he tell them, "You're all wrong. This is the U.S.A., Earth, Greeneville, New York, and it's June, nineteen hundred fifty-four, all right—but there isn't any space travel yet except an experimental rocket that's going to land later tonight. And dollars are the currency and not credits, even if they've got Fred M. Vinson's signature and Washington's picture—and those purple monsters walking down your main street can't possibly be there, and a guy named L. A. Borden—if you can find him better than I can—will explain who I am. I hope."

Impossible, of course. From what he'd seen and heard, there was only one person *here* who would believe any of that. That one person's name was Keith Winton and he would be promptly locked up in the nearest nuthouse.

No, he couldn't possibly go to the authorities with what would seem to them an utterly incredible story. Not yet, anyway. Not until he'd had time to orient himself a little better and to find out and figure out what had happened and where he was.

Somewhere, blocks away, sirens wailed. They came closer.

If those sirens meant the same thing *here* that they did in a more familiar universe, then they were police cars and probably after him.

The fact that there was blood on his coat, if no other reason, decided him against the main street. Quickly he crossed the quiet side street, went through another alley and then, keeping in the shadows as much as possible, put another few blocks between himself and the main street.

He shrank back into the shadow of another areaway as a squad car turned the corner with siren shrieking.

It went past.

Maybe they were looking for him, maybe they weren't, but he didn't dare risk that. He had to find sanctuary somewhere; he couldn't wander about very long with blood on his sleeve and—he remembered now—with the back of his coat torn where the purple monster had ripped it.

Across the street there was a sign, *Rooms for Rent.* Did he dare take a chance on trying to rent a room? The feel of blood running down past his elbow told him he'd have to.

He made sure no traffic was coming and then crossed the street. The building with the sign looked like a cross between a rooming house and a cheap hotel. It was a red-brick building flush with the sidewalk. He looked through the glass of the door.

There wasn't any clerk at the desk in the tiny lobby. On a corner of the desk was a pushbell and a sign, *Ring for Clerk.* He opened the door as quietly as he could and closed it the same way. He tiptoed to the desk and studied the rack behind it. There was a row of boxes, some with mail, a few with keys in them.

He looked around carefully and then leaned across the desk and picked the key out of the nearest box; it was numbered 201.

He looked around again. No one had seen him.

He tiptoed to the stairs. They were carpeted and didn't creak. And he couldn't have picked a better room key. Room 201 was right at the head of the stairs.

Inside the room he locked the door and turned on the light. If only the occupant of 201 didn't come in within the next half hour, he had a chance.

He stripped off his coat and shirt and studied the wound. It was going to be painful, but not dangerous unless it became infected. The gouge was quite deep but the bleeding had already started to slow down.

He made sure by looking in the dresser drawers that the missing occupant of 201 had shirts—and luckily within half a size of his own—and then he ripped apart the shirt he had just taken off and used it to bandage the arm, winding it around and around so that the blood would soak through slowly if at all.

Then he appropriated a dark-blue shirt from the dresser—choosing a dark one because his own shirt had been white—and a necktie from the rack.

He explored the closet and found three suits hanging inside it. He chose an Oxford gray to contrast with his own light-tan suit—the coat of which was hopelessly torn and bloodstained anyway. There was a straw hat in the closet. At first he thought it was too big for him but, with a little paper folded under the sweatband, it served. With a complete change of clothes and a hat—he had been hatless before—he doubted if even the druggist would recognize him at a distance on the street. And the police would be looking for a man in a torn tan coat. The druggist could not have missed seeing that tear.

He made a quick estimate and translation of the value of the things he had taken and left a five hundred credit note on the bureau. Fifty dollars should be ample; the suit, which was the main item, was neither expensive nor new.

He made his own clothes into a bundle, wrapped with some newspapers that had been in the closet. Much as he wanted to study and read those newspapers, no matter how old they might be, he knew that getting out of here and to a safer place came first. The man whose room he was using might return at any moment.

He opened the door and listened. There was still no sound from the little lobby downstairs. He went down the steps as silently as he had come up them.

He hesitated in the lobby, wondering if he should now ring the bell and ask for a room in the ordinary way. No, he decided, not here. The clerk would notice that he had on an Oxford gray suit and a straw hat and carried a bundle; if, during the evening, the owner of those garments came home, noticed what was missing and told the clerk, the clerk might connect the two facts.

He went out the door to the street. Now, as soon as he got rid of the bundle in some place where it would not attract immediate attention, he should be comparatively safe for a while. Safe as long as he didn't talk to anyone and make a break of some sort. And making a break would be all too easy until he'd learned the ropes. If giving a man a half dollar dated nineteen forty-three made him try to kill you as a spy—and *had* the druggist really said *Arcturian* spy?—then who could even guess what other pitfalls there might be in the most ordinary conversation? He was glad now he hadn't talked much to the man who'd given him the lift into Greeneville; surely he'd have made a bad break sooner or later.

He walked toward the main street now, pretending a confidence that he was a long way from feeling. At the very corner of the main street he got rid of his bundle into a convenient trash receptacle.

And now, he decided, with his appearance reasonably changed, he dared look for sanctuary for the night. Sanctuary and a place where he could study at leisure the two magazines in his pocket. He had a hunch those two magazines, carefully studied, might give him at least a clue to what it was all about.

He walked in the direction opposite that of the drugstore where disaster had so nearly befallen him. He passed a men's haberdashery, a sporting goods store, a theater at which was playing a picture he had seen in New York two months before, and everything seemed normal and ordinary. The people about him seemed normal and ordinary.

For a moment he wondered if possibly everything *was* normal and ordinary and he'd been imagining the differences. Possibly the druggist had been insane, possibly there was some reasonable explanation for everything, even the purple monsters.

Then he came to a newsstand with a rack of newspapers in front of it. Both local Greeneville papers and New York newspapers were displayed. All very ordinary looking, until he happened to notice a headline. It read:

ARCS ATTACK MARS, DESTROY KAPI
EARTH COLONY UNPREPARED
DOPELLE VOWS VENGEANCE

He stepped closer to read the date. It was today's issue of the *New York Times,* typographically as familiar as the palm of his hand.

He picked the top copy off the rack and went into the store with it. He handed the news dealer a hundred-credit note and got ninety-nine credits in change—all in bills like the ones he had, except for the denominations. He stuffed the paper into his pocket and hurried out.

A few doors farther on was a hotel. He checked in, signing—after a second's hesitation while he pretended to fumble with the pen—his right name and address.

There wasn't any bellhop. The clerk handed him a key and told him where to find his room, at the front end of the corridor on the second floor.

Two minutes later, with the door closed and locked behind him, he took a deep breath of relief and sat down on the bed. For the first time since whatever had happened in the drugstore, he felt really safe.

He took the newspaper and the magazines from his pocket and put them on the bed. Then he got up and hung his coat and hat on the hanger, and as he did so he noticed two knobs and a dial on the wall beside the doorway, above a six-inch circular area of cloth—obviously a built-in radio with the cloth covering the speaker outlet.

He turned the knob that looked like a rheostat, and it was one. A faint hum immediately came from the speaker. He turned the tuning dial until a station came in clear and strong, then turned down the volume a little. It was good music—sounded like Benny Goodman, although he didn't recognize the tune.

He went back to the bed, took off his shoes to make himself comfortable and propped pillows up against the head of the bed. He picked up, first, his own magazine, *Surprising Stories*. He studied again, with growing wonder, the cover—the cover that was incredibly the same picture, incredibly different.

He'd have stared at it for minutes had not a sudden thought occurred to him that made him open the magazine quickly to the contents page. He looked at the fine type at the bottom and read:

Published by Borden Publications, Inc. L. A. Borden, Editor and Publisher. Keith Winton, Managing Editor...

He found he'd been holding his breath until he saw his name there. He belonged here, then—wherever *here* was, he still had a job. And Mr. Borden was here, too, but what had happened to Borden's summer estate, the estate that had seemingly literally fallen out from under him a few minutes before seven o'clock this evening?

Another thought struck him, and he grabbed up the love story book and almost tore it getting it open to the contents page. Yes, Betty Hadley was Managing Editor. But there was something puzzling—the fact that the magazine was published by Borden Publications, Inc. This issue, the July one, should have shown the imprint of Whaley Publishing Company—it was only a matter of days since Borden had bought the magazine. Even the August issue should still bear the Whaley imprint. But that was a minor matter.

The important thing was that—whatever mad universe this was—Betty Had-ley was here.

He sighed with relief. With Betty Hadley here, this couldn't be too bad a place, even if it contained purple monsters from the moon. And if he, Keith Winton, was still editor of his favorite science-fiction magazine, *Surprising Stories*, then he still had a job and could still eat, and he didn't care too much if they paid him in credits instead of in dollars.

The tune on the radio stopped suddenly, as though someone had shut off a record. A voice cut in:

"*Special news bulletin. Second warning to citizens of Greeneville and surrounding territory. The Arcturian spy reported half an hour ago has not yet been apprehended. All railway stations, roads and spaceports are being closely guarded and a house-to-house search is being instituted. All citizens are requested to be on the alert.*

"*Go armed. Shoot on sight. Mistakes may and will be made but again we remind you that it is better that a hundred innocent people die than that the spy escape to cause the loss, perhaps, of millions of Terrestrial lives.*

"*Shoot on the slightest suspicion!*

"*We repeat the description. . ."*

Scarcely breathing, Keith Winton listened to that description.

"*...about five feet nine, one hundred sixty pounds, tan suit, white sport shirt open at the collar, wears no hat. Brown eyes, brown wavy hair, appears to be about thirty years old..."*

He let his breath out slowly. They hadn't discovered his change of clothes. And there was no mention of his being wounded. The druggist, then, had not known that one of the shots he'd fired had been a hit.

The physical description was fairly close, but that couldn't be too dangerous if they didn't know what clothes he was wearing now or the fact that his upper arm would be bandaged.

Of course he'd be in much greater danger if the man whose room he had burgled at the rooming house came home and reported that his Oxford gray suit and straw hat were missing. And despite the fact that he'd been left five hundred credits to cover his loss, he probably *would* report them if he had heard the broadcasts. He was sorry now that he'd left the money; an ordinary thief would attract less attention than would a thief who left money to cover what he took. He should, he realized, have made it appear to be the ordinary rifling of a room, have stolen other objects as well. He could have taken all three suits in a suitcase that had been on the floor of the closet; then they could have taken only a guess as to which of the three he was wearing.

As it was, if they tied in what had happened at the rooming house, they'd have a good description of him again.

But—ye gods, what had he walked into?—*Shoot on sight!* And he had seriously considered giving himself up!

Well, that "shoot on sight" order definitely ended any possibility of his going to the authorities. Somehow, he was in such deadly danger here that there wouldn't even be a chance to explain—if he knew *how* to explain. Even with the roads and stations watched, he'd have to get back to New York and orient himself. But what would New York be like? As he knew it, or otherwise?

It was getting hot and stuffy in the hotel room. He went to a window and opened it, then stood looking out on the street below. So ordinary a street, such ordinary people. Then he saw three of the tall purple monsters, arm in arm, come out of the theater lobby across the street. And nobody paid any attention to them.

He stepped back suddenly from the window, for one of the purple things might, for all he knew, be the same one that had seen him in the drugstore. The monsters all looked alike to him, but if they were used to human beings— as they seemed to be—then the one that had seen him once would undoubtedly be able to recognize him again.

The sight of the purple monsters made him tremble a little at a sudden thought— *was* he insane? Could it be that? If so, it was the craziest form of insanity he'd ever heard of, and he'd taken a course in abnormal psych at college.

And, if he really was crazy, which was the delusion—the world in which he now found himself, or all of his memories?

Could his mind have conceivably built itself a set of false memories of a world without spaceships, without purple monsters from the moon, with dollars instead of credits, no spies from Arcturus and no Earth colonies on Mars?

Could it be that this world was the one he'd lived in all his life and that the world which seemed familiar, the world of his memories, was a phantom of his mind?

But if this *were* the real world, if his memories—up to seven o'clock tonight— *were* false, then where did he fit into things? *Was* he an Arcturian spy? That seemed no more impossible than anything else.

There were footsteps suddenly along the corridor just outside his door, heavy footsteps of several people. There was a loud, authoritative knock on the door.

A voice said, "Police."

MAD MANHATTAN

Keith took a deep breath and thought fast. The radio had just told him that a house-to-house search was being made; probably that was all this was. As someone who'd just checked into the hotel he'd be investigated first, naturally. Aside from his time of checking in, they could have no grounds for suspicion.

Was there anything on him that would give him away if he was searched? Yes, his money. Not the credit bills the druggist had given him, but his change and the bills that were in his wallet in dollar denominations.

Quickly he took from his pocket the change he had left—a quarter, two dimes and some pennies. From his billfold he took the bills—three tens and some singles—that weren't credit bills.

The knocking was repeated, more loudly and insistently.

Keith wrapped the change in the bills, making a small tight wad, and reached out through the window, putting them on the corner of the window ledge out of sight.

Then he took a deep breath and went and opened the door of the room.

Three men, two of them in police uniform, stood there. The uniformed ones held drawn revolvers in their hands. It was the other, the man in a gray business suit, who spoke.

He said, "Sorry, sir. We're making a routine checkup. You've heard the broadcasts?"

"Of course," Keith said. "Come in."

They were coming in anyway, even before he spoke. They came in, ready and alert. The muzzles of both of the pistols were aimed at his chest and they didn't waver a bit. The cold, suspicious eyes of the man in gray didn't waver from Keith's face, either.

But his voice was carefully polite. "What is your name?"

"Keith Winton."

"Occupation?"

"Editorial work. I'm managing editor of *Surprising Stories.*" Keith gestured casually at the magazine lying on the bed.

The muzzle of one of the two revolvers aimed at him dropped a little, maybe as much as an inch. A broad grin spread across the round, flat face of the man behind it.

"The hell," he said. "Then you must be the guy who runs the Rocketalk Department, huh? The Rocketeer?"

Keith nodded.

"Then maybe," said the uniformed man, "you remember my name. I'm John Garrett. I've written you four letters and you've published two of them."

Quickly he transferred the pistol to his left hand—but kept it aimed squarely at Keith—and stuck out his right hand.

Keith shook it. "Sure," he said, "you're the guy who keeps trying to talk us into running color on our inside illustrations, even if we have to raise our price a d—" He caught himself quickly. "—a credit."

The man's grin got broader and his pistol dropped to his side. "Sure," he said, "that's me. I've been a fan of your magazine ever since—"

"Raise that gun again, Sergeant," snapped the man in the gray suit. "Don't get careless."

The gun came up again, but the sergeant kept on grinning. He said, "This guy's all right, Captain, If he wasn't what he said he was, he couldn't have known what was in my letters to the magazine, could he?"

The captain asked, "Were your letters published?"

"Well—yes, but—"

"Arcturians have prodigious memories. If he prepared himself for the role of an editor, he'd have studied back issues of the magazine he was going to claim to edit."

The sergeant frowned. He said, "Well, yeah, but—" He pushed back his hat with his right hand and scratched his head.

The captain had closed the door of the room and leaned against it, looking from Keith's face to the sergeant's. He said, "But the idea's a good one, Sergeant, if you can check up on Mr. Winton's genuineness in some way that hasn't been in print. Can you?"

The sergeant looked even more puzzled, but Keith said, "Sergeant, do you remember the last letter you wrote us? About a month ago, I believe."

"Sure. You mean the one where I said—"

"Don't say it," Keith interrupted him. "Let me. You said that comic books could run pictures in color and could sell even cheaper than pulp magazines, so you couldn't understand why we couldn't run our stuff in color and still hold to the same price."

The muzzle of the gun dropped again. The sergeant said, "That's right, Captain. That's just what I said, and that letter's not been published yet. So this guy's all right or he wouldn't know about it. He couldn't. Unless—" He glanced again at the magazine lying on the bed. "Unless it's in that issue. I haven't seen that one yet. It's a new one, must've hit the stands today."

"That's right," Keith said. "But your letter isn't in it; go ahead and take a look."

Sergeant Garrett glanced at his superior officer and got a nod. He stepped around Keith and picked up the magazine, leafed through it to the Rocketalk Department at the back and tried to read and keep his eyes on Keith at the same time.

The man in gray smiled thinly and took a short-barreled revolver from a shoulder holster. He said, "Put away your gun and concentrate on what you're doing, Sergeant. Burke and I will stand guard."

Sergeant Garrett said, "Sure, Captain. Thanks," and holstered his gun. With both hands and both eyes for the task, he could handle the magazine easily.

As he hunted for the correspondence department, Garrett said, "I still think you oughta use color inside, Mr. Winton. It'd sure make the Bems show up better."

Keith smiled. "Wish we *could* afford it, Sergeant. But our books couldn't compete with the others if we did."

The captain looked from one to the other of them curiously. "What are you guys talking about?" he asked. "What are Bems? And why talk about books? Those are magazines."

Keith said, "Calling their magazines books is a common habit among pulp editors and publishers, Captain. Possibly because they wish the magazines *were* books. As for Bems, that's slang among the fans. It's the initials of *bug-eyed monsters*. That's a Bem on the cover of the issue Sergeant Garrett's looking at."

"And a good one," said the sergeant. "One of them things on the third planet of Arcturus, ain't it?"

"If I remember the story," Keith said, "it's a Venusian."

The sergeant laughed heartily, as though Keith had made a very funny joke. If he had, Keith didn't know what it was, but he grinned too. The sergeant kept turning pages through the Rocketalk department.

A minute later he looked up. "Say, Mr. Winton, about this letter from the guy in Provincetown who doesn't like the lead novels Bergman writes. Don't pay any attention to guys as dumb as that. Bergman's your best writer, outside maybe of—"

"Sergeant!" The captain's voice was icy. "We're not here to listen to your likes in fiction. Just look at the signatures or headings of those letters to be sure yours isn't in that issue. And don't take all evening to do it."

The sergeant turned red and turned pages.

"No," he said, a minute later. "It ain't in here, Captain."

The man in gray smiled at Keith. He said, "Guess you're all right then, Mr. Winton. But, as routine, do you have identification?"

Keith nodded and started to reach for his wallet. But the man in gray said, "Wait. If you don't mind—"

And whether Keith minded or not, he stepped around behind Keith and ran his hands swiftly over all of Keith's pockets. Apparently he felt nothing in any of the pockets that interested him except the wallet. He took that out and examined the contents quickly, then handed it back.

He said, "Okay, Mr. Winton. Looks all right, but—"

He went to the closet, opened the door and looked inside. He opened the dresser drawers, looked under the bed, made a quick but reasonably thorough search of the room.

There was a touch of suspicion in his voice again. "No luggage, Mr. Winton? Not even a toothbrush?"

"Not even a toothbrush," Keith said. "I didn't expect to stay in Greeneville overnight. But the business I came on took me longer than I expected."

The man in gray finished his search. He said, "Well, sorry to have bothered you, sir. But we have to be thorough and not take any chances—and you'd just registered here. Good thing you and Sergeant Garrett got together on a proof of who you are or we'd have to check up even more thoroughly. But as it is—"

He nodded to the other uniformed man, who shoved his pistol back into its holster.

Keith said, "Quite okay, Captain. I understand you can't take any chances at all."

"You're plenty right there. Not with a spy loose somewhere around. Well, he won't get out of Greeneville. We've got a cordon that a mosquito couldn't get through. And we'll keep it here till we get the Arc, too."

"Think I'll have any trouble getting back to New York?" Keith asked.

"Well—they're screening pretty fine at the stations. Guess you can talk them into letting you through." He smiled. "Especially if you find one of your fans among the guards."

"And that isn't too likely, Captain. You know, I've been thinking about going back in the morning. It'll get me to the office so late that I think I really ought to change my mind and go back tonight. I was pretty tired when I decided to stay over here, but I'm feeling better now. Do you know offhand when's the next train for New York?"

"Half past nine, I believe," the captain said. He glanced at his wrist watch. "You'll have time to make it, but I don't know if you'll have time to have them check up on you and let you through. And the next train's at six in the morning."

Keith frowned. "I'd like to make the nine-thirty one. Say, Captain, wonder if you'd do me the favor of phoning whoever's going to be in charge at the station and vouching for me so they won't have to hold me up and make me miss the train. Or is that too much to ask?"

"Guess not, Mr. Winton. Sure, I'll put in the phone call from here."

Ten minutes later Keith was in a taxi bound for the railroad station; half an hour later he was on an uncrowded train bound for New York City.

He breathed a deep sigh of relief; the worst immediate danger seemed to be over. Surely he'd be safe in New York City. The main thing was that he was through the cordon. Not only that, but he'd dared—after the policemen had left his room—to recover his money from the window sill. He'd believed, and correctly, that the call Captain Whoever-he-was had made to the officials at the railroad station would spare him being searched again when he showed proof of his already-established identity.

And he hated to give up those bills and coins until he knew what things were all about. Presumably they were all dangerous but some of them were valuable. The druggist had given him the equivalent of two hundred dollars for one coin, and possibly others would be even more valuable. Why, the druggist had admitted that the quarter was worth more than he'd paid for it!

But the half dollar— He shrugged mentally. No use trying to guess; he'd just have to wait until he could find out what it was all about, and be as careful as possible meanwhile. After paying for his hotel room and the railroad ticket, he still had about a hundred and forty dollars' worth of credits; that would last him for a while. For quite a while, if he was careful with it. And the little wad of non-credit currency and coins was carefully stuffed into the fob pocket of his trousers so he wouldn't inadvertently offer the wrong coinage to pay for a purchase. The coins were tightly wrapped in the bills so they wouldn't rattle together and give him away.

Oh, it was undoubtedly dangerous to hang onto them, but he had a reason stronger even than their possible value. They were a straw to which his hope of sanity clung. His memories might be figments of his imagination, but those coins were hard physical objects. They were *proof*, in a way, that at least part of what he remembered was really true. The slight bulge in his fob pocket was, in some measure, reassuring.

Watching out the window of the train as it gathered speed, he saw the lights of Greeneville become less and less frequent, and then they were out in the darkness of the country.

At least for the moment, he was safe. And with a little over two hours of leisure to look through the two magazines and the newspaper he had bought.

The newspaper came first.

ARCS ATTACK MARS, DESTROY KAPI

That was the news, the big news. He read it carefully. Kapi, it would seem, was an Earth colony on Mars established in 1939, the fourth of the seven colonies established there. It was the smallest of the colonies; there had been eight hundred and forty-odd Terrestrial colonists. All had been killed, it was believed, as had an estimated hundred and fifty Martian laborers.

Then, Keith realized, there must be native Martians, as distinguished from the colonists, the emigrants from Earth. What were the native Martians like? There wasn't any clue in the brief news article, which read like a front-line dispatch from a more familiar war. Possibly "Lunan" really had been a name, after all; perhaps the purple monsters were Martians and not inhabitants of the moon.

But there were more important things to wonder about than that. He read on.

A single ship of Arcturians had somehow got through the cordon of space-guards and had launched a single torpedo before the Dopelle fighters had detected it. They had attacked at once and, although the Arctunan vessel had switched to interstellar drive, they had caught up with it and destroyed it.

Preparations, said *The New York Times,* were being made for a counterraid. The details were, of course, a military secret.

There were a lot of names and things that meant nothing to Keith as he encountered them in the course of reading the article. Somehow, it seemed stranger when he came across a familiar name in an unfamiliar context—a mention, for example, of General Dwight D. Eisenhower, in charge of Venus sector.

The end of the article concerned increased defense measures proposed for the more vulnerable cities, and was quite obscure to Keith Winton. There were frequent references that meant nothing at all to him—a recurring phrase "all-city mistout" and several references to "the renegades" and "the Nighters."

The main article—about two columns of it—out of the way, he went through the paper from front to back, reading every headline and at least part of any story that looked interesting or unusual. There seemed to be amazingly little difference in the minutiae of life, almost no difference in the domestic scene.

The society news was there, and he recognized many of the names and would undoubtedly have recognized most of them had he been in the habit of reading society news. St. Louis was leading in one major league and New York in the other—and that, too, was as he remembered it, although he couldn't be sure whether the exact percentage figures were the same. The ads were for the same familiar products and brands that he knew—except that the prices were given in credits instead of dollars and cents. There were no ads for spaceships, no Little Wonder Atomic Kits for the kiddies.

He studied the want ads particularly. The housing situation was considerably better than he remembered it, and a probable explanation of that lay in the fact that an occasional flat or house was offered with the comment "Emigrating to Mars." One Pets for Sale ad offered a Venus coline, whatever that was, and another offered a moonpup.

At a little after one o'clock, on schedule, the train pulled into Grand Central. Keith folded the newspaper for more detailed study later. It had occupied his attention so strongly that he hadn't even glanced at the two magazines.

Gradually, as the train slowly crawled into the station, Keith became aware of something unusual, something different that he couldn't put his finger on, something in the atmosphere of the place. It wasn't lack of lights; there were the usual lights on in the station, perhaps more of them than he remembered.

He realized, too, that the car he was leaving was only a fourth full, perhaps not that much. And as he left it, he saw that it was the only train unloading and that all the redcaps seemed to have gone off duty.

Just ahead of Keith, a little man was struggling to carry three suitcases, one in each hand and one under an arm. He was having heavy going.

"Give you a hand with one of those?" Keith asked.

The little man said, "Sure, thanks," with real gratitude in his voice. He relinquished one of the heavy suitcases to Keith and they started down the cement walk between the tracks.

Keith said, "Not much traffic tonight, is there?"

"Guess that was the last train in. Really shouldn't run 'em *that* late. What's the use of getting in if you can't go home? Oh, sure, you get a better start in the morning, but in the long run what good does it do you?"

Keith said, "Not much, I guess," and wondered what they were talking about.

"Eighty-seven killed last night!" the little man said. "At least that many bodies found; nobody knows how many more went in the river."

"Awful," Keith said.

"And that's one night, an average night. Say there were at least a hundred killed. And that's only the ones killed outright. Heaven knows how many got dragged down alleys and beat up but not killed." He sighed. "I remember when it was safe even on Broadway."

He stopped suddenly and put down the suitcases. "Got to rest a minute," he said. "If you want to go on, just leave that other one."

Keith was glad of a chance to put down the case he'd been carrying; his wounded left shoulder prevented him from changing hands with it. He flexed his right hand, cramped from the handle of the suitcase. "I'm in no hurry," he said. "I'm in no hurry to get home."

The little man laughed as though something very funny had been said. Keith allowed himself a noncommittal smile.

"That's a good one," the little man said. "In no hurry to get home." He slapped a hand against his thigh.

Keith said, "Uh—I haven't heard a newscast for a while. Have you? Is there anything new?"

"Damn right there is!" The little man's face got suddenly scared and deadly serious. "There's an Arc spy in the country. But maybe you heard that—it was on early in the evening." He shuddered slightly.

"No, hadn't heard that," Keith said. "Remember any of the details?"

"Upstate in Greeneville, town we came through. Don't you remember? They kept all the train doors locked, nobody on except people they checked. Whole station full of cops and guards."

Keith said, "Guess I must have dozed through our stop at—you said Greeneville?"

"Yeah, Greeneville. Glad I didn't have to get off there. They'll turn that town upside down."

"How was he spotted?" Keith asked.

"Tried to sell someone some banned coinage, and the coin was an Arc counterfeit—one of the wrong-dated ones."

"Oh," said Keith. It *had* been the coin then; he'd felt pretty sure of it. Maybe he'd be smart to get rid of the rest of them, regardless of their value or potential value, as soon as he had a chance to put them into a sewer or somewhere. Or maybe he should have left them on the window sill of the hotel room he'd had in Greeneville.

No, that would have been bad, for if they were found they'd be traceable to him; he'd registered in that hotel book by his right name and had—fortunately, for other reasons—given his right name to the policemen who'd come up to the room. Yes, finding of those coins on the window ledge outside that room would lead to a search for Keith Winton in New York to explain how they got there. He hadn't thought of that when he'd recovered them from the ledge—he'd thought, in fact, that he was being a little foolhardy in continuing to take a chance with them. Now he sweated a little, realizing how lucky it had been that he had taken that chance.

He asked, "If they spotted the spy on this coin business, how come they didn't catch him?"

"*Catch him!*" The little man shook visibly with emotion. "Lord, mister, you don't *catch* Arcturians; you kill 'em. And they did try to kill him—a druggist and a moonie that the druggist yelled to for help—but he got away from both of 'em."

"Oh," said Keith.

"Bet twenty or thirty people have been killed in Greeneville by mistake since then," the little man said gloomily. He rubbed his palms together and picked up the suitcases. "Guess I can make it the rest of the way now, if you can."

Keith picked up the other suitcase and they resumed their way toward the station lobby.

"Hope there are cots left," the little man said.

Keith opened his mouth and shut it again. Any question he might ask could be one that would give away his ignorance on some point he should know about. He said, "Probably won't be," in a humorously pessimistic voice, so it could be taken for a joke if it was the wrong thing for him to have said.

But the little man merely nodded gloomy assent. They were nearing the lobby now, and a redcap came toward them. The little man sighed with relief as he and Keith surrendered the three suitcases to the redcap.

"Cots?" the redcap asked. "There are a few left."

"Sure, swell. Two of them," said the little man. Then he hesitated and looked at Keith. "Didn't mean to speak for you. Some people rather sit up."

Keith felt as though he were walking a tightrope in the dark. What was this business about a choice between a cot or sitting up? He didn't want to do either.

He said hesitantly, "Guess I'll mosey along."

He looked in surprise—for they had just come through the doors into the main room of the station—at the cots. Long, orderly rows of army-type cots, closely spaced. Except for aisles left for walking between the rows of them, they covered the entire floor of the tremendous room. On most of the cots people lay asleep.

Could the housing shortage be *this* desperate? No, it couldn't; not from the number of for-rent ads in *The New York Times* in his pocket. But—

The little man touched his shoulder—his bad shoulder, as it happened—and Keith jumped. But the little man didn't notice that. He was saying, "Just a minute, porter," to the redcap, who was several steps ahead of them.

He leaned closer to Keith. "Uh—if you're short of creds to get yourself a cot, mister, I could—uh—lend you a few."

"Thanks," Keith said. "But I think I'd better run along."

"You don't mean you're going *out,* do you?" There was horror and surprise on the man's face.

He'd said something wrong again, but he couldn't guess what it was, or why the cots were there in Grand Central, or why it seemed to matter whether he stayed here. Anyway, he'd better get away from the little man before he aroused his suspicions, if he hadn't already.

"Of course not," he said. "I'm not that foolish. But someone was supposed to meet me here and I want to look around for him. Maybe I'll take a cot later, but I don't think I can sleep anyway. Don't worry about me. And thanks for offering to lend me credits, but I've got plenty."

He got away quickly before he could be asked any more questions. The lighting here in the main room of the station was dim, undoubtedly so people could sleep without bright light glaring in their eyes. Keith threaded his way through the dimness, walking as quietly as he could so as not to awake the sleepers he passed, and headed toward the Forty-second Street entrance.

As he neared it, he saw that two policemen were posted at each of the doors.

But he couldn't stop now. The ones he was approaching had seen him coming and were watching him. He'd been walking directly toward the door they were covering, and he couldn't turn aside now without attracting their attention even more strongly than if he kept walking. If it turned out that he wouldn't be allowed to leave—for what reason he couldn't remotely guess—he could pretend that he'd strolled up to the door merely to look through the glass.

So he walked up to them casually, noticing that the door had been painted black on the outside of the glass.

The bigger of the two policemen spoke as Keith came near. But his voice was respectful.

He asked, "Are you armed, sir?"

"No."

"It's pretty dangerous out there. Well, we haven't the authority to make you stay; all we can do is advise it."

Keith's first reaction was one of relief; he wasn't, as he had feared, going to be kept in here. Whatever the reason, he didn't want to waste a night in Grand Central.

But what did the policeman mean? Dangerous? What sort of danger was it that he knew nothing about but that kept these thousands of people, the late arrivals on the last trains from here and there, inside the station? What had happened to New York?

Well, it was too late for him to back out now. Besides, he thought grimly, he was in danger *anywhere* until he knew the score and the ropes a lot better than he did.

He said as casually as he could, "Haven't far to go. I'll be all right."

"It's your business," said the cop.

The other one grinned. "We hope it ain't your funeral. Okay, mister." He opened the door.

Keith almost stepped back. It hadn't been black paint on the outside of the glass of the doors. It had been—blackness. A kind of utter black darkness he'd never seen before. Not a glimmer of light showed anywhere. The dimmed lights inside the station didn't seem to cut into that blackness at all. Looking down, he could see the paving of the walk for only a foot or two beyond the edge of the open door.

And—was it his imagination, or was a little of that outside blackness drifting into the station itself through the doorway, as though it weren't darkness at all but a palpable blackness, a gaseous blackness? As though it were something more than mere absence of light?

But, whatever was out there, he couldn't admit now that he hadn't *known* about it. He had to go through that open doorway now, whatever it led into.

He walked through and the door closed behind him. It was like walking into a closet. This was a blackout beyond blackouts. It must be—he remembered a phrase from the *New York Times*—the mistout.

He looked up and there wasn't a sign of a star or the moon and it had been, in Greeneville, at least, a brightly moonlit night.

He'd taken two steps outside the door and now he turned to look back at it. He couldn't see it. There should be a lighted pane of glass there. However dimly lighted, it should be visible for a long way in darkness like this. Unless, of course, the glass really *had* been painted black on the outside. He stepped closer and he could see it, a very dim rectangle, close enough now that he could reach out and touch it. It wasn't visible any farther away than that.

He took a step back and it was gone. He fumbled a box of matches out of his pocket and struck one of them. Held at arm's length, he could see only a faint spot of light. At two feet from his eyes, he could see it clearly. But no farther.

It burned down almost to his fingertips and he dropped it; he didn't know whether it went out when it hit the sidewalk or not. Maybe it was still burning down there on the concrete.

He wished now that he had taken a cot back inside the station, but it was too late to turn and go in again. He'd attracted enough attention going out. But why hadn't he followed the little man's lead? He'd have to remember that it was safer to imitate others than not.

Reaching out to touch the building and trailing his hand along it as he walked, groping with his free hand before him, he started walking west, toward the Vanderbilt Avenue corner. He kept his eyes open, straining against the black, but he might as well have closed them for all the good they did him. He knew now how a blind man felt. A cane, to tap ahead of him on the invisible sidewalk, would have been welcome. A seeing-eye dog, though, would have been useless; he doubted if even a cat could see more than a foot or so into this black mist.

His trailing hand encountered emptiness, the corner of the building. He paused a moment, wondering if he should go on at all. He couldn't go back into the station, but why not just sit down here on the walk, his back to the building, and wait for morning?—if morning *did* bring dissipation of the black mist.

Certainly getting to his bachelor apartment down in the Village was completely out of the question. Taxicabs *couldn't* be running. And reason told him that no other form of transportation would be running either. Only utter fools or people as ignorant as himself—and surely there couldn't be another in that category—would try to get anywhere in stuff like this.

But he decided against the sidewalk. There might be police patrols that would question him, wanting to know why he was outside the so-near sanctuary of the station. No, if he did sit down to wait out the night, it couldn't be here, so near his starting point. If he was picked up farther away, he could at least say he'd been *trying* to get home from the station.

So with only his shuffling feet to guide him now, he made his way from the building to the curb and out into the street. If there was any traffic—but there *couldn't* be, unless it operated on radar. That thought hurried him across the second half of the street: how did he know they didn't operate on radar?

He found the curb on the far side by falling over it. He got up and shuffled across the sidewalk until he was again able to touch solidity with a guiding right hand as he groped along Forty-second Street.

Forty-second Street, only a few blocks from Times Square and Broadway, and he might as well have been on the—no, not on the moon, for on the moon there'd be purple monsters to keep him company. *Were there any here?*

He tried not to wonder about that.

His ears strained but couldn't pick up a sound except for the soft shuffle of his own footsteps, and he realized that, for no conscious reason, he was walking on tiptoe to disturb the awful quiet as little as possible.

He completed the short block to Madison, crossed it, and began to grope his way toward Fifth Avenue.

Where, he wondered, was he going? To Times Square? Why not? The Village was out of the question, too far to reach in a full night of snaillike progress like this. But he had to be heading somewhere, so why not for the center of things? If there was anything open anywhere in New York, it would be there.

To get in, *anywhere,* out of this palpable blackness!

He started trying doors as he passed them. They were all locked. Trying them reminded him that he had a key to the Borden Publishing Company office in his pocket, and that it was only three blocks south. But no, the outer door of the building would surely be locked, and he didn't have a key to that.

He crossed Fifth Avenue. Across the street from him, to his left, would be the Public Library. He considered crossing the street and spending the rest of the night on the steps there, but decided not to. Might as well keep on to Times Square, now that he'd picked that as a destination. Surely there'd be some sanctuary at the hub of the universe, even if it was only a lighted subway station.

From Fifth Avenue to Sixth Avenue—he wondered if they'd tried to name it Avenue of the Americas here—is a long block. But in all its length there wasn't an unlocked door. He tried them all.

He crossed Sixth Avenue, was halfway to Broadway.

He tried another door, it was locked as had been all the others. But in the brief instant when his footsteps paused as his hand tried the knob, he heard a sound, the first sound other than ones he had made himself since he'd left Grand Central.

It was the sound of footsteps, as soft and cautious as his own had been. Stealthy footsteps; something inside told him that there was danger in them, deadly danger.

THE NIGHTERS

He stood rigid as the footsteps shuffled closer. Whoever, whatever it was, there wasn't any way of avoiding a meeting, unless he turned and worked his way back in the other direction. It was, it seemed suddenly to Keith, a one-dimensional world. There was only a forward and a backward in it as long as each of them—he and the unknown—groped their way along the building fronts. Like ants crawling along a string they must meet and pass unless one of them turned.

And before he had made up his mind to turn, it was already too late. A groping hand touched him and a whining voice was saying, "Don't rob me, mister. I ain't got no credits."

Keith sighed with relief. "Okay," he said. "I'll stand still. You go around me."

"Sure, mister."

Hands touched him lightly, and a strong alcoholic breath almost made him gasp as the man groped past him. There was a chuckle in the darkness.

"Just an old space dog on a spree," the voice said. "And rolled already, mister, two hours ago. Look, mister, I'll give you a tip. The *Nighters* are out. The whole gang of 'em, over Times Square way. You better not keep on the way you're goin'. I'm warnin' you."

The man was past him now, but his hand still touched Keith's sleeve to maintain contact.

"They're the ones who robbed you?" Keith asked.

"*Them?* Mister, I'm alive, ain't I? Would I be alive if the Nighters had got me? I ask you."

Keith said, "That's right; I forgot that. So maybe I'd better not go that way. Uh—are the subways open?"

"The *subways?* Man, you really want trouble, don't you?"

"Where *is* a safe place to go?"

"Safe? Long time since I heard that word. What's it mean?" He gave a drunken laugh. "Mister, I was on the Mars-Jupe run in the days of the plat-rush, when they said the last rites over us before they closed the airlocks. I'd damn near as soon be back there as messing around this mistout and playing tag with Nighters."

Keith asked, "How'd you know I wasn't a Nighter?"

"You kidding? How could one guy be a Nighter when they go in armlocked gangs from building to building and you can hear 'em tapping? We're fools to be out in this. You and me, both of us. If I wasn't drunk— Say, got a match?"

"Sure, a box of them. Here. Can you—?"

"I got the shakes, mister. From Venus swamp fever. Would you light one for me? And then when I get a fag going, I'll tell you a safe enough place where you and me can hide out the rest of the night."

Keith scraped a match along the side of the box and struck it. The sudden flame made gray dimness out of the black mist for a radius of a couple of feet.

It revealed a hideous, leering, scarred face—and above it a club raised to strike. The club started to come down the instant the match flared.

There wasn't time to duck that blow. Keith stayed alive in that second by acting instinctively, instantaneously. He stepped in under the blow, thrusting the flaming match into that ugly face. The man's forearm, not the club, struck Keith's head a glancing blow. The impact of it jarred the club from his hand, and the club struck the sidewalk with a thud.

Then they were struggling, wrestling in the dark, with strong hands trying for Keith's throat, foul breath in his face and fouler words in his ears. He managed to jerk free of those strangling hands. He stepped back and struck. His fist connected solidly in the dark.

He heard his assailant fall—not knocked out, though, for he was still cursing. Under cover of the sound, Keith took three light, quick steps backward, out into the open blackness away from the wall; he stood there quietly, not making a sound.

He heard the man scramble to his feet, breathing hard. For half a minute, perhaps, that breathing was the only sound in the world.

And then there was another sound, a new one. It was a different kind of sound altogether—it was the distant, soft tapping of a hundred blind men's canes. As though a company of blind men were coming tapping through the dark. The sound came from the direction in which Keith had been going, the direction of Broadway and Times Square.

He heard a subdued mutter, "Nighters!" and then the quick shuffle of footsteps as his former assailant started off. His voice, no longer cursing or even belligerent, came back out of the dense dark: "Run, pal. *Nighters!*"

The shuffle and scuffle of his footsteps died away as the tapping sounds got louder and nearer. They came nearer incredibly fast.

What were Nighters? Human beings? He tried to piece together the few things he'd heard about them, or read about them. What had the man with the scarred face said about them?—"They go in armlocked gangs from building to building and you can hear 'em tapping." Human or otherwise, they must be an organized gang of killers that scoured the streets of the mistout— a long row of them from building to building with their arms locked together, tapping canes to guide them.

Were the canes weapons, too, or did they carry other things besides the canes they tapped with?

The tapping sound was only yards away now, coming closer faster than men can walk in the dark, almost at a run. They had a system, somehow, that gave them speed.

Keith didn't wait any longer; he turned and ran diagonally toward the line of building fronts until his hand, outthrust, made scraping contact, and then ran parallel to them, and despite the risk of falling over some object he couldn't see, he *ran*.

The danger behind seemed greater than the danger of running blindly in darkness. The fear that had been in the voice of the men with the scarred face was contagious. That man, however foul he was, had been no coward. And he had *known* what the Nighters were and he'd been afraid of them, plenty afraid. Killer himself, he was jackal to a pack of lions when that tapping sound had come.

Keith ran thirty or forty paces and then stopped to listen. The sounds behind him were a little farther away; they weren't coming as fast as he had dared to run. Then, from the opposite direction, from the direction in which he'd been running, came a horrible, hoarse scream. He thought, he felt sure, that it was the voice of the man with the scarred face. The scream rose to a high pitch of agony and then subsided into a rattle and silence.

What had the man with the scarred face run into? *What* could cause a man to die—and Keith had no doubt but that the scarred man was dead—in that great an agony? It was as though the jackal running from the lions had stepped into the coils of a boa constrictor. Crushed in a monster serpent's coils, a man might scream like that—and for about that long, before he died.

The hair at the back of Keith Winton's neck prickled. He'd have given, at that instant, his right arm for *light,* no matter what that light might reveal. He knew now what fear was; he could taste it in his throat.

Behind him, the tapping. He'd gained on it in that sprint; it was about twenty yards away instead of five or ten. He could outdistance it if he ran again and kept running. But *what* was he running toward?

Scar-face had been running along the building fronts; whatever had got him must be there. Keith diagonaled out toward the curb and down it into the street. Then, turning to run parallel to the curb, he started again away from the tapping row of Nighters. He ran another thirty or forty paces and again stopped to listen. Yes, again the tapping was farther behind him.

Or *was* it? For a moment, he was confused as to direction and thought he'd got turned around in the dark. Then he realized the truth. There was tapping behind him; there was also tapping in the opposite direction, ahead of him.

Two lines of them, coming from opposite directions, and he was in between. That was their method of hunting, of treeing whatever quarry might be on whatever block they were working. He'd wondered how they managed to catch anybody when their progress by tapping gave them away and warned their quarry to run. But he understood now.

He stopped, his heart beating wildly. The Nighters—whatever Nighters were—had him in the middle. There was no way to run.

He stood there hesitating until the tapping from behind him—nearer than the tapping in front—came so close that he *had* to do something. Standing still meant being caught within a minute. Running either forward or backward meant being caught sooner than that.

He turned at right angles and ran for the building fronts on the south side of the street—the side opposite from the point at which Scar-face had met his death. He didn't worry about the curb; there wasn't time to grope for it with his feet. He found it by falling over it, scrambled to his feet, and made the few more steps across the sidewalk to the nearest building front. He paused only a fraction of a second to listen. The tapping was equidistant to his right and to his left.

He groped his way into a doorway. He found the handle of the door—not because he expected to find it unlocked, but because he needed to locate it in order to open it from the inside. He swung his fist at the glass beside it.

He should have cut his knuckles badly, but he didn't. As though luck had decided to give him a break at last, a small area of glass fell neatly inward. The rest of the pane didn't crack or fall out of the door frame.

He had a glimpse of light inside as a thick curtain drawn down over the glass of the door swung inward from the blow of his fist. He reached quickly through the opening, turned the knob from the inside, and stumbled through the door.

The light inside almost blinded him as he slammed the door shut behind him. A voice said, "Stop or I'll shoot!"

Keith stopped and raised his hands shoulder high. He blinked until he could see again. He was in the lobby of a small hotel. Across the desk, a dozen feet in front of him, leaned a white-faced very frightened-looking clerk, holding a re-peating shotgun the muzzle of which looked as big as a cannon and was aimed straight at Keith's chest. The clerk was breathing harder than Keith.

His voice trembled a little. "Don't come any closer. Get out, get back out right away. I don't want to have to shoot you, but—"

Without moving in either direction and without lowering his arms, Keith said, "I can't. The *Nighters* are right outside. If I open the door to go out, they'll come in."

The clerk's face got even whiter. For a second, he was too scared to speak and in that second they both heard the sound of tapping.

The clerk's voice was just above a whisper when he found it. "Back up against that door. Hold the curtain fast against the break, so no light shows."

Keith took a step backward and leaned against the door.

He and the clerk were both very silent. Keith was sweating. Would the Nighters see—or, groping, feel— that hole in the glass? Was a knife or a bullet or something going to come through that hole into his back? His skin crawled. Time crawled.

But nothing came through the hole.

For a moment there was louder tapping, muffled voices. He thought they were human voices, but he wasn't sure. Then the sounds died away.

Neither Keith nor the clerk moved or spoke for at least three minutes after the last sound from outside. Then the clerk said, "They've gone. Now get out."

Keith kept his voice pitched as low as he could and still make it audible to the clerk. He said, "They're still near; they'll get me if I go out again. I'm not a robber. I'm not armed. And I've got money. I'd like to pay for that window-pane I broke—and I'd like to rent a room if you've got one. If you haven't a room, I'll even pay a fair price to sit in your lobby all night."

The clerk studied him uncertainly, without lowering the gun.

Then he asked, "What were you doing—out there?"

Keith said, "I came in from Greeneville—last train into Grand Central. I'd had word my brother was seriously sick and I took a chance on getting home— a dozen blocks. Hadn't realized quite how bad it was out there. Now that I've seen it—well, I'll settle for getting home in the morning."

The clerk studied him closely. Finally he said, "Keep your hands up." He lowered the shotgun down to the counter, but kept his hand on it and his finger inside the trigger guard while, with his free hand, he took a pistol out of a drawer behind the desk.

He said, "Turn around, your back toward me. I'll be sure you're not armed."

Keith turned around and stood still while he heard the clerk come around the end of the counter. He stood even stiller while the business end of a pistol pressed into the small of his back and the clerk's hand ran over his pockets lightly.

"Okay," the clerk said. "I guess you're all right; I'll take a chance on it anyway. I'd hate to send a dog out into—that."

Keith sighed with relief and turned around. The clerk was walking behind the desk again and no gun was pointed at him.

He asked, "How much do I owe you for the windowpane? And how much for a room, if you've got one?"

"Sure, we got a room. A hundred creds will cover both. But first give me a hand with something. Let's move that rack of magazines and pocket books— give me a hand to put it in front of the door. It's high enough to block off that break in the glass. Anyway, it'll keep the curtain from swinging in, and you couldn't see the break from outside as long as the curtain stays flat."

Keith said, "Good idea." He took one end of the rack and the clerk took the other and they slid it against the door without having to lift it.

Keith's eye was caught by the titles of some of the pocket editions of books in the magazine rack. One in particular—a book called *Is the Mistout Worth It?* He'd take a few of those books up to his room with him. He noticed the price— 2½ cr. Apparently the rule of one credit to ten cents held pretty true.

And that meant that a hundred credits—ten dollars—for the pane of glass and for a hotel room seemed plenty reasonable, almost a bargain. Almost? Hell, it *was* a bargain. He'd have paid all the credits he had left—well over a thousand of them— rather than go out into the mistout on Forty-second Street again tonight.

That reminded him of a minor mystery. He was pretty sure that there wasn't any hotel on the south side of Forty-second between Sixth Avenue and Broadway. Especially a cheap small hotel like this one. That is, there wasn't any such hotel here where *he* came from. That is—

He quit that-is-ing and followed the clerk back to the desk and signed a registration card. He took a hundred-credit note from his wallet and then put a fifty-credit note on top of it.

He said, "I'm going to pick out two or three of those pocket books to read. You keep the change." That would give the clerk a four-dollar-plus tip.

"Sure, thanks, Mr. Winton. And here's your key. Three-oh-seven—that's third floor front. You'll have to walk up and find it yourself. You see, we lock up at sunset, so there aren't any bellboys on. And I have to stay here on guard."

Keith nodded and pocketed the key. He walked back to the rack of books and magazines.

First he picked *Is the Mistout Worth It?* No doubt at all about his wanting that one.

His eye ran over the other titles. Some of them were familiar, others were not.

H. G. Wells' *Outline of History* he grabbed quickly. He could get a lot that he needed to know out of that book.

And what for third choice? There was plenty of fiction, but he wanted redder meat than that. Something that would give him more concentrated information.

There were, he noticed, half a dozen books about somebody named Dopelle. Where had he heard that name before? Oh yes, in the *New York Times*—the general in charge of all the Terrestrial space fleets.

Dopelle, the Man. The Story of Dopelle. Dopelle, Hero of Space. And several others.

If there were that many books about him out of the slim assortment of non-fiction titles in the rack, then Dopelle was someone he should know something about. He picked *The Story of Dopelle,* and wasn't even surprised to notice that it had been written by Paul Gallico.

He held up the books so that the clerk could see how many he was taking and then headed for the stairway before he was tempted to pick more of them or to choose some magazines to add to the two he still had: the ones he'd bought in Greeneville and hadn't looked at beyond the covers and title pages.

Already he had more reading matter than he could do justice to in the remainder of the night, no matter how lightly he skimmed it or how little he slept.

And he'd have to get *some* sleep, no matter how interesting the reading matter was. The walk up to the third floor showed him how tired he was. His wounded shoulder was aching rather badly by now. And the knuckles of his right hand were beginning to hurt like the very devil; the glass had not cut them but they were badly bruised and so sore that it hurt him to flex the fingers of his right hand.

He found the room by the dim light in the hallway, went in and turned on the light. It was a pleasant, comfortable room, with an inviting-looking bed that he stared at longingly. But he didn't dare get into it until he'd found out a few things that he might learn from the books he'd bought. Things that might save him, tomorrow, from making some blunder as bad as the one he'd made tonight in leaving Grand Central Station. Only by sheer good luck had he survived *that* blunder.

He undressed enough to be comfortable and sat down to read, deliberately picking the less comfortable of the two chairs in the room, so he could stay awake longer. He knew that, if he lay down on the bed to read, he wouldn't be able to keep awake for half an hour.

He chose first, *Is the Mistout Worth It?* That one was going to get a once-over lightly, but at least he was going to find out what the mistout *was.*

Luckily, the history of the mistout was fairly well summarized in the first chapter. It had been perfected, he learned, by a German professor in 1934, shortly after the destruction—by Arcturian spaceships—of Chicago and Rome. The destruction of Chicago, in which nearly nine million people had perished, had happened early in 1933, the destruction of Rome a few months later.

Immediately after the destruction of Chicago, every large city in the world had enforced a strict blackout—but the blackout had not saved Rome.

Rome, although its blackout had been perfect, had gone the way of Chicago. Fortunately, however, that particular Arcturian ship—the one that destroyed Rome—had been captured by Dopelle with a few members of its crew alive.

Through the intervention of someone or something called Mekky (the author of *Is the Mistout Worth It?* assumed that all of his readers knew all about Mekky and therefore failed to explain) it had been learned from the surviving Arcturians in the ship that they had detectors which picked up hitherto unknown rays—not light rays—emitted by electrical incandescence.

They could thus locate a city through their detectors even though lights were burning inside closed buildings, for the buildings were as transparent to the so-called epsilon rays as they were to radio waves.

For a while it seemed that the only safety for Earth's cities lay in going back to candles or gaslight for illumination at night. (Electrical lighting could safely be used for interior lighting by day, for sunlight damped out the epsilon rays before they left the atmosphere.)

But Dopelle had retired to his laboratory and worked on the problem. He had discovered the nature of epsilon rays and had issued daily bulletins of his work to scientists all over the world who were, under his orders, trying to find some method of damping out these rays by night as effectively as sunlight damped them out by day.

The German professor had come up with the only practicable answer that had yet been found—the epsilon gas which formed the mistouts which were now required by the Greater Earth Council for all cities larger than a hundred thousand population.

It was a substance of strange properties indeed, this discovery of the Herr Professor Kurt Ebbing. Odorless, harmless to all forms of animal and vegetable life, it was impervious to light and to epsilon rays. It was inexpensively made from coal tar; one plant could turn out enough in a few hours each evening to mix with the air and completely blanket a city. And at dawn sunlight disintegrated it within the space of ten or fifteen minutes.

Since the discovery of the mistout, other Arc ships had been through the cordon but no major city of Earth had been attacked. The mistout worked.

A dozen smaller cities had been destroyed. Granting that the Arc ships would have chosen for attack the largest cities that their detectors showed, then a dozen large cities had been saved. Balancing the losses in the dozen smaller cities against the losses that *would* have been sustained had a dozen large cities been destroyed—as they would have been without their mistouts—it could be shown that the mistout had saved a probable ten million lives or more at a very minimum. Had New York or London been among the cities that, without the mistout, would have been destroyed, then the number of lives saved might have run many times that minimum figure of ten million.

But the mistout had taken lives, too. Law-enforcement agencies in most major cities had found themselves completely helpless to combat growing crime waves. Under cover of the mistout, the streets of most of the biggest cities had become no-man's-lands after dark. In New York, five thousand policemen had been killed before the police department—what was left of it—had abandoned the attempt to patrol the streets at night.

Vigilante methods had been tried and had failed.

The situation was aggravated by the strong tendency of combat veterans who had fought in space to turn to crime, a psychosis to which possibly a third of them succumbed.

In most of the largest cities—particularly in Paris, New York and Berlin—all attempt to keep order at night had finally been abandoned. After dark, the gangs and criminals held sway. Respectable citizens remained off the streets and stayed at home. Public transport service did not operate.

Strangely—but fortunately—most of the criminals confined their depredations to the open air. Burglaries were no more common than in the pre-mistout days. The citizen who stayed at home behind locked doors and windows was in no more danger than he had ever been. The nature of the *mistout psychosis,* as it was called, that underlay most urban crime, seemed to require that depredations be done under cover of that dense and dreadful dark.

There were both lone-wolf criminals and gangs, but the gangs were worse. Some gangs, such at the Nighters of New York, the Bloodies of London and the Lennies (Keith wondered if the name came from Lenin's) of Moscow, had adopted specialized techniques and seemed highly organized.

Hundreds died nightly in the biggest cities. The situation would have been even worse except for the fact that the hoodlums robbed and killed one another more often than honest citizens who stayed home.

The mistout was, the book admitted, a big price to pay for immunity of big cities to space attack. Possibly a million people had died in crimes in the mistout—but a minimum of ten million lives had undoubtedly been saved. Because of the mistout, the twelve flaming hells since Chicago and Rome had been small—expendable—cities. *Is the Mistout Worth It?* Yes, said the author, to the tune of at least nine million lives and probably many more than that.

Keith shivered a little as he put down *Is the Mistout Worth It?* If he'd bought that book in Greeneville and read it on the train, he'd have known better than to have left Grand Central Station. He'd have taken a cot there—or slept on the floor if all the cots were gone.

Very obviously, night life on Broadway wasn't what it had been where *he* came from.

He walked to the window and stood looking—well, not *out,* exactly, but at the blank blackness that was beyond the pane. The curtain wasn't pulled down, but that didn't matter on any but a first-floor window.

A few feet away, outside, one wouldn't be able to see the lighted window at all. It was an uncanny kind of blackness; he wouldn't have believed it if he hadn't been out in it.

And what was going on right now down there in the darkness of Forty-second Street, only half a block from Times Square, the center of the universe?

He shook his head in blank bewilderment. Criminals taking over Forty-second Street! Purple denizens of the moon walking down the main drag of Greeneville! General Eisenhower in charge of Venus Sector of Earth's space fleet in the war with Arcturus!

What mad universe was he in?

THE SEWING MACHINES RAMPANT

Well, whatever universe this was, he was here and he was stuck with it; and he was going to be in continuous danger until he learned the ropes well enough so he wouldn't risk making a fatal break every time he did or said anything.

Breaks just weren't safe in a spot where you could get yourself shot on sight as a spy on no provocation at all, where you could get yourself killed by being foolish enough to try to walk from Grand Central Station to Times Square after dark.

He'd better stay awake long enough to read some more.

Resolutely, he picked up the pocket edition of H. G. Wells' *Outline of History.* He was too tired by now to sit up any longer. He'd lie on the bed to read and, if he went to sleep, well, he'd read as long as he dared in the morning before he went out to face New York by day. And whatever New York was like by day, it would be an improvement over New York by night.

He folded the pillow under his head and started in on H. G. Wells. He skimmed lightly through the opening chapters, reading only key sentences here and there, turning pages rapidly, usually several at a time.

He'd happened to reread the book only a few months before and was quite familiar with it. There was nothing different about this copy of it—so far. Even the pictures were the same.

The dinosaurs, Babylon, the Egyptians, the Greeks, the Roman Empire, Charlemagne, the Middle Ages, the Renaissance, Columbus and America, the American Revolution, the Industrial Revolution—

Into Space.

That was the chapter heading, nine-tenths of the way through. He quit skimming and leafing over pages and started to read.

The year nineteen hundred and three. Professor George Yarley, an American scientist at Harvard University, had discovered the spacewarp drive.

Accidentally!

He had been working on, of all things, his wife's sewing machine, which had been broken and discarded. He was trying to rig it up so the treadle would run a tiny home-made generator to give him a high-frequency low-voltage current that he wanted to use in some class experiments in physics.

He'd finished making his connections—and fortunately he remembered afterwards just what they'd been and where he'd made his mistake—and he'd worked the treadle a few times when his foot stamped unexpectedly on the floor and he nearly fell forward out of his chair.

The sewing machine, treadle and generator and all, just wasn't there any more.

The professor, Wells humorously pointed out, had been sober at the time, but he'd quickly remedied that. After he'd sobered up, he borrowed his wife's new sewing machine and carefully duplicated the generator that was to run off the treadle. This time he saw the error in wiring which he'd made the first time and deliberately made the same mistake again.

He worked the treadle—and the new sewing machine was gone.

He didn't know what he had, but he knew he had *something*. He drew money from his bank account and bought two more sewing machines. One was for his wife to sew with. The other one he rigged exactly as the first two had been rigged.

And this time he got witnesses, including the president and the dean of the university. He didn't tell them what they were going to witness; he just told them to watch the sewing machine.

They did, and then the sewing machine wasn't there any more.

He had a little trouble convincing some of them that it wasn't a trick of prestidigitation, but when they were convinced—by the disappearance of the dean's wife's sewing machine from her own sewing room—they all admitted that he had something.

They relieved Yarley of his teaching duties and gave him a grant to finance further experimentation. He lost half a dozen more sewing machines and then he quit using sewing machines and began to get the thing down to the essential minima.

He found he could use a clockwork motor—connected in one particular way—to run the misconnected generator. The treadle wasn't essential—but an electric motor running the generator canceled something out and the thing wouldn't work. He found that he didn't need a bobbin or a flywheel but that the shuttle was necessary, and it had to be made of ferrous metal.

He found that he could use anything except electricity to run the generator. Besides foot power through a treadle and the clockwork motors, he tried a water wheel and his son's toy steam engine (and had to buy him a new one).

And he finally got it down to a comparatively simple layout of stuff mounted on a box—boxes were cheaper than sewing machines—powered with an inexpensive toy windup motor, the whole thing costing less than five dollars and taking only a few hours to make.

All he had to do then was wind the motor, push the lever, and—well, it went *somewhere*. Where it went or why it went he didn't know. But he kept experimenting.

Then one day there was a news story about something at first thought to be a meteor that had struck the side of a tall building in Chicago. Upon subsequent examination it proved to be what was left of a wooden box and some oddly assorted clockwork and electrical apparatus.

Yarley took the next train to Chicago and identified his handiwork.

He knew then that the thing had moved through *space,* and he had something to work on. Nobody had timed the striking of the object against the

Chicago building to an exact second, but as nearly as a time could be assigned to it, Yarley decided that the object had traveled from Cambridge to Chicago in approximately nothing flat.

The university gave him assistants, then, and he began experimenting in earnest, sending out the things in considerable numbers, each with an identifying serial number on it, and with an accurate record kept of variations in the number of windings, the exact number of turns given the clockwork motor, the direction in which it had been facing, and the time—to a fraction of a second—of its disappearance.

Also, he publicized what he was doing and got people watching for them all over the world.

Two, out of the thousands he sent, were reported. By comparison with his records he learned some crucial things. First, that the machine traveled in the exact direction of the axle of the generator part; second, that there was a relationship between the number of windings and the distance it traveled.

Now he could really go to work. By 1904 he had determined that the distance the machine traveled was proportionate to the cube of the number of turns or fractional turns on the generator and that the duration of the trip was actually and exactly zero seconds.

And by cutting the generators down to thimble size, he could send a machine for a comparatively short measured distance—a few miles—and make it land in a particular field outside of town.

It might have revolutionized transportation in general except for the fact that the machines were always damaged seriously, internally and externally, when they landed. Generally there was barely enough of them left for identification, not always that much.

And it wasn't going to make much of a weapon; explosives sent never arrived. They must have exploded en route, somewhere in the warp.

But in three years of experimentation they got it worked out to a nice formula and even began to understand the principles back of it as well as being able to predict the results.

They determined that the reason things were destroyed was their sudden materialization, at the end of the journey, in *air*. Air is pretty material stuff. You can't displace a quantity of it in nothing flat without damaging whatever does the displacing—not only damaging it as an object, but damaging its very molecular structure.

Obviously, the only practical place to which an object could be sent, and arrive intact, was space, open space. And since the distance increased as the *cube* of the number of windings it wouldn't take a very large machine to reach the moon, or even the planets. And even interstellar travel would not take a really monster one, especially as the thing could be done in several hops, each taking no longer in time than it took the pilot to press a button.

Furthermore, since time was a zero factor, no trajectories needed to be calculated. Simply aim directly at a destination, adjust the distance factor, press the button and there you were, materializing in space a safe distance from the planet, ready to descend and land.

Of course the moon was the first objective.

How to land took them a few years to work out. The science of aerodynamics hadn't been worked out very well yet—although two brothers named Wright had successfully flown a heavier-than-air machine at Kitty Hawk, N.C., a few years before—in the same year, in fact, in which Professor Yarley had lost his first sewing machine. And anyway there wasn't supposed to be any air on the moon.

But the method of landing was solved, and in 1910 the first man landed on the moon and returned safely.

The habitable planets were all reached within the next year.

The next chapter was *The Interplanetary War,* but Keith couldn't read it. It was three-thirty in the morning. He'd had a long day and things had happened to him. He simply couldn't hold his eyes open.

He didn't even undress any farther than he already had; he simply reached out and turned off the light, and was asleep almost before his head dropped back on the pillow.

It was nearly noon when he awakened. He lay there for a moment before opening his eyes, thinking of the crazy dream he'd had about a world with space travel—via sewing machine—and war with Arcturus and mistouts over New York.

He rolled over and his shoulder hurt so badly that he opened his eyes and saw an unfamiliar ceiling over his head. That was a shock, and it awakened him fully. He sat up in bed and looked at his wrist watch. Eleven forty-five! Hours late for his job.

Or was he?

He was horribly mixed up, disoriented. He got out of bed—a strange bed—and walked over to the window. Yes, he was on Forty-second Street, on the third floor, looking down at a normal street scene. Normal traffic and the sidewalks as crowded as ever, with ordinary-looking people wearing ordinary clothes. It was the New York he knew.

It *must* have been a dream, all of it. But then how did it happen that he was here on Forty-second Street?

He stood there, puzzling, trying to fit in his being here in New York into the scheme of things. The last thing he remembered that really made sense was sitting in a chair in Mr. Borden's garden. After that—

Could he have returned to New York other than in the way he seemed to remember—and have supplied, somehow, a nightmare to substitute for his memory of the trip? If so, he was overdue to see a psychiatrist.

Was he crazy? He must be. Yet *something* had happened to him. Unless he accepted the unacceptable, he couldn't remember how he got back to New York from Mr. Borden's estate, nor could he account for the fact that he was in a hotel room uptown instead of in his own diggings down in the Village.

And his shoulder was really sore. He put a hand to it and felt the bandage under his shirt. He'd been injured somehow, but surely not in the fantastic manner of his nightmare.

Well, he'd get out of here, go home and—he couldn't plan any farther than that just yet. He'd go home first and then decide.

He turned around and walked to the chair where he'd put some of his clothes. Something on the floor beside the bed caught his eye. It was a copy of the pocket edition of H. G. Wells' *Outline of History.*

His hands shook a little as he picked it up and opened it to the contents page. He looked at the names of the last three chapters. In order, they were: *Into Space, The Interplanetary War,* and *Struggle Against Arcturus.*

The book dropped out of his hand. He reached to pick it up and saw another one that had slid partly under the bed. It was named *Is the Mistout Worth It?*

He sat down in the chair and didn't do anything for a few minutes except to try to think, to adjust his mind to the fact that it hadn't been a nightmare; it had been reality.

Or a reasonable facsimile thereof.

Either he was stark mad or it had all really happened. Being chased by the purple monster. The mistout with its jungle savagery.

He reached for the hip pocket of the trousers hanging over the chair and got his wallet. The bills in it were credits, and not dollars. A little over a thousand credits.

He dressed slowly, thoughtfully, and walked back over to the window. It was still Forty-second Street and it still looked ordinary, but it didn't fool him now. He remembered what it had been like at one o'clock last night, and he shuddered a little.

And, looking for them, he began to notice things he hadn't noticed before. Most of the store fronts were familiar, but others were strange and he was almost sure they hadn't been there before.

Then, to top it off, he caught a flash of purple in the crowd. It was a purple monster, all right, walking into a novelty store across the street. And nobody was paying any more attention to it than to any of the human beings in the street.

He sighed deeply and got ready to leave. Packing consisted in putting the *Outline of History, The Story of Dopelle* and the two pulp magazines into various pockets. He decided not to take along the copy of *Is the Mistout Worth It?;* he'd got all he needed out of that. Nor the copy of yesterday's *New York Times.*

He went downstairs and out through the lobby. A different clerk was on duty and didn't even glance at him. The front door gave him pause for a moment because the glass in it was intact; then he noticed the fresh putty around the edges of the glass.

Now that he was fully awake he was hungry. Eating was the first order of business; he hadn't eaten since noon yesterday. He walked east until he found an inviting-looking little restaurant across from the Public Library.

He took a little table for one at the side and studied the menu. There was choice of a dozen entrees and all but three of them were familiar. The other three were all expensive items at the bottom of the list—Martian *zot à la Marseille,* roast *krail* with *kapi* sauce, and *gallina de luna.*

That last, if Keith remembered his Spanish, meant moon chicken. Some day, he decided, he was going to eat moon chicken, Martian *zot* and roast *krail,* but right now he was too hungry to experiment. He ordered goulash.

Goulash, for one thing, didn't require concentration. And while he ate, he skimmed through the final two chapters of the *Outline of History.*

H. G. Wells was bitter about the interplanetary war. He saw it purely as a war of conquest, with Earth the aggressor.

The inhabitants of the Moon and of Venus had proved friendly and exploitable, and they had been exploited. The intelligence of the tall, purple Lunans was about that of an African savage, but the Lunans were much more docile. They made excellent laborers and still better mechanics, once they had been introduced to the mysteries of machinery. The more industrious among them saved their wages and made sightseeing trips to Earth, but they never stayed here; two or three weeks was the maximum time one of them could remain healthy on Earth. For this same reason, employing them on Earth was impractical—and was forbidden by law after thousands of them had died within a few months of being imported to work as laborers here. The life span of a Lunan was about twenty years, on Luna; elsewhere— Earth, Venus, Mars, Callisto—none had ever lived longer than six months.

The Venusians, although almost as intelligent as Terrestrials, were creatures of a quite different nature. Interested solely in philosophy, the arts, and abstract mathematics, they had welcomed Earthmen, avid for the exchange of cultures and ideas. They had no practical civilization, no cities (or even houses), no possessions, machines or weapons.

Few in number, they were nomads who, aside from the life of the mind, lived as primitively as animals. They offered no barrier and every assistance— short of work—to man's colonization and exploitation of Venus. Earth had established four colonies there, aggregating a little short of a million people.

But Mars had been different.

The Martians had the silly idea that they didn't *want* to be colonized. They had, it turned out, a civilization at least equal to ours, except that they had not discovered space travel—possibly because, wearing no clothes, they had not developed sewing machines.

The Martians had greeted the first arrivals from Earth gravely and courteously (the Martians did everything gravely; they had no sense of humor) and had suggested that they return home and stay there. They had killed the second arrivals and the third.

And, although they had captured the spaceships in which these parties (except the first) had arrived, they had not bothered to use or copy the machines. They had no desire to leave Mars, ever. In fact, Wells pointed out, no Martian had ever left Mars alive, even during the interplanetary war.

A few, captured alive and put on Earth-bound ships for demonstration and study here, had willed themselves to death even before the ships had left the thin atmosphere of Mars.

This unwillingness or inability to live, even for minutes, off their own planet extended to Martian animals and plants. No single specimen of Martian fauna or flora graced zoos or botanical gardens of Earth.

The so-called interplanetary war, therefore, had been fought entirely on the surface of Mars. It had been a bitter struggle in which the Martian population had been several times decimated. They had, however, capitulated short of annihilation and had permitted colonization of Mars by Earthmen.

Of all the planets and their satellites in the Solar System, only four—Earth, the Moon, Venus, and Mars—had turned out to be inhabited by intelligent life. Saturn supported plant life of a strange sort and a few of the moons of Jupiter bore plant life and wild animals.

Man had met his match—an aggressive, colonizing race of intelligent beings—only when he went beyond the Solar System. The Arcturians had had the space drive for many centuries. It was only by chance—for the galaxy is very wide indeed—that they had not yet visited the Sun's planets. When they learned of us through an encounter near Proxima Centauri, they set about to remedy that omission.

The current war with Arcturus was, on Earth's part, a defensive war—although it involved such offensive tactics as we could muster. And thus far the war had been a stalemate, defensive tactics on both sides being adequate to block any sustained offensive action. Only occasional ships of either side managed to penetrate defensive cordons and to wreak damage.

By fortunate early capture of a few Arc ships, Earth had quickly overcome the technological handicap of several centuries under which it had started in the war.

Currently, thanks to the genius and leadership of Dopelle, Earth had a slight advantage in some ways, although basically it was still a war of attrition.

Dopelle! That name again. Keith put down the H. G. Wells book and started to take *The Story of Dopelle* from his pocket when he realized that he had long since finished eating and had no further excuse for sitting there.

He paid for his meal and went out. The steps of the library across the street looked inviting. He could sit there and read some more.

But there was his job to be considered.

Did he work for the Borden Publishing Company—here and now—or didn't he? If he did, having missed a Monday morning might not be unforgivable. Missing a whole day might be.

And it was well after one o'clock already.

Should he call up first and try to get as much information as he could before he dared make a personal appearance? It seemed the logical and sensible thing to do.

He went into the cigar store on the next corner. There was a short line waiting in front of the phone booth. Annoying as waiting in line was, it enabled him to solve the minor question of how pay telephones were operated in a coinless country. As each caller ahead of him in the line left the phone booth he walked to the cash register and made payment in paper currency of the amount that showed on a register on top of the phone booth. When payment had been made, the cashier pressed a button and the register reverted to zero.

Probably there had been such a register atop the booth in the drugstore in Greeneville and he had failed to notice it. And since his call there had not been completed, the dial pointers had remained at zero.

Fortunately, none of those ahead of him made long calls and he reached the booth in a few minutes.

He dialed the Borden Publications number, realizing as he did so that he really should have looked it up in the directory while he was waiting; it might or might not be the same number that he knew.

But a voice that sounded like that of Marion Blake, the receptionist, said, "Borden Publications."

Keith said, "Is Mr. Winton there? Mr. Keith Winton?"

"No, sir. Mr. Winton is not here. Who is calling, please?"

"Never mind. I'll call tomorrow."

He hung up quickly before she could ask any more questions. He hoped she hadn't recognized his voice; he didn't think she had.

He paid half a credit at the cash register, and he realized now that he could and should have got more value for that half credit. He should have asked whether Keith Winton was out to lunch or out of town—or if they didn't know where he was. But it was too late now unless he wanted to stand in line again.

And suddenly he was in a hurry to get there and find out the worst, no matter how dangerous it might be.

He walked rapidly the few blocks to the office building in which Borden Publications occupied all of the tenth floor.

He took the elevator up, and took a deep breath as he stepped out of it.

A COCKTAIL FROM CALLISTO

He stood before that familiar, beautiful door that he had always admired so. It was one of the very modern ones that look like nothing more than a sheet of glass with a futuristic chrome handle on it. The hinges were either hidden or invisible. The lettering *Borden Publications, Inc.* was just below eye height, small and chaste, in chrome letters that were suspended right inside the thick glass.

Keith took the handle very carefully, as he always did, so he wouldn't fingerprint that beautiful sheet of nothingness, opened the door and went in.

There was the same mahogany railing, the same pictures—hunting prints—on the walls. And the same plump little Marion Blake with the same pouting red lips and upswept brunet hair-do, sitting at the same stenographer-receptionist desk back of the railing. She was the first person he'd seen that he *knew* since—Lord, was it only since seven o'clock yesterday evening? It seemed like weeks. For a dizzy moment he wanted to jump over that railing and kiss Marion Blake.

He'd seen familiar things and familiar places, but not a familiar person, until now. True, the address on the contents page of the copy of *Surprising Stories* (at 2 cr.) had told him that the Borden Publications was still here, still in business at the same old stand, but he found now that he hadn't really believed it until he saw that Marion Blake was still receptionist.

For just a second, the familiar sight of her there, and the fact that everything else about the office was just as he remembered it made him doubt his memory of the past eighteen hours.

It couldn't be, it simply *couldn't*—

Then Marion had turned and was looking up at him and there wasn't a trace of recognition in her face.

"Yes?" she asked, a bit impatiently.

Keith cleared his throat. Was she kidding? Didn't she know him, or was she just acting funny?

He cleared his throat again. "Is Mr. Keith Winton in? I'd like to speak to him, please."

That could pass as a gag to counter hers; if she grinned now, he could grin back. She said, "Mr. Winton has left for the day, sir."

"Uh—Mr. Borden. Is he in?"

"No, sir."

"Is Bet—Miss Hadley in?"

"No, sir. Nearly everybody left at one o'clock. That's the regular closing time this month."

"The reg— Oh." He stopped himself in time before he could pull a boner by being incredulous about something he undoubtedly should know. "I forgot," he finished lamely. He wondered why one o'clock in the afternoon would be the regular closing time and why this month in particular.

"I'll be in tomorrow then," he said. "Uh—what would be the best time to catch Mr. Winton?"

"About seven."

"*Sev*—" He caught himself starting to echo her again. Did she mean seven in the morning or seven in the evening? Must be the morning; seven m the evening would be almost time for the mistout.

And then suddenly he guessed the answer and it was so simple he wondered why he hadn't thought of it sooner.

Of course working hours would be different in a city with the mistout, a city in which the streets were sudden death after dark, a city without normal night life. The hours of work would *have* to be different in order to give employees any personal lives at all.

It would change things completely when one had to be home before dark, probably well before, in order to assure safety. The working day would be from six or seven in the morning—an hour or so after the early sunshine dissolved the mist—until one or two o'clock in the afternoon. And that would give people afternoons as the equivalent of evenings, for recreation.

It would have to be that way, of course. He wondered why he hadn't thought of it when he was reading the book on the mistout.

And it was good news. It meant that Broadway wasn't necessarily as dead as he had pictured it. There would be shows and dances and concerts, but they'd all be in the afternoon instead of the evening. Probably matinees were held in the morning. And instead of night clubs there'd be afternoon clubs.

Everybody would be safely home in bed by, say, seven or eight o'clock and would sleep till four or five o'clock so they'd be up and dressed by dawn.

And since dawn and darkness didn't come at the same times all the year around, working hours would be varied according to the season of the year. That's why one o'clock was the closing time *this* month. Probably it was regulated by local ordinance, because Marion had expected him to know it and had appeared surprised when he didn't.

Marion, he noticed, was putting things into the drawer of her desk, getting ready to leave. She looked up again as though wondering why he was still there.

He said, "Isn't your name Blake? Marion Blake?"

Her eyes widened a little. "Why, yes. But I don't—"

"I thought I remembered you, but I wasn't sure right away," Keith said. He was thinking fast, remembering things he'd heard Marion say about herself, girl friends he'd heard her mention, where she lived, what she did.

He said, "A girl named Estelle—I forgot her last name—introduced us at a dance in—wasn't it Queens?" He laughed a little. "I was with Estelle that night. Isn't it funny, that I can't remember her last name, but I remember both of your names, when I danced with you only once?"

She dimpled at him for that compliment. She said, "You must be right, even if I don't remember it. I live in Queens and go to dances there. And I've got a girl friend named Estelle Rambow. So you couldn't have made that all up, I guess."

"I wouldn't expect you to remember my name," Keith said. "It was months ago. I'm Karl Winston. I'm sure you made an impression on me, though, because I still remember that you told me you worked for a magazine publisher. Only I'd forgotten which one, so I wasn't expecting to see you when I came in here. And I remember you told me that you wrote—poetry, wasn't it?"

"I wouldn't really call it poetry, Mr. Winston. Just verse, really."

"Call me Karl," Keith said, "since we're old friends, even if you don't remember me. You're leaving now?"

"Why, yes. I just had two letters to finish after one o'clock and Mr. Borden said if I'd finish them I could come in half an hour late tomorrow morning." She glanced at the clock over her desk and smiled ruefully. "Guess I got hooked on the deal, though. The letters were long ones; took me almost an hour."

"Anyway, I'm glad you were still here," Keith said. "Will you have a drink with me?"

She hesitated. "Well—just one drink. I've got to be out in Queens by two-thirty. I've got a date then."

"Fine," Keith said. He was glad she did have a date, because over one drink he could find out a few things he wanted to know and yet he didn't want to be stuck with Marion for the whole afternoon.

They took the elevator down and he let Marion choose the place, which turned out to be a little bar around the corner on Madison, one he'd never been in before.

Over a pair of Callisto cocktails (Keith had ordered one when Marion had; he found it too sweet but not undrinkable), he said, "I think I mentioned to you that night that I'm a writer—doing feature stuff up to now. But I've decided to take a flyer at some pulp fiction. I've done a little of it already."

"Oh. That's why you came up to the office?"

"Yes, I wanted to talk to Winton—or to Mr. Borden or Miss Hadley—to find out what kind of stuff is needed right now. And what lengths and so on."

"Well, I can tell you some of it. I think they're fairly well stocked on both westerns and detective stories. Miss Hadley is looking for shorter lengths for her love book and I understand they can use both short and long stuff for the adventure books."

"How about science-fiction? I think I'd be best at that."

Marion Blake looked at him in surprise. "Oh, you've heard about that, then?"
"About what?"

"That Borden's going to start a science-fiction magazine."

Keith opened his mouth—and closed it again quickly before he could put his foot in it. He mustn't be surprised at anything. So he took a slow sip of his Callisto cocktail and thought instead. There was a catch somewhere.

Why would Marion say that Borden was starting *a* science-fiction magazine? Borden published *Surprising Stories* all right; he had a copy in his pocket to prove it, and he'd seen that it had the Borden imprint. Why wouldn't Marion say Borden was starting *another* science-fiction magazine, then?

Since he didn't know why, he answered cautiously, "I did hear a rumor to that effect. Is it true?"

"It's true, all right. They've got one issue dummied up and ready to go to press. They'll start it as a quarterly with a fall issue, and if it sells well on the stands they'll make it a monthly. And they do need material for it; all they've got beyond the first issue is one lead novel and a short or two."

Keith nodded and took a sip at his drink. "What do you think of the science-fiction field?" he asked.

"I think we should have put out a science-fiction magazine a long time ago. It's the only important field we haven't got a magazine in."

Keith casually reached into his back pocket and took the folded copy of *Surprising Stories* from it—the copy he'd bought in Greeneville and hadn't had time to read yet, because he'd given precedence to the *New York Times, Is the Mistout Worth It?* and H. G. Wells.

Casually he put it down on the table to see what comment Marion would make about it, just after she'd said that Borden didn't have a book in the science-fiction field.

He watched her closely and saw her glance at the cover of the magazine.

She said, "Oh, I see you've been reading our top adventure book."

As simple as that, Keith thought. And again, why hadn't he had sense enough to think of the answer himself? Why, of course. In a world where interplanetary travel and interstellar war and purple moon monsters were actual fact, cold reality, then stories about such things would be *adventure* stories, and not science-fiction at all.

But if stuff like that was merely adventure, then what in hell would science-fiction be? He made a mental note to buy some science-fiction magazines the very first chance he had. They would really be something to read.

He looked back at *Surprising Stories.* "It's a good magazine, all right," he said. "I'd like to write for it."

"Mr. Winton needs material, I guess. He'll be glad to talk to you if you come in tomorrow morning. Do you have any stories ready?"

"Not exactly. I've got a lot of half-baked ideas, and I thought I'd like to talk to him first before I go ahead with any of them. So I don't bake the wrong ones."

"Do you know Mr. Winton, Mr. Winston? Say, your names are a lot alike, aren't they? Keith Winton, Karl Winston. Maybe that won't be too good."

He answered the question first. "No, I've never met Mr. Winton. Yes, our names are a lot alike—same initials, too, since I spell Karl with a K. But why may that not be too good?"

"Sounds a little like a pen name, that's all. I mean, if stories by Karl Winston appear in Keith Winton's magazines, a lot of people are going to think they're his own stuff under a thinly disguised pen name. And probably he wouldn't like that."

Keith nodded. "I can see that, now that you mention it. Well, it doesn't matter because I'll probably do fiction under a different name anyway. My feature stories are under my own name, except of course things I've ghost-written. But I'd already decided to use a pen name for fiction."

He took another sip of the almost sickeningly sweet Callisto and decided he'd never order another one.

He asked, "Can you tell me something about this Keith Winton, by the way?"

"Why—what do you want to know?"

He gestured vaguely. "Oh, anything to give me a line on him. What he looks like. What he eats for breakfast. How tough an editor he is."

"Well—" Marion Blake frowned thoughtfully. "He's tallish, a little taller than you, and slender. Dark. Wears shell-rimmed glasses. About thirty, I think. Kind of serious-looking." She giggled a little, suddenly. "Guess he's more serious than usual lately, but you can't blame him for that."

"Why not?"

She said archly, "He's in love—I think."

Keith managed a smile. "With you?"

"*Me?* He never even *sees* me. No, with our new love book editor, the super-beautiful Miss Betty Hadley. Not that it does him any good, of course."

Keith wanted to know why, but that "of course" warned him off. When people say "of course" they mean one is already supposed to know. But how—since he had already said he didn't know Keith Winton and hadn't said he did know Betty Hadley—could he be expected to know why being in love with Betty Hadley wasn't going to do Keith Winton any good?

Still, if he could keep Marion talking, he might find out without asking.

"Kind of tough on him, huh?" he said.

"I'll say." Marion sighed deeply. "Gee, I guess any girl in the world would give her eye teeth and her right arm to swap places with Betty Hadley."

He couldn't ask why, but he could keep fishing. He asked, "Would you?"

"Would *I?* Are you kidding, Mr. Winston? To be fiancée of the greatest man in the world? The smartest, the handsomest, the bravest, the most romantic, the most—*golly!*"

"Oh," said Keith, a bit flatly in spite of himself.

He gulped the rest of his drink and almost gagged on it. He raised a finger to the waitress and, as she came toward the booth, asked Marion, "Have another?"

"I'm afraid I haven't time." She glanced at her watch. "No, I haven't. Anyway, I've got almost half of this one left. You go ahead and have another, but not me."

Keith looked up at the waitress. "One Manhattan, please."

"Sorry, I don't believe I've ever heard of that one, sir. Is it a new drink?"

"Martini?"

"Oh, sure. The blue or the pink?"

Keith suppressed a shudder. "Do you have straight whiskey?"

"Of course. Any particular brand?"

He shook his head, not wanting to tempt fate any farther than that. He hoped the whiskey would be neither pink nor blue.

He looked back at Marion, wondering how he could keep her talking and get her to tell who Betty Hadley's fiancée was. Apparently he was supposed to know. And maybe he *did* know, for that matter; at least, a horrible suspicion had come to him.

Marion confirmed it without further prodding. A dreamy look came into her eyes.

"Gee," she murmured. *"Dopelle!"* It sounded reverent; almost like a prayer.

MEKKY

Well, Keith thought, now he knew the worst. And anyway, she was only engaged and not married. Maybe there was still a chance, no matter how slim a chance.

Marion sighed again. She said, "I think she is a fool, though. Agreeing to wait until after the war is over. And who knows how long the war will last? And insisting on keeping her job as an editor, when Dopelle has as much money as he wants to have, and—still, I suppose she'd go nuts waiting if she didn't have a job to handle. Golly, I'd go nuts waiting for *Dopelle,* even if I *had* a job."

"You have got a job."

"But I haven't got Dopelle." Marion took a sip of her drink and sighed so deeply that Keith was afraid she'd attract attention to their table.

Keith's whiskey came, and it was amber and not blue or pink. Furthermore, a sip of it convinced him that it not only tasted like whiskey, but *was* whiskey. He downed it neat as Marion took the last sip of her Callisto cocktail. It made him feel a little better. Not much better.

Marion stood up. "Got to go," she said. "Thanks for the drink, Mr. Winston. You'll be in at the office tomorrow?"

"Tomorrow or the next day," Keith said. He'd already decided he might as well have a story with him when he went in. Two or three, if he could turn them out fast enough—and he thought he knew a way in which he could turn them out that fast.

He walked with Marion to the subway, and then headed for the public library.

That wasn't where he wanted to go. He wanted to go back to the bar he'd just left—or any other bar—and hang one on. But common sense told him that would be fatal. Probably quite literally fatal. He could get into enough trouble here when he was cold sober.

But he'd just taken two very tough punches. First, he *didn't* have a job here; the Keith Winton who worked for Borden not only wasn't he but didn't even look like him. He was about the same age, and that was all. Second, Betty

Hadley was not only engaged but engaged to someone so incredibly romantic that—that it was incredible.

In the library, he went upstairs to the general reading room and took a seat at one of the tables. He didn't send in a slip for books; he had with him more than he could read in one afternoon. And besides his reading, he had plans to make.

He took out of his pockets the three publications he'd bought and hadn't read yet—the copies of *Surprising Stories* and *Perfect Love Stories* and Paul Gallico's *The Story of Dopelle*.

He frowned at the pocket edition. From the little he'd heard and read about Dopelle—and it was little only because he'd been in this screwy place less than twenty hours—the guy had the whole Solar System in his pocket. He practically ran the place—and he had Betty Hadley too.

He picked up the book and put it down again. Once he started it, he wanted to read it through, and that would take more time than he could afford this afternoon.

Since he wasn't a pulp magazine editor, he had a living to make, and he had to start making it right suddenly; the money he had left from the Greeneville episode wasn't going to last him very long. And his idea for making a living was contingent upon his study of these two—and other—magazines.

He took up *Surprising Stories* first. He studied the contents page, comparing it with his memory of the contents he had sent to press for the July issue. All of the authors were the same, right down the line. Some of the story titles were the same, others had been changed.

Before he started reading, he skimmed through, glancing at the illustrations. In each of them was the same subtle difference he had noticed in the cover picture. They had been done by the same artists—or by artists having the same names and the same general styles—but they were more vivid, had more action. The girls were more beautiful and the monsters were more horrible. Horribly more horrible.

He started in on the shortest of the short stories and read it carefully, analytically. The plot was as he remembered it, but there were differences in the setting and in the surrounding circumstances. He finished it still vaguely puzzled, but with the glimmerings of an idea.

He sat and thought a few minutes and the idea clarified. He didn't read the other stories, but he skimmed them, paying little attention to the plots or characters, concentrating on settings and background.

His idea had been right. The difference between these stories and the ones he remembered putting in the issue was that the backgrounds, the settings of these stories coincided. Each writer described Martians the same way, Venusians the same. Spaceships all worked on the same principle—the one he'd read about in the H. G. Wells book. The only space-war stories concerned either the Earth-Mars war of the early planetary colonization days or the current Earth-Arcturus conflict.

Marion Blake had been right, of course, in classifying *Surprising Stories* as an adventure magazine, not one in the science-fiction field. The backgrounds were—in this mad universe he found himself in—*true*. Situations and settings were authentic, and consistent with one another.

Adventure stories, pure and simple.

He smacked the book down on the table in front of him, drawing a reproving glance from the librarian.

But, he thought, there must *be* science-fiction magazines here or Borden wouldn't be starting one. And, if these stories were not science-fiction, what would science-fiction be? He'd buy some and find out.

He picked up the Dopelle book and stared at it bitterly again. *Dopelle!* He hated the guy. But anyway, he knew now how to pronounce his name, having heard Marion say it; it was pronounced as though it were French—Dough-PELL, only two syllables and the accent on the second.

He frowned at it. That book, much as he was going to hate it, came next on his course of reading. But should he start it here and now? He glanced at the big library clock and decided not. There were even more important things to do and they all had to be done before dark, before the mistout.

He had to find a place to stay and a way to make money so he could keep on eating. He didn't dare let himself get down to the end of his resources until he had a way to bring in more money.

He took out his wallet and counted what he had left out of the two thousand credits—the two hundred dollars, approximately—the Greeneville druggist had given him. There was just about half of it left.

Enough, maybe, to last him a week if he was careful. Certainly not longer than that, since he'd have to buy some clothes and toilet articles and heaven knew what else, starting from scratch.

Or did he, in this universe, still have a closet and a bureau full of clothes in a nice little two-room bachelor apartment down on Gresham Street in Greenwich Village?

He considered the possibility and discarded it as too slight to consider seriously. The Keith Winton who had his job probably had his apartment too. He knew by now that this universe didn't have any neat niche for him to fit into. He'd have to make one for himself. And a precarious job it was going to be.

But *where* was he? *How* did he get here? *Why?*

He shoved those wonderings resolutely aside. There must be an answer, maybe even a way back. But survival came first, and his mind must be free to plan—and to plan intelligently. How best could he parlay a hundred bucks' worth of credits into a future?

He thought and planned, and after a while he went to the desk and borrowed a pencil and paper from the librarian. He returned to his table and began to make a list of the things he'd need. Its length appalled him.

But when he put down approximate figures and added them up, it wasn't as bad as he'd feared. He could do it all for about four hundred credits and have six hundred to live on. If he picked a cheap hotel and ate at inexpensive restaurants, he could hold out for ten days, possibly even two weeks, on that much.

He went out of the library and headed first for the tobacco store across from it whose telephone he had used a few hours before.

Might as well, he thought, eliminate the remote possibility first. He looked up Keith Winton in the phone book; the name was listed and the telephone number and address were the same.

He went into the booth—there was no line in front of it now—and called the number.

A voice said, "Keith Winton speaking."

He hung up quietly. That was that.

He headed for the nearest dime store and started his buying there, realizing that he couldn't afford to be fastidious if he was going to stay within his means. He started with a small cardboard suitcase, the cheapest that he could find, at twenty-nine and a half credits. He went on down the list—socks, handkerchiefs, razor, toothbrush—

Gauze bandage and an antiseptic for his shoulder, pencil, eraser, a ream of white paper and a ream of yellow—the list seemed almost endless. And when he'd added a few shirts from a cheap haberdashery, the suitcase was almost full.

He had the suit he was wearing sponged and pressed while he waited in a cubicle at the back of a cleaner's shop. He had his shoes shined.

His final purchase, and it left him a little under six hundred credits, was a dozen pulp magazines of various kinds. He took his time picking them out, with a special purpose in mind.

It was while he was in a drugstore making that final purchase that the crowd must have gathered. When he came out of the store the edge of the sidewalk was lined half a dozen deep and, from a block or so down the street, came the sound of wild cheering.

Keith hesitated a moment and then stood still, backed against the window of the drugstore. He wanted to see what was coming, but he stood a better chance of seeing from there, over the heads of the crowd, than if he tried to work his way nearer to the curb, especially impeded as he was with suitcase and magazines.

Something or someone was coming. The cheering grew nearer. Keith saw that all traffic had stopped and pulled toward the curbs. Two policemen on motorcycles came along and behind them was a car with a uniformed man at the wheel.

There wasn't anyone in the back seat of the car but, above it, floating in mid-air about ten feet above the car and keeping pace with it, was *something*.

It was a round, featureless, blank metal sphere a little larger than a basketball.

The cheering grew as it came nearer. Auto horns honked and the din became almost deafening.

He heard words now that were part of the cheers and recognized one of them. "Mekky! *Mekky! MEKKY!*" And someone beside him yelled, "Get the Arcs for us, Mekky!"

And then the incredible thing happened.

Over or under the cheering, Keith suddenly heard a voice that wasn't a cheering, yelling voice. It was a calm, clear voice that seemed to come from everywhere or nowhere.

"An interesting situation, Keith Winton," it said. *"Come see me sometime and we'll investigate it."*

Keith started violently and looked around him. No one near him was looking at him. But the suddenness with which he turned made the man next to him turn and look.

"Did you hear that?" Keith demanded.

"Hear what?"

"Something about—about a Keith Winton?"

"You're crazy," the man said. His eyes left Keith's and went to the street again, and he yelled at the top of his voice, "Mekky! 'Ray for Mekky!"

Keith stumbled out from against the building to the narrow open area of sidewalk between the crowd at the curb and the crowd at the back of the sidewalk. He tried to keep pace with the car and the thing that floated above it, the basketball-sized sphere. He had the strangest feeling that it was that *thing* that had spoken to him.

If so, it had called him by name and no one else had heard it. Now that he thought of it, that voice hadn't seemed to come from outside at all; it had been inside his head. And it had been a flat mechanical-sounding voice. Not a human voice at all.

Was he going crazy?

Or was he already crazy?

But whether or not, and whatever the explanation, he had a blind impulse not to lose sight of—of whatever that basketball was. *It had called him by name.*

Maybe it knew the answer to why he was here, to what had happened to the world as he, Keith Winton, knew it—to the sane world in which there'd been two world wars but no interplanetary ones, to the world in which he'd been editor of a science-fiction magazine which—*here*—was an adventure magazine and was edited by someone who had the name of Keith Winton but didn't even look like him.

"Mekky!" the crowd was roaring. "Mekky! Mekky!"

Mekky must be the name of the sphere. And maybe Mekky had the answers. Mekky had said, *"Come see me sometime"*!

Sometime, hell! If there were answers, he wanted them now.

He stumbled into people, his suitcase banged legs. He drew sharp looks and sharp words. But he paid no attention to either; he kept going, not quite keeping up with the pace of the car out in the street, but not losing much ground either.

And the voice came inside his head again. *"Keith Winton,"* it said. *"Stop. Don't follow. You'll be sorry."*

He started to yell his answer over the roar of the cheering. "Why?" he yelled. "Who are—?"

And then he realized that people were hearing him, even over the sounds of their own voices, and were turning to stare.

"Don't attract attention," the voice said. *"Yes, I can read your thoughts. Yes, I am Mekky. Do as you have planned and see me about three months from now."*

"Why?" Keith thought, desperately. "Why so long?"

"A crisis in the war," said the voice. *"The survival of the human race is at stake. The Arcturians can win. I have no time for you now."*

"But what shall I do?"

"As you have planned," the voice said. *"And be careful, more careful than you have been. You are in danger every moment."*

Keith tried desperately to frame within his mind a question that would give him the answer he sought. "But what has happened? Where am I?"

"Later," said the voice within his mind. *"Later I will try to solve your problem. I do not know the answer now, although I perceive the problem clearly, through your mind."*

"Am I insane?"

"No, and do not make one fatal error. This is real; it is not a figment of your imagination. Your danger here is real and this world is real. If you are killed here, you will be very dead."

There was a second's pause, then: *"I have no more time for you now. Please stop following."*

Abruptly, in Keith's mind, before he could frame another frantic question and before he could again hear the sounds of cheering voices and tooting auto horns, there was a sensation of silence. Whatever had been in his mind had withdrawn. He knew that without knowing how he knew, and he knew that thinking further questions would be useless; there'd be no answers.

Obedient to the last order he stopped walking. He stopped so suddenly that someone bumped into him from behind and snarled at him.

He caught his balance and let the man past, then stood staring down the street, over the heads of the crowd, at the sphere that was floating away from him, out of his life.

What was it? What kept it up there? Was it alive? How could it have read his mind?

Whatever it was, it seemed to know who he was and what his problem was—and it had said that it could solve that problem.

He didn't want to let it go. Wait three months? Impossible, when there was even a remote chance of getting the answer now!

But the sphere was already half a block away; he couldn't possibly keep up with it, through that crowd on the sidewalk, while he was burdened with the suitcase and the armful of magazines. He looked about him wildly and saw that he was in front of a cigar store.

He darted in and put the suitcase and magazines down on a soft drink cooler near the entrance.

He said, "Back in just a second. Thanks for watching these," and ran out again before the proprietor could protest. Possibly he'd lose all the stuff he'd just bought, taking a chance like that, but right now following that sphere was the most important thing in his life.

Outside again he could go faster. Pushing his way ruthlessly as fast as he could walk, he held his ground half a block behind the car and the motorcycles and even gained a little.

They turned south on Third Avenue, went south to Thirty-seventh Street and turned east again. Just around the corner there was a big crowd gathered. The motorcycles and the car stopped just at the edge of the crowd.

But the sphere that had floated above the car didn't stop. It floated on and up, over the heads of the cheering people. Up, up, to an open window in the fourth floor of an apartment building on the north side of the street.

A woman was leaning out of the window. She was Betty Hadley.

Keith Winton got to the edge of the crowd and didn't try to push his way into it; he could see better from here than closer in against the building.

The cheering was tremendous. Besides the cheers for Mekky, he could hear cheers for Betty Hadley and for Dopelle. He wondered if Dopelle was here—but couldn't see anyone who seemed likely to be the world's greatest hero. All eyes of the crowd were on Mekky, the sphere, or on Betty Hadley, leaning out of the window, smiling. And looking more beautiful, more desirable than he had ever seen her.

She was dressed, what he could see of her, in the sort of costume heroines wore on the covers of science-fiction magazines—a scarlet bra that outlined perfect hemispheres, bare (and perfect) shoulders and arms, bare midriff, and below that—well, he presumed she had on something below that, but she wasn't leaning far enough out of the window for him to tell.

The sphere floated upward until it was level with and just beside the open window from which Betty Hadley leaned; it poised there, a few inches from her white shoulder. It hovered there; whether it was facing Betty or the crowd below, in the case of a featureless sphere, Keith found it impossible to guess.

It spoke. This time, from the very first word, Keith knew somehow that it was speaking in the minds of the entire crowd, not to him individually. The cheering didn't stop; there was no need for it to slacken for everyone to hear; the words were heard through the mind and not through the ears. One could hear both the cheering and the words of the sphere, and one didn't interfere with the other.

"*Friends,*" said the voice, "*I leave you now to bear a message from my master and creator, Dopelle, to Miss Hadley. It is a private message, naturally.*

"*I thank you for the reception you have given me. And, from my master, I bring this message to all of you: The situation is still critical and we must all do our best. But be of good cheer. There is hope for victory. We must and we shall win.*"

"Mekky!" the crowd roared. "Dopelle!" "Betty!" "Victory!" "Down with Arcturus!" "Mekky, *Mekky, MEKKY!*"

Betty Hadley, Keith saw, was still smiling, her cheeks flushed with embarrassment at the adulation of the crowd. She bowed once more and then withdrew her head and shoulders inside the window. The sphere floated in after her.

The crowd began to disperse.

Keith groaned. He tried to hurl a thought at the sphere, but he knew it was too late. It would pay no attention to him even if it received the thought.

Well, it had warned him. If it had been inside his mind it knew how he felt about Betty Hadley and it had warned him not to follow. It had known how he would react to seeing Betty again under circumstances like that. It tried to save him from the bitterness and despair he was feeling now.

It hadn't meant much—not too much, that is—when Marion Blake had told him that Betty was engaged. As long as she wasn't actually married, he'd thought, there was still hope. He'd dared to think he could make her forget this Dopelle.

But—what a chance! Far more than anything he'd read or heard about that magnificent hero, the exhibition he'd just seen had made him realize what a personage Dopelle must be. "My master and creator," Mekky, the miraculous sphere, had called him. And all New York cheering him when he wasn't even there!

What chance had he, Keith Winton—less than a nonentity, an *un*entity, in this universe—to take away the fiancée of a guy like that!

THE DOPE ON DOPELLE

He walked back moodily to the cigar store where he'd left his suitcase and magazines. They were still there and he apologized to the proprietor for the manner of his leaving them, and bought a carton of cigarettes to make amends.

The streets were beginning to empty when he came out of the cigar store. He realized that it must be getting near dusk and that he must find a place to stay.

He hunted until, on Eighth Avenue near Fortieth Street, he found an inexpensive little hotel where, for a hundred and twenty credits in advance, he took a room for a week. He left his suitcase and magazines in the room, went down again to eat in a cheap chili restaurant, and then returned to his room for a long evening of reading and study.

He picked up one of the pulp magazines. Now to test the feasibility of his plan. If, that is, it needed testing; it must be sound since Mekky, the sphere, had told him to go ahead with it.

For a while, a long while, he couldn't really concentrate. Betty Hadley's face, with its aura of golden blond hair, its smooth creamy skin and kissable red lips, kept getting in the way. Not to mention Betty Hadley's beautiful body as he had seen it at her window, clad (as far as he could tell) only in a form-fitting scarlet bra.

Why hadn't he had sense enough to obey the sphere's orders not to follow it—and get himself in a mood like this, just when he had to be able to think more clearly than he'd ever thought before.

For a long time Betty kept getting between him and the magazine, and the hopelessness of his ever getting her made what he was trying to do seem futile and useless. But after a while, in spite of himself, he began to get interested in his reading. And he began to see that what he had hoped to do might be really possible.

Yes, he ought to be able to make himself a living writing—for some of these magazines, if not for others. Five years earlier, before he'd started working for Borden, Keith had done quite a bit of free-lancing. He'd sold a number of stories, and he'd written a number that hadn't sold.

In fact, his batting average had been about fifty-fifty, and—for a writer who wasn't too prolific and who had difficulty in plotting—that hadn't been too good. Besides, his stories hadn't come easily; he'd had to sweat them out. So when a chance at an editorial job had come, he'd taken it.

But now, with five years of editing under his belt, he thought he could do better at stories than he had before. He could see now what a lot of his mistakes had been—laziness among them. And laziness is curable.

Besides, this time he had plots to start with—the plots of all the unsold stories he could remember. He thought he could do better with them now than he'd done five years ago, a lot better.

He went through magazine after magazine of the pile of them that he had bought, skimming all the stories, reading some of them. Darkness fell outside and the blank blackness of the mistout pressed against the pane of his window, but he kept on reading.

One thing became increasingly obvious to him—he couldn't, and didn't dare try to, place stories in a setting with which he was as unfamiliar as he was with the world about him. He'd make mistakes, little mistakes if not big ones, that would give him away, that would show his unfamiliarity with the details of life here. Stories of the present were definitely out.

Fortunately, that still left him two fields. From his reading of Wells' *Outline of History* he knew that the differences here all dated from those vanishing sewing machines of 1903. He'd be on sure ground on any story written as a costume piece and placed before 1903. Luckily, he'd been a history major at college and was pretty familiar with the eighteenth and nineteenth centuries, particularly in America.

He noticed with satisfaction that the pulp magazines carried a fair percentage of historical stories, costume pieces; a far higher percentage of them than had pulp magazines of where he'd come from. Possibly because, here, there was a wider difference between life of today and life of the colonial and pioneer times, the settings of the eighteenth and nineteenth centuries were quite popular in some of the adventure magazines. *Surprising Stories* was an exception to that rule, seeming to specialize exclusively in modern adventure in space. To balance it, Borden published another pulp adventure magazine, *Romantic Adventure Stories,* which specialized exclusively in historicals—Civil War and Revolutionary War stories predominating. He noticed that it, also, was edited by Keith Winton.

Even the love pulps, he was both surprised and pleased to learn, carried a fair percentage of love stories in historical settings. That was a field he hadn't counted on; it made three fields available to him.

The other was, of course, science-fiction. He studied three science-fiction magazines and found he couldn't go wrong on them; they were stories of adventures in far and unexplored galaxies, stories of the distant future or the remote, mythical past, stories of time travel, unexplored powers of the mind, even pure fantasies of the werewolf-vampire type in historical settings. He'd be on safe ground there.

He finished his study of the magazines by ten o'clock and, from then until midnight, he sat at the little desk in his room, pencil in hand and paper before him. Not writing yet—he'd need a typewriter for that—but jotting down notes of all the stories he could remember having written and not sold.

He could remember, in that length of time, twenty such stories. There were others he'd be able to think of later. Of those twenty, six had been historical adventures or romances; those six were *in,* particularly the four that had been short and could be rewritten comparatively quickly. Another six he picked out as being fairly easy to translate into historical or fantastic settings.

A dozen stories, then, to start on, as soon as he could get hold of a typewriter. If one or two out of the dozen could be sold quickly, he'd be all right. Of course he couldn't keep on rewriting stories indefinitely; sooner or later he'd have to start turning out new ones. But with his experience in editing back of him he thought he could do that, also, once he had a start. And having the backlog of unsold stories to begin on would get him off with a bang.

If he couldn't sell a story before he went broke, well—he'd have to look into the possibility of getting some money out of the coins in his pocket. A quarter had got him two thousand credits in Greeneville—but it also got him into a terrific jam. He wasn't going to take a chance on that again unless he had to, and even then not without studying up on the subject to see what the pitfalls were.

By midnight he was too sleepy to remember any more plots of his unsold stories. But he hadn't finished all he wanted to do yet. He picked up the copy of *The Story of Dopelle* by Paul Gallico and started to read.

Now to find out what the competition really was.

The competition, he learned within the next hour, was more than terrific. It was impossible.

Dopelle (he didn't seem to have a first name at all) was simply unbelievable. He seemed to combine all the best characteristics—and none of the bad ones—of Napoleon, Einstein, Alexander the Great, Edison, Don Juan, and Sir Lancelot. He was twenty-seven years old.

The sketch of the first seventeen years of his life was brief. He'd been brilliant in school, skipped a lot of grades and had been graduated *(magna cum laude)* by Harvard at the age of seventeen, president of his class and the most popular man of his class despite his comparative youth.

Prodigies aren't usually popular, but Dopelle had been an exception. He hadn't been a grind. His high standing in his classes was due to his ability to remember perfectly everything he read or heard, obviating the necessity for hard study.

Despite his heavy schedule of classes (he'd taken about everything Harvard had to offer) he'd had time to captain an undefeated and untied football team. He had worked his way through school, and had become financially independent in the process, by writing in his spare time six adventure novels which had become best sellers at once and which still rated as top classics in their field.

The wealth these books (all of which, of course, were made into top-ranking motion pictures) brought him enabled him to own his own private space cruiser and his own laboratory where—during his last two years of college—he had already made several important improvements in the techniques of space travel and space warfare.

That was Dopelle at the age of seventeen, just an ordinary young fellow, comparatively speaking. His career had really started then.

He'd gone from Harvard to a Space Officers' Training School, had emerged a lieutenant, and had jumped grades rapidly for a year or so. At twenty-one he was in charge of counter-espionage, and was the only man who had ever been to the Arcturian System as a spy and had returned alive. Most Terrestrial knowledge about the Arcs had been obtained by him on that trip.

He was an incredibly good spacefighter and spacepilot. Time and again his squadron had turned back Arcturian attacks—with Dopelle spearheading the fighting as well as directing it. Because of his invaluable scientific knowledge, the brass had begged him not to fight personally. But—apparently by this time he was already above authority—he fought anyway, every chance he got. He seemed, however, to bear a charmed life. His bright red spaceship, the *Vengeance,* was never hit.

At twenty-three he was general of all the Solar forces, but command seemed to be the least important of his activities. Except during times of crisis he delegated authority and spent his time having exciting adventures in espionage or in working in his secret laboratory on the moon. It was his work there that enabled Earth to keep technologically equal to, or slightly ahead of, the Arcs.

The list of his accomplishments in that laboratory was almost unbelievable.

The greatest of them, perhaps, was the creation of a mechanical brain, Mekky. Into Mekky Dopelle had put mental powers beyond those of human beings. Mekky wasn't human, but he (Gallico pointed out that although Mekky was actually an *it,* he was always referred to as *he*) was, in some ways, superhuman.

Mekky could read minds and could speak to people, individually or *en masse,* telepathically. He could even, at close range, read Arcturian minds. Human telepaths had tried that, but invariably had gone insane before they could report their findings.

Also, Mekky could solve—as an electronic calculating machine can solve—any problem, however difficult, if all the factors could be given him.

Into Mekky also was built the ability to teleport—to transfer himself instantaneously through space without the necessity of having a spaceship to ride in. This made him invaluable as an emissary, enabling Dopelle, wherever he was, to keep in touch with his space fleets and with the governments of Earth.

Briefly and touchingly, near the end of the book, Gallico told of the romance between Dopelle and Betty Hadley. They were, it seemed, engaged and deeply in love with one another, but had decided to wait until the end of the war to marry.

Meanwhile Miss Hadley continued to keep her job as editor of the world's most popular love story magazine, the job she had held when she and Dopelle had met and fallen in love—while he was in New York incognito on an espionage job. Now the whole world loved the lovers and eagerly awaited the end of the war and the day of their marriage.

Keith Winton swore as he put down the book. Could anything possibly be more hopeless than his loving Betty Hadley?

But somehow it was the very hopelessness of things that gave him hope. The cards just couldn't possibly be stacked *that* badly against him. There might be a catch somewhere.

It was after one o'clock when he undressed for bed, but he phoned the desk of the hotel and left a call for six. Tomorrow was going to be a busy day. It had to be, if he were to keep on eating after a week or so.

He went to sleep, and dreamed—the poor goof—of Betty. Of Betty dressed (more or less) as he had seen her in the window of her apartment on Thirty-seventh Street, but being chased across the wild, weird landscape of some other world by a bug-eyed monster forty feet long, with nine legs on each side and green tentacles a yard thick.

Only somehow, in the mixed-up manner of dreams, he, Keith, was the green Bem that was chasing Betty, and he was thwarted when he almost caught her by a tall dashing romantic young man who had muscles of steel and who must be Dopelle, although he looked uncommonly like Errol Flynn.

And Dopelle picked up the green monster that was Keith Winton and said, "Back to Arcturus, spy!" and threw him out into space. And there he was spinning heels (all eighteen of them) over head out into the void, among the planets and then among the stars. Going so fast that there was a ringing sensation in his ears. The sound got louder and louder until he quit being an Arcturian and realized that the ringing was the telephone.

He answered it and a voice said, "Six o'clock, sir."

He didn't dare lie down again or he'd have gone back to sleep, so he sat on the bed a while, thinking, remembering the dream—which, after all, wasn't any sillier than most of what else had been happening to him.

What *did* Dopelle look like? Like Errol Flynn, as in his dream? Why not? Maybe Dopelle *was* Errol Flynn. If he remembered to do it, he'd check and see whether there *was* an Errol Flynn here.

He wouldn't be surprised if there wasn't.

Could this be some fantastic movie or story or book he'd tangled himself into on some quasi-plane of reality? Why not? Dopelle, he thought, was too perfect, too fantastic a character to be true. He didn't even sound like something out of a pulp magazine. No editor in his right mind would accept a story dealing with so improbable a character. Certainly no editor editing anything above the mental level of a comic book would accept Dopelle as a character.

And if this universe he found himself in was too screwy for fiction, how could he accept it as reality?

And yet hadn't the mechanical brain, Mekky, in brief contact with him, anticipated that very thought?

"...do not make one fatal error. This is real; it is not a figment of your imagination. Your danger here is real and this world is real..."

Mekky—fantastic as Mekky himself had been—had anticipated the very things he was thinking now. And Mekky was right. This universe and the spot it had put him in were plenty real, and if he doubted that fact, the best proof to the contrary was his hunger, at this moment, for breakfast.

He dressed and went out.

At six-thirty in the morning the streets of New York were as busy as—where he'd come from—they would have been at ten or eleven o'clock. The short day necessitated by the mistout demanded an early start.

He bought a paper and read it while he ate breakfast.

The big news story, of course, was the visit of Mekky to New York, and the reception given him. There was a picture splashed over a quarter of the first page showing the sphere poised in mid-air outside the open window and Betty Hadley leaning out of the window, bowing to the crowd below.

A boxed item in ten-point boldface type gave the words Mekky had spoken, telepathically, to the crowd, just as Keith had heard them there, inside his head. *"Friends, I leave you now to bear a message from my master and creator, Dopelle, to..."*

Yes, word for word. And apparently that had been the only public statement made by the mechanical brain. An hour later it had returned to "Somewhere in Space" as the news story put it.

He skimmed the rest of the paper. There was no news of the war, no mention of the crisis which Mekky had said (privately to Keith) was impending in the war.

If things were going badly, obviously it was being kept from the public. If Mekky had told him a military secret it must have been because Mekky—during Mekky's brief investigation of his thoughts before Mekky had spoken to him *("An interesting situation, Keith Winton..."*)—had recognized that Keith was in no spot to spread the secret farther, even if he wished to.

An item on an inside page about a man being fined five thousand credits and cost for possession of a coin interested him. He read it carefully, but failed to find any answer to the problem of why the possession of coins was illegal. He made a mental note to look up coins in the public library as soon as he had time to do so. But not today. He had too much to do today already.

First thing was to rent a typewriter.

Before he left the restaurant he used the classified directory to locate the nearest typewriter rental agency.

By taking a chance on using the name Keith Winton, for which he still had identification in his wallet, he got one without having to leave a deposit and took it to his room in the hotel.

He put in the hardest day's work he'd ever done in his life.

At the end of it—he was dead tired by seven o'clock and had to quit then— he'd finished seven thousand words. A four-thousand-word story and a three-thousand-word one.

True, they were both rewrites of stories he'd written before, long ago, but he'd done a better job on them this time. One was a straight action story in a Civil War setting. The other was a light romance set against the background of early pioneer days in Kansas.

He fell into bed, too sleepy to phone down to the desk and leave a call for the morning. He knew he wouldn't sleep longer than twelve hours, and seven o'clock would be early enough for him to get up.

But he awoke early, just after five o'clock, in time to watch from his window the action of the sunlight in dissipating the blackness of the mistout. He watched, fascinated, while he dressed and shaved.

He had breakfast at six, and then back in his room he read over the two stories and was more than satisfied with them. They were *good*. What had been wrong with them before, the reason they hadn't sold the first time he'd written them, hadn't been the plots. His plots had always been sound. It had been the writing and the treatment. And five years as an editor had really taught him something.

He could make a living writing; he was sure of that now. Not that he could keep on batting out two stories every day except when he was rewriting his old stuff from memory. But he wouldn't have to do it nearly that fast. Once he'd rewritten the dozen or so stories that would be rewrites, he'd have a backlog. After that, two shorts or one novelette a week would be enough to keep the wolf from the door—even if, as before, his sales average would be fifty-fifty. And it should be better than that now, because these stories were better, definitely better.

One more story, he decided, and he'd start out to peddle them. And start, of course, with Borden Publications. Not only because he knew the ropes better there, but because they were good for quick checks if they liked the stories. Often, to oblige a writer who needed money quickly, he had put through a voucher and got a check into the mail within twenty-four hours after he'd read and accepted the story.

For his third rewrite job, he picked a science-fiction plot he'd tried once, one that had run only two thousand words. He had the plot clear in his mind and knew he could knock out the yarn in a couple of hours. And Marion Blake had told him Borden was in the market for science-fiction for their new magazine in that field, so the chances of a sale should be excellent.

The story required no major changes at all. It was a time-travel story about a man who went back to prehistoric times—told from the point of view of the cave man who encountered the time traveler. None of it was in a modern setting, so it couldn't go wrong.

He started pounding the typewriter again and finished by nine o'clock, despite the fact that the story had run a bit longer this time; he'd put in more characterization and atmosphere and had made it a much stronger and more vivid story. He felt damned proud of himself.

Half an hour later he was smiling at Marion Blake across the mahogany railing in the outer office at Borden Publications.

She smiled back. "Yes, Mr. Winston?"

"Brought in three stories," he said proudly. "One I want to leave with Miss Hadley for her love book. And one—who's running this new science-fiction book you told me about?"

"Keith Winton. Temporarily, anyway. After it's really on the stands they may put someone else on it."

"Good. I'll leave one with him. And who's running *Romantic Adventure Stories?*"

"Mr. Winton runs that, too. That and *Surprising Stories* are his regular books. I think he's free now; I'll see if he can talk to you. Miss Hadley's busy right now but maybe she'll be free by the time you've talked to Mr. Winton, Mr. Winston. Oh, by the way, did you decide on a pen name for yourself?"

He snapped his fingers in annoyance. "Forgot it. Put Karl Winston as a by-line. Well, we'll see if Mr. Winton minds. I'll mention it to him and tell him

I've not used my right name on anything but feature articles, so it's perfectly okay if he wants me to use a *nom de plume* instead."

Marion had already pushed a plug into a hole in the switchboard. She talked a moment into the mouthpiece; Keith couldn't hear what she was saying.

She pulled the plug and smiled up at him again. "He'll see you," she told him. "I—uh—told him you were a friend of mine."

He said "Thanks a lot," and meant it. He knew that little things like that mattered sometimes. Not that an *in* of any kind would enable him to sell an unsalable story. But it would help in getting a quick reading and—if the story was accepted—a quick check for it.

After he'd started for Keith Winton's office he realized that he wasn't supposed to know the way until Marion had directed him, but it was too late by the time he remembered, so he kept on going.

A moment later Keith Winton sat down opposite Keith Winton, reached across the desk to shake hands with him and said, "I'm Karl Winston, Mr. Winton. Have a couple of stories to leave with you. I could have mailed them in, of course, but I thought I'd like to meet you while I'm in town."

SLADE OF THE W.B.I.

Keith was studying Winton as he spoke. Winton wasn't a bad-looking guy. He was about Keith's age, an inch or so taller but a few pounds lighter. His hair was darker and a bit curlier. Facially, there wasn't any noticeable resemblance at all. And he wore shell-rimmed glasses, fairly thick ones. Keith had never worn glasses in his life and had perfect vision.

"You don't live in New York?" Winton was asking him.

"Yes and no," Keith said. "I mean, I haven't been, but I may decide to stay here from now on. Or I may decide to return to Boston. I've been working on a paper there and doing quite a bit of free-lancing on the side." He'd thought out his story and didn't have to hesitate. "Got a leave of absence for a while and, if I can make a go of free-lancing here in New York, I probably won't go back.

"I brought in two shorts I'd like you to consider—one for *Romantic Adventure* and one for the new science-fiction book Marion tells me you're starting."

He took two of his three stories from the envelope and handed them across the desk.

"I know it's imposing on you to ask it," he said, "but I'd greatly appreciate a reading as quickly as you can get to it. Because I want to write some more I have planned along these lines. And I don't want to start them until I know—from your reaction to these—whether I'm on the right track or not."

Winton smiled. "I'll keep them out of the slushpile."

He glanced at the top right-hand corners of the title pages of the two scripts. "Three and four thousand. Well, those are lengths we need, and both books are wide open if the stories fit."

"Fine," Keith said. He decided to crowd his luck a little. "I happen to have an appointment here in the building on Friday, day after tomorrow. Since I'll be so close, do you mind if I drop in to see whether or not you've had time to read them?"

Winton frowned slightly. "Can't promise for sure that I'll get to them that soon, but I'll try to. If you're going to be in the building anyway, you might as well drop in."

Keith said, "Swell, thanks." Despite the lack of a promise he knew it was odds-on that the stories would be read by Friday. And if one or both of them rated acceptance, then would be the time to bring up the matter of putting through a voucher for a quick check. He'd have a story ready to account for his need of money in a hurry.

"Oh, by the way," he said. "About a by-line—" And he pointed out the similarity between Karl Winston and Keith Winton, and explained his willingness to use a pen name if Winton thought he should.

Winton smiled. He said, "It's not really important. If Karl Winston's your name, you have every right to use it. And I'm not doing any writing myself—and who notices the name of the editor of a magazine?"

"Other editors do," Keith said.

"And if you're really going in for pulp, you'll be sending stories to them, so they'll know Karl Winston's not a pen name of mine. So don't worry about it unless you *want* to pick up a *nom de plume* for your fiction work."

"And also," Keith said, "unless I sell a story to put a by-line on." He stood up. "Thanks a lot. And I'll drop in Friday about this same time. Good-bye, Mr. Winton."

He went back to Marion Blake's desk.

She said, "Miss Hadley's free now; you can go in, I think, as soon as I ring her." But she didn't push a plug; she looked at him curiously. "How did you know which door was Mr. Winton's office?"

He grinned at her. "I'm psychic."

"Seriously. I'm curious."

"Seriously, you glanced at that door the first time we mentioned Mr. Winton's name. Maybe you don't remember it, but you did. So I thought it was his, and if I'd been wrong you'd have called me back."

She dimpled at him; he'd passed *that* examination with flying colors. But, he thought, he'd have to remember to be on guard every second. Little mistakes like that could spoil everything.

She'd put in a plug and again was talking inaudibly into the mouthpiece. She pulled the plug out again. "Miss Hadley will see you," she told him.

And this time Keith remembered to wait until she pointed out the proper door to him.

On the way to it, he felt as though he was wading through thick molasses. He thought, "I shouldn't do this; I should have my head examined. I should leave the story for her, or mail it in, or take it to another love story magazine editor."

He took a deep breath and opened the door.

And then he *knew* he should have stayed away. His heart did a double somersault when he saw her sitting there at her desk, looking up at him with a slight, impersonal smile.

Incredibly, she was wearing a costume like the one she'd been wearing when he'd seen her at the window of her Thirty-seventh Street apartment. That is, she was wearing a green bra this time; nothing else showed above the top of the desk.

And, at close range, she was twice as beautiful as he remembered her to be. But of course that was silly—

Or *was* it silly? This was, somehow, a completely different universe. It had a completely different Keith Winton in it. Why couldn't it have at least a slightly different Betty Hadley? A few days ago he couldn't have imagined an edition of Betty more beautiful than the original. But this one *was*. The costume, of course, didn't make her any less attractive, but it was more than that.

And he was twice as much in love with this one as with the original.

Without realizing that he was staring at her, he stared, wondering just what the difference was. Feature for feature, she was the same. Of course, with this Betty Hadley, more features were visible because of the costume, but even that didn't account for it.

It was as subtle as the difference between the girls on the magazine covers back there and the ones on the covers here. Here they had more—well, you name it.

And it was like that with Betty; she was the same girl but subtly twice as beautiful and twice as desirable, and he was twice as much in love with her.

But slowly her smile faded and when she asked, "Yes?", he realized how long he'd been staring at her.

He said, "My name is Kei—Karl Winston, Miss Hadley. I—uh—"

She saw, obviously, how badly he was floundering and helped him out. "Miss Blake tells me you're a friend of hers and a writer. Won't you sit down, Mr. Winston?"

"Thank you," he said, taking the chair opposite her desk. "Yes, I brought in a story which..." And, once started, he managed to continue to talk intelligibly, telling her substantially the same story he'd told Keith Winton.

Even though his mind wasn't on what he was saying at all.

And then, somehow, he was making his getaway without falling over his own feet, and the interview was over, and he was out of the door.

But he decided then and there that he'd never again torture himself by coming that close to her. Not that it wouldn't be worth the torture if there was a chance in a million— But there wasn't; there couldn't be.

He was so miserable that he almost walked past the switchboard blindly and without speaking, but Marion Blake called out, "Oh, Mr. Winston!"

He turned and managed to make himself smile. He said, "Thanks a lot, Miss Blake, for telling both of them that I'm a friend of yours, and—"

"Oh, don't mention that. That's all right. But I have a message for you from Mr. Winton."

"Huh? But I just talked to him."

"Yes, I know. He just left, a minute ago, to keep an important appointment. But he said there was something he wanted to ask you, and he'll be back by half past twelve. And could you phone him then—that is, between then and one o'clock, when we close?"

"Why, sure. I'll be glad to. And again, thanks a lot."

He should, he knew, invite her out for another drink or ask if he could take her to a show or a dance or something. He would, in fact, if even one of the three stories he'd just left turned out to be a sale. Until then, his dwindling capital didn't let him chance repaying the favor she'd done him.

He walked to the door, wondering what Keith Winton wanted to talk to him about so soon. He'd been in Betty's office less than fifteen minutes; Winton couldn't possibly have read even one of the two stories.

But—well, why wonder? He'd phone at half past twelve and find out.

As he walked toward the elevators in the hallway outside Borden Publications, Inc., the door of an up elevator slid open. Mr. and Mrs. L. A. Borden came out and the door slid shut behind them.

Caught unaware, Keith nodded and spoke to them. Each of them nodded slightly and Mr. Borden murmured something inaudible, as one does when spoken to by someone one cannot recall.

They went past him and entered the offices he'd just left.

Keith frowned as he waited for a down elevator. Of course they didn't know him, and he shouldn't have spoken. It was a very slight slip, but he'd have to be on the alert to avoid even slight ones.

He'd almost made a bad one back in Betty's office, too, when he'd started to introduce himself as Keith Winton instead of Karl Winston. And, now that he thought of it, Betty had given him a very peculiar look when he'd started to make that slip, when he'd got as far as "Kei—" before he caught himself. Almost as though—but that was silly. He put the thought out of his mind.

Why, though, did Betty Hadley wear that costume, or lack of a costume, even at the Borden offices? He hadn't seen any other women dressed that way—and surely he'd have noticed. It was one of the most puzzling of the minor mysteries he'd encountered. He wondered how he could find the answer without asking.

Such wide differences, and such amazing similarities. And it came to him again, as he walked into the elevator, that the similarities of this universe might be more dangerous to him than the differences; familiar things might trap him into unconsidered reactions, like speaking to the Bordens.

That particular one undoubtedly didn't matter, but how easy it would be to make a similar mistake that did matter, that would give him away completely as the fake and phony he had to be in order to survive. The ever-present possibility of making a *big* mistake worried him.

He'd have worried about it more if he'd known that he already had.

He stood for a moment outside the building, wondering what he should do next. He didn't feel up to going back to his hotel and grinding out another story, not just yet. Late this afternoon and during the evening—when he'd have to stay indoors anyway on account of the mistout—would be time enough. Three stories—even though they were all rewrites and all fairly short—was plenty for two days' work. And he knew those stories were good; it would be better to keep up the quality rather than to drive himself and turn out junk. Yes, he'd take the afternoon off and resume writing this evening.

If he did a story tonight and another tomorrow he'd have something more to take with him when he kept his appointment at Borden. It seemed funny, he thought, to be on the other side of the fence there, to be taking stories in instead of having writers and agents bring them to him. Maybe he should get himself an agent—no, let that wait until he had a sale or two he could report, and a foot inside the door. And right now he could push his first stories harder than any agent would.

He strolled over to Broadway and north to Times Square. He stood looking up at the Times Building, wondering what was strange about it; then he realized that the strips of current news headlines in electric lights weren't flashing around as they should have been. Why not?

Probably because New York used a minimum of electric lighting by day. Probably because those whatever-they-were rays emitted by electrical incandescence and detectable by Arcturian spaceships weren't as completely blanked out by sunlight as they were by the mistout at night.

And that would account for the comparatively dim lighting he'd noticed in restaurants and offices and stores by day. Come to think of it, there'd been just about an irreducible minimum of lighting in all of them.

He'd have to watch little things like that, to keep from giving himself away. He'd had the electric light on in his hotel room most of the time he'd worked or read by day. Luckily, he hadn't been called on it. But hereafter he'd move the desk and chair over to the window and leave the light off except at night.

He walked past a newsstand slowly and read the headlines:

FLEET BLASTS ARCTURIAN OUTPOST
BIG VICTORY FOR SOLAR FORCES

That ought to give him a kick, Keith thought, but it didn't. He couldn't hate Arcturians; he didn't even know what they looked like. And this war with Arcturus might be real, but it couldn't *seem* real to him; he couldn't believe in it yet. It still seemed like a dream to him, a nightmare that he'd wake up from, despite the fact that he'd waked up four times here and the war with Arcturus was still on.

He stood staring moodily at a window of hand-painted neckties. Something touched his shoulder, and he turned around. He jumped back, almost into the glass of the window. It was one of the tall, purple, hairy Lunans.

It said, in a shrill voice, "Pardon me, sir; do you have a match?"

Keith wanted to laugh, and yet his hand trembled a little as he handed over a package of matches and then took it back when the Lunan had lighted a cigarette.

It said, "Thank you," and walked on.

Keith watched its back and the way it walked. Despite bulging muscles, it walked like a man wading through waist-deep water. Heavy gravity, of course, Keith thought. On the moon, it'd be strong enough to throw Gargantua around. Here on Earth it was slumped down, pulled together, by a gravity several times what it was used to. Not an inch over eight feet tall; on the moon it would probably stand eight and a half or nine feet.

But wasn't there supposed to be no air on the moon? That must be wrong—or at least not true here. Lunans must breathe or they couldn't smoke cigarettes. No creature can smoke without breathing.

Suddenly—and actually for the first time—something occurred to Keith Winton. He could go to the moon if he wanted! *To Mars! To Venus!* And why not? If he was in a universe that had space travel, why shouldn't he take advantage of the fact? A little chill of excitement went down his spine. Somehow he hadn't, in the few days he'd been here, thought of space travel in connection with himself. Now the very thought of it excited him.

He couldn't do it right away, of course; it would take money, probably lots of money. He'd have to write plenty. But why shouldn't he?

And there was another possibility, once he'd learned the ropes enough to take a chance on it: those coins he still had. If a quarter picked at random had brought him two thousand credits, maybe one of the others would turn out to be really rare—valuable enough to finance a vacation on the planets. Come to think of it, the Greeneville druggist had admitted that the quarter was worth more than two thousand, but had said that was all he could afford to pay for it.

There must be a black market somewhere for those other coins. But it was too dangerous, until he'd learned more about them.

He strolled up Broadway as far as Forty-sixth and then saw by a clock in a window that it was almost twelve-thirty. He went into a drugstore and phoned Keith Winton at Borden Publications.

Winton's voice said, "Oh, yes, Mr. Winston. I thought of something else I wanted to talk to you about, something you might be able to do for us. You say you've done quite a bit of feature and non-fiction writing?"

"Yes."

"There's a non-fiction feature I've been wanting to run, and I'd like to talk to you about it to see if you'd care to tackle it for me. Only I'll need it within a day or two. Would you be interested? And could you do it that quickly?"

Keith said, "If I can do it at all, I can do it that quickly. But I'm not sure—What is the subject matter?"

"A bit complicated to explain over the phone. Are you free this afternoon?"

"Yes."

"I'm leaving here pretty soon; hardly be time for you to come back here. But I wonder if you'd mind dropping around to my place in the Village? We can have a drink and talk it over."

"Fine," Keith said. "Where and when?"

"Four o'clock all right? And I'm in Apartment 6 at three-one-eight Gresham, down in the Village. You'd probably better take a cab unless you know the district down there."

Keith grinned, but kept his voice serious. "I think I can find it all right," he said.

He ought to be able to. He'd lived there for four years.

He put the receiver back and went out to Broadway again, this time walking south. He stopped in front of the window of a travel agency.

"Vacation Trips," the sign read. *"All-Expense Tours to Mars and Venus. One Month. 5,000 Cr."*

Only five hundred bucks, he thought. Dirt cheap, as soon as he could earn enough to get five hundred bucks ahead. And maybe it would help take his mind off Betty.

Suddenly he was impatient to start writing again. He went back to his hotel, walking fast. He could get in about three hours' work before he had to leave for his appointment with Keith Winton.

He jerked paper and carbon into the typewriter and started working on the fourth story. He worked until the last minute, then hurried out and caught a downtown subway train.

He wondered what kind of a feature article Keith Winton wanted written in a hurry; he hoped it was something that he could handle, for it would mean a reasonably sure and reasonably quick check. Only if the feature was to be about something he didn't know anything about—like the training of space cadets or conditions on the moon—he'd have to have an explanation ready to enable him to turn down the assignment. Of course, he wouldn't turn it down if there was any chance of his handling it, possibly with the aid of a morning spent in research at the public library.

But he spent the subway ride and the walk from the subway to Gresham Street thinking up some plausible excuses to use in case the article was about something he didn't dare tackle.

The building was familiar and so was the name *Keith Winton* on the mailbox of Apartment 6 in the hallway downstairs. He pressed the button and waited, with his hand on the latch, until the lock clicked.

Keith Winton—the *other* Keith Winton—was standing in the doorway of the apartment as Keith walked back along the hail.

"Come in, Winston," he said. He stepped back and opened the door wider. Keith walked in—and stopped suddenly.

A big man with iron-gray hair and cold iron-gray eyes was standing there in front of the bookcase. There was a deadly looking forty-five caliber automatic in his hand and it was pointed at the middle button of Keith's vest.

Keith stood very still, and raised his hands slowly.

The big man said, "Better frisk him, Mr. Winton. From behind. Don't step in front of him. And be careful."

Keith felt hands running lightly over him, touching all his pockets.

He managed to keep his voice steady. "May I ask what this is all about?"

"No gun," Winton said. He stepped around where Keith could see him again, but kept out of the line between Keith and the automatic in the big man's hand.

He stood there looking at Keith with puzzled eyes. He said, "I guess I owe you an explanation, sure. And then you owe me one. Okay, Karl Winston—if that's really your name—meet Mr. Gerald Slade of the W.B.I."

"Glad to know you, Mr. Slade," Keith said. What, he wondered, was the W.B.I.? World Bureau of Investigation? It seemed like a good guess. He looked back at his host. "Is that all the explanation you owe me?"

Where, he wondered desperately, had he made a mistake that had led to this?

Winton glanced at Slade and then back at Keith. He said, "I—uh—thought it best to have Mr. Slade here while I asked you certain questions. You brought me two stories this morning at the Borden office. Where did you get them?"

"Get them? I wrote them. And this business about wanting me to write a feature article for you—was that a gag?"

"It was," Winton said grimly. "It seemed the easiest way to get you out here without making you suspicious that we wanted to question you. Mr. Slade suggested it, after I called him and told him what you'd done."

"And what, may I ask, have I done?"

Winton looked at him curiously. "The only legal count thus far is plagiarism—but plagiarism in such an incredible manner that I thought the W.B.I. should look into it to find out *why* you even tried it."

Keith looked at him blankly. "Plagiarism?" he echoed.

"Those two stories you left were stories *I* wrote, five or six years ago. You did a nice rewrite job on them; I'll say that for you. They're better than the originals. But what made you think you could get away with selling me two of my own stories? It's the most unbelievable thing I've ever run into."

Keith opened his mouth and closed it again. The roof of it felt dry and he thought that if he tried to say anything only a croaking noise would come out. And what was there to say?

It was so completely obvious, now that he thought of it. Why *shouldn't* the Keith Winton who lived here—who had his job and lived in his apartment—have written the same stories?

He damned himself for a fool for not having thought of the possibility.

The pause was getting too long. He moistened his lips with his tongue. He had to say something, or silence would be construed as admission of guilt.

GUN JUMP

Keith Winton moistened his lips with his tongue a second time. He said, weakly, "Lots of stories have similar plots. There have been lots of cases where—"

Winton interrupted him. "These aren't just cases of similar plots. That I could understand. But too many of the minor details are identical. In one of the two stories the *names of both of my main characters* are the same. One of the stories has the same title as I used for it. And throughout both of them, there are too many little things that are identical. Coincidence won't wash, Winston; coincidence could account for similarities—even pretty close similarities— in basic plots, but not for so many names and minor things being identical.

"No, those stories were *plagiarized.*" He waved a hand toward a file cabinet standing beside the bookcase. "I've got copies of the original versions in my file there to prove it."

He frowned at Keith. "I suspected something before I finished reading the first page of one story. When I'd read all of both stories I was sure of it—but what I was sure of puzzled me. I don't get it. Why would a plagiarist have the colossal gall to try to sell stolen stories to the very man who wrote them? However or whenever you stole them—and that puzzles me too—you must have known I'd recognize them. And another thing— Is Winston your real name?"

"Of course."

"That's funny, too. A man calling himself Karl Winston offering stories written by a man named Keith Winton. What I can't understand is why, if it's a fake name, you didn't pick one that wasn't so close—same initials and one letter added in the last name."

Keith wondered about that himself. His only excuse was that he'd had to think of a name on the spur of the moment while he was talking to Marion Blake. Even so, he should have had a better name ready, just in case he had to use one.

The man with the automatic asked, "Got any identification with you?"

Keith shook his head slowly. He had to stall, somehow, until he could figure an out—if there was one. He said, "Not with me. I can prove my identity, though. I'm staying at the Watsonia Hotel. If you phone there—"

Slade said dryly, "If I phone there I'll be told there's a Karl Winston registered. I know that; I phoned there already. You gave that return address on the stories you left with Mr. Winton." He cleared his throat. "That doesn't prove a thing except that you've been using the name Karl Winston during the two days you've registered there."

He clicked the safety catch on the big automatic. His eyes hardened. He said, "I don't like to shoot a man in cold blood but—"

Keith took an involuntary step backwards. "I don't get it," he protested. "Since when is plagiarism—even if I were guilty of it—something to shoot a man for?"

"We're not worried about plagiarism," Slade told him, grimly. "But we're under orders to shoot on sight anybody suspected of being an Arc spy. And there's one loose, last seen in Greeneville upstate. We got a kind of punk description, but such as it is, you could fit it. And if you can't account for yourself any better than you have—"

"Wait a minute," Keith said desperately. "There's a simple explanation of this somewhere. There's *got* to be. And if I *were* a spy, wouldn't pulling a dumb stunt like stealing an editor's stories and trying to sell them back to him be the last thing I'd do?"

Winton said, "He's got something there, Slade. That's what puzzles me most about the whole thing. And I don't like the idea of shooting him down unless we're sure. Let me ask him one or two more questions before you shoot."

He turned to Keith. "Look, Winston, you can see this is no time to stall. It won't get you anything but bullets. Now if you're an Arc, heaven only knows why you'd have brought me those stories. Maybe I was supposed to react differently—do something else besides call in a W.B.I. man.

"But if you're *not* an Arc, then there must be some explanation. And if there is, you'd better give it quickly."

Keith licked his lips again. For a desperate moment—although an idea had come to him—he couldn't remember any of the places where he'd submitted those stories after he'd first written them five years ago. Then he remembered one.

He said, "There's only one possibility I can think of. Did you ever submit those stories to the Gebhart chain of pulps in Garden City?"

"Ummm—one of them, anyway. Probably both. I've got a record of it."

"About five years ago?"

"Yes, about that."

Keith took a deep breath. He said, "Five years ago I was a reader for Gebhart. I must have read your stories when they came in. I must have liked them—and probably passed them—but the managing editor who gave the final readings must not have bought them. But my subconscious mind must have remembered them—even the small details you say I had the same."

He shook his head as though bewildered. "If that's true, I'd better quit writing. Fiction, anyway. When I wrote those stories recently, I thought they were originals. If it was my subconscious memory of stories I'd read that long ago—"

He saw with relief that Slade's grip on the pistol wasn't quite so tight.

Slade said, "Or you could have taken notes on those stories intending to swipe them sometime later."

Keith shook his head. "If it had been deliberate plagiarism, wouldn't I have changed at least the names of the characters?"

Winton said, "That makes sense to me, Slade. The subconscious mind can do funny things. I'm inclined to believe him. As he says, if he were plagiarizing deliberately, he'd at least change the names of the characters. And he wouldn't have kept the same name for one of the stories. He'd have changed more than he did—of the things that don't matter—all the way down the line."

Keith sighed with relief. The worst was over, if he could make the story stick. He said, "Better tear up the stories, Mr. Winton. I'll tear up my carbons. If my mind can play tricks like that on me, I stick to feature writing."

His host was looking at him curiously. He said, "The funny thing is, Winston, that those stories—as you've rewritten them—are plenty good enough to use. And, since the plots are mine and the writing is yours, damned if I'm not tempted to buy and print them, on a collaboration basis. In other words, to split with you. I'd have to explain things to Borden, but—"

"Just a minute, please," Slade interrupted. "Before you gentlemen get down to business, *I'm* not convinced. Or anyway I'm only ninety per cent convinced, and that's not enough. On a ten per cent doubt, I'm supposed to shoot—and you both know that."

Winton said, "We can check his story, Slade. Part of it, anyway."

"That's what I'm leading up to. And I'm not taking this gun off him until we check it forty ways from Sunday. For a start, do you want to put through a call to Garden City to check—no, they'd be closed hours ago; they're in the area that follows New York working hours even though they're out of the mistout."

Winton said, "I've got an idea, Slade. When I frisked him a few minutes ago, I was looking only for a gun. I didn't feel one, but I did feel a billfold."

Slade's eyes got even harder than they'd been before as he stared at Keith. His fingers were again white on the gun.

"A billfold?" he said coldly. "And no identification in it?"

There was, Keith thought, plenty of identification in it—but not as Karl Winston. Would Slade hesitate even a second to shoot when he saw that the identification in the billfold would seem to indicate that he had impersonated or intended to impersonate Keith Winton?

That identification had saved his life in Greeneville; it was going to cost him his life in New York City. He should have gotten rid of it the minute he quit using the name Keith Winton. He saw now, clearly, the string of mistakes he'd been making ever since his first trip to the Borden office.

And it was too late now to correct any of them. Probably he had only seconds to live.

The W.B.I. man wasn't waiting for him to explain why there wasn't identification in the wallet. It had been a rhetorical question. He said to Winton, without taking his eyes off Keith: "Get behind him again and get the wallet. And see what else is in his pockets. This is the last chance I'm going to give him—and I'm softhearted and softheaded to do that much."

The other Keith Winton circled to approach him from the back.

Keith took a deep breath. This was going to be *it*. Besides the identification in the wallet, he still had the incriminating coins wrapped in the paper money—probably equally incriminating—so it wouldn't rattle. He hadn't dared leave the stuff in his hotel room, and it was still in a tight little wad in the fob pocket of his trousers.

Not that it would be needed. The contents of the wallet would be enough.

Yes, this was *it*. Either he was going to die here and now or—he'd have to try to jump that gun. Heroes in the stories he had bought—back in a sane universe where he'd been a Borden editor instead of an Arcturian spy—always managed to jump a gun whenever it became necessary.

Was there a chance in a thousand that it could really be done?

The other Keith Winton was behind him now. Keith stood very still with the muzzle of the pistol aiming right at him. His mind was going like a mill-race, but it wasn't thinking of anything that offered much promise of keeping him from being shot within the next minute or two. As soon as that wallet was opened and the identification in it was read...

All Keith's attention was on the automatic. A gun like that, he knew, shot steel-jacketed bullets that would go right through a man at close range. If Slade fired now he'd probably kill both of them, both Keith Wintons.

And then what? Would he wake up back on Borden's farm in Greeneville, in a sensible world? No, not according to Mekky, the mechanical brain. *"This is real... Your danger here is real. If you are killed here..."*

And, wildly improbable as Mekky himself was, Keith knew somehow that Mekky was dead right. Somehow there were two universes and two Keith Wintons—but this one was just as real as the one he'd grown up in. The other Keith Winton was just as real as he was, too.

And would the fact that one shot would probably kill them both while the other Winton was behind him delay the W.B.I. man's finger on the trigger for a single second? It might, or it might not.

A hand was reaching into his hip pocket. It came out, and he felt the billfold coming out with it. Keith found that he was holding his breath. A hand went into his side trouser pocket; apparently his host was going to finish the search before studying any of the objects he found.

Keith quit thinking and moved.

His hand closed on Winton's wrist, and he pivoted and swung Winton around in front of him, between himself and Slade. His trouser pocket ripped. Over

Winton's shoulder he saw the W.B.I. man moving to the side to get a clear shot. He moved, keeping Winton between them.

Out of the corner of his eye he saw one of Winton's fists coming for his face and he jerked aside, letting the fist pass over his shoulder. Then—with Winton still between him and Slade—he stepped in low, butting his head against Winton's chest. And, with both hands and with all the weight of his body and the momentum of his forward rush, he bulled Winton backward against Slade, following close.

Slade stumbled backward into the bookcase and glass crashed. The automatic went off, making a noise like a blockbuster in the confined space of the room.

Keith clung with both hands to Winton's lapels while, alongside Winton's legs, Keith's foot kicked upward at the automatic. He missed the gun but the toe of his shoe hit Slade's wrist and the automatic went out of Slade's hand.

It clunked against the carpeted floor. Keith gave a final shove against Winton, pushing him and Slade back against the tottering bookcase, and then dived for the gun. He got it.

He backed off, holding the gun to cover both of them. He was breathing hard and, now that the immediate action was over, his hand was trembling. It had worked; a gun *could* be jumped, just as in the stories he used to buy, when the gun-jumper had nothing to lose in trying.

There was a knock on the door.

Keith moved the gun menacingly and both Winton and Slade stood still.

A voice called out, "Are you all right, Mr. Winton?" Keith recognized the voice—that of Mrs. Flanders, who lived in the adjoining apartment.

He tried to make his voice sound as much as possible like the other Keith Winton's, trusting to the muffling action of the door to disguise any difference in the overtones. He called, "Everything's okay, Mrs. Flanders. Gun went off while I was starting to clean it. The recoil knocked me over."

He stood still, waiting, knowing she'd be wondering why he didn't open the door. But all his attention had to be on the two men in front of him and he didn't take his eyes off them for a second.

He saw the puzzled look in Winton's eyes; Winton was wondering how he had known Mrs. Flanders' name and how he had recognized her voice.

There was a few seconds' silence and then Mrs. Flanders' voice came through the door again. "All right, Mr. Winton. I just wondered—"

He considered calling out again, to tell her he couldn't open the door because he wasn't dressed. But he decided not to. This time she might be listening more critically to the sound of his voice and realize that it wasn't that of the Keith Winton she knew. And besides it wasn't too logical that he'd be cleaning a gun while he was undressed.

Better to let her wonder and to quit while he was ahead. He heard her walking back to her own apartment and from the slowness of her steps, he knew she *was* wondering. Why he hadn't opened the door, and why there'd been so much noise just from his falling over from the recoil.

He didn't think she'd call a copper right away; she'd keep on wondering a while first. But some other tenant might be calling right now to report the

sound of a gunshot. He had to do something quickly about Winton and the
W.B.I. man, so he could get away before the police came.

It was something of a problem. He couldn't just shoot them—nor could he
simply walk out and leave them to start an immediate pursuit. Tying up would
take too long and be too risky.

But he needed at least a few minutes' grace to start his getaway. Getaway to
where? he wondered; then shoved that thought out of his mind. Right now he
couldn't afford to figure more than minutes ahead.

"Turn around," he ordered, making his voice sound grim and deadly—as
grim and deadly as Slade's voice had sounded when Slade had had the gun.

He stepped in close when they had turned, keeping the muzzle of the gun
in the W. B. I. man's back; he was much more afraid of Slade than of Winton.
His left hand felt Slade's hip pockets. Yes, there was a pair of handcuffs there,
as he had hoped. He took them and stepped back again.

He said, "All right, step over by that post in the archway. You, Winton,
reach through it. Then cuff yourselves together. First, toss me your keys, Slade."

He watched their every move until he heard the cuffs click twice.

Then he backed to the door and slid the gun into his pocket, keeping his
hand on it, but throwing on the safety catch with his thumb. He looked back
at his prisoners as he opened the door, thought of telling them not to yell, but
didn't bother. They'd yell anyway.

They started almost as soon as he pulled the door shut from the outside.
Doors started popping open on either side as he strode along the hallway to
the front. He walked fast, but wouldn't let himself run. Nobody, he thought,
would actually try to stop him, although phone calls to the police were undoubtedly being made right now in more than one apartment.

Nobody did stop him. He made the street and kept up his fast walk. He
was a block away when he heard sirens. He slowed down instead of hurrying
faster, but he turned off Gresham Street at the next corner.

A squad car passed him, heading toward the apartment, but he knew he
didn't have to worry about it just yet; within five or ten minutes they'd have
his description and that would be a different matter. But by that time he could
be on Fifth Avenue, walking north from Washington Square, and they wouldn't
be able to pick him out of the crowd even if they came that way. Or better yet,
if he could get a taxi—

One came along, empty, and he started to hail it, then put his hand down
quickly and stepped back to the curb before the driver saw him. He swore at
himself, remembering now that he'd forgotten, in the excitement, to get his
wallet back from Winton.

On top of everything else, now, he was broke! He couldn't even take the
subway!

He swore at himself again when he realized that he might just as well have
taken advantage of the situation back there, while he'd held the upper hand,
to augment his fortunes. Why hadn't he taken Winton's billfold—and even
Slade's—as well as his own? Ordinary rules of honesty scarcely apply when one
is already wanted for an offense that carries a shoot-on-sight penalty!

With the combined contents of his own, Winton's and Slade's wallets, he'd have been solvent. And even if he had money, his situation was desperate enough now. He couldn't even go back to his hotel to get his pitifully few clothes and possessions.

He kept walking north, and by the time he'd crossed Fourteenth Street, he began to feel fairly safe from the squad cars that would be looking for him. Several might have passed; he studiously kept from watching the traffic that streamed past on Fifth Avenue.

The sidewalks were still crowded—possibly a little more so now than at any other time since he'd started walking. It might have been because he was a little nearer the center of town, but he didn't think that was the reason.

Also, he noticed, there was a change in the way people were walking. There were no strollers; everybody walked as though in a hurry to get somewhere. Unconsciously, he'd increased his own pace to match, to avoid being conspicuous as the only stroller. There seemed to be hurry in the air.

And suddenly he realized why. Twilight was falling, and all these people were hurrying to be home before dark.

Before the mistout.

GIRL OF SPACE

All these people were hurrying-scurrying to get home and under cover, to lock and bar the doors of their apartments, and to leave the streets to blackness and to murder.

And for the first time since he'd made his getaway from the apartment he stopped and wondered seriously where he was going, where he *could* go.

If only he'd had the sense not to give his right address on those manuscripts he'd turned in, then they wouldn't be waiting for him at his hotel. A minor annoyance that seemed major was the fact that he was paid in advance there for the rest of the week.

It looked as though he were going to have to try to capitalize on the coins in his pocket. If it were only earlier in the day, he could go to the library and study up on coinage, try to find out what it was all about. Why hadn't he done that while he was in the library, while he had the chance? Why, for that matter, hadn't he done a lot of things he hadn't?

Aside from getting capital by disposing of the coins, there was just one possibility he could think of. If only he could get in touch with Mekky! Mekky had been inside his mind. Mekky could vouch for him, could assure the forces of law and order that he was not an Arcturian spy, whatever he was.

And surely, if he could get a message through to Mekky, Mekky wouldn't refuse to help him *in extremis*.

He was still walking northward, in the Twenties, when he realized where he must go. He started walking faster.

It was dusk when he reached the apartment house on Thirty-seventh Street; the few people left on the streets were almost running now in their haste to beat the mistout.

A janitor was just reaching to lock the outer door as Keith opened it. The man's hand went quickly to his back pocket, but he didn't draw the gun or whatever was there. He asked suspiciously, "Who do you want to see?"

"Miss Hadley," Keith said. "Just staying a minute."

"Okay." The janitor stepped aside and let him past.

Keith started back for the door of what looked like a self-service elevator, but the janitor's voice came back after him. "You'll have to walk. Juice is off already, mister. And hurry back down if you want me to take a chance of opening the door to let you out."

Keith nodded and took the stairs instead. He ran up them so fast that on the landing of the fifth floor he had to stop, panting, to get his breath back so he'd be able to talk.

After a minute he rang the bell of the front apartment. There were footsteps toward the door and Betty Hadley's voice called out, "Who is it?"

"Karl Winston, Miss Hadley. Sorry to bother you, but it's important. It's— a matter of life and death."

The door opened on the chain and Betty's face looked at him through the three-inch opening. Her eyes looked a little frightened.

He said, "I know it's awfully late, Miss Hadley—but I've got to get in touch with Mekky right away. It's terribly important; is there any way it can be done?"

The door started to close and for a moment he thought she was going to shut him out without speaking again; then he heard the rattle of the chain and knew that she'd pulled the door nearer shut only so that she could unbolt the chain.

The bolt slid out of the groove and the door opened.

Betty said, "Come in, *K-Keith Winton.*"

He didn't even notice at first that she'd called him by his right name. She still wore the costume she'd worn at her desk that morning at the Borden offices. Yes, there were green trunks to go with the green bra. They were very brief trunks, very well shaped. Green leather boots came halfway up shapely calves. Between the boots and the trunks, the bare golden flesh of dimpled knees and rounded thighs.

She stepped back and, scarcely daring to breathe, Keith went into the room. He closed the door behind him and stood leaning against it, staring at Betty, not quite believing.

The room was dim, the shades already pulled down. The light came from a pair of candles in a candelabrum on the table behind Betty. Her face was shadowed, but the soft light behind her made a golden aura of her blond hair and silhouetted her slim, beautiful body. An artist could not have posed her better.

She said, "You're in trouble, Keith Winton? They found out— about you?"

His voice surprised him by being a bit hoarse. "How—how did you know my name?"

"Mekky told me."

"Oh. Just what did Mekky tell you?"

Instead of answering, she asked, "You haven't mentioned Mekky to anyone else? No one would think of your coming here?"

"No."

She nodded, and then turned, and Keith saw for the first time that a colored maid was standing in the far doorway. Betty said, "It's all right, Della. You may go to your room."

"But, Miss—" The maid's voice was worried.

"It's all right, Della."

The door closed quietly behind the maid and Betty turned back to Keith.

He took a step toward her, and then made himself stop. He asked, "Don't you remember—I don't understand. *Which* Betty Hadley are you? Even if Mekky told you—how could you have known—"

It sounded inarticulate and confused, even to him.

Her voice was cool, but friendly. She said, "Sit down, Mr. Winton. I'm going to call you that to avoid confusing you with the Keith Winton I know. What happened? Was it Keith who found you out?"

Keith nodded gloomily. "Yes, the two stories I gave him were his own stories. I didn't even try to explain they were mine, too. It wouldn't have made sense to him; it doesn't make much sense to me, either, even though I know it's true. And I'd have been shot long before I got halfway through trying to tell the truth."

"Do you know what the truth *is?*"

"No. Do you? Did Mekky tell you?"

"He doesn't know either. What about the stories? What do you mean, he wrote them and you wrote them too?"

"Something like that. In the universe I came from, I am—I was—Keith Winton. Here *he's* Keith Winton. Our lives were approximately parallel up to last Sunday evening.

"But about my stories— Please tear up that one I left with you this morning. Technically, it's plagiarized. But—about reaching Mekky. I've *got* to. Is there any way?"

She shook her head. "You can't possibly reach Mekky. He's with the fleet. The Arcs are—" She stopped short.

"The Arcs are going to attack," Keith said. "Mekky told me there was a crisis in the war. That the Arcs might win." He laughed a little, bitterly. "But I can't get excited about the war. I can't believe in it enough to get excited about it. I can't seem to believe in anything here, really, except— No, I don't even believe in you—in that costume. What is it? Do you wear it all the time?"

"Of course."

"Why? I mean, other women here—"

She looked at him in bewilderment. "Not all of them, of course. Only a very few in fact. Only the space girls."

"Space girls?"

"Of course. Girls who work, or have worked, on spaceships. Or ones who are fiancées of space men. Being Dopelle's fiancée would entitle me to wear it, even if I hadn't done exploring in space, on leaves of absence from Borden."

"But *why?*" He floundered. "I mean, is it so hot in a spaceship that such an—an abbreviated costume is necessary? Or what?"

"I don't know what you mean. Of course it isn't hot in spaceships. Mostly we wear heated plastic coveralls."

"Transparent plastic?"

"Naturally. Mr. Winton, what are you getting at?"

He ran a hand through his hair. "I wish I knew. The costumes. Transparent plastic— Like the covers on *Surprising Stories.*"

"Why, of course. Why would cover pictures like that be *put* on *Surprising Stories* unless we really wore such costumes?"

He tried to think of an answer to that; there wasn't any.

And anyway, he could stay here only a few minutes and there were important things he had to know. Things that might make the difference of his being alive or dead twenty-four hours from now.

Resolutely he looked *at* her costume instead of the parts of her that weren't covered by it. That helped a little. A damned little.

He asked, "What did Mekky tell you about me?" That was safer ground, and besides he had to know.

"He didn't know much himself," she told him. "He said he hadn't time to go really deep under the surface of your mind. But he learned that you really were from—somewhere else. He didn't know where, or how you got here or what had happened. He said that if you tried to explain yourself to anyone else, you'd be judged insane, but that you weren't. He could tell that."

"He knew that where you came from you were called Keith Winton and were an editor—although you don't look like the Keith Winton you found here, and you were smart enough to use a different name."

"But not smart enough," Keith said, "to use a completely different one. And not smart enough not to try to sell Keith Winton his own stories. But go on."

"He knew you were in a jam here because—well, because you don't know enough about things not to make mistakes. He knew you'd get yourself shot for a spy unless you were awfully careful. He said he warned you about that."

Keith leaned forward. "What *is* Mekky? Is he really only a machine, a robot? Or did—Dopelle put a real brain into a sphere?"

"He's a machine—not a real brain in the sense you mean it. But he's more than a machine, somehow. Even *Dopelle* doesn't understand all of that part of it, how *he* did it, but Mekky has emotions. He even has a sense of humor."

Keith noticed the almost reverent way she'd said *Dopelle* and the way she'd emphasized the personal pronoun, almost capitalizing it. Damn him, he thought, she almost worships him.

He closed his eyes a second and when he opened them he didn't look at her. But looking away made him think of her even more strongly, and he hardly knew that she was talking again until he realized she was asking a question.

"What can I do? Mekky told me he saw in your mind that you might come to me for help if things got hopeless for you. And he said it would be all right for me to help and advise you if I didn't take any risk myself."

Keith said, "I wouldn't let you do that. I wouldn't have come here if anybody could have followed me, or even have suspected that I might come to you. But what I wanted was to find out how to get in touch with Mekky. My masquerade here has blown up higher than a kite, and I haven't any believable answers for the questions the cops would ask me—even if they stopped to ask questions. I hoped Mekky could do something."

"But there's no way you could get in touch with Mekky unless you could get to the fleet."

"And where is the fleet?"

She hesitated, frowning, before she decided to speak. "I guess it doesn't matter if I tell you. It's not exactly public knowledge, but a lot of people know. It's near Saturn. But you couldn't possibly get there; you'll have to wait it out until Mekky returns. Do you have any money?"

"No, but I don't— Wait, there's something you can tell me, I hope. I could look it up at the library tomorrow, but if you can tell me now, it'll save time. What's the score on coinage—metal coins?"

"Metal coins? There haven't been any since nineteen thirty-five. They were called in then, at the time of the change over from dollars-and-cents currency to credits."

"Why?"

"The change to credits? To establish a world-wide monetary standard. All countries made the change at the same time, so the war effort would be—"

Keith interrupted. "Not that; I mean why no metal coins?"

"The Arcs were counterfeiting them—and nearly succeeding in upsetting our economy by doing so. Counterfeiting paper currency, too. They discovered Earth was a capitalist economy and—"

"All of it? Russia?"

"Of course, all of it. What do you mean about Russia?"

"Never mind," Keith said. "Go on."

"They were able to make counterfeit money that couldn't be told from real— not even by experts. It started an inflation that looked like it was going to lead to a smashup of the whole world economy.

"So the war council of the nations appealed to the scientists, and a group of scientists worked out a kind of paper currency that the Arcs couldn't counterfeit. I don't know what the secret of the currency is; nobody does except a few top men in the various countries' bureaus of engraving."

"Why can't it be counterfeited?" Keith asked.

"The paper. Something secret—a process, rather than an ingredient that the Arcs could analyze—makes the paper give off a faint yellowish glow in the dark. Anybody can spot counterfeit money now, just by holding it somewhere in a deep shadow. And no counterfeiters, including the Arcs, can duplicate the paper that gives off that glow."

Keith nodded. "And that was when the change was made from dollars to credits?"

"Yes, in all countries simultaneously when the new paper was introduced. Each country backs its own currency, but it's all in credits and all kept at par so it's interchangeable."

"And they called in all the old money, and made it illegal to possess any?"

"Yes. And there's a pretty stiff fine—a jail sentence, in some countries—for possessing any. But there are coin collectors, a great many of them, who are willing to take a chance because they're so enthusiastic about their hobby. And, because the traffic in coins is black market, they bring high prices. Collecting coins is illegal and dangerous, but it's not considered really a moral crime by most people."

"Like drinking during Prohibition?"

Betty looked puzzled. "Like what?"

Keith said, "Never mind." He took the little wad of money out of his pocket, the coins wrapped in the bills. He opened them out and studied them, first the bills and then the coins.

He said, "I've got five coins here and two bills that are dated before nineteen thirty-five. Got any idea what they might be worth?"

He handed them to Betty, who held them near the candle to look at them closely. She said, "I don't know just what prices are paid; it depends on the dates and the condition. But very roughly, I'd guess they're worth ten thousand credits—a thousand dollars by the old scale."

"Is that all?" Keith asked. "A druggist in Greeneville gave me two thousand credits for just one coin, and he said it was worth a lot more than that."

She handed the money back to him. "It was probably a rare date. Of course, one of these could be rare, too. I just made a guess on a basis of their being about average as far as rareness of dates is concerned. But one of them alone might be worth ten thousand credits if it's a rare date. What are those other bills and coins you separated these from?"

"The ones that could have got me in real trouble. They're all dated after nineteen thirty-five."

"Then they must be counterfeits, Arc counterfeits. You'd better get rid of them and not have any of them found on you."

Keith said, "That's what I don't understand. These *aren't* Arc counterfeits, but why would the Arcs have counterfeited coins of dates after the Earth governments quit *making* coins?"

"They do stupid things as well as brilliant ones. After the currency change cut off their chance of counterfeiting in the ordinary way, they had their spies here raise money for their operations by selling coins to collectors. Only they pulled the stupid boner of continuing to make coins and bills of the obsolete type but of current dates.

"About twenty Arc spies have been caught because they tried to sell misdated coins to collectors. Why, just last Sunday, somewhere upstate, an Arc spy tried to—" She stopped and stared at him. "Oh. That would have been you, wouldn't it?"

"That would have been I," Keith said. "Only I'm not an Arc spy, and the coin wasn't a counterfeit—Arc or otherwise."

"But if it wasn't counterfeit, how *could* it have been dated after thirty-five?"

Keith sighed. "If I knew that, I'd have answers to a lot of other questions. Anyway, I'll drop the unsalable coins and bills out of this lot down the first sewer after I leave here. But look—about Arcturian spies. Are Arcturians human beings? Are they so like us physically that they can pass as humans?"

The girl shuddered. "They're *horribly* different. Monsters. More like insects in appearance, bigger of course, and as intelligent as we are. But evil. Back in the early days of the war, they captured quite a few human beings alive. And they can—*take over* people, put their minds into human bodies and use them as spies and saboteurs.

"There aren't so many now. Most of them have been killed. Sooner or later they give themselves away because their minds are alien and they don't completely understand the details of our civilization. They make some mistake that exposes them."

"I can see how they'd do that," Keith said grimly.

"Anyway, it's a diminishing danger. Our defenses are good enough now that it's been years since any human beings have been captured alive. Sometimes they can get through to kill, but not to capture. And they can't have many left alive out of the people they captured early in the war."

"But even so," Keith said, "why shoot on suspicion? Why aren't they arrested? If their minds are really alien, a psychiatrist should be able to tell for sure whether they're Arcturians or not. Don't a lot of innocent people get killed because of that shoot-on-suspicion business?"

"Of course. Maybe a hundred for every real spy that's killed. But—well, they're so dangerous, so capable of doing things that can result in the death of a million or more people, that it's better, *really* better, not to take the slightest chance with one. Even if a thousand humans were killed to get one Arc spy, it'd be worth it.

"You see if they got even a few of our scientific secrets to add to their own science it would change the tide of the war—and it's pretty evenly balanced now. That is, I thought it was pretty even until Mekky told me, as he told you, that there's a crisis right now. Maybe they have an edge already. And if we lose the war, it means annihilation for the human race. They don't want even to rule us; they want to exterminate us and take over the Solar System for their own use."

"That would be nasty of them," Keith said.

Betty's face flamed with sudden anger. "Don't joke about it. Do you think the end of the human race is a joke?"

"I'm sorry," Keith said contritely. "It's just that somehow I can't— Let's skip that. I guess I see what you mean about how dangerous a spy can be. But I still don't see what's to lose by being sure before you shoot one. If you've got a gun on him, he can't get away."

"Oh, but he can, a good fraction of the time. They tried arresting them until too many escaped on the way to jail or even while they were locked up. They've got special powers, physical and mental. Having a gun on one of them isn't enough."

Keith grinned wryly. "So one of them could take a gun away from a W.B.I. man who was holding it on him. Well—in my case, if they had any doubts before this afternoon, they haven't now."

He stood up. For a long moment he stared at Betty, at the gleam of candle-light on her golden hair and golden skin, at the incredible beauty of her face and the incredible wonder of her body. He stared at her as though he might never see her again—as, indeed, seemed very probable.

He formed a mental picture of her that he would carry with him, he knew, for the rest of his life—whether the rest of his life was forty minutes or forty years. The former seemed the more likely.

He turned his head and looked at the window, the window from which Betty had leaned on the occasion of Mekky's visit. The pane of the window was black, blank.

The mistout had started.

He said, "Thank you, Miss Hadley. Good-bye."

She stood up, and her eyes went to the window, as his had. "But where are you going to go? You might take a chance for a block or two if you're careful, but—"

"Don't worry about me. I'm armed."

"But you haven't any place to go, have you? You can't stay here, of course; there's just Della and I. But there's a vacant apartment on the floor below. I can fix it with the janitor so—"

"*No!*"

Keith's answer was so explosive that he felt foolish after he had said it.

She said, "But tomorrow I can talk to the W. B. I. I can explain to them that Mekky vouched for you to me. Until Mekky gets back a few months from now, it won't be safe for you to be running loose—but on my word they might hold you in protective custody until Mekky does come back."

It made sense and a shade of doubt must have showed on Keith's face. Little as he liked the idea of several months in protective custody, it wouldn't last forever, and it was better to be alive than to be dead.

She must have seen she was gaining her point. She said, "I'm almost sure they'll believe me—at least enough to give you the benefit of the doubt. As Dopelle's fiancée—"

"No," Keith said. She couldn't have known it, but it had been the wrong thing to say. He shook his head very definitely.

"I can't stay," he said. "I can't explain—but I can't stay."

He looked at her again, filling his eyes with her for what would quite likely be the last time. "Good-bye," he said.

"Good-bye, then." She held out her hand to him but he pretended not to see it. He didn't trust himself to touch her.

He got out quickly.

On his way down the stairs he began to realize how foolish he had been, and to be glad that he'd been foolish. He was glad he hadn't accepted any help from Betty Hadley. Advice, yes; that was all right. And answers to questions he couldn't have asked anyone but her or Mekky. His picture of this universe was a lot clearer now, especially his understanding of the coinage matter.

Other things were still puzzling. That matter of the costume she wore. Didn't she know she must drive men crazy, dressing like that? And yet the costume had seemed to her so natural that she was puzzled why he had wondered about it.

Well, that matter would have to be filed away for future curiosity. Maybe Mekky would be able to explain a lot of minor things to him, if and when he ever got to Mekky, and if and when Mekky condescended to give him enough time to solve his major problem.

Anyway, he was glad he'd had the guts not to accept Betty's offer of help.

It was silly not to have, but he was tired, very tired, of being pushed around by this mad universe of disguised Arcturians and flying sewing machines.

The more cautious and careful he'd tried to be, the more slips he'd made and the more trouble he got into. He was mad, now. And he had a gun in his pocket, a big gun, a forty-five automatic that would stop even an eight-foot purple Lunan.

He was in a mood to use that gun, too. Anybody who gave him any trouble in the mistout was going to get some trouble back. Even if he ran afoul of the Nighters, he'd get a few of them before they got him.

The hell with being cautious. What did he have to lose?

The janitor was still in the downstairs hallway. He looked in amazement as Keith came down the stairs.

"Y'ain't going *out*, are you, mister?" he wanted to know.

Keith grinned at him. "Got to. Got to see a man about a sphere."

"You mean *Mekky?* You going to see *Dopelle?*" There was awe in the man's voice. He went to the door to open it, drawing a revolver from his hip pocket as he did so. He said, "Well, if you know *him*—and I shoulda guessed it, since you was seeing Miss Hadley—maybe you know what you're doing. I hope so."

Keith said, "We both hope so."

He slid through the doorway into the blackness and heard the door quickly slammed shut and bolted after him.

He stood there, just outside the door, and listened. After the scrape of the bolt going shut, there wasn't a sound. The silence was as dense as the darkness.

Finally, he took a deep breath. He couldn't stand there all night; might as well get going. This time he was going to take a smarter way of traversing the mistout, though, than the one he'd used Sunday night after his arrival from Greeneville.

He felt his way out to the curb and sat down on it long enough to take off his shoes, tie the laces of them together, and hang them around his neck. Without them, he wouldn't make enough noise for anyone to hear and stalk him.

He stood up and found that it was easy, if awkward, to follow the curb line by walking with one foot on the curbing and the other foot down in the gutter.

The feel of a sewer grating under his foot reminded him of the misdated coins and bills he had to get rid of. He'd put them back in a different pocket from the others so he didn't have to strike a match to identify them as he took them out and shoved them through the grating of the sewer. He heard them splash into water several feet down.

With that out of the way, he went on, listening. He shifted the forty-five automatic to his right coat pocket and kept his hand in the pocket and on the gun, his thumb ready to flick the safety catch.

He wasn't afraid now, as he'd been the last time he'd been in the mistout. Having the gun was a factor in that, but it wasn't all of the explanation. Nor was it because the last time the mistout itself had been a mystery and now he understood what it was and why it was there.

The difference was simpler than that: last time, he had been the hunted and this time he was the hunter. His role now was active, not passive, and the mistout was his friend and not his enemy.

His plans were necessarily vague and would have to adapt themselves to circumstances, but the first step was clear. The first thing he needed was money, a chance to sell several dollars' worth of dollars for ten thousand credits, more or less. And anyone he would encounter would be a criminal—since only criminals were abroad in the mistout—and could be persuaded, with a forty-five if not otherwise, to lead him to a fence who'd buy the illegal coins and bills from him.

Yes, it felt good to be the hunter and not the hunted, and to be taking some more positive action than writing stories merely to survive. He'd always hated writing, anyway.

Hunting was much better. And this kind of hunting, especially. He'd never hunted men before.

JOE

He turned south on Fifth Avenue. For the first few blocks, he might have been groping through the ruins of Chichen Itzá or Ur of the Chaldees. Then, suddenly, he heard his quarry.

It was not the sound of footsteps; whoever it was either was standing still against the front of a building or else had, like Keith, taken off his shoes to walk silently. The sound Keith heard was a slight, barely audible sniffle.

He stood very still, scarcely breathing, until he heard it again, and then he knew the man was moving, going south. The second sniffle had come from further away, in that direction.

He hurried his steps, almost running, until he was sure that he was well ahead of his quarry. Then he cut diagonally across the sidewalk and groped with his hands ahead of him until he came to the building fronts. Then, facing the direction from which his victim was approaching, he drew the automatic from his pocket and stood waiting.

The instant something bumped into the muzzle of the pistol, Keith reached out with his left hand and caught the front of a coat to keep the man from pulling away.

"Don't move," he said sharply. Then, "All right, turn around, very slowly."

There'd been no answer but a sharp intake of breath. The man turned slowly; Keith's hand kept contact with him. When the man's back was toward

Keith, Keith's left hand groped, crossed over, and took a revolver out of a right hip pocket. He slid it into his own left coat pocket and quickly put his hand on the man's shoulder again. The most dangerous part was over.

He said, "Don't move yet. We're going to talk. Who are you?"

A tight voice said, "What do you care who I am? All I got on me is about thirty credits and that rod. You got the rod; take the dough too, and let me go."

"I don't want your thirty credits," Keith told him. "I want some information. If I get it straight I might even give you your rod back. Do you know your way around?"

"What do you mean?"

Keith said, "I just got in town, from St. Louis. I don't know the ropes here, and I got to find me a fence. Tonight."

There was a pause, and the voice was a little less tight now. "Jewelry? Or what?"

"Coins. And a few bills. Pre-thirty-five dollars. Who handles the stuff here?"

"What's in it for me?"

Keith said, "Your life, for one thing. Maybe your gun back. And—if you don't try to cross me—maybe a hundred credits. Two hundred, maybe, if you take me to somebody who'll give me a good price."

"Peanuts. Make it five hundred."

Keith laughed. "You're in a swell position to bargain. I'll make it two hundred and thirty, though. You've already got the thirty on account; consider that I took it away from you and gave it back."

Surprisingly, the man laughed, too. He said, "You win, mister. I'll take you to see Ross. He won't cheat you any worse than anybody else would. Come on."

"One thing first," Keith said. "Turn back this way and strike a match, I want a look at you. I want to know you again, if you make a break."

"Okay," the voice said. It was relaxed now, almost friendly.

A match scraped and flared.

Keith's captive, he saw, was a small, slender man of about forty, not too badly dressed but in need of a shave and with slightly bleary eyes. He grinned, a bit lopsidedly.

"You'll know me," he said, "so you might as well have a handle. It's Joe."

"Okay, Joe. How far is this Ross guy?"

"Couple of blocks. He'll be in a poker game." The match died. "Look, St. Louie, how much is this stuff worth, about?"

"Somebody told me ten thousand credits."

"Then you might get five. Ross is square. But listen, gun or no gun, you'll do better to cut me in. There'll be other guys there. We could take you easy, unless I'm on your side."

Keith thought a minute. Then he said, "Maybe you've got something there. I'll cut you in for ten per cent—five hundred if I get five thousand. Fair enough?"

"Yeah, fair enough."

Keith hesitated only a second. He'd need a friend, and there was something in Joe's voice that made him think he could take a chance. His whole plan was a desperate gamble anyway, and a slight risk now might save having to take bigger ones later.

Impulsively, he took Joe's revolver out of his pocket, groped for Joe's hand, and gave the gun back to him.

But there wasn't any surprise in Joe's voice when he said, "Thanks. Two blocks south. I'll lead the way and you stick with me. Better keep a hand on my back."

They single-filed along the building fronts, locked arms while they crossed two streets.

Then Joe said, "Stick close now. We go back in the areaway between the second and third buildings from the corner. Keep touching me or you'll go on past."

Back in the areaway, Joe found a door and knocked three times and then twice.

It opened and a light blinded Keith momentarily. When he could see again, a man in the doorway was lowering a sawed-off shotgun. He said, "Hi, Joe. This mug all right?"

Joe said, "Sure. Pal of mine from St. Louie. We got some business with Ross. Is he in the game?"

The man with the shotgun nodded. "Go on in."

They went along a narrow hallway. Around the corner of it was a man with a submachine gun aimed toward them, standing in front of a chair near a closed door. He said, "Hi, Joe," and sat back down in the chair with the gun in his lap. "Bring a sucker for the game?"

Joe shook his head. "Nope, business. How go things?"

"Ross is going hot tonight. Better not sit in unless you feel plenty lucky."

"I don't. Glad Ross is winning, though; maybe he'll give us a good price."

He opened the door beside which the gunman was sitting, and went into a room that was blue with smoke. Keith followed him.

Five men were sitting around a green poker table. Joe walked up to one of them, a fat man with very thick glasses and no hair whatsoever. He jerked his thumb at Keith.

"Friend of mine from St. Louie, Ross," he said. "Got some coins and bills. I told him you'd give him a square price."

The thick glasses turned on Keith and Keith nodded. He took the coins and bills from his pocket and put them on the green table in front of the fat man.

Ross glanced at each one and then looked up. "Four grand," he said.

"Make it five and it's a deal," Keith said. "They're worth ten easy."

Ross shook his head and took up the cards that had just been dealt him. "Open for a yard," he said.

Keith felt a touch on his arm. Joe pulled him back a step from the table. He said, "I should have told you. Ross is one-price. If he offers you four thou, he won't give you four thousand and one. Any price he makes is strictly take-it-or-leave-it. Won't do any good to argue."

"And if I leave it?" Keith asked.

Joe shrugged. "I know a couple more guys. But it means a lot of traveling in the mistout to get to 'em; we might get there or we might end up in the gutter. And probably they wouldn't give you any more than Ross would. Was whoever told you the coins were worth ten gees an expert on pre-cred?"

"No," Keith admitted. "Okay, I'll take it. He'll give us the cash now, won't he? He carries that much?"

Joe grinned. "Ross? If he's got less than a hundred gees on him, I'll eat an Arc. Don't worry about getting cash on the line. Four grand's peanuts to him."

Keith nodded and turned back to the table. He waited until the hand was over and then said, "Okay. Four grand is all right."

The fat man pulled a fat wallet from his pocket and counted out three thousand-credit bills and ten hundred-credit ones. He folded Keith's coins carefully inside the bills again and put them into his vest pocket.

"Sit in on the game a while?" he asked.

Keith shook his head. "Sorry. Something I got to do."

He glanced at Joe as he finished counting the money and Joe shook his head almost imperceptibly to indicate that he didn't want to take his cut here.

They went out again, past the man in the hallway with the submachine gun in his lap and the man at the outer door with the sawed-off shotgun. The latter bolted the door after them.

In the mistout again, they moved out of earshot of the door and then Joe said, "A tenth of four gees is four yards. Want me to light a match so you can count it?"

"Okay," Keith said. "Unless you know somewhere we can have a drink and talk a few minutes. Maybe we can do some more business."

"An idea," Joe said. "Guess I can take off this evening anyway, with four hundred in the sock. That'll hold me tomorrow and I got some coming tomorrow night. Gawd, I was down to thirty snicks."

"Which way, Joe?"

"Just keep your hand on my shoulder. I won't lose you—not till you pay off, anyway." He sighed. "Man, I can sure use a snort of moonjuice."

"Me too," said Keith, ungrammatically and not quite truthfully; he wondered what moonjuice was and hoped it didn't taste anything like a Callisto cocktail.

He groped with his hand and found Joe's shoulder as Joe said, "All right, pal. Here we go." They went out of the areaway and turned south. Only half a block farther—they hadn't crossed any streets this time—Joe stopped and said, "This is it. Wait a sec."

Again he knocked on a door, this time twice and then three times. This time the door swung inward into a dimly lighted hallway. No one was in sight.

Joe called out, "It's me, Rello. Joe. And a friend." He walked in and down the hallway. Keith followed him.

"Rello's a Proxie," Joe explained as Keith followed him along the hallway. "On a shelf over the door. Gets you in the back as you go down the hall here, if he don't know you."

Keith turned and looked over his shoulder, and wished that he hadn't. Whatever was on the shelf over the door was in deep shadow and he couldn't see it clearly, but maybe that was just as well for his peace of mind. It looked like a large turtle with tentacles like a devilfish, and with bright red luminous eyes like flashlight bulbs behind big red lenses. It didn't have any weapon that he could see—but he had a hunch it wouldn't need one.

Was a Proxie a being from Proxima Centauri? He wished he could ask Joe about it; maybe he could lead the conversation around to Rello without showing his ignorance on the subject, after they were sitting down drinking.

He turned back and felt chills down his spine all along the hallway until they came to a door with a peephole in it. Just like Prohibition, he thought—and almost said, until he remembered Betty's blank reaction to a mention of Prohibition and stopped himself in time.

Joe knocked two and three again and they were examined through the peephole. Joe jerked a finger over his shoulder and said, "With me, Hank. He's okay," and the door opened for them.

They went into the back room of a tavern; through an open doorway Keith could see the bar, dimly lighted with green and blue neons. The room they were in was filled with tables; card games were going on at three of them.

Joe waved at several men who looked up as they came in, then looked back at Keith. "Sit in here?" he asked. "Or shall we go in the bar? Guess we can talk better in there, and you said something about business."

Keith nodded. "Bar sounds better," he said.

They went through the doorway into the blue and green lighted barroom. Except for a bartender on duty and three women sitting on stools at the bar, it was empty. The three women looked up as they came in; one, Keith noticed, was dressed in the exceedingly brief costume that Betty had been wearing, bra and shorts of blue silk and blue leather calf-boots; nothing else. But she looked nothing like Betty otherwise; she was at least twenty years older, fat, blowsy and slightly drunk. The blue-green light made her look ghastly.

Joe waved at her and said, "Hi, Bessie," then went to the farthest booth and slid into one of the seats. Keith took the seat opposite him.

Keith took out his wallet to take out the four hundred credits for Joe, but the little man said quickly, "Not yet, pal. Wait till the gals have been here."

The gals were coming already, Keith saw. Not the one in the space-girl costume—or lack of costume—but the other two. They were young and not unattractive, both of them, despite what the blue-green light did to their complexions.

Fortunately, Joe stalled them before they could sit down. He said, "We got business to talk, girls. Maybe we'll call you down later, if you're not busy then. Tell Spec to give you each a drink on me, meanwhile, huh? And one for Bessie."

One of them said, "Sure, Joe," and they went back to their stools at the bar.

Keith took out his wallet again and had succeeded in handing over the four hundred credits by the time the bartender came down to see what they wanted. Joe left one of his hundred-credit bills on the table.

He said, "Bring us a couple of moonjuices, Spec. And one around for the gals. How's Little Rello doing tonight?"

The bartender chuckled. "Not bad, Joe. We had to sweep the hallway twice, and it's early yet."

He went away back of the bar and Keith took a chance. He said, "Rello interests me, Joe. Tell me something about him." That was general enough not to get him in trouble.

Joe said, "Rello's a rennie, and just about the toughest of the bunch. He's the toughest in New York, anyway. He was one of the first Proxies to change sides during the little squabble out at Centauri. Want to meet him?"

"Not especially," Keith said. "I was just wondering." He wondered, but not aloud, if rennie was slang for renegade. And if Rello had been one of the Proxima Centaurians to change sides during a war, his being a renegade would make sense.

Joe said, "Don't blame you. But you'd better, if you want to come back here sometime. He can get you with one eye at twenty feet and if he quares through both eyes—brother, there won't be enough of you left to bother mopping. I'll give you a tip."

"Yes?"

"Speak to him *as* you come through the door. Don't wait till you're far enough in for him to see you or maybe it'll be too late. I think that's what happens to most of these mugs they have to sweep up here."

Joe shoved his hat back on his head and grinned. "Telling you all this because you're a right guy—I think. I hope we can do more business."

"About that—"

"Not yet," Joe interrupted. "Not till we've had anyway one moonjuice, Dunno, at that, whether I ought to string with you or do business with you. You trust people too much; you'll get in trouble."

"You mean giving you back your rod?"

Joe nodded.

Keith said, "And if I hadn't?"

Joe's hand rubbed his stubbly chin with a raspy sound. Then he grinned. "Damn if you're not right at that, St. Louie. If you hadn't, I'd have taken you. All I'd have had to do was give the signal, back there where you talked to Ross. But on account of your giving me back my rod, I didn't. Even here, pal, if I didn't want you to, you wouldn't last longer than—"

He broke off as Spec came with two shot glasses of a slightly milky fluid. He picked up Joe's hundred-credit bill and put down some change in paper currency.

Joe lifted his glass. "Death to the Arcs," he said, and took a sip.

"And suddenly," Keith said. He watched Joe carefully, saw that he took only a sip of the milky liquid, and did the same. It was just as well that he did; even one sip burned its way down his throat with the heat of, say, half a tumbler of gin. It was hot as chili powder and, paradoxically, it was cool, too. It was thick as syrup but not sweet; it left a faint mint taste in his mouth, once his tongue had cooled.

"Real stuff," Joe said. "Right off the space freighter. Get much of it out your way?"

"Some," Keith said cautiously. "Not much of it this good, though."

"How are things out that way?"

"Fair," Keith said. He wished he could talk more, but giving more than monosyllabic answers could be dangerous. He stared into his glass of moonjuice and wondered what it was and what effect it was going to have. He felt none, as yet, from the single sip he'd taken.

"Where you staying here?"

Keith said, "Nowhere yet. Just blew in. I should have holed in before the mistout, not knowing the ropes here, but didn't have sense enough to. And I got in a game and lost all the credits I had—that's why I had to cash in on those coins tonight; I was flat broke outside of them. I'd intended to hang onto them and try to get a good price direct from a collector."

That, he thought, would give Joe an explanation of why he'd been alone in the mistout, broke except for coins he had to sell right away. And apparently it was all right. Joe nodded. He said, "Well, if you want to hole in for the night later, I can fix it for you here. A room with or without."

Keith didn't ask with or without what. He said, "Later, maybe. The evening's a pup." And he was surprised to realize that it really was; it couldn't be over an hour and a half since darkness had fallen.

Joe laughed heartily. He said, "The evening's a pup. That's a good one. Never heard that before, but it's a good one. You know, pal, I like you. Well, you ready?"

Keith wondered, for what? He said, "Sure."

Joe picked up his glass. "Then here we go. See you when we get back."

Keith picked his up and said, "Happy landing."

Joe howled with laughter. "That's another good one. Happy landing. You think 'em up, pal; you really think 'em up. Here's mud in your ear."

He tossed the drink down. And held the pose, rigid, glass to his lips. His eyes looked glazed, although they were still open. Keith had brought his own glass to his lips but hadn't yet downed the drink. He didn't, now. He stared across the table, fascinated, at Joe. Joe wasn't seeing him; Joe wasn't seeing anything in this world.

Keith glanced quickly down the bar and saw that neither the bartender nor any of the three women was looking his way. He reached under the table and poured the rest of the moonjuice on the floor, then put the glass back to his lips.

He was just in time. Joe's eyes flickered once and then, as suddenly as it had come, the rigidity was gone. He put the glass down and sighed deeply.

He said, "Gawd, I was back on Venus again. In one of the slimy swamps, but I loved it. There was a space girl—" He shook his head wonderingly.

Keith watched him, curiously. There seemed to be no after-effect whatsoever. He'd been completely paralyzed for ten or twenty seconds; now he was completely normal, no different in any way than he'd been before.

Joe took cigarettes out of his pocket and passed one across to Keith. He said, "One more, huh? Then if you want to talk business, okay."

"If it's on me, all right," Keith said. He glanced down the bar and this time caught the bartender's eye. He held up two fingers and the bartender nodded. Apparently that was a signal that couldn't be misunderstood anywhere. Even here.

Keith put a bill of his own on the table. He was aware of a mounting excitement in him as he realized that he'd decided that this time he was going to down the milky liquid as Joe had done; he was going to find out what had happened to Joe during those ten or twenty seconds. Joe had come out of it all right and if Joe could, he could. And being cautious had its limits.

The moonjuice came and he got seventy credits change out of his bill.

Joe picked up his glass and so did Keith, but Joe merely took a sip and smacked his lips, so Keith did likewise. Apparently the preliminary sip and then a bit of conversation was ritual. Probably it would be rudeness to down the drink right away.

The second sip tasted better than the first one had; it burned less and he found out that the aftertaste wasn't quite mint after all; it was something he couldn't identify.

Since there was to be an interval anyway, he thought it wouldn't hurt to lead around gradually to the business he had in mind. He leaned a little across the table. "Joe," he said, "do you happen to know where I can find an ex-space-pilot who'd like to make a little dough on the side?"

Joe started to laugh, and then his eyes narrowed a little. He asked, "You kidding?"

That meant it had been a bad question, but Keith couldn't see why. And anyway, he had to go through with it now; whatever he'd said wrong, he didn't know how to back out.

Casually he let his hand drop toward the pocket in which he had the automatic. He wondered what his chances of shooting his way out of this place—by any door except the one guarded by Rello the Proxie—would be. They wouldn't be too good, he decided, if Joe gave the signal. But maybe, if something was really wrong, he could get the drop on Joe again before Joe could give a signal.

He stared at Joe coolly, his fingertips already touching the butt of the automatic. "Why should I be kidding?" he demanded.

SPACEWARD HO

To Keith's relief, Joe grinned. He jerked a thumb at the lapel of his coat. Keith saw an emblem there about the size and shape of the ruptured duck he himself had worn for a while.

"You're blind, St. Louie," Joe said.

Keith's hand moved away from his pocket; he hadn't made a major boner after all. He said, "Didn't notice it, Joe. Guess I *am* blind. But we've been in the mistout most of the time; it didn't show up so well out there. How long you been out?"

"Five years. Most of the time I was in, I was based on Kapi, Mars. Glad I wasn't there a few days ago." He shook his head slowly. "Nothing left of Kapi now."

Keith said, "We'll get back at them for that."

"Maybe."

"You sound pessimistic, Joe."

Joe lighted another cigarette from the butt of his last one and took a deep drag. He said, "There's a showdown coming, St. Louie. A big one. Oh, I don't *know* anything or I wouldn't be talking about it. Anyway, I know just what I read between the lines. But when you've been out there bucking the Arcs you get the feel of things. There's a full-scale attack coming. I think the Arcs are going to make it. I think the stalemate is over, and the war's going to be over too, one way or the other. What I'm afraid of—"

"Yes?" Keith prompted.

"What I'm afraid of is that they've got something new. We're so evenly balanced, that one new weapon— You know what I mean."

Keith nodded gravely. He remembered he'd better stick to the point and talk as little as possible. He couldn't discuss the war intelligently, so he'd better get Joe to safer ground—and closer to the point he wanted to lead up to. And he wanted to know if Joe could really pilot a ship or if he'd been just a gunner or something.

He asked, "Been to the moon recently?"

"A year ago." Joe's lips twisted. "Hadn't started mistouting yet, then. I fought it longer than most of the boys. Like a chump, I thought I could make an honest living. But about the moon—yeah, I piloted a rich guy there in his own boat. What a brawl that was!"

"Bad?"

"Good. Six of 'em in the party and all as drunk as gracchi miners on a holiday. A six-year-old kid can peelot one of those Ehrling jobs, but none of 'em in the party was sober enough to do it. They'd have ended up in the Pleiades without a paddle.

"I was driving a cab, picked 'em up one afternoon on Times Square and drove 'em to their private port over in Jersey. Guy that owned the boat saw my copper chicken and offered me a thousand to pilot them. I hadn't been off Earth for two whole years and I was itching to hitch a ganser—even in a kiddy-car like an Ehrling. So I just left my cab on the road in Jersey—and that cost me my job and license and put me in the mistout after I got back—and took 'em to the moon. And what a party it was. We went to the Pleasure Caves."

"Like to go there sometime," Keith said.

"Better than Callisto. But don't try the Pleasure Caves unless you've got plenty of what it takes. We were there two weeks." He grinned crookedly. "My thousand credits lasted me exactly a day and that was because they did all the buying. But they kept me with them all the time we were there, and paid everything."

Keith pulled him back to the point at issue. "Those Ehrlings much different from the hot jobs?"

"Same difference as between a roller skate and a racing car. The Ehrlings are all visual. Direct sight on your objective, push the button. Takes you just outside the air, so you spread your wings and coast in. Automatic compensation, automatic gyros, automatic everything. Complicated as drinking moonjuice. Which reminds me. Ready?"

"Right." Keith lifted his glass. "Death to Arcturus!"

"Here we go, then. Happy landing!"

Keith downed the liquid this time; it didn't burn at all, maybe because there was too much of it in a full drink to burn. All that happened was that a sledge hammer hit him under the chin at the same time a rope around his neck yanked him upward through the ceiling, through the blackness of the mistout and clear up into the cold blue sky above it, so that looking down he could see the mistout itself like a huge black disk. On one side of it the moon shone on towns and fields and on the other it glimmered brightly on the flat expanse of the Atlantic Ocean.

Then the noose around his neck loosened and was gone, but he was going higher and higher, whirling as he went, so that sometimes he could see the Earth, sometimes the stars and the great crescent of the moon. The Earth dwindled to a ball, a monstrous dark ball lighted on one side, a crescent Earth, getting smaller as the moon grew larger. And some of the stars were so bright that they looked like disks, little disks of colored fire.

The moon, when he faced it in his turnings, was a ball now, too. Not as big as the Earth, but bigger than he had ever seen it before. He knew that he was well out of the atmosphere now, in space, but there wasn't any of the cold of space that he'd always read about. It was warm, pleasant, and there was music such as he had never heard before, wonderful music that kept time to his turning—or he was turning in time to the music; it didn't matter which. Nothing mattered except the wonderful sensation of floating and spinning and being freer than he had ever been before.

And then, as he turned again, he saw that something occulted the moon, something long and cigar-shaped that could be only a spaceship. Yes, as he turned again, he saw that there were several lighted ports in it and that it had retractable wings folded along the sides.

And he was going to crash into it.

He did, but it didn't hurt. He went right through the walls of one side of it and there he was sitting, unharmed, on the thickly carpeted floor of what looked like a small but beautifully decorated and tastefully furnished *boudoir*. A boudoir in a spaceship? Partly recessed into one white-painted metal wall was a bed with black silk sheets turned back as though ready for occupancy.

He stood up quickly. It was wonderfully easy to get up and to stand there; he felt as though he weighed a little less than half his usual weight and that he was more than twice as strong as he had ever felt before. He felt as though he could move mountains, and wanted to. Light gravity, he thought.

And then he quit thinking, because a door had opened, a steel panel set into the steel wall. Through it Betty Hadley stepped.

She was dressed, again, in the costume that she had told him was the prerogative of a space girl. This time it was of white silk. Narrow—but marvelously twin-rounded—white silk bra. Very short white silk trunks, so tight-fitting that they might have been painted on—and by the brush of a very great artist. And gleaming white patent-leather boots halfway up beautifully molded calves.

Nothing else—except Betty Hadley, Betty Hadley's golden skin and golden hair; her wide blue eyes and soft red lips in a face more beautiful than an angel's.

She was so incredibly beautiful, so incredibly desirable, that, looking at her only a few feet away, he could hardly breathe.

She had come through the door, apparently, without noticing that he was there. Now she saw him and her face became radiant. She raised her white arms toward him and said, *"Darling—oh, my beloved!"*

She ran to him; her arms were around him and her body pressed tightly against his. For an instant her face was buried in his shoulder, and then she lifted her lips for his kiss, her eyes misty with love—

"My Gawd," said Joe. "You were gone forty-fifty seconds. Hadn't you drunk moonjuice before, St. Louie?"

The glass was still at his lips and there was a burn of fire in his mouth, down his throat, under his diaphragm. His eyes slowly focused on Joe's ugly mug. Gradually his body felt the feel of the bench under him, the table on which his elbows rested; gradually, again, his weight changed, this time increasing until he weighed what he had before and felt no stronger.

And the light was blue-green neon, through which he stared blankly at the little ex-spacepilot.

"You hadn't, had you?" Joe asked.

It seemed a full minute before he knew what Joe was talking about, and another minute before he could decide to shake his head, and it seemed that it took him another full minute to get it into motion.

Joe grinned. He said, "It's funny stuff, all right. The more of 'em you've drunk, the shorter a time they knock you out but the longer a time you're gone. Now me, I've been drinking it—whenever I got the dough—for years, and I'm under only five-ten seconds, but I'm gone two-three days. Funny thing is, you came back so quick the first time you took one, a few minutes ago. But that happens, too, on a first try. Sometimes, the first time a guy drinks one, nothing happens at all; he just blacks out. That what happened to you the first time?"

Keith nodded.

"And the second? Did you get as far as the moon?"

Keith found his voice would work again. He said, "Halfway."

"Not bad. And what happened there? None of my damn business, I suppose." He looked at Keith's face and then laughed. "How right I am. And the first few times, you always come back too soon. How well I remember."

He leaned across the table. "Let me give you one chunk of advice, pal; don't have any more of that stuff tonight. You take more than one or two the first time you try it, and the top of your head comes off."

Keith said, "I don't *ever* want to try it again, Joe."

"Next time, you might not come back so soon."

"That's why I don't want to try it again. I want what I want, Joe—but I don't want it in a pipe dream."

Joe shrugged. "Some guys feel that way. I used to be like that myself. Well, that's your business. And speaking of business, you still haven't told me. Let's have a whiskey chaser and then you can spill it."

Joe turned around and called to Spec, and the bartender brought them two shots of whiskey. They were three-ounce shots, but Keith downed his like water.

After the moonjuice, it made him feel better. He saw that Joe downed his as quickly and as easily.

Then Joe's face got businesslike. "All right. What is it?"

Keith said, "I want to get to the moon."

Joe shrugged. "What's tough about that? Every hour on the hour—daytimes—from Idlewild. Three hundred credits round trip. Twelve credits for a passport."

Keith leaned forward and lowered his voice. "Can't do it that way, Joe. I'm hot. There are dodgers out on me from St. Louis, and they've got a good description, even fingerprints."

"They know you headed for New York?"

"If they're smart, they know it."

Joe said, "That's bad. They'll be watching the spaceports, all right. Far as the passport's concerned, I could get you a good forgery job done. But you're dead right; you better stay away from spaceports."

Keith nodded. He said, "And there's another angle. Some friends of mine—on the other side of the fence—are on the moon. They might be watching the spaceports for me there."

Joe said, "That would be bad."

"It wouldn't be good. I'd rather land unannounced—not at a spaceport—in one of these little Ehrlings. Then I could walk in by the back door on the guys who're looking for me. You know what I mean."

"I can guess."

Keith said, "It's a close guess, then. Listen, how good are Ehrlings on distance?"

"Why? If you're going only to the moon, what's the difference how good they are?"

"Might find the moon a little hot for me; that's all."

"Well, an Ehrling'll take you anywhere in the Solar System. Might have to make a few dozen jumps to get to an outer planet, but since a jump takes nothing flat, so what? Only—unless you know navigation, and you're a liar if you do—don't try to get out of the system with one of them. You might get wherever you wanted to go, but you'd never find Sol to get back."

Keith reassured him. "Don't worry; I wouldn't want to get out of the system. Probably nowhere but the moon, for that matter, but I just wondered what an Ehrling would do in an emergency."

"Well, pin it down, St. Louie. Just what do you want me to do?"

"Get me an Ehrling."

Joe whistled softly. "Do you mean fake the registry so you could buy one, or do you mean steal one?"

"What's the matter with that one you know about over in Jersey, the one the rich guy has? Could we get it?"

Joe looked at him thoughtfully. "And would you want me to take you there?"

"Not if you could show me the controls and tell me how to operate it."

"That I could do in ten minutes. But swiping a boat, pal—that isn't peanuts. It's ten years on Venus if we're caught; ten years in the swamps. That is, if you live that long."

Keith laughed. "You wander around in the mistout, and worry about a risk like that? You risk your life out there to pick up a few credits in somebody's pocket, and then squawk at swiping an Ehrling?"

Joe frowned at him. "How much?"

Keith had three and a half thousand credits besides the change left from the moonjuices. He said, "Two or three thousand credits."

"What do you mean, two or three thou? That's a funny way to put it."

Keith said, "Three thousand if I get the Ehrling tonight. Two thousand if I get it tomorrow. That's what I mean."

Joe sighed deeply. "I was afraid that might be what you had in mind, St. Louie. And the money's not enough, either way. But three thou is better than two, so tonight it is. Even though getting out of town from under the mistout is going to be almost as dangerous as swiping the boat—and a hell of a lot harder. Means I got to steal a car too."

"Can you do it?"

"You being funny? But we'll have to crawl in the car, not much faster'n walking. The mistout doesn't taper off until three or four miles into Jersey, either. It'll take us a good three hours to get that far."

"Sounds like good time to me," Keith said.

"Not many guys could do it," Joe said modestly. "You were lucky you picked me, St. Louie. I'll show you a trick not many guys know—how to pilot a car through a mistout by dead reckoning. And a compass. What time is it?"

Keith looked at his watch. "About half past ten."

"Say it'll take me half an hour to get a car; that's eleven. Three hours under the mistout—and if we get out of it at all that'll be two. Half an hour's driving to get to the private spaceport, half an hour to get inside it and show you the controls—that makes three o'clock. Time to the moon, nothing flat. Say ten minutes to land. You'll be on the moon by three-ten tonight."

It was hard for Keith to believe.

He asked, "What about the plane, though? I mean, the spaceship. What if he's using it?"

"Naw. I saw his picture in the paper today. He's under fire from a Congressional committee, so he'll be in Washington. You must have read about it. He makes rajiks."

"Oh," said Keith, as though that explained everything. Maybe it did. Apparently Joe thought that it did.

"One more whiskey, huh? And then we'll go."

Keith said, "Okay, but make mine a short one this time."

But when it came, he rather wished he'd ordered a long one. He was getting a little scared again.

He was still on Manhattan, and Saturn—and Mekky and the fleet—seemed a long, long way off. Thus far, he'd been lucky, unbelievably lucky. But how long would luck like that hold?

It held to the extent that they didn't have to pass Rello, the rennie, on the way out. A man with a pump-action shotgun under his arm let them out a back door into an areaway, out into the impenetrable blackness again.

Again he put his hand on Joe's shoulder and followed. They reached the sidewalk of Fifth Avenue and turned south. At the corner Joe stopped.

He said, "You better wait here. I can make better time swiping a car by myself. I think I know where I can get one, about two blocks from here. Stick right here till you hear me coming in the car."

"How can you drive it in soup like this?"

"I'll show you," Joe said. "Come to think of it, you better not wait here, along the buildings. There's a lamppost out on the corner there. Drape yourself around it; there's less chance of your getting slugged or shot if somebody comes along this way."

He was off again through the blackness, walking so silently that Keith couldn't hear a sound except, once, that faint sniffle that had enabled him to catch Joe in the first place. And catching Joe had been the luckiest thing that had happened to him since last Sunday evening. Joe was turning out to be a godsend.

Keith groped his way to the curb and found the lamppost to lean against. He tried to keep himself calm, not to worry about the slimness of his chances of actually reaching the fleet near Saturn—his real destination, rather than the moon, as he had told Joe in order not to make Joe suspicious of him. And he tried not to worry about the very high probability of his being blown out of space, Ehrling and all, by the first ship of the fleet he approached within a thousand miles.

In fact, there were so many things he tried not to think about that concentrating away from one of them always brought him to another that was just as bad or worse. But, all in all, it made the time go more quickly.

At any rate, it seemed like much less than half an hour before he heard a car coming toward him, inching along the curb, occasionally scraping rubber lightly against the curbstone.

It stopped short of the corner, about a dozen feet from him as nearly as he could judge from the sound. He walked toward it, one foot on the walk and the other in the gutter to enable him to stay along the curb, until his shin cracked painfully into a car's bumper.

"Joe?" he called softly.

"Right, St. Louie. Your chariot awaits. Get the hell in here so we can get going. Took me longer than I thought and I want to get to that spaceport while it's still dark."

Keith groped his way around the car and found the handle of the door. He opened it and got in.

Joe said, "It's slow going when you got to guide by a curb, but with two of us we can make better time, once I show you how. Take this flashlight."

The flashlight poked him in the ribs and Keith took it. He flicked the switch and found he could see Joe's face, a few feet away, and he could see the windshield—but not far enough through the windshield to make out the radiator cap.

"Not that way, stupid," Joe told him. "Aim it down at the floor boards, and keep it aimed down there. Now take this chalk and draw a line parallel with the wheelbase of the car, front to back. Make it as straight as you can."

Keith had to bend over to see the floor clearly, but it was easy to draw the line straight; there was a straight-line pattern in the linoleum or whatever it was that covered the floor boards.

Joe bent down and looked, too. He said, "Good. I didn't know that line was there; we'll have it easy with a line we know is dead straight. Now here's the compass. Put it down smack in the center of the line."

Keith did. He said, "Now what?"

"Nothing, yet. I'm going to the corner and turn west. How far back did you walk from the lamppost to the car? About ten steps?"

"Twelve or fifteen, I think."

"Okay, then I can make the corner and the turn all right and get going west. And I think I can make it over to Sixth Avenue by the seat of my pants. We're going south on Sixth Avenue, and we'll start navigating there."

Joe started the car and inched it forward, this time deliberately scraping the curb until the curb wasn't there to scrape. Then he turned right and straightened the car out as nearly at right angles to the direction they'd been going as he could judge. He went forward slowly until a tire—this time the one on the opposite front side of the car—scraped the curb again. He said, "Got it, now." And went a little faster after he'd moved a little out from the curb.

It seemed to Keith that the car had gone several blocks before Joe stopped it.

Joe said, "We ought to be close to Sixth Avenue now. Get out and catch a house number."

Keith got out and made his way to the building fronts and got a number. He remembered that he wasn't supposed to know New York well, so when he got back into the car he merely gave Joe the number without comment.

"Then we overshot by about two buildings," Joe said. "I'll back up and cut to the right, and we'll be heading south on Sixth Avenue."

He did, and then drove forward a bit and stopped the car again. He told Keith, "See how far I am from the curb on your side."

Keith got out again and this time, on his return, reported they were about six feet from the west curb.

"Good," Joe said. "Now we get down to business with the flashlight and the compass, and we can make ten miles an hour. Look, that line you drew is the line of direction of the car, see? And Sixth Avenue runs about southeast by south—all the straight streets do. At Minetta Place it turns a trifle more east and then we go straight again to Spring Street; that's where we turn for the tunnel.

"You watch the compass and keep us headed right. I got another flashlight and I'll watch the tenths of miles on the speedometer, so I'll know where we are, roughly. You may have to get me a house number once in a while but not often."

"What if we run into something?"

Joe said, "Won't kill us at ten miles an hour. Worst that could happen is that we'll have to swipe another car. We'll waver from one side of the street to the other, but if you keep good guard over that compass, we shouldn't scrape curbing oftener than about once a block. And they're not our tires."

They started. Joe was a skillful pilot and, as an ex-taxi driver, knew the streets perfectly. They scraped rubber only twice on the long stretch to Spring Street, and only twice did Keith have to get out and check house numbers; the second check he made showed them only a few buildings off where they should be for the turn to the Holland Tunnel.

They scraped rubber quite often in the tunnel itself and once, about under the middle of the river, they heard another car go by them, heading in from Jersey. But they were lucky and didn't even scrape fenders.

Joe knew the Jersey side too and kept them on straight streets where they could navigate by compass. After a couple of miles, he turned the headlights on and Keith could see that they penetrated ten or twelve feet into the blackness.

Joe said, "Okay, pal; it tapers off from here. You can give me back the compass."

Keith straightened his aching back and twisted his neck until the kinks were out of it, and by that time they were in the clear, completely out from under the black mist.

Then, between towns, they were in open country. And through the window on his side of the car, Keith saw the moon and the stars in the blackness of space.

He thought: this is a dream, and I'm not really going there.

But something inside told him: it *isn't*, and you *are*.

And suddenly the very thought of it scared him, scared him worse than purple monsters, the Nighters, Arcturus and the W. B. I. all put together.

But it was too late to back out now. He'd committed himself. For better or worse, he was spaceward bound.

THE MOON. SO WHAT?

At two-forty by Keith's watch, Joe pulled the car to the side of the road and turned off the lights. He said, "We're here, pal. End of the line."

He took the flashlight from Keith. "Across the fields there, quarter of a mile back. It's pretty isolated; we won't even have to be careful. Hope nobody steals this car on me before I get back to it."

They climbed a fence and started across the fields, Joe leading the way with the flashlight until they were through a row of trees that was just inside the fence. After that they could see well enough by moonlight to cross the level fields beyond.

Keith asked, "How'll you get back into town in the car by yourself? Can you manage the car and the compass both?"

"Might, in a pinch, if I went slow enough. But I guess I won't go back to New York tonight. I'll drive the car into Trenton or somewhere and shack up there for the rest of the night. And I probably better not go back tomorrow in that stolen car. It might be reported early. I'll let them find it in Trenton."

They climbed another fence into another field and Joe pointed ahead. "It's just past those next trees."

He used the flashlight again going through the grove, but this time kept it carefully shaded and pointed only at the ground under their feet. Under the shadow of the final clump of trees he turned it off and pocketed it.

Just ahead of them was what looked like a big greenhouse; there were two spaceships inside, both clearly visible through the glass in the bright moonlight. They looked, to Keith, more like airplanes than spaceships; they were not even remotely similar to the cigar-shaped spaceship he'd seen in his moonjuice dream. The bigger one of these two was about the size of a transport plane; the smaller wasn't much bigger than a Piper Cub. The wings didn't appear to be foldable or retractable, and he wondered why he'd imagined that they would be.

Joe said, "Wait here. I'll walk once around and be sure the coast's clear."

When he came back, he nodded and motioned to Keith to join him. They went around a corner of the glass enclosure and came to a small door.

"Hold the flash," Joe told him, "till I get this thing open."

He took a little picklock from his pocket and had the lock open in about two minutes. They stepped inside and Joe closed the door after them.

Keith looked up at the roof over his head; there didn't appear to be any door in it. But the far end of the hangar was a big double door. They'd have to take one of the ships out through it and Keith wondered why Joe hadn't picked the lock on the double door right away and come in through it.

And then he realized, before he asked why, that they wouldn't have to wheel the ship out. It could go right through the solid roof—and that was why the hangar was made of glass. Like the professor's sewing machines, the spaceships would—in effect—dematerialize and go right through a solid wall or roof to rematerialize at their destination. The reason the hangar was transparent was to enable one to take a direct sight on the objective without having to wheel the ship outside.

That made him wonder why the double doors were necessary at all and he almost asked that before he realized that the operation didn't work both ways. Returning to Earth, a spaceship had to materialize outside the atmosphere and then glide down to its landing field on its wings and be wheeled—or taxi itself—into a hangar.

Joe said, "They're both Ehrlings—ten-passenger Skymaster and two-passenger Starover. Which do you want?"

"The little one, I guess. Don't you think so?"

Joe shrugged. "The big one doesn't cost any more, pal. Of course, though, you can't sell it when you're through; they're under tight registry. Whichever you take, you'll just have to abandon it when you're through using it."

"Controls are the same? One handles as easy as the other?"

"Exactly the same," Joe said. "The little one's a bit easier to handle in air, though, and doesn't need as big a field to land in."

Keith said, "The little one it is, then."

He walked around it, seeing that, at close range, it looked less like an airplane than he'd thought. The wings were shorter and stubbier. There wasn't any propeller. The outside of the fuselage, which had looked like canvas, felt more like asbestos.

Joe joined him on the far side of the ship. He said, "Here's the airlock. Just turn this handle; and it has a handle just like it on the inside. But if you have to open it in space for any reason, better put a space suit on first. There's one inside under each seat. And if you open it in space, open the valve in the door first to let the air out gradually or the air'll whoosh out and you with it. And if you let your air out, it takes the airmaker—I'll show you that—about fifteen minutes to build it back up again after your airlock's closed. Get on in and I'll show you."

Keith got in and sat at the controls while Joe, in the other seat, explained them to him. The gliding controls consisted of a stick and a pair of rudder pedals just about like those on a lightplane. Since Keith had flown a lightplane almost a hundred hours he didn't anticipate any difficulty with that part of it.

"Here's the sighter," Joe was saying. "Just aim that where you want to go. And these dials set the distance. Big one's in hundred-thou-mile units; your top jump is five hundred of them—that's fifty million miles. It'd take you quite a few jumps to get to one of the outer planets; that's the disadvantage of one of these little Ehrling jobs for long-range stuff.

"The next dial is in thousand-mile units, and on down to the little vernier in tenths of a mile. Now about the moon—you said you wanted to land on this side of it, didn't you?"

"Yes."

"Then just sight on where you want to go. Set the distance for—wait a minute." He opened a compartment in the instrument panel similar to the glove compartment of an automobile and took out a thick paper-bound volume about the size and format of a *World Almanac*. He looked at the date on it and said, "Good. For a minute I was worried for fear Old Man Eggers might not have the current edition of the *Astrogators Monthly* in here, since he hasn't been using the ship. But it's all right; this is the current one. It's got tables; you can look up the distance from anything in the Solar System to anything else in the Solar System for any given minute of time during the month."

He flipped it open. "Here are the Earth-moon tables. You pick, say, three-fifteen for your starting time and look up the distance in here and set your dials for then. At three-fifteen you push the button. Got it so far?"

"But maybe my watch is a few minutes off. What then? Would I maybe go too far and end up materializing inside the moon instead of outside it?"

Joe snorted. "You don't use your watch, stupid. That clock on the panel. And it's dead accurate to the fraction of a second; it's got to be. It's rhodomagnetic."

"It's what?"

"Rhodomagnetic," said Joe patiently. "Anyway, you couldn't crash into the moon because you've got a safety factor—this repulsor dial. If you want to materialize ten miles above the moon—and that's about the right distance—you set your repulsor for ten miles and it stops you ten miles short of the objective you're sighted on. You set your repulsor according to how thick an atmosphere you're aiming for. Ten miles for the moon, about twenty-five for Earth, thirty for Venus, fifteen for Mars, and so on. Catch?"

"You push the button and you're there," Keith said. "And then what?"

"Soon as you materialize you start falling, but the gyro keeps you level. You put the nose down in a steep glide and let yourself fall until the wings begin to take hold as you get into the atmosphere. Soon as you've got enough air under your wings you glide in and land. That's all.

"If you see you're going to miss what you're aiming for or make a bad landing—well, you have your finger on the button and you push it. The repulsor flashes you back ten miles high again so you start over. That's all, St. Louie. Got it?"

"Sure," Keith said. It sounded simple enough. And besides he saw a clip on the inside of the airlock door with a book entitled *Manual of Instructions* under it, so he could pick up anything he'd missed or forgotten to ask.

He took out his billfold and counted out the three thousand credits he'd promised Joe. It left him only five hundred and seventy, but then he probably wasn't going to need any money anyway. By morning he'd either be dead or he'd have reached Mekky and, he hoped, have the answer to his problem.

"Better give me your gun, too, St. Louie. Don't forget you can't teleport explosives. They go off in the warp—and that's not comfortable when it happens in your pocket."

Keith remembered what he'd read in Wells' book and knew that Joe was telling the truth about that. He said, "Thanks, Joe, for reminding me. I'd probably have forgotten—and blown myself up. Thanks."

He handed the forty-five automatic to Joe.

"Okay, pal," Joe said. "Thanks—and good luck. Happy landing."

They shook hands solemnly.

After Joe had gone, Keith reached for the *Manual of Instructions* and studied it carefully for over half an hour.

The manual explained things better than Joe had, and it seemed unbelievably simple. According to the instructions, there really wasn't any point—unless you wanted to be fancy—in using the distance tables in the *Astrogators Monthly.* One could leave the dials set for maximum distance—fifty million miles—at all times and use the repulsor to stop the ship at the proper distance from the objective. Exact distances and verniers were really necessary only when one spaceship was maneuvering to approach another in space. And he could take care of that, Keith figured, by staying still and letting the other spaceship do the maneuvering.

Gliding in didn't seem any tougher than making a dead-stick landing in a lightplane—and with the added advantage that, if it didn't look as though the landing was going to be a good one, you could flash back up and start over again.

He looked up through the glass panel in the top of the spaceship and the glass roof of the hangar, through the atmosphere of Earth and the nothingness of space—at the stars and the moon.

Should he hunt for Saturn now, or should he go to the moon first, for practice?

The moon seemed so near, and so easy. A step, comparatively. There wasn't any important reason for him to go there. The fleet, near Saturn, was his destination. And yet he knew his chances of getting through to Mekky alive weren't any too good and he knew that if he did reach Mekky, and his hopes were realized, he'd go from there back to his own world, the world he'd left last Sunday evening. And he'd probably never again have the opportunity—in either case—to set foot on the moon or on a planet. And what difference did half an hour or so make?

Yes, he'd be willing to skip the planets, but just once, while he had the chance, he wanted to set foot on soil that was not the soil of Earth. And the moon offered little risk. The *Manual of Instructions* he'd just read had stated, in a paragraph about the moon, that the fertile lands and all the settlements were on the far side where there was water and where the air was denser. On the near side were only barren desert country and mountains.

He took a deep breath and strapped himself into the pilot's seat in front of the controls. It was a few minutes before half past three and he looked up the distance of the moon at that time in the *Astrogators Monthly* and set his dials. At a few seconds before three-thirty he put the sights dead center on the moon, watched the second hand of the rhodomagnetic (whatever that was) clock, and then pressed the button.

Nothing happened, nothing at all. He must have forgotten to turn a switch somewhere.

He realized that he'd closed his eyes when he pressed the button and he opened them again to look over the instrument panel. Nothing was wrong that he could see.

He looked at the sighter to see if it was still centered on the moon. It wasn't. The moon wasn't there any more, anywhere that he could see. But up over his head was a big ball, shining along one edge, that was several times as big as the moon. And it didn't *look* like the moon. With sudden shock, he realized that it wasn't. It was Earth, up there over his head—about two hundred and forty thousand miles over his head. And all through the sky were stars, thousands of stars, several times brighter than he'd ever seen stars before. Brilliant, beautiful stars.

But where was the moon?

Suddenly he was aware, too, of a difference of sensation. A feeling of lightness, of falling, of going down in a very fast elevator.

He remembered that there was a glass panel in the floor between the rudder pedals. He looked down through it and saw the moon rushing up at him, filling the panel, only miles away. The little Starover had turned over—as he had known that it would, had he stopped to think—under the gyro controls so that he would be right side up with reference to his objective when he reached it.

His heart was pounding with excitement as he quickly set the dials again, ready to flash him back again to a point ten miles high if he pressed the button; then he took the stick and put his feet on the rudder pedals. He put the nose down. A forward push of the stick did it; the stick must have been connected to the gyro because there couldn't have been enough air purchase on the tail surfaces as yet to have nosed down the plane as he pushed forward on the wheel.

And then, just as the plane was nosing down, the wings began to catch air and he was in a steep glide for the moon.

But it had been too sudden, too unexpected, he hadn't been ready. He pressed the button.

Again nothing happened, apparently, except that the surface of the moon was a little farther away.

This time he waited it out, going into a glide. He kept his finger on the button until he cleared the edge of a crater and saw he was heading for a flat level plain on which even a dub couldn't miss making a good landing.

He made a perfect one, and rolled to a stop.

Slowly he unstrapped himself. He hesitated just a moment with his hand on the latch of the door, wondering if there really was air outside. Its presence on the moon was against all good opinion on the subject back where he'd come from—but then so were a lot of other things.

And then he realized how silly he'd been even to wonder. If there wasn't any air, then what had he glided down through?

He opened the door and stepped out. Yes, there was air. Thin, cold air, about like that on top of very high mountains on Earth. But breathable. He looked around him, shivering a little, and at first felt disappointed. He might have been standing on a barren desert on Earth, with mountains in the distance. It didn't look any different.

It felt different, though. He felt unbelievably light. He took an experimental little hop that wouldn't have taken him higher than six inches on Earth, and it took him several feet into the air. He came down more slowly and lightly than he'd expected. But doing it gave him a queasy feeling at the pit of his stomach and he didn't feel inclined to try it again.

He was on the moon—and he felt horribly disappointed. It wasn't, somehow, anything like as exciting as he'd expected it to be.

He looked up, wondering what was wrong in that direction. The Earth was still there, but it didn't look nearly as bright and impressive as it had when he'd seen it from the little spaceship, ten miles high above the moon. But that, of course, was because he'd not been looking through an atmosphere then, and he was now.

He wondered if the scientists back in his own universe were wrong about there being no air on the moon. Or was the presence of air on the moon here merely another one of the many variant conditions he'd found?

The stars, from here, looked a little brighter than he'd ever seen them from Earth, but not much. That, too, was because of the presence of air.

The sharp feel of cold air in his throat and lungs reminded him that he'd freeze if he stood out here much longer. It was well below zero and he was dressed for summer weather in New York.

He shivered and looked once more around him at the bleak, uninviting landscape. He was on the moon, he thought and so what? He didn't like it.

He knew now, beyond all doubt, what he did want. He wanted to get back to his own universe, a universe where men hadn't yet reached the moon. And, if he got back there, be damned if he'd suggest to any scientists that they quit trying rocket propulsion and start hitching generators to sewing machines.

He got back into the ship—much more eagerly than he'd got out of it—and closed the airlock. The air inside was cold and thin now, too, but now that the airlock door was closed the airmaker unit and the heater would bring it back to normal in a few minutes.

He strapped himself back in the pilot's seat, thinking, "Well, I'm glad I'm disappointed."

He was glad because—if he hadn't done this—he'd never have been quite satisfied with his own universe again, even if he ever got back there. He'd have thought, all the rest of his life, how he'd been in a place where space travel was possible, and hadn't taken advantage of it.

Now he had, and that was that.

Maybe, he thought, he was too old to readjust himself to something like this. If it had happened when he was under twenty instead of over thirty, and if he'd been heart-free instead of really, deeply in love, then he'd have thought that this universe was just what he wanted.

But it wasn't, now. He wanted back.

And there was only one mind—a mechanical mind—that might possibly help him get there.

He set the pointer at Earth and the dial at a hundred and twenty thousand miles, halfway between Earth and the moon. Out there in space he could take his time about locating Saturn.

He pressed the button.

THE THING FROM ARCTURUS

By now he was used to nothing seeming to happen when he pressed the button. This time something did happen, almost right away, and it surprised him. It was a strange sensation that didn't come all at once. At first he felt almost normal, and then, as the Starover—midway between Earth and the moon—overcame its inertia and started falling toward Earth, he became completely weightless.

It felt utterly strange. Through his floor port he could see Earth, twice as big a ball as it had seemed from the moon. And through the glass port in the top he could see the moon, twice as big as it looked from Earth.

He knew he was falling toward Earth, but that didn't worry him. It would take him a long time to fall a hundred and twenty thousand miles. And if he hadn't located Saturn by the time he was dangerously close, he could always jump himself back a hundred and twenty thousand miles away again.

Of course, if Saturn happened to be on the other side of the sun he'd have a bit of a problem on his hands, although he didn't doubt that he could solve it with the aid of the *Astrogators Monthly*. But first he might as well see if he could spot it with the naked eye.

He began, first through one panel and then another, to scan the sky. He thought the rings would be visible. Out here in space, with no atmosphere to blunt vision, the stars were monstrous compared to the way they looked from Earth. Mars and Venus, he had noticed, were tiny disks rather than spots of light. He had heard that even on Earth rare people with gifted eyesight were sometimes able to see the rings of Saturn. Normal eyesight ought to do it easily, out here in space.

And even though he didn't know Saturn's present position, he wouldn't have to search the entire sky. He knew enough of elementary astronomy to recognize the plane of the ecliptic and Saturn would be in that plane, somewhere along a single line across the sky.

It took him a minute to get his bearings because there were so many more stars than he was used to seeing. They didn't twinkle; they looked like shining diamonds on a piece of black velvet and the fascination of their brightness prevented him from recognizing the constellations.

But he found the Dipper and then the belt of Orion and, after that, it was easy to locate the constellations of the zodiac, the belt around which the planets revolve.

He followed it carefully, studying each celestial object near the imaginary line of the ecliptic. He found again the reddish disk of Mars and thought this time that he could see faint crackly lines of the canals.

He followed the line through about thirty degrees, and there was Saturn. The rings were almost edge on, but they were unmistakable.

He reached for the *Astrogators Monthly* and looked up the Earth-Saturn tables. He was still over a hundred thousand miles from Earth despite however many miles he'd fallen toward Earth since his jump from the moon, but that was negligible compared to the total distance; the Earth-Saturn table would be close enough. He looked tip the distance, as of half past four; it was 968,700,540 miles.

Nineteen jumps at his maximum range of fifty million miles. He set the dials for maximum distance and pressed the button nineteen times, pausing a second or so between jumps to be sure the sighter remained on the ringed planet.

Saturn was gorgeously beautiful at the end of the nineteenth jump, still over eighteen and a half million miles away. He set the dials for eighteen million—this time setting the repulsor for a hundred thousand as a factor of safety—and pushed the button again.

He didn't have to look for the fleet; it found him the very second he got there.

A voice startled him by saving, "Do not move." It was a physical, actual voice, not one inside his head, as Mekky's had been. This wasn't Mekky.

The voice continued. "You're under arrest. Pleasure craft are forbidden outside the orbit of Mars. What are you doing here?"

This time he located the source of the voice while it was speaking. It came out of a tiny speaker set into the instrument panel. He had noticed a grating there but had not even wondered what it was. There were two of the gratings; the other, he realized, probably covered a pickup mike. At any rate, since the voice had asked him a question, there was undoubtedly some equipment that would enable the speaker to hear his answer.

He said, "I must see Mekky. It's important."

While he spoke, he looked out through the vision panels and saw his captors; half a dozen oblong objects that globed him in at close range, occulting big chunks of sky. How big they were he couldn't guess; without knowing their distance he couldn't judge their size, and without knowing their size he had no idea as to their distance.

The voice said sternly, "Under no circumstances whatsoever are civilians or occupants of civilian craft permitted to approach the fleet. You will be escorted back to Earth and turned over to the authorities there for punishment. Do not attempt to touch the controls or your craft will be destroyed instantly. Your ship is pinned anyway; you couldn't move it—but our instruments will show if the controls are touched, and we shall construe it as an attempt to escape."

"I don't want to escape," Keith said. "I came here on purpose so you'd capture me. I want to see Mekky. I've *got* to see him."

"You will be returned to Earth. We are about to enter your ship; one of us will take you back. Are you wearing a space suit?"

"No," said Keith. "Listen, this is important. Does Mekky know I'm here?"

"Mekky knows you're here. He ordered us to englobe and capture you. Otherwise you would have been destroyed within a decisecond of your arrival here. Here are your orders: Put on a space suit so you can let the air out of your ship and open the lock. One of us will enter and take over operation of your ship."

Keith didn't even hear the last part, because he had no intention of obeying it, anyway. Getting sent back to Earth meant sure death; he might as well die arguing.

And Mekky knew he was here. That meant Mekky must have been, probably still was, in mental contact with him.

He spoke directly to Mekky, knowing it didn't matter whether he spoke aloud— but doing so, anyway, because it enabled him to concentrate better.

"Mekky!" he said. "Aren't you forgetting one thing? My death means nothing to you, or to your universe; I don't blame you for not caring about that. But aren't you forgetting that I come from a different—place? That, although we haven't space travel, we might have *something*, some weapon or defense, that might be important to you in—in what you say is coming? I haven't heard anyone here mention radar. Do you have radar?"

The voice that answered him this time was different. Strangely, it spoke both ways at once, inside his head *and* through the speaker on his instrument panel.

"Keith Winton," it said, "I told you not to come here. Yes, we have radar. We have instruments of detection your universe never dreamed of."

Keith said, "But, Mekky, I had to come now or never. The plans—the ones you read in my mind—went wrong. And even you aren't omniscient or you'd have known they couldn't go right—my submitting stories to the man who wrote them! So you haven't been deeply into my mind, or you'd have known that! You can't be sure I haven't got something that would help you. How do you know what you've missed— and that I wouldn't recognize? All you know is my surface thoughts.

"And you're in a jam here right now. You're afraid of the next Arc attack. How can you overlook a bet, however slight a chance it might be?"

"Your universe is relatively primitive. You haven't—"

Keith interrupted. "How do you *know*? You don't even know how I got here; whatever mechanism activated *that* is something that you haven't got, or you'd know about it. And you said you didn't."

A calm voice that Keith hadn't heard before spoke out of the speaker in the instrument panel. It said, "Maybe he's got something there, Mekky. When you told me about him, you told me you didn't know what the score was— except that he was sane and on the level. So why not bring him over to the fleet? You can psych him in ten minutes—and the lines we've been working along haven't been very productive."

It was a youthful but deep voice; authority and confidence were in it. What it had said had been worded as a suggestion, yet, hearing it, one knew that it was an order that would be carried out.

Keith knew that it must be the voice of Dopelle—the great Dopelle, with whom Betty Hadley, *his* Betty Hadley, was so hopelessly in love. The magnificent Dopelle who held this universe—except for the Arcturians—in the palm of his hand.

Damn him, Keith thought.

Mekky's voice said, "All right. Bring him to the fleet. To the flagship."

There was dull knocking on the outside of the airlock. Keith quickly unstrapped himself from the pilot's seat. He said, "Just a minute. Getting a space suit on."

He lifted the seat next to his and found a suit. It was thick and awkward to handle, but—except for the confined space he had to work in—there wasn't any difficulty about getting into it. It worked with zippers—perfectly ordinary zippers except that there was a gummy feeling to them that indicated some coating that made them airtight.

The helmet clicked automatically into place against the neck ring. There was a little box over the chest that looked as though it would be the airmaker. He flicked the switch on it before he closed the face plate of the helmet.

Then he opened the valve in the airlock that would release the air in the ship. When it quit hissing, he opened the door.

A man wearing a space suit even thicker and more cumbersome than his own came in. Without speaking he sat down in the pilot's seat and began to work the vernier controls. A few seconds later he pointed to the airlock, and Keith nodded and opened it.

They were against, almost touching, the side of a big ship. From so close, Keith couldn't even guess how big it was.

An airlock the size of an average room stood open, and Keith stepped across into it, and the door closed behind him. A ship this size, he realized, would have to have an intermediate chamber from which air could be exhausted to admit someone to the ship from space; from such a small craft as the one he'd come here in, it was more practical simply to let the air out of the whole ship.

The outer door swung shut behind him. Something started to hiss, and when the hissing had stopped, a door at the inner end of the room opened.

A tall, very handsome young man, with black curly hair and flashing black eyes, stood just inside the inner door, smiling at Keith. Beyond doubt, it was Dopelle.

He didn't look like Errol Flynn, but he was even more dashing and romantic. Keith knew that he ought to hate him, but somehow he didn't. He rather liked him.

Dopelle stepped forward quickly and helped Keith take off the helmet. He said, "I'm Dopelle. And you're this Winton or Winston Mekky told me about. Let's hurry and get that suit off of you."

His voice was cheerful, but with worry showing through. "We're really in a tough jam. I hope you're right and that you've got something we can use. Otherwise—"

Slipping out of the space suit in the doorway, Keith looked around him. The ship was big all right. The room he was about to enter must be the main chamber; it was about a hundred feet long by thirty or thirty-five feet wide. There were a lot of men in it, mostly working down at the far end in what looked like a completely equipped experimental laboratory.

His eyes went back to Dopelle, but they didn't stay there. For just above Dopelle's head hung Mekky, the basketball-sized sphere that was a mechanical brain.

Inside his head came Mekky's voice. It said, "You just could be right, Keith Winton. I see something about a thing called—in your world—a potentiomotor. Something invented by a man named Burton. It had something, vaguely, to do with a rocket to the moon. Whatever it is, it isn't known here. But do you know the details, the wiring diagram?

"Don't answer aloud. Just think. It's faster that way, and time counts... Try to remember...

"Yes, you've seen diagram and formula—the equation. You don't know them consciously, but they're there in your subconscious. I think I can get to them under light hypnosis. You are willing?"

"Yes, of course," Keith said. "What's the score?"

"The score is this," said Dopelle, answering for Mekky. "The Arcs are going to attack soon. We don't know the exact time, but it will be within hours.

"And they've got something new. We don't know how to buck it yet—we got some things about it from an Arc prisoner we managed to capture, but he didn't know the details.

"It's a single ship, not a fleet—but their whole effort for years has gone into it. And, in one way, that's good news; if we can destroy this ship the way will be clear for us to take the fleet to Arcturus and end the war. But—"

"But what?" Keith asked. "Is this one ship too big for you to handle?"

Dopelle waved a hand impatiently. "Size doesn't matter—although this one is really a monster. Ten thousand feet long, ten times the size of anything we've ever tried to build. But that isn't the point.

"It's coated with a new metal, something impervious to anything we know. We can A-bomb it all day and not scratch the finish."

Keith nodded. He said, "We had that stuff, too—in our science-fiction magazines. I used to edit one of them."

Dopelle's face lighted with sudden interest. "I used to read them," he said, "when I was younger. Used to be crazy about them. Of course now—"

Something in the expression on Dopelle's face registered.

Keith had seen a face that looked like that somewhere—not long ago. No, he hadn't seen the face either; it had been a photograph. A photograph of a much younger and far less handsome edition of—

"*Joe Doppelberg!*" he said. His mouth fell open.

"What?" Dopelle looked at him in bewilderment. "What do you mean?"

Keith's mouth snapped shut. He stared at Dopelle for seconds.

Then, "I know you now," he said. "At last I've got a clue to this setup and some of it makes sense. You're Joe Doppelberg—or Doppelberg's Doppelgänger."

"And who is Joe Doppelberg?"

Keith said, "A science-fiction fan of—of back where I came from. You look like him—and you're what he would want to be! You're older, of course, and a thousand times handsomer and more romantic and more intelligent—

"*You're* just what he'd have dreamed himself to be. You—he—used to write me long letters, full of corny humor, to my Rocketalk Department, and you called me Rocky and you didn't like our covers because the monsters weren't horrible enough, and—"

He stopped, and again his mouth fell open. Dopelle's forehead was creased with lines of puzzlement. He said, "Mekky, he's insane. You won't get anything out of him. He's stark crazy."

"No," the mechanical voice said, "he isn't insane. He's *wrong*, of course, but he isn't insane. I can follow his thought processes and see why he thinks what he just said—and it isn't illogical; it's merely wrong.

"I can straighten him out on it; I see most of the truth now, except the diagram and the formula that we need. And that is the thing that comes first, before explanations, or none of us may survive."

Mekky floated down from over Dopelle's head to a point just in front of Keith Winton. He said, "Come, stranger from another universe, and follow me. You must go under light hypnosis so I can get from your mind, from your deep subconscious, what we need. Then, after we have started work on it, I'll tell you everything you need to know."

"How to get back?"

"Possibly. I'm not sure of that. But I can see now that the thing you know that we do not know—the Burton potentiomotor which, in your universe, was attached to the first moonbound rocket—may be the means of saving Earth from Arcturus.

"And I tell you again that you are wrong; that this world is as real as the one you came from, and is not the dream of someone in your world. And that if the Arcturians win here, you will not survive even to try to get back where you came from. Do you believe me?"

"I—don't—know."

"Come, let me show you what you may be saving Earth from. Would you like to see an Arcturian? A live Arcturian?"

"Why— Sure, why not?"

"Follow."

The sphere that was Mekky floated across the room, and Keith followed. The voice was saying inside his head, "This is one we captured near Alpha Centauri, in a scouting ship. It's the first we've captured alive in a long time. It was from its mind—if one can call it a mind—that I learned of the monster ship that is to come, the ship that is capable of destroying our entire fleet unless we destroy it first, and of the armament and the defensive hull it will have. Perhaps, after you see it—"

A door swung open, revealing, just beyond it, a second steel-barred door that led to a cell. With the opening of the door a light flashed on just inside the cell.

"That," said the voice of Mekky, "is an Arcturian."

Keith took a step closer to look through the bars. He stepped back—several steps—even more quickly. He felt as though he were going to be sick at his stomach. He closed his eyes and swayed dizzily. Horror and nausea almost blanked him out.

And he'd had only a quick, indistinct glimpse of part of the Arcturian. He didn't really know, even now, what an Arcturian looked like. But he knew that he didn't *want* to know; that even seeing one behind bars and helpless might drive a human being mad.

It was alien beyond all imagining. Even Joe Doppelberg couldn't have imagined *that*.

The steel door swung shut.

"That," said Mekky, "is an Arcturian in his own body. Possibly now you will understand why an Arcturian spy—one of *those*—disguised in the body of a human being is shot on suspicion. Back in the early days of the war, a few Arcturians were taken to Earth and shown there, to steel Earth for the long and bitter struggle it faced to avoid annihilation.

"People of Earth have seen *those*. They know the power a disguised Arcturian, one who has taken over the body of a captured human, has. That is why Earthmen shoot at possible Arcturian spies on mere suspicion. Do you understand, now that you have seen?"

Keith's throat was dry and his lips were dry. He said, "Yes," and his voice was almost a croak. He was still filled with the horror and loathing that even a quick glimpse of the monster had given him; he was scarcely conscious of what Mekky was saying.

"*That,*" said Mekky, "is what will destroy the human race and populate the Solar System, unless we can destroy the monster ship that will be here soon.

"Come, Keith Winton."

HUCKLEBERRY INFINITY

Keith Winton felt a little dazed. He felt as though he'd been drunk and was just sobering up, or as though he'd been under ether and hadn't quite come out of it yet.

But it wasn't quite like either of those things. Though he felt physically lethargic, his mind was clear, crystalline, in fact. It was just that too much strong meat was being fed to it all at once. It was having difficulty absorbing more.

He sat on a little steel-railed balcony, looking out over the big room of the flagship, watching Dopelle and a varying number of other men swiftly and efficiently making something that looked like a tremendously large and quite modified edition of something he'd seen a picture of in a science magazine back on Earth, his own Earth. It was a Burton potentiomotor. And it had been in the science magazine that he'd seen the wiring diagram and the formula that covered the electrical field.

The sphere that was Mekky floated above the operation, just over Dopelle's shoulder and a good fifty feet away from Keith. But it was talking to Keith, inside Keith's mind. Apparently distance didn't make any difference to Mekky.

And Keith had a hunch that Mekky was carrying on more than one of those telepathic conversations at the same time, for it was pretty obvious that Mekky was directing Dopelle and the workmen even while he talked to Keith.

"You find it difficult to grasp, of course," Mekky's voice was saying. "Infinity is, in fact, impossible fully to grasp. Yet there is an infinite number of universes."

"But where?" Keith's mind asked. "In parallel dimensions—or what?"

"Dimension is merely an attribute of a universe," Mekky said, "having validity only within that particular universe. From otherwhere, a universe—itself an infinity of space—is but a point, a dimensionless point.

"There are an infinite number of points on the head of a pin. There are as many points on the head of a pin, therefore, as in an infinite universe—or in an infinity of infinite universes. And infinity to the infinite power is still only infinity. Do you understand?"

"Almost."

"There are, then, *an infinite number of coexistent universes.* They include this one and the one you came from. They are equally real, and equally true. But do you conceive what an infinity of universes means, Keith Winton?"

"Well—yes and no."

"It means that, out of infinity, *all conceivable universes exist.*

"There is, for instance, a universe in which this exact scene is being repeated except that you—or the equivalent of you—are wearing brown shoes instead of black ones.

"There are an infinite number of permutations of that variation, such as one in which you have a slight scratch on your left forefinger and one in which you have purple horns and—"

"But are they all me?"

Mekky said, "No, none of them is you—any more than the Keith Winton in this universe is you. I should not have used that pronoun. They are separate individual entities. As the Keith Winton here is; in this particular variation, there is a wide physical difference—no resemblance, in fact.

"But you and your prototype here had roughly the same history. And you found, to your sorrow, each of you wrote the same stories once. And there are similarities between my master, Dopelle, here and a science-fiction fan named Doppelberg in your universe, but they are *not* the same person."

Keith said thoughtfully, "If there are infinite universes, then all possible combinations must exist. Then, somewhere, *everything must be true.* I mean, it would be impossible to write a fiction story—because no matter how wild it sounds, that very thing must be happening somewhere. Is that true?"

"Of course it's true. There is a universe in which Huckleberry Finn is a real person, doing the exact things Mark Twain described him as doing. There are, in fact, an infinite number of universes in which a Huckleberry Finn is doing every possible variation of what Mark Twain *might* have described him as doing. No matter what variation, major or minor, Mark Twain might have made in the writing of that book it would have been true."

Keith Winton's mind staggered a little.

He said, "Then there are an infinite number of universes in which we—or our equivalents—are making Burton outfits to defeat attacking Arcturians? And in some of them we'll succeed and in others we'll fail?"

"True. And there are an infinite number of universes, of course, in which we don't exist at all—that is, no creatures similar to us exist at all. In which the human race doesn't exist at all. There are an infinite number of universes, for instance, in which flowers are the predominant form of life—or in which no form of life has ever developed or will develop.

"And infinite universes in which the states of existence are such that we would have no words or thoughts to describe them or to imagine them."

Keith closed his eyes and tried to visualize universes which he could not visualize because he couldn't even imagine them. He snapped his eyes open again when Mekky said:

"All possible combinations must exist in infinity. Therefore there are infinite number of universes in which you're going to die within the next hour, piloting a rocket against the monster ship from Arcturus. As you are going to pilot one here."

"*What?*"

"Of course. At your own request. It may get you back to your own universe. And you want to get back there; I can see that very clearly in your mind. You will be given the chance if you wish. But do not ask me whether you will succeed in this particular universe. I cannot read the future."

Keith shook his head to clear it again. There were still a million questions he wanted to ask. He went back to the beginning, and asked again one of the first questions he'd asked after the hypnosis. Maybe, with a little better basis of overall understanding, the answer to it would mean more now than it had the first time.

"Will you please explain again, Mekky, how I got here?"

"The moon rocket from your Earth must have fallen back and landed very near you. Probably within a few yards. The Burton machine functioned upon landing—not exactly an explosion, although some of the effects were similar. But I can see, from my study of the machine, that some of the electrical effects would be peculiar. Anyone caught in the flash—directly in it, and not at the edges—is not killed. He is simply knocked out of his universe and into another one of the infinite number of universes."

"But how can you *know* that, if the Burton effect is new here?"

"Partly by deduction from what happened to you. Partly by analysis—a much deeper analysis than could have been given to it on your Earth—of the Burton formula and the Burton effect. The first alone would be enough, without the theoretical justification. You were there; you are here. Q.E.D.

"And, from your mind, I can see why, out of an infinity of universes, you landed in this one."

"You mean it wasn't random?"

"Nothing is random. It is because you chanced, at the exact instant of the flash, to be *thinking* about this particular universe. That is, you were thinking about your science-fiction fan, Joe Doppelberg, and you were wondering what kind of a universe he would dream about, what kind of a universe he would really *like*. And this is it.

"That doesn't mean that this isn't a real universe, as real as your own. Neither Joe Doppelberg nor you *thought up* this universe. It was; it existed. But it is *the* universe out of infinite universes which happens to be the one exactly like what you were thinking of at the time of the flash—thinking of, that is, as the universe you thought Joe Doppelberg would dream up."

Keith said, "I think I understand now. And it explains a lot of things. Such as why 'space girls' wear the costumes they wear here. Joe *would* think of that— or I would have thought he would. And—"

He thought of so many things at once—and all of them fitted—that he couldn't say them all.

Dopelle was *exactly* what Doppelberg would have dreamed himself to be. Down to the romanticizing of his name.

And so many little things were explicable now. Joe Doppelberg had been at the Borden office in his, Keith's absence. Therefore he had never seen Keith and didn't know what he looked like. But he'd had a mental picture of him, from having corresponded, and the Keith Winton of this universe would be like that mental picture—taller, more slender than Keith, more studious-looking because of the glasses—more typically an editor, in brief. If Joe had seen Keith, then the picture would have corresponded; Keith Winton here would have been the physical double of Keith Winton there. Or, more accurately, Keith would have been transported to the universe (otherwise identical to this one) in which Keith Winton *was* his physical double.

Joe Doppelberg had undoubtedly seen Betty Hadley at the Borden offices. He hadn't known she'd worked there only a few days so, in this universe, that wasn't true. He hadn't known of Borden's Greeneville estate and so, here, Borden's estate wasn't in Greeneville, whererever it was. He must have one somewhere.

Yes, it *all* fitted—even to the improvement of the bug-eyed monsters on the covers of *Surprising Stories*—Bems with the subtle horror that Doppelberg demanded of them.

And otherwise—in so many ways—this was the universe that a space-stricken adolescent would dream up. Jalopies and spaceships. The Nighters. Air on the moon. Ordinary forty-five automatics on Earth, and God knows what weapons in intragalactic warfare. Moonjuice and the W.B.I.

And Doppelberg as Dopelle, master of a universe except for the opposition of Arcturus. Dopelle, superscientist, creator of Mekky, the only man who'd been to Arcturus and returned alive.

Dopelle, fiancée of Betty Hadley. Of course he'd fallen in love with her on sight, the day he'd seen her at the Borden office. And that was one thing Keith couldn't blame him for.

Universe *à la* Doppelberg.

Again Keith corrected himself: Universe *à la* Doppelberg as he, Keith, could have conceived it, consciously and subconsciously. Joe himself really didn't have anything to do with it at all. This was merely the universe Keith had imagined that Doppelberg would dream up. Even to the details he hadn't thought out.

Mekky was right; it fitted too well to be wrong.

The men in the big room down below the balcony were now putting the finishing touches on the thing they were making—a thing of complicated coils that only vaguely resembled the picture he'd once seen of the Burton potentiomotor. Obviously Mekky had, once he understood the principle, made it vastly more powerful and more efficient.

Mekky floated up to the balcony now and hovered near Keith's shoulder.

He said, "Now they'll install it as a warhead on a lifeboat—a rocket-propelled craft. I cannot foresee what effect a teleported space hop would have on the Burton field, so we cannot chance putting it on anything larger. And there is no time for experimentation.

"Someone—and you will have the first privilege of volunteering—must take the lifeboat out of its mother ship, this ship, and run it around awhile until a sufficient charge is built up in the Burton apparatus. It will be a tremendous charge."

"How long will that take?" Keith asked. He knew already that he was going to volunteer.

"Only minutes. To be exact, it will be fully charged within four and a quarter minutes. Running the rocket ship longer than that will neither add to nor diminish the potential that has been built up.

"Thereafter the rocket must hover near the flagship—which will be the first objective of the monster ship from Arcturus. And when it materializes here to attack us, the rocket ship must crash into the Arcturian monster.

"The Arcturian ship will be inertialess; any other ship we have can crash into it without harming it. Nothing in our armaments can touch it. It will blaze a path of death and destruction through the fleet—and then the planets, including Earth, after it has destroyed the fleet. Unless the Burton apparatus—which is as new to them as it is to us—can destroy it."

"But *can* it?"

If it was possible for Mekky's mechanical voice to be grim, then it sounded grim in Keith's mind. "I think it will. You will know when you crash the lifeboat. I see in your mind that you do volunteer to do that—as a chance to get back to your own world.

"It is a great privilege. Every man in the fleet would volunteer, if you did not wish to."

"Will I be able to operate the lifeboat? I have no idea of the controls; I've never even seen one. Are they more difficult than an Ehrling?"

"That is irrelevant," Mekky's voice said. "I shall implant knowledge of how to operate it in your mind before you enter. You will have automatic reflexes that you won't even have to think about. In fact, you *must* have them if you are to get back to your own universe—instead of merely out of this one. Your mind must be free from the necessity of concentration on the rocket controls."

"Why?"

"Because you must concentrate on the universe that you wish to get back to, remember things about it. Concentrate on the very spot, in fact, where you were a week ago when the moon rocket landed near you. Not on that *time,* of course, allow for the time lapse. Else you may get back there just in time to be blown away again by the flash of the moon rocket's landing.

"You can explain your absence for this week by pretending that you have had amnesia as a result of the shock of the landing of the rocket. And from Greeneville you can go to New York and to Betty Hadley—*your* Betty Hadley, if you can win her."

Keith reddened a little. There was a disadvantage to having one's mind read so thoroughly, even by a mechanical brain.

The men were wheeling off the thing they had made.

"Will it take them long to install it on the rocket ship?"

"Ten minutes or less. Relax now and close your eyes, Keith Winton. I shall implant in your mind the knowledge of how to control the craft you will operate."

Keith Winton closed his eyes and relaxed.

THE OLE ROCKETEER

The rocket-driven lifeboat hovered, half a million miles out from Saturn. A hundred miles from the flagship of the Earth fleet. Keith could see the flagship in his visiplate and he knew that everyone on the flagship who could get near a visiplate was watching him.

Right now, however briefly, he was the hero of this universe. For this brief moment he was greater even than Dopelle. He was about to do what Dopelle had never quite been able to do—destroy the might and menace of Arcturus.

Nothing, he thought sardonically (and a bit plagiaristically), that he had done in this universe had become him as would the manner of his leaving it.

Come to think of it, he'd done all right here. From a hunted suspect to be shot on sight, he'd become the hero who had a chance of saving the human race. Only he'd not be here to know whether he'd saved it or not; whether or not the flash of the Burton effect destroyed the monster ship from Arcturus, it would either kill Keith Winton or blow him—somewhere. Back to his own universe, he hoped.

He wondered if statues would be erected to him, if all went well. If Keith Winton's Birthday would be a national holiday—an international—an interplanetary holiday. But how confusing that would be to the other Keith Winton, the one who belonged here and who undoubtedly had the same birthday. People would have to call one of them Keith Winton Two.

Out of an infinity of Keith Wintons in an infinity of universes plus an infinity of universes in which there wasn't any Keith Winton plus at least one universe—rather, plus an *infinity* of universes again—in which Keith Winton had been but was missing after a rocket flash...

But *this* universe was a real one now. For a while, at least.

And he, alone in this tiny cigar-shaped rocket only thirty feet long by six in circumference, might be able to do what the whole Earth fleet couldn't do.

He wondered. But Mekky thought it would work and Mekky should know if anybody or anything should know. No use worrying about it. It would work or it wouldn't and, if it didn't, he wouldn't be alive to know that it hadn't.

He tested the controls, sending the rocket in a tight little circle only a mile across, coming back to a dead stop at exactly the point from which he'd started. A difficult maneuver, but easy for him now; he was an expert, thanks to Mekky.

The Ole Rocketeer, he thought, remembering the way he'd signed his Rocketalk Department in *Surprising Stories.* If only the fans who wrote to that department could see him now! He grinned.

Inside his head, Mekky's voice said, "It's coming, I can feel vibrations in the subether. Get ready, Keith Winton."

He looked hard at the visiplate. There was a black dot just off the center of it. He touched the controls, got the dot on dead center, and then slammed on all the rocket's full power.

The black dot grew, slowly at first; then it filled the screen. It filled the screen although the objective for which he was aiming was still a long way off. It must be tremendous!

He could see the gun ports of the monster ship; guns were trying to swivel around toward him. But there wouldn't be time for them to get in a single shot; he was only a split second away.

A fraction of a second now!

Quickly, desperately, he remembered to concentrate on Earth, *his* Earth, on the spot near Greeneville, New York. On Betty Hadley. Above all, on Betty Hadley. On currency in sensible dollars and cents, and night life on Broadway without the mistout. On everything he'd known and loved back home.

A whole series of pictures was flashing through his mind, as is supposed to happen to a drowning man (but doesn't, really). He thought, "But good God, why didn't I think of it sooner? It doesn't have to be exactly like the world I left. It can be *better!* I'm missing from an infinity of universes; I can pick one that will give me at least a few improvements. I can pick a universe *almost* exactly like mine, except that—my job—Betty—"

Of course all those thoughts weren't going through his mind just in that form, word following word, in the fraction of a second in which he had to think them. They weren't that coherent; it was just a blinding flash of realization— of what he might have done had he had time to think things out.

And then, as the rocket hit the monster ship on dead center, there was another blinding flash. A different kind of blinding flash.

Again there was no sense of a time lapse. And again, Keith Winton was lying flat on the ground and it was early evening. There were stars in the sky and a moon. It was a quarter moon, he noticed, not the narrow crescent of last Sunday evening.

He looked down and around him. He was in the middle of a big charred and blackened area. Not far away were the foundations of what had been a house, and he recognized the size and shape of it. He recognized, too, the blackened stump of a tree beside him.

And things looked—as they should—as though the explosion and fire had taken place nearly a week ago.

"Good," he thought. "Back at the right time and place."

He stood up and stretched, feeling a bit stiff from his confinement in the little rocket ship. He walked out to the road—a familiar road, this time, the same road that had been outside the estate.

But he still felt uneasy. *Why* had he taken the chance of letting his mind wander a trifle just at that last second? He could all too easily have made a horrible mistake doing that. What if—?

A truck was coming along and he hailed it, getting a lift into Greeneville. The driver was taciturn; they didn't talk at all on the way in.

Keith thanked him as he got off on the main square of town.

He ran quickly to the newsstand to look at the headline of the current newspaper displayed there. "Giants Beat Bums," it read. Keith sighed with relief. He realized that he'd been sweating until he'd seen that headline.

He wiped the perspiration off his forehead and went into the newsstand. "Got a copy of *Surprising Stories?*" he asked. That was the next hurdle.

"Right here, sir."

He glanced at the cover, at the familiar cover, and saw that the girl and the monster on it were as they should be and that the price said 20¢ and not 2 cr.

He sighed with relief again, and then reached into his pocket for change and remembered there wasn't any. And there'd be only credit bills—to the tune of about five hundred and seventy credits, if he remembered rightly—in his wallet. No use pulling them out.

Embarrassed, he handed the magazine back. "Sorry," he said. "Just realized that I came away without any money."

"Oh, that's all right, Mr. Winton," the proprietor said. "Pay me any time. And—uh—if you came away without your money, could I lend you some? Would twenty dollars help?"

"It surely would," Keith said. That would be more than enough to get him to New York. But how did the proprietor of this little place in Greeneville know him? He folded the magazine and put it in his pocket while the proprietor opened the cash register.

Keith said, "Thanks a lot. But—uh—just give me nineteen eighty, so I won't owe you for the magazine too."

"Sure, might as well keep it even. Gee, I'm glad to see you, Mr. Winton. We thought you were killed when the rocket hit. All the papers said so."

"I'm afraid they made a mistake," Keith said. Of course, he thought; that was how the man knew him. His picture had been in the newspaper as one of the visitors of Borden who was presumed to be killed by the rocket.

"Sure glad the newspapers were wrong," the proprietor said.

Keith pocketed the change from twenty dollars and went out again. It was getting darkish now, just as it had been on last Saturday night. Well, now to—now to what? He couldn't phone Borden.

Borden was dead—or maybe blown into some other universe. Keith hoped it was the latter. Had the Bordens and the others who were on the estate been near enough the center of the flash to have had that happen to them? He certainly hoped so, for all their sakes.

An unpleasant memory made him walk on past the corner drugstore where— it seemed like years ago—he'd seen his first purple Bem and had been shot at by the druggist. It wouldn't happen that way this time, of course, but just the same he kept on walking to the next drugstore, a block farther on.

He went back to the phone booth and—yes, there was a coin slot in it. Should he try calling the Borden offices in New York? Often someone worked late there, far into the evening sometimes. Maybe someone would be there now. And if not, all the call would cost him would be a report charge.

He went back to the tobacco counter and got a handful of change for two of the dollar bills the newsstand proprietor had given him, and returned to the phone booth.

How did one dial a long-distance operator from a Greeneville phone? He picked up the Greenville directory dangling from the chain to find out, and idly flipped it open to the B's first. The last time he'd opened one of these things, there hadn't been any L. A. Borden listed, as there should have been. And that had been the start of his troubles.

So this time—just to reassure himself—he ran his finger down the column where the name should be.

It wasn't. There wasn't any L. A. Borden listed.

For just a minute he leaned against the back of the phone booth and closed his eyes. Then he looked again. It wasn't any different.

Had some vague embryonic thoughts of his at the very last moment changed things and brought him back to a universe that wasn't exactly the same as the one he'd left? If so, this was the first sign, unless one counted the newsstand man calling him by name—and that was easily explained. But—no Borden?

Quickly he yanked the copy of *Surprising Stories* out of his pocket and opened it to the contents page. He ran his finger down the fine print to the point where it said—

Ray Wheeler, Managing Editor.

Not Keith Winton. Ray Wheeler. Who the hell was Ray Wheeler?

Quickly his eyes swung to the name of the publisher to see if that, too, was wrong. It was.

It didn't read Borden Publications, Inc.

It read *Winton Publications, Inc.* He stared at it blankly and it took him a full five seconds to figure out where he'd heard the name *Winton* before.

When he finally recognized it as his own name, he grabbed the phone book again, and this time looked under the W's. There was a Keith Winton listed, Cedarburg Road, and a familiar phone number, Greeneville 111.

No wonder the news dealer had known him! And he *had* changed things after all, during that last split second! In this universe, Keith Winton owned one of the biggest chains of publications in the country and had owned a Greeneville estate. He must be a millionaire!

The last things he'd thought of had been his job—and Betty.

He almost broke a finger getting a coin into the nickel slot of the telephone. He still hadn't looked up how to get a long-distance call through, but he dialed the zero and asked for a long-distance operator. It worked.

He said, "New York, please. And have the New York operator see if there is a Betty Hadley listed, and get her for me if there is. Quickly, please!"

A few minutes later she told him how much to deposit and then said, "Your party, sir."

Betty's cool voice was saying, "Hello."

"Betty this is Keith Winton. I—"

"Keith! We thought you— The papers said— What happened?"

He'd thought that out, back in the rocket, along the lines Mekky had suggested. "Guess I must have been in the explosion, Betty, but at the edge of it. Must have been knocked out but not hurt except that the shock gave me amnesia. I've probably been wandering around and just came to myself. I'm in Greeneville."

"Oh, Keith, that's wonderful! It's—I just can't say it! You're coming right to New York?"

"As soon as I can get there. There's a small airport here—I'm pretty sure—and I'll take a taxi there right away and charter a plane for New York. Should be there in an hour or so. Want to meet me at Idlewild Airport?"

"Do I *want* to? *Darling—oh, my beloved!*"

A moment later, Keith Winton, with a dazed and somewhat silly look on his face, hurried out of the drugstore to find a taxi.

This, he thought, was a universe he'd really settle for.

The Lights in the Sky Are Stars

The Lights in the Sky Are Stars

1997

I'd been intending to stay a few more days but, that afternoon, something changed my mind. It was the sight of myself in the mirror in my brother Bill's bathroom. Stark naked, dripping wet, standing on one leg because I have only one leg to stand on, water running noisily out of the tub behind me, I decided to leave that very night.

Time was running out of me like the water out of that bathtub. The sight of myself in the long mirror on the door showed me that, all too clearly.

A mirror doesn't lie to you. If it tells you that you look your fifty-seven years, then by God you do. And if there's something you want to do, somewhere you want to go, then you'd better start the doing and the going. You'd better start using the time that's left in you, because you can't stop it from running out. You can stop water from running out of a tub by putting the plug back in, but there isn't any plug that can stop time from running out of you. Oh, you can slow it down. By living right. By letting the medics give you the works in geriatrics you can baby yourself past the century mark, but brother you're still old at seventy.

In thirteen years I'd be seventy, I thought. Maybe *I'd* be old sooner than that, what with the way I'd lived most of the time, what with one foot—hell, one leg up to the knee—in the grave already.

It's indecent and inhuman to put full length mirrors in bathroom doors. They cause narcissism in the young and unhappiness in the old.

After I dried myself and before I put my prosthetic leg back on, I hopped up on the bathroom scale and weighed myself. A hundred and twenty-six. Not too bad, I thought; I'd gained back seven of the fourteen pounds I'd lost. If I took even reasonable care of myself I'd have the rest of it back in another few weeks and I didn't have to stay here until I had all of it back.

I looked at myself in the mirror again and this time it wasn't so bad. It still had strength in it, that body, the wiry strength that's better in the long run than heavy musculature. And now that the magnelite leg was back on it was a whole body, or looked like one.

147

The face above it wasn't bad either; it too had a kind of strength in it.

I dressed and went downstairs, but I didn't tell them yet. I waited until after dinner, until after Merlene went upstairs to put Easter and Bill Junior to bed. I knew there'd be an argument and I didn't want the kids in on it. Bill Senior and Merlene I could handle; I could just agree with everything they said but tell them I was leaving anyway. But what can you do with *Uncle Max, please don't go* stuff from kids.

Bill sat watching the viddy.

My kid brother, Bill. My kid brother with graying hair and a bald spot and no imagination. But a nice guy. Happily married, although he'd married late. A good steady job, good steady opinions.

But no taste whatsoever. He liked cowboy music. He was sitting listening to it now.

Out of space it came, that program. From Earth's second artificial satellite, from the telestation twenty-two thousand miles out in empty space, revolving around Earth once a day as Earth turns once a day under and with it, staying always over Kansas, always twenty-two thousand miles over the tall corn of Kansas.

In full color, that program, tri-dimensional and out of space to Earth. And it was a man in a cowboy hat strumming a guitar and singing in a Texas accent:

Give me the lone pray-ree,
And a stallion wild and free...

I'd rather have given him a gelding than a stallion, but I'd have given him anything to shut up.

Bill liked it.

I wandered over to the picture window and stood looking out into the night. A fine view of Seattle, Bill had, from this window facing it and thirty miles away, atop a hill. A fine view especially on a clear night like this one, one of those rare but wonderful warm, bright evenings that can happen in the fall of the year.

Below, the lights of Seattle; above, the lights in the sky.

Behind me, a cowboy singing. Then the song ended and Bill flicked the toggle switch on the arm of his chair that cut off sound while the commercial was on.

In the sudden and blessed silence I said, "Bill, I'm leaving."

He did what I'd hoped he wouldn't do, but had known that he would. He walked over and shut off the viddy completely.

Cowboy music he was giving up. Just to argue with me, to try to talk me into staying longer.

To make it worse Merlene came back into the room just then. The kids must have gone to bed without putting up even a token battle about it. I'd counted on having Bill worn down by the time Merlene came downstairs to reinforce him. Now I had both of them at once. And Merlene had heard what I'd said.

She said "No." Firmly. She sat down on the sofa and looked at me.

I said "Yes." Mildly.

"Max Andrews, you've been here less than three weeks. You're about half-way well now. You need at least another two weeks of rest and you know it."

"Not full time rest," I said. "I'll take things easy for a while."

Bill was back in his chair. He said, "Listen, Max—" I turned toward him but he bogged down. He turned to Merlene and I turned too.

Merlene said, "You're not well enough to leave here yet and you know it."

"Then I'll no doubt fall down just outside. If I do, you can drag me back in and I'll stay. Okay?"

She glared at me. Bill cleared his throat and I looked at him. He got as far as "Listen, Max—" and bogged down again.

Merlene said, "You and those itchy feet of yours."

"Just one of them itches," I told her. "Now, children, if this argument must continue, will you please sit together so I don't get dizzy turning around to face whichever one of you is talking. Bill, will you please sit on the sofa by your wife?"

He got up and moved over. Not gracefully; he stumbled. But grace has never been one of Bill's strong points. Opposite of Merlene; she'd been a dancer before they were married and every movement she made was graceful. She could change Easter's diapers as though it were part of a ballet—and with no conscious knowledge that she was making a dance out of it; that was what made it so wonderful to watch.

Merlene said, "Please understand this, Max. We like having you here. We like *you*. It isn't as though you are imposing on us, or anything like that. And you're paying your own way, which helps the budget a lot."

"It can't help your budget," I pointed out, "when you insist on charging me cost only and figuring it down to the penny. If you'd let me pay you a flat fifty a week, as I'd suggested—"

"Will you stay two more weeks if we let you pay it that way?"

I'd walked into that one. I said, "No, darling, I'm sorry."

I counterattacked. "Listen," I said, "you're only two to one against me, but you can increase the odds. You know I'm crazy about Easter and Billy, and they can't possibly be asleep yet. Why don't you get them here too and tell them I'm leaving so they can cry about it and soften me with their salty little tears?"

Merlene glowered at me. "You—you—"

I grinned at Bill. "The reason she's speechless is that she was thinking about doing just that and now she can't. She was probably wondering already what pretext she could use for bringing them back downstairs." I looked at Merlene. "But it really wouldn't be fair, honey. I don't mean to me—that doesn't matter. I mean it wouldn't be fair to them. It might disturb them emotionally, and to no purpose. Because no matter how much it disturbs either them or me I'm leaving tonight. I've got to."

Bill sighed. He sat there looking at me sadly, my kid brother with his temples turning gray. He said, "I don't suppose, then, that it'll do any good to tell you I've been working at wangling you a job with Union Transport. A good job."

"I'm a rocket mech, Bill. Union Transport doesn't use rockets."

"It would be administrative work, Max. From that point of view what's the difference between rockets and stratojets?"

"I don't like stratojets. That's the difference."

"Rockets are going out, Max. And besides—my God, you can't be just a mech all your *life.*"

"Why can't I? And damn it, rockets are *not* going out. Not until we get something better."

Bill laughed. "Such as sewing machines?"

I'll never live that sewing machine episode down.

I smiled back at him, though, because by now it was funny to me too. Maybe it had been funny even then. It had cost me nearly two weeks' time and nearly a thousand dollars cash but a really good joke on yourself is worth at least that.

Bill cleared his throat again, but Merlene saved me. She said, "Oh, let him alone, Bill. He's going, whatever we say, so why spoil the last evening?"

I walked across the room and patted her shoulder. "My angel," I said. "Can we have a drink to that?"

For a moment she looked doubtful. I said patiently, "It's all right, darling. I am not an alcoholic—at least not in the sense that I can't do normal social drinking or even get pixilated once in a while without it 'starting me off.' Now in celebration of my imminent departure, may I mix us a round of martinis?"

She jumped up. "I'll make them, Max." She walked out of the room and her walk was a dance. Both Bill's eyes and mine followed her.

"Good gal," I told him.

"Max, why don't you get married and settle down?"

"At my age? I'm too young to settle down."

"Seriously."

"I'm serious."

Bill shook his head slowly. Well, that's the way I felt about him and his way of life.

Merlene spared us pitying one another further by bringing in the drinks. We touched glasses.

"Luck to you, Max," Merlene said. "Decided where you're going?"

"San Francisco."

"Rocket mech on Treasure Island again?"

"Probably, but not right away. I meant what I said about resting up a little first."

"But why not stay here until you're ready to go back to work?"

"Something happening there I want to look in on, maybe give a hand with. News item I heard on the viddy last night."

Bill said, "Bet I know which item. That crazy dame who's running for senator and wants to send a rocket to Jupiter. My God, *Jupiter.* What have Mars and Venus got us?"

My poor little brother, my poor brother who was rich in money and bereft of vision, my blind blind brother.

I said, "Listen, children, I'm going to catch the two A.M. jet plane. And it's only eight o'clock now, so that's six hours away. Here's a suggestion. You two haven't taken advantage of having an expert baby sitter since I've been here and this is your last chance. Why don't you rev up the hellie and run into Seattle for an evening out. Night club or something, see some live entertainment. If you get back by one-thirty or so Bill can run me to the stratoport in plenty of time to make the plane."

Merlene looked reproachful. "Your last evening here and you think we'd rather—"

"Whatever you'd rather," I told her, "*I'd* rather you did. I've got some thinking to do and some planning. And some packing. Off with you."

I talked them into it.

My suitcase by the door, ready. It wasn't heavy; I travel lightly and live lightly. Physical possessions tie you down and God knows we're tied down enough without them.

I went back upstairs to my bedroom, or to the room that had been my bedroom for the past three weeks and which was the guest room again now that all my things were out of it. This time I didn't turn on the light. I tiptoed across the room quietly—as I had packed quietly, because it was right next to the room Billy and Easter were sleeping in—opened the window and stepped through it onto the railed upper porch.

It was a beautiful night. Warm and clear. Mount Rainier in the distance, the near distance.

Overhead and in the far distance the lights in the sky that are stars. The stars they tell us we can never reach because they are too far away. They lie; we'll get there. If rockets won't take us, *something* will.

There's got to be an answer.

We got to the moon, didn't we? And Mars and Venus—

Thank God I was in on that, back in the glorious sixties when man erupted suddenly into space, the first step, the first three steps toward the stars.

I was there, I was in on it. Spaceman First Class Max Andrews.

And now? What are we doing now to reach the stars?

The stars—listen, do you know what a star is?

Our sun is a star and all the stars in the sky are suns. We know now that most of them have planets revolving about them, as Earth and Mars and Venus and the other planets of the solar system revolve around our sun.

And there are a hell of a lot of stars.

That isn't profanity; it's understatement. There are about a thousand million stars in our own galaxy. A thousand million stars, most of them with planets. If they average only one planet apiece that's a thousand million planets. If one out of a thousand of those planets happens to be Earth-type—one with a breathable atmosphere, about the same size and distance from its sun as Earth so its temperature and gravity would be similar—then there ought to be at least a million planets in our own galaxy which man can colonize and on which he can live a normal life, on which he can be fruitful and multiply.

A million worlds for us to reach and take and live on.

But that's going to be only the start, the beginning. That's only *our own galaxy,* as tiny in relation to the universe as our little solar system is to our galaxy.

There are a hell of a lot of galaxies. There are more galaxies of stars in the universe than there are stars in our own galaxy. At least a thousand million times a thousand million suns.

A million times a million planets, habitable by man. Do you know how that figures out? To twenty-five planets or so apiece for every member of the human race, every man, woman and child.

Since no one can populate a planet all by himself let's say fifty planets per couple. Fifty planets, and if we hold the average population density down to three billion per planet, times fifty—we'll have to get there first of course, but when we do it's going to take a lot of multiplying to populate all those worlds. Well, the human race has always been good at that, hasn't it?

Or maybe we'll find some of them already populated. Well, that will be interesting too. Just *what* will they be populated with?

San Francisco at three-fifteen in the morning. The damn stratojet was late. They always are.

I bought a tabloid at the jetport on Angel Island and caught a helicab to Union Square, the only place right downtown where they'll let the hellies land. To try my strength I walked up Nob Hill to the Mark; it winded me a little but not too badly.

The Mark's an old hotel, run-down, and cheap—you can get a single for as little as fifteen a day. When I was a kid it was famous for its view of the harbor and the bridges; now there are mostly higher buildings around it. But if you can get a room above the seventh floor and on the California-Mason corner you can still see northeast over the low buildings of the Chinese section and you can see Treasure Island, where the rockets land. Maybe there'd be one going out or coming in tonight and even from a distance the sight of a rocket taking off or landing in the dark is a beautiful thing. I hadn't seen a rocket for some months now and I was lonesome for the sight of one. I'd been away from them too long. So I asked for a high room in the right corner of the building.

The clerk told me they didn't have one there, but for ten bucks he looked again and told me someone had checked out an hour ago, in the middle of the night, and that if I wanted to take a room that hadn't been made up yet I could have it. I took it.

The room was a mess all right; the someone who'd just checked out had been a couple and obviously they'd done a lot of drinking and had had a fight in addition to using the bed and several of the towels. They'd got their money's worth even if they'd stayed only half the night.

But I didn't give a damn about that. I pulled a chair over to the window and sat there, keeping watch on the lights of Treasure and the sky over it while

I read the tabloid I'd bought on Angel. Skimmed it, rather, since there wasn't anything in it on what I was interested in, the special election.

I put it down after a while and just watched for a rocket, and I thought about a lot of things. I thought about Bill's son, Billy. At six, he still had the Dream; he still wanted to be a spaceman. He wanted the stars. I wondered if I'd helped make him that way or whether it had been space opera on the viddy, and then I decided that it didn't matter. As long as he had the Dream, and if he kept it. One more starduster he'd be. One more crackpot. And every one of us counts. When there are enough of us—

Fog began to drift over the harbor as the sky grayed with dawn and I knew I wouldn't be able to see a rocket any more if one took off or landed, so I went to sleep. There in the chair, not wanting to lie in or even on that rumpled messy bed. But I slept soundly.

The maid woke me, trying the door.

There was bright sunshine out the window and my wrist watch told me it was eleven o'clock and that I must have slept about seven hours. I was stiff when I got up out of the chair.

But I went to the door before she got away and told her I was going out for a short while and would appreciate it if she cleaned the room. Stiff, dirty and un-shaven, I went downstairs for breakfast. Cleaning up and shaving could wait till the bathroom was cleaned up and had fresh towels. I wondered if the maid would think I messed up the room like that and then I decided it didn't matter what she thought.

When I came back the room was clean and orderly and I took a shower and shaved. The stiffness was gone and I decided I felt pretty good.

I phoned Treasure Island and asked for the head mech, Rory Bursteder. His voice came on and I said, "This is Max, Rory. How's everything?"

He said, "Max who?"

"Max No Difference," I told him.

Rory roared, "Max Andrews! You son of a bitch you, where you been the last year?"

"Here and there. Mostly New Orleans."

"Where you calling from?"

I told him.

"Get the hell over here fast. Start you right in."

I said, "I don't want to start work for about a week yet, Rory. Something I want to look into here, first."

"Oh. The election, maybe?"

"Yeah. I just heard about it yesterday, up in Seattle. What's the score?"

"Come on over and I'll tell you. Or—wait a minute, got any plans for this evening?"

"Nope."

"Then eat with me and the old lady. We're still in Berkeley so this is halfway there for you. I'm off at six; meet me at the gate then and we'll go the rest of the way together."

"Swell," I said. "But listen, what take-offs or landings are there this afternoon?"

"Only one. Paris rocket takes off at five-fifteen. Okay, I'll leave word at the gate to get you in at five."

Rory's wife Bess is a wonderful cook. Not that I hadn't enjoyed the meals at Bill's, but Merlene is a little on the fancy side as a cook, worries as much about how a dish looks as how it tastes. Bess Bursteder's cooking is old-fashioned and German, but she makes dumplings so light they need the thick rich gravy to keep them from rising off the plate and floating away, and the meat was so tender that it must have come from Circassian virgins, young ones.

We washed it down with ale and then sat back and relaxed. I couldn't have got up if I'd wanted to.

I said, "Now tell me about the election deal, Rory."

"Well—it looks like a fair chance."

"That's not what I meant, although I want to hear that too. Listen, all I heard was a few sentences of a newscast yesterday. All I know is some dame named Gallagher is running for senator from California and if she gets in she plans to introduce and back a bill making an appropriation to cover an expedition to go around Jupiter."

"That's right."

"But damn it, that's *all* I know. What are the details? First, how come a special election? I thought the governor of a state could appoint someone to finish the unexpired term of a senator who dies while in office."

"You're ten years out of date. Revised Statutes of nineteen eighty-seven—if a senatorship is vacated by death with more than half of the unexpired term remaining a special election must be held at a date to be set before the next session of Congress."

"Oh. Well, that answers that. Now, who the hell is this Gallagher woman?"

"Ellen Gallagher, forty-five, widow of Ralph Gallagher who died while he was mayor of Los Angeles six or seven years ago. She struck out on her own in politics after that—she'd been active in them before, but only to work in her husband's interests. Two terms in the California assembly since then, now running for senator. Next question."

"What makes her tick? Is she a starduster?"

"No. But she's a friend of Bradly of Caltech. Know of him?"

"I've read some of his stuff. A little stodgy, but good."

"One of us, within limitations. He still kowtows to the relativists, thinks we'll never exceed the speed of light. But anyway he sold the Gallagher dame on the Jupiter run—only hell, why didn't she keep her hatch shut about it until after she got in? California's pretty conservationist and jetting off may cost her the election."

"We'll have to see it doesn't. Who's bucking her?"

"Guy named Layton, Dwight Layton, of Sacramento. Ex-mayor there and has a machine. Crooked as they come. Conservationist."

I shuddered. "Is that all?"

"He's buying a lot of viddy time and he's a smooth talker. He says mankind is wasting its most valuable resource, uranium, spending it in prodigious quantities to maintain valueless minor colonies on a dead moon and dead Mars. Earth is impoverishing itself in the futile effort to make a long-since-proved-impractical dream come true. Over a hundred billion dollars spent on Mars alone, and what is there of value to us on Mars? Sand and lichens, not enough air to support human life, bitter cold. Yet we spend more millions every year to supply a few dozen people who are mad enough to try—"

"Shut up," I said. "That's enough."

Bess said, "Scram, you boys. I want to clear the table."

We helped her. Afterward, over some ale in the living room, I said to Rory, "All right, I've got the picture now. What can I do about it?"

He sighted. "Well—to start with, you can vote. Got here just in time to register; tomorrow's the last day. You'll have to come over to Berkeley again to do it because you'll have to claim a year's residence to vote, see, and you can give this address; we'll say you've been rooming with us that long."

"Good," I said.

Bess said, "Except that it's silly for you to go back across the bay tonight and then come back here just to register. Stay with us tonight and register in the morning before you go back."

"Swell; thanks, Bess."

Rory said, "Should have thought of that myself. Well, to get back to what you can do about the election; you've got plenty of friends in San Francisco so you can register in a few precincts over there. You can probably be set to cast three or four votes next Tuesday."

"Can do. Five or six maybe."

"And make sure your friends have registered. We don't have to worry which way they'd vote, or they wouldn't be friends of yours. And every vote will help, Max."

"Sure, every vote will help. But even if I can swing a couple of dozen votes that's peanuts. Damn it, isn't there anything more than that?"

"Damn if I know what, Max. You're no speaker. If you get yourself a soap box or even buy viddy time, you'll get het up and sound like a fanatic—which you are—and probably alienate more people than you'll convince."

I sighed. "'Fraid you're right on that. Still, maybe there's *something*. I can look up the Gallagher and ask her—like to meet her anyway."

"Don't think she's in town. But you could look up her campaign manager. Richard Shearer. Got a suite at the St. Francis for campaign quarters. I talked to him on the phone yesterday."

"What about?"

"Heard he was going to send a speaker over to Treasure to talk to the boys during lunch hour. Told him not to waste the speaker; he had the Treasure Island vote solid anyway and might as well send the guy where it could help him."

"Right," I said. "I'll see him first thing Thursday; I'll spend tomorrow getting registered myself and making sure my friends are."

I set my alarm for half past three on Thursday. Not to see Richard Shearer that early, but because the Moscow rocket was due to land at three-forty, the first rocket to land or take off at night since I'd been there. Night rocket flights are relatively infrequent; why risk night landings when a few hours will take you as far as a terrestrial rocket need go in one flight, halfway around the earth? But night landings are beautiful to watch.

From the window, standing there in my room in the dark, I watched it. You've seen a rocket sit down on its fiery tail; I don't have to describe it for you. It's the most wonderful fireworks that ever were, the fireworks that gave us the moon and Mars and Venus and that can and will take us to other and farther planets.

Rockets are going out, Bill had said.

They *are* going out, but not far enough. We took the first steps and then we lost our guts. Temporarily—it *must* be temporarily—we've lost our drive, or most of us have.

Not all of us, thank God, not all. Millions of us, millions besides me, want the stars. But right now there are more millions who don't—or who mildly do but think it's impossible anyway in our lifetimes, and that it's not worth the money it would cost to try.

Worst of all there are the reactionaries, the conservationists, the shortsighted tightwads with no vision at all, who think everything we have done is wasted time and effort just because it hasn't yet yielded any financial return.

Of course they haven't, but they're only steps, the first steps, and even when we took them we knew from our astronomers what to expect to find there. But Jesus, when you're climbing a staircase to a room—an infinite room—filled with all the treasures of the universe, should you stop climbing just because you don't find a handful of treasure on the first two or three steps?

Conservationists, millions of them, calling us crackpots, stardusters. Taxes they worry about, money they worry about. We've gone into debt enough, they say, and why go any farther? The planets are worthless and the stars—why, if we can reach them at all, it might take us thousands of years.

I'll buy part of that. It *may* take us thousands of years, and it damn well will unless we keep trying with everything we've got. But if we do keep trying it can happen suddenly too. It can come as unexpectedly as our reaching Mars came in 1965, four years ahead of our schedule for reaching the moon. Suddenly we'd found the A-drive and the chemical fuels we'd been working with and figuring on were obsolete. We were in the situation of a man trying to cross the ocean in a rowboat, when only a few miles out from shore he is suddenly given a supersonic-speed airplane to use instead of his rowboat.

Maybe it'll be the same way when we try for the stars, for let's face it that even an A-drive rocket is a rowboat when it comes to interstellar distances. We may find something new that will make the stars as relatively easy as the A-drive made the planets, but damn it, we'll find it only when we're *trying,* all out, to get there with what we've got. Like we were *trying* for the moon, all out, with chemical rockets when we found the A-drive.

At nine o'clock I walked into Suite 1315 of the St. Francis. *Gallagher for Senator Headquarters*, the sign on the door read. A blonde receptionist was spreading papers around on her desk. She looked up when I came in and liked what she saw or she'd been told to smile at everybody; anyway, she smiled.

I thought I'd first check Rory's information that the candidate herself wasn't in town. "Is Ellen Gallagher in?"

"Mrs. Gallagher won't be in. She's on a speaking tour in the northern part of the state. I'm sorry."

"Why should you be sorry? Richard Shearer in?"

"He'll be in any moment. Would you care to sit down and— Oh, here he is. This gentleman wants to see you, Mr. Shearer."

The man who'd just come in was a big redhead with a moon face. I introduced myself and he shook hands. "What can I do for you, Mr. Andrews?" His voice was deep and slow, almost a drawl.

"Tell me how I can help Ellen Gallagher get elected."

"Come in my office." He led the way to an inner room, showed me a chair and sat at a desk, one of the old-type all-plastic automatics.

"You're a friend of Mrs. Gallagher's, Mr. Andrews?"

"Sure," I said. "I've never met her, but if she's going to back an appropriation for a rocket to Jupiter I'm a friend of hers."

"Oh, a starduster." He grinned. "Well, we can use starduster support; in fact, we'll certainly need it now that our candidate has stuck her neck out about that rocket."

"Which you don't approve of?"

"I approve of the rocket. I think it's about time we tried another step out. But I'm afraid her statement to the press about it, just before the election, was a political mistake that will cost her more votes than it will win her."

"Enough to lose her the election?"

"I don't know, Mr. Andrews. But we'll certainly need the solid starduster vote, now that we're committed."

I said, "Don't worry about the starduster vote. You'll get it—several times over in at least some cases."

He smiled faintly. "I'm afraid to ask you just what you mean by that, so let's forget it, or still better let's say I didn't hear you."

"All right, I didn't say it. But you just said you didn't *know* whether she'd win. What do you *think*?"

He was silent so long that I decided to say it for him. "So she's going to lose, as things stand."

"I'm afraid it does look that way. Unless something unexpected happens—"

"Such as a sudden and unexpected accident to this Dwight Layton?"

He'd been slouching forward on his desk. Now he sat up straight as suddenly as though someone had just pushed a ramrod up him.

He said, "You're not suggesting—" He stared at me. "By Christ I believe you are and I believe you'd try to *arrange* one."

"Consider it a hypothetical question but answer it. Would it help Gallagher's chances?"

He got up and started pacing the length of the office slowly, thinking. Five times, and then he stopped and faced me. "No, it would be the worst thing that could happen for her—even if Layton had a *genuine* accident."

"Why?"

"Because Dwight Layton is a damned crook, although nobody can prove it. But plenty of people, even in his own party, suspect it, and it's going to cost him some votes. Not as many, I'm afraid, as Ellen's unfortunate statement is going to cost her, but it'll help. With any other candidate bucking her—even someone run in at the last minute whom the public had never heard of, she'd have even less chance. Besides, if Layton had an accident of such a nature that there could be even a remote suspicion that it had been arranged by a fanatical starduster—my God, man, don't you see the damage that would do to *your* cause, all over the country, besides what it would do to Ellen?"

"You're right," I said. "Forget it. In what way is Layton a crook? What's he done?"

"As mayor of Sacramento, he got rich awfully suddenly. The rumor is that it was kickbacks on public construction contracts. But it's covered up damned well. The income tax boys investigated him last year on the strength of the rumors and had to give him a clean bill of health."

"Must have a good accountant."

"He *is* a good accountant. Was near the top in that field before he got into politics. He's clever, and there isn't a thing against him. If we even intimate there is, he can sue the bejesus out of us."

"What if *I* intimate it? Hire viddy time with my own money, having no connection with the Gallagher campaign? What if I accuse him openly and don't mind being sued?"

He shook his head slowly. "It would still react against Ellen. You can't attack one candidate in an election without automatically associating yourself with the other one. No, I'm afraid there's not a thing you can do, Mr. Andrews, that won't do us more harm than good. Nothing on a large scale, that is. Of course we'll appreciate your vote and whatever votes you can swing among your friends."

And he held out his hand to me, showing the interview was over.

I wandered around a while, thinking. I wanted to do some thinking, plenty of it, before I settled for anything as weak as voting a few times myself and helping swing a few or even a few dozen other votes. Even a few hundred votes wouldn't help much, the way her campaign manager had talked when he'd finally leveled with me.

I found myself passing Union Square. There was a platform in the middle and a guy on it talking; his voice was amplified and you could hear it all over the square.

"Jupiter," he said, as though it was a swear word. "This woman proposes to spend our money—and it would take at least a billion dollars of it—to send a rocket around Jupiter. A billion dollars that we'll have to pay, money out of our pockets, bread out of our mouths!

"A billion dollars, and what are we buying for it? Another worthless planet? Not even that. Just a closer *look* at another worthless planet. The rocket wouldn't even land. It couldn't land."

There was a small crowd around the platform, but people all over the square, passing on every side of it, were listening, hearing, even though they walked on about their business.

I thought of going up to the platform, climbing up on it and slapping him silly. My hands itched to do it. But it wouldn't help and it would only land me in jail so I couldn't even vote myself.

So I didn't. For once I was sensible.

"The planet *Jupiter.* Four hundred million miles away, more than *eight times* as far as Mars, a planet on which man can never land. It has a poisonous atmosphere of methane and ammonia, so thick that at the bottom it is liquid under pressures so great that the strongest rocket would be crushed like an eggshell, an atmosphere thousands of miles deep and in constant turbulence. Below that atmosphere? A layer thousands of miles thick, under terrific pressure. Our telescopes tell us these things about Jupiter, tell us that it is not fit for man. We already know that this giant planet has so strong a gravitational pull that a spaceship cannot even approach it closely without crashing—or should I say splashing?—into it. We already know that its moons are more barren, colder, more inhospitable than our own. And yet Mrs. Gallagher wants to waste a billion dollars of our money to..."

Hands balled in my pockets, I made myself stand there quietly and listen, just so I'd get mad enough to try to do what I'd decided would give Ellen Gallagher her only chance to win the election.

It was noon when I got to Sacramento. The jetport was jammed—I think it was because of a convention of some kind—and I had a lot of trouble getting a helicab into town. But by half past one I was in front of the building on K Street in which Dwight Layton had his office suite.

A minute later I was in the outer office of the suite.

The receptionist was tough, but not too tough; I fast-talked my way past her on the story that my business was highly personal and that it concerned the campaign and seriously affected Mr. Layton's chances. And no, it wasn't anything I could take up with his campaign manager or his secretary or anybody but Mr. Layton himself.

He was busy just then and I had to wait twenty-seven minutes, but I got in.

I gave him a phony name and started an excited crackpot spiel about unfair tactics that the God damned stardusters were using against him in the campaign. Still talking excitedly, I let him ease me out within a minute.

I could have held out longer, but a minute had been long enough for me to get a look at the layout of his office, the kinds of locks on the inner and outer doors, and the make and size of his safe. It was a big but old-fashioned job that any good mech could open in ten minutes with the right tools.

I bought all the things I'd need and a brief case to carry them in. I killed time until nine o'clock and then burgled Layton's office.

No burglar alarm; that's the one chance I'd taken.

I didn't even have to open the safe. I tried the desk first. It had one locked drawer and in the drawer, the only thing in it, was a red ledger. The entries in it were in Layton's handwriting—I compared it with the writing on other papers in the desk to make sure. Names, dates and amounts, even notations of what sales to the city of Sacramento they represented percentages of. Enough evidence to send him to jail half a dozen times over.

Strange and systematic is the mind of an accountant.

There might have been money in the safe and it wouldn't have hurt my conscience to take it, but I didn't want to risk tarrying. I had what I'd come for and it was more important than money. I didn't want to crowd my luck.

I mailed it in a plain wrapper to Richard Shearer at the St. Francis.

I went back to San Francisco and to bed.

Just before noon I phoned Shearer.

"Did you get a package?" I asked him.

"God yes. Who is this?"

"The man who sent it. Leave us name no names, particularly over the telephone. Have you done anything with it yet?"

"I'm still deciding the best way to use it. I'm sweating."

"Quit sweating," I said. "Turn it over to the state police, that's all. But in front of an office full of reporters, to whom you furnish photographic copies of a few of the juiciest pages."

"But where do I say I got it?"

"Where *did* you get it? It was mailed to you a plain wrapper from Sacramento. You can turn the wrapper over to the cops too. It hasn't any fingerprints on it and the address is in block lettering. Your hunch is that somebody in Layton's organization hates his guts. And that's what Layton himself will probably figure, if that matters. He won't find any evidence of a burglary and he probably hasn't even missed it yet."

"Listen, what do you want out of this? What can we do for you?"

"You can do two things for me. The first is to buy me a drink and over that I'll tell you the second. I'll be in the Big Dipper Bar in fifteen minutes. I'll know you if you don't know me."

"I think I'll know you. Didn't you imply in my office yesterday that you were going to vote several times?"

"Quiet," I said. "Don't you know that voting more than once is against the law?"

I'd picked the Big Dipper for its name; I'd been past it but had never gone in. It turned out to be a nice quiet spot, though. I took a booth and a few minutes later Shearer came in.

He looked both excited and worried. He said, "I guess your suggestion about the state police, with reporters watching, is the best bet. I'd thought of it too. But I'll wait until tomorrow, Saturday, late in the day; that'll break it in the Saturday evening newscasts and the Sunday papers, and give it the best coverage. It'll be a shoo-in, a boat race."

"How will you account for the delay? The postmark shows you got it today."

"Easy. I still don't know whether it's the McCoy or not. How do I know if that's really Layton's handwriting or if someone is trying to hoax me out on a limb?"

I frowned. "You don't really think there's a possibility I'm pulling something like that on you, do you?"

"Hell, no. But if it had really come to me cold, as I'm going to have to tell it, I'd have been plenty suspicious. Anyway it's going to take me until tomorrow afternoon to make sure and some photographs will be taken in the process; that's how come I'll have them on hand for the reporters. Okay, what's the one thing you want besides this drink?"

"It can wait till after the election. Ellen Gallagher will be busy until then. But I want you to tell her who really got you that ledger and fix an appointment with her for me. Think she'll talk to me?"

"Talk to you? Man, she ought to sleep with you. Okay, what else?"

"Nothing you can promise me. I'll have a favor to ask the Gallagher. That's why I want her to know I've got one coming."

He sipped his drink and looked at me. "You can't ride that rocket, you know, even if Ellen would want you to. Top age for pilots—"

I held up a hand to stop him. "Do you think I'm crazy? I know better than you do what the top age for spacemen is. Thirty, and I'm fifty-seven. No, I can't ride it. But I can help push it and that's all I want."

He nodded. "I know Ellen well enough to say she'll get you the best job on the project you're qualified for. If it goes through, of course; I wouldn't give it over one chance out of ten myself."

"What chance would you have given Ellen Gallagher to be elected, up to the time you got that ledger?"

"About the same. But getting a bill through Congress is something else again. You can't burgle the office of every congressman who's going to vote against it."

I grinned at him. I said, "I can try."

The election was a shoo-in, a boat race. The story had broken at just the right time and both viddy and the papers had made the most of it. Layton's party had made a desperate last-minute effort; Layton himself had appeared on the viddy claiming innocence but announcing his withdrawal from the race until he could clear himself of the charges against him, in favor of someone else whose name nobody bothered to listen to. The last-minute substitute carried six precincts in Sacramento and Ellen Gallagher carried everything else.

At eight o'clock that evening Bess, Rory and I watched the opposition concede defeat. We left the viddy on, turned low, because we all wanted to see Ellen Gallagher and hear what she had to say. It had been announced that she

was leaving Los Angeles to fly to San Francisco by stratojet and would be inter-
viewed on its landing at Angel Island at eight thirty-seven.

Bess got the bottle of champagne from the refrigerator; we'd held off opening it until the election had been formally conceded.

We poured drinks around and toasted victory.

We drank and talked. At thirty-five minutes after eight I saw the viddy screen
switch to an interviewer at the jetport so I went over and turned up the sound.

"...very thick fog," he was saying. "Visibility is just about zero out there on
the field so we'll wait until Senator Gallagher is inside here to interview her.
You wouldn't be able to see the jet land anyway; it will have to come in on
instruments. But it's coming down now, exactly on time. I can hear it."

I said, "My God, Rory, those jets are lousy on instrument landings. What
if—"

And we heard the crash.

I started to rush out to go there but Rory pulled me back. He said, "We'll get the
news here quicker."

It came in gradually, a piece at a time. The plane had cracked up badly,
many of the passengers had been killed outright and none of them had escaped
injury. The copilot had survived and was conscious when they pulled him out.
He said that both the radar and the radio had gone out simultaneously when
they were only yards off the ground, too late to pull up again.

One at a time they got the others out. Richard Shearer, Mrs. Gallagher's
campaign manager, dead. Dr. Emmett Bradly of Caltech, dead.

"God damned stratojet," Rory said.

The Gallagher was alive. Unconscious and badly injured, but alive. She was
being rushed to the Angel Island emergency hospital and further reports on
her condition would be given as soon as possible.

Wailing of ambulance sirens in the fog. Damn San Francisco, damn fogs,
damn stratojets, damn everything.

We sat and waited. The champagne was warm and flat. Rory poured it out
in the sink and got us cold beer instead. I didn't touch mine.

It was after eleven before there was further word on Senator Gallagher. She
was alive and expected to live, but very seriously injured. Two operations had
been performed. She would be hospitalized for months. But eventual recovery
was reasonably certain.

I wondered if Richard Shearer had told her yet the real story of how he'd
got that ledger. He *must* have. She'd certainly have asked him about it and he'd
have had no reason to stall on telling her—except that he might not have been
alone with her and he couldn't have told her in front of others.

Yes, it could all too easily have happened. She'd had a party of seven with her,
five others besides Shearer, who had flown down to join her only that afternoon in
Los Angeles, and Bradly. It was all too possible she hadn't been alone with Shearer.

Finally I drank the glass of beer Rory had poured for me. It was as warm by
then as the champagne had been, and flatter.

The next morning I started working at Treasure Island under Rory.

1998

Working on rockets. Working on rockets that were going out, but not far enough out. Only a few hundred miles out, these rockets, and then back to Earth again. The rockets for New York and Paris and Moscow and Tokyo and Brisbane and Johannesburg and Janeiro. Not even for the moon or Mars, these rockets out of San Francisco. Those rockets, the *real* rockets, take off from bases in New Mexico and Arizona. The government runs them, and the government has silly ideas about rocket mechs. The government thinks rocket mechs should not be over fifty. The government thinks rocket mechs should have both legs made of flesh and bone. Oh, I've worked on the interplanetaries despite that latter ruling, times when friends of mine have been in a position to get me special dispensation on the leg. But not since I'd passed the fifty mark seven years ago; that's one rule that's really enforced at the government bases. A few times since I passed fifty I've worked short periods at the interplanetary bases, but not as a rocket mech, not working on the rockets but just to be near them, to see them, to touch one occasionally and to watch take-offs and landings. But never for long periods; there's no future, no pathway to the stars, in working in a commissary or being a feather merchant. It's better actually to work on rockets, even if they're only the terrestrial ones that take off from Earth to come down again.

So, San Francisco—and besides, Senator Gallagher was there. Still in the hospital, but now recovering. She'd live all right, my gal whom I'd never met. She'd live and be completely well in a few months, just a matter of time. Just a matter of time to Jupiter, the next outward step. Just a matter of time, and time running out.

Oh, I accomplished something that January. I got an idea that slightly cut down the weight of a gyro-stabilizer. I got a thousand-dollar bonus for it and it would save the terrestrial rocket lines quite a few thousand a year. That wasn't important, though; the important thing was that the improvement could be and would be on the interplanetaries too. A tiny saving in mass-ratio, an inch closer to the stars. That's what mattered. Rory and Bess and I spent a hundred of my thousand bonus on a spree.

The good news, the big news, came a few weeks later, in February. A letter from Senator Gallagher, at last. I was moving around a bit, hadn't yet found quarters I really liked, so I was getting my mail at the Bursteders', and Bess called me at work one day to tell me the letter had come. Of course I told her to tear it open and read it quick. Pause for tearing envelope, unfolding letter.

"*Dear Mr. Andrews,*" Bess read: "*At long last I am allowed to dictate answers to some of the letters I have received, and yours is of course among the first.*

"*Yes, Ricky Shearer told me it was you who supplied the bombshell that won me the election and I am deeply aware of my indebtedness to you. His telling me was, as it happened, one of the last acts of his life; we were sitting together in the stratojet and he told me just as we were coming in for the landing at Angel.*

"It is not yet certain, although the doctors are hopeful, whether or not I shall take my place in the current session of Congress, which will probably adjourn in May this year, but I shall certainly be completely recovered by mid-summer and more than ready for the nineteen ninety-nine session starting next January.

"Meanwhile, and long before then, I hope to meet you and to be able to discuss the Jupiter project with you. Yes, I know your interest is in the project and not in me personally, and I shall do my best to push that project and, if at all possible, to give you an active part in it if the appropriation is approved. I know that is what you want and I know that it is the only adequate way I can thank you for what you did for me in the election campaign.

"I shall write you again, probably in about a month. By that time I shall be able to have visitors and hope you will be able to call on me."

"Wonderful," I told Bess.

And wonderful I meant. I was still in. Dear Richard Shearer, Ricky, had come through. He'd lived long enough to tell the Gallagher the truth about that ledger. Dear Ricky, I loved him. I loved everybody. I was still in.

And the rockets still went out and I worked on them. Up they went, even though down they came, down at other cities two thousand miles or more away. That's the minimum distance it's worth while sending a local rocket. You can't take off and land one in much less than that. And if you could, the time saving over a stratojet plane wouldn't be great enough to matter much.

Even on short hauls like New York and Mexico City the saving in time is only a few hours. Let's face it that there's no *great* saving in time on runs shorter than, say, the Paris run. That takes eighteen hours by stratojet, with the two refueling stops it has to make, and less than four hours by rocket. Fourteen hours is worth saving, but even so only the rich can afford to save it because the rocket fare is more than ten times as much. Thank God for the rich. Thank God for the rich because they keep the local rockets going. And it's important that they be kept going because the interplanetaries, the ones that really matter, benefit by every small technical improvement that the operators of the locals make, and there have been thousands of such improvements. Not big ones, mostly, but each one of them counts because it will add however slightly to the pay load an interplanetary job can carry. Or cut the time of its journey by a few minutes or increase its safety factor by a fraction of a percent. Not to mention that the locals give jobs to rocket mechs who because of age or some other silly technicality can't work on the government jobs. All the puddle-jumper operators care about is whether you're technically qualified and physically able to do the work.

Yes, thank God for the rich.

Senator Gallagher didn't write a second time. She phoned instead, one evening in late March. She still had Rory's address for me and called there; luckily I was spending the evening with them so the call didn't have to be relayed.

Bess answered the phone. "For you, Max," she told me. "A strange woman. Maybe it's—"

And it was.

"Mr. Andrews? This is Ellen Gallagher. I'm home now and feeling much better. I'm allowed visitors, with half an hour time limit. Would it be convenient for you to call soon?"

"Any time," I told her. "Right now, for that matter—or wait, you say you're home again. Does that mean you're calling from Los Angeles?"

"No, I'm still in San Francisco. By 'home' I mean an apartment I've taken here for a month or two so I can stay in close touch with the doctor who's been treating me. It's on Telegraph Hill."

"If tonight's okay, I can be there in half an hour."

She laughed. It was a nice laugh; I was going to like her. Like her? Hell, I loved her already. She said, "You really are in a hurry, Mr. Andrews. And you sound and talk just as Ricky described you. But I really shouldn't have company tonight. Are you free tomorrow? Could you come at about two in the afternoon?"

I told her I was free and would see her then—and of course I was free as soon as I explained to Rory and arranged with him to knock off work at noon. That would give me plenty of time after lunch to clean up, dress up and get there.

A private nurse let me into the apartment and took me to the room where Ellen Gallagher was sitting up in bed, waiting for me.

She looked pale but prettier than the pictures of her I'd seen; maybe that was because the only pictures I'd run across were black-and-whites and her chestnut hair, almost red, was much more striking than it had photographed. She didn't look forty-five, either; she could have passed for anywhere in the thirties. Her eyes were dark, wide apart. Her mouth, too, was wide and generous. On second thought, second look, she wasn't pretty; I'd used the wrong word there. But she was attractive, and she was all woman.

"Not bad," I said.

She laughed. "Thank you, Mr. Andrews."

"Max to you, Ellen," I said.

"All right, Max. Sit down and quit pacing like that. The rocket isn't ready to take off yet."

I hadn't known I'd been pacing. I sat down. "When?" I asked.

"You know how long a government project takes."

Yes, I knew that. I knew it would take at least a year to get started after the appropriation went through. Longer than that unless somebody behind it pushed and kept pushing. And, as a government job, at least two years to build a new type rocket. Private industry could do it in about half the time.

I asked, "What, honestly, do you think your chances are of getting it through Congress?"

"Pretty good, Max. I can make it look good, get it good publicity, get statements from all the top scientists about the value to science of a close examination of Jupiter. Of course that's window dressing. Actually, since it's a comparatively small appropriation, I'll put it through by horse trading."

"Horse trading? How do you mean?"

She looked at me and shook her head wonderingly. "You really don't know how Congress operates?"

"No. Tell me."

"It's like this, Max. Every congressman has some bill he personally wants to put through, usually something he wants to get for his home state, for his constituents, so they'll vote him back into office. Senator Cornhusker, let's say, from Iowa wants a new and higher parity price on corn. We horse trade. I vote for his bill and he votes for mine."

"Good God," I said. "There are a hundred and two senators. You mean you'll have to make a hundred and one—"

"Max, you're not thinking straight. Fifty-two votes is a majority. I can count on at least thirty-five—there are that many who'll vote for it in any case. That leaves only seventeen—or twenty to play safe—votes I'll have to trade for."

"But the House of Representatives—"

"Will be tougher. But the starduster lobby will help. They'll know exactly which votes can be counted on anyway and how to swing enough others. They'll handle the liaison work, fix it so I can trade for blocks of votes there—one vote in the senate is worth eight house votes since the last reapportionment. And I won't have to do all the trading myself, either; the lobby can line up at least a few representatives who'll want that bill through badly enough to do some trading themselves."

"That sounds like it will take time. Is there any chance of getting it through this coming session? I mean, if you get well fast enough to get there say a month before adjournment?"

She shook her head definitely. "Max, even if I hadn't been injured, even if I was there now, I wouldn't try pushing it through this session. This is ninety-eight, a presidential election year. President Jansen will run for re-election—and probably win. He's mildly on our side; he'll not veto the bill if it comes to him after re-election. But just *before* election he'd almost have to."

"What if he's not re-elected?"

"I think he will be, but it shouldn't matter too much to us if he isn't. Whoever'd beat him would be almost certain to be a middle-of-the-roader who'll approve a small expansionist bill like ours even though he'd veto, as Jansen would, any really big new move—like trying to colonize another planet or trying to build a star-ship."

"How can you be sure? Sure, I mean, that he'd be a middle-of-the-roader?"

"Because neither party would dare run a deep-dyed conservationist any more than they'd dare run a rabid starduster. Luckily the split there isn't on party lines—and the starduster vote is big enough that neither party would dare have it solidly in opposition. And be glad it's that way, Max, for right now. If party lines were drawn that way, we'd be in the minority."

"I can see that. But one thing I can't see. Woman, since you're smart enough to figure politics like that, how come you were dopey enough to let Jupiter become an issue in that special election? Telling those reporters you were going to back a new rocket damn near lost you the job."

"I know. I would have lost it except for what you did. But it wasn't really my mistake, Max. Brad—Dr. Bradly of Caltech—made it. He let it slip that he'd worked out details of the project and that I was going to back it in Congress if I got in. The reporters came to me for confirmation—and I couldn't let Brad down, could I? I couldn't call him a liar."

"No, you couldn't," I said. "But why did *he* do such a damn fool—"

"Max!" Her voice was a little sharp. "Brad's dead, remember. And anyway it was he who sold me on the project. It was his idea."

"I'm sorry," I said.

She smiled again. "All right, let's forget it. Tell me—"

She looked toward the doorway as we heard footsteps coming toward it. The nurse appeared there. "It's been half an hour, Mrs. Gallagher. You told me to remind you."

"Thanks, Dorothy." She looked back at me. "Max, what I was just going to ask you will take quite a bit of time for you to answer. So for now let's just arrange a time for you to come back."

We set it for Friday evening at seven.

I bought a pair of six-inch optical glass blanks to grind myself a lens for a reflecting telescope. I wanted to be able to do a lot of looking, without having to go to an observatory to do it, at Big Jupe and his moons.

I'd have lots of time to look if there wasn't a chance of the project getting started for at least another year.

I started grinding. It's a long, tedious job, but it would help pass the time for me.

Friday evening Ellen Gallagher was sitting up in a chair, wearing a housecoat. She looked better, less pale.

She said, "Sit down, Max. All right, we'll start where we left off. I was going to bring the conversation around to you. What do you want?"

"You know damn well what I want. I want to ride that rocket. But we both know damned well that I can't, so that's that. Next to riding it, I want to help you get it through Congress, help build it, watch it take off, and then live long enough to watch it land again. I want to know that we've taken one more step out toward where we're going."

"That's what I thought. Yes, I can fix it for you to work on the rocket. But as for your helping get it through Congress—no, definitely not. That's not your department. It's my job and I can do it."

"I don't seem to recall having done too badly—"

"Max, that was different. You didn't get me elected, you know. You got my opponent defeated. Sure, the result was the same. But something like that wouldn't help a bill through Congress. What would you do? Burglarize congressmen's offices to get something to blackmail them with?"

"I could argue with people."

"Max, you'd do more harm than good in Washington. Stay away from the place. Promise me you will?"

"All right. I guess you're right."

"Good. Now about what kind of a job we can get you on the project, once it's started—well, Ricky Shearer told me you were a rocket mech and that he thought but wasn't sure that you were an ex-spaceman. Are you?"

I nodded.

"Honorable discharge? Where's your discharge button?"

"In a drawer someplace. I don't wear it. Don't feel I should wear it for something I did so many years ago."

"Start wearing it. Your having been a spaceman will help. Now start from scratch and tell me your background and your qualifications."

"All right," I said. I sighed. "Scratch was in the year nineteen hundred and forty, in Chicago, Illinois. I was the son of poor but honest parents."

"No corn, Max. Tell this straight. It may be important."

"Okay, sorry. Well, I was seventeen in fifty-seven when work was started on the space station project, the space station that was to be our first step toward the moon and then the planets.

"I was space-nutty, of course, like a few million other kids. Hell, in those days all kids were space-nutty. Of course I wanted to be a spaceman. Every seventeen-year-old in his right mind wanted to be a spaceman.

"But I was smarter than most of them because I figured out—or guessed—the right way to get in, ahead of the rush. I enlisted in the air corps, for pilot training, just before the rush started. Only a month later the word got around that when a space corps was formed, spacemen would be drawn from the air force, the pick of the best pilots would be the first chosen. And suddenly over a million kids tried to enlist in the air force all at once."

I grinned. "And of course the air force could take only a few of them and it got to be harder to get into the air force than—than to get elected to Congress. They were able to take just about one out of every thousand applicants.

"But there I was with my little piccolo, already in pilot training. And I made the grade. Got to be a hot ship pilot, a jet pilot—and knew I'd get into the space corps eventually. But not in the first class, because there were several hundred pilots ahead of me, ones who had priority over me because they'd been in the air force longer. There were three hundred in the first class at space school, the class that started in fifty-eight, while the rockets they'd be flying were still on the drafting board. Those big three-step deals, tall as a ten story building and able to lift only a few hundred pounds of pay load up to the orbit they were going to put the space station in.

"That first class, or the half of it that didn't get washed out, graduated in sixty-two. Ready, just in time, for the rockets that were ready to start putting the space station up there in the sky. But there were still more spacemen than rockets and it looked bad when I graduated in the second class in sixty-three."

I laughed. "Only the top two dozen of the *first* class had ever actually got off Earth. I was near the top of my class but there were still over a hundred ahead of me. And I was getting old—I was twenty-three! In those chemical rocket days rocketing was so rough that twenty-seven was the top age for active duty and it looked like those other four years might go by before I'd get up there, even on a ferry trip to the space station! Woman, I nearly went nuts worrying."

"I'll bet you did. It could have happened."

I said, "Sure, it could have happened. But something else happened first, thank God. Nineteen sixty-four happened—and the lid blew off. So suddenly that it seemed overnight, although they'd been working on it for years, the Los Alamos boys came up with the micropile and we had atomic energy for rockets.

"Those old chemical fuel rockets were all of a sudden as obsolete as ox carts. Sure, we still needed fuel tanks but because of the high exhaust velocities atomic energy gave us, relatively small ones. And just to carry any inexpensive liquid, even water, for the micropile to turn into exhaust gases. We could go to the moon in one trip, to Mars and Venus with only an orbital refueling. The space station was obsolete and unnecessary before it was a third finished and we landed on the moon five years ahead of schedule.

"Oh, we finished the space station, but on a smaller scale than planned, and mostly just as an observation station for the meteorologists. And we put the second one, the twenty-four hour one, up there just for telecasting. And meanwhile—"

"Max, I've read rocket history. You're telling me your own experiences and background, remember?"

"Oh, sure. Well, suddenly I wasn't so far down the line. The atomic rockets were being built in quantity. They really worked, and thirty of them were finished in sixty-five, forty more in sixty-six, and they were getting into the four-man jobs by then and so I was in. I got to the moon in late sixty-six, co-pilot and navigator on a two-man rocket with a five-ton pay load for the observatory that we were starting to build there. Co-piloted once more, to Mars in the next year, and then I was made spaceman first class and full pilot. I was twenty-six, but they'd extended active duty age to thirty, where it is now, so I still had four years ahead of me.

"But damn it, I got retired at twenty-seven just the same. An accident on a routine surface exploration trip to Venus—the eighth trip we'd made there; I never got a first."

"What kind of an accident, Max?"

"We'd finished our mission; we were checking the rocket for take-off. I was outside, climbing up to check the solars, but the co-pilot thought I was inside and fired a short test burst from the steering jets. I had a leg in front of one of them and that was the end of that leg, from just below the knee. They got me back to Earth alive and I lived, but that was the end of my being a spaceman."

She said, "Oh," quietly, and then, "I'm sorry, Max."

"I'm not," I said. "I mean, I wouldn't have the leg back at the expense of not having made the six trips I made into space. A lot of the early spacemen paid with their lives for one trip. I was lucky. Six trips for only a leg."

"Yes, you'd feel that way. Go on."

"Go on where? That's all."

She laughed a little. "You were only twenty-seven then and you're fifty-seven now. What happened to you in between?"

"I made myself a rocket mech. I could have had a pension but turned it down in favor of their giving me all the courses they had in atomics and rocket mech work. And I've been a rocket mech ever since. That's all."

I thought a moment. "No, by God, that isn't all. If I'm trying to give you the full picture I've got no business being modest. I made myself into a *good* rocket mech, one of the best in the country. And I've kept abreast of improvements in them; I know them inside out and I can fix anything that ever went wrong with one. I'm not a nuclear physicist as far as theory goes but I've got a thorough working knowledge of applied atomics. I know and have worked on commercial passenger rockets, mail rockets and interplanetaries.

"I haven't worked on the interplanetaries since I passed the government's age limit for mechs seven years ago, but I've kept up with every change that's been made in them—and I've even had a few minor suggestions of my own for improvements accepted and used."

I said, "This will sound like I'm bragging, but I've worked at every one of the twelve commercial rocket ports in this country and I can work at any one of them again any time I want to, starting at one minute's notice and whether they're short of men or not. And even though I'll never ride a rocket again, I've kept up on every new technique in astrogation that's been tried out or used. I'm a fair amateur astronomer, and not just the star-gazing kind that can tell one celestial object from another. I can calculate orbits and trajectories and eclipses."

"Do you have an engineering degree?"

"No, just a bachelor of science degree—that came with graduation from space school in those days, and don't think we didn't earn it. But as far as knowledge goes, I'm a rocket engineer. Might have to bone up on a few points to get an engineering degree, but I could get one. I just never bothered because I like mech work better. I like to work on rockets themselves, not on pictures of rockets on paper."

"You've never done administrative work, then?"

"No. I don't like it."

"But would you do it on Project Jupiter?"

"I'll sweep floors if I have to, to get on. But I'd rather be head mech."

"Would you like to be assistant director?"

I took a deep breath. I said, "Yes."

"Max, I may be able to swing it for you—on a couple of conditions. And it would mean you'd really be running the project. The project director will have to be a political figure; there's no out on that. But the assistant director won't have to be, and he'll be the one who runs things—with the director as a figurehead. Would you like that, Max? To run the project and build and send the rocket?"

"Woman, don't ask crazy questions. And the two conditions are granted. What are they?"

"You're not going to like them," she said. "And I'm not going to tell you now, because it might lead to argument."

"It won't," I said. "I'll agree to anything, even cutting off my other leg. Or my head, for that matter."

"You'll need your head. And as for cutting off your other leg, this may hurt worse. But Max, we've talked pretty long and I'm getting tired. Want to come back again tomorrow evening, same time?"

I wanted to.

Back home I started to do some grinding on the reflector for my telescope, but grinding is painstaking and ticklish work so I quit when I found that my hands were trembling.

Not that I could blame them for trembling. They had a chance now, an outside chance, a thousand-to-one-against chance, of going to Jupiter, of piloting a rocket that was going out into space eight times as far as Mars, eight times as far into space as a rocket had ever been before.

A chance in a thousand. But yesterday it had been a chance in a million. A few months ago a chance in a billion, or no chance at all.

No, I didn't blame my hands for trembling.

"The conditions?" I asked Ellen Gallagher.

"Let's have the amenities first. May I offer you a drink, Max, to fortify you?"

"The conditions, woman. Quit stalling."

"First, a degree in rocket engineering. You said you could get one if you wanted it. Can you get one before the project appointments are made? Say within a year?"

I groaned. "I can, but it will mean some tough slogging. I'll have to pass examinations in about ten subjects. Six of them I can pass as of right now, but four will take me some pretty heavy studying. They're things I know from the practical side, but I'm going to have to absorb some theory. Yes, I can do it in a year. Maybe less. And what's the other condition?"

"That you get into administrative work, now. And between now and the time the appointments are made work yourself up to as high a spot as you can."

I groaned again.

She said, "Here's why, Max. The project will be set up so the project director appoints his own assistant—but it will have to be subject to presidential approval; you'll have to look good to pass that."

I said, "But if the President appoints the director, how'll you swing any weight as to who the director makes his assistant?"

She smiled. "Because it will be a deal. I'll pick my figurehead for director—someone with a big name but out of a job and looking for one—and I'll offer to recommend him for the job on the condition that he appoint you his assistant. If he wants the directorship badly enough, he'll agree—up to a point. But I still won't be able to sell him a simple, barefoot rocket mech, Max. You can see that."

"I'm afraid I can. How high will I have to get?"

"The higher the better. But any responsible administrative job with a big rocket port ought to do it. That and your being an accredited rocket engineer. Not to mention the glamour of your being an ex-spaceman."

"And if I go through all that and then the President does his own picking out of a project director?"

"A chance you take. But I think I can make my recommendation stick—by the simple expedient of picking a man who'll be completely acceptable to the President, whom he might pick anyway if I didn't make a recommendation. And there are other angles. Complicated to explain—but I'm pretty sure I can swing it. If you can get that degree and get yourself into a job with a good sounding title. Can you?"

"I can," I said. "I fear that I can. Any other conditions?"

"No."

"Then I'll have that drink you offered me. I need it. Where is it?"

"In that cabinet in the corner. Make anything you want and please pour me a glass of the sherry."

I took sherry too. I had some heavy thinking coming up.

I said, "Los Angeles Rocket Port is my best bet. It's one of the biggest, for one thing. For another, the superintendent there is a friend of mine, the closest friend I've got among the brass. He came up from being a mech himself and we talk the same language.

"And he's been heckling me for years to wash the grease off my hands and get into the office end. He'll start me in as a department head if there's an opening. If there isn't, he'll give me the best thing open and swing me up as fast as he can. I might, with luck, even get to be assistant superintendent within a year. In fact—"

I thought a minute. "In fact, if we want to be Machiavellian about it, and why shouldn't we, I can tell him the score and why I need the title for a front. And he can probably fix it for me to be holding the title temporarily just while the appointments to Project Jupiter are being made. Hell yes, he'll do that for me. And by then I can have saved up enough so we can give his regular assistant a month or so off with my paying his salary for the period I hold his job for a front. Sure, Klockerman will do that."

"Assistant superintendent would be fine. Even your being a department head might be enough. How soon can you start?"

"A day or two, I guess. Luckily we're slack on work at Treasure so I won't be leaving Rory in a jam—and even if I was, he'd understand when I tell him the score. Sure, I can leave here tomorrow. I'll call up Klockerman tonight after I get home and talk to him. And I'll see Rory tonight and catch the first jet out."

She laughed a little. "The thing I like about you, Max, is that you don't do things by halves. Returning favors aside, I really want you to run Project Jupiter. You'll do a good job of it."

"I'll do my best," I said. "Damn you, Senator, I ought to hate you for making the next year of my life the miserable one it's going to be, but I love you instead. How soon are you going to be well enough for me to make a pass at you?"

She laughed again. "You'd do even that for a chance to run the project?"

"I'd do even that," I said. "But we'll postpone discussion of it now. And let's consider my plans settled and quit talking about me. Tell me something about the project, about the rocket itself. Bradly had it all figured out?"

"To the last decimal, Max. A detailed prospectus. But the prospectus is in my safe in Los Angeles and you can see it after I go back home there. I could tell you a few things about it, but I've no head for technical details and I might get some of them wrong. You might as well wait till you can read the prospectus and get the whole thing at once."

"All right," I said. "How soon will you be in L.A.?"

"Within a month if I keep on improving as fast as I have, and with no setbacks. About the first of March, maybe. As soon as you're settled there, write me so I'll have your address and phone and can let you know when I'm coming."

"Fine," I said. "Will do. But won't you tell me even a few simple things about the rocket now, so I can be thinking about them?"

"Please don't ask me to, Max. I'm getting tired now and you've stayed pretty long. If we get started talking about the rocket now it'll be hard to stop. And everything about it is in Brad's prospectus that you'll be seeing. It was Brad's baby."

It was Brad's baby, and she was carrying it. I wondered if that meant anything and decided it was none of my business if it did. I'd just been kidding about making that pass. Or had I been kidding? She was a damned attractive woman.

I went straight to Rory's instead of back to my room, and as soon as I'd told Rory the score I phoned Klockerman. It was okay. He wanted me. Best he could do right off was to give me charge of the tool room but he had a couple of department heads who weren't too satisfactory and he thought that within a month at the outside he could move me up. I didn't, over the phone, tell him my real reason for switching from mech work or how high and fast I wanted to rise. Time enough for that later, over a drink or two.

I offered Rory the optical blanks I'd started to grind; it takes a lot of evenings to grind a good reflector for a scope and my evenings were going to be busy for a long time. I still wanted a scope to look at Jupiter with but now I'd have to buy one instead of making it. Rory wanted the blanks and drove me to my room so he could pick them up. He waited while I packed and then took me to the square where I could catch a helicab to the stratojet field on Angel. I was in Los Angeles by midnight.

February, March I worked days, studied nights.

But I was making progress both ways. At the rocket port I was head of a department, maintenance. Dull stuff, but it gave me a title. And I gave it all I had and was doing well; it looked like I might get that first assistantship honestly, without finagling, and within the year. I hadn't leveled with Klockerman yet; I'd decided that if I could get as far as that assistantship on my own, finagling might get me even farther. If I got to be his assistant honestly, before I told Klocky what I was really working for, then he might let me pull a real coup by taking a month or so off at the crucial time and leaving me as acting superintendent of the third largest rocket port in the world.

On the scholastic front I was down to four subjects, the four tough ones. I'd learned there were only nine subjects I'd have to pass examinations in to get that engineering degree and three of them were so easy I didn't even need refreshing in them. I got those three out of the way the first week. A week's study took care of the next two. Of the four I had left, two were subjects I knew but hadn't used for so long I was pretty rusty in them. But I could bone up on them myself and take the exams within another month.

That would get me down to the two, the ones that were going to be toughies for me. Extreme-temperature metallurgy and unified field theory. Neither of them are things I'd ever figured a rocket engineer needed to know. You can take the characteristics of all metals and all common alloys from charts that have been worked out to the tenth decimal; what's the advantage of being able to calculate them yourself? Unified field theory is even worse; nobody yet has worked out a unified field theory that's *more* than a theory or has any practical application to rocket engineering. Besides, it's got to be approached through relativity, and relativity sets my teeth on edge because it tries to set limits; I don't believe in limits.

Yes, when I got to those two subjects I'd need tutoring, but there are plenty of Caltech instructors and even professors willing to pick up some money on the side by giving the kind of help I'd need, and with a good salary coming in and no free time to spend any of it, I had money to burn.

Senator Gallagher returned in early April. I met her at the jetport but there were others meeting her too and I didn't join the entourage that escorted her home; I just managed to talk to her long enough to make an appointment for the first evening she had free. She seemed to be almost completely recovered and told me she expected to go to Washington within another month to take her place in the Senate for the final month or so of the current session.

My appointment was for two evenings later and she promised to hold the whole evening for me so we'd have time to go over the prospectus for the rocket.

"Drink, Max?"

"Woman," I said. "Show me that prospectus. I've been waiting months now to see it."

Ellen shook her head wonderingly. "Even administrative work doesn't civilize you, Max. You're a savage. And you have a strictly one-track mind."

"Exactly," I told her. "And it's on the prospectus. Let's see it."

"Not until we've had a drink and a minimum of fifteen minutes of civilized conversation. You've waited months and a few more minutes won't kill you."

I made us drinks. And I made myself be polite and patient, even beyond the time she'd set. I waited twenty-two minutes before I again asked to see the prospectus.

She brought it to me.

I took a quick glance at the sketch of the rocket and I screamed. Not aloud, but inside my mind. I leafed over to the recapitulation of the costs and wanted to tear my hair out by the roots.

My face must have shown how I felt. Ellen asked, "What's wrong, Max?"

"A step-rocket!" I said. "Shades of nineteen sixty-two, a step-rocket! Ellen, it doesn't take a step-rocket to go to Jupiter, not with atomics! And the cost—

three hundred and ten million! I can send a rocket to Jupiter and back for a tenth that much. Fifty million at the very most. This is crazy."

"Are you sure, Max? Brad was a rocket engineer, too—and one of the top ones."

"Sure, but—wait, give me a few minutes to skim through this to see where he went off the beam."

I skimmed, and shuddered.

I said, "Point one. He's using a two-man rocket. Why? One man's plenty. One man can do all the necessary recording and observing and have time on his hands to boot, even while he's rounding Jupe."

"Brad and I talked about that. He said that an entire year alone in space is too much for any—"

"Nuts," I said. "The first trip to Mars, circle and return without landing, was made by Ortman in sixty-five and he was alone in space four hundred and twenty-two days. The living compartment in that rocket was three feet in diameter by six and a half feet long, just a good roomy coffin. And there wasn't a cadet in space school who didn't envy him every minute of that trip.

"Woman, this trip to Jupiter is another *first,* and the first in more years than any spaceman likes to think about. A thousand qualified men will be fighting for the privilege of making that trip, no matter what the conditions are, no matter how tough it's going to be."

I looked at the prospectus again. "A ten-foot-diameter living compartment, that's what Brad figured here. Now even if it had to be a two-man rocket, which it doesn't, that's silly for a *first*. He picked that because it's standard on a two-man Mars rocket, but Mars is a milk run. One man, a four-foot-diameter compartment, that's plenty. That's luxury. And it cuts down the weight of that part of the rocket by about 70 per cent."

Ellen shuddered. "I know I'd hate to spend a year in a space that size."

"Sure, but you're not a spaceman. Spacemen are tough, mentally and physically. They've got to be to get *into* space school, let alone get through it and graduate.

"And one of the first things they psych them for, Ellen, is claustrophobia. And if they've got the faintest touch of it they're out unless it can be completely cured. They're trained to be alone with themselves for long periods when necessary. Why, with the psychoanalysis they put them through today a trip like that one is a breeze."

I grinned. "Ellen, when I entered space school back when, psychoanalysis wasn't what it is today. Know how they tested us for claustrophobia, our first week in? Each of us would be locked up in a dark closet exactly two feet square— you couldn't even sit down in it—and each of us had to stay in one of those closets forty-eight hours, and stay awake. There was a button he had to press every hour on the hour—he had a watch with a radium dial so he'd know the time—to prove that he was awake and okay. Or if a guy felt himself getting scared or starting to go crazy, he could give three quick rings on the same button and they'd come and let him out—out of the closet and the school both. That was just *one* of the cute little mental and physical endurance tests we had to go through in those days, and not the worst one by a long shot."

"But Max, Brad *did* try figuring a one-man rocket, and he said it would have to be a step-rocket anyway so the cost would be only slightly more to make it a two-man ship so—"

"Quiet," I said. "I'm reading some more of this horrible document. Aha— here's the big joker, Ellen. Here's why he thought he'd need a step-rocket even for a one-man ship; he's figuring on carrying the eagle for the whole trip, the round trip!"

"The eagle?"

"Slang for E.G.L., exhaust gas liquid. You see, Ellen, an atomic rocket doesn't have to carry fuel—unless you count the consumption inside the micropile and that's negligible weight-wise—in the same sense that an old-type chemical rocket had to carry fuel. But an atomic rocket has to carry tanks of some liquid for the heat pile to turn into gases, the gases that come out of the exhaust vents and drive the rocket."

"I understand that. But why *doesn't* the rocket have to carry exhaust gas liquid for the whole trip? It's a circle trip."

I was pacing the floor with that damned prospectus in my hand. I said, "Sure, it's a circle trip as far as Jupiter is concerned. But Jupiter's got twelve moons, any one of them easy to land on and take off from because of low gravity. And at least seven of them lousy with frozen ammonia. For free, all you want."

"But would ammonia work?"

"Any reasonably inert liquid works. Ammonia works fine. It's been tried, on the test block. The only strike against it is that at ordinary temperatures, it's a gas unless it's kept under pressure in the tank. A pressurized tank has to be a heavier tank; it adds to the weight of the rocket and so cuts down the pay load."

"But in that case, Max—"

"The difference in rocket weight, though, in using pressurized tanks is slight, almost negligible, compared to the weight difference of having to carry exhaust gas liquid for the round trip. That's big enough to make the difference between a one-stage rocket and a three-stage. Between fifty million and three hundred million."

Ellen leaned forward. "Max, that would make a tremendous difference. If it can be done as cheaply as that— Are you *sure?*"

I said, "I'll make sure. Right now. I'll be back tomorrow evening. Same time." I stood up.

"Don't rush off—"

I rushed off. Home. Limbered up my slide rule on a few preliminaries and then realized I didn't have all the data I'd need to work it out thoroughly. Klockerman would have it all, either in his head or his library. And he'd be better than I, particularly in figuring costs; that was where I'd be weakest.

I called him and explained, told him we'd better work at his place because all the data would be there. I called a helicab.

We worked all night.

We figured it. Not exactly, but to one decimal place, near enough to show that it would work, and easily. And I'd guessed high on the cost. Klocky figured it to be twenty-six million, less than a tenth the cost of Bradly's step-rocket.

We topped the coffee we'd been drinking all night with breakfast and benzedrine and went to work.

That night I gave the results to Ellen. She studied them wonderingly. Especially the table of costs and its total.

"You say Klockerman worked with you on this?"

"It's more his work than mine."

"He's good, isn't he?"

"The best," I said. "The best, that is, outside of a few boys in government service, at Los Alamos and White Sands. And of course they'll go over those specifications later, before the rocket's actually started. But I'll guarantee you, Ellen, they'll find nothing fundamentally wrong. They may make minor changes, may insist on upping a few safety factors slightly, but they won't up the estimate more than 10 per cent at the very most, and that's still under thirty million."

She nodded slowly. "Then this is the rocket we'll use. Now, Max, make us a drink and we'll drink to it."

We drank to it. I gave us each a straight drink first that we could down as a toast, and then I made a pair of highballs for leisurely sipping.

Ellen sipped hers thoughtfully. "Max, this is going to change things a lot. It gives me an idea. I'm going to Washington in two weeks. I'm well now, but I'm going to take two more weeks for a little more rest and some planning. And do you know what I'm going to do as soon as I get to the Senate?"

"Sure. Since this is only a tenth what you thought you'd have to ask for, you'll try to get it through this session. Right?"

"Wrong. This year it would be vetoed regardless of amount and even if I could get it through that quickly, and I couldn't. No, I've got an idea that will get this through like a shot next session, early next session. As soon as I get to Washington I'm going to put an appropriation bill in the hopper based on Brad's step-rocket."

"My God," I yelled. "Why?"

"Quiet." She grinned. "Yes, the three hundred ten million dollar rocket. But I'll also make sure that it stays in committee and doesn't get voted on. Early next session, the first week, I go to the committee and offer to withdraw that bill in favor of a substitute one—one tenth the size. Max, I'll have it through both houses and past the President in a month!"

I said, "Senator, I love you."

She laughed. "It's the rocket you love. The rocket and Jupiter."

"And the stars. But you too, Senator Ellen Gallagher."

Suddenly it came to me that I'd *meant* what I'd just said.

I loved her, and because she was a woman, not because she was pushing a rocket.

I went over and sat beside her on the sofa, put my arm around her and kissed her. And again, and this time her arms came up around me, pulling me to her tightly.

"You damned fool," she said, "why did you wait so long to do that?"

I decided that a couple of weeks off studying would do me more good than harm in the long run. I was ahead of schedule on my studies and I was pretty sure that I'd get the degree in plenty of time; a little rest would keep me from getting stale.

So I spent most of my evenings those two weeks with Ellen. A few nights too, but we were discreet about it. A scandal wouldn't have helped Ellen's career.

And marriage was definitely out of the question, if for no other reason than that it would have kept me off the Jupiter project. Nepotism had become a nasty word in government by the nineties; the old days when congressmen got their relatives on government payrolls, even in minor capacities, were gone. With Ellen sponsoring the Jupiter project she couldn't possibly have sponsored a husband for a job on it.

Klockerman knew about Ellen and me, but he was one of the family by then. We'd even leveled with him about my real reason for taking an administrative job under him, and he'd told me that he'd guarantee my being acting superintendent of the port at the time the project appointments came up, that he'd take as much time off as necessary, even six months, and leave me in charge. He said he was due for a long vacation anyhow and that there were places he wanted to see and things he wanted to do.

Life was suddenly being very good to an aging ex-spaceman. I was happier than I'd been for more years than I liked to think about.

Ellen went to Washington the third week in April. She'd be gone at least a month, possibly as long as two, depending on how long Congress stayed in session.

I missed her like hell. Funny how quickly you can get used to a woman. Here I'd hardly thought about one for several years, and now after only two weeks of Ellen there was a big hole in my life when she went away, even though she'd be back soon.

Back to my studies. The rest from them had sharpened my mind and had done me good. Two weeks saw me through the two subjects I'd been refreshing myself in, both those examinations out of the way. Down to the two toughies. I found myself a Caltech boy who knew extreme-temperature metallurgy and with him tutoring me four evenings a week, I dived in. Two other evenings a week I'd study alone. One evening a week, usually Sunday, I spent at Klocky's place, playing chess, drinking a little beer, talking.

On the study nights, either alone or after my tutor had left, I'd read until my eyes would start to blur. Then I'd quit and if it was a clear night with good seeing I'd go up on the roof and rest my eyes by looking far with them for a while, through the telescope I'd bought myself and had mounted up there.

Jupiter was nearing opposition, coming almost as close to Earth as he ever gets. Only four hundred million miles away he'd be in another few weeks, not much more than that now. Big Jupiter, the giant of the solar system, eleven times as big as Earth in diameter, three hundred times as great in mass. More than twice as big as all the other planets in the system put together.

Big Jupiter with its twelve moons. Four of them visible through my telescope. The others all tiny, a hundred miles or less in diameter. It takes a big scope to find them.

But four of them I could see, the four that are as big as Earth's moon or bigger, the four that Galileo had discovered in 1610, with the first crude telescope he made.

Four moons, four cold but lovely moons which man had never reached but which man was going to reach and set foot upon. Soon. Damned soon.

Io. Europa. Ganymede. Callisto.

Which would I land upon? Or would I ever land on any? Max, I told myself, Max you silly fool you dreamer, it's still a thousand to one chance. The rocket is going, yes, the rocket will be built and you'll supervise the building of it. But Max you ass, your chance of stealing it? It's going to be a government project with guards, with hundreds of people working on it. Sure, you can arrange *some* of the things you'll have to arrange; you can have it fueled and loaded and ready to take off twenty-four or forty-eight hours before actual take-off time; you can arrange somehow to have the orbital refueling rocket up there already, ahead of time—yes, you can give reasons for that; you can finagle something that will get the director himself off the grounds so you'll be in full charge at the crucial time. But still so many things could go wrong, so many things...

Still a chance in a thousand. But a chance to go on eight times as far as Mars, ten times as far out into space as man had ever been before.

A little closer to the stars, the far far stars that someday we're going to reach, the billion billion billion stars that are waiting for us.

Ellen came back in the middle of July.

We saw one another, of course, the night she got back, but then not again for a week. I was so close to being ready for my exam in metallurgy that we agreed not to see one another again until I had it over with. That gave me a double incentive to burn midnight oil and I really burned it. The seeing was bad that week, too, so I wasn't even tempted to the roof, and I skipped my usual evening with Klocky.

So it was just seven days on the head after Ellen's return that I was able to phone Ellen that I'd passed my second last exam and had only one subject left between me and the degree.

"Wonderful, darling," she said. "And you're not going to start the last subject right away, are you? You're way ahead of schedule."

"Right, Ellen. And here's another item of good news. Klocky has been more than satisfied with the way I'm handling the maintenance department. Says he'll use my getting that degree as occasion for making me assistant supervisor. That'll give me at least several months of experience before he takes off for a while and leaves me as acting super."

"Max, things are really working out. Just as they are in Washington. Coming over tonight to celebrate?"

"Is that a new word for it?"

"Don't be vulgar, darling. I've got some champagne. Does that tempt you?"

"It would, except that I've got a better idea. I can take a week off at the rocket port, starting as of now. What are your plans?"

"Why—I have a few appointments, one viddy appearance, a meeting or two—"

"Could you cancel them? We could run down to Mexico City for a week. We can be there in time for dinner this evening."

We went down to Mexico City for a week.

It was a wonderful week, and also a restful one. We were both tired and got plenty of sleep, slept till noon every day and sometimes even later. Evenings, but never into the small hours of the night, we saw the sights and went the round of the bright spots. Ellen wore a skin mask, of course—one of the new Ravigos that can hardly be detected even in daylight—whenever we were outside our suite. The price of being famous.

I really got to know Senator Ellen Gallagher that week. She told me just about everything important that had ever happened to her.

She'd had a kind of rough early life. She'd been born Ellen Grabow, and she'd never seen her father; he'd been a casualty in fifty-two in that mess we were embroiled in then in Korea, just a few weeks before she was born. Her mother had died two years later; the grandparents on her father's side had tried to take care of her but they were too poor to have a nurse or governess, too old and one of them too ill to raise her themselves. They'd had to put her in an orphanage.

She'd been an ugly duckling, a sickly, unattractive child with chronic skin trouble and frequent colds. Also, she admitted, pretty much of an unmanageable brat because of her dissatisfaction with herself and her overcompensations for her feelings of inferiority. She'd been adopted on a trial basis three times between the ages of three and eight and turned back to the orphanage at the end of the trial period or before.

The fourth offer, when she was ten, she effectively turned down herself with a tantrum that frightened off the prospective adopters. She stayed at the orphanage until she was fifteen; she was then released—on parole, as it were—to take a job, on the conditions that she must live at a girls' club until she was of age and that she must continue her studies at night school until she had a high school diploma. Her job was in the package room of a department store and she stuck at it two weeks until she got her first pay check. All of this had been in Wichita, Kansas.

She so thoroughly hated Wichita and the conditions of her parole that she used that first money she got to jump parole and take a bus to Hollywood. She was enamoured of acting and wanted to get into the booming viddy field. (That was the year they'd built the second space station, the telestation for viddy only, and it had gone up right over her head in Kansas.) She was still unattractive at fifteen and knew it, but thought she had a great acting ability and that she could do character parts and brat roles, possibly even become a comedienne.

Perhaps, she admitted, thinking of herself as being funny or potentially funny had been her defense against her own unattractiveness during adolescence. Instead of admiring herself in her mirror, she used to practice making funny faces at herself.

"Intermission," I said.

I got up and made us each a drink, brought them back to bed. Ellen had propped up pillows for us and we lay back against them. We sipped our drinks.

"Have I been boring you, Max?" she asked.

"You never have and you never will," I told her. "Go on."

She went on. She went on, to California and to what she hoped would be sudden success in the viddies.

But two years in Hollywood, working as a waitress, convinced her that she wasn't going to get a chance to try; then she did get a couple of chances and failed to get either part or any encouragement whatsoever, and that convinced her she'd better start looking for something more likely than a viddy career.

Something more likely turned out to be Ray Connor, a young man only a year older than she, who wanted to marry her. At eighteen he was an orphan too, but a recent one who had a little money and a small income from his parents' estate. He wanted to become a lawyer and a statesman, and he was just starting to put himself through law school. When they were married he suggested that she enter college too and was a little horrified to learn that she was a year and a half short of having finished high school. Ellen was beginning by then to be aware of the shortcomings of her education and readily agreed to study high school subjects at home, with her husband's help, until she could take college entrance examinations.

She was surprised to find that she enjoyed studying and learning, now that she was doing it because she wanted to and not because she had to. She made the college examinations in only six months—sooner than she'd have gotten a diploma if she'd stayed in Wichita and had continued going to night school there. She entered college only a term behind her husband and she too decided to study law. She'd become interested in it through his interest and had begun to see herself as a Portia, perhaps even as a stateswoman; that was in the early seventies when women were going more and more into politics.

She made up the term she was behind Ray and they graduated together in seventy-five; she was twenty-three then and he was twenty-four. And it was right in the middle of the Depression and there were no jobs or partnerships for young and inexperienced lawyers; even the older ones were barely hanging on, like people in every other profession except psychiatry. And Ray's money was gone. They had to look for any kind of work they could get, just to keep eating. Ellen was the first to get a job because of her experience as a waitress and the comparatively rapid turnover in waitress work even in depression times. It took Ray three months of hunting before he got any kind of work at all. It was a construction job. On his third day at it he fell from a girder four stories in the air and was killed.

"Did you love him, Ellen?" I asked.

"Yes, by then, very much. I'm afraid I married him mostly for practical reasons, but in five years I'd come to love him very deeply."

"Have you loved many men, Ellen?"

"Four, only four. Three besides you."

Ralph Gallagher was the second.

She met him four years later when she was a law clerk in the firm of Gallagher, Reyoll and Wilcox. He was older than she, but not too much older, forty-one to her twenty-seven. He was already becoming prominent in politics and was well on his way to being a big man. He'd been married once but had been divorced several years.

Ellen had admired him, looked up to him. When, several months after she started work there, he began to notice her and be friendly to her, she was pleased. When he'd taken her out a few times, she was even more pleased to learn that he was looking for a wife and not a mistress, and that he thought she would be just right for the job.

She married him. And for the ten years they had together before his death she merged her own ambitions with his; she made being his wife her career. She learned how to entertain for him. She learned politics, the practical kind, and used them to help him. She helped make him mayor of Los Angeles and an almost certain winner in the next election for the governorship of California.

But coronary thrombosis got him first.

And Ellen got another shock. She was broke again, flat broke. Familiar as she had been with his political affairs she had paid no attention to his financial ones, and he had stupidly put all his eggs into one basket, a basket with no bottom in it. His estate, after final expenses were paid out of it, was barely going to break even.

Ellen had had a law education but had never practiced; it would have been late for her to start at thirty-seven. But she knew politics and she bore a name that was respected in California, especially in Los Angeles.

She ran for city council and won easily, won a second time by an even bigger vote two years later, was made president of the council. Then two terms in the state assembly. And after that she was talked by the leaders of her party into running in the special election to fill the unexpired portion of the Senate term of a man who had died in office.

"And would have been miserably defeated, Max, if you hadn't pulled a rabbit out of a hat."

"Out of your opponent's office, my love. But you skipped over man-I-loved number three. Was it Bradly?"

"Yes, it was Brad. For about a year, a couple of years ago. It ended then, sort of by mutual consent and without even a quarrel, so I guess it couldn't have been too serious."

"But he came to you with the Jupiter project? Or had he sold you on that before?"

"A little of both. He'd talked about it before, while we were in love or thought we were, but just in a general way. When he heard I was running for the Senate he came to me with the specific plans, the prospectus, and asked me to try to get it through if I won. I told him I would, never dreaming he'd make the political mistake of talking about it to reporters just before the election. If I'd foreseen that, I'd never have agreed."

I said, "You don't mean that. You mean you'd have warned him to keep his yap shut. Or—do you mean you weren't really enthusiastic about the project itself? That it was just your friendship with Bradly that made you agree?"

"Well, it was partly that. Oh, I liked the idea of a rocket going out to Jupiter. I wanted to see man take another step out, in my lifetime. But it wasn't really important to me and I certainly wouldn't have staked my political career on it. You want to know, Max, when I got really enthusiastic about that rocket? The evening I first met you. The look in your eyes, the way you talked, the way you thought. I guess a little stardust rubbed off on me that evening. I found myself talking about horse trading that bill through Congress as though it was the most important legislation in the world—and suddenly it was."

"And did you know that evening what was going to happen between us?"

"Of course. Almost as soon as you walked in the doorway."

I shook my head wonderingly. "Would you like a drink?" I asked her.

She would. I got up and made one for each of us.

Back in bed, sitting up with drinks in our hands, we talked some more.

"Max, do you *really* think we'll ever reach the stars? They're light years away, and a light-year is a frightening distance."

"It is, if you let it frighten you,"

"How far is the nearest one? I've heard, but I've forgotten."

"Proxima Centauri is about four light years. And we still don't know how far the farthest ones are because the galaxies keep on going for all the billions of light years our telescopes show us. Maybe the relativists' finite universe is wrong and they go on forever. Maybe there *is* an infinity."

"And an eternity?"

"You're in the middle of that now. This talk about the age of the universe being a specific figure—two billion years, four billion years—nuts. Can you think that suddenly somebody or something wound up a clock and started it running, that there wasn't any *time* before a certain specific moment? Time can't be stopped or started, damn it. If this particular universe does have a definite age, isn't eternal and constantly renewing itself by some process we don't yet understand, then there must have been universes before this one. In eternity there could be an infinite progression of universes, an infinite number of them past and an infinite number to come.

"Maybe, Ellen, there was a universe umpteen billion years ago in which two people were sitting up beside one another in bed, just as we are, with maybe the same names we have, drinking the same drinks, saying the same things—except that maybe they were wearing different colored pajamas because that was a different universe."

Ellen laughed. "But half an hour before, then, they weren't wearing any pajamas at all so you couldn't have told the difference. But Max, leaving time and eternity out of it, do you really believe the relativists are wrong about the universe being finite in volume, space curving back on itself? Even finite, they allow for it being pretty big, you know."

I took a sip of my drink. I said, "I hope they're wrong, because no matter how big they decide it is, if it's finite then there must be a farthest star, and I don't like to think there is. Where would we go from there?"

"But if space curves on itself, wouldn't the farthest star be the nearest one too?"

"Woman," I said, "that is *really* a frightening thought. It makes me dizzy. I refuse to buy it, or even examine it. Let's get back to a finite universe. If this one is finite, there could still be an infinite number of universes like it, an infinity of finites. Like drops of water. Maybe we are like animalculae in a drop of water that happens to be separate from other drops of water, a universe in itself. Do you suppose the animalculae ever suspect that there are other drops of water besides theirs?"

"One of them might. *You* just did. But Max, what if *our* drop of water is on the slide of a microscope or some equivalent of a microscope and what if Something is looking at us right now?"

"Let it look," I said. "As long as it behaves itself. And if it doesn't, I'll slap it down."

Back to Los Angeles, back to maintenance, back to study.

Not quite so strict a regime this time, now that I was down to one subject, with the degree in sight. Ellen convinced me that all work and no play would make me a dull boy and I didn't want to be a dull boy. I studied four evenings a week, two of them solo and two of them with coaching. Two evenings a week I saw Ellen or Klocky or both of them, one evening I just read and rested. Usually my evenings with Ellen were quiet ones at her apartment but occasionally we took in a show or a concert. It didn't matter if we were seen together once in a while as long as we avoided the plush places frequented by the gossip columnists and commentators; we didn't want our names coupled in print or on the viddy because even a suggestion of romance between us would be bad when the time came for Ellen to use pressure to get me on the project.

July, August, September.

I was making a new friend, too, in the man who was coaching me in unified field theory. His name was improbable, Chang M'bassi, but he himself was much more improbable than his name.

Chang M'bassi was the last, or believed to be the last, of the Masai tribesmen who, until the late sixties, had lived in east equatorial Africa. They don't live there any more because they're all dead except M'bassi; at least there is no other authenticated case of a survivor among them. They were perhaps the most colorful of all the African tribes and the fiercest and bravest warriors. They were the tall ones, averaging well over six feet in height. Their sport was hunting lions with spears; no youth became a full member of the tribe until he had killed his lion. They did not hunt other game and seldom ate meat; they were herders as well as warriors. They had great herds of cattle and their staple diet, almost the only food they ate, was a mixture of milk and cattle blood. That diet proved fatal to them in the great plague, the sudden disaster that struck equatorial Africa in, if I have the year right, 1969, killing fifteen or sixteen million people within a few weeks. The plague came the year following the first large-scale attempt to exterminate the tsetse fly in that area. The attempt was almost but not completely successful; a few of the tsetses proved immune or developed immunity to the new "wondercide" that was being used against them. They came back the next year greatly diminished in number but they had in them a new or hitherto unknown virus with which they infected cattle, and a strange triple-play death struck the region. The cattle showed no outward signs of illness from the infection, nor did human beings who were infected directly by the tsetse flies. But in the blood and in the milk of infected cattle the virus underwent a change that made it deadly to humans. Eating meat, blood or milk from an infected cow was fatal. Vomiting started in hours, helplessness within a day, death within three to four days.

When the plague struck, less than a week after the tsetses had swarmed in from their breeding places, the Masai hadn't had a chance. They'd all been infected, almost simultaneously; all of them, except a boy named M'bassi, were ill before the epidemiologists could get there, all of them except M'bassi were dead before an effective treatment could be found. The epidemiologists had quickly isolated the virus and its source and had immediately spread the warning to avoid beef and milk. Because of these warnings and because within a week the epidemiologists had found an effective treatment for the disease itself, no other tribes had casualties higher than half their numbers. Not even those tribes who were also primarily herdsmen; their herds had not been as quickly and as thoroughly infected as those of the Masai.

M'bassi's survival had been accidental or providential, whichever way you want to look at it. A Chinese medical missionary, one Chang Wo Sing, a Buddhist, had just arrived among them to try to convert them to the Eightfold Path. He would have had a tough job doing it because his particular sect of Buddhism, besides being evangelical, preached rigid vegetarianism and was against the killing of animals. To embrace the philosophy he brought to them, the Masai—well, it's anybody's guess now whether they would have been more horrified at the thought of eating vegetables or the thought of giving up their passionate devotion for hunting lions. He might have had more luck making non-violent vegetarians out of the lions.

But in a limited way—limited to one person—Chang Wo Sing had actually succeeded in converting the entire Masai people to his way of thinking. M'bassi, last of the Masai, was a Buddhist.

M'bassi had been eleven years old then, a son of the chief of the particular Masai village upon which Dr. Chang had benevolently descended. And on the very day of the good doctor's arrival there M'bassi had been badly mauled by a lion about half a mile outside the village. He had been brought in mercifully unconscious but more nearly dead than alive, with very little blood left in him. His father the chief, no doubt giving the boy up for dead in any case, had shown no hesitancy in letting the Chinaman try to save his life.

Dr. Chang had tried and succeeded. But M'bassi a few days later was still an awfully sick Masai boy, and being sick saved his life. His throat had been injured badly—a claw had just missed the jugular vein—and he was being fed intravenously, with a nutrient solution that was purely vegetable in origin.

The other Masai in the village, in all the Masai villages, fell ill and began to die. Dr. Chang guessed at least part of the answer even before the arrival of the epidemiologists and tried to save them, or some of them, but the disease was new to him and he wasn't a bacteriologist. His advice to them to stop eating food from cattle was good advice but it came too late—and would have been ignored even had it come in time. Most of the victims were too far gone to be eating anyway and the entire tribe, except for one badly damaged boy, was already infected and doomed. The medical reinforcements that arrived found Dr. Chang in a village peopled by the dead and the dying.

But M'bassi lived. After the last other Masai in the village had died and had been buried and after the other doctors had moved on to where they hoped they might still be useful, the Buddhist medical missionary stayed on, alone with the boy, for two weeks longer, until M'bassi could be moved. First to Nairobi for a month in the hospital there, then, convalescent, by rail to Mombassi and by ship back to China.

Back in his native land the good doctor had prospered. He had raised the boy like a son and had been able to send him abroad for an education. To London, to Tibet, to the Massachusetts Institute of Technology.

Meet M'bassi. Six feet five inches tall, and slender. Black as the Venusian night. About forty years old now. Quiet, contemplative eyes set in a fierce African face made fiercer looking by deep scars from the claws of a lion, claw marks that ran from up in his kinky hair the full length of his face, having miraculously missed both eyes. A soft gentle voice that makes any language it speaks sound sweet and melodious. Buddhist, mystic, mathematician, and a wonderful guy.

I'd been steered to him by Ellen. She knew him because he had been a friend of Brad's and had suggested him months before, when I'd first mentioned that field theory was one of the subjects I'd need coaching in. Chang M'bassi—he'd taken his foster father's name and, in the Chinese manner, put it ahead of his given name—was an instructor in higher mathematics at the University of Southern California.

"But don't," Ellen had told me, "let the 'instructor' part fool you. He can have a full professorship any time he wants one. It's just that he doesn't want the responsibility and doesn't want to put in that much time; he'd rather be an instructor because he can put in less time at it, have more time for his own work."

"In that case," I said, "why would he be interested in coaching me?"

"He might not, Max. For purely monetary considerations I'm sure he wouldn't. But if you got to know him first and the two of you liked one another—"

The two of us liked one another.

God knows why. Except for one thing—and that one thing was something I didn't learn about until I'd known M'bassi a long time—we seemed to have nothing, absolutely nothing, in common. Mysticism bored me to tears. Science, except for the pure realms of higher mathematics, held no interest for him.

But somehow we became friends.

In October I took my degree in rocket engineering.

We had dinner and a party, quite a party, in a suite at the Beverly. Rory and Bess Bursteder flew down from Berkeley for it, Bill and Merlene from Seattle. Klockerman and his wife. Chang M'bassi, stag. Ellen of course. Nine of us.

Bill enjoyed himself, but I think he was a little baffled at most of the conversation. Still, he was pleased and happy to be there. Pleased not so much by the degree I was celebrating as by the fact that I'd finally got the dirt and grease off my hands, that I finally was holding down a responsible position and getting somewhere. Kiockerman's little speech announcing that arrangements had been made for me to become assistant director at the rocket port got a big hand from Bill. But I caught Merlene looking at me curiously and I winked at her to make her even more curious. It does a woman good to be curious and it served her right for being smart enough to realize that a leopard doesn't change its spots without reason.

Christmas eve alone with Ellen, at her place. I'd shot the works on a present for her, a pearl necklace. I'd been, for almost a year now, earning more money than I'd ever earned before. And behaving myself, with little chance to spend much of it. Money piling up in the bank had begun to worry me and this was a wonderful excuse to get rid of a chunk of it.

Ellen gave me a beautiful cigarette case, a black one studded with chip diamonds in a random design. Random? I looked again and it was a familiar pattern. The Big Dipper, Ursa Major, pointing to Polaris, the North Star.

She said, "The only way, darling, I could find to give you the stars."

I wanted to cry. Maybe I did cry a little; my vision blurred.

1999

From Ellen in Washington, late January: *"Oh, my darling, my darling, I wish you were here with me tonight. Or that I were there with you.*

"Then this tiredness and this dull headache would go away. Then I'd be happy and relaxed. But headache or no, I've got to tell you what I accomplished today.

"I picked my victim and my timing perfectly. The victim: the Gentleman from Massachusetts who is the leader of the conservationists and the head of the appropriations committee, Senator Rand. The timing: a tête-à-tête lunch for which I cleverly lured him to a spot where neither of us was known, so there would be no interruptions.

"And while we ate I bored him stiff, telling him the advantages to science and humanity of a close-up look-see at big Jupiter. But that was just the surface subject. Underneath it I kept dropping stronger and stronger hints that I could and would push that bill through despite opposition. I intimated that I already had enough votes lined up to carry it—not true, but he'll never find out now—and that his opposing it wasn't going to do him any good. I watched him get sourer and sourer about it while I kept mentioning how small a figure three hundred and ten million dollars was for such a project. To keep that figure fresh in his mind, I mentioned it half a dozen times.

I waited till we'd finished lunch and were sipping brandy; Rand always tops off a meal, even lunch, with a brandy so I did too this time. While he was savoring the warmth and flavor of his first taste of it, I mentioned casually that there was another way of getting a rocket to Jupiter, much more cheaply and with the additional advantage of a landing on one of the moons. I took your prospectus, the one you and Klocky did together, from my purse and showed it to him. He didn't look at anything but the figures, but he really stared at their total, only twenty-six million. And then he stared at me. 'Senator Gallagher,' he said, 'if it can be done this cheaply, why on Earth or Jupiter did you introduce a bill based on a figure twelve times as high?'

"I'd known that would come, of course, and had my answer ready—that the technique for doing it more cheaply had not been worked out at the time I presented the bill now in the hopper and that the step-rocket covered in the original bill had the advantage of being a two-man rocket and provided more space and comfort for the spacemen who would man it. But that in spite of those factors I would be willing to withdraw the original bill and substitute one based on the inexpensive one-man rocket if, but only if, I had his personal word that the conservationists would let the substitute bill go through without delay and without opposition. They wouldn't have to vote for it, I pointed out; they could abstain or take a walk in the corridor while the bill was being voted on.

"He stalled a while, trying to tell me that he could promise nothing more than that he himself would not oppose the bill, but I pooh-poohed that and flattered him a bit by telling him I knew how much influence he had with the conservationists in both houses and telling him I knew they all looked to him for leadership. He still demurred and I got on my high horse; I told him that if we were going to have a fight on our hands anyway we'd make the fight on the basis of the original and more expensive proposal, and fall back on the alternative only if the original bill lost out. He saw the light, finally. He promised to do his best to see that there was no active conservationist opposition if I withdrew the original bill and introduced the substitute. And Senator Rand, whatever you may think of him otherwise, is a man of his word.

"The bill is practically passed, Max. It was already drafted and I turned it in this afternoon. It'll be reported out of committee next Monday. We'll get it voted on in the Senate within a few days, get it through the House of Representatives within a month at the outside.

"And it won't be vetoed. We have President Jansen's private assurance of that, and given on the basis of the original bill. He'll sign the substitute one like a shot. And be so pleased to get off so cheaply that I'm sure he'll agree to appoint whoever I suggest, provided he's politically qualified, for project director. And before I suggest anyone for the appointment, Max, I'll have the suggested one's private promise to make you his assistant director.

"So in about a month, say around the first of March, I suggest you have Klocky start that vacation of his and leave you in charge. A three months' leave should be ample time; your appointment should be made and confirmed by then, although the project itself isn't likely to get started, even on the drafting board, until fall. The boys at White Sands are going to have to vet the plans and that will take time. There is, there had to be, a provision in the bill that makes the feasibility of the rocket subject *to their approval before the appropriation is actually made and the project set up for operation.*

"But I don't anticipate that they'll cause any trouble. In fact, I'm reasonably sure they'll not only go along but be enthusiastic about giving us all the help they can. General Rudge, the big noise there, was in Washington last week end and strictly off the record and in confidence, I showed him your prospectus. And he told me, also unofficially, that it looked good to him, although of course they'll have to check the figures forty ways from Sunday and I have a hunch they're going to insist on upping a few of the safety factors a little.

"Well, that's the score to date, darling. Wish it wasn't so long till the midsession recess, seven long weeks. But by then probably the bill will be passed and signed—with luck your appointment will have been made and confirmed. Then we can really celebrate, no?

"Meanwhile, don't forget to Write Your Congressman."

I wrote my congressman that I missed her like hell.

And I *was* missing her like hell. Being away from her was showing me that I really loved her and that what was between us was something deep and important, not just an affair, like others I'd had. Sometimes I almost damned Project Jupiter for keeping us apart.

Alone—and I'd never felt alone before—I found that there were too many evenings in a week.

It was a very rainy rainy season in Los Angeles, but I walked a lot, sometimes having to wade in flooded streets. I read a lot. As often as I could without boring them I spent evenings with Klocky or M'bassi, arguing or playing chess. I heard an occasional concert, took in a few shows. Still there were too many evenings. Seven of them a week.

Why did I love Ellen? It was like asking why I had five fingers on each hand.

The days rushed by, at work, and the evenings crawled.

From Ellen, early February: *"My telegram of yesterday told you that the bill passed the Senate, darling. Quite probably, if you were sticking as close to the viddy for news as I suspect, you knew it even before my telegram got there.*

"But I doubt that any of the newscasts carried a breakdown of the vote, so you probably don't know how close a thing it was. It scared us, and it's changed our plans a little.

"Max, it passed by a margin of only three votes.

"And it wasn't because Rand crossed us up. He didn't. Of the approximately twenty-five votes in the Senate that make up the conservationist bloc, only a few went against us; nearly all of them either were absent at the time of the voting or abstained.

"And we had twenty-five certain votes lined up on our side—the fifteen we can always count on and ten more that we'd traded for. We'd figured that, as usual, the other fifty votes, the in-betweeners, would divide about equally. And if that had happened we'd have had almost a two to one majority with the conservationists abstaining.

"But even with no organized opposition, with no speeches against the project, those in-between votes went heavily against us. The actual vote was 36-33, which means that out of forty-four votes cast besides the twenty-five we were sure of, we got only eleven, one vote out of four.

"Since then we've found out why, by talking to some of the in-betweeners who usually vote our way, who are usually willing to go along with any expansionist project in reason. There'd been a sudden change of sentiment because of that Mars rocket crash last week, the three-million-dollar rocket carrying cargo and six men for the Mars colony that was hit by a meteor and crashed on Deimos.

"I'd heard about it at the time, of course. I'd even known that there was what I'd thought was a mild popular furor over it, but I'd never suspected that men supposedly intelligent enough to be sent to the Senate of the United States would be swayed by that furor. As though we'd curb surface transport because of one train crash, no matter how much money it cost or how many people it killed!

"So although, thank God, the bill did go through, we got a scare that showed us how overconfident we'd been. And we learned that before we let that bill be reported out of committee and voted on in the House, we've got to plan carefully and move cautiously. We've got to go in for horse trading on a big scale.

"And we're going to have to wait, in any case, at least until after the recess and possibly even a month or so longer, until that rocket crash is less fresh in the minds of the representatives and their constituents. If, God forbid, there's another rocket crash within the next couple of months, we'll simply have to keep that bill in committee until we can try to jam it through on the closing day of the session. And it would be pretty much of a gamble even then.

"So if Klocky hasn't made irrevocable arrangements to start his leave on the first of March, it will be better if he waits a month and starts the first of April. Please ask him to, because I've got a selfish reason, too, for wanting it that way. The midsession recess this year will be the second two weeks in March, from the sixth through the twenty-first. If Klocky leaves the first of March you'll be holding down his job and I know you wouldn't be able to take those two weeks off. But if he stays on through March, could you possibly, so soon (although it seems so long) after the week we had in Mexico City?

"I still have this damned headache, although it isn't as bad now as when I wrote you last. Now that the excitement about the appropriation bill is temporarily over, I think I'll go to a doctor about it; hope it isn't migraine, although they've got pretty good techniques for taking care of that now so it'll be nothing to worry about seriously even if that's what it is.

"Do let me know as soon as you can about those weeks, so we'll have time to make plans if you'll be free."

It was all right with Klockerman; he'd made arrangements and plans to start his leave the first of March, but it wasn't too late for him to change them. I telephoned Ellen that evening and we had a long talk. We picked Havana, Cuba; we arranged to meet there on the sixth of March.

The narrow vote in the Senate and the delay necessary before the bill could be brought before the House didn't worry me seriously at all. If anything they made me more optimistic. Things had been going too smoothly, too easily, I'd felt. A hitch or setback of some sort had been due and overdue. Now that there'd been one and it hadn't been a fatal one, I felt better.

Lunch one Sunday with M'bassi, rabbit food for him and a steak for me. Afterwards since it was a sunny afternoon and unseasonably warm for February even in Los Angeles, we went to one of the nudist beaches to sun ourselves for an hour or two. I, to get an early start on the tan I wanted to acquire. M'bassi because he loved the sun and its warmth; God knows he didn't need a tan.

We talked of lions. M'bassi brought them up.

"Yesterday afternoon," he said, "I did a thing that I have never done before. I went to a zoo. I went there to look at a lion. I had not seen a lion for thirty years. I saw one."

"What did it look like?"

"It looked like a lion. It looked very much like a lion. But for a while I suspected that it was not one, because it looked so different, so utterly different, from the lions I had seen as a boy in Africa, so utterly different from the lion that had saved my life by mauling me. Then I realized that the difference was not in the lion but in my perspective on the lion. It was an odd experience. I am glad that I went."

"The difference in perspective," I said, "could be due to either of two things. The difference between a free lion and a caged one, or the difference between the viewpoint of a boy and the viewpoint of a man. Which was it, M'bassi?"

"It was neither of those things, Max. It was the difference between the viewpoint of a savage—for at eleven years I was a savage—and that of a civilized man. It was more than the difference between the viewpoint of a boy and a man because had I remained a savage, continued tribal life, that viewpoint would not have changed."

"How would you define that viewpoint? That of the savage, I mean."

"Admiration, respect, and the desire to kill. The need to pit my manhood against his lionhood in combat, to prove to myself that I was not afraid of him."

"But I thought the Masai were so brave they were not afraid of lions."

"Of course they were brave. And of course they were afraid or there would have been no bravery in their lion hunts. Where there is no fear there can be no bravery."

"And your attitude toward a lion, as a civilized man?"

"Admiration, respect, and compassion."

"It's easy to feel compassion for a caged lion. What if it had been charging you in Africa?"

M'bassi sighed. "I would have defended myself, if possible, with regret. The Hsin philosophy is not fanatical; it recognizes that although all life is important a human life is more important than that of an animal."

"Then it wouldn't be a sin to kill a charging lion. But it would be to hunt one?"

"Under certain circumstances that too might be necessary. If, for example, a lion has become a man-killer. What would be wrong would be to hunt or to kill for pleasure, to take joy in the death of any living creature."

Living creatures, sea gulls, soaring lazily and gracefully overhead. Living creatures, a group of girls, walking by, giggling and jiggling. The lazy rhythm of the waves, the sun's warmth and the sky's blueness.

I waved my arm at it. "All this, M'bassi. All this and the stars too. Isn't it enough without having to invent a religion and a God?"

"It might be, if we could *have* all this and the stars too without a religion. You have science. I have religion. You back your horse to take you to the stars; I'll back mine."

I didn't dream, then, that he meant it.

I pretended that I was rich and took the Miami rocket, flew the rest of the way to Havana. Ellen's jet landed two hours later and I was able to have a hotel suite ready for us by the time I met it.

Ellen had seen a doctor about her headaches; he'd fixed them up and everything was fine. But she seemed tired the first few days.

"Damn it, woman," I told her, "you've been working too hard. You've done more than your share on the Jupiter project already. Let the starduster lobby jockey it through the House."

"I'll be pushing it too, Max. I'll be all right, all rested up, by the time I have to go back. And my tiredness isn't *all* from pushing a rocket toward Jupiter. That Buckley Dam bill—I've got to get it through for California or I won't have a ghost of a chance of being re-elected."

"And why do you want to be re-elected? Ellen, it was you who pushed me into administrative work but I'll have to admit I'm through disliking it, and it pays well. Well enough to let me afford a senator of my own. Why don't we get married as soon as my appointment is set?"

"We can talk about it then, darling."

"We can *do* it then," I said. "We can *talk* about it now. There's no charge for talking. Ellen, are you in politics because you really want to be, because you really want a career for yourself? Or just to make a living?"

"I—Max, I honestly don't know. It's probably a little of both and right now I'm too mixed up to analyze my feelings about politics or about getting married. In any case I wouldn't want to marry you until after I've finished the term I was elected to—and that's another two years. It's a long time."

"Damn right it is. And we're not getting any younger."

"No, but we're not missing anything either, are we? We're together almost as much as if we were married. Max, even if we married sooner than two years from now I wouldn't resign from the Senate, so I'd still have to be in Washington six or seven months a year."

"At least you wouldn't have to wear that damn mask in public."

"I don't mind it. And think how nice it is to take it off when we're in private. Will you make us drinks?"

She sipped hers and then lay back against the pillow and closed her eyes. "Talk to me, darling."

"About what? About how much I love you?" I frowned at her. "Damn it, woman, do you know this is the first time in fifty-eight years I've ever asked a woman to *marry* me? And I can't even get a straight answer out of her."

"I love *you*, Max. I'm yours. Isn't that enough? Why, you're a part of me. What do a few words and a piece of paper matter?"

"It isn't the words and the paper. It's—oh, hell, I guess it's selfish of me, when you make me analyze myself. It's probably mostly because I want to be able to brag about having you, not have to keep it secret."

"Secret, except for the few people you really care about. Klocky, the Bursteders, your brother and sister-in-law, M'bassi, a few others—"

"All right," I said, and tried to think of another reason, one that would make sense.

Ellen beat me to the punch. She sat up and reached for her drink again. "Max, let me explain you to yourself. I'll believe that you never asked another woman to marry you, but don't ask me to believe you've never loved another woman. You must have, more than once, and at least as much as you love me. Now admit that much."

"Sure, I've loved other women. But never as *much;* you're wrong there. This is different."

"Max, I'll tell you what's different about it. You're space-nutty and you have been ever since you were old enough to know what love was. By the time you did know, the stars came first and the woman second. Marriage would have tied you down and kept you from trying to go where you wanted to go. Now and for the first time, you've got the two things in one package—a woman you love and through her a chance to help send a rocket farther out into space than one has ever gone before."

There was a hell of a lot of truth in that.

She said, "If you doubt that, I can prove it to you. Suppose I offered to marry you right now, here in Havana, but only on the condition that you'd quit looking up at the stars and dreaming about them."

"You wouldn't ask that. You wouldn't be *you* if you did."

"Of course not. But you see my point just the same. Oh, Max, let's not talk about marriage tonight. Let's not *us* talk about anything. Just you talk, and let me listen."

"All right. What shall I talk about?"

"The only thing you talk well about, the stars. Do you really think we'll ever reach them?"

"You're just baiting me, darling. You know perfectly well that I really think we'll reach them—and that we really will. It's only a question of time. Don't ever sell mankind short by saying there's *anything* he can't do, ever, or anything that he isn't going to do.

"The stars are there waiting for him and he's going to take them. Someday, and maybe suddenly, he's going to explode into deep space as he exploded into the solar system in the sixties. Only let's hope this time he doesn't have to wait until he's scared into it."

"Scared into it?"

I said, "Yes, like the Germans and the Japs scared us into developing the A-bomb. Like the Commies scared us into starting the space station and shooting for the moon. Sometimes it looks as though we have to have the bejesus scared out of us before we're willing to tackle anything that has to be tackled on a big scale and that takes a lot of billions of dollars to accomplish.

"The Nazis and the Japs in the forties—before your time. You know why we developed the A-bomb? To save money. The Nazis we could have licked without it—in fact, we did, because it wasn't developed in time. But the Japs were set for a long bitter defense of their homeland and it would have cost us more billions than the A-bomb cost us, to defeat them with lesser weapons. Wait, that's not entirely true—although it worked out that way. When we *started* developing the A-bomb we weren't thinking about saving money; we were thinking about saving our way of life and maybe our lives; we were scared to the point where money didn't matter.

"And it was in the fifties and the early sixties that the Commies gave us an even worse scare—before the rift between Russia and China in sixty-five and the counter-revolutions in the other satellite countries ended our worries about them. But in the late fifties—and I'm old enough to remember them—we were scared spitless of the Commies. They had A-bombs too, so that wasn't enough. That's when we really started pouring money into trying for controlled atomic energy, energy that could be used for power and propulsion as well as for sheer destruction.

"And before we'd even got it we were shooting the moon by starting work on the space station, starting to put it up there in the sky with chemical fuel rockets, Ellen, primitive three-stage affairs that stood as tall as a ten-story building, and whose pay load was only a fraction of a per cent of their take-off weight. It took us three years and four or five billions of dollars to get the *first* ton of pay load up in that orbit. All of that on chemical fuel rockets before the nuclear boys came through and step-rockets were as obsolete as crossbows—and so was the space station, for military purposes, before we had it well started. Why, instead of one space station up there we could have orbited thousands of rockets with H-heads, controlled by radio and ready to blast a whole continent off the earth if we wanted to.

"Only before we put them up there, there wasn't any need to. Communism came apart at the seams and we weren't scared."

"But we went on to the moon and Mars just the same, Max."

"And Venus," I said. "Our momentum carried us that far and no farther. We weren't scared any more, and big spending stopped. An observatory on the moon, a small experimental colony on Mars. A few looks under the clouds of Venus. And there we stopped."

"Maybe just to catch our breath, Max. That was a big and sudden jump."

"Forty years is too long a time just to catch your breath in. We're overdue to push on. Not just to Jupiter and the outer planets, but to the stars. We should be trying for the nearest star anyway."

"But could we, Max? Right now, I mean, with what we've got, with what we know?"

"We could, yes. It would cost plenty—maybe as much as the atom bomb and all our planetary rockets put together. It would have to be a *big* ship, assembled out in an orbit like the space station was. It would have to be big enough to hold at least half a dozen families, to be practical, because by the time that ship made the four light-years to Proxima Centauri at our present speeds, it would be their descendants several generations later who'd get there."

"Yes, I remember now reading about how it could be done. But I'm afraid, darling, people aren't ready for anything like that yet. Spending all that money, all that effort, and then never knowing what the result would be because they'd be a century dead before the results could be known—if they ever were."

"I know," I said. "It could be done, but I know it won't be done. Not for centuries, anyway, if that's the way it has to *be* done. I wouldn't vote for it myself."

Ellen opened her eyes. "*You* wouldn't?"

"No, I'd rather see those billions thrown into developing an ion drive. Why, if the government put the money and effort into that that it put into developing the A-bomb—why, they might find it in a few years! And you and I might be still alive when the first ship came back from a star!"

Ellen's eyes were bright. "Maybe, if something spectacular comes from the Jupiter trip—"

"What— Wait, something spectacular could come at that, Ellen. Uranium—our resources aren't too high on that, and if we found a lot of it on one of Jupe's moons—that could be one thing. Or intelligent life. I think that would be better than uranium. To *know* there was intelligent life—waiting for us out in the galaxy—Ellen, that would stimulate our curiosity, our drive to get there, more than anything else would."

"Would it? Mightn't it work the other way? Make us afraid we might find life *more* intelligent than ours?"

"I don't think so. Men may be cowards individually, but collectively maybe that's just the challenge we need. God, if we'd only found canals on Mars, proof that another race besides ours *had* lived!

"Just for lack of fuel to feed it on the first few places we reached, are we forgetting our big dream? Are we forgetting where we started to go?

"Jesus, do we have to wait till it's a matter of survival for us to do it? Until we get scared again? Until a space ship from some other star system comes here and starts shooting us up so we've got to have star ships to fight back? Or until our astronomers tell us that our own sun is going to nova and explode, and give us a deadline date to get away from it? Or—a dozen million years from now—decide our own sun is getting so cold we'd better find another one before we freeze to death? Ellen, do we have to wait for one of those things?"

She didn't answer and I looked over at her. She was breathing slowly and regularly. Sound asleep.

I turned out the lights and got quietly into bed without waking her.

The second week she felt much better, much less tired. We went out more that week, saw the town. Neither of us cared for dancing but we both liked good modern Cuban music, the quarter tone stuff that America had imported in the seventies and discarded in the eighties but that was still going strong in Havana. We liked Cuban dancing, too; I guess we were both old-fashioned.

We took a couple of boat trips on the sunniest days, renting skitterbugs, those little skimmers that are so fast you have to wear bathing suits because of the spray. Out of sight of shore we'd stop and let it rock in the waves while we took off our suits and sunbathed on the flat part of the deck. There aren't any nudist beaches in Cuba; people of Spanish descent are for some reason awfully prissy about nudity, like Americans used to be.

It was a good vacation and we both felt fine, all rested up, when it ended, as it had to end. Ellen back to Washington, I back to the L.A. Rocket Port.

And to a plenty busy week. Klocky's last week before his vacation leave, one week to show me the various things I still didn't know about taking over his job while he was gone. We worked late every evening as he'd remember one thing after another that I should learn about.

It's a big job, I was learning, running the Los Angeles Rocket Port, plenty of responsibility and a hell of a lot to know about every department under you. Until Klocky got back I was going to be up to my ears in work.

He left for Africa on the first of April. I saw him off in a gray dawn. "Keep in touch with me, Max, so I'll know when the appointment is set and it's okay for me to come back. But not sooner than three months, damn it. I want at least that much time off. And—good luck."

For a while, until I got things licked into shape so I could handle them, I was too busy to worry about my luck. But it was still holding.

I heard from my congressman late in May:

"Hold thumbs, darling. We're going to run the bill through the House late this week, Thursday or Friday. That's definite, unless, of course, some rocket disaster, interplanetary or local, should happen sooner. We'll postpone a showdown if that should happen; we don't want another near thing such as happened in the Senate. We want to be sure; we want at least a sixty per cent majority.

"And we've been working hard and we're sure we'll get it and without waiting any longer.

"So that you won't be distracted these last few days, spending all your time watching the viddy for news, count on a telephone call from me the minute we know for sure. My call will be made before you'll get even a flash in the viddy, because it's not a big enough deal—to the commentators—for them to put on a flash until the vote is final, but I'll phone you as soon as we know it's in the bag and not wait for the exact count or the last few votes.

"The bill won't be voted on before ten in the morning nor after five in the after-noon, Washington time, and that's 7 A.M. and 2 P.M. your time, so be within reach of a telephone between those hours on Thursday and Friday if you want the news as quickly as I can get it to you. If the call is before nine (your time) I'll try your apart-ment first, after that I'll call you at the port.

"It's going to be good news, darling, believe me. And here's another item of good news. I was at the White House yesterday, with two other senators and talking to the

President on another matter, but I managed to get a few minutes alone with him after we'd finished what, to everybody else concerned, was the main order of business. I brought up the Jupiter project and reminded him of his assurance to us that he'd sign the bill if Congress passed it. He remembered and reassured me that he would.

"And he said he'd heard about it when it had passed the Senate and had been surprised at the fact that the appropriation figure was only twenty-six million, that he didn't remember the exact figure that had been mentioned when the bill had first been discussed with him but he had the impression that it had been a lot more than twenty-six million.

"That gave me a perfect opportunity, Max, to start laying my groundwork for your appointment. I told him something about you and gave you full credit—except that I told him Klockerman had checked your prospectus and figures—for working out the less expensive way of doing the job.

"And while the iron was hot I did a little more ironing with it then and there. I told him that I thought you should be, and deserved to be, director of the project. I admitted, though, that it might be wiser to have a politician for that job, one who knows the ropes and the red tape, as the nominal director, but that whoever got the directorship should get it with the understanding that he should make you his next in command, with the title of project superintendent, and let you handle the actual construction of the rocket.

"He agreed with me, darling! He said that any man who could figure how to cut a three hundred million dollar project down to less than a tenth of that amount certainly deserved to work on that project if he wanted to, and in the highest ranking job he was capable of filling.

"In fact I had to fast-talk him out of deciding then and there to make you director instead of superintendent. And that wouldn't have worked, darling, and here's why: his appointee to the directorship will have to be approved by the Senate and there's too much of a chance for a wheel to come off in that deal. You're not a known political figure and so there'd be sniping at you by some senator or other who wanted to get the job for someone he owed a political obligation to.

"And the sniping would take the form of questioning your qualifications and you know where that would lead. It would bring out the fact that your engineering degree is less than a year old and that until only a year and a half ago you'd had no experience in administrative work at all. And that would mean to the Senate, and to the President too when the word got back to him, that you're not qualified to direct a multimillion dollar project. It's much too big a risk to take. And your being suggested for the directorship and turned down would make it awfully rough for me in getting you the job of project superintendent, if I could do so at all.

"So I told Jansen I didn't think you'd even want the directorship; I told him you'd be much more interested in the actual engineering and construction, that you cared more about rockets than about paper work. I told him you'd been both a spaceman and a rocket mech and knew rockets from the ground up to as high as Mars and that, anyway, a politically known figure ought to front for the project as director.

"He asked if I had anybody in mind for the top spot and I said I'd thought of several good possibilities but that I'd rather not make a specific suggestion until after passage of

the bill by the House, and I told him when that was scheduled.

"He asked if its passage was certain and when I told him that it was, he called in his secretary and his appointment calendar and made a date for me to see him at two o'clock Wednesday, a week from tomorrow.

"By that time I'll have picked out the stuffed shirt I'm going to recommend for director and also have a second-string one in reserve in case Jansen makes any objection to the first. And I'll have talked to both of them, with cards on the table, and will have told each that if I recommend him for the job it's going to be in exchange for the promise to name the man I suggest as his project superintendent and that if he won't promise I won't recommend him for the directorship.

"He'll promise all right; I worked out that bill so that the directorship is a plump political plum (How's that for alliteration?) with good pay. And the prospects I have in mind are going to want it badly enough not to quibble about the single condition I attach to recommending them for it.

"Things are snowballing to a fast finish, darling. Hold thumbs."

I held thumbs. Ellen's letter had come by rocket mail and special delivery; it reached me early afternoon of the day she'd written it, Tuesday.

So I had two days of thumb-holding to face if the bill came to a vote on Thursday, three if it held over till Friday.

And I really held thumbs. I was getting scared again, now that it was so close.

So many things could go wrong.

What if there was another rocket crash? There hadn't been, since the Deimos one which had come so close to wrecking the passage of the bill through the Senate. I'd caught a late roundup newscast every night so I was sure. But what if there'd be one now, in the last few days before the bill was passed? It would stall things till next session for sure and might even change the whole picture. At the best, almost a year's delay. And I wasn't getting any younger; I'd just passed my fifty-ninth birthday. Sixty coming up.

Those last few days I kept a pocket viddy on my desk at work, catching every newscast that came on. Especially Thursday, while I was expecting a call from Ellen. After all, she might have trouble getting a call through and the viddy might beat her to the news. I didn't stir out of my office without first making sure my secretary would know exactly where to reach me if a call came from Washington. But none came.

I waited until I got back to my apartment to phone Ellen; it would be nine in Washington then and she'd be sure to be home. She was.

"Everything okay, darling?" I asked her.

"Everything's fine. Bill's scheduled for tomorrow, third on the agenda. The first two are pretty routine matters so it ought to come up by eleven o'clock; that's eight A.M. your time. You'll still be home then, won't you?"

"Yes, but—but if you call much later than that I'd be on my way between home and the office. So here's what I'll do. I'll go to the office early, get there at seven o'clock, say. Then whenever you call I won't be enroute between the two places."

Her soft laughter came over the wire. "All right, I'll call the office then. But you needn't get there before half past seven; I'm sure the bill won't be passed any sooner than that. And then only if we can keep it routine and avoid debate."

"Fine. I'll be at the office from seven-thirty till I hear from you. Ellen, your voice sounds tired. Are you all right?"

"I *am* tired. Outside of that, I'm all right."

"No more headaches?"

"No more headaches. And I'll rest up now. I'm going to bed early tonight. Tomorrow I'm not going to the Senate. I'll be in the gallery of the House, watching, until I phone you, and then I'll take the rest of the day off."

"And rest?"

"And rest. Oh, maybe I'll go somewhere in the afternoon, just for relaxation, if the bill goes through in the morning session. Tell you what I'll do. Go to the zoo and watch the monkeys. After a morning of watching the House of Representatives, that will soothe my nerves. And restore my faith in human nature. Or simian nature, if there's any difference. Darling, I wish I had your faith in humanity."

"You have more than I. You're just overtired. And I won't keep you any longer. Good night, darling."

I tried to go to bed early that night, myself, but I was too keyed up, too worried, to get sleepy. After a while I gave up, put on a lounging robe and went up on the roof to use my telescope a while. Jupiter was below the horizon but Saturn was beautiful that night, at just the angle that best shows off the rings. Spectacular Saturn, next out beyond Jupiter, our next step outward after Jupe.

And tomorrow would tell the tale of whether we'd be going to Jupiter soon. Would the bill go through, or would a wheel come off?

No wheel came off.

Ellen's call came a few minutes before nine o'clock. "All okay, darling," she said, "it's going through."

"Wonderful."

"A comfortable margin. It's a roll call vote, still going on. Only about three-fourths of the House has been polled but we've got a majority already—a majority of the total number of votes that will be cast, I mean. So it's really passed already. If you're interested in the final count I can phone again in about twenty minutes."

"It doesn't matter," I said. "Ellen, you still sound tired. You'd better go home and rest up. Or were you being serious about going to the zoo this afternoon to watch the monkeys?"

"I was about halfway serious when I said it, but I guess I'll go home and get some sleep instead. I've got a dinner-date tonight. It's time I start lining up my recommendations for the directorship."

"Who, tonight?"

"Whitlow. William J. Whitlow. He's my first choice. Does the name mean anything to you?"

"It sounds familiar but I can't place him. Brief me."

"Ex-congressman from Wisconsin. Jansen's own party. He lost out in the last election but it wasn't his fault; he ran well ahead of his ticket, got more Wisconsin votes than Jansen did. There was that scandal out there, remember, about the dairy interest briberies. Whitlow wasn't involved but too many of his party were and too many straight ticket votes went against him. In the House two years ago he led the fight for the Alaskan reclamation bill—it had his name on it, the Burns-Whitlow Act. That's where you probably heard of him."

"What's he doing now?"

"One of the undersecretaries of state. That was the best job Jansen could hand him after the election, but it's not much of a job compared to the directorship of the project, pays about half as much and gets him only a fraction as much publicity. He'll jump at the Jupiter project. And Jansen will be glad of a chance to move him up; I'm sure of that."

"Nothing against him that might come up when the Senate has to approve him?"

"Not a thing. He's kept his nose clean. Dull and almost disgustingly honest. He won't get a single challenge in the Senate. He's a natural, Max."

"Sounds good. But how about conservationist tendencies?"

"I've checked his voting record carefully. He's better than middle of the road. Hasn't been active in pushing any expansionist bills, but he hasn't voted *against* a single rocket or colony bill. That makes him a lot better for the job—more politically acceptable, I mean—than if he was known as a fanatical expansionist."

"Right. What's he like personally?"

"Well, a bit stuffy, I'm afraid. But don't worry; you'll be able to handle him and he won't interfere with you. He doesn't know the first thing about engineering or rockets, not even about construction. He'll be glad to take the glory and supervise the paper work while you do the real job. I'll do a good job of selling you to him tonight. No, come to think of it, I won't mention your name tonight. I'll just get his irrevocable promise to make the person I name his assistant in exchange for my recommending him for the directorship."

"Why work it that way?"

"I've got a scheme that ought to make it doubly sure. Really Machiavellian. If I hold off on telling him your name until after he's talked with Jansen about the job, just maybe Jansen will remember some of the things I told him about you and suggest you on his own hook to Whitlow. And a recommendation from Prexy would make Whitlow think he's in an embarrassing spot because of his promise to me. And then when I recommend the same man Jansen had recommended, just look what it will do to your stock with Whitlow! He'll be so happy to be able to keep his promise to me and still take Jansen's advice that you'll own the project; he'll be afraid to cross you on anything. And if Jansen doesn't mention your name, nothing's lost."

"Good girl," I said. "Don't let him keep you out late tonight."

"I won't. Won't have to. I'll be offering him a deal he'll jump at, not trying to sell him something. I won't even have to be nice to him, let alone try to seduce him."

"You'd better not. But that reminds me—don't you think this deserves a celebration? Today's Friday; I can fix things to be off tomorrow and Sunday. If you sleep all this afternoon, all night tonight and all day tomorrow do you think you'd be rested up enough for a celebration, just the two of us, tomorrow night? I could take a stratojet there tomorrow afternoon and catch one back Sunday afternoon."

"It sounds wonderful—but Max, let's wait until we can *really* celebrate, until your appointment has been made. If I really push things that could be as soon as next week end, and isn't that worth waiting for?"

I sighed. "I suppose so. But it's damned lonesome here, with Klocky gone too. I see M'bassi once in a while, but I can hardly celebrate with him this week end. He won't drink anything stronger than wine and only a glass or two of that."

Ellen laughed. "Doesn't sound very festive, does it, darling? Why don't you run up to Berkeley tomorrow night and hang one on with Bess and Rory? They're wonderful people."

"They are, and I will," I said.

"Oh, and don't miss tonight's papers, Max. We've got a really good publicity man and he's worked out fine press releases on the project. We've been holding them back until it went through the House, but he'll release them this afternoon."

"I'll watch for them," I said. "All right, darling, I won't keep you talking any longer. I hope I'll see you next week end then, and keep me posted."

"I'll let you know the minute there's any further news. 'Bye now."

I intended to phone Rory that evening to make sure he and Bess would be at home and free the following night and that they'd want me to come up. But Rory beat me to the punch. He phoned me at the office just before quitting time.

"Max, can you run up here for tomorrow evening?"

I said that I could.

"We're throwing a wing-ding to celebrate Project Jupiter," he said. "About fifty of us in on it so far, mostly the boys at Treasure, but there'll be more. We're taking a suite, or as many suites as we'll need, at the Pleiades Hotel and it's going to be quite a brawl."

It was quite a brawl all right. It lasted till dawn. I found that I was the guest of honor because the newspaper releases had given me most of the credit for working out the plans for the rocket. I had to make a speech and botched it badly, but nobody seemed to care.

The publicity hadn't hurt my stock at the L.A. Rocket Port either. I found that out Monday morning when I went back to work. If there'd been any resentment—and I'd thought there had been at least a little—about the way Klocky had jumped me up so fast, over other people's heads, it was gone now. I was hero for a day now, and I could do no wrong. I could feel the difference.

No word from Ellen Monday or Tuesday. No reason why she should have called or written, of course. A newscast Tuesday afternoon mentioned that the

President had signed the Jupiter Project bill and that it was now officially enacted. But that had been anticipated so there was no reason why Ellen should have called me about it.

But Wednesday was the date of Ellen's appointment with Jansen, and I knew she'd phone me, or at least send a telegram, as soon as she left him. If she'd made the deal with Whitlow and if Whitlow was definitely going to get the appointment, then I was in.

Her appointment was at two o'clock, eleven Pacific time, so after eleven I stayed in my office so as not to miss a call. When it hadn't come by noon I sent out to have a lunch brought in to mc and stuck by the telephone. By one o'clock I was getting a little worried; surely her appointment with Jansen wouldn't have lasted more than fifteen minutes. Then I decided she must have had to hurry back to the Senate and had decided to call me this evening.

But five o'clock, when I was ready to leave work, was eight o'clock for her and still there'd been no call. Don't be a damned fool, I told myself; no news is good news. Everything went okay and she's waiting till you're home to phone you so the conversation can be leisurely without interrupting your work.

I ate hurriedly enroute and was home by six. At seven I phoned Ellen's apartment in Washington and got no answer. I tried again every hour until it was two o'clock there, eleven to me, and gave up for the evening. If she wasn't home by two she was staying elsewhere for the night. But why hadn't she called me? Surely she'd know that I was waiting for a call and might call her if she didn't call me, and that I'd wonder and worry when I found she wasn't home.

I set the alarm for five and turned in. I got a little sleep off and on, but I got up at four-thirty and made myself coffee. I tried her apartment again at five; if after spending the night out she came home to change clothes or get papers to take to the Senate with her, that was the time she'd be home, an hour before the Senate opened. No answer; she hadn't come home at all.

I made myself wait an hour and a half, then I phoned the Senate, now half an hour in session, and got the sergeant-at-arms. I had to pull my rank as director of the port to convince him my call was important enough for him to go to her desk on the floor of the Senate right away. I told him, though, that if she was there he didn't have to pull her away to answer the phone if she was busy, but that he could give her a message to call me back as soon as convenient, and that I'd hold the phone until he came back and told me whether he'd found her or not. He came back on in ten minutes and said that Senator Gallagher had not yet come in, but that he'd watch for her and give her my message when she did come.

I thanked him and hung up.

Should I try the Washington police? If she'd been in an accident it would have been last night, in all probability, and they'd know by now. But if everything was all right, if there was a simple explanation for her absence, a call to the police might start an inquiry that would prove embarrassing to her, might even make the newspapers or a telecast before she turned up.

I sat staring at my phone. It rang.

Washington was calling. I breathed again, thinking Ellen had just reached the Senate, had had my message from the sergeant-at-arms, and had called right away.

But it was a man's voice. "Mr. Andrews?"

I said yes.

"This is Dr. Grundleman of Kerry Hospital. I am calling on behalf of Senator Ellen Gallagher, who is a patient here and who asked me to make this call."

"What's wrong? Is she badly hurt?"

"It was not an accident, Mr. Andrews. She is to undergo an operation later today for the removal of a brain tumor. She asked me to tell you—"

"Save the message for a minute. How dangerous is the operation?"

"It is a serious one but the chances are fairly good. They would have been much better had the operation been performed ten days ago when the condition was first diagnosed. But I think we can bring her through."

"What time's the operation? Can I get there in time to talk to her before it?"

"It's scheduled for half past two; we'll have to start preparing her for it at two and it's nine-fifty here now, our time, so that means there's only four hours and ten minutes. I suppose a chartered rocket would do it, but that would be terribly expen—"

"Tell her I'll be there," I said. I slammed down the receiver.

I picked it up and dialed the house number of my secretary. After a few minutes she answered sleepily.

"This is Max, Dotty," I said. "Snap awake because this is an emergency. Got paper and a pencil handy?"

"Yes, Mr. Andrews."

"Good. Write these things down so you won't slip up on any of them, and start doing them the second I hang up. First, call the port and tell them to get the charter rocket ready to take off the minute I get there; it'll be within twenty minutes. If there's more than one pilot on stand-by, I want Red. Landing clearance at Washington. Got that?"

"Yes, Mr. Andrews."

"Second you've finished that, get a helicab to pick me up here. Emergency priority, pilot to land on the roof. If he gets in trouble for it, I'm responsible. I'll be on the roof in ten minutes after I finish this call. Listen, get those things started happening while I get dressed, then phone me back and I'll give you a few more."

I threw on clothes. Dotty called back just as I finished. The rocket was being readied and the helicab was coming. I gave her instructions about the port itself this time, who'd be in charge and what to tell him, things like that.

Then I ran up three flights to the roof, got there two minutes before the helicab landed to pick me up.

We took off from the rocket port at seven-twelve, just twenty-two minutes after I'd hung up on my long distance call from the hospital. The trip to Washington—with maximum acceleration and deceleration allowed on a passenger flight—should have taken two and a quarter hours. But Red didn't figure me for a passenger, when I told him that every minute counted. We let down in an hour and fifty minutes. And there was a hellie waiting for me; it came right out on the field to pick me up the moment we'd landed. I hadn't thought of that, but Dotty had.

So I reached the hospital by noon, Eastern time, two hours before they'd start preparing her for surgery.

At the desk they wouldn't tell me Ellen's room number. Dr. Grundleman had left orders that I was to be shown to his office on arrival. I was shown to his office.

He was red-faced, short and stocky, bald as the nose of a rocket; he looked more like a bartender or a wrestler than like a doctor. He held out a hand and I took it but I didn't hang onto it long. I hadn't come to see him, but to see Ellen, and would he please have me taken to her.

"You made excellent time getting here, Mr. Andrews. There's no hurry."

"You're not in a hurry, but I am. Where is she?"

"Please sit down, Mr. Andrews. You won't lose any time with her by sitting down a moment here. It's almost two hours before we must start preparing her, and I cannot possibly let you have more than an hour with her. Even to let you spend that long is stretching things. And wouldn't you rather have the last hour, from one until two, so you can be with her right up to the time when we'll have to start preparing her?"

"All right," I said. "Providing you let her know right away that I'm here and that I'll be with her at one, so she won't lie there wondering if I'll make it in time or not."

"She already knows. The desk phoned me while you were being brought here and I immediately relayed word of your arrival to Senator Gallagher; she knows that you are here and that you'll spend the hour from one to two with her. Now will you sit down?"

I sat down. I said, "Sorry, Doctor, I'm edgy."

"Which is another reason why I'd rather you didn't see her immediately. I want you to be calm, not excited, when you talk to her. Do you think you can be?"

"I think I can pretend to be," I said. "What happened? When and how was she brought here? How long has this been going on?"

"The tumor must have started developing at least a year ago. The first symptom, headaches, started developing in January. At first they were intermittent and not too severe; Senator Gallagher went to a doctor for treatment late in March, about two months ago."

I nodded. That would have been immediately after our vacation in Havana. She'd probably been more ill then than she'd let me know.

Grundleman was saying, "The doctor she went to diagnosed the trouble as migraine and treated it as such. No fault of his; the location of the tumor is such that the symptoms at that time were almost identical with those of migraine. And for a while she seemed to be recovering. Until ten days ago there was a sudden setback, one that made her doctor suspect his original diagnosis and suggest that she come here immediately for a thorough examination. We discovered and located the tumor and I advised an immediate operation. She insisted, however, on waiting two weeks, despite the increased danger the wait would entail, until she had finished with some legislative business she considered extremely important."

I closed my eyes. Jupiter project. She'd considered it important enough to risk her life for. Or had it been the project itself, rather than my driving interest in the project and her love for me? "Go on," I said.

He shrugged. "There was nothing I could do. We scheduled the operation for this coming Saturday. Arranged to have Dr. Weissach—do you know of him?"

I shook my head.

"Probably the best brain surgeon in the world. Lives in Lisbon, but has no practice of his own, just operates. Where possible people are flown to Lisbon for him to operate on, but in an emergency case like that of Senator Gallagher he will come to the patient, although at a much higher fee."

"Any question of money?"

"Oh, no. Senator Gallagher can meet all expenses. Dr. Weissach is already here. He arrived this morning and has made his preliminary examination and arrangements. He is resting now. Is there anything else I can tell you?"

"Yes. What are her chances?"

"With a surgeon like Weissach, I would say they are excellent."

"How long after the operation before she is out of danger, *completely* out of danger?"

"I would much rather answer that question after the operation."

"All right. I'll have to phone my office to let them know how long I'll be gone, but that can wait."

I walked into Ellen's room at one o'clock exactly.

She looked pale, otherwise no different from the way she'd looked when I'd last seen her. She smiled up at me. I didn't kiss her, not yet, not just then; I just stood looking down at her. Striking, her chestnut hair on a white pillow.

She must have realized that it was. "Take a last look at the hair, darling," she said. "They're going to shave it off, you know."

"To hell with your hair," I said. Maybe not a romantic first remark, but she knew what I meant and smiled again.

"Woman," I said, "why didn't you let me know this was happening? You've known for ten days you were going to have an operation."

"I didn't want you to worry. Oh, I wanted you here, wanted to see you once more before the operation—in case. But the operation was to be this coming Saturday; I was going to phone you Friday evening and have you come on a night plane and be with me Saturday morning, and Sunday you could have gone back. This way—I'm sorry it was such short notice, darling. But I'm so glad you came anyway. Aren't you going to kiss me?"

I kissed her very gently, tenderly.

She said, "Now Max, pull up that chair. Sit and let me talk till I've brought you up to date. Dr. Grundleman said you didn't even let him give you my message."

"I didn't want to waste time, that's all. I just wanted to get here. What was the message?"

"That President Jansen will appoint Whitlow, and that Whitlow has made the promise I asked him to make."

"Woman, why didn't you have that operation ten days ago when Grundleman said you should have it? That Jupiter rocket is going to take a couple of years to build anyway, so what difference would a few more weeks make?"

"I couldn't have stalled it then, Max. It was lined up to go through the House, everything set and ready. It would have gone through from there without me."

"But then why didn't—"

"Don't you see, darling? I'd have been out of circulation at just the wrong time, when the appointments were being made. And I wanted you to have that job. Besides, I thought Grundleman was exaggerating the danger and the need for rushing into an operation. I thought two weeks more wouldn't matter, that it wouldn't involve any additional risk. And if it was going to kill me anyway, I wanted to make sure you'd have what you wanted, what we both wanted you to have."

"Quit talking as though you're going to— Damn it, woman, you're going to be okay."

"Of course I am. But I had to consider the other chance. Here's what happened yesterday. I saw Prexy at two and I took a short cut by bringing Whitlow with me. Of course I left him out in the anteroom when I went in. I got right down to business by telling Prexy who I thought would be the best man for the job and he was pleased. He said he thought Whitlow would be ideal and that he deserved a better spot than the one he had in the State Department. Yes, he'd be glad to appoint Whitlow to the directorship. He'd ask his secretary to make an appointment for Whitlow to see him.

"I grinned at him and told him I'd been so sure he'd like the idea that I'd taken a chance and brought Whitlow with me, that he'd allowed fifteen minutes for my appointment and only two had been used up and why couldn't he save himself another appointment by telling Whitlow now? So he had his secretary bring Whitlow in, and that was that. Except, darling, for the best part! Prexy remembered about you and suggested you to Whitlow for the supervisor job, gave you quite a build-up. While he was doing it—" Ellen giggled a little. "—I could see Whitlow beginning to sweat because he'd promised to appoint whoever I suggested for the job and here was Prexy putting the pressure on him. Then he happened to glance toward me and I nodded. You should have seen the relief on his face, Max. He almost stuttered, he was so eager to tell Jansen that he'd appoint you."

I said, "That's wonderful, Ellen. But why didn't you phone me—I don't mean about that, but when you decided to have the operation today instead of Saturday?"

"I didn't decide. When we left the White House Whitlow offered to drop me home in the cab he was taking and I took him up on it. I passed out in the cab and the next thing I knew was when I woke up here this morning. Whitlow had had the cab rush me to an emergency hospital; at the hospital they found a receipted bill from Dr. Grundleman in my handbag and phoned him right away for instructions. He arranged to have me transferred here and phoned Weissach in Lisbon to come as soon as he could. When I woke up this morning everything was arranged. All I could do was to ask Grundleman to phone you right away, as he did. I hoped you'd come and could get here in time, but in case you couldn't make it I wanted you to know that everything was set about your job on the project."

I said, "Thank God I got that message in time to come."

"I'm glad you did, but we could have talked anyway. After I knew you were coming, after it was too late, I realized that I could have had them run an extension phone in here and that I could have told you myself. If you hadn't been coming, I'd still have had them arrange for the phone call."

"This is better," I said. "I couldn't have kissed you over the phone."

"Nor held my hand. Hold it, Max, because now that you're here there are still a few things I want to tell you."

I moved my chair closer and held her hand in both of mine.

"They can wait till afterward," I said. "For now, just tell me again that you love me."

"You know that already. I've never been as close to anybody as I have been, still am, to you. It's—it's almost as though I'm you and you're me; we're part of one another."

"I know," I said. "I feel it too."

"But if I should—if I don't come through the operation, don't let it throw you, darling. You've got a job to do, whether I'm with you or not."

"Woman, don't talk about—"

"Max, we've got to face the fact that there is a chance I won't come through. Whether it's one chance in ten or one in a hundred, there are a couple of things I want you to know. Will you let me say them, and then we won't talk about the possibility any more."

"All right," I said. "Get them over with. I'll listen." I tightened my grip on her hand.

"First, about my will. I wish I could change it in your favor, but—"

"My God, woman," I said, "I don't want to hear about your will."

"You said you'd listen. I want you to understand why I didn't change it, despite the fact that it's in favor of two distant relatives with whom I'm only on casually friendly terms, although they're the closest relatives I have, even though they're both relatives by marriage, Ralph Gallagher's brother and sister.

"The main reason is the fact that if, when my will is probated, the news gets out that I left you my money, such as it is, it would prejudice your chances of getting that job. If some columnist picked it up and made something of it—"

"Okay, I understand."

"And besides it's not going to be enough to get excited about after paying for this operation, and after funeral expenses and—"

"My God, woman!"

"We're discussing *ifs,* darling, and if I die there's going to have to be a funeral. And that's the other thing I want to tell you about. I don't want you to go to it."

"Why not? There'd be hundreds of people. Nobody would couple our names just because—"

"That's not why, Max. It's just that I wouldn't want you to. I hate funerals, think they're pompous and silly and disgusting. I hate the thought of having one myself even though I won't know about it while it's happening. Since I'm a public figure I suppose there'll have to be one, but I don't want the only person I really love there sharing in it. If I die, I don't want you to see me dead, either here or in a funeral parlor. I don't want you to remember a dead body or even the outside of a coffin. I want your last memory of me to be as I am now, alive. I don't want you even to think about a funeral or send flowers. Will you promise me those things, Max?"

"Yes, if you'll quit talking about them."

"All right, I'm through being macabre. From now on we'll be bright and cheerful. How much time have we got left?"

I glanced at my watch. "Nearly half an hour."

"Good. Now you do the talking for a while. Tell me a story."

"A story? I'm no good at telling stories."

"A true story. There's one you promised to tell me once and never have. Do you remember?"

I shook my head.

"Last October when you got your degree and we had a party to celebrate and your brother Bill and his wife came down from Seattle, remember? Bill made a crack about sewing machines and you laughed with him, and when I asked you what the joke was you said it was a long story, about something crazy you'd done once, and that you'd tell me sometime but not just then. I never remembered to ask you about it afterwards until this morning I thought of it for some reason after I knew you were coming and decided to ask you if we had time."

I laughed. "It's not much of a story, Ellen. I just didn't want to take out time to tell you in the middle of a party. It started with a book I read in my teens, one of the early science fiction novels. I forget who wrote it but it was called *Mad Universe* or something like that. One of those alternate time-track stories, where the hero gets switched somehow to another universe that's been identical with his up to a certain point in history and at that point there's a split in the time-track; something happens in one universe that doesn't happen in the other and they go in different directions.

"In this one the change had started early in the nineteenth century with the accidental discovery of a method of interstellar travel by a scientist who was trying to rig a little low-voltage generator out of an old treadle sewing machine. Had a couple of small coils mounted, the treadle to turn one inside the other, and started it going—and the sewing machine disappeared. He'd had it hooked up wrong—wrong for a generator, that is—but he was able to figure out where he'd make his mistake and tried it again, on his wife's good sewing machine. He lost that too.

"But he kept on experimenting and losing sewing machines until he had the secret of the instantaneous space-warp drive. Ever happen to read the book, Ellen?"

She shook her head slowly.

"You might get a kick out of it, while you're getting better, if I can find a copy, but I doubt if I can. It's probably been out of print for forty or fifty years and I'm not even sure of the exact title. Only way I could get hold of it would be a through a collector of early science fiction.

"But anyway, I read it in my teens and didn't think about it again until I was in my early forties, when I happened to get hold of an old copy and read it again. And one thing about it looked different to me then, because I was different and things were different.

"I was a pretty bitter guy about that time, Ellen. I was bitter about the fact that I was only a one-footed rocket mech and would never get into space again and that I wasn't getting anywhere, but I was still more bitter about the fact that *we* weren't getting anywhere. We'd got to the moon and Mars and Venus, and because we hadn't found plains strewn with gold and diamonds or alien aborigines or civilizations, we'd almost lost interest. We weren't going any farther, it looked like, in my lifetime, and in particular we weren't shooting for the stars, weren't even trying to work out a stellar drive. The conservationists were worse then, Ellen, than they are now. We're gradually, I can see now, getting our second wind and getting ready to try again. But that was about the worst point of reaction against space travel and the government seemed on the verge of even pulling in the outposts we already had. Even terrestrial rocketry was at its lowest ebb. A big passenger rocket had just crashed into a crowded Paris street and had killed over a hundred people besides all its own passengers, and there was even talk of banning rockets completely for terrestrial travel. That was in—I think it was in nineteen eighty-four."

I frowned at the way I was telling it. I said, "Damn it, I'm trying to tell you something funny, something crazy I did, and I'm going at it all wrong. But now that I've messed it up anyway I might as well finish filling in the rest of the background. I was drinking a lot then, regularly and heavily. Well on my way to becoming a lush. Rory was trying to straighten me out, and so was Bill—Bill was still single then and living in San Francisco—but I was pretty blue and discouraged and neither of them was having much luck working on me.

"And then one night, getting drunk alone in my room, I happened to reread that ancient book with the thing about the sewing machines in it. And I got to thinking, why not? We didn't, and still don't for that matter, know the basic principle of any form of interstellar drive except the rocket, but there must be one. And since we don't know how it will work we're quite as likely as not to come across it accidentally, aren't we? Only we might speed up the time of that accidental discovery by deliberately messing around with screwy coils and hook-ups.

"I had half a bottle of whisky left when I decided that. I poured it down the drain and went to bed. And the next morning I went to the bank and drew out every cent I had, about a thousand bucks. I quit my job by telephone and I moved to another room in a different part of town so neither Rory nor Bill could find me.

Then I went out and bought—God help me, Ellen, but this is the truth—three used sewing machines. One of them an electric portable and two old-fashioned treadle ones I had to find in antique shops and pay fancy prices for. And a flock of electric and electronic stuff, wire, coils, condensers, vacuum tubes, transistors, switches, crystals, batteries, everything I could think of.

"I holed in that room and tried random crazy circuits and contraptions fifteen or sixteen hours a day for two weeks. I went out only to eat, and I didn't take a single drink." I grinned. "Maybe that was what was wrong. Maybe I'd have been more lucky—or more intuitive—if I'd combined that spree with a drinking spree, but I didn't. You'd think I'd have found *something*, if not an interstellar drive, out of the tens of thousands of crazy things I tried, but I didn't. At the end of the two weeks all I'd accomplished was to go broke and burn myself a few times with a soldering iron.

"And that was when Bill finally found me and walked in on me. I started explaining to him what I'd been doing or trying to do, and I started laughing because suddenly I was seeing the whole thing in perspective—or maybe seeing it through Bill's eyes—and I realized how howlingly funny it was, so I howled, and after a while Bill got the joke and was howling with me.

"Anyway, it cured me of the long black depression I'd been in, and somehow it brought Bill and me closer than we'd ever been before. That evening, after I'd fixed things to start back to work the next day and had borrowed money from Bill to live on until I got a pay check again, Bill got a little drunk with me, something he doesn't often do. But it was a happy drunk I had, and a mild one, not the escape drinking I'd been doing up to two weeks before. I was out of that."

I grinned at Ellen. "Well, that's the story of the sewing machines. It's been a joke between Bill and me ever since, and he seldom misses a chance to kid me about it. Now you can kid me too."

Ellen smiled. "I love that story, darling, but not because it's funny—although I suppose it is. I love it because it's *you,* and I love you so I love it. Only you're wrong about one thing."

"What's that?"

"We *have* got an interstellar drive. It's in you, and people like you. It's even in me a little, now that I've caught it from you. It's in Klocky, in Rory, in almost everybody that works with rockets. Even in M'bassi."

"M'bassi?" I must have looked blank. "He's no starduster. He's a mystic."

She smiled again. "Maybe you've never asked him what he's mystical about. Try it next time you see him."

There was a light tap on the door and Grundleman came in. "Just another minute," he said. "Thought I'd give you that much warning." He stepped out and closed the door again.

"Max, darling, promise me something?"

"Anything," I said.

"If I die—we know I won't, but if I do—promise me that you won't let it throw you, won't let it start you drinking."

"I promise."

The door opened again, this time not Grundleman but a nurse and an orderly. The orderly said, "I'm sorry but you'll have to leave now, sir. We're to prepare the patient."

To prepare her, to shave her hair, her lovely chestnut hair so beautiful against the white pillow. I bent down and kissed her hair, and then her lips.

Dr. Grundleman came to me in the waiting room.

"They're taking her into Operating now, Mr. Andrews," he said. "Dr. Weissach is ready. But she may be on the table a long time, and you won't be able to see her for at least twenty-four hours after the operation, if that soon. You'll be more comfortable at a hotel, and I can phone you as soon as—"

"I'll wait," I said.

I waited.

I wished that I could pray. Then I did pray, *"God, I don't believe that you exist, and I believe that if you do exist you're an impersonal entity and that if you notice the fall of sparrows you don't do anything about it, on request or otherwise, but if I'm wrong, I'm sorry. And in case I'm wrong I pray to you that..."*

Years later, Grundleman came back. He was smiling. Thank God, he was smiling.

He said, "A beautiful operation. Weissach worked a miracle. I think she'll live."

I stared at him. "You think she'll live! A beautiful operation but you only think she'll live."

He quit smiling. "Yes, she has an even chance now, or slightly better than even. But she won't be completely out of danger for three or four more days."

Jesus God, I thought, what had the odds been before? What had the odds against her been while I was talking to her only two and a half hours ago? What does a doctor mean when he says a patient's chances are excellent? That it's one chance in a hundred or one in a thousand?

"Will I be able to see her tomorrow?"

"Perhaps. It's too soon for me to promise that for sure. Phone me tomorrow morning."

"I'll phone you as soon as I check in somewhere, so you'll know where to reach me."

He nodded.

In my room at the hotel I discovered how tired I was. I hadn't slept much the night before and the strain of worry is more tiring than physical labor.

But before I let go, I phoned the rocket port and talked to the man I'd put in charge there, told him I'd probably be away a week, and made sure everything was going smoothly and that he'd know where to reach me if he needed help or advice.

I called the hospital to let them know where I was, and then I slept. But fitfully; every slight sound from outside wakened me because my ear was tuned to the telephone, listening for it to ring, hoping it wouldn't.

It didn't.

But even fitful sleep adds up over a long enough period, and morning found me rested and feeling better. And hungry as hell because, I realized now, I'd completely forgotten to eat the day before.

I called the hospital and was told Ellen had had a quiet night and that her condition was good. Grundleman hadn't come in yet so I couldn't ask about visiting Ellen. I left word to have him call me as soon as he came in.

I phoned room service and had a triple-sized breakfast sent up to my room so I wouldn't have to get away from the telephone. I ate all of it.

Grundleman phoned a little after nine o'clock. He told me that Ellen was "resting nicely."

"Is that double-talk or does it mean that the odds are better?"

"Much better. They're definitely, strongly in her favor now."

"Will I be able to see her this afternoon?"

"Probably. Want to phone me about one o'clock? Or are you going to stay in your room where I can reach you?"

"Both," I said. "I'll be here if you want to reach me, and I'll phone you at one if I haven't heard from you sooner."

I knew he wouldn't be calling back right away so it was a good time for me to try to reach Klockerman in Africa, which might tie up my phone for a while. I knew he'd want to know about Ellen and I thought too that I'd better let him know that I was playing hooky from the job he'd given me. He might even want to rocket back and take over himself if he didn't think the man I'd put in charge there could handle things.

I knew he was in Johannesburg and told the operator she could probably find out where he was staying by checking with the American embassy there. She could and did; within twenty minutes I was telling him what had happened.

"Thank God," he said, when I'd brought him up to date on Ellen. "It's odds-on now, then?"

"Definitely. But what about the job? I left Gresham in charge. Can he handle it?"

"Hell yes; don't worry about it. I'm not going to. Just keep me posted on Ellen. Call me again if there's any change or let me know when she's out of danger. How's everything on the Jupiter deal? I know it went through okay— we got that news even over here. But I mean your tie-in with it. All okay?"

I told him it was and explained how Ellen had endangered herself by holding off on the operation until she had everything wrapped up for me.

He said, "She's a wonderful woman, Max."

As though he was telling me something I didn't know.

Grundleman beat me to the punch. I'd been watching the time to call him at one o'clock and my phone rang three minutes sooner.

He said, "She's doing fine and she's awake now. You can have half an hour with her whenever you get here. But please stop in my office first; I want to talk to you."

"You're talking to me now. Tell me whatever it is now and save me worrying on the way over. Is anything wrong?"

"Not exactly. Physically, she's doing fine, considering the operation was what it was and was less than twenty-four hours ago. But something's wrong with her morale. For some reason she's feeling depressed and pessimistic, much more so than she was before the operation—and God knows there was cause for it then. That's why I'm allowing you as much as half an hour with her. I want you to cheer her up, tell her I told you that the operation was a complete success and that she's past all danger. I told her that myself, but she doesn't quite believe me."

"I'll tell her. But *is* she out of danger?"

"Almost."

"I don't know what *almost* means. Quote me odds."

"Well—as of this moment I'd say she has three chances out of four."

"Right," I said. "That's language I can understand. And I'll do my best to cheer her up. Only I've got a suggestion I want you to consider."

"What is it?"

"That you let me tell her the truth. If I try to lie to her, as you did, she'll know it even more surely than she knew you were lying. Let me level with her and tell her she now has three chances out of four. She'll not only like that but she'll believe it, and it'll do her more good than all the lies I could tell her."

"Hmmm. Maybe you've got something there, Mr. Andrews. Only let's stretch it a little. Say nine chances out of ten."

"The truth or nothing. She'll know if I stretch it."

"All right then, the truth. But remember, don't get excited about anything while you're with her, and don't let her get excited either. If you want to kiss her, do so lightly, and don't let her move her head. But she knows about that."

Thick white bandages this time instead of chestnut hair. But she smiled up at me. "Hope I haven't worried you too much, darling."

"You've been worrying me plenty, but don't worry *about* me. How are you feeling? Any pain?"

"No pain, but I feel awfully weak. You'd better do most of the talking."

I pulled up a chair close. "Fine. What shall I talk about?"

"First, have they told you the truth about my chances as of now?"

"Yes," I said, and told her in detail about my conversation with Grundleman on the phone.

Her eyes brightened a little. "Fine, Max. Yes, you were right. It's a lot better to know the real odds, when they're three to one in my favor, than to be handed a line and have to wonder. Three chances out of four; that's better than I'd guessed. I feel better to know the truth."

"I knew you would. All right, anything special you want me to talk about?"

"About yourself, darling. What you told me yesterday, the sewing machine episode, made me realize how little I knew about you except while you were a spaceman or learning to be one. Before you were seventeen and after you became a rocket mech. What was your childhood like?"

"Nothing very exciting. I was horn in Chicago, as I told you, in nineteen-forty. In a four-room third-story flat over a paint store on State Street ten blocks south of the Loop; that was a tough district then.

"I was second of three children; had a sister two years older than I; she died about twenty years ago. And one brother five years younger—Bill. Our old man was a street-car conductor, and a pretty heavy drinker.

"I grew up as a tough kid, ran with a gang that committed petty crimes and a few that weren't so damn petty. A lot of my childhood playmates ended up behind bars, and I don't mean as bartenders. I guess only one thing saved me from going the same way.

"From the time I could read, I read all the science fiction I could lay my hot little hands on. Comic books—remember them? Then magazines and novels. There was wonderful stuff being written then—or it seemed wonderful to me. Adventures on Mars and the other planets and across the galaxy and to the farthest galaxies. They knew space travel was coming, the boys who wrote those early science fiction yarns. They had the Dream, and they gave me the Dream. There was stardust in what they wrote, and it got in my eyes. I knew space travel was coming and I knew I was going to be a spaceman.

"That's what kept me in line, kept me from going too far astray. I knew I had to keep my name off the police blotter, keep out of the reformatory, or they wouldn't let me in the space corps when one was formed. That's what kept me in school when my friends stayed out, because I was able to figure even then that I'd have to have an education to go where I wanted to go.

"God, the fights I had because I wouldn't duck school with the kids I ran with and they thought I was sissy, or when they thought I was yellow because I wouldn't risk getting a record by helping them roll drunks or burgle stores. Did me good, though; toughened me up and taught me that nothing is easy and you have to fight for what you want. I wanted space, and I fought for it.

"And all the while we were growing up and living under the shadow of the A-bomb, under the threat of all-out atomic war any minute—and I was glad of it, reveled in it. I loved it because I could see even then that it was fear and fear only that would ever make a government spend the billions it would have to spend to get us the space station and the moon and the planets. I didn't care how big a risk we were taking, didn't care how afraid we got to be, if being afraid got us started toward the stars.

"It did get us started, and it's going to get us there. It's in the cards, Ellen. It's something we've got to do, unless we want to become extinct like the dinosaurs. And we won't, because we're smarter than dinosaurs. We're past the stage already where changing conditions can lick us, as it licked them, because we can change conditions ourselves. We can do more to nature right now than nature can do to us. And we ourselves won't retrogress because we've already got a science of genetics—and give us a few more centuries to educate people up to having it applied and the race will never slide backward either physically or mentally. We'll keep it getting stronger and stronger and smarter and smarter until we're gods. Or as near to being gods as we'll ever want to be; we'll have to keep a little of the devil in us to keep us from boring ourselves and one another.

"Ellen, we'll reach the stars all right. If we have to, it'll be by slower-than-light ships that take generations for a crossing, or that send colonists in suspended animation for centuries enroute. But I don't think we'll have to. Relativity tells us we can't exceed the speed of light, but relativity is just a theory, arid there's a short cut somewhere. Hyper-space, sub-space, whatever you want to guess it'll be. But if it's there, that short cut, we'll find it. Don't sell us short."

Ellen was smiling at me. "I wouldn't even sell *you* short, Max. And—it's nice to be able to believe with you. I didn't really, at first, but I do now." There was an almost childlike note of wonder in her voice. "We really *are* going there."

"Damn right we are. It's just a matter of time, like our taking the next step out in the solar system, to Jupiter, was just a matter of time. A damn short time now, thanks to you."

"Thanks to both of us, darling. That's *our* rocket. I only wish I could ride it with you."

"Ride it with—?" I stared at her.

She smiled again. "Don't you think I know you by now, Max? Don't you think I know every bit of you and the way your mind works? Don't you think I know you'd give your other leg and both of your arms—not to mention your life—to pilot that rocket yourself, and that you've got enough confidence in yourself to know you could do it? And don't you think I know that you're going to try?"

I didn't answer.

She said, "It's all right, Max. I *want* you to, if you can get away with it. Even if you're going to kill yourself doing it, I want you to have that chance, to die that way."

I squeezed her hand. There wasn't anything I could think of to say, anything at all.

"Max, if I die—"

"Damn it, woman, you're not going to. Don't talk about it."

"All right, after this I won't. But—there's an envelope on the stand there. Put it in your pocket."

I picked it up. "What is it?"

"A little of my hair I asked them to save. I didn't want to tell them what a sentimental fool I was, so I told them I wanted a sample so that in case my new hair grew in gray I could have it dyed to match what it had been. But I wanted it for you, Max. I want you to take it with you if you get to make that trip. I want part of me to go too, and I want you to leave it on—wherever you land, whichever moon of Jupiter. You don't think that's silly of me, do you, Max?"

I shook my head because I didn't quite trust my voice.

She said, "You see, darling, if I die, I want you to think of me when you're out there in space, rounding Jupiter. I want to be with you, as nearly as I can."

I said, "Ellen, you're going to live. Get that through your head. But whether you do or not, if I get away with that rocket you'll be with me on the trip every minute, every second, whether I'm awake or asleep. You'll be with me, Ellen, you'll be with me."

I still wanted to stay by the phone until Ellen was completely out of danger. So I had dinner sent up to my room again that evening, and some magazines to kill time until I felt ready to sleep again.

The evening passed slowly.

I went to bed and to sleep around midnight and the phone wakened me at three-fifteen in the morning.

Ellen, the phone told me, had just died.

I was sitting at a bar. There was a drink in my hands; they were shaking so badly I had to use both of them to hold it. I hadn't tasted the drink yet. I'd just picked it up.

I stared down into it.

I shouldn't taste it, I told myself. If, as I felt now, I took even a sip, I was gone. I'd take a second sip and a second drink, and.

Not this way out, this time. Not the little death of temporary oblivion, the familiar escape. Not this time.

I owed too much.

Ellen had given me too much. Her love. Her life. Our rocket. The rocket would be built now. It would go to Jupiter. But she had wanted me to build it, and she had wanted me to ride it if I could.

I couldn't let her down by starting to drink now at a time when starting to drink would mean keeping on drinking and would cost me everything that she had wanted me to have.

And besides, I suddenly remembered, I had promised. I had specifically promised Ellen that if she died I would not let her death do to me what, a moment ago, it had been about to do.

I put the glass back on the bar, and I walked out. I went back to my hotel, back to my room. It was midmorning, ten o'clock. I think I had walked all those hours since three-fifteen, until I had found myself about to drink and the finding had unnumbed my mind.

From my room I phoned Klockerman. I told him.

"My God, Max," he said. "What can I say?"

"Nothing," I said. "Don't try to. I just wanted you to know."

"I'll catch the next rocket back."

"Don't, Klocky," I said. "If it's the funeral you have in mind, she wouldn't want you there because she made me promise not to come to it. And if it's the port you mean, please don't. Let me get back to it and run it a while, for as long as you want to stay away."

"Are you sure that's what you want to do, Max?"

"It's what I've got to do. It's the only thing I can do, Klocky. I'm catching the next scheduled rocket back. I want to get back to work, to work like hell."

I never did find out whether Ellen's funeral was held in Washington or back in Los Angeles. I dived right into my job and worked myself crazy, read no newspapers, took sleeping pills every night to knock myself out until I could start working again the next day.

It was almost a month before I began to think clearly about anything except work, the work I'd been using as an anodyne, as a less harmful anodyne than alcohol.

The ache was still there; it would always be there. But I could think now despite it or around it. I began to want to see people again. M'bassi, Rory, Bill had all phoned me but I'd put them off. Klocky had been phoning weekly, ostensibly to check with me on how things went at the port, but actually just to talk to me, to see how I was doing and when I'd be ready to have him come back. The fourth time he called, about the middle of July, I told him, "Okay, Klocky. No hurry on my end, but come back any time you're ready." He said that was swell, that he'd take another two weeks and be back by the first of August.

M'bassi was out of town when I phoned him. The woman he roomed with said he'd gone to Tibet and would be back in another week or two. Rory was home when I phoned Berkeley that evening and sounded happy when I asked him if I might run up to see him and Bess over the coming week end.

Meanwhile, I decided, I'd better brief myself on what, if anything, had been happening on Project Jupiter. I stopped downtown on my way home from work that evening and picked up back copies of *The Times* and *The Herald* for the past month and took them home with me. After dinner I went through them.

The appointment of William J. Whitlow to the project directorship by the President had been announced three weeks before; confirmation of the appointment, without opposition, by the Senate only a week ago.

That was the extent of the news, but there'd been two Sunday supplement stories about the project, one with diagrams and drawings of the rocket that weren't too far off the track, the other quoting various astronomers and astrophysicists about what conditions would be found on the various Jupiter moons and which would be the best one for the ammonia pick-up landing. Also some wild guesses of the writers about what form intelligent life would take on Jupiter's moons if any of them held intelligent life. The usual crap.

I decided to phone Whitlow and ask him how soon things were going to get started, and then I reconsidered and decided to wait until Klocky was back; after that I could tell him I was ready to take off on an hour's notice any time he was ready for me.

Klocky got back two days early, rested up and ready to go. As soon as I was his assistant again, and expendable, I phoned Whitlow.

"William J. Whitlow speaking." A dry, pedantic voice.

"Max Andrews here," I said. "Just wondering when we're going to get started on Project Jupiter, when I should give notice here that I'm quitting."

There was a slight pause, not long enough to make me worry. Then he said, "There's no hurry, Mr. Andrews. The first steps are purely administrative and are being taken here in Washington. You aren't needed for them since your job will be the supervising of construction in the field. That will not start till next year."

"Why not?"

"Why *not?* Mr. Andrews, you do not seem to realize the complexities of organizing a project of this magnitude. The financial arrangements alone..." His voice trailed off as though he had decided explanation was hopeless.

"What financial arrangements?" I wanted to know. "Congress appropriated twenty-seven million dollars. The President signed the bill and made you director. Is the Treasury too broke to turn the money over to the project?"

"You are being facetious, Mr. Andrews. You know perfectly well that a government project takes time to get into operation."

"Yes, I do know. And I've always wondered why."

I could hear him sigh, over two thousand miles away.

He said, "My dear man, these things involve complicated procedures, very complicated procedures. Forms must be printed—"

"And tape must be dyed red, I suppose. But seriously, can't we get construction started before next year?"

"I am afraid not. In fact, if we get actual construction, past the drafting board stage, started *early* next year, we'll be doing very well indeed. Don't forget that approval of our plans must be obtained on three levels before we can even go to the drafting board."

I groaned. "All right, if it's early next year then it's early next year, but let's move it up if we can. In any case, let's not let it be any later than that. The job itself will take a full year."

"Longer that that, I am afraid."

"It can't take longer than that without overrunning our appropriation," I said. "The cost estimate was based on the job being done within a year. Listen, Mr. Whitlow, there are a lot of details I want to talk to you about—too many to discuss over the phone. How's about my coming to Washington some week end soon? When can you spare me an afternoon of your time?"

"Well—not this coming week end, or the next. The one after that?"

"If that's the soonest. All right, let's make it definite. To save me phoning you again. Time and place?"

"I don't ordinarily go to my office on Saturday, but I suppose I could."

I supposed he could, too; if I was coming all the way from Los Angeles to see him he could travel as far as his office to see me.

I said, "Your office, then. Or—wait, if I catch the early stratojet I'll get in just about noon. Why don't we meet somewhere for lunch, and then go on to your office after we've eaten."

"I already have a luncheon engagement for that day, Mr. Andrews. Can you be at my office at two?"

I told him I could be at his office at two.

Well, Ellen had warned me that he was a little stuffy, hadn't she? Not that I gave a damn about his stuffiness. What was getting me down was the terrific speed with which the Jupiter rocket was not taking off.

Well, I'd argue with him some more about that when I saw him. At least he hadn't shown any signs of forgetting his promise to make me his project supervisor.

Still the ache, still the empty feeling as though part of me, the most important part of me, was gone. But now, with Klocky back and the pressure of work off me at the port, it began to drive me to seek company instead of solitude. Some evenings with Klocky, sometimes playing chess, sometimes talking. We worked out a rough sketch and rough plans for a rocket that would make the round trip to Saturn, next from the sun after Jupiter. The mysterious ringed planet; we still didn't know much about those rings and wouldn't until we could observe them at close range. But Saturn, like Jupiter, has moons with ammonia on them, and the same general plan as that for the Jupiter trip could be used. Saturn's a lot farther than Jupiter but we were surprised and pleased to find that a Saturn rocket would cost only about three times as much as the Jupiter one—still peanuts compared to the three hundred million dollar estimate Bradly had made on the plans for the original Jupiter rocket, the step-rocket one. But Saturn would have to wait until the Jupiter rocket had made the round trip and proved itself a success.

The next week end, the one before my date with Whitlow, I flew to Seattle to spend a day with Merlene and Bill. It was good to see them again. Now, with Ellen dead, I'd probably never have a home of my own, and Bill's house would be as near to one as I'd ever know. God, I thought, if I only had a couple of kids like Easter and Billy, Jr. But it had been too late for that even when I'd met Ellen.

Or had it? Ellen, at forty-five, probably couldn't have had children, but if she'd lived and if she had felt about it as I did, we might have adopted one, maybe one about Billy's age. We weren't too old for that; Ellen at least would have lived to see him grow up.

I thought of trying to talk Bill and Merlene into moving to Los Angeles so I could see more of them and the kids, but I remembered that I'd be there myself only a few months longer, until I could get started on Project Jupiter. After that I'd be at the project site, wherever that would be. I wondered if it had been chosen yet and I made a mental note to ask Whitlow about it. If none had been arranged for, I'd be able to make some suggestions.

After dinner that evening Merlene took Easter upstairs first and I kidnapped Billy and took him out on the front porch in the early dark, with the stars just coming out. We sat on the steps and looked at them.

"Uncle Max."

"Yes, Billy."

"Have you got to a star yet?"

"No, kid. Nobody's got to a star yet. But we will. You want to get there, don't you?"

"Gee, sure. Like Rock Blake on the viddy. He gets to lots of them and has fights and everything. Only Daddy says that's fick-shun, it doesn't really happen."

"He means that it hasn't happened yet, Billy."

"And he says it's a punk, junky program for me to watch, but he lets me watch it. Do you think it's a punk, junky program?"

"I don't know, Billy. I've never watched it. But whether it's punky-junky or not, if watching it makes *you* want to go out to the stars like Rock Blake does, then it's a good program for you to watch."

"Gee, I think so too, Uncle Max. And the Captain Space program too. Gee, this afternoon he was fighting with green people with heads like lions on a plan-net of Sir—Sir—"

"Sirius?"

"That's it, Sirius. Do you think there are really green people like that up there?"

I grinned at him. "I'll show you where you can go to find out, Billy."

And I pointed out Sirius to him, the brightest star in the sky.

M'bassi got back the following Wednesday evening. I went to the field to meet his stratojet. I grinned at the way he towered over the other passengers walking up the ramp from the landing area. "Hi, Licorice Stick," I said.

He smiled and his big white teeth flashed. "Max. It is good to see you." Then his face sobered. "I heard the news, about Ellen. I cannot say how sorry I am."

We had a drink at the airport bar. Wine for M'bassi; he drinks only wine and in moderation. Then I suggested my apartment for a game of chess, and we went there.

We took off our coats, and through the almost transparent nylon shirt M'bassi wore I could see that he'd lost weight; his ribs stood out like the ridges of a washboard.

He guessed what I was thinking and smiled. "It is nothing, Max. A ten-day fast, but I ended it four days ago. I am beginning to regain. You've lost a little weight yourself, my friend."

I had, from hardly eating the first few weeks after Ellen's death. But I was beginning to regain now, too.

I got the chessboard and men and while M'bassi set them up I poured us each a small glass of sauterne to sip at while we played.

Pawn to the king's fourth, he moved. I reached for my king's pawn and then remembered.

"M'bassi," I said, "when I talked to Ellen in the hospital she said that even you had an interstellar drive, and that some time I should ask you what you were mystical about. What did she mean?"

"She spoke truly, Max. Our goals are the same. We travel different roads in trying to reach them."

"You mean you're a *starduster?* Why didn't you ever tell me?"

"You never asked me." He smiled gently. "And you would not understand my road because you call it mysticism and call me a mystic; and those words form a curtain through which you cannot see. To call the study of the spirit and its capabilities mysticism is to say that the body of a man is something which we are capable of understanding whereas the mind of man must ever be a mystery to us. And that is not true, my friend."

"But what's that got to do with getting to the stars?"

"Your plan for reaching the stars is to send your body there, causing your body to carry your spirit—I'll call it your mind, so you will not object to the terminology, my materialistic friend—along with it. Mine is to send my mind there, causing it to carry my body along."

I opened my mouth and shut it again.

M'bassi said, "The idea should not be new to you. You have read early science fiction, I know. Certainly you must have read Edgar Rice Burroughs, who wrote the stories of John Carter on Mars—*Princess of Mars,* I believe, was the first, and there were at least half a dozen sequels to it."

"I read them," I said. "They were Godawful tripe."

"If they were Godawful tripe why did you read them?"

"Because I read them before I was old enough to know how bad they were. While I was a kid. M'bassi, you're not trying to tell me you think those stories were *good* ones, are you?"

"No, I am not, Your estimate of their literary quality is, I will admit, entirely correct. But do you recall that there was one thing about them that distinguished them from all of the other early space stories?"

"Not offhand, M'bassi. What was it?"

"The method by which Burroughs' protagonist John Carter reached Mars. Do you remember that?"

I had to think hard—it had been damn near fifty years ago, back around nineteen fifty, that I'd read Burroughs.

I said, "I remember. He just looked up at Mars one night and wished he was there, and suddenly he was. Of all the—"

I started to laugh and made myself stop because I didn't want to hurt M'bassi's feelings.

"Laugh if you wish," M'bassi said. "It does sound funny if you put it that way. And certainly Burroughs' method was an oversimplification, but what if it was an oversimplification of something that will someday be possible for us to do? Let me translate into language that will not offend your materialism by calling it *teleportation,* the ability to transport a physical body through space without physical means."

"But there's been no authenticated case of teleportation, M'bassi."

"Nor has there been an authenticated case of travel by means of sub-space or a space-warp or any of the other shortcut methods science fiction writers have predicated to enable themselves to write about interstellar travel. But there is a considerable body of evidence in support of telekinesis, the ability of the mind to affect physical objects without physical means—to control dice, for example. Teleportation is merely an extension of telekinesis, Max. If one is possible then the other is."

"Maybe," I said. "I'll take rockets. I know rockets work."

"Rockets work. For planetary travel, they work. But for the stars, Max?"

"When we get the ion drive—"

"With any drive a rocket cannot even closely approach the speed of light. Unified field theory proves that, Max, no matter how mystical you think unified field theory is. And what of the stars that are hundreds of thousands of light years away? Are we going to take hundreds of thousands of years to reach them?"

He took a sip of his wine and put the glass back down. He said, "Thought is instantaneous, my friend. If we can learn to travel with the power of thought we then travel with the speed of thought, not like snails at the speed of light or less. If we solve the secret of teleportation, we can travel to the farthest galaxy in exactly the same length of time it would take us to travel a single inch."

The chess game stood forgotten, one pawn moved, for the rest of the evening while we talked. M'bassi told me about his trip to Tibet. It had been to see a famous *guru* there who was studying teleportation. He had studied and fasted with the *guru*.

"And did he teleport for you?" I asked.

"I—would rather not answer that question, Max. Something happened, or else I imagined that something happened, on the ninth day of our fast together. But hallucinations are common after extended fasting. The thing that happened, if it really happened, my *guru* was unable to repeat, so we have no proof and of what I am not certain myself that I really saw, I would rather not talk. You will forgive me?"

I damn well had to forgive him, because I couldn't talk him into changing his mind. The only other facts about it that I could get out of him were that on the tenth day of fasting the *guru* had become so weak that further abstinence became too dangerous for him and the experiment had ended.

"And he is a very old man, Max, one hundred and seven years old. It may be impossible for him ever to try again, in that manner. But if he does I shall have word from him and I shall go to him again immediately, even if I must spend all my life's savings on a chartered rocket to enable me to reach him in time."

I stared at him. "M'bassi, damn your beautiful jet hide, how could you possibly have not told me these things before I asked you? Look at all the time we've spent together and wasted playing chess or talking about unimportant things. Why didn't you tell me?"

"At first, Max, there was a reason. Ellen suggested it when she arranged for me to coach you in field theory. She said that if I let myself be drawn into arguments about interstellar travel, I'd get no coaching done. Since then—well, we had fallen into the habit of discussing other things and it did not occur to me to change things. And I knew that I could never bring you to my way of thinking any more than you can ever bring me to yours. Not that I disapprove of your way. I may be wrong, and your way of reaching the stars may be the only one we shall ever know."

He sighed. "I wish only that I had your faith. It is you, my friend, who of the two of us is a mystic."

And then Washington, D.C., two o'clock on Saturday afternoon, Whitlow's office. William J. Whitlow looked exactly as his voice had sounded over the phone. He was small, dapper, precise, stuffy. Middle aged, but old; he'd been born old, you could tell that by looking at him.

"When," I asked him first, "shall I give notice that I'm leaving the rocket port?"

"The first of the year would be a convenient time, Mr. Andrews," he said. He tented his fingers over the immaculate blotter on the desk in front of him and looked at me over them. "I could get you on the pay roll sooner, perhaps, but there is little if anything you can do until we're ready to start construction. And putting you on the pay roll sooner would not benefit you financially. As the project is set up your job will pay no more than you are undoubtedly earning as Mr. Klockerman's assistant meanwhile."

"I don't care about that," I said. "All I want is to get going on that damn rocket."

"We are setting up things as rapidly as we possibly can, I assure you. And once you start, there will be plenty of work for you to do. Perhaps—ah—this idea would appeal to you. I could put you on the pay roll as of, say, the first of November, and you could end your employment with the rocket port as of that date. But since there would be little or nothing you could do during those extra two months it would give you a chance to rest up, to take a vacation, as it were, on pay, before you would start—"

"I don't want a rest or a vacation," I cut in. "And I'm not in the slightest interested in getting on the pay roll before I can start building the rocket. Have you chosen a site yet?"

"No. I've been intending to ask your advice on it. Do you have any specific recommendation?"

"Not a specific one, but I'd suggest either New Mexico or Arizona. And the site should be within easy commuting distance of a fairly large city—Albuquerque, Phoenix, Tucson, El Paso—a city large enough to absorb all the workers on the project and provide living quarters for them without special construction. If we build out in the middle of nowhere, or even near a small town, we'll have to spend money building living quarters for a couple of hundred people, and that would take a big bite out of our budget. One that wasn't figured in."

He nodded. "That sounds sensible. Of the cities you mentioned, Albuquerque has one advantage over the others. It has the biggest stratojet port, with several scheduled flights a day to and from Washington. And I'll have to be going back and forth frequently, so that would be a considerable advantage."

"Good," I said. "Then we should give Albuquerque first choice. Besides, the government owns a lot of land around there and we might find something we can use without buying—not that it'll cost much if we have to buy. There's plenty of land around there too poor even to grow sagebrush; you can buy it for almost nothing. The one thing we'll want to watch out for is to find a good tract that's near a main highway, so we won't have to waste a lot of money on road building. Want me to look over some places on my way back? I'll have all day tomorrow and I might find something. If I do we can go ahead and sew it up and quit worrying about a site."

"If you would care to, certainly, Mr. Andrews. But—I'm afraid we haven't a setup yet to reimburse you for whatever expenses you incur."

"Don't worry about that. It's on my way back and stopping over won't cost enough extra to bother about. Okay, I'll do that and let you know if I find anything. And I'll give notice at the port that I'm leaving as of the end of the year. Anything else we ought to talk about now?"

There wasn't. All the talking we'd done could have been over the phone and much more cheaply. But I'd wanted to see Whitlow and size him up in person.

I wasn't impressed with him, but I was pleased. He wasn't the type of guy who'd get in my hair much once the thing was under way. I had a hunch he'd be spending most of his time in Washington, especially when he found out how damned hot it can get out on those badlands.

I flew to Albuquerque and got there by dusk. I checked in at a hotel that had hellie service and a landing field on the roof, and arranged to rent a hellie for the next day.

It was nearly noon when I found it. I knew at sight that it was perfect. I was flying south along the main highway, 85, about twenty-five miles south of Albuquerque, about five miles north of Belen.

It was to the left of the highway, not far back. An area flat as a lunar *mare*, about a quarter of a mile square, surrounded on all sides by low hills that would give it shelter from sand-laden winds.

A side road, two lane, already led back to it from the main highway and at the end of the road, the near side of the flat area, was a group of half a dozen buildings of assorted sizes. They looked deserted but not dilapidated. It would be almost too good to be true if that site was obtainable and the buildings already on it usable, even if they needed repairs and alterations.

I flew low and once around the perimeter. It was *fenced*, fenced with a high metal barrier just like a rocket launching area. But it hadn't been that; there weren't launching platforms.

The buildings looked like construction sheds, warehouses, one like a power station. I landed near the buildings and walked over. They weren't in as good shape as they'd looked to be from the air, but they weren't bad either; it would cost only a fraction as much to make them usable as it would cost to build new ones.

But what had this site been?

Suddenly it came back to me; I remembered. The G-station!

Remember? If you're old enough to remember the seventies you remember the plans for the G-station and the wide publicity it got.

A super-luxury space station to be put in the seven hundred mile orbit by a cartel of the biggest of the gambling syndicates, a super-duper gambling club for millionaires who wouldn't mind a thousand dollar ferry charge to get up to it for an evening's recreation.

The gamblers had already thrown a few million bucks into the project, in acquiring this site and putting up these buildings for constructing the ferry rockets that would put the space station up in its orbit piece by piece and which would later be converted into passenger ferries to bring up the customers.

They'd just started the first rocket when the crackdown came, when the Harris-Fenlow bill broke the gambling syndicates, and broke a lot of the gamblers too. The project folded before a single rocket had been finished.

But God what a break for Project Jupiter! Why hadn't I thought of this? Why hadn't *someone* thought of it?

Here was at least a two million dollar saving for us in money, not to mention the saving in time in having our site leveled and fenced, our buildings already built and needing only repair.

And either the federal government or the State of New Mexico must own it, on tax foreclosure. It was a thousand to one that no one had kept up taxes on it for over twenty years.

What a break for Project Jupiter.

I spent a couple of hours walking around, looking around. The buildings were all boarded up tightly and nailed shut but I could get a good enough idea of them from the outside, and I got more and more excited at the idea.

I flew back to Albuquerque and parked my hellie on the roof without turning it in, went down to my room and started phoning. A helpful long distance operator got me Governor Romero at his home just north of Santa Fe at Tesuque. He said yes, the state owned the old G-station site. And yes, he'd give me a little time to talk to him about it if I flew up right away. Yes, there was a field adjacent to his home where a hellie could land; he gave me instructions how to find it.

Half an hour later I was talking to him in person; an hour and a half later I was back at the hotel and had Whitlow on the phone to tell him about it.

"Governor Romero thinks it's a wonderful idea," I told him. "It'll take an act of the legislature so he can't make a definite promise, but he says he feels sure we can lease it for free, or for a purely nominal rental, for as long as we need it. Jupiter Project'll bring quite a few millions into the state that gets it and I hinted that if we didn't get the G-station site we'd probably take a site we were considering in Arizona, near Phoenix."

"A good point, Mr. Andrews. A very good point. And you might also have reminded him of the fact that the property, when we turn it back to him after the project is finished, will be considerably more valuable than it is now because of the repairs, renovations and additional construction we'll put on it."

"I did," I said. "Although the only new construction we'll need is the launching platform, and maybe a crane or two. They didn't get as far as cranes or launching platforms. But there's at least as much building and office space as we'll need."

"It sounds very attractive, Mr. Andrews. I'll look into it. Some time within the next month I'll fly out there and make a personal inspection. If it even approximates what you say it is, I'll get in touch with Governor Romero and make the formal application for a lease."

"Why not strike while the iron is hot? Write him airmail tomorrow and make the request formal, so he can go to work on the legislature while he's enthusiastic himself. Nominal rental means a dollar a year. If we get the lease before you make a personal inspection and then you decide I gave you a bum steer, I'll pay the dollar. So what have you got to lose?"

"Perhaps you have a point there, since it may be at least a month before I can find time for a personal inspection. However, I prefer to wait to write to the governor until I have a full report and description of the property from you, in writing. Will you send me such a report after your return to Los Angeles?"

I told him I would, but I did better.

There were still several hours of daylight left. First, I had the manager of the hotel recommend a good private detective and had the switchboard operator get him for me. I told him I wanted a legal description of that property and wanted it right away—I knew Whitlow well enough by now to know that he wouldn't make a move until he had a *legal* description of the property—and that I didn't care how he got it. I told him this was his bailiwick and not mine and that if he didn't know where such things were kept he could find out. And that if he didn't know whose palm to grease to get access to such records on a Sunday afternoon he could find that out too. All I wanted was that legal description, right away.

Then I rented a big fancy job of an Instaprint camera and hellied out to the G-station site again and took pictures, lots of them. Half a dozen from the air, at different heights and angles. Close and distant shots of the various buildings, the fence, the road, from the ground.

It was just getting dark when I got back. The detective was waiting for me. He'd done better than copying off the bare legal description; he'd worked as fast as I had. He had photostats of the tax liens and the foreclosure papers. A plat map with the property marked off on it; it included, I was pleased to learn, quite a bit of extra surrounding land besides the fenced in area, including almost a mile of frontage on the highway. And best of all he had construction plans of the buildings, showing interior layout. My photographs hadn't been really necessary, except insofar as they showed present condition.

A good man, that detective. I not only paid him off; I took him to dinner with me. I'd skipped lunch in the excitement and I was plenty hungry by then.

After dinner I got myself a public stenographer and dictated a full report, including details of my conversation with Governor Romero, to go with the documents and photographs.

I checked Washington-bound stratojets while she typed, and when she'd finished and we'd made the works into an impressive sized package, I got it to the jetport in time to make the stratojet that took off at nine-forty. I put special delivery stamps on it, sent it to Whitlow's home address.

I grinned to myself, wondering what Whitlow would think when that completely documented report woke him up in the middle of the night, only hours after he suggested that I send it, presumably at my leisure, after my return to Los Angeles. Well, he'd have no excuse now for not writing to Romero the first thing in the morning.

I'd missed the last jet for Los Angeles, but that didn't matter. The first one in the morning would get me there in time if I went right to my job instead of going home first.

Before I went back to the hotel and to bed, I had myself a drink; I thought I'd earned it.

Project Jupiter was looking up. Unless Whitlow muffed the ball, and I didn't see how he could or why he would, Project Jupiter had a site, and to me, a site was a start.

M'bassi lived in the Hollywood slums, in one of those hideous dozen-story apartment buildings on Sunset. Dark, gloomy hallways and an old rattling elevator instead of a tube. The whole third floor, about sixteen rooms, had once been a single palatial apartment, now rented and sublet by a strange woman whose grandmother had been a movie star and who lived in the glory of the past, when Hollywood had been a fabulous place instead of a tenderloin. But once you were inside the four connected rooms at the back which M'bassi rented from her, you forgot about the district you were in.

The big main room was completely oriental, beautifully furnished and ornamented with things he'd brought back from his various trips to China. It was a room as exotic as his study was utilitarian—a medium sized room lined on all sides from floor to ceiling with shelves of books and, besides them, containing only a chair and a desk. Another room combined the functions of bedroom and kitchen. The fourth room was tiny and contained absolutely no furniture at all, not even carpeting. It was the monastic cell in which M'bassi did his meditating and thinking.

Over the soft background music—Scriabin this evening—that M'bassi loved to have going while we talked, M'bassi was answering my questions, or trying to.

"*How* does one teleport himself? Max, Max, if I knew that, do you think I would be here?"

"But damn it, M'bassi, you're trying to learn how to do it; you must know how you go about *trying.*"

"A thousand ways. All difficult to explain to someone who has not studied the field. Could you explain, to someone who knew absolutely nothing of physical science, how a rocket works?"

"Certainly I could, in a general way. Atomic energy turns liquid into a gas under high pressure which shoots out of the back of the rocket and pushes it."

"Now explain to me how a space-warp drive works."

"You know, damn it, we haven't got a space-warp drive yet. But we'll get one."

"And you know equally well that I cannot yet teleport myself. So how can I tell you how it is done?"

"What makes you think it can *be* done?"

"There are two reasons why I think it can be done, Max. One is that it is only a logical extension of the already proved and accepted telekinetic powers of the mind. The other reason is that I believe teleportation has happened. Three people whom I know and trust, under whom I have studied, have experienced it in one form or another. They have succeeded in teleporting themselves, but only—how shall I say it?—without fully knowing how they did it, without being able to repeat the act at will, without finding the key. No matter how closely they tried to reproduce the exact mental and physical conditions that existed at the time of their successful teleports, they were unable to repeat."

"Are they *sure* they did it the first time?"

"Is one ever sure of anything, my friend? There is always the possibility that one is hallucinating or otherwise mistaken. Are you sure that I am here, talking to you now?"

"But you believe they really teleported?"

"I do. For instance, the *guru* with whom I spent time, under whom I studied, this summer in Tibet, tells me he is certain that he has teleported twice. He is an honest man."

"Let's grant that. Tell me why you think he isn't a mistaken one."

"Because he is a wise man, wise enough to have taken precautions against self-delusion. He told me the precautions he had taken and I believe them sufficient."

"Do you take precautions when you experiment, M'bassi?"

"Of course. Otherwise how would I know that I succeed, if I do succeed? If I am experimenting in the room you call my monk's cell, I lock the door on the inside; that lock can be worked only from the inside. Suppose I succeed—find myself elsewhere. In this room for example. I return and see if that door is still locked from the inside. If it is, then I could not possibly have let myself out, somnambulistically, walked into this room and awakened here."

"You'd have to break the door down to get back in the cell."

"It would be worth it, would it not?"

I said, "I guess it would. But listen, what's fasting got to do with teleportation?"

"The body, Max, affects the mind in various ways. Food or the lack of it, overweariness, stimulants and depressants, all these things and many others affect our ability to think and our manner of thinking. For many centuries wise men—and some stupid men as well—have known that fasting can bring clarity of thought, sometimes vision."

"And sometimes visions, otherwise hallucinations. So can alcohol. I've seen—well, never mind things I've seen a time or two. But I'm sure they weren't there."

"True. Yet, Max, at just a certain stage of intoxication have you never had the feeling that you were just on the *verge* of understanding something of vast importance, of— You know what I mean."

"Damn right I know what you mean," I said. "But it's always the verge; you never cross the verge."

"Is it not possible that under special conditions one might? Although I believe there is more hope in drugs than in alcohol. I intend to experiment with drugs soon."

"You've already experimented with alcohol?"

"Yes. And with smoking opium. I believe I came closer with opium."

"That's dangerous experimenting, M'bassi."

"Rockets are safe?" He smiled as I involuntarily looked down at my prosthetic leg. He said, "Max, I know you'd take *any* chance to get somewhere you want to go. Why shouldn't I?"

That night I went home with an armful of books from M'bassi's library, ones he said were elementary ones.

They weren't elementary to me. They were gibberish as far as I was concerned. At three o'clock in the morning I gave up and went to sleep. M'bassi could try his methods; I'd have to stick to mine. I was too old a dog to learn such new tricks.

Besides, although I hoped M'bassi had something and I respected him for trying, I couldn't quite believe it.

Project Jupiter, Project Saturn, Project Pluto, Project Proxima Centauri—that was for me. The one-fold path, not the eight-fold path.

In October Project Jupiter was in the news again. It had leased the old G-station rocket construction and launching site from the State of New Mexico.

It was in the news just briefly on the Wednesday when it was announced but the Sunday papers and roundup-casts gave it a big play, reviving in some detail the story of the G-station's fall from space before it had risen there. There were photographs with some of the stories and I recognized two of them as ones I'd taken from the hellie. I got a credit line on them, "Foto: Max Andrews," but no mention in the story. On the other hand Whitlow was mentioned only incidentally as director of the project; he hadn't given me credit for the idea of using the G-station, but he hadn't claimed it for himself either. That was all right for publicity. The main thing was that Whitlow hadn't muffed the ball.

Project Jupiter had a home.

It wouldn't be long now, and once the project got started I'd be working on it about twenty-four hours a day and that would be good for me, very good for me.

Not that things were too bad now, except for my impatience. I was coming to accept my loss of Ellen and in that acceptance finding that, in a sense, it brought her back to me. Because I could now think about her and remember her with less pain, she was more constantly with me than before, while bitterness and pain had clouded my thoughts and warped my thinking. Now, sometimes, I even talked to her; imaginary conversations, not aloud. I could go to her now, in my mind, for help and comfort when I needed them. And at times I could even think of her as though we were merely temporarily apart, as when she'd been in Washington and I in Los Angeles; think of her as though she was still alive and waiting for me somewhere. And in a sense she was; she lived in my memory and would live there as long as I myself lived.

Even her death, I was learning, could not take her away from me completely. And with that knowledge came peace.

November, getting near December. I began to get impatient to get going on that project. I thought, surely by now things in Washington are shaping up to the point where there are discussions going on, plans being made, that I ought to be in on. So I wouldn't be on the pay roll until the first of the year, but to hell with that if I could be helping get things started.

I asked Klocky if I'd be leaving him in a jam if I left sooner than the notice I'd given.

He laughed at me. "What the hell makes you think you're indispensable? I've known you were leaving the first of the year anyway; I've been getting Bannerman ready to take over your job. Damn it, Max, you've been disappointing me the last month or so, up to now. I thought you'd be heading there even sooner. What's been holding you down?"

"Damned if I know," I said. "Maybe the thought that I'd get there and find nothing to do. That'd be worse than sitting it out here."

"If there's nothing you can do, come back. How's about doing it this way? I'll give you a leave of absence—let's see, today's Wednesday—for the rest of this week. Fly to Washington and beard Whitlow in his den, find out if there's anything you can start doing. If there is, call me up and quit. If there isn't, come back and start in again next Monday, work another month, or however long it's going to be."

"Klocky, you're a swell guy."

He snorted. "You're just finding that out? What are you going to do about your apartment, though? And your books and your tapes and stuff?"

I hadn't thought of it. I groaned a little, suddenly realizing how much junk I'd accumulated in the last two years. "Damn if I know," I said, "about the books and stuff. There's no problem about the apartment; I've already given notice for the end of the year and paid up till then."

"Give me a key, Max. I'll take care of it, have the stuff sent to you at Washington. Or Albuquerque, if you want to wait for it until you're working at the site."

I breathed a sigh of relief. "Swell," I said. "Listen, I won't want it in Washington; I know that. And if I'm not going to be in Albuquerque until after the rent runs out, just send a moving company around to crate the stuff and hold it in storage."

"How's about the telescope? It still up on the roof?"

I nodded. "I'll bring it down this evening. And I'd better either leave a note or tag stuff, so the movers'll know which stuff is mine. Otherwise they might miss something, like those Bonestell originals."

"Don't worry about that, Max. I know which stuff is yours and I'll supervise the crating. Good idea, though, to bring the telescope down off the roof. Why not do it this afternoon, though? You can catch the late afternoon jet for Washington, be there this evening ready for a good start tomorrow morning."

"You mean you don't mind if I take off right now?"

"Hell, no." He looked at his watch. "It's twenty of twelve. Start your leave as of noon, twenty minutes from now. Just time for you to have a stirrup cup with me."

He flicked the switch of the intercom that put him through to his secretary. "Dotty," he said into it, "don't let anybody in here for twenty minutes. We're going to be doing something strictly against the rules. Don't even put through a phone call for that long. If anybody calls, tell him I'm out."

He flicked the switch again, and then took a bottle and glasses out of the bottom drawer of his desk. He poured us drinks and handed me mine.

"To Jupiter, Max."

We drank. Then he looked at me and for God's sake there was mist in his eyes. His voice was quiet. "Do you think you'll make it, Max?"

I hadn't told him. He'd guessed, as Ellen had. He knew me too.

I said, "I think there's a chance, Klocky."

"Jesus but I envy you that chance, Max. No matter how slim it is. I'd give everything I've got—"

He refilled our glasses.

I packed two suitcases, enough stuff to last me for a couple of months if I had to be in Washington that long before I could get going on the site.

I dismounted the telescope, brought it down and disassembled it ready for crating.

Bad, I thought, looking around me, that I'd accumulated so much. A man should never own more stuff than he can carry in his hands at a dead run. It was bad, but it had happened.

Stratojet to Washington. Helicab to a hotel, and by then it was evening. I considered calling Whitlow at his home, but decided against it.

Tomorrow, in his lair.

I turned in early and got a good long night's sleep.

Thursday, nine. Whitlow, William J. Whitlow, my master Whitlow, behind that big mahogany desk, looking at me across it. Then staring down to doodle with a ball-point pen on a block of foolscap.

Saying, "I'm sorry you came, Mr. Andrews."

Not ready for me yet, damn him. I said, "I don't give a damn about the pay. There must be *something* I can start doing."

"It isn't that. I wrote you a letter yesterday. I'm sorry, for your sake, that you came before you received it."

For Christ's sake, for my sake. Did the bastard mean—? Would I hit him, beat him to a pulp with my fists, or get my suddenly aching hands around that fat neck and strangle him, which?

"Your appointment was to have been announced soon. Naturally though, Mr. Andrews, we made a routine investigation of your qualifications. And when the report came in— Naturally, in view of my promise to Senator Gallagher, and of President Jansen's own recommendation of you, I consulted him and he fully agrees with me that—"

I knew, I remembered, I realized, and I died again, and Whitlow wasn't there any more, no face to beat, no neck to strangle, just a Voice, a gray voice out of grayness.

And the Voice was saying it. The Voice was saying "...do not know whether you are a psychopathic liar or whether you thought you could get away with a fraudulent claim, but in either case..."

The Voice was saying, "...true that you graduated from space school as you claimed, in nineteen sixty-three, but the accident that cost you a leg was on Earth, shortly after you graduated, and not on Venus. And because of it you never left Earth, not even as far as the moon, not even as far as a space station."

The Voice said, "I cannot understand, Mr. Andrews, in view of your other qualifications, why you made such ridiculous claims in the face of fact, because they would have been unnecessary. Your degree in rocket engineering, your responsible position at the Los Angeles Rocket Port, despite how recent both of them are, would have fully qualified you for the job, which after all is the construction of a rocket and not the piloting of one.

"But the President agrees with me fully—and so, I am certain, would Senator Gallagher had she known the facts—that your making claims to have been in space when you have not is indicative either of basic dishonesty or of psychopathic tendencies, and in either case..."

The Voice said, the Voice said.

There was a bar and there were other bars, and then I was in a hotel room with a bottle part full and another bottle empty, and the room was gray as Whitlow's office had been gray, and Ellen was there with me although I could not see her through the grayness.

"Darling," I was telling her, "darling, it's true, I know it's true, what the Voice said and is saying, but I want you to understand that I didn't *mean* to deceive you, I didn't *mean* to lie to you. And that I knew that I was lying and yet I didn't know, because I'd been lying to others and to myself so long that—that—"

"You don't have to explain, Max. I understand."

"But Ellen, *I* don't understand. Am I mad, or was I mad? How can a man come to believe something that he knows is a lie? And at the same time not believe it, know that it is a lie, but that it is a lie he has told others and himself for so long that he has forgotten, that he has accepted—"

I said, "Ellen, I must have been mad, insane, after that accident that kept me out of space just when I was on the threshold of it. It was an hour, darling, *only an hour,* before what would have been my first trip into *space.* A month out of school and my first trip came up, and it happened just like I told it to you except that the rocket was getting ready to take off to Venus instead of from Venus back to Earth.

"To Venus, I was going to Venus. Not just to the moon like most first trips, but to another planet, to Venus. And then the accident—and it wasn't the pain or the physical shock; it was the shock of learning that I was Earth-bound, that I'd never leave Earth, never be a real spaceman.

"And the years, the long years. and the fantasy building up in my mind, my mind not able to take the knowledge that I'd come so close to space and missed by a single hour, a single accident that wasn't my fault.

"I was space-nutty, darling. It was too much to take. I still don't know whether I became a psychopath or a fraud. I don't know, maybe something of both. But I didn't mean to lie to *you.* To myself, to others, it didn't matter. But I should never have lied to you."

"I understand, Max. I would have understood then."

"But since I did lie to you, thank God you didn't find out that I was lying. Don't tell me that you could have loved me still had you learned that I was a fraud. Thank God you never learned."

Her hand on my face. Or a curtain blowing?

"Max, I would have loved you still. I would have believed in you still. It wasn't your fault, Max, that you didn't leave Earth. You tried. And kept trying, all your life."

"Not always, darling. At times—always at times like this when I've known, when I've remembered—I've drunk, like I'm drinking now. For bitter weeks, even months, when I've been sane, when the curse of clarity is upon me and I know myself for what I am. Dozens of times, darling, like this time. I was pulling out of one of them, staying in Seattle with Bill and Merlene, when I first heard of you, when I heard you were going to send a rocket farther out, and I came to help you send it."

"And we've sent it, Max. Don't ever forget, that's our rocket, and it's going out, it's going whether you help build it or whether you ride it. A rocket farther out,

Max, a rocket to Jupiter, and it would not be going there—not for another decade anyway—if it had not been for *you*. Isn't that enough for one man, one lifetime?"

"No," I said. "The rocket's going, but I'm not."

"Max, put your arms around me, find comfort in me."

I sought her in the grayness and she wasn't there, she was dead and she wasn't there, she wouldn't be there ever again and I could never find comfort in her again. Ellen, beloved, you are dead and your voice is in my mind and only in my mind.

Other rooms, a room with hideous big purple flowers in the wallpaper. And in it I had the dream that always led into the nightmare, the dream and the nightmare that I hadn't had for years now. The nightmare the same, as always; the dream that led to it varied a little each time.

This time, of course, Ellen was in it. We were both young, about the same age, and it was back in the early sixties; I'd graduated from space school and I was a spaceman ready for my first trip out; we were to be married after my return from that first trip.

I was kissing Ellen good-by and then she wasn't there any more and I was helping ready the big beast—we called rockets beasts in those days—and with a rag in my pocket I was climbing the outside rings because from inside I had noticed that the forward observation port had a dead gnat stuck on it. Our rise through the atmosphere would probably get it off but there'd be a smear left, and I didn't want to have to look at a smear all the way to Venus. I was going to wipe it off and polish that port.

And then the sudden roaring sound and agonizing pain, and without transition the nightmare. I was in a white room, a hospital room. A doctor had the covers folded back from the foot of the bed, doing something down there, changing a dressing.

I raised my head and looked down.

And went into the frozen moment that lasted an eternity, as it always did.

I woke up trembling, soaking wet with sweat.

I got out of there, out of that room with the purple flowers in the wallpaper. Because there'd be no more sleep for me that night, little sleep for nights to come. Once the nightmare had started, it would be there waiting for me, just past the edge of unconsciousness. That frozen instant that lasted till the end of time, waiting for me. Only complete and utter exhaustion could carry me safely past it.

Streets and joints. A bar and a jukebox that was playing the Cuban quarter tone stuff Ellen and I had loved in Havana.

And the Voice. Over the music the Voice. "Cannot understand, Mr. Andrews, in view of your other qualifications, why you made such ridiculous claims in the face of fact, because they would have been unnecessary. Your degree in rocket engineering, your responsible position..."

Every word I remembered, every word ran through my head in quarter tones to Cuban rhythms.

"Afraid I can't sell you any more, pal. Might cost me my license, pal. You're pretty drunk."

Not drunk enough, pal, not drunk enough.

Over street noises, the Voice. Over other voices, over the whirring whirling of the Earth in space, the Earth my spaceship carrying me even now through the void but to nowhere, until some day it would be my revolving coffin.

Snow and gay decorations and somebody saying Merry Christmas to you, my buying someone a drink, his buying back, his face coming suddenly into focus. Guy about fifty, with a beautiful-ugly face, broken nose, wide clear eyes, eyes that had seen the naked stars, the stars from space, steady and untwinkling. A spaceman.

He said, "You'd better straighten out, matey, before it gets you down for keeps. Anything I can do?"

"I'm not your matey. I'm not a spaceman."

"Don't gimme. You're Max Andrews."

"I'm Max No Difference," I said. "I'm a fake. I'm not anybody."

"Matey, I know you. You're the best mech in the game, and you're a spaceman." He leaned forward and his eyes, those wide clear eyes, got bright. "Listen, matey, things have looked lousy for a while, but they're looking up again. We're sending one farther out. To Jupiter."

"The hell we are," I said. "Listen, you got me mixed with somebody else. I never heard of a Max Andrews."

He said, "If you want it that way."

"It *is* that way."

I woke from the nightmare of the frozen instant again and sat up, struggling into awakeness to dispel the spell.

A hotel room again, but no purple flowers. A bigger room, a nicer room, with two beds. And my friend of last night, the spaceman whose name I didn't know, sleeping in the other bed. He'd brought me here to pull me out of it.

But not yet, not yet.

Necessity gave me the steadiness to dress very quietly, making not a single sound, so as not to waken him.

I didn't want to argue with him, because he was right. He was a good guy, this spaceman who knew me but whom I didn't know or didn't remember, and he'd brought me here to help me. He was right by his standards and his standards were right for him, but they weren't right for me because I was wrong. I was wrong and I wouldn't be right until this ran its course, if it ever did.

But how could I explain to him? How can you show someone else your nightmares?

I checked money in my wallet. Plenty of it. I must have wired back for some, got some somehow. I took out enough to pay for the room and left it on the dresser, and I got out of there quickly and quietly.

I needed a drink worse than I needed anything else, except maybe to die and get it over with, and my friend probably had a bottle there somewhere, knowing I'd need at least a pickup shot in the morning. But it was hidden and I didn't dare search for it. Spacemen, even ex-spacemen, are always light sleepers.

Eight o'clock in the morning, but I found a liquor store open.

Other bottles, other rooms. Day and night and crowds and solitude. Bars and drinks and a fight, blood on my face and on my knuckles.

Devils and a cold wind, and phantoms of the living and dead. Arguing with my father, with Bill, pleading with Ellen.

"Darling, darling, you understand, don't you? I've got to do this, I've got to let it run its course, I can't stop now. Even if this is the big one, the last one, I've got to ride it through."

Ellen didn't argue about the drinking; she understood.

Sometimes in semi-sober moments I wondered whether she would have, really.

But the dead must understand everything if they understand anything at all.

And one night, one unexpected night, street noises again and cheerful voices, happy voices.

People laughing, people blowing horns, people celebrating.

Suddenly more noises, crescendo.

Sirens and whistles, bells ringing. Bells tolling.

Somebody yelling at me, and the words came through, *Happy New Year.*

The bells and the sirens and the whistles and the yelling and the crowds and a big clock beginning to toll *bong, bong, bong.*

Suddenly it came to me what this was. Not just another damn new year after another Christmas; it was more than that. It came to me through the noise, through the gently falling snow, this is the turn of the century and the turn of the millennium, Jesus God, this isn't just another year, this is the year two thousand, the year *two*

2000

thousand! Something to celebrate, something really to celebrate! Yell Happy New Year, Happy New Millennium. A bar with people crowding up to it three and four deep. I tried to push my way in, couldn't. Drinks being passed back. Somebody had an extra one in his hand, looking around for someone he'd been with. He shrugged, handed me the drink. "Luck, Old-timer!"

Buying drinks for others, being bought drinks, caught in the frantic frenetic gaiety of a *fin de siècle,* the manic madness of a *fin de mille.* Back-slapped and slapping backs, shaking hands meaninglessly, in and out of focus. Then the crowd thinning, melting away, the last of us put out at closing hour, out into the night, now a windless night, cold, clear and still.

Staggering away somewhere, up streets and down streets, across turf in what seemed to be a park.

A bridge over a pool, over a still dark pool.

I staggered onto the bridge, stood looking down over the low railing into the black water, the water so still and so black that I could see the stars reflected in it, gently dancing, light years below the still dark surface. Water in which life developed, the water wherein we were born and grew and whence we crawled out into air and onto land and looked up with animal eyes, seeing lights in the sky. Now drunkenly watching lights in water, the reflected stars.

I was falling toward the sky, toward the stars.

The white room again, but this time not a nightmare, just a dream. Or was it even that? Someone was bending over me, someone with chestnut hair. But my eyes and my mind came in focus and it wasn't Ellen. It was a nurse, white-uniformed, with chestnut hair the shade of Ellen's, but not Ellen.

Her voice wasn't Ellen's voice and it wasn't speaking to me. "I believe he's conscious, Dr. Fell."

Dr. Fell; it rang a bell; I do not like you, Dr. Fell. How did that ancient rhyme go? *I do not like you, Dr. Fell. The reason why, I cannot tell. But this I know and know right well: I do not like you, Dr. Fell.*

The nurse had stepped back and I turned my head and could see him. A big man with iron gray hair and clear gray eyes, a face that, except for the broken nose, looked a lot like the face of the spaceman who'd taken me to the hotel.

"Up to talking?" he asked me. His voice was deep, resonant; the voice of a man you could have confidence in.

I said, "I think I like you, Dr. Fell."

He grinned at me. "All of my patients think of that damn rhyme, one way or the other. I should have changed my name." He said, over his shoulder, "You may go now, Miss Dean."

To me, "How are you feeling?"

"I don't know yet. Was anything wrong with me, outside of—?"

"Exposure, pneumonia, malnutrition, delirium tremens. That's about all. Do you remember what happened?"

"I remember falling into a pool. That's all. Did I get out by myself?"

"You crawled out, yes. It was only a foot deep. But you lay there near the edge, wet and freezing, for God knows how long before anybody found you. But I'll tell you one thing; if it had been even half an hour longer, you wouldn't be here. And another thing—one more drinking bout like that one will be your last, even if you don't fall into anything. Do you understand that?"

"Yes," I said.

"Luckily for you, you're not an alcoholic, so I don't have to warn you against doing normal, social drinking—after you're up to it again. But another extended drinking bout—"

I said, "I understand. How do you know I'm not an alcoholic?"

"From your brother and from a friend of yours, Mr. Klockerman. They've both been here. Your brother's still around; he'll be back during visiting hours this afternoon."

"You mean they both came all the way here from the coast? Or—wait, am I still in Washington?"

"This is Denver. You're at the Carey Memorial Hospital in Denver."

"How long have I been here? What's the date?"

"You've been here eleven days. You were brought in at five A.M. on New Year's day, and it's now January 11th, a Tuesday."

"What year?" I just wanted to hear him say it.

He looked at me strangely and then from the way he spoke, he must have got the idea.

"Two thousand," he said. "The year two thousand."

The new millennium, I thought, when I was alone again. The twenty-first century, in the third millennium.

The future. I'd always thought of two thousand as the future. When I was in my teens back in the nineteen fifties, it had been the unbelievably distant future, a date so far ahead that it didn't mean anything.

Here it was. Here it was and I was in it.

And here and now I had to make peace with myself if I was to keep on living in it. I had to make myself face the truth, and face it without concealment and without bitterness. With not too much bitterness, anyway.

I must recognize that I was getting old, too old ever to get out into space, not even to the planets, that I'd had my chance and missed when I was young, that I'd had a miraculous second chance—no matter how slim a chance—in my late fifties, and I'd missed that too. And I was practically sixty now, and there wouldn't be another chance. So what? Lots of people are space-nutty all their lives and never even come close. They keep on living, don't they?

Accept that, I told myself, and you'll be all right from here on in. Nothing really bad can ever happen to you again, because you'll never come close again, to be disappointed. Nor will you ever love again, as you loved Ellen; if nothing so wonderful as her love can ever happen to you again, then neither can anything so terrible as her death.

Remember, never forget, that you've never left Earth and that you never will. Remember that, and it's a downhill coast.

You expected too much. More for yourself than one man has any right to hope for. And you expected mankind to accomplish more in your lifetime than you had any right to hope for.

He'll reach the stars, and in this millennium. Where was he at the start of the last millennium, the year *one* thousand? Fighting mistaken crusades with swords and spears and bows and arrows. And before the end of that millennium he'd left the Earth and reached the nearest planets.

And where will he be before the end of *this* millennium?

No, you won't see it. But you're *part* of it, as you're part of mankind, and you can help. For as long as you live, you can help push, since you can't ride. You can help push rockets and men toward the stars.

The chestnut-haired nurse brought my lunch and I found that I was pretty weak, but able to feed myself and to eat a little.

When she took the tray away I asked her when visiting hours were, wondering if I'd have time for a nap before Bill came. But there was only half an hour, so I didn't.

I thought about M'bassi instead. Chang M'bassi.

What if he and not I had the right idea? Well, it was possible. Nothing is impossible. Who, here and now, can define the limitations of the human mind, the things man may be able to do now or eventually with that wonderful and mysterious thing that is his mind?

Who, here and now, knows even the exact relationship between mind and matter? A man is a chunk of matter in which is imprisoned a mind, and when either dies—I think—the other dies with it. But the body can move the mind, and who am I to say that, now or eventually, the power of the mind cannot carry the body, and with the speed of thought.

If that's the right road, I thought, more power to M'bassi and may he be the one to find the road and take at least a step along it.

But it's not for me. I'd be kidding myself if I even tried it, and I've kidded myself enough. Rockets are my racket, and I'll stick to them. And settle for pushing them, improving them.

Bill said, "Hiya, Max. Glad to see you're back with us."

I shook hands with him and said, "All the way back, Bill." He'd know what I meant by that, and he'd know he could quit worrying about me, if he'd been worrying.

He pulled up a chair.

I said, "Let's get details over with first. How am I set for money? Who's paying for this?"

"You're all right. Kiockerman's got your stuff—he's holding it for you—and he checked your bank book and says there's enough left to pay your full bill here and get you back again."

"Did he check with the bank to see whether—?"

"Sure. You'd wired them for money twice and they'd sent it, but that's figured in. Oh, by the time you get back to work you may owe one or the other of us a couple of hundred or so, but nothing enough to worry about."

"Good," I said. "Another thing. I talked to Fell, but forgot to ask him how much longer I'd have to stay here. Has he told you?"

"Checked with him on my way in just now. He says about ten more days and you'll be able to travel, but that you shouldn't go back to work for at least a month after that. Will you come and stay with us in Seattle? Merlene and the kids'll be crazy to have you, and so will I."

"I—do I have to decide that right now, Bill?"

"Of course not. I didn't mean to push you. And I ought to tell you you've got alternatives. Klocky, M'bassi and Rory have all put in bids for you. You've got some swell friends, Max."

"And swell relatives, Bill." I turned and looked at him squarely. "Listen, Bill," I said. "In case I do decide to come to Seattle there's one thing I want to talk out with you first, and while we're alone."

"Shoot."

"It's about Billy. Do you mind if I—" I'd started to say, *if I try to give him the Dream,* but that wouldn't be Bill's language. "Do you mind if I talk space to him, try to make a starduster out of him?"

"Merlene and I have talked that over," he said quietly. "And the answer is no, we don't mind. It's up to Billy what he wants to do and be." He grinned suddenly. "Unless he changes when he grows up, he won't *need* any pushing from you. He's almost as bad as you used to be, Max."

"Good," I said. "In that case, Bill, I'll probably spend part of that month's rest-up with you. Not the first two weeks, probably, because I'll be—well, the second two weeks, when I'm stronger, will be better for me to be with the kids. They're pretty strenuous for an old man, when he's down."

"Great. I'll tell Merlene we'll have you the second two weeks. About the others, know yet who you want to spend time with first? I can let him know for you and save you writing."

"No, I haven't decided yet. But I'll appreciate it if you'll do this, Bill. Wire or phone all three of them that I'm out of it, and okay. All the way okay. Will you do that?"

"Sure."

"And keep a tab of how much the wires or calls cost. Also how much your trip here cost."

He laughed. "The calls, sure, but don't be silly about the trip. A vacation from my family, and hell I've always wanted an excuse for a trip to Denver. Max, this used to be a cow town. About the biggest one, I think. And they've got museums of the Old West here, and I'll bet you can't guess where I've been staying."

"My God," I said, "don't tell me there are still such things as dude ranches."

There were, and he was staying at one and having the time of his life. Probably almost sorry I'd recovered consciousness and coherence because now he'd have to grow up again and go home to his family.

My kid brother, riding a horse, playing cowboy, living in the past. My wonderful kid brother.

Letters came. One from Merlene saying how glad she and the kids would be to see me, that Billy especially was all excited because I was coming.

Letter from Bess Bursteder. *"I'm writing because Rory's awfully busy. He's changing jobs, Max. He's not been too happy at Treasure Island for quite a while now. He's been having trouble with the directors, doesn't see eye to eye with them on a lot of things. So he's taking another job and we're moving there this week end. It's still a head mech's job, but at a smaller rocket port and it won't pay quite so much. That doesn't matter, though, if he's happier in the work, and he will be, since they're giving him full authority over the mechanical end, no restrictions on whom he hires and fires, nor on the time he allocates* to each job—and that's the big beef he's had with the port directors here; they've been trying to get him to cut corners and save a few dollars.

"I know you'll be glad to know where we're going—because it's Seattle. Now and from now on you can kill two birds with one rocket blast in your visiting because we'll be living in the same city as your brother and his family. We hope to get to know them better, too. I liked your sister-in-law an awful lot the one time I met her. At the party in Los Angeles when we celebrated your getting your degree, remember?

"We're not buying a house there until we've had time to look around, but we both flew up there last week end and rented an apartment to live in meanwhile—and it's got a guest room for you. We're moving in Saturday and Sunday and we'll be settled down and ready for you by the time you get here. You are coming; don't give us any argument about that. Wait a minute; Rory's here looking over my shoulder and he says if I'm through he wants to add something. I'll turn it over to him. Bess signing off."

Rory's stubby handwriting took over. "Swell you're going to be with us, Max. Suppose you'll be going back to your old job at L.A. but if you don't want to, there'll be one for you in Seattle any time you want it. You just read what Bess wrote about the hiring and firing. Keep your chin up."

It put my chin up, to get a letter like that. And it decided me on Seattle.

Another letter the next day undecided me. It was from M'bassi and it was a brief hurried scrawl. A paragraph telling me I should by all means come and stay with him while I was convalescing, and then:

"Max, I think—I hope—that I'm on the verge of success. I want your help. Please come here."

That put a different look on things.

What did he mean, he was on the verge of success—that he could teleport himself, or that he thought he could do it soon?

And how the hell could I help?

Or, damn his wonderful black hide, was that just bait to get me there, by arousing my curiosity?

But Jesus, what if—?

It was hard to make up my mind, until two days later a letter came from Klocky.

"Max," he said, "I'm worried as hell about M'bassi. He's off on one of his mystical sprees. He's been fasting and taking drugs, and that's a hell of a dangerous combination. He's so thin he doesn't throw a shadow, and he won't listen to any common sense I try to talk to him. He can't go on like that much longer.

"If you feel up to it by the time you leave there—and I won't blame you if you don't—I think you ought to take him up on his invitation, just so you can be with him and try to get him straightened out. He's crazy to try whatever he's trying. If he doesn't starve himself to death he'll end up as a drug addict—no, I guess he has too much will power for that. But what he's doing is dangerous, just the same.

"God knows why, but you've got as much influence on him as anybody except Gautama Buddha, and I think he needs you.

"If you decide to stay with him, let me know when you're coming and I'll pick you up in my hellie so we can have a talk before I take you around."

That made up my mind for me, all right. It also got me out of the hospital three days short of the ten Dr. Fell had predicted. Maybe I did a little exaggerating to him about how well and strong I felt, but I got away with it.

Klocky looked just as he did the day I left him. I don't know why that surprised me, after only two months, but it did. Maybe because those two months had seemed like twice that many years.

He gripped my hand so hard it hurt. "Good you're back, Max. Missed you. Let's go to the coffee shop for a few minutes and talk before we go to my hellie."

I remembered Klocky never liked to talk while he piloted, or even while he drove a ground car. I nodded.

Over coffee, I asked him about M'bassi.

"Nothing new that I know of. Haven't seen him for two days—but listen, before we talk about M'bassi, let's talk about you a minute. You're coming back to your job with me, aren't you?"

"I—I don't know, Klocky. I don't think so."

"It's open. I marked you down for indefinite leave of absence. And I need you, Max."

I grinned at him. "That isn't what you said the day I left. But seriously, I want to mech a while again, I think. It's what I need—for a while anyway. Grease and oil and grit and soot on my hands. Physical work."

"Max, you're not getting any younger. You can't do mech work all your life."

"For another few years I can. After that—I'll see. But don't keep that job open for me, Klocky."

He shrugged. "It's your business. I'll keep it open for a while, though, in case you change your mind. And I'll give you a mech job meanwhile, but damn it—"

I shook my head. "Not at L.A., Klocky. It would be embarrassing for both of us to have your former assistant working as a grease monkey. I know where I'm going to work." I told him about Rory's change of jobs and his offer.

"Okay, if that's the way you want it." I could see that he was relieved that I didn't intend to mech at the L.A. port.

"Klocky," I said, "I haven't been reading the papers much. Has the appointment been announced?"

He knew what appointment I meant. He nodded. "Kreager, Charlie Kreager."

The name didn't register, but apparently Klocky knew who he was. "Good man?" I asked.

"Damn good."

That was what I wanted to hear and I let it go at that. How much Klocky knew or guessed of the details of what had actually happened, I didn't know, didn't want to ask. We let it go at that, but it knocked a worry out of my mind to know that a good man would be supervising the construction of the Jupiter rocket.

I said, "Now about M'bassi."

"On second thought, Max, there's nothing else I need to tell you. You'll know the score the minute you see him. Maybe better if I don't tell you any more than I have—not that there's much more to tell."

"We're wasting time then. Let's go there," I said.

No answer to our knock. A square pink corner sticking out from under the door. I pulled it out and opened the pink telegram envelope. It was the telegram I'd sent the day before telling M'bassi when I'd arrive. It must have been delivered to his rooms twenty-four hours ago at least.

The door wasn't locked; we went in. Knowing, both of us, that we were too late, knowing what had happened.

Inside, the light layer of dust over the smooth surfaces.

The door to the little room, the room without furniture, the cell, was bolted on the inside. I knocked only once; then Klocky and I looked at one another and I nodded. He's fifty pounds heavier than I; he backed up and ran at it, throwing his shoulder against it. The bolt snapped.

M'bassi was smiling, lying there.

He lay on his back on a strip of canvas, wearing only a breechclout. His rib case looked like a bird cage. His eyes, wide open, stared fixedly through pin-point pupils upward.

We made the routine checks before we made the routine phone calls. But we'd known, both of us, from the moment that our knock on the outer door hadn't been answered, that we were too late.

M'bassi wasn't there. His body was there, but M'bassi?

I wished that I could believe that M'bassi had gone *somewhere,* not just that M'bassi had gone.

I wish that I could believe not in mortality but in reincarnation or individual im-mortality; I wish that I could be living again in another body or, God help me, even watching from the edge of a fleecy cloud in Heaven or out through the dirty win-dowpane of a haunted house or through the dull eyes of a dung beetle or on *any* terms. On *any* terms I want to be watching, I want to be there, I want to be around, when we reach the stars, when we take over the universe and the universes, when we become the God in whom I do not believe as yet because I do not believe he exists as yet nor will exist until we become Him.

But I've been wrong so I can be wrong. *Make* me wrong, damn You, show me that I'm wrong, show me that M'bassi had cause to smile.

Show Yourself, God damn You, make me wrong.

2001

"We'll see better from here, Billy," I said.

I'd parked the hellie behind the hill and we'd walked up it, one of the low hills that ringed the site. Five o'clock of a clear October evening, the sun getting low.

Three hours before the take-off of the Jupiter rocket, but there were others there even before us, finding good spots on the best hills. By three minutes after eight, take-off time, these hills would be filled with people.

"You're sure, Uncle Max, that down by the fence—?"

"Not nearly as good, believe me." I grinned at the boy. "I know you want to get close, but don't worry; you'll be closer to rockets than you'd get to that one at the edge of the launching site."

Forty-three feet tall it stood, and beautiful. God, how beautiful. Sleek and slender, shiny and Oh God there aren't any words for a rocket, a new one-man rocket that's going where no rocket has been before, to another world, farther out. Nearer where we're going.

I saw the disappointment in Billy's freckled face. I said, "Okay, there's lots of time. Go down to the fence and look at it from there, but then come back. The take-off will look better from here."

I watched him run down the hill. Ten now, he was. God, how fast the four years had gone since I'd first heard of this rocket, since I'd first heard of Ellen Gallagher. God, how fast the years go when they near the end. Constant acceleration, like a falling object. Be with you soon, Ellen, I thought; whether it's a couple of years or thirty years, they'll go like a flash. The speed of light? It's nothing to the speed of time.

I spread the blanket and sat on it, watching the rocket, watching Billy. He stood now at the high steel-mesh fence, pushing his face against it to be as close as he could.

I saw myself at ten, although there weren't interplanetary rockets to look at then, back in nineteen fifty. But I'd have looked at one like that, had there been one to look at.

I looked at one now, and I wanted to cry because I wouldn't be on it when it went to Jupiter. But sixty-one is too old to cry. You're a big boy now, I told myself.

Sun going down. Son coming up; not my son, but the nearest I'd ever have to a son of my own, plodding up the hill toward me, his eyes filled with stardust. Sitting on the blanket beside me.

The lost, longing look in his eyes. The look of a spaceman Earth-bound. The caged look.

Dusk, and more people gathering. Silent, most of them. Most of us. Silent in wonder at the thing that was to happen.

Dusk and the bright floodlights down there, down where it was going to start to happen, down there where a man with a light in his eyes like the light in Billy's eyes was getting ready to leave Earth, to escape from this poor two-dimensional surface upon which we three-dimensional beings crawl.

Escape, God how we all need escape from this tiny here. The need for it has motivated just about everything man has ever done in any direction other than that of the satisfaction of his physical appetites; it has led him along weird and wonderful pathways; it has led him into art and religion, asceticism and astrology, dancing and drinking, poetry and insanity. All of these have been escapes because he has known only recently the true direction of escape—*outward,* into infinity and eternity, away from this little flat if rounded surface we're born on and die on. This mote in the solar system, this atom in the galaxy.

I thought of the distant future and the things we'd have, and discounted my wildest guesses as inadequate. Immortality? Achieved in the nineteenth millennium X.R. and discarded in the twenty-third because it was no longer necessary. Reverse entropy to rewind the universe? Obsolete with the discovery of nolanism and the concurrent cognate in the quadrate decal. Sounds wild? How would the word *quantum* or the concept of a matter-energy transformation sound to a Neanderthaler? *We're* Neanderthalers, to our descendants of a hundred thousand years from now. You'll sell them short to make the wildest guess as to what they'll do and what they'll be.

The stars? Hell, yes. They'll have the stars.

Dark now. "What time is it, Uncle Max?" "Four minutes to go, Billy."

The floodlights go off. There is a breathless hush. Thousands of people and a breathless hush.

Oh God, Ellen, if you could be here with me, to watch our rocket take off. *Our* rocket. But more yours than mine. You died for it.

Here waiting in the breathless dark I feel humble before it and before you, before man and his future, before God if there is a God before mankind becomes one.

Martians, Go Home

Martians, Go Home

Prologue

If the peoples of Earth were not prepared for the coming of the Martians, it was their own fault. Events of the preceding century in general and of the preceding few decades in particular should have prepared them.

One might say that preparation, in a very general sort of way, had been going on much longer than that, for ever since men had known that Earth was not the center of the Universe but only one of a number of planets circling about the same sun, men had speculated as to whether the other planets might not be, like Earth, inhabited. However, such speculation, for lack of evidence pro or con, remained on a purely philosophical plane, like speculation as to how many angels could dance on the point of a pin and whether Adam had a navel.

So let's say that preparation really started with Schiaparelli and Lowell, especially Lowell.

Schiaparelli was the Italian astronomer who discovered the *canali* on Mars, but he never claimed that they were artificial constructions. His word *canali* meant channels.

It was the American astronomer Lowell who changed the translation. It was Lowell who, after studying and drawing them, set afire first his own imagination and then the imagination of the public by claiming they were canals, definitely artificial. Proof positive that Mars was inhabited.

True, few other astronomers went along with Lowell; some denied the very existence of the markings or claimed they were only optical illusions, some explained them as natural markings, not canals at all.

But by and large the public, which always tends to accentuate the positive, eliminated the negative and sided with Lowell. Latching onto the affirmative, they demanded and got millions of words of speculation, popular-science and Sunday-supplement style, about the Martians.

Then science fiction took over the field of speculation. It took over with a resounding bang in 1895 when H. G. Wells wrote his superlative *War of the*

247

Worlds, a classic novel describing the invasion of Earth by Martians who bridged space in projectiles fired from guns on Mars.

That book, which became tremendously popular, helped greatly in preparing Earth for invasion. And another Welles, one Orson, gave it a big assist. On Halloween eve in 1938 he put on a radio program that was a dramatization of Wells' book—and proved, although unintentionally, that many of us were even then ready to accept invasion from Mars as a reality. Thousands of people all over the country, having tuned in the program late and having missed the announcement that it was fiction, believed it as fact, believed that Martians had actually landed and were licking the hell out of us. According to their natures, some of these people ran to hide under their beds and others ran out into the street with shotguns to look for Martians.

Science fiction was burgeoning—but so was science itself, so much so that it was becoming increasingly difficult to judge, in science fictions, where the science ended and the fiction started.

V-2 rockets over the channel into England. Radar, sonar.

Then the A-bomb. People quit doubting that science could do anything it wanted to do. Atomic energy.

Experimental space rockets already pushing outside the atmosphere above White Sands, New Mexico. A space station planned to revolve around the Earth. Pretty soon the moon.

The H-bomb.

The flying saucers. Of course we know now what they were, but people didn't then and many believed firmly that they were extraterrestrial.

The atomic submarine. The discovery of metzite in 1963. Barner's theory proving Einstein's wrong, proving speeds faster than light were possible.

Anything could happen and a great many people expected it to.

Not only was the Western Hemisphere affected. People everywhere were becoming ready to believe anything. There was the Jap in Yamanashi who claimed to *be* a Martian, and got himself killed by a mob that believed him. There were the Singapore riots of 1962, and it is known that the Philippine Rebellion of the following year was sparked by a secret cult among the Moros which claimed to be in mystic communication with the Venusians and acting under their advice and guidance. And in 1964 there was the tragic case of the two American army flyers who were forced to make an emergency landing of the experimental stratojet they were flying. They landed just south of the border and were immediately and enthusiastically killed by Mexicans who, as they stepped from their plane still wearing space suits and helmets, took them to be Martians.

Yes, we should have been prepared.

But for the *form* in which they came? Yes and no. Science fiction had presented them in a thousand forms—tall blue shadows, microscopic reptiles, gigantic insects, fireballs, ambulatory flowers, what have you—but science fiction had very carefully avoided the cliché, and the cliché turned out to be the truth. They really *were* little green men.

But with a difference, and *what* a difference. Nobody could have been prepared for that.

Because many people still think that this might have a bearing on the matter,
it may be well to state that the year 1964 started out in no important way
different from the dozen-odd years that preceded it.

If anything, it started a trifle better. The relatively minor recession of the
early sixties was over and the stock market was reaching for new highs.

The Cold War was still in the deep freeze, and the deep freeze showed no
more signs of imminent explosion than at any other time since the China crisis.

Europe was more nearly united than at any time since World War II and a
recovered Germany was taking its place among the great industrial nations. In
the United States business was booming and there were two cars in most ga-
rages. In Asia there was less starvation than usual.

Yes, 1964 *started* well.

Part One — The Coming of the Martians

CHAPTER ONE

TIME: Early evening of March 26, 1964, a Thursday.
PLACE: A two-room shack in desert country, near—but not too near; it was
almost a mile from its nearest neighbor—Indio, California, about a hundred
and fifty miles east and slightly south of Los Angeles.

On stage at rise of curtain: Luke Devereaux, alone.

Why do we start with him? Why not; we've got to start somewhere. And
Luke, as a science fiction writer, should have been much better prepared than
most people for what was about to happen.

Meet Luke Devereaux. Thirty-seven years old, five feet ten inches tall, weighing, at this moment, a hundred and forty-four pounds. Topped with wild red
hair that would never stay in place without hair dressing, and he would never
use hair dressing. Under the hair, rather pale blue eyes with, quite frequently,
an absent-minded stare in them; the kind of eyes that you're never sure are
really seeing you even when they're looking right at you. Under the eyes, a
long thin nose, reasonably well centered in a moderately long face, unshaven
for forty-eight hours or more.

Dressed at the moment (8:14 P.M., Pacific Standard Time) in a white T-
shirt emblazoned Y.W.C.A. in red letters, a pair of faded Levis and a pair of
well-scuffed loafers.

Don't let the Y.W.C.A. on the T-shirt fool you. Luke has never been and
will never be a member of that organization. The shirt belonged or had belonged to Margie, his wife or ex-wife. (Luke wasn't exactly sure which she was;
she'd divorced him seven months ago but the decree would not be final for
another five months.) When she had left his bed and board she must have left

the T-shirt among his. He seldom wore T-shirts in Los Angeles and had not discovered it until this morning. It fitted him all right—Margie was a biggish girl—and he'd decided that, alone out here in the desert, he might as well get a day's wear out of it before considering it a rag with which to polish the car. It certainly wasn't worth taking or sending back, even had they been on more friendly terms than they were. Margie had divorced the Y.W.C.A. long before she'd divorced him and hadn't worn it since. Maybe she'd put it among his T-shirts deliberately as a joke, but he doubted that, remembering the mood she'd been in the day she'd left.

Well, he'd happened to think once during the day, if she'd left it as a joke, the joke had backfired because he'd discovered it at a time when he was alone and could actually wear it. And if by any chance she'd left it deliberately so he'd come across it, think of her and be sorry, she was fooled on that too. Shirt or no shirt, he thought of her occasionally, of course, but he wasn't sorry in the slightest degree. He was in love again, and with a girl who was the opposite of Margie in almost every way. Her name was Rosalind Hall, and she was a ste-nographer at the Paramount Studios. He was nuts about her. Mad about her. Crazy about her.

Which no doubt was a contributory factor to his being alone here in the shack at this moment, miles from a paved highway. The shack belonged to a friend of his, Carter Benson, who was also a writer and who occasionally, in the relatively cooler months of the year, as now, used it for the same purpose for which Luke was using it now—the pursuit of solitude in the pursuit of a story idea in the pursuit of a living.

This was the evening of Luke's third day here and he was still pursuing and still hadn't caught up with anything except the solitude. There'd been no lack of that. No telephone, no mailman, and he hadn't seen another human being, even at a distance.

But he thought that he had begun this very afternoon to sneak up on an idea. Something as yet too vague, too diaphanous, to put on paper, even as a notation; something as impalpable, perhaps, as a direction of thinking, but still *something*. That was a start, he hoped, and a big improvement over the way things had been going for him in Los Angeles.

There he'd been in the worst slump of his writing career, and had been going almost literally insane over the fact that he hadn't written a word for months. With, to make it worse, his publisher breathing down his neck via frequent airmails from New York asking for at least a *title* they could list as his next book. And how soon would he finish the book and when could they schedule it? Since they'd given him five five hundred dollar advances against it, they had the right to ask.

Finally sheer despair—and there are few despairs sheerer than that of a writer who must create and can't—had driven him to borrow the keys to Carter Benson's shack and the use of it for as long as he needed it. Luckily Benson had just signed a six months' contract with a Hollywood studio and wouldn't be using the shack for at least that long.

So here Luke Devereaux was and here he'd stay until he had plotted and started a book. He wouldn't have to finish it here; once he'd got *going* on one he knew he could carry on with it back in his native habitat where he'd no longer have to deny himself evenings with Rosalind Hall.

And for three days now, from nine in the morning until five in the afternoon he'd paced the floor, trying to concentrate. Sober and almost going crazy at times. Evenings, because he knew that driving his brain for even longer hours would do more harm than good, he allowed himself to relax, to read and to have a few drinks. Specifically, five drinks—a quantity which he knew would relax him but would neither get him drunk nor give him a hangover the next morning. He spaced those five drinks carefully to last the evening until eleven. Eleven, on the dot, was his bedtime while here at the shack. Nothing like regularity—except that thus far it hadn't helped him much.

At 8:14 he had made his third drink—the one which would last him until nine o'clock—and had just finished taking his second short sip of it. He was trying to read but not succeeding very well because his mind, now that he was trying to concentrate on reading, wanted to think about writing instead. Minds are frequently that way.

And probably because he wasn't trying to he was getting closer to a story idea than he'd been in a long time. He was idly wondering, what if the Martians...

There was a knock at the door.

He stared at it for a moment in blank surprise before he put down his drink and got up out of the chair. The evening was so quiet that a car couldn't possibly have approached without his having heard it, and surely no one would have *walked* here.

The knock was repeated, louder.

Luke went to the door and opened it, looked out into the bright moonlight. At first he saw no one; then he looked downward.

"Oh, no," he said.

It was a little green man, about two and a half feet tall.

"Hi, Mack," he said. "Is this Earth?"

"Oh, *no,*" Luke Devereaux said. "It *can't* be."

"Why can't it? It must be. Look." He pointed upward. "One moon, and just about the right size and distance. Earth's the only planet in the system with one moon. My planet's got two."

"Oh, God," said Luke. There is only one planet in the solar system that has *two* moons.

"Look, Mack, straighten up and fly right. Is this Earth or isn't it?"

Luke nodded dumbly.

"Okay," said the little man. "We got that settled. Now, what's wrong with *you?*"

"G-g-g," said Luke.

"You crazy? And is this the way you welcome strangers? Aren't you going to ask me in?"

Luke said, "C-come in," and stepped back.

Inside the Martian looked around and frowned. "What a lousy joint," he said. "You people all live like this or are you what they call white trash? Argeth, what stinking furniture."

"I didn't pick it out," Luke said defensively. "It belongs to a friend of mine."

"Then you've got lousy taste in picking friends. You alone here?"

"That," Luke said, "is what I'm wondering. I'm not sure I believe in you. How do I know you're not an hallucination?"

The Martian hopped lightly up on a chair and sat there with his feet dangling. "You don't know. But if you think so you got rocks in your head."

Luke opened his mouth and closed it again. Suddenly he remembered his drink and groped behind himself for it, knocked the glass over with the back of his hand instead of getting hold of it. The glass didn't break but it emptied itself across the table and onto the floor before he could right it. He swore, and then remembered that the drink hadn't been a very strong one anyway. And under the circumstances he wanted a drink that *was* a drink. He went over to the sink where the whiskey stood and poured himself half a tumbler of it straight.

He drank a slug of it that almost choked him. When he was sure that it was going to stay down he came back and sat, glass in hand, staring at his visitor.

"Getting an eyeful?" the Martian asked.

Luke didn't answer. He was getting a double eyeful and taking his time about it. His guest, he saw now, was humanoid but definitely not human. A slight suspicion that one of his friends had hired a circus midget to play a joke on him vanished.

Martian or not, his visitor wasn't human. He couldn't be a dwarf because his torso was very short proportionate to the length of his spindly arms and legs; dwarfs have long torsos and short legs. His head was relatively large and much more nearly spherical than a human head, the skull was completely bald. Nor was there any sign of a beard and Luke had a strong hunch that the creature would also be completely devoid of body hair.

The face—well, it had everything that a face should have but again things were out of proportion. The mouth was twice the size, proportionately, of a human mouth and so was the nose; the eyes were as tiny as they were bright, set quite close together. The ears were very small too, and had no lobes. In the moonlight the skin had looked olive green; here under artificial light, it looked more nearly emerald green.

The hands had six fingers apiece. That meant he probably had twelve toes too, but since he wore shoes there was no way of verifying that.

The shoes were dark green and so were the rest of his clothes—tight-fitting trousers and a loose blouse, both made of the same material—something that looked like chamois or a very soft suede. No hat.

"I'm beginning to believe you," Luke said wonderingly. He took another pull at his drink.

The Martian snorted. "Are all humans as stupid as you? And as impolite? Drinking and not offering a guest a drink?"

"Sorry," Luke said. He got up and started for the bottle and another glass.

"Not that I want one," said the Martian. "I don't drink. Disgusting habit. But you might have offered."

Luke sat down again, sighed.

"I should have," he said. "Sorry again. Now let's start over. My name's Luke Devereaux."

"A damn silly name."

"Maybe yours will sound silly to me. May I ask what it is?"

"Sure, go ahead."

Luke sighed again. "What is your name?"

"Martians don't use names. Ridiculous custom."

"But they're handy to call someone. Like—say, didn't you call me Mack?"

"Sure. We call everyone Mack—or its equivalent in whatever language we're speaking. Why bother to learn a new name for every person you speak to?"

Luke took some more of his drink. "Hmmm," he said, "maybe you've got something there, but let's skip it for something more important. How can I be sure you're really there?"

"Mack, I told you, you got rocks in your head."

"That," said Luke, "is just the point. Have I? If you're really there I'm willing to concede that you're not human and if I concede that there's no reason why I shouldn't take your word as to where you're from. But if you're not there, then I'm either drunk or hallucinating. Except that I know I'm not drunk; before I saw you I'd had only two drinks, weak ones, and I didn't feel them at all."

"Why'd you drink them then?"

"Irrelevant to what we're discussing. That leaves two possibilities—you're really there or I'm crazy."

The Martian made a rude noise. "And what makes you think those possibilities are mutually exclusive? I'm here all right. But I don't know whether or not you're crazy and I don't care."

Luke sighed. It seemed to take a lot of sighing to get along with a Martian. Or a lot of drinking. His glass was empty. He went and refilled it. Straight whiskey again but this time he put in a couple of ice cubes.

Before he sat down again, he had a thought. He put down his drink, said, "Excuse me a minute," and went outside. If the Martian was real and was really a Martian, there ought to be a spaceship somewhere around.

Or would it prove anything if there was, he wondered. If he was hallucinating the Martian why couldn't he hallucinate a spaceship as well?

But there wasn't any spaceship, hallucinated or real. The moonlight was bright and the country was flat; he could see a long way. He walked around the shack and around his car parked behind it, so he could see in all directions. No spaceship.

He went back inside, made himself comfortable and took a sizable swallow of his drink, and then pointed an accusing finger at the Martian. "No spaceship," he said.

"Of course not."

"Then how'd you get here?"

"None of your damned business, but I'll tell you. I kwimmed."

"What do you mean?"

"Like this," said the Martian. And he was gone from the chair. The word "like" had come from the chair and the word "this" came from behind Luke.

He whirled around. The Martian was sitting on the edge of the gas range. "My God," Luke said. "Teleportation."

The Martian vanished. Luke turned back and found him in the chair again.

"Not teleportation," the Martian said. "Kwimming. You need apparatus to teleport. Kwimming's mental. Reason you can't do it is you're not smart enough."

Luke took another drink. "You got here all the way from Mars that way?"

"Sure. Just a second before I knocked on your door."

"Have you kwimmed here before? Say—" Luke pointed a finger again, "I'll bet you have, lots of you, and that accounts for superstitions about elves and—"

"Nuts," said the Martian. "You people got rocks in your heads, that's what accounts for your superstitions. I've never been here before. None of us has. We just learned the technique of long-distance kwimming. Just short-range before. To do it interplanetary, you got to savvy hokima."

Luke pointed a finger again. "Got you. How come, then, you speak English?"

The Martian's lip curled. It was a lip well adapted to curling. "I speak all your simple silly languages. All of them spoken on your radio programs anyway, and whatever other ones there are I can pick up in an hour or so apiece. Easy stuff. You'd never learn Martian in a thousand years."

"I'll be damned," Luke said. "No wonder you don't think much of us if you get your ideas about us from our radio programs. I'll admit most of them stink."

"Then so do most of you or you wouldn't put them on the air."

Luke took a firm grip on his temper and another drink from his glass. He was beginning, finally, to believe that this really was a Martian and not a figment of his own imagination or insanity. And besides, it struck him suddenly, what did he have to lose in assuming so? If he was crazy, that was that. But if this was really a Martian, then he was missing a hell of an opportunity for a science fiction writer.

"What's Mars like?" he asked.

"None of your damn business, Mack."

Luke took another pull at his drink. He counted ten and tried to be as calm and reasonable as he could.

"Listen," he said. "I was rude at first because I was surprised. But I'm sorry and I apologize. Why can't we be friends?"

"Why should we? You're a member of an inferior race."

"Because if for no other reason it'll make this conversation more pleasant for both of us."

"Not for me, Mack. I like disliking people. I like quarreling. If you're going to go namby-pamby and pally-wally on me, I'll go find someone else to chin with."

"Wait, don't—" Luke suddenly realized that he was taking exactly the wrong tack if he wanted the Martian to stay. He said, "Get the hell out of here then, if you feel that way."

The Martian grinned. "That's better. Now we're getting somewhere."

"Why did you come to Earth?"

"That's none of your business either, but it'll be a pleasure to give you a hint. Why do people go to zoos here on your lousy planet?"

"How long do you plan to stay?"

The Martian cocked his head sidewise. "You're a hard guy to convince, Mack. I'm not *Information, Please*. What I do or why I do it is none of your business. One thing I didn't come here for is to teach kindergarten."

Luke's glass was empty again. He filled it.

He glared at the Martian. If the guy wanted to quarrel, why not? "You little green wart," he said, "damned if I don't think I ought to—"

"You ought to what? Do something to me? You and who else?"

"Me and a camera and a flash gun," Luke said, wondering why he hadn't thought of it sooner. "I'm going to get at least one picture of you. Then when I get it developed—"

He put down his glass and hurried into the bedroom. Luckily his camera was loaded and there was a bulb in the flash gun; he'd stuck them in his suitcase, not in the expectation of shooting a Martian but because Benson had told him coyotes often prowled quite close to the shack at night and he'd hoped to get a shot of one.

He hurried back, set the camera quickly, raised it in one hand and the flash gun in the other.

"Want me to pose for you?" asked the Martian. He put his thumbs in his ears and waggled his ten other fingers, crossed his eyes and stuck out a long greenish-yellow tongue.

Luke took the shot.

He put another bulb in the gun, wound the film, aimed the camera again. But the Martian wasn't there. His voice, from another corner of the room, said, "One's enough, Mack. Don't crowd your luck by boring me any worse."

Luke whirled and aimed the camera that way, but by the time he'd raised the flash gun, the Martian was gone. And a voice behind him told him not to make more of an ass of himself than he already was.

Luke gave up and put down the camera. Anyway, he had one shot on the film. When it was developed, it would either show a Martian or it wouldn't. Too bad it hadn't been color film, but you can't have everything.

He picked up his glass again. Sat down with it, because suddenly the floor was becoming just a bit unsteady. He took another drink to steady it.

"Shay," he said. "I mean, say. You catch our *radio* programs. What's the matter with television? You people behind the times?"

"What's television, Mack?"

Luke told him.

"Waves like that don't carry that far," the Martian said. "Thank Argeth. It's bad enough to listen to you people. Now that I've seen one of you and know what you look like—"

"Nuts," said Luke. "You never invented television."

"Of course not. Don't need it. If anything's going on anywhere on our world that we want to see, we just kwim there. Listen, did I just happen to find a freak, or are *all* people here as hideous as you are?"

Luke almost choked over a sip he was taking from his drink. "Mean to shay—say, you think *you're* worth looking at?"

"To any other Martian, I am."

"I'll bet you drive the little girls wild," said Luke. "That is, if you're bisexual like us and there *are* Martian girls."

"We're bisexual but not, thank Argeth, like you. Do you people really carry on in the utterly disgusting way your radio characters do? Are you in what you people call love with one of your females?"

"None of your damn business," Luke told him.

"That's what *you* think," said the Martian.

And he vanished.

Luke stood up—not too steadily—and looked around to see if he had kwimmed to another part of the room. He hadn't.

Luke sat down again, shook his head to clear it, and took another drink, to fuddle it.

Thank God or Argeth, he thought, that he'd got that picture. Tomorrow morning he'd drive back to Los Angeles and get it developed. If it showed an empty chair he'd put himself in the hands of a psychiatrist, but fast. If it showed a Martian—Well, if it did, he'd decide then what he was going to do about it, if anything.

Meanwhile, getting drunk as fast as he could was the only sensible thing he could do. He was already too drunk to risk driving back tonight and the faster he drank himself to sleep the sooner he'd wake up in the morning.

He blinked his eyes and when he opened them again, there was the Martian back in the chair.

Grinning at him. "I was just in that pigsty of a bedroom, reading your correspondence. Foo, what trash."

Correspondence? He didn't have any correspondence here with him, Luke thought. And then he remembered that he did have. A little packet of three letters from Rosalind, the ones she'd written him while he was in New York three months ago, seeing his publisher and talking him out of more money on the book he was now trying to start. He'd stayed a week, mostly to renew his acquaintances among magazine editors while he was there; he'd written Rosalind every day and she'd written him three times. They were the only letters he'd ever had from her and he'd saved them carefully, had put them in his suitcase thinking to reread them here if he got too lonely.

"Argeth, what mush," said the Martian. "And what a damned silly way you people have of writing your language. Took me a full minute to break down your alphabet and correlate the sounds and letters. Imagine a language that has the same sound spelled three different ways—as in true, too and through."

"God damn it," said Luke, "you had no business reading my mail."

"Chip, chip," said the Martian. "Anything's my business that I make my business and you wouldn't tell me about your love life, Sweetie-pie, Darling, Honeybun."

"You really did read it then, you little green wart. For a dime, I'd—"

"You'd what?" asked the Martian contemptuously.

"Toss you all the way back to Mars, that's what," Luke said.

The Martian laughed raucously. "Save your breath, Mack, for making love to your Rosalind. Bet you think she meant all that hogwash she fed you in those letters. Bet you think she's as dopey about you as you are about her."

"She *is* as dopey—I mean, God damn it—"

"Don't get an ulcer, Mack. Her address was on the envelope. I'll kwim there right now and find out for you. Hold your hat."

"You stay right—"

Luke was alone again.

And his glass was empty so he made his way across to the sink and refilled it. He was already drunker than he'd been in years, but the quicker he knocked himself out the better. If possible, before the Martian came back or kwimmed back, if he really was coming or kwimming back.

Because he just couldn't *take* any more. Hallucination or reality, he couldn't help himself, he *would* throw the Martian right through the window. And maybe start an interplanetary war.

Back in the chair he started on the drink. This one should do it.

"Hey, Mack. Still sober enough to talk?"

He opened his eyes, wondering when he had closed them. The Martian was back.

"Go 'way," he said. "Get lost. Tomorrow I'll—"

"Straighten up, Mack. I got news for you, straight from Hollywood. That chick of yours is home and she's lonesome for you all right."

"Yeah? Tole you she loved me, didden I? You li'l green—"

"So lonesome for you she had someone in to console her. Tall blond guy. She called him Harry."

It partly sobered Luke for a second. Rosalind *did* have a friend named Harry, but it was platonic; they were friends because they worked in the same department at Paramount. He'd make sure and then tell off the Martian for tattling.

"Harry Sunderman?" he asked. "Slender, snappy dresser, always wears loud sport coats—?"

"Nope, this Harry wasn't that Harry, Mack. Not if he always wears loud sport coats. This Harry wasn't wearing anything but a wrist watch."

Luke Devereaux roared and got to his feet, lunged at the Martian. With both hands extended he grabbed at a green neck.

And both hands went right through it and closed on one another.

The little green man grinned up at him and stuck out his tongue. Then pulled it in again. "Want to know what they were doing, Mack? Your Rosalind and her Harry?"

Luke didn't answer. He staggered back for his drink and gulped the rest of it down.

And gulping it down was the last thing he remembered when he woke up in the morning. He was lying on the bed; he'd got that far somehow. But he was atop the covers, not under them, and fully dressed even to his shoes.

He had a God-awful headache and a hellish taste in his mouth.

He sat up and looked around fearfully.

No little green man

Made his way to the living room door and looked around in there. Came back and looked at the stove, wondering if coffee would be worth the effort of making it.

Decided that it wouldn't since he could get some already made on his way back to town, less than a mile after he got on the main highway. And the sooner he got there and the sooner thereafter he got back to town the better. He wouldn't even clean up or pack. He could come back later and get his stuff. Or ask someone to come and get it for him if he was going to be in the looney bin for a while.

Right now all he wanted was *out* of here and to hell with everything else. He wouldn't even bathe or shave until he was home; he had an extra razor in his apartment and all of his good clothes were still there anyway.

And after that, what?

Well, after that he'd worry about what after that. He'd be nearly enough over his hang-over to think things out calmly.

Walking through the other room he saw the camera, hesitated briefly and then picked it up to take along. Might as well, before he did his heavy thinking, get that picture developed. There was still a chance in a thousand that, despite the fact that his hands had passed through it, an actual Martian and not an hallucination had been in that chair. Maybe Martians had stranger powers than being able to kwim.

Yes, if there *was* a Martian on that photograph it would change all his thinking, so he might as well eliminate the possibility before making any decisions.

If there wasn't—well, the sensible thing to do if he could bring himself to do it would be to phone Margie and ask her the name of the psychiatrist she'd tried to get him to go to several times during their marriage. She'd been a nurse in several mental institutions before they were married and she'd gone to work in another one when she'd walked out on him. And she'd told him that she'd majored in psychology at college and, if she could have afforded the extra years of schooling, would have tried to become a psychiatrist herself.

He went out and locked the door, walked around the house to his car.

The little green man was sitting on the car's radiator.

"Hi, Mack," he said. "You look like hell, but I guess you earned the right to. Drinking is sure a disgusting habit."

Luke turned and went back to the door, let himself in again. He got the bottle and poured himself a pickup drink and drank it. Before, he'd fought off the idea of taking one. If he was still hallucinating, though, he needed one. And, once his throat had quit burning, it did make him feel better physically. Not much, but a little.

He locked the house again and went back to his car. The Martian was still there. Luke got in and started the engine.

Then he leaned his head out of the window. "Hey," he said, "how can I see the road with you sitting there?"

The Martian looked back and sneered. "What do I care whether you can see the road or not? If you have an accident it won't hurt *me.*"

Luke sighed and started the car. He drove the stretch of primitive road to the highway with his head stuck out of the window. Hallucination or no, he couldn't see through the little green man so he had to see past him.

He hesitated whether or not to stop at the diner for coffee, decided that he might as well. Maybe the Martian would stay where he was. If he didn't, if he entered the diner too, well, nobody else would be able to see him anyway so what did it matter? Except that he'd have to remember not to talk to him.

The Martian jumped down when he parked the car and followed him into the diner. There weren't, as it happened, any other customers. Just a sallow-faced counterman in a dirty white apron.

Luke sat on a stool. The Martian jumped up and stood on the adjacent stool, leaned his elbows on the counter.

The counterman turned and looked, not at Luke. He groaned, "Oh, God, another one of 'em."

"Huh?" said Luke. "Another what?" He found himself gripping the edge of the counter so tightly that it hurt his fingers.

"Another Goddam Martian," said the clerk. "Can't you *see* it?"

Luke took a deep breath and let it out slowly. "You mean there are *more* of them?"

The counterman stared at Luke in utter amazement. "Mister, where *were* you last night? Out on the desert alone and without a radio or TV? Jesus, there are a *million* of them."

CHAPTER TWO

The counterman was wrong. It was estimated later that there were approximately a billion of them.

And let's leave Luke Devereaux for a while—we'll get back to him later—and take a look at things that were happening elsewhere while Luke was entertaining his visitor at the Benson shack near Indio.

As near as matters, a billion Martians. Approximately one to every three human beings—men, women and children—on Earth.

There were close to sixty million in the United States alone and an equivalent number relative to population in every other country in the world. They'd all appeared at, as near as could be determined, exactly the same moment everywhere. In the Pacific time zone, it had been at 8:14 P.M. Other time zones, other times. In New York it was three hours later, 11:14 P.M., with the theaters just letting out and the night clubs just starting to get noisy. (They got noisier after the Martians came.) In London it was 4:14 in the morning—but people woke up all right; the Martians wakened them gleefully. In Moscow it was 7:14 A.M. with people just getting ready to go to work—and the fact that many of them actually went to work speaks well for their courage. Or maybe they were more afraid of the Kremlin than of the Martians. In Tokyo it was 1:14 P.M. and in Honolulu 6:14 P.M.

A great many people died that evening. Or morning or afternoon, depending on where they were.

Casualties in the United States alone are estimated to have run as high as thirty thousand people, most of them within minutes of the moment of arrival of the Martians.

Some died of heart failure from sheer fright. Others of apoplexy. A great many died of gunshot wounds because a great many people got out guns and tried to shoot Martians. The bullets went right through the Martians without hurting them and all too frequently came to rest embedded in human flesh. A great many people died in automobile accidents. Some Martians had kwimmed themselves into moving vehicles, usually on the front seat alongside the driver. "Faster, Mack, faster," coming from what a driver thinks is an empty seat beside him is not conducive to his retaining control of the car, even if he doesn't turn to look.

Casualties among the Martians were zero, although people attacked them—sometimes on sight but more frequently after, as in the case of Luke Devereaux, they had been goaded into an attack—with guns, knives, axes, chairs, pitchforks, dishes, cleavers, saxophones, books, tables, wrenches, hammers, scythes, lamps and lawn mowers, with anything that came to hand. The Martians jeered and made insulting remarks.

Other people, of course, tried to welcome them and to make friends with them. To these people the Martians were much more insulting.

But wherever they arrived and however they were received, to say that they caused trouble and confusion is to make the understatement of the century.

CHAPTER THREE

Take, for example, the sad sequence of events at television station KVAK, Chicago. Not that what happened there was basically different from what happened at all other television stations operating with live broadcasts at the time, but we can't take *all* of them.

It was a prestige program and a spectacular, rolled into one. Richard Bretaine, the greatest Shakespearean actor in the world, was enacting a condensed-for-television version of *Romeo and Juliet,* with Helen Ferguson playing opposite him.

The production had started at ten o'clock and by fourteen minutes after the hour had reached the balcony scene of Act II. Juliet had just appeared on the balcony and Romeo below was sonorously declaiming that most famous of romantic speeches:

> But, soft! what light through yonder window breaks?
> It is the east, and Juliet is the sun!
> Arise, fair sun, and kill the envious moon,
> Who is already sick and pale with grief,
> That thou her maid...

That was just how far he got when suddenly there was a little green man perched on the balcony railing about two feet to the left of where Helen Ferguson leaned upon it.

Richard Bretaine gulped and faltered, but recovered and went on. After all, he had no evidence yet that anyone besides himself was seeing what *he* was seeing. And in any case the show must go on.

He went bravely on:

> ...art far more fair than she:
> Be not her maid, since she is envious;
> Her vestal livery is but sick and green—

The word *green* stuck in his throat. He paused for breath and in that pause he heard a collective murmur that seemed to come from all over the studio.

And in that pause the little man said in a loud clear sneering voice, "Mack, that's a lot of bull, and you know it."

Juliet straightened up and turned and saw what was on the railing beside her. She screamed and slumped in a dead faint.

The little green man looked down at her calmly. "What the hell's wrong with *you*, Toots?" he wanted to know.

The director of the play was a brave man and a man of action. Twenty years before he had been a lieutenant of marines and had led, not followed, his men in the assaults on Tarawa and Kwajalein; he had earned two medals for bravery beyond the call of duty, at a time when bravery within the call of duty was practically suicide. Since then he had put on sixty pounds and a bay window, but he was still a brave man.

He proved it by running from beside the camera onto the set to grab the intruder and carry him off.

He grabbed, but nothing happened. The little green man gave a loud raspberry, Brooklyn style. Then he jumped to his feet on the railing and, while the director's hands tried in vain to close around his ankles and not through them, he turned slightly to face the camera and raised his right hand, put thumb to nose and wiggled his fingers.

That was the moment at which the man in the control room suddenly recovered enough presence of mind to cut the show off the air and nobody who wasn't in the studio at the time knows what happened after that.

For that matter, only a fraction of the original half million or so people who had been watching the show on their television sets saw the show even up to that point, by a minute or two. They had Martians of their own to worry about, right in their own living rooms.

CHAPTER FOUR

Or take the sad case of honeymooning couples—and at any given moment, including the moment in question, a lot of couples are on honeymoons, or some reasonable if less legal equivalent of honeymoons.

Take, for random example, Mr. and Mrs. William R. Gruder, ages twenty-five and twenty-two respectively, who that very day had been married in Denver. Bill Gruder was an ensign in the navy, stationed as an instructor on Treasure Island, San

Francisco. His bride, Dorothy Gruder, nee Armstrong, was a want-ad taker for the Chicago *Tribune.* They had met and fallen in love while Bill had been at the Great Lakes Naval Training Station near Chicago. After Bill's transfer to San Francisco they had decided to get married on the first day of a week's leave Bill had coming, and to meet each other halfway, in Denver, for the purpose. And to spend that week in Denver as a honeymoon, after which he'd return to San Francisco and she'd go with him.

They had been married at four o'clock that afternoon and, had they known what was going to happen within a few hours, they would have gone to a hotel immediately to consummate their marriage before the Martians came. But of course they didn't know.

At that, they were lucky in one way. They didn't happen to draw a Martian immediately; they had time to prepare themselves mentally before they saw one.

At 9:14 that evening, Mountain time, they had just checked into a Denver hotel (after having had a leisurely dinner and then killing time over a few cocktails, to show themselves and each other that they had the will power to wait until it was decently time to go to bed and that anyway they hadn't got married *just* for *that)* and the bellboy was just putting down their suitcases in the room.

As Bill was handing him a somewhat overgenerous tip, they heard the first of what turned out to be a series of noises. Someone in a room not too far away screamed, and the scream was echoed by other and more distant screams, seemingly coming from several different directions. There were angry shouts in masculine voices. Then the sound of six shots in rapid succession, as though someone was emptying a revolver. Running footsteps in the corridor.

And other running footsteps that seemed to come from the street outside, and a sudden squeal of brakes and then some more shots. And a loud voice in what seemed to be the room right next to theirs, too muffled for the words to be clear but sounding very much like swearing.

Bill frowned at the bellboy. "I thought this was a quiet hotel, a good one. It used to be."

The bellboy's face was bewildered. "It *is,* Sir. I can't imagine what in the world—"

He walked rapidly to the door and opened it, looked up and down the corridor. But whoever had been running there was out of sight around a turn.

He said over his shoulder, "I'm sorry, Sir. I don't know what's happening, but *something* is. I better get back to the desk—and I'd suggest you bolt your door right away. Good night and thank you."

He pulled the door shut behind him. Bill went over and slid the bolt, then turned to Dorothy. "It's probably nothing, honey. Let's forget it."

He took a step toward her, then stopped as there was another fusillade of shots, this time definitely from the street outside, and more running footsteps. Their room was on the third floor and one of the windows was open a few inches; the sounds were clear and definite.

"Just a minute, honey," Bill said. "Something *is* going on."

He strode to the window, threw it up the rest of the way, leaned out and looked down. Dorothy joined him there.

At first they saw nothing but a street empty save for parked cars. Then out of the doorway of an apartment building across the street a man and a child came running. Or was it a child? Even at that distance and in dim light there seemed to be something strange about him. The man stopped and kicked hard at the child, if it was a child. From where they watched it looked for all the world as though the man's foot went right *through* the child.

The man fell, a beautiful prat-fall that would have been funny under other circumstances, then got up and started running again, and the child stayed right with him. One of them was talking, but they couldn't hear the words or tell which it was, except that it didn't sound like a child's voice.

Then they were out of sight around the corner. From another direction, far off in the night, came the sound of more shooting.

But there was nothing more to see.

They pulled their heads back in, looked at one another.

"Bill," Dorothy said, "something's— Could there be a revolution starting, or—or what?"

"Hell, no, not here. But—" His eyes lighted on a quarter-in-the-slot radio on the dresser and he headed for it, fumbling loose coins out of his pocket. He found a quarter among them, dropped it in the slot and pushed the button. The girl joined him in front of it and they stood, each with an arm around the other, staring at the radio while it warmed up. When there was a humming sound from it, Bill reached with his free hand and turned the dial until there was a voice, a very loud and excited voice.

"...Martians, definitely Martians," it was saying. "But *please,* people, do not panic. Don't be afraid, but don't try to attack them. It doesn't do any good anyway. Besides, they are harmless. They can't hurt you for the same reason that you can't hurt them. I repeat, they are harmless.

"I repeat, you can't hurt them. Your hand goes right through one, as through smoke. Bullets, knives, other weapons are useless for the same reason. And as far as we can see or find out, none of them has tried to hurt any human being anyway. So be calm and don't panic."

Another voice was cuffing in, more or less garbling what was being said, but the announcer's voice rose in pitch to carry over the new voice. "Yes, there's one on my desk right in front of me and he's talking to me but I'm keeping my mouth so close to the mike that—"

"Bill, that's a gag, a fiction program. Like the time my parents told me about— back twenty years ago or so. Get another station."

Bill said, "Sure, honey. Sure it's a gag." He turned the dial a quarter of an inch.

Another voice. "...don't get excited, folks. A lot of people have killed one another or hurt themselves already trying to kill Martians, and they just don't kill. So don't try. Stay calm. Yes, they're all over the world, not just here in Denver. We've got part of the staff monitoring other stations, covering as many of them as they can, and we haven't found a station yet that's operating that isn't reporting them, even on the other side of the world.

"But they won't hurt you. I repeat, they won't hurt you. So don't get excited, stay calm. Wait, the one that's on my shoulder—he's been trying to say something to me but I don't know what because I've been talking myself. But I'm going to put the mike up to him and I'm going to ask him to reassure you. They've been being—well, impolite here to us, but I know that when he knows he's talking to millions of listeners, he'll, well— Here, fellow, will you reassure our great audience?" A different voice spoke, a voice a little higher pitched than the announcer's. "Thanks, Mack. What I've been telling *you* was to screw yourself, and now I can tell *all* these lovely people to—"

The station went dead.

Bill's arm had fallen from around Dorothy and hers from around him. They stared at one another. Then she said faintly, "Darling, try another station. That just *can't*—"

Bill Gruder reached for the dial, but his hand never got there.

Behind them in the room a voice said, "Hi, Mack. Hi, Toots."

They whirled. I don't have to tell you what they saw; you know by now. He was sitting cross-legged on the window sill they had been leaning over a few minutes before.

Neither of them said anything and a full minute went by. Nothing happened except that Bill's hand found Dorothy's and squeezed it.

The Martian grinned at them. "Cat got your tongues?"

Bill cleared his throat. "Is this the McCoy? Are you really a—a Martian?"

"Argeth, but you're stupid. After what you were just listening to, you ask that."

"Why, you damn little—"

Dorothy grabbed Bill's arm as he let go of her hand and started forward. "Bill, keep your temper. Remember what the radio said."

Bill Gruder subsided, but still glared. "All right," he said to the Martian, "what do you want?"

"Nothing, Mack. Why should I want anything *you* could give me?"

"Then scram the hell out of here. We don't want company."

"Oh, newlyweds maybe?"

Dorothy said, "We were married this afternoon." Proudly.

"Good," said the Martian. "Then I do want something. I've heard about your disgusting mating habits. Now I can watch them."

Bill Gruder tore loose from his bride's grip on his arm and strode across the room. He reached for—and right through—the Martian on the window sill. He fell forward so hard that he himself almost went through the open window.

"Temper, temper," said the Martian. "Chip, chip."

Bill went back to Dorothy, put a protecting arm around her, stood glaring. "I'll be damned," he said. "He just isn't *there.*"

"That's what *you* think, Stupid," said the Martian.

Dorothy said, "It's like the radio said, Bill. But remember he can't hurt us either."

"He's hurting *me,* honey. Just by sitting there."

"You know what I'm waiting for," the Martian said. "If you want me to go away, go ahead. You people take your clothes off first, don't you? Well, get undressed."

Bill took a step forward again. "You little green—"

Dorothy stopped him. "Bill, let me try something." She stepped around him, looked appealingly at the Martian. "You don't understand," she said. "We—make love only in private. We can't and won't till you go away. *Please* go."

"Nuts, Toots. I'm staying."

And he stayed.

For three and a half hours, sitting side by side on the edge of the bed they tried to ignore him and outwait him. Not, of course, ever saying to one another that they were trying to outwait him, because they knew by now that that would make him even more stubborn in staying.

Occasionally they talked to one another, or tried to talk, but it wasn't very intelligent conversation. Occasionally Bill would go over to the radio, turn it on, and fiddle with it for a while, hoping that by now someone would have found some effective way of *dealing* with Martians, or would give some advice more constructive than simply telling people to stay calm, not to panic. Bill wasn't panicky but neither was he in any mood to stay calm.

But one radio station was like another—they all sounded like poorly organized madhouses—except for those that had gone off the air completely. And nobody had discovered anything whatsoever to do about the Martians. From time to time a bulletin would go on the air, a statement released by the President of the United States, the Chairman of the Atomic Energy Commission, or some equally important public figure. The statements all advised people to keep calm and not get excited, that the Martians were harmless, and that we should make friends with them if possible. But no station reported a single incident that indicated that anyone on Earth had succeeded in making friends with a single Martian.

Finally Bill gave up the radio as a bad job for the last time and went back to sit on the bed, forgot that he was ignoring the Martian and glowered at him.

The Martian was seemingly paying no attention whatsoever to the Gruders. He had taken a little fifelike musical instrument out of his pocket and was playing tunes to himself on it—if they were tunes. The notes were unbearably shrill and didn't form any Earthly musical pattern. Like a peanut wagon gone berserk.

Occasionally he'd put down the fife and look up at them, saying nothing, which was probably the most irritating thing he could have said.

At one o'clock in the morning, Bill Gruder's impatience exploded. He said, "To hell with this. He can't see in the dark, and if I pull down the shades before I turn off the light—"

Dorothy's voice sounded worried. "Darling, how do we *know* he can't see in the dark. Cats can, and owls."

Bill hesitated, but only a moment. "Damn it, honey, even if he can see in the dark he can't see through blankets. We can even undress under the covers."

He went over to the window and slammed it down, then pulled the shade, taking angry pleasure in reaching right through the Martian to perform both operations. He pulled down the other shade and then turned off the light. Groped his way to the bed.

And, although their feeling of a need for silence inhibited them in some ways, and they didn't feel it right even to whisper to one another, it was a wedding night after all.

They'd have been less happy about it though (and *were* less happy about it the next day) had they known, as everyone found out within a day or two, that not only could Martians see in the dark, but they *could* see through blankets. Or even walls. Some kind of X-ray vision or, more likely, some special ability like kwimming, enabled them to see right through solid objects. And very good vision it was too, for they could read the fine print on folded documents in closed drawers or in locked safes. They could read letters or even books without opening them.

As soon as this was learned, people knew that they could never again be *sure* of privacy as long as the Martians stayed. Even if there wasn't a Martian in the room with them, there might be one in the next room or outside the building watching them through the wall.

But that is getting ahead of ourselves, because few people learned or guessed it the first night. (Luke Devereaux, for one, should have guessed it, because his Martian had read Rosalind's letters in a closed suitcase—but then at that moment. Luke didn't yet know that the Martian couldn't have simply opened the suitcase and handled the letter. And after Luke *did* have those two facts to couple together he was in no shape to do any effective coupling.) And that first night, before most people knew, the Martians must have seen plenty. Especially the thousands of them that happened to kwim into already darkened rooms and found themselves interested enough in what was going on there to keep their mouths shut for a while.

CHAPTER FIVE

America's second most popular indoor sport took an even worse beating that night, and became impossible then and thereafter.

Take what happened to the gang that played poker every Thursday night at George Keller's place on the beach a few miles north of Laguna, California. George was a bachelor and retired; he lived there the year round. The others all lived in Laguna, held jobs or owned shops.

That particular Thursday evening there were six of them, counting George. Just the right number for a good game, and they *played* a good game, all of them, with the stakes just high enough to make it exciting but not high enough to hurt the losers seriously. Dealer's choice, but dealers chose only between draw poker and five-card stud, never a wild game. With all of them poker was more nearly a religion than it was a vice. Thursday nights from around eight until around one—or sometimes even two—in the morning were the highlights in their lives, the shining hours to which they looked forward throughout the duller days and evenings of the week. You couldn't call them fanatics, perhaps, but you could call them dedicated.

By a few minutes after eight they were comfortable in shirt sleeves and with neckties loosened or taken off, sitting around the big table in the living room ready to start play as soon as George had finished shuffling the new deck he had just broken out. They'd all bought chips and they all had tinkling glasses or opened beer cans in front of them. (They always drank, but always moderately, never enough to spoil their judgment or the game.)

George finished his shuffle and dealt the cards around face up to see who'd catch a jack for the first deal; it went to Gerry Dix, head teller at the Laguna bank.

Dix dealt and won the first hand himself on three tens. It was a small pot, though; only George had been able to stay and draw cards with him. And George hadn't even been able to call; he'd drawn to a pair of nines and hadn't improved them.

Next man around, Bob Trimble, proprietor of the local stationery store, gathered in the cards for next deal. "Ante up, boys," he said. "This one'll be better. Everybody gets good cards."

Across the room the radio played soft music. George Keller liked background music and knew which stations to get it on at any given hour of a Thursday evening.

Trimble dealt. George picked up his hand and saw two small pairs, sevens and treys. Openers, but a bit weak to open on right under the gun; someone would probably raise him. If someone else opened he could stay and draw a card. "By me," he said.

Two more passed and then Wainright—Harry Wainright, manager of a small department store in South Laguna—opened the pot for a red chip. Dix and Trimble both stayed, without raising, and George did the same. The men who'd passed between George and Wainright passed again. That left four of them in the game and gave George an inexpensive draw to his two small pairs; if he made a full house out of them he'd probably have the winning hand.

Trimble picked up the deck again. "Cards, George?"

"Just a second," George said suddenly. He'd turned his head and was listening to the radio. It wasn't playing music now and, in retrospect, he realized that it hadn't been for the past minute or two. Somebody was yammering, and much too excitedly for it to be a commercial; the voice sounded actually hysterical. Besides, it was around a quarter after eight and if he had the program he thought he had, it was the *Starlight Hour,* which was interrupted only once, at the half hour, by a commercial break.

Could this possibly be an emergency announcement—a declaration of war, warning of an impending air attack, or something of the sort?

"Just a second, Bob," he said to Trimble, putting down his hand and getting up out of his chair. He went over to the radio and turned up the volume.

"...little green men, dozens of them, all over the studio and the station. They say they're Martians. They're being reported from all over. But don't get excited—they can't hurt you. Perfectly harmless because they're impal—im— you can't *touch* them; your hand or anything you throw at them goes right through like they weren't there, and they can't touch you for the same reason. So don't—"

There was more.

All six of them were listening now. Then Gerry Dix said, "What the hell, George? You holding up the game just to listen to a science-fiction program?"

George said, "But is it? I had the Goddam *Starlight Hour* tuned in there. Music."

"That's right," Walt Grainger said. "A minute or two ago they were playing a Strauss waltz. *Vienna Woods,* I think."

"Try a different station, George," Trimble suggested.

Just then, before George could reach out for the dial, the radio went suddenly dead.

"Damn," George said, fiddling with the dials. "A tube must have just conked out. Can't even get a hum out of it now."

Wainright said, "Maybe the Martians did it. Come on back to the game, George, before my cards get cold. They're hot enough right now to take this little hand."

George hesitated, then looked toward Walt Grainger. All five of the men had come out from Laguna in one car, Grainger's.

"Walt," George said, "you got a radio in your car?"

"No."

George said, "Damn it. And no telephone because the lousy phone company won't run poles this far out from— Oh, hell, let's forget it."

"If you're *really* worried, George," Walt said, "we can take a quick run into town. Either you and me and let the others keep playing, or all six of us can go, and be back here in less than an hour. It won't lose us too much time; we can play a little later to make up for it."

"Unless we run into a spaceshipload of Martians on the way," Gerry Dix said.

"Nuts," Wainright said. "George, what happened is your radio jumped stations somehow. It was going on the blink anyway or it wouldn't be dead now."

"I'll go along with that," Dix said. "And what the hell, if there *are* Martians around let 'em come out here if they want to see us. This is our *poker* night, Gentlemen. Let's play cards, and let the chips fall where they may."

George Keller sighed. "Okay," he said.

He walked back to the table and sat down, picked up his hand and looked at it to remind himself what it had been. Oh, yes, sevens and treys. And it was his turn to draw.

"Cards?" Trimble asked, picking up the deck again.

"One for me," George said, discarding his fifth card.

But Trimble never dealt it.

Suddenly, across the table, Walt Grainger said, "Jesus Christ!" in such a tone of voice that they all froze for a second; then they stared at him and quickly turned to see what *he* was staring at.

There were two Martians. One was sitting on top of a floor lamp; the other was standing atop the radio cabinet.

George Keller, the host, was the one who recovered first, probably because he was the one of them who'd come nearest to giving credence to the report they'd heard so briefly on the radio.

"H-hello," he said, a bit weakly.

"Hi, Mack," said the Martian on the lamp. "Listen, you better throw that hand of yours away after the draw."

"Huh?"

"I'm telling you, Mack. Sevens and threes you got there, and you're going to have a full house because the top card on the deck's a seven."

The other Martian said, "That's straight, Mack. And you'd lose your shirt on that full because *this* slob—" He pointed to Harry Wainright, who had opened the pot. "—opened on three jacks and the fourth jack is the second card from the top of the deck. He'll have four of them."

"Just play the hand out and see," said the first Martian.

Harry Wainright stood up and slammed his cards down face up on the table, three jacks among them. He reached over and took the deck from Trimble, faced the top two cards. They were a seven and a jack.

As stated.

"Did you think we were kidding you, Mack?" asked the first Martian.

"Why, you lousy—" The muscles of Wainright's shoulders bunched under his shirt as he started for the nearest Martian.

"Don't!" George Keller said. "Harry, remember the radio. You can't throw them out if you can't touch them."

"That's right, Mack," said the Martian. "You'll just make a worse ass out of yourself than you are already."

The other Martian said, "Why don't you get back to the game? We'll help all of you, every hand."

Trimble stood up. "You take that one, Harry," he said grimly. "I'll take this one. If the radio was right we can't throw them out, but damned if it'll hurt to try."

It didn't hurt to try. But it didn't help either.

CHAPTER SIX

Human casualties in all countries that night—or, in the opposite hemisphere, that day—were highest among the military.

At all military installations sentries used their guns. Some challenged and then fired; most of them just fired, and kept on firing until their guns were empty. The Martians jeered and egged them on.

Soldiers who didn't have guns at hand ran to get them. Some got grenades. Officers used their side arms.

All with the result that carnage was terrific, among the soldiers. The Martians got a big bang out of it.

And the greatest mental torture was suffered by the officers in charge of really *top secret* military installations. Because quickly or slowly, according to how smart they were, they realized that there no longer *were* any secrets, top or otherwise. Not from the Martians. Not, since the Martians loved to tattle, from anyone else.

Not that, except for the sake of causing trouble, they had any interest in military matters per se. In fact, they were not in the slightest degree impressed by their examination of secret armed-rocket launching sites, secret A- and H-bomb stock piles, secret files and secret plans.

"Peanut stuff, Mack," one of them sitting on the desk of a two-star general in charge of Base Able (up to then our really top military secret) told the general. "Peanut stuff. You couldn't lick a tribe of Eskimos with everything you got if the Eskimos knew how to vahr. And we might teach them to, just for the hell of it."

"What the hell is vahring?" roared the general.

"None of your Goddam business, Mack." The Martian turned to one of the other Martians in the room; there were four of them altogether. "Hey," he said, "let's kwim over and take a look at what the Russkies got. And compare notes with them."

He and the other Martian vanished.

"Listen to this," one of the two remaining Martians said to the other. "This is a real boff." And he started reading aloud from a supersecret document in a locked safe in the corner.

The other Martian laughed scornfully.

The general laughed too, although not scornfully. He kept on laughing until two of his aides led him away quietly.

The Pentagon was a madhouse, and so was the Kremlin, although neither building, it must be said, drew more than its proportionate share of Martians, either at the time of their arrival or at any time thereafter.

The Martians were as impartial as they were ubiquitous. No one place or type of place interested them more than did another. White House or cathouse, it didn't matter.

They were no more or less interested in big things like, say, the installations in New Mexico where the space station was being worked on than they were in the details of the sex life of the humblest coolie in Shanghai. They sneered equally at both.

And everywhere and in every way they invaded privacy. Privacy, did I say? There no longer was such a thing.

And it was obvious, even that first night, that for as long as they stayed there would *be* no more privacy, no more secrecy, either in the lives of individuals or in the machinations of nations.

Everything concerning us, individually or collectively, interested them—and amused and disgusted them.

Obviously the proper study of Martiankind was man. Animals, as such, did not interest them, although they did not hesitate to frighten or tease animals whenever such action would have the indirect effect of annoying or injuring human beings.

Horses, in particular, were afraid of them and horseback riding, either for sport or as a means of transportation, became so dangerous as to be impossible.

Only a foolhardy person, while the Martians were with us, dared try to milk a cow that was not firmly secured with its feet tied down and its head in a stanchion.

Dogs became frenetic; many bit their masters and had to be put away.

Only cats, each after an initial experience or two, became used to them and took them calmly and with aplomb. But then cats have always been different.

Part Two — Landscape with Martians

CHAPTER ONE

The Martians stayed, and no one knew or could guess how long they might stay. For all we knew, they might be here permanently. It was none of our business

And little if anything was learned about them beyond what was obvious within a day or two after their arrival.

Physically, they were pretty much alike. Although not identical, they averaged considerably less physical variation from one of them to another than human beings, of the same race and sex, average.

The only important difference among them was a difference in size; the largest among them was as tall as three feet and the smallest as short as two feet, three inches.

There were several schools of thought, among human beings, as to the explanation of this difference in height among them. Some people thought that they were all adult males—which, judging from their faces, they appeared to be—and that variation in height among them was as natural among them as is variation in height among human beings.

Other people thought that the difference in height indicated a difference in age; that probably they were all adult males but that, with them, growth did not cease at adulthood and that the short ones were relatively young and the tall ones relatively old.

Still other people thought that the tall ones were probably males and the shorter ones females, and that sex differences between them, whatever they might be, didn't show except in height when they had their clothes on. And since no one ever saw a Martian with his clothes off, this possibility, like the others, could be neither proved nor disproved.

And then there was the theory that all Martians were alike sexually, being either bisexual or having no sex at all, as we understand sex, and that possibly they reproduced by parthenogenesis or some means we couldn't even guess at. For all we knew they grew on trees like coconuts and dropped off when they were ripe, already adult and intelligent, ready to face their world, or to face and sneer at ours. In that case, the smallest among them could have been babies, as it were, just off the tree but fully as hateful as the bigger and older ones. If the smallest among them weren't infants, then we never saw a Martian infant.

We never learned what they ate or drank or even whether they did eat or drink. They couldn't have eaten Earth food, of course; they couldn't even pick it up or handle it, for the same reason that we couldn't handle them. Most people thought that, since their kwimming seemed to be an instantaneous process, a Martian would simply kwim to Mars and back again any time he felt the need for food or drink. Or for sleep, if Martians slept, since no one had ever seen a Martian sleeping on Earth.

We knew amazingly little about them.

We didn't know for sure that they were really *here* in person. Many people, and especially scientists, insisted that a life form that is noncorporeal, without solidity, cannot possibly exist. And that therefore what we saw weren't the Martians themselves but *projections* of them, that the Martians had bodies as solid as ours and left their bodies back on Mars, possibly in a trance state, that kwimming was simply the ability to project an astral body that was visible but not corporeal.

If true, that theory explained a lot, but that there was one thing it didn't explain even its most ardent proponents had to admit. How could a noncorporeal projection talk? Sound is the physical movement or vibration of air or other molecules so how could a mere projection that wasn't really there create a sound?

And they certainly created sounds. Actual sounds, not just in the mind of the listener; the fact that the sounds they made could be recorded on wax or tape was proof of that. They could really talk and they could also (but seldom did) knock on doors. The Martian who knocked on Luke Devereaux's door on what came to be called Coming Night had been an exception in that particular respect. Most of them had kwimmed their way, without knocking, right into living rooms, bedrooms, television stations, night clubs, theaters, taverns (there must have been some wonderful scenes in taverns that night), barracks, igloos, jails, everywhere.

They also showed clearly on photographs, as Luke Devereaux would have found out had he ever bothered to have that roll of film developed. Whether they were there or not, they were opaque to light. But not to radar, and scientists tore their hair over that.

They all insisted that they had no names, or even numbers, and that names were ridiculous and unnecessary. None of them ever addressed a human being by name. In the United States they called every man *Mack* and every woman *Toots;* elsewhere they used local equivalents.

In one field at least they showed tremendous aptitude—linguistics. Luke's Martian hadn't been bragging when he said he could learn a new language in an hour or so. The Martians who appeared among various primitive peoples whose tongues had never been broadcast by radio arrived without knowing a word of the language, but they were speaking it adequately within an hour, fluently within a few hours. And whatever language they spoke, they spoke it idiomatically, even slangily, with none of the stiffness and awkwardness with which human beings speak a new language which they have recently acquired.

Many words in their vocabulary were obviously *not* learned from radio broadcasts. But that isn't difficult to account for; within seconds of their arrival they, or many of them, had plenty of opportunity to pick up a liberal education in profanity. The Martian, for example, who had broken up *Romeo and Juliet* on television with his vulgar comment on Romeo's balcony scene speech was no doubt one who had first kwimmed into, say, a tavern but had sought greener pastures within a matter of seconds when he had found too many others of his kind had kwimmed into the same place.

Mentally, the Martians were even more alike than they were physically, although again there was minor variation—some of them were even worse than others.

But one and all they were abusive, aggravating, annoying, brash, brutal, cantankerous, caustic, churlish, detestable, discourteous, execrable, fiendish, flippant, fresh, galling, hateful, hostile, ill-tempered, insolent, impudent, jabbering, jeering, knavish killjoys. They were leering, loathsome, malevolent, malignant, nasty, nauseating, objectionable, peevish, perverse, quarrelsome, rude, sarcastic, splenetic, treacherous, truculent, uncivil, ungracious, waspish, xenophobic, yapping, and zealous in making themselves obnoxious to and in making trouble for everyone with whom they came in contact.

CHAPTER TWO

Alone again and feeling blue—there wasn't even a Martian present or he'd have felt bluer—Luke Devereaux took his time unpacking two suitcases in the little room in a cheap rooming house he'd just taken in Long Beach.

It was just two weeks after Coming Night. Luke had fifty-six dollars left between himself and starvation and he'd come to Long Beach to look for a job, any kind of job that would keep him eating after that fifty-six dollars was gone. He'd given up even trying to write, for a while.

He'd been lucky in one way, very lucky. He'd been able to sublet his hundred-dollars-a-month Hollywood bachelor apartment, which he'd furnished himself, for the same figure by renting it furnished. That left him free to cut his living expenses and still hang onto the bulk of his possessions without having to pay storage on them. He couldn't have sold them for enough to bother about anyway because the most expensive items were his television set and his radio, and both of those were utterly worthless at the present moment. If the Martians ever left, they'd be valuable again.

So here he was in the cheapest district of Long Beach and all he'd brought with him were two suitcases of clothes and his portable typewriter, the latter for writing letters of application.

He'd probably have to write plenty of them, he thought gloomily. Even here in Long Beach the situation was going to be tough. In Hollywood it would have been impossible.

Hollywood was the hardest hit spot in the country. Hollywood, Beverly Hills, Culver City and the whole movie colony area. Everybody connected in whatever capacity with the movie and television and radio businesses was out of work. Actors, producers, announcers, everyone. All in the same boat, and the boat had sunk suddenly.

And by secondary reaction everything else in Hollywood was being hit hard. Bankrupt or failing were the thousands of shops, beauty parlors, hotels, taverns, restaurants and call houses whose clientele had been mostly among movie people.

Hollywood was becoming a deserted village. The only people staying there were those who, for one reason or another, couldn't get out. As he, Luke, wouldn't have been able to get out, except by walking, if he'd waited much longer.

Probably, he thought, he should have gone farther from Hollywood than Long Beach but he hated to cut deeply into his dwindling hoard for long-distance transportation. And anyway, things were tough all over.

Throughout the country—except Hollywood, which simply gave up— BUSINESS AS USUAL had been the slogan for a week now.

And in some businesses it worked, more or less. You can get used to driving a truck with a Martian sneering at the way you drive or jumping up and down on the hood—or if you can't get used to it, at least you can *do* it. Or you can sell groceries across a counter with a Martian sitting—weightlessly but irremovably—on top of your head and dangling his feet in front of your face while he heckles you and the customer impartially. Things like that are wearing on the nerves but they can be done.

Other businesses did not fare so well. As we have seen, the entertainment business was the first and hardest hit.

Live television was particularly impossible. Although filmed television shows were not interrupted that first night, except at some stations where technicians panicked at the sight of Martians, every live television broadcast was off the air within minutes. The Martians *loved* to disrupt live broadcasts, either television or radio ones.

Some television and radio stations closed down completely, for the duration, or forever if the Martians stayed forever. Others were still operating, using only canned material, but it was obvious that people would tire soon of seeing and hearing old material over and over again—even when a temporary absence of Martians in the living room permitted them to see and hear it without interruption.

And, of course, no one in his right mind was interested in buying *new* television and radio sets, so there went a good many more thousands of people out of work all over the country, all of those engaged in the manufacture and sale of television and radio sets.

And the many thousands who had worked in theaters, concert halls, stadiums, other places of mass entertainment. Mass entertainment of any sort was out; when you brought together a mass of people you brought together a mass of Martians, and whatever was supposed to be entertainment ceased to be such even if it was possible for it to continue at all. Scratch baseball players, ticket sellers, ushers, wrestlers, projectionists…

Yes, things were tough all over. The Great Depression of the nineteen thirties was beginning to look like a period of prosperity.

Yes, Luke was thinking, it was going to be a tough job to find a job. And the sooner he got at it the better. He tossed the last few things impatiently into the dresser drawer, noticing somewhat to his surprise that Margie's Y.W.C.A. T-shirt was among them—why had he brought that?—felt his face to remind himself that he'd shaved, ran his pocket comb quickly through his hair, and left the room.

The telephone was on a table in the hall and he sat down at it and pulled the phone book over. Two Long Beach newspapers came first. Not that he had any real hope of getting on one, but reporting was the least onerous type of work he could think of, and it wouldn't cost him anything to try, except for a couple of dimes in the telephone. Besides he knew Hank Freeman on the *News,* which might give him an in on one of the two papers.

He dialed the *News.* There was a Martian at the switchboard jabbering along with the switchboard girl, trying to foul up calls and sometimes succeeding, but he finally got through to Hank. Hank worked on the city desk.

"Luke Devereaux, Hank. How are things?"

"Wonderful, if you don't care what you say. How are the Greenies treating you, Luke?"

"No worse than anybody else, I guess. Except that I'm looking for a job. How are chances of getting on the *News?*"

"Zero point zero. There's a waiting list as long as your arm for every kind of job here. Plenty of 'em with newspaper experience, too—left newspaper work to go into radio or TV. You never worked on a newspaper, did you?"

"I carried a route when I was a kid."

"You couldn't even get a job doing *that* now, pal. Sorry, there isn't a ghost of a chance of anything, Luke. Things are so tough we're all taking pay cuts. And with so much high-powered talent trying to get in, I'm afraid of losing my own job."

"Pay cuts? With no competition from newscasts, I'd think newspapers would be booming."

"Circulation is booming. But a newspaper's revenue depends on advertising, not on circulation. And that's way down. So many people are out of work and not buying that every store in town's had to cut its advertising budget with a dull ax. Sorry, Luke."

Luke didn't bother to phone the other newspaper.

He went out, walked over to Pine Avenue and south into the business district. The streets were full of people—and Martians. The people were mostly glum and silent, but the strident voices of the Martians made up for that. There was less auto traffic than usual and most drivers drove very cautiously; Martians had a habit of kwimming suddenly onto the hoods of cars, right in front of windshields. The only answer to that was to drive slowly and with a foot on the brake pedal ready to stop the instant vision was cut off.

It was dangerous, too, to drive *through* a Martian, unless you were sure that he wasn't standing in front of some obstacle to block your view of it.

Luke saw an example of that. There was a line of Martians part way across Pine Avenue just south of Seventh Street. They seemed to be very quiet, for Martians, and Luke wondered why—until a Cadillac came along at about twenty miles an hour and the driver, with a grim look on his face, suddenly speeded up and swerved slightly to drive through the line. It had been masking a two-foot-wide trench dug for laying sewer pipe. The Cadillac bounced like a bronco and the right front wheel came off and rolled ahead of it down Pine Avenue.

The driver broke the windshield with his head and got out of the wrecked car dripping blood and profanity. The Martians yelled with glee.

At the next corner, Luke bought a newspaper. And, seeing a shoeshine stand, decided to get a shine while he looked at the ads. His last paid-for shine until after he was solvent and working again, he told himself; hereafter he'd keep his own shoes shined.

He turned to the want ads, looked for MALE HELP WANTED. At first he thought there weren't any such ads, then he found a quarter of a column of them. But there might as well have been none, he realized within a few minutes, as far as he was concerned. Jobs offered were in two categories only—highly skilled technical jobs demanding a special training and experience, and NO EXPERIENCE NEEDED sucker ads for house-to-house canvassers on straight commission. Luke had tried that toughest of rackets years before when he was in his twenties and just getting a start at writing; he'd convinced himself that he couldn't even give away free samples, let alone sell anything. And that had been in "good times." No use his trying it again now, no matter how desperate he got.

Folding back the paper to the front page, he wondered if he'd made a mistake in picking Long Beach. Why *had* he? Not, certainly, because the mental hospital his ex-wife Margie worked at was here. He wasn't going to look her up; he was through with women. For a long time, anyway. A brief but very unpleasant scene with the fair Rosalind the day after his return to Hollywood had shown him that the Martian hadn't been lying about what had happened in her apartment the night before. (Damn them, they never lied when they tattled; you *had* to believe them.)

Had Long Beach been a mistake?

The front page of the paper told him that things were tough all over. DRASTIC CUT IN DEFENSE SPENDING, the President announced. Yes, he admitted that that would cause more unemployment, but the money was desperately needed for relief and would go farther that way. And relief—with people starving—was certainly more important than defense spending, the President told the press conference.

In fact, defense spending wasn't important at all, just at the moment. The Russians and the Chinese were having troubles of their own, worse than ours. Besides, by now we knew all their secrets and they knew all ours—and, the President had said with a wry smile, you can't fight a war *that* way.

Luke, who had served a three-year hitch as an ensign in the navy ten years before, shuddered at the thought of fighting a war with the Martians gleefully helping both sides.

STOCK MARKET STILL ON TOBOGGAN, another article told him. But entertainment stocks, like radio, moving pictures, television and theater, had staged a slight comeback. After being considered completely worthless the week before, they were now being bid for at about a tenth of their former value, as a long-shot long range gamble, by people who thought and hoped that the Martians might not stay long. But industrials reflected the defense spending cut with a sharp drop, and all other stocks were down at least a few points. The big drops, all down the line, had happened the week before.

Luke paid for his shine and left the paper on the seat.

A line of men and a few women, that led around a corner caused him to turn the corner to see where the line led. It was an employment agency. For a moment he considered going back and joining the line; then, in the window, he saw a sign that read REGISTRATION FEE $10, and decided the hell with it. With hundreds of people being registered the chance of getting a job through that agency certainly wasn't worth ten bucks of his dwindling capital. But hundreds of people were paying it.

And if there were any employment agencies that didn't charge registration fees, they'd be mobbed even worse.

He drifted on.

A tall elderly man with fierce eyes and a wild gray beard stood on a soapbox at the curb between two parked cars. Half a dozen people stood listening listlessly. Luke stopped and leaned against a building.

"...and *why,* I ask you, do they never tell lies in their meddling? *Why* are they truthful? *Why?* So that, since they tell no small lies, you will believe their BIG LIE!

"And what, my friends, is their BIG LIE? *It is, that they are Martians.* That is what they want you to believe, to the eternal damnation of your souls.

"Martians! They are DEVILS, devils out of the foulest depths of hell, sent by SATAN, as is predicted in the Book of Revelations!

"And, O my friends, you are damned, damned unless you see the TRUTH and pray, on your bended knees every hour of the day and night, to the ONE BEING who can drive them back whence they came to tempt and torment us. O my friends, pray to GOD and to His Son, ask forgiveness for the EVILS of the WORLD that loosed these demons..."

Luke drifted on.

Probably, he thought, all over the world religious fanatics were taking that line, or a similar one.

Well, they could even be right. There wasn't any proof that they were Martians. Only thing was, he personally believed that there *could* be Martians and he didn't believe in devils and demons at all. For that reason, he was willing to take the Martians' word for it.

Another queue, another employment agency.

A boy walking along with a pile of handbills handed Luke one. He slowed down to glance at it. "GREAT OPPORTUNITIES IN NEW PROFESSION," he read. "BECOME A PSYCHOLOGICAL CONSULTANT."

The rest was in smaller type and he stuffed it into his pocket. Maybe he'd read it later. A new racket, probably. A depression breeds rackets as a swamp breeds mosquitoes.

Another line of people leading around a corner. It seemed longer than the two other lines he'd passed and he wondered if it might be a public employment agency, one that wouldn't charge a registration fee.

If so, it wouldn't hurt to register, since he couldn't think of anything more constructive to do at the moment. Besides, if his money ran out before he got a job, he'd have to be registered there before they'd let him go on relief. Or even get on any of the WPA-type projects that the government was already getting ready to organize. Would there be a Writers' Project this time? If so, he could certainly qualify for that, and it wouldn't take creative writing, just boondoggling along on something like a history of Long Beach, and even if he was burned out as a writer he could do that. In his sleep.

And the line seemed to be moving fairly fast, so fast that he decided they must be just handing out blanks for people to fill out and mail in.

Just the same, he'd check the head of the line first and make sure that was what was going on.

It wasn't.

The line led to an emergency soup kitchen. It led through a doorway into a big building that looked as though it had once been a skating rink or a dance hall. It was filled now with long tables improvised from planks laid over sawbucks; hundreds of people, mostly men but a few women, sat at the tables hunched over bowls of soup. Scores of Martians ran up and down the tables, frequently stepping—but without other than visual effect, of course—into the steaming bowls and playing leapfrog over the diners' heads.

The odor of the soup wasn't bad, and it reminded Luke that he was hungry; it must be at least noon and he'd skipped breakfast. Why shouldn't he join the line and husband his dwindling financial resources? Nobody seemed to be asking any questions; anybody who joined the line got a bowl.

Or did they? For a moment, he watched the table on which stood a big kettle of soup, from which a big man in a greasy apron ladled soup into bowls; he noticed that quite a few people turned down the bowl offered them and, with a slightly sickish or disgusted look on their faces, turned and headed out again.

Luke put his hand on the arm of a man walking past him after declining a bowl. "What's the matter?" he asked. "The soup look that bad? It smells all right."

"Go look, chum," said the man, disengaging his arm and hurrying outside.

Luke stepped closer and looked. There was a Martian, he could see now, sitting or squatting in the middle of the bowl of soup. Every few seconds he would bend forward and stick a tremendously long chartreuse tongue into the soup in front of him. Then he'd pull his tongue back and pretend to spit out the soup, making a very disgusted and very disgusting noise in the process. The big man with the ladle paid no attention, dipping soup right out through the Martian. Some of the people in the line—the ones who'd been here before, Luke suspected—paid no attention either, or walked past with eyes carefully averted.

Luke watched a minute longer and then went outside. He didn't join the line. He knew perfectly well that the Martian's presence in it had no effect whatsoever on the soup. But just the same, he wasn't that hungry yet, and wouldn't be while his money lasted.

He found a little five-stool diner, empty of customers and, for the moment at least, also happily empty of Martians. He ate a hamburger sandwich and then ordered another one and a cup of coffee.

He'd finished the second sandwich and was sipping at the coffee when the counterman, a tall blond kid of about nineteen, said, "Let me hot it up for you," and took the cup to the coffee urn, filled it and brought it back.

"Thanks," Luke said.

"Want a piecea pie?"

"Uh—I guess not."

"Blueberry pie. It's on the house."

"At that price," Luke said, "sure. But how come?"

"Boss is closing up the place tonight. We got more pie than we'll sell by then. So why not?"

He put a slab of pie and a fork in front of Luke.

"Thanks," Luke said. "Is business really that bad?"

"Brother, things are tough," said the counterman.

CHAPTER THREE

Brother, things were tough. Nowhere tougher than in the fields of crime and law enforcement. Offhand, you'd say that if things were tough for the cops they'd be good for the crooks, or vice versa, but it didn't work out that way at all.

Things were tough for the forces of law and order because crimes of passion and sudden violence were up, way up. People's nerves were already wearing thin. Since it did no good to attack or quarrel with Martians—or even to *try* to attack or quarrel with them—people quarreled with and fought with one another. Street fights and domestic fights were a dime a dozen. Murders—not the premeditated variety but ones committed in sudden anger or temporary insanity—were two bits a dozen. Yes, the police had their hands full and their jails even fuller.

But if the cops were overworked, professional criminals were underworked, and hungry. Crimes for gain, whether of stealth or violence, *planned* crimes, were down, way down.

The Martians tattled so.

Take, for random but typical example, what happened to Alf Billings, Cockney pickpocket, right while Luke Devereaux was eating his lunch in the Long Beach diner. It was early evening, of course, in London. Let's let Alf tell it in his own words.

Take it, Alf.

"Well, Guv'nor, 'ere Hi am fresh from a moon in a flowery, and Hi'm poppin' out of an oozer after a pig's ear that took my last smash. Blimey, Hi'm on the rib. So when I gets a decko at this connaught ranger takin' a pen'worth of chalk down the frog lookin' like 'e'd 'ave a dummy full of bees and honey, 'e looks ripe for a buzz. Hi takes a decko around—no bogies. Hi see a greenie on a jam-pot near but 'ow'd Hi know 'e was a grass? Hi *got* to speel or there's no weeping willow for my Uncle Ned. So I closes up and uses my fork to blag—"

Wait, Alf. Maybe you'd better let *me* tell what happened, in *my* words.

Here was little Alf Billings, fresh from a month in jail, coming out of a pub after just having spent his last change for a glass of beer. So when he saw a prosperous-looking stranger walking down the street, he decided to pick his pocket. Nobody in sight looked like a policeman or detective. True, there was a Martian sitting on top of a parked automobile nearby, but Alf hadn't learned much about the Martians yet. And, in any case, Alf was flat broke; he had to take a chance or he wouldn't be able to afford a place to sleep that night. So he closed up on the man and picked his pocket.

That's what Alf just told you, but I thought it better to repeat. And to go on from there:

Suddenly there was the Martian on the sidewalk beside Alf, pointing to the wallet in Alf's hand and chanting delightedly, "Yah, yah, yah, yah, yah, look 'oo blagged a dummy!"

"Nark it, you bloody barstard," Alf growled, shoving the wallet quickly out of sight into his own pocket and turning to slouch away.

But the Martian didn't nark it. He kept pace with poor Alf, and kept up his delighted chanting. And with a quick look over his shoulder, Alf saw that his victim had turned, was feeling in his hip pocket and getting set to start after Alf and his little companion.

Alf ran. Around the nearest corner and right into the blue-clad arms of a bobby.

You see what I mean.

It wasn't that the Martians were against crime or criminals, except in the sense that they were against everything and everybody. They loved to make trouble and catching a criminal either planning a crime or in the act of committing one gave them such a beautiful opportunity.

But once a criminal was caught, they were equally assiduous in heckling the police. In court they would drive judges, lawyers, witnesses and juries to such distraction that there were more mistrials than completed ones. With Martians in a courtroom, Justice would have had to be deaf as well as blind in order to ignore them.

CHAPTER FOUR

"Damn good pie," Luke said, putting down his fork. "Thanks again."

"More coffee?"

"No, thanks. I've had plenty."

"Nothin' else at all?"

Luke grinned. "Sure, a job."

The tall young man had been leaning both hands on the counter. He suddenly straightened. "Say, that's an idea, brother. Would you take one for half a day? From now till five o'clock?"

Luke stared at him. "You serious? Sure I would. Better than wasting the afternoon looking for one."

"Then you got yourself one." He came around from behind the counter, pulling his apron off as he came. "Hang up your coat and put this on." He tossed the apron on the counter.

"Okay," said Luke, not yet reaching for the apron. "But what's it all about? What's the score?"

"I'm heading for the hills, that's the score." And then at the expression on Luke's face, he grinned. "All right. I'll tell you all about it. But let's introduce ourselves. I'm Rance Carter." He stuck out his hand.

Luke said "Luke Devereaux," and shook it.

Rance sat down on a stool, one stool away so they could face one another. He said, "Wasn't kidding about being a hillbilly; anyway I was one till two years ago when I came to California. Paw and maw got a little farm—bottom land, too—near Hartville, Missouri. Wasn't satisfied there then, but with what's happenin' now—and me outa work fer God knows how long, reckon I shore want back there now." His eyes were shining with excitement—or homesickness—and with every sentence his accent slipped farther and farther back into the hillbilly.

Luke nodded. "Good idea. At least you'll eat. And there'll be fewer Martians around a farm than in a city."

"You said it. Made up muh mind tuh go back soon as the boss said he was closin' up. Sooner the better and I been gettin' in a hellfire hurry all mornin' and your askin' about a job give me an idea. Promised the boss I'd keep the place open tell five uh-clock—when he gets down—an' guess I'm too damn honest tuh jest close up an' walk out on him. But it cain't make no deffrence ef I let you do it instead, can it?"

"I guess not," said Luke. "But will he pay me?"

"I'll pay you. Get ten a day besides mah eats, an' I'm paid through yesterday. Ten bucks comin' for today. I'll take it out uh the register an' leave a note, give you five bucks an' keep five bucks."

"Fair enough," said Luke. "It's a deal." He stood up, peeling off his suit coat, and hung it on one of the hooks on the wall. He put the apron on, tied the cords.

Rance had put on his own suit coat and was at the register back of the counter, taking out two five dollar bills

"Cal-eye-for-nee, here Ah go—" he caroled, and then paused, obviously at a loss for a second line.

"Right back home to Hartville, Mo!" Luke supplied.

Rance stared at him in open-mouthed admiration. "Hey, guy, did you think uh that jest like *that?*" He snapped his fingers. "Say, you oughta be a writer, or somethin'."

"I'll settle for being something," Luke told him. "By the way, anything I should know about this job?"

"Nah. Prices are on the wall there. Everything that ain't in sight's in the 'frigerator there. Here's the five and thanks to hell and back."

"Good luck," said Luke. They shook hands and Rance went out singing happily, "Cal-eye-for-nee, here Ah go—right back home to..."

Luke spent ten minutes familiarizing himself with the contents of the refrigerator and the prices on the wall. Ham and eggs looked to be the most complicated thing he might have to prepare. And he'd done that often enough for himself at home. Any writer who is a bachelor and hates to interrupt himself to go out to eat becomes a fairly good short order cook.

Yes, the job looked easy and he hoped the boss would change his mind about closing the place. Ten bucks a day, with his meals furnished as well, would be plenty for him to get along on for a while. And with the pressure off maybe he could even start writing again, evenings.

But business, or the lack of it, killed that hope long before the afternoon was over. Customers came in at the rate of about one an hour and usually spent fifty cents or less apiece. A hamburger and coffee for forty cents or pie and coffee for thirty-five. One plunger brought the average up a little by shooting ninety-five cents for a hamburger steak, but it was obvious, even to a non-businessman like Luke, that the take wasn't covering the cost of food plus overhead, even if his own pay was the only item of overhead involved.

Several times Martians kwimmed into the place, but, as it happened, never while a customer was eating at the counter. Finding Luke alone, none of them tried to do anything seriously annoying and none stayed longer than a few minutes.

At a quarter of five Luke wasn't hungry again as yet but decided he might as well save a little money by stocking up for the evening. He made himself a boiled ham sandwich and ate it. Made himself another, wrapped it and put it into the pocket of his coat hanging on the wall.

As he put it there his hand encountered a folded paper, the handbill that had been given to him on the street earlier in the day. He took it back to the counter and unfolded it to read while he had a final cup of coffee.

"BEAT THE DEPRESSION

WITH A NEW PROFESSION,"

the handbill told him. And in smaller type, "Become a Consulting Psychologist."

Neither heading was in flagrantly large type. And the body type was ten-point Bodoni with wide margins; the effect as a whole was very conservative and pleasing for a handbill.

"Are you intelligent, presentable, well-educated—but unemployed?" the handbill asked him. Luke almost nodded a yes before he read on.

> If you are, there is an opportunity now for you to help humanity, and yourself, by becoming a consulting psychologist, by advising people how to remain calm and to stay sane despite the Martians, for however long they stay.

If you are properly qualified, and especially if you already have a fair lay knowledge of psychology, a very few lessons, perhaps as few as two or three, will give you sufficient knowledge and insight to help first yourself and then others to withstand the concerted attack upon human sanity which is being made by the Martians today.

Classes will be limited to seven persons, to permit free discussion and the asking of questions after each class. The fee will be very moderate, five dollars per lesson.

Your instructor will be the undersigned, Bachelor of Science (Ohio State, 1953), Doctor of Psychology (U.S.C., 1958), subsequently with five years' experience as an industrial psychologist with Convair Corporation, active member of American Association of Psychologists, author of several monographs and of one book, *You and Your Nerves*, Dutton, 1962.

Ralph S. Forbes, Ps. D.

And a Long Beach telephone number.

Luke read it again before he folded it and put it in his pocket. It didn't sound like a racket—not if the guy really had those qualifications.

And it made sense. People *were* going to need help, and need it badly; they we cracking up right and left. If Doc Forbes had even a piece of the answer—

He glanced at the clock and saw that it was ten minutes after five, and was wondering how late "the boss" might be, and whether or not he should just lock the door and leave, when the door opened,

The middle-aged stocky man who came in looked at Luke sharply. "Where's Rance?"

"On his way back to Missouri. You the owner?"

"Yeah. What happened?"

Luke explained. The owner nodded and came around the counter. He opened the register, read Rance's note, and grunted. He counted the cash in the register—it didn't take long—and pulled a strip of paper out of the side to check the reading on it. He grunted again and turned back to Luke.

"Business really that lousy?" he asked. "Or did you drag down a few bucks?"

"Business was really that lousy," Luke told him. "If I'd taken in even ten bucks I might have been tempted. But not when I took in less than five. That's less than my minimum price for being crooked."

The owner sighed. "Okay, I believe you. Had your dinner?"

"Had a sandwich. And put another in my pocket."

"Hell, make a few more. Enough to last you tomorrow. I'm going to close up now—what's the use of wasting an evening?—and take home what grub's left. But it's more'n my wife and I can eat before it starts to spoil."

"Thanks, guess I might as well," Luke said.

He made himself three more cold sandwiches and, when he left, took them along; they'd save him from having to spend money for food for another day.

Back in his room, he carefully looked the sandwiches in the tightest closing one of his suitcases to protect them from mice and cockroaches—if there were mice or cockroaches around; he hadn't seen any yet, but he'd just taken the room that morning.

He took the handbill from his pocket to read it again. Suddenly a Martian was perched on his shoulder reading it with him. The Martian finished first, howled with laughter, and was gone.

It made sense, that handbill. At least enough sense to make him want to gamble five dollars on *one* lesson from the psychology prof. He took out his wallet and counted his money again. Sixty-one dollars; five more than he'd had left after paying a week's room rent this morning. Because of his lucky break at the lunch counter, he was not only richer by that five bucks, but he'd had to spend no money on food today nor would he have to spend any tomorrow.

Why not gamble that five bucks and see if he could parlay it into a steady income? Hell, even if he never followed through and made any money out of it, he might get five bucks' worth of information on how to control his own temper and his own reactions toward the Martians. Possibly even to the point where he could try writing again soon.

Before he could weaken and change his mind he went to the telephone in the hall and dialed the number on the handbill.

A calm, resonant male voice identified itself as that of Ralph Forbes.

Luke gave his own name. "I've read your handbill, Doctor," he said, "and I'm interested. When are you holding your next class, and is it filled yet?"

"1 haven't given a class yet, Mr. Devereaux. I'm starting my first group this evening at seven, about an hour from now. And another group at two o'clock tomorrow afternoon. Neither group is filled as yet; as it happens I have five reservations for each, so you may have your choice."

"In that case, the sooner the better," Luke said. "So put me down for this evening please. Are you having these classes at your home?"

"No, I've taken a small office for the purpose. Room six-fourteen in the Draeger Building on Pine Avenue just north of Ocean Boulevard. But just a moment; before you hang up, may I explain something to you and ask a few questions?"

"Go ahead, Doctor."

"Thank you. Before I enroll you I hope you'll forgive my asking a few questions about your background. You see, Mr. Devereaux, this is not a—ah—racket. While I hope to make money from it, naturally, I'm also interested in helping people, and a great many people are going to need a great deal of help. More people than I can hope to advise individually. That is why I have chosen this method, working through others."

"I see," Luke said. "You're looking for disciples to make into apostles."

The psychologist laughed. "Cleverly put. But let's not carry the analogy any farther—I assure you that I do not consider myself a messiah. But I do have enough humble faith in my ability to help others to make me want to choose my pupils carefully. Especially since I'm keeping my classes so small, I want to be sure to confine my efforts to people who—ah—"

"I understand perfectly," Luke cut in. "Go ahead with the questions."

"Do you have a college education, or equivalent?"

"I went to college two years, but I think I can claim to have the equivalent of a college education—an unspecialized one, that is. I've been an omnivorous reader all my life."

"And how long, may I ask, has that been?"

"Thirty-seven years. Wait, I mean that I'm thirty-seven years old. I haven't been reading *quite* that long, by a few years anyway."

"Have you read much in the field of psychology?"

"Nothing technical. Quite a few of the popular books, the ones written for laymen."

"And what, may I ask, has been your principal occupation?"

"Fiction writing."

"Indeed. *Science* fiction? Are you by any chance *Luke* Devereaux?"

Luke felt the warm glow a writer always feels when his name is recognized. "Yes," he said. "Don't tell me you read science fiction."

"But I do, and love it. At least I did until two weeks ago. I don't imagine anyone is in the mood to read about extraterrestrials right now. Come to think of it, there must be quite a sharp break in the science-fiction market. Is that why you're looking for a new—ah—profession?"

"I'm afraid that even before the Martians came I was in the worst slump of my writing career, so I can't blame it all on them. Not that they've helped, of course. And you can say what you said about the science-fiction market again and a lot more strongly. There just isn't any such market any more, and there may not be one for years after the Martians leave—if they ever leave."

"I see. Well, Mr. Devereaux, I'm sorry you've run into bad luck with your writing; needless to say, though, I'll be more than glad to have you in one of my classes. If you'd happened to mention your first name as well as your last when you identified yourself a moment ago, I assure you my questions would have been needless. I'll see you at seven this evening, then?"

"Right," Luke said.

Maybe the psychologist's questions had been needless, but Luke was glad he'd asked them. He was sure now that this was not a racket, that the man was everything he claimed to be.

And that the five dollars he was about to spend might be the best investment he'd ever made. He felt certain now that he *was* going to have a new profession, and an important one. He felt sure that he was going to follow through and take as many lessons as Forbes would decide he needed, even if it was more than the two or three that Forbes' advertisement had said might be enough. If his money ran out first, no doubt Forbes—already knowing him by name and admiring him as a writer—would be willing to let him have the last few lessons on credit and let him pay for them after he was making money helping others.

And between lessons he'd spend his time at the public library or reading books taken home from it, not just reading but actually studying every book on psychology he could lay his hands on. He was a fast reader and had a retentive memory, and if he was going in for this thing he might as well do it whole hog and make himself into as near to a real psychologist as it was possible to become without the accolade of a degree. Even that, maybe, someday. Why not? If he was really through as a writer it would be better for him really to shoot, no matter how tough the shooting might be at first, for a foothold in another legitimate profession. He was still young enough, damn it.

He took a quick shower and shaved. Nicking himself slightly when a sudden Bronx cheer sounded right in his ear as he was in the middle of a stroke; there hadn't been a Martian around a second before. It wasn't a deep cut, though, and his styptic pencil stopped the bleeding easily. Could even a psychologist, he wondered, ever become sufficiently conditioned to things like that to avoid the reaction that had made him cut himself? Well, Forbes would know the answer to that. And if there wasn't a better answer, an electric razor would solve the problem. He'd get himself one as soon as he was solvent again.

He wanted his appearance to back up the impression his name had made, so he put on his best suit—the tan gabardine—a clean white shirt, hesitated over the choice between his Countess Mara tie and a more conservative blue one, and chose the blue.

He left, whistling. Walked jauntily, feeling that this was a turning point in his life, the start of a new and better era.

The elevators in the Draeger Building weren't running, but it didn't discourage him to have to walk up to the sixth floor; it exhilarated him instead.

As he opened the door of six-fourteen, a tall slender man in Oxford gray, with thick shell-rimmed glasses, rose and came around from behind a desk to shake hands with him. "Luke Devereaux?" he asked.

"Right, Doctor Forbes. But how did you know me?"

Forbes smiled. "Partly by elimination—everyone who's signed up was already here except yourself and one other. And partly because I've seen your picture on a book jacket."

Luke turned and saw that there were four others already in the office, seated in comfortable chairs. Two men and two women. They were all well-dressed and looked intelligent and likable. And there was one Martian, seated cross-legged on a corner of Forbes' desk, doing nothing but looking bored at the moment. Forbes introduced Luke around—except to the Martian. The men were named Kendall and Brent; the women were a Miss Kowalski and a Mrs. Johnston.

"And I'd introduce you to our Martian friend if he had a name," said Forbes cheerfully. "But they tell us they do not use names."

"—you, Mack," said the Martian.

Luke chose one of the unoccupied chairs and Forbes went back to his swivel chair behind the desk. He glanced at his wristwatch. "Seven exactly," he said. "But I think we should allow a few minutes for our final member to arrive. Do you all agree?"

All of them nodded and Miss Kowalski asked, "Do you want to collect from us now, while we're waiting?"

Five five-dollar bills, including Luke's, were passed up to the desk. Forbes left them lying there, in sight. "Thank you," he said. "I'll leave them there. If any of you is not satisfied when the lesson is over, he may take his money back. Ah, here is our final member. Mr. Gresham?"

He shook hands with the newcomer, a bald middle-aged man who looked vaguely familiar to Luke—although Luke couldn't place the name or where he'd seen him—and introduced him around to the other class members. Gresham saw the pile of bills on the desk and added his, then took the vacant seat next to Luke's. While Forbes was arranging some notes in front of him Gresham leaned over toward Luke. "Haven't we met somewhere?" he whispered.

"We must have met," Luke said. "I had the same feeling. But let's compare notes afterwards. Wait, I think I—"

"*Quiet,* please!"

Luke stopped and leaned back abruptly. Then flushed a little when he realized that it was the Martian who had spoken, not Forbes. The Martian grinned at him.

Forbes smiled. "Let me start by saying that you will find it impossible to ignore Martians—especially when they say or do something unexpectedly. I hadn't meant to bring up that point right away, but since it is obvious that I am going to have 'help' in this class tonight, perhaps it is best that I start with a statement which I had intended to lead up to gradually.

"It is this: your life, your thoughts, your sanity—as well as the lives, thoughts and sanity of those whom I hope you will advise and teach—will be least affected by them if you choose the middle way between trying to ignore them completely and letting yourself take them too seriously.

"To ignore them completely—rather, to try to ignore them completely, to pretend that they aren't there when so obviously they are, is a form of rejection of reality that can lead straight to schizophrenia and paranoia. Conversely, to pay full attention to them, to let yourself become seriously angry with them can lead straight to nervous breakdown—or apoplexy."

It made sense, Luke thought. In almost anything, the middle way is the best way.

The Martian on the corner of Forbes' desk yawned mightily.

A second Martian suddenly kwimmed into the room, right in the middle of Forbes' desk. So close to Forbes' nose that he let out an involuntary yip. Then smiled at the class over the Martian's head.

Then he glanced down to look at his notes; the new Martian was sitting on them. He reached a hand through the Martian and slid them to one side; the Martian moved with them.

Forbes sighed and then looked up at the class. "Well, it looks as though I'll have to talk without notes. Their sense of humor is very childlike."

He leaned to one side to see better around the head of the Martian sitting in front of him. The Martian leaned that way, too. Forbes straightened, and so did the Martian.

"Their sense of humor is very childlike," Forbes repeated. "Which reminds me to tell you that it was through the study of children and their reaction to Martians that I have formulated most of my theories. You have all no doubt observed that, after the first few hours, after the novelty wore off, children became used to the presence of Martians much more easily and readily than adults. Especially children under five. I have two children of my own and—"

"Three, Mack," said the Martian on the corner of the desk. "I saw that agreement you gave the dame in Gardena two thousand bucks for, so she wouldn't file a paternity suit."

Forbes flushed. "I have two children *at home,*" he said firmly, "and—"

"And an alcoholic wife," said the Martian. "Don't forget *her.*"

Forbes waited a few moments with his eyes closed, as though silently counting.

"The nervous systems of children," he said, "as I explained in *You and Your Nerves,* my popular book on—"

"Not so damned popular, Mack. That royalty statement shows less than a thousand copies."

"I meant that it was written in popular style."

"Then why didn't it sell?"

"Because people didn't buy it," snapped Forbes. He smiled at the class. "Forgive me. I should not have permitted myself to be drawn into pointless argument. If they ask ridiculous questions, do not answer."

The Martian who had been sitting on his notes suddenly kwimmed into a sitting position atop his head, dangling legs in front of his face and swinging them so his vision was alternately clear and blocked.

He glanced down at his notes, now again visible to him—part at the time. He said, "Ah—I see I have a notation here to remind you, and I had better do so while I can read the notation, that in dealing with the people whom you are to help, you must be completely truthful—"

"Why weren't *you,* Mack?" asked the Martian on the corner of the desk.

"—and make no unjustified claims about yourself or—"

"Like you did in that circular, Mack? Forgetting to say those several monographs you mention weren't ever published?"

Forbes' face was turning beet red behind its pendulum of green-clad legs. He rose slowly to a standing position, his hands gripping the desk's edge. He said, "I—ah—"

"Or why didn't you tell them, Mack, that you were only an assistant psychologist at Convair, and why they fired you?" And the corner-of-the-desk Martian put his thumbs in his ears, waggled his other fingers and emitted a very loud and juicy Bronx cheer.

Forbes swung at him, hard. And then screamed in pain as his fist, passing through the Martian, struck and knocked off the desk the heavy metal desk lamp which the Martian had been sitting over and concealing.

He pulled back his injured hand and stared at it blankly through the pendulum of the second Martian's legs. Suddenly, both Martians were gone.

Forbes, his face now white instead of red, sat down slowly and stared blankly at the six people seated in his office, as though wondering why they were there. He brushed his hand across his face as though pushing away something that was no longer there, and which couldn't have been pushed away while it was.

He said, "In dealing with Martians, it is important to remember—"

Then he dropped his head into his arms on the desk in front of him and started sobbing quietly.

The woman who had been introduced as Mrs. Johnston had been seated nearest the desk. She stood up and leaned forward, put her hand on his shoulder. "Mr. Forbes," she said. "Mr. Forbes, are you all right?"

There was no answer except that the sobbing stopped slowly.

All the others were standing now too. Mrs. Johnston turned to them. "I think we'd better leave him," she said. "And—" she picked up the six five-dollar bills. "—I guess we've got these coming back." She kept one and passed the others around. They left, very quietly, some of them walking on tiptoe.

Except for Luke Devereaux and the Mr. Gresham who had sat next to him. "Let's stay," Gresham had said. "He may need help." And Luke had nodded.

Now, with the others gone, they lifted Forbes' head from the desk and held him straight in the chair. His eyes were open but stared at them blankly.

"Shock," Gresham said. "He *may* come out of it and be all right. But—" His voice sounded doubtful. "Think we'd better send for the men in the white coats?"

Luke had been examining Forbes' injured hand. "It's broken," he said. "He'll need attention for that, anyway. Let's phone for a doctor. If he hasn't come out of it by then, let the doc take the responsibility for having them come and get him."

"Good idea. But maybe we won't have to phone. There's a doctor's office next door. I noticed when I came here, and the light was on. He must either have evening hours or be working late."

The doctor had been working late, and was just leaving when they caught him. They brought him into Forbes' office, explained what had happened, told him it was his responsibility now, and then left.

Going down the stairs, Luke said, "He was a good guy, while he lasted."

"And had a good idea, while *it* lasted."

"Yeah," Luke said. "And I feel lower than a mole's basement. Say, we were going to figure out where we've seen or met one another. Have you remembered?"

"Could it have been at Paramount? I worked there six years up to when they closed two weeks ago."

"That's it," said Luke. "You wrote continuity. I put in a few weeks there a few years ago, on scripts. Didn't do so hot, and quit. What talent I've got is for the written word, not for scripting."

"That's it, then. Say, Devereaux—"

"Make it Luke. And your first name's Steve, isn't it?"

"Right. Well, Luke, I feel lower than a mole's basement, too. And I know how I'm going to spend the five bucks I just got back. Got any idea about yours?"

"The same idea you have. After we buy some, shall we go to my room or yours?"

They compared notes on rooms and decided on Luke's; Steve Gresham was staying with his sister and her husband; there were children and other disadvantages, so Luke's room would be best.

They drowned their sorrows, drink for drink; Luke turned out to have the better capacity of the two of them. At a little after midnight, Gresham passed out cold; Luke was still operating, if a bit erratically.

He tried and failed to wake up Gresham, then sadly poured himself another drink and sat down with it to drink and think instead of drinking and talking. But he wanted to talk rather than to think and almost, but not quite, wished a Martian would show up. But none did. And he wasn't crazy enough or drunk enough to talk to himself. "Not yet anyway," he said aloud, and the sound of his voice startled him to silence again.

Poor Forbes, he thought. He and Gresham had deserted; they should have stayed with Forbes and tried to see him through, at least until and unless they found out it was hopeless. They hadn't even waited for the doctor's diagnosis. Had the doc been able to snap Forbes out of it, or had he sent for the men in the white coats?

He could phone the doctor and ask him what had happened.

Except that he didn't remember the doctor's name, if he had ever heard it.

He could call Long Beach General Mental Hospital and find out if Forbes had been taken there. Or if he asked for Margie, she could find out for him more about Forbes' condition than the switchboard would tell him. But he didn't want to talk to Margie. Yes, he did. No, he didn't; she divorced him and to hell with her. To hell with all women.

He went out in the hallway to the phone, staggering only slightly. But he had to close one eye to read the fine type in the phone book, and again to dial the number.

He asked for Margie.

"Last name, please?"

"Uh—" For a blank second he couldn't remember Margie's maiden name. Then he remembered it, but decided that she might not have decided to use it again, especially since the divorce wasn't final yet. "Margie Devereaux. Nurse."

"One moment please."

And several moments later, Margie's voice. "Hello."

"Hi, Marge. S'Luke. D' I wake you up?"

"No, I'm on night duty. Luke, I'm glad you called. I've been worried about you."

"Worried 'bout *me*? I'm aw right. Why worry 'bout me?"

"Well—the Martians. So many people are— Well, I've just been worrying."

"Thought they'd send me off my rocker, huh? Don't worry, honey, they can't get *me* down. Write science fiction, 'member? Wrote it, I mean, I *invented*

Martians."

"Are you sure you're all right, Luke? You've been drinking."

"Sure, been drinking. But I'm aw right. How're *you?*"

"Fine. But *awfully* busy. This place is—well, it's a madhouse. I can't talk long. Did you want anything?"

"Don't wanna thing, honey. I'm *fine.*"

"Then I'll have to hang up. But I do want to talk to you, Luke. Will you phone me tomorrow afternoon?"

"Sure, honey. Wha' time?"

"Any time after noon. 'Bye, Luke."

"'Bye, honey."

He went back to his drink, suddenly remembering that he'd forgotten to ask Margie about Forbes. Well, the hell with Forbes; it didn't matter. He was either okay or he wasn't, and nothing could be done about it if he wasn't.

Surprising, though, that Margie'd been so friendly. Especially since she'd recognized that he was drunk. She wasn't a prig about drinking—she herself drank moderately. But always got mad at him if he let go and drank too much, like tonight.

Must really have been worried about him. But why?

And then he remembered. She'd always suspected him of not being very stable mentally. Had tried to get him to have analysis once—that was one of the things they'd quarreled about. So naturally now, with so many people going nuts, she'd think him likely to be one of the first to go.

To hell with her, if she thought *that.* He was going to be the last to let the Martians get him down, not the first.

He poured himself another drink. Not that he really wanted it—he was plenty drunk already—but to defy Margie and the Martians. He'd show 'em.

One was in the room now. One Martian, not one Margie.

Luke leveled an unsteady finger at it. "Can't get me down," he said. "I 'nvented you."

"You're already down, Mack. You're drunk as a skunk."

The Martian looked disgustedly from Luke to Gresham, snoring on the bed. And must have decided that neither of them was worth annoying, for it vanished.

"See. Told you so," Luke said.

Took another drink from his glass and then put the glass down just in time, for his chin fell forward on his chest and he slept.

And dreamed of Margie. Part of the time he dreamed of quarreling and fighting with her and part of the time he dreamed—but even while the Martians were around, dreams remained private.

CHAPTER FIVE

The Iron Curtain quivered like an aspen leaf in an earthquake.

The leaders of the People found themselves faced with an internal opposition that they could not purge, could not even intimidate.

And not only could they not blame the Martians on the Capitalist warmongers but they soon found out that the Martians were *worse* than Capitalist warmongers.

Not only were they not Marxists but they would admit to no political philosophy whatsoever and sneered at all of them. They sneered equally at all terrestrial governments and forms of government, even theoretical ones. Yes, they themselves had the perfect form of government but they refused to tell anyone what it was—except that it was none of our business.

They weren't missionaries and had no desire to help us. All they wanted was to know everything that went on and to be as annoying and irritating as they possibly could.

Behind the trembling curtain, they succeeded wonderfully.

How could one tell the Big Lie or even a little one, with a third of a billion Martians gleefully ready to punch holes in it? They loved propaganda.

And they tattled so. No one can guess how many people were summarily tried and executed in Communist countries during the first month or two of the Martians' stay. Peasants, factory superintendents, generals, Politburo members. It wasn't safe to do or say *anything*, with Martians around. And there seemed always to be Martians around.

After a while, of course, that phase of things eased up. It had to. You can't kill everybody, not even everybody outside the Kremlin, if for no other reason than that then the Capitalist warmongers could march in and take over. You can't even send everybody to Siberia; Siberia would hold them all right, but it wouldn't support them.

Concessions *had* to be made; minor variations in opinion had to be permitted. Minor deviations from the party line had to be ignored if not actually winked at. These things were bad enough.

But what was worse was that propaganda, even *internal* propaganda, was impossible. Facts and figures, in speeches or in print, had to be honest. The Martians *loved* it when they found even the slightest misstatement or exaggeration, and told everybody.

How could you run a government that way?

CHAPTER SIX

But the Capitalist warmongers were having their troubles too. Who wasn't?

Take Ralph Blaise Wendell. Born at the turn of the century and now sixty-four years old. Tall but becoming a little stooped; slender, with thinning gray hair and tired gray eyes. Although it had not seemed a misfortune at the time, he had had the misfortune to have been elected President of the United States in 1960.

Now and until the November elections brought surcease he was president of a country that contained a hundred and eighty million people—and about sixty million Martians.

Now—now being an evening in early May, six weeks after the Coming—he sat alone in his big office, brooding.

Completely alone; there wasn't even a Martian present. Such solitude was not unusual. Alone, or with only his secretary present, he had as good a chance as anyone else of not being bothered, The Martians haunted presidents and dictators no more than they haunted file clerks and baby sitters. They were no respecters of persons; they were no respecters of anything at all.

And now, at least for the moment, he was alone. The day's work finished, but loath to move. Or too tired to move. Tired with the special weariness that comes from the combination of great responsibility and a feeling of utter inadequacy. Tired with defeat.

He thought back bitterly over the past six weeks and of the mess things had become. A depression that made the so-called Great Depression of the thirties look like prosperity beyond the dreams of avarice.

A depression that had started—not with a stock market crash, although that had followed quickly enough—with the sudden loss of employment of millions of people all at once. Almost everyone connected with entertainment; not only the entertainers but stagehands, ticket takers, scrubwomen. Everyone connected in any capacity with professional sports. Everyone connected with the movie industry in any capacity whatsoever. Everyone connected with radio and television except a few technicians to keep transmitters running and to handle the already-filmed or already-taped replays. And a few, a very few, announcers and commentators.

Every orchestra and dance band musician. Shades of Petrillo!

Nobody had guessed how many millions of people had made their living one way or another, directly or indirectly, from sports and entertainment. Not until they all lost their jobs at once.

And the fall to almost zero of entertainment stocks had set off the stock market crash.

And the depression had pyramided, and was still pyramiding. Automobile production down 87 per cent over the same month a year ago. People, even those who still had jobs and money, weren't buying new cars. People were staying at home. Where was there to go? Sure, some of them had to drive to work and back but for that purpose the old car was plenty good. Who would be silly enough to buy a new one in a depression like this and especially with the used car market glutted with almost-new cars people had been forced to sell? The wonder was not that automobile production was down 87 per cent but that any new cars were being made at all.

And with cars being driven only when necessary—pleasure driving being no longer a pleasure—the oil fields and the refineries were hard hit too. More than half of the filling stations had closed.

Steel and rubber were hit. More unemployment.

Less construction because people had less money and they weren't building. More unemployment.

And the jails! Jammed to overflowing, despite the almost complete disappearance of organized crime. But they'd become jammed before criminals had discovered that their trade was no longer practical. And what to do now with the thousands of people being arrested daily for crimes of violence or desperation?

What to do with the armed forces, with war no longer a possibility—disband them? And increase unemployment by several more million? Just that afternoon he had signed an order that would grant immediate release to any soldier or sailor who could prove that he had either a job waiting for him or sufficient capital to guarantee his not becoming a public charge. But a pitifully small percentage would be able to qualify.

The national debt—the budget—the make-work programs—the army—the budget—the national debt—

President Wendell dropped his head in his hands on the desk in front of him and groaned, feeling very old and very futile.

From a corner of the room came an echoing groan, a mocking one. "Hi, Mack," said a voice. "Working overtime again? Want help?"

And a laugh. A nasty laugh.

CHAPTER SEVEN

Not *all* business was bad.

Take the psychiatrists. Going crazy trying to keep other people from going crazy.

Take the morticians. With the death rate, due to the increase in deaths from suicide, violence and apoplexy, still several times normal, there was no depression among the coffin stuffers. They were doing big business, despite the increasing trend toward simple burial or cremation without anything that could really be called a funeral. (It was all too easy for Martians to make a farce out of a funeral, and they especially loved to kibitz a minister's eulogy whenever it strayed from strict fact about the virtues of the deceased or glossed over any of his vices. Whether from previous observation, from eavesdropping or from having read hidden letters or records, the Martians who attended funerals were always able to pounce gleefully on any deviation from the truth in a funeral oration. It wasn't always safe even when the loved one was thought to have led a truly blameless life; all too often the mourners learned things about him that shocked them silly.)

Drugstores did a land-office business in the sale of aspirin tablets, sedatives and ear stopples.

But the biggest boom of all was in the industry in which you'd expect the biggest boom to be, the liquor industry.

Since time immemorial alcohol has been man's favorite gateway of escape from the routine vicissitudes of everyday life. Now man's everyday life had little green vicissitudes a thousand times worse than the routine ones had been. Now he *really* had something to escape from.

Most drinking, of course, was done in homes.

But taverns were still open, and they were crowded in the afternoon and jammed in the evening. In most of them the backbar mirrors were broken as a result of people throwing glasses, bottles, ash trays or what have you at Martians, and the mirrors weren't replaced because if they were they'd be broken again the same way.

But the taverns still operated and people thronged to them. Sure, Martians thronged to them too, even though Martians didn't drink. The owners and frequenters of taverns had found a partial answer—noise level. Juke boxes were kept going at top volume and most taverns had at least two of them. Radios helped add to the din. People who talked had to yell in their neighbors' ears.

Martians could only add to the volume of sound and the volume was already such that addition was practically superfluous.

If you were a solitary drinker (and more and more people were becoming solitary drinkers) you had less chance of being bothered by Martians in a tavern than anywhere else. There might be a dozen of them about but if you stood bellied up to the bar with a glass in your hand and your eyes closed, you could neither see them nor hear them. If, after a while, you opened your eyes and saw them, it didn't matter because they really didn't register.

Yes, taverns were doing all right.

CHAPTER EIGHT

Take *The Yellow Lantern* on Pine Avenue in Long Beach. A tavern like any tavern, but Luke Devereaux is in it, and it's time we got back to Luke because something big is about to happen to him.

He's bellied up to the bar, with a glass in his hand. And his eyes are closed so we can look him over without disturbing him.

Except that he looks a little thinner, there's no great difference in him since we saw him last, which was seven weeks ago. He's still clean and neatly shaven. His clothes are still good and are in good shape, although his suit could use pressing and the wrinkles in his shirt collar show that he is now doing his own laundry. But it's a sport shirt and doesn't look too bad.

Let's face it; he's been lucky, until tonight. Lucky in that he had been able to make his original fifty-six dollars, supplemented by occasional small earnings, last him these seven weeks and hasn't had to go on relief. As yet.

Tomorrow, he had decided, he would.

And he'd made the decision while he still had six dollars left, and for a very good reason. Since the night when he'd got drunk with Gresham and had phoned Margie, he had not had a single, solitary drink. He had lived like a monk and had toiled like a beaver whenever he'd found anything to toil at.

For seven weeks his pride had kept him going. (The same pride, incidentally, had kept him from phoning Margie again as he had drunkenly promised to do that night. He'd wanted to, but Margie had a job and, he wasn't going to see or even talk to her until and unless he himself had one.)

But tonight after the tenth consecutive completely discouraging day (eleven days ago he'd earned three dollars helping a man move a houseful of furniture) and after paying for a frugal meal of day-old buns and discouraged cold frankfurters to eat in his room, he had counted his dwindling capital and had found it to be exactly six dollars, to the penny.

And had decided to hell with it. Unless a miracle happened, and he thought that no miracle was going to happen, he'd have to give up and go on relief within a few more days in any case. If he decided now to go on relief tomorrow he had enough left for one final binge first. After seven weeks of total abstinence and on a not too full stomach, six dollars was enough to get him plenty drunk even if he spent it all in a tavern. Or if he didn't enjoy the tavern he could spend only part of it there and the rest on a bottle to take back to his room. In either case he'd awaken horribly hung over, but with empty pockets and a clear conscience in going on relief. It would be less unpleasant, probably, with a hang-over than otherwise.

And so, having decided that no miracle could happen to him, he had come to *The Yellow Lantern,* where the miracle awaited him.

Stood at the bar with his fourth drink in front of him and his hand clasped around it. A bit disappointed that he didn't feel the first three drinks more. But there was still money for quite a few more—in his pocket, of course; you don't leave money on a crowded bar and stand in front of it with your eyes closed. And for the same reason, you keep your hand around your glass.

He took another sip from it.

Felt a hand on his shoulder and heard a voice scream, "Luke!" in his ear. The scream could have been a Martian, but not the hand. Somebody here knew him, and he'd wanted to get drunk alone tonight. Damn. Well, he could brush the guy off.

He opened his eyes and turned around.

It was Carter Benson, grinning like a Cheshire cat. Carter Benson, from whom he'd borrowed the use of the shack near Indio where, a couple of months ago, he'd tried to start that science-fiction novel that hadn't got started and never would get started now.

Carter Benson, nice guy, but looking as prosperous as he always looked and probably still in the chips, and the hell with him, tonight. Any other time okay, but tonight Luke didn't want even Carter Benson's company. Not even if Carter bought him drinks, as he no doubt would if allowed to. Tonight he wanted to get drunk alone so he could feel sorry for himself for what was going to happen tomorrow.

He nodded to Carter and said, "The Jabberwock with eyes of flame came whiffling through the tulgey wood," because Carter would see his lips moving but wouldn't be able to hear a word anyway, so why did it matter what he said? And nodded again before he turned back to his drink and closed his eyes. Carter wasn't a stupe; he'd get the idea and go away.

He had time to take one more sip from his drink and sigh once more, deeply, in sorrow for himself. And then the hand was on his shoulder again. Damn Carter, couldn't he take a hint?

He opened his eyes. They were blocked by something in front of them. Something pink, so it wasn't a Martian. It, whatever it was, was too close to his eyes and made them cross. So he pulled back his head to look at it.

It was a check. A very familiar type of check, although he hadn't seen one like it for a long time. A check of *Bernstein Publishers, Inc.,* his own publisher as well as Carter Benson's. Four hundred and sixteen dollars and some cents. But what the hell was Carter showing it to him for? To show off that he was still making money writing and wanted help in celebrating. To hell with him. Luke closed his eyes again.

Another and more urgent tap on his shoulder and he opened them again. The check was still there in front of them.

And he saw this time that it was made out to Luke Devereaux, and not to Carter Benson.

What the hell? He owed Bernstein money, on all those advances he'd had, not the other way around.

Just the same, he reached up with suddenly trembling fingers and took the check, held it at the proper distance from his eyes to examine it properly. It looked real all right.

He jerked back and dropped it as a Martian who was running and sliding the length of the bar as though it were an ice slide slid right through his hand and check. But Luke picked it up again without even being annoyed and turned again to Carter, who was still grinning.

"What the hell?" he asked, this time forming words exaggeratedly so Carter could read his lips.

Carter pointed to the bar and held up two fingers, then mouthed, "Want to step outside?"

It wasn't an invitation to fight, as, in happier times, that sentence had been when spoken in a bar. It had a new meaning that had developed because of the deafening din that prevailed in post-Martian drinking places. If two people wanted to talk for a minute or a few minutes without having to scream at one another or read lips, they'd step outside the front or back door onto the sidewalk or into an alley, and walk a few paces away, taking their drinks with them. If no Martian followed them or kwimmed suddenly to join them they could talk undisturbed. If a Martian did bother them they could go back inside to the maddening noise and they'd lost nothing. Bartenders understood and didn't mind people going outside with their drinks; besides, bartenders were usually too busy to notice.

Quickly Luke slid the check into his pocket and got the two drinks Carter's two fingers had signaled for and then as unobtrusively as possible led the way out the back door and into a dimly lighted alley. And luck, having bit Luke so hard and suddenly, stayed with him; no Martian followed them.

"Carter, thanks a million. And forgive me for trying to brush you off—I was just starting out on a final and solitary jag and—well, skip it. But what the hell's the check *for?*"

"Ever read a book called *Hell in Eldorado?*"

"Read it? I wrote it. But that was twelve or fifteen years ago, and it was a stinking Western."

"Exactly. Except for the *stinking;* it was a fairly good Western, Luke."

"But it's dead as a dodo. You don't mean Bernstein is reissuing it?"

"Not Bernstein, no. But Midget Books is bringing out a new pocket edition. The market in Westerns is booming and they're desperate for them. And they paid a very sweet advance guarantee to reissue your old Western."

Luke frowned. "What do you mean, Carter? Not that I want to act as though I'm looking a gift horse in the proverbial, but since when is four hundred bucks a very sweet advance on a pocket book deal? Not that it isn't a fortune to me right now, but—"

"Down, boy," Carter said. "Your share of that advance was three grand, and that's damn good for a pocket book reissue. But you owed Bernstein over two and a half grand on all those advances you've been getting, and they deducted. That check you've got there is clear and you don't owe anybody anything."

Luke whistled softly. That made it different all right.

Carter said, "Bernstein—Bernie himself—called me up last week. Mail was being returned from where you lived before and he didn't know how to reach you. I told him if he wanted to send the check care of me, I'd find you somehow. And he said—"

"How *did* you find me?"

"Found out from Margie you were in Long Beach—seems you called her some weeks ago but then never called back, and you hadn't given her an address. But I've been coming over here evenings, making the rounds of the taverns. Knew I'd run into you sooner or later."

"Miracle you did," Luke said. "My first time in one since that night I called Margie. And my last one for—I mean, it *would* have been my last time for God knows how long if you hadn't found me. But now go on about what Bernie said."

"Said to tell you to forget the science-fiction book. Science fiction's dead. Extraterrestrial stuff is just what people want to escape from right now. They've *got* Martians, in their hair. But people are still reading and there's a big swing to mystery and a bigger one to Westerns. Said to tell you that if you've actually started that science-fiction book— Have you, by the way?"

"No."

"Good. Anyway, Bernie was fair about it; he said that he'd commissioned it and given you advances against it and that if you actually did have any of it done, he'd pay you a word rate for however much you've actually done—but that you can then tear it up and throw it away. He doesn't *want* it, and he wants you to stop work on it."

"Not hard when I haven't got even an idea for it. I think I had one once, in that shack of yours, but it slipped away. The night the Martians came."

"What are your plans now, Luke?"

"Tomorrow I'm going on—" Luke stopped suddenly. With a check for over four hundred dollars in his pocket he wouldn't be going on relief tomorrow after all. What *were* his plans? With the depression drop in prices he could live for months on that much money. Solvent again, he could even look up Margie. If he wanted to. Did he want to?

"I don't know," he said, and it was the answer to Carter's question and his own.

"Well, *I* know," Carter said. "I know what you're going to do if you've got any sense. You think you're burned out as a writer because you can't write science fiction any more. But you're not. You just can't write *science fiction*—and for the same reason you and everybody else doesn't want to *read* it any more. It's dead. But what's wrong with Westerns? You wrote one once—or was it only one?"

"One novel. A few short stories and novelettes. But— I don't *like* Westerns."

"Do you like digging ditches?"

"Well—not exactly."

"Look at this." Carter Benson's wallet was in his hand again and he took something from it and handed it to Luke.

It looked like another check. It *was* another check. There was barely enough light for Luke to read it. One thousand dollars, made out to Luke Devereaux, signed by W. B. Moran, Treas., Bernstein Publishers, Inc.

Carter reached across and took the check out of Luke's hand. "Not yours yet, son. Bernie sent it to me to give to you as an advance on another Western novel—if you agree to write one. He says to tell you that if you do, and if it's no worse than *Hell in Eldorado* you'll make at least five thousand out of it."

"Gimme," Luke said. He took back the check and stared at it lovingly.

His slump was over. Ideas were beginning to crowd him toward his typewriter. A lonely Western plain at dusk, a cowboy riding...

"Attaboy," Carter said. "Now do we hang one on to celebrate?"

"Hell, yes—or—wait a minute. Would you mind awfully if we didn't? Or at least postponed it?"

"Whatever you say. Why? Feel like diving in?"

"Exactly. I feel hot and think I should get that novel going while the mood lasts. And I'm still sober so far; this is only my fourth drink, so it's not too late. You don't mind, do you?"

"Hell, no. I understand, and I'm glad you feel that way. Nothing like the sudden turn of a new leaf." Carter put down his glass on a window sill beside him and pulled out a notebook and pencil. "Just give me your address and phone number while we're together."

Luke gave him both. Then stuck out his hand. "Thanks to hell and back. And you won't have to write to Bernie, Carter. I'll write him tomorrow—and tell him the Western's already started."

"Attaboy. And listen, Margie's been worrying about you. I could tell from the way she talked when I called her. And I had to promise I'd give her your address if I found you. Is that okay?"

"Sure, but you won't have to. I'll call her myself tomorrow." He wrung Carter's hand again and hurried off.

He felt so exhilarated and excited that it wasn't until he was on the stairs going up to his room that he discovered that he still had a half-full glass of whiskey and soda in his hand and that, fast as he'd walked, he'd carried it so carefully for ten blocks that he hadn't spilled a drop.

He laughed at himself and stopped on the landing to drink it off.

In his room he took off his suit coat and necktie and rolled up his sleeves. Put the typewriter and a stack of paper on the table and pulled up a chair. Ran paper in the typewriter. Yellow paper only. He'd already decided to do rough draft on this one so he wouldn't have to stop to look up anything. Whatever points came up that might indicate a spot of research could be taken care of on the final version.

Title? You didn't need a good title for a Western. Just so it indicated action and *sounded* like a Western. Something like *Guns Across the Border* or *Guns Across the Pecos.*

Sure, he'd settle for the *Guns Across* part except that he didn't want to write a border story again—*Hell in Eldorado* had been a border story—and he didn't know anything about the Pecos country. Better take something in Arizona; he'd traveled quite a bit around Arizona and could handle the descriptions much better.

What rivers were there in Arizona? Hmmm, the Little Colorado, but that was too long. The name, not the river. And a Trout Creek, but *Guns Across the Trout* would sound silly. *Guns Across the Date* would sound worse.

He had it. The Gila. *Guns Across the Gila.* It would even seem alliterative, to people who didn't know it was pronounced Heela and not Gilla. And even if one pronounced it right it was still a plenty good title.

He centered it in caps at the top of the page.

Under it, "by Luke Devers." That was the by-line he'd used on *Hell in Eldorado* and a few other Westerns he'd written, the shorts and the novelettes. Devereaux had seemed a little fancy for the horse-opera trade. Bernie probably would want him to use it again. If he didn't, if he figured the reputation Luke had built in science fiction under his own name would carry over and help sales on a Western, that was all right too. Bernie could use either by-line he wanted to, for a thousand advance and another four thousand in eventual earnings. That was better than he'd averaged on his science-fiction novels.

A little farther down he centered "Chapter I," then spaced down a few more lines and shoved the carriage to the left. Ready to start writing.

And he was going to start right now and let the plot, or at least the details of the plot, work themselves out as he wrote.

There aren't many plots for Westerns anyway. Let's see; he could use the basic plot he'd used in one of his novelettes, *Thunder on the Range.* Two rival ranches, one run by the villain and one by the hero. And one ranch, this time, would be on each side of the Gila River and that would make the title perfect. Villain, of course, has a big ranch and hired gunmen; the hero a small ranch with maybe a few cowpokes who aren't gunmen.

And a daughter, of course. For novel length there's got to be a dame.

The plot was coming fast now.

Changing point of view. Start out with the point of view—over the shoulder—of a gunslinger hired by the villain, just coming to join up at the big ranch. But the gunslinger is a good guy at heart and is going to fall in love with the good rancher's daughter. And change sides and save the day for the right side when he finds out that—

Tried and true. A lead-pipe cinch.

Luke's fingers poised over the keyboard, hit the tab key for a paragraph indention, then started typing:

```
    As Don Marston drew nearer the figure that
waited for him on the trail, the figure re-
solved itself into a grim-eyed hombre whose
hands held a stubby carbine crosswise on the
pommel of his saddle and...
```

Back and forth the typewriter's carriage, slowly at first and then faster and faster as he got into the swing of it. Forgotten in the click of keys everything but the rush of words.

And suddenly a Martian, one of the smaller ones, was sitting astride the typewriter carriage, riding it.

"Whoopie!" he yelled. *"Hi-yo, Silver! Away!* Faster, Mack, faster!"

Luke screamed.

And—

CHAPTER NINE

"Catatonia, Doctor?" the interne asked.

The ambulance physician rubbed his lantern jaw for a moment, staring down at the still figure that lay on Luke's bed.

"Very strange," he said. "Catatonic state at present, certainly, but it's probably only a phase, like the other phases." He turned to Luke's landlady, who was standing in the doorway of the room. "You say you heard a scream first?"

"That's right. An' I thought it was from *his* room and I come out in the hall to listen, but there was his typewriter banging away so I thought he was aw right and went back. An' then, two-three minutes later, glass crashed and *that* time I opened his door and went in. And there was his window busted and him laying outside it on the fire escape. Good thing for him there *was* a fire escape, throwing hisself out the window thataway."

"Strange," the doctor said.

"You're gonna take him, ain't you, Doctor? Especially him bleeding like that."

"We'll take him all right. But don't worry about the bleeding. It's superficial."

"Not on my bedclothes it ain't. An' who's going to pay for that busted window?"

The doctor sighed. "That is not within my province, Madam. But we'd better stop the bleeding from those cuts before we move him. I wonder if you would be so kind as to boil us some water?"

"Sure, Doctor."

When the landlady had left the interne glanced curiously at the doctor. "Did you really want her to boil water or—?"

"Of course not, Pete. I wanted her to boil her head, but she wouldn't have agreed to that. Always ask women to boil water if you want to get rid of them."

"It seems to work. Shall I clean up those cuts with alky here or should we take him in first?"

"Clean them up here, please, Pete. I want to look around a little. And there's a chance he might come out of it and be able to walk down those two flights under his own power."

The doctor walked over to the table on which stood a typewriter with paper in it. He started to read and stopped a moment at the by-line. "By Luke Devers," he said. "Sounds vaguely familiar, Pete. Where have I heard the name Luke Devers recently?"

"I don't know, Doc."

"Start of a Western. A novel, I'd say, since he put down *Chapter I*. Reads all right for three paragraphs—and then here's a place where a key punched right through the paper. I'd say that's how far he got when something happened to him. A Martian, no doubt."

"Is there any *other* reason why people go crazy, Doc?"

The doctor sighed. "There used to be other reasons. I guess they're not worth going crazy over, now. Well, that must have been when he screamed. And then— the landlady's right; he kept on typing for a few more lines. But come over and read them."

"In a second, Doc. This is the last cut I'm working on."

A minute later he went over to the typewriter.

"It makes sense up to there," the doctor said, pointing. "That's where a key punched through. And after that—"

"HI YO SILVER HI YO SILVER HI YO SILVER HI YO SILVER HI YO SILVER AWAY HI YO AWAY SILVER HI SILVER YO AWAY AWAY DOWN SOUTH IN THE LAND OF SILVER HI YO AWAY," the interne read.

"Sounds like a telegram the Lone Ranger might send his horse. Make anything out of it, Doc?"

"Not much. I'd guess it ties in somehow with whatever happened to him, but I can't guess how. Well, I'm new on this run, Pete. Any red tape or do we just take him in?"

"We check his wallet first."

"What for?"

"If he's got any money, any quantity of it, he'll have to go to one of the private sans. And if he's got 'in case of accident notify' identification, we notify first; maybe his relatives will foot the bill for private care and we're out from under. We're so overcrowded we have to look for an out before taking anybody."

"Is his wallet on him?"

"Yeah, hip pocket. Just a second." The interne rolled the motionless figure on the bed far enough over to take the wallet from the pocket. He brought it to the light to open it. "Three bucks," he said.

"Aren't those folded papers checks?"

"Maybe they are." The interne took them out and unfolded first one and then the other. He whistled softly. "Over fourteen hundred bucks. If they're good—"

The doctor was looking over his shoulder. "They are, unless they're forgeries. That's a reputable publishing company. Say—Luke *Devereaux* they're made out to. Luke Devers must be just a pen name, but even so it was close enough to sound familiar."

The interne shrugged. "I still haven't heard it. But then I don't read much fiction. Haven't time."

"I didn't mean it was familiar that way. But there's a girl, a nurse over at General Mental, who's been passing the word around to every doctor and psychiatrist in Long Beach to let her know if one of them gets a Luke Devereaux for a patient. He's her ex-husband, I believe. Her name is Devereaux too—I forget the first name."

"Oh. Well, then we got someone to notify all right. But how about these checks? Is he solvent or isn't he?"

"With fourteen hundred dollars?"

"But is it? They aren't endorsed. And right now he's in no shape to do any endorsing."

"Ummm," said the doctor thoughtfully. "I see what you mean. Well, as I said, I think the catatonia is a temporary phase, in his case. But if he's pronounced insane, would his endorsement be valid?"

"You got me, Doc. But why worry about it, at least until after you've talked to this dame, his ex-wife. She must have something in mind, and maybe it's to take responsibility—and that would let us off the hook."

"Good idea. And I think I remember there's a phone right out in the hall on this floor. Hold the fort, Pete. And keep an eye on him—he could snap out of that at any time."

The doctor went out into the hall and came back five minutes later. "Well, we're in the clear all right," he said. "She's taking over. A private san—at her expense if there's any difficulty about those checks. And a private ambulance will come get him. All she asks of us is we wait ten or fifteen minutes till it gets here."

"Good deal." The interne yawned. "Wonder what made her suspect he *would* end up this way. Instable personality?"

"Partly that. But she was especially afraid something would happen if he went back to writing—seems he hasn't been doing or even trying any writing since the Martians came. And she said that when he really gets into a story and is working hard and fast on it, concentrating, he used to jump ten feet and fly into a violent tizzy at even a slight interruption. When he was writing, she used to have to go around the house on tiptoe and—well, you see what I mean."

"I guess some guys are like that, when they concentrate hard on something. Wonder what a Martian did to him tonight?"

"Your guess is as good as mine. Whatever it was, it happened in the heat of creation just when he was getting started on a novel. I *would* like to know what happened though."

"Why don't you ask me, Gentlemen?"

They whirled around. Luke Devereaux was sitting up, on the edge of the bed. There was a Martian in his lap.

"Huh?" said the doctor, not very brilliantly.

Luke smiled and looked at him through eyes that were, or at least seemed, perfectly calm and sane.

He said, "I'll tell you what happened, if you're really curious. Two months ago I went insane—I think from pressure of trying to force myself to write when I was in a slump and couldn't. I was in a shack on the desert and I started hallucinating about Martians. I've been having hallucinations ever since. Until tonight, when I snapped out of it."

"Are you—are you *sure* they were hallucinations?" the doctor asked. At the same time he put his hand quietly on the interne's shoulder. As a signal, a signal to keep quiet. If the patient, in this frame of mind, should look down too suddenly, the trauma might happen all over again, and worse.

But the interne didn't get the signal. "Then what," he asked Luke, "do you call that creature in your lap?"

Luke looked down. The Martian looked up and stuck out a long yellow tongue right into Luke's face. He pulled the tongue back with a loud slurping noise. Then stuck it out again and let its tip vibrate just in front of Luke's nose.

Luke looked up and stared at the interne curiously. "There's nothing in my lap. Are you *crazy?*"

CHAPTER TEN

The case of Luke Devereaux, upon which a monograph was later written by Dr. Ellicott H. Snyder (psychiatrist and proprietor of the Snyder Foundation, the asylum for the mentally deranged to which Luke was committed), was probably unique. At least no other case has been authenticated by a reputable alienist in which the patient could both see and hear perfectly but could neither see nor hear Martians.

There were, of course, a great many people who had the combined afflictions of blindness and deafness. Since Martians could not be felt, smelled or tasted, these otherwise unfortunate people could have no objective or sensory proof of their existence and had to take the word, communicated by whatever means, of those about them that there were such things as Martians. And some of them never did fully believe; one cannot blame them.

And, of course, there were millions, many millions—sane and insane, scientists, laymen and crackpots—who accepted their existence but refused to believe that they were *Martians.*

The most numerous of these were the superstitious and the fanatically religious who claimed that the self-styled Martians were really banshees, brownies, daemons, demons, devils, elves, fairies, fays, gnomes, goblins or hobgoblins; imps, jin, kobolds, peris, pixies, powers of darkness or powers of evil; sprites, trolls, unclean spirits or what-have-you.

All over the world, religions, sects and congregations split over this issue. The Presbyterian Church, for example, found itself split into three separate denominations. There was the Demonist Presbyterian Church, which believed they were devils out of Hell sent to punish us for our sins. There was the Scientific Presbyterian Church, which accepted that they were Martians and that the invasion of Earth by them was no more—or no less—an Act of God than are many of the earthquakes, tidal waves, fires and floods by which, from time to time, He keeps in His hand. And the Revisionist Presbyterian Church, which accepted the basic doctrine of the Demonists but took it a further step and accepted them also as Martians by simply revising their concept of the physical location of Hell. (A small splinter group of Revisionists, calling themselves the Rerevisionists, believed that, since Hell is on Mars, Heaven must be located beneath the everlasting clouds of Venus, our sister planet on the opposite side.)

Almost every other denomination found itself divided or dividing along similar—or even more startling—lines. The two outstanding exceptions were the Christian Scientists and the Roman Catholics.

The Church of Christ, Scientist, held most of its membership (and those who did wander away joined other groups rather than form a new group) by proclaiming that the invaders were neither devils nor Martians but the visible and audible product of *human error* and that if we refused to believe in their existence they would go away. A doctrine, one might note, with considerable parallel to the paranoiac delusion of Luke Devereaux, except that *his* theory worked, for him.

The Roman Catholic Church likewise maintained its integrity and a good ninety per cent of its membership due to the common sense or the Infallibility, as you prefer, of the Pope. His proclamation was to the effect that a special diet composed of Catholic theologians and Catholic scientists would be called to determine the position of the Church and that until an official announcement was made Catholics might hold opinions either way. The Diet of Cologne convened within a month and was still in session; since a condition of its adjournment was that a unanimous decision be reached, its deliberations promised to continue indefinitely and meanwhile schism was averted. True, in various countries young girls had Divine if conflicting revelations as to the nature of the Martians and their place and purpose in the universe, but none of them was recognized by the Church or gained more than local adherents. Not even the one in Chile who could show stigmata, the prints of small six-fingered hands, green, in the palms of her own hands.

Among those who inclined more to superstition than to religion, the number of theories about the Martians was as near as matters infinite. As were suggested methods of dealing with or exorcising them. (The churches at least agreed that, whatever the nature of the Martians, prayer to God to free us from them was indicated.)

But among the superstitious, books on sorcery, demonology, and black and white magic sold prodigiously. Every known form of thaumaturgy, demonomancy and conjuration was tried, and new forms were invented.

Among the soothsayers, the practitioners of astrology, numerology and the myriad other forms of prediction from the reading of cards to the study of the entrails of sheep, predicting the day and hour of the departure of the Martians became such an obsession that at no matter what hour they might have left us hundreds of the diviners must have been proved right. And any prognosticator who predicted their departure at any hour within a few days could gain followers, for a few days.

CHAPTER ELEVEN

"The strangest case of my entire experience, Mrs. Devereaux," said Dr. Snyder.

He sat at his expensive mahogany desk in his expensively furnished office, a short, stocky man with piercing eyes in a bland moon face.

"But why, Doctor?" asked Margie Devereaux. She looked very pretty, sitting straight in a chair made for lounging. A tall girl with honey hair and blue eyes. Slender, but she filled a nurse's uniform (she had come to the sanitarium directly from her job at the hospital) beautifully in the right places. "I mean, you say you diagnose it as paranoia."

"With hysterical blindness and deafness to Martians, yes. I don't mean the *case* is complicated, Mrs. Devereaux. But he is the first and only paranoiac I have ever known who is ten times as well off, ten times as well adjusted, as though he were sane. I envy him. I hesitate to *try* to cure him."

"But—"

"Luke—I've got to know him well enough to call him by his first name— has been here a week now. He's perfectly happy—except that he keeps demanding to see you—and is working beautifully on that Western novel. Eight and ten hours a day. He has completed four chapters of it; I've read them and they are excellent. I happen to enjoy Westerns and read several a week and I am a good judge of them. It's not hack work; it's fine writing, up to the best of Zane Grey, Luke Short, Haycox, the other top writers in the field. I managed to find a copy of *Hell in Eldorado,* the one other Western Luke wrote some years ago— Was that before he and you were married?"

"Long before."

"—and read it. The one he's writing now is infinitely superior. I wouldn't be surprised if it turned out to be a best seller, or as near to a best seller as a Western can become. Best seller or not, it should definitely become a classic in its field. Now if I cure him of his obsession—his purely negative obsession that there are no Martians—"

"I see what you mean. He'd never finish it—unless the Martians drove him insane again."

"And happened to drive him again into exactly the same form of aberration. A chance in thousands. Is he going to be happier seeing and hearing Martians again and being unable to write because of them?"

"So you suggest *not* curing him?"

"I don't know. I'm puzzled, Mrs. Devereaux—and that's putting it mildly. It's completely unethical to care for a patient who might be cured without attempting to cure him. I've never considered such a thing, and I shouldn't be considering it now. Nevertheless—"

"Did you find out about those checks?"

"Yes. I telephoned his publisher, Mr. Bernstein. The smaller of the two, the four hundred dollar one, is money his publisher owed him. It will be all right for us to have him endorse that and deposit, or use, it for him in any case. At the hundred dollars a week I charge here, it alone will cover the past week and the next three. The—"

"But your own fee, Doctor?"

"My own fee? How can I charge a fee if I don't even try to cure him? But about the other check, the thousand-dollar one; it was an advance against a Western novel. When I explained the circumstances to Mr. Bernstein—that Luke is definitely insane but still working well and rapidly on the novel—he was skeptical; I fear he didn't trust my literary judgment. He asked me to borrow the manuscript from Luke, telephone him back collect and read him the first chapter over the phone. I did so—the call must have cost him well over a hundred dollars—and he was enthusiastic about it. He said that if the rest of the book held up to that level, it would earn Luke at least ten thousand dollars and possibly many times that. He said that of course Luke could cash and keep the check for the advance. And that if I did anything to Luke that would stop him from finishing it, he would personally fly out here and shoot me. Not that he meant that literally, of course, and even if I thought he did I couldn't let it affect my decision, but—"

He spread his hands apologetically and a Martian appeared, sitting on one of them, said "—you, Mack," and disappeared again.

Dr. Snyder sighed. "Look at it this way, Mrs. Devereaux. Take ten thousand dollars as the minimum figure *Trail to Nowhere*—he changed the title as well as the opening from the one he originally projected—will bring Luke. The four chapters he has written in the week he's been here constitute approximately one-fourth of the book.

"On that basis, he's earned two and a half thousand dollars within the past week. If he keeps on producing at that rate, he will have earned ten thousand dollars within a month. And, even allowing for vacations between books and for the fact that he's writing unusually rapidly at present as reaction against not having been able to write at all for so long—well, he should earn at least fifty thousand dollars within the next year. Possibly a hundred or two hundred thousand if, as Mr. Bernstein said, the book may earn 'many times' the minimum figure. Last year, Mrs. Devereaux, I cleared twenty-five thousand dollars. And *I* should cure *him?*"

Margie Devereaux smiled. "It rather frightens me to think of it myself. Luke's best year thus far, the second year of our marriage, he made twelve thousand. But one thing I don't understand, Doctor?"

"And what is that?"

"Why you sent for me. I *want* to see him, of course. But you said it would be better if I didn't, that it might disturb or distract him and cut down or even stop his production. Not that I *want* to wait any longer, but if at the rate he's writing he can finish that novel within another three weeks, might it not be wiser for me to wait that long? To make sure that, even if he—changes again, he'll at least have *that* book finished?"

Dr. Snyder smiled ruefully. He said, "I'm afraid I was given no choice, Mrs. Devereaux. Luke went on strike."

"On strike?"

"Yes, this morning he told me he wouldn't write another word unless I phoned you and asked you to come to see him. He meant it."

"Then he lost a day's writing today?"

"Oh, no. Only half an hour—it took me that long to get you on the phone. He started working again the moment I told him you'd promised to come this evening. He took my word for it."

"I'm glad. Now before I go up to see him, any instructions, Doctor?"

"Try not to argue with him, especially about his obsession. If any Martians come around, remember that he can neither see nor hear them. And that it's quite genuine; he isn't pretending in the slightest."

"And ignore them myself, of course. But you know perfectly well, Doctor, that isn't always completely possible. If, for instance, a Martian suddenly shouts in your ear when you're not expecting it—"

"Luke knows that other people still see Martians. He won't be surprised if you start suddenly. Or if you have to ask him to repeat something he just said, he'll know it's because a Martian must have been yelling louder than he was talking—that is, that *you think* a Martian is yelling."

"But if a Martian should make noise while I'm talking to him, Doctor, how is it that—even if his subconscious won't let him hear the sound the Martian makes—he can hear me clearly despite it? Or can he?"

"He can. I've checked that. His subconscious must simply tune out the Martian by pitch and he hears you clearly even though you're whispering and the Martian is screaming. It's similar to the case of people who work in boiler factories or other noisy places. Except that it's long practice rather than hysterical deafness that lets them hear and understand ordinary conversation over, or rather under, the noise level."

"I understand. Yes, I see now how he could hear despite interference. But how about *seeing?* I mean, a Martian is opaque. I don't see how even someone who doesn't believe in them can see *through* one. Suppose one got between him and me when he's looking at me. I can see how he might not see it as a Martian—as a blur, maybe—but he couldn't possibly see through it and he'd have to know *something* was there between us."

"He looks away. Common defense mechanism of specialized hysterical blindness. And his is specialized of course since he is not blind to anything but Martians.

"You see, there is a dichotomy between the conscious mind and the subconscious mind, and his subconscious mind is playing tricks on his conscious one. And it makes him turn away, or even close his eyes rather than let him find out that there's something in his direct range of vision he can't see through."

"But why does he think he turns away or closes his eyes?"

"His subconscious provides him an excuse for it, somehow. Watch and study him any time there are Martians around and you'll see how. Watch what happens any time a Martian gets in his direct range of vision."

He sighed. "I made a careful check of that the first few days he was here. I spent quite a bit of time in his room, talking with him and also in reading or pretending to read while he worked. Several times a Martian got between him and the typewriter while he was typing. Each time he'd put his hands behind his head and lean backward staring up at the ceiling—"

"He always does that when he's writing and stops to think."

"Of course. But these times his subconscious stopped his flow of thought and *made* him do it, because otherwise he'd have been looking at his typewriter and unable to see it. If he and I were talking, he'd find an excuse to get up and move if a Martian got between us. And once a Martian sat on top of his head and blocked his vision completely by letting its legs hang in front of his face. He simply closed his eyes, or I presume he did—I couldn't see through the Martian's legs either—because he remarked that his eyes were pretty tired and asked my pardon for closing them. His subconscious just wouldn't *let* him recognize that there was something there he couldn't see through."

"I'm beginning to understand, Doctor. And I suppose that if one used such an occasion to try to prove to him that there *were* Martians—told him there was one dangling its legs in front of his eyes and challenged him to open his eyes and tell you how many fingers you were holding up or something—he'd refuse to open his eyes and rationalize it somehow."

"Yes. I can see you've had experience with paranoiacs, Mrs. Devereaux. How long have you been a nurse at General Mental, if I may ask?"

"Almost six years altogether. Just ten months this time—since Luke and I separated—and for about five years before we were married."

"Would you mind telling me—as Luke's physician, of course—what caused the breakup between you?"

"I wouldn't mind at all, Doctor—but could I tell you another time? It was—a lot of little things rather than one big thing and it would take quite a while to explain it, especially if I try to be fair to both of us."

"Of course." Dr. Snyder glanced at his wrist watch. "Good Lord, I had no idea I'd kept you this long. Luke will be chewing his fingernails. But before you go up to see him, may I ask you one very personal question?"

"Of course."

"We're very shorthanded on nurses. Would you by any chance care to quit your job at General and come here to work for me?"

Margie laughed.

"What's personal about that?" she asked.

"The inducement I had in mind to get you away from them. Luke has discovered that he loves you very much and knows now he made a bad mistake in letting you get away from him. I—ah—gather from your concern that you feel the same way about him?"

"I—I'm not sure, Doctor. I feel concern, yes, and affection. And I've come to realize that at least part of the trouble between us was my fault. I'm so—so damn normal myself that I didn't sufficiently understand his psychic problems as a writer. But as to whether I can love him again—I'll want to wait until I've seen him."

"Then the inducement applies only if you decide that you do. If you decide to work and live here, the room next to his has a connecting door. Ordinarily kept locked of course, but—"

Margie smiled again. "I'll let you know before I leave, Doctor. And I guess you'll be glad to know that if I do so decide, you won't be condoning an illegality. Technically, we're still married. And I can call off the divorce at any time before it becomes final, three months from now."

"Good. You'll find him in room six on the second floor. You'll have to let yourself in; the door opens from the outside but not from the inside. When you wish to leave, just press the service buzzer and someone will come to open the door for you."

"Thanks, Doctor." Margie stood.

"And come back here, please, if you wish to talk to me on your way out. Except I hope that—ah—"

"That you won't be up that late?" Margie grinned at him and then the grin faded. "Honestly, Doctor, I don't know. It's been so long since I've seen Luke—"

She went out of the office and up thickly carpeted stairs, along the corridor until she found the door numbered six. Heard from beyond it the fast clicking of a typewriter.

Knocked gently to warn him, and then opened the door.

Luke, with his hair badly mussed but his eyes shining, jumped up from the typewriter and hurried to her, catching her just inside the door as she closed it behind her.

He said, "Margie! Oh, Margie!" and then he was kissing her. Pulling her tight against him with one arm while the other reached over her shoulder to the light switch, plunging the room into darkness.

She hadn't even had time to see if there was a Martian in the room.

Nor, she decided a few minutes later, did she care. After all, Martians weren't human.

And she was.

CHAPTER TWELVE

A lot of people were deciding, by that time, that Martians weren't human—when it came to letting their presence or possible presence inhibit the act of procreation.

During the first week or two after the coming of the Martians, many people began to fear that if they stayed long enough the human race might die out within a generation from lack of propagating itself.

When it became known, as it very quickly did become known, that Martians could not only see in the dark but had X-ray vision that could see through sheets, quilts, blankets, comforters and even walls, there is no denying that, for a while, the sex life of the human being—even his legitimate marital sex life—*did* take an awful beating.

Accustomed, except in the case of the degenerate and depraved, to complete privacy—except of course for his partner in the act—for even the most legal and laudable satisfaction of the flesh, people could not adjust themselves, at first, to the possibility or even probability that they were being *watched*, no matter what precautions they took. Especially since—whatever their own method of procreation—the Martians seemed to be excessively interested in, amused by and disgusted at *our* method.

The extent to which their influence proved inhibiting is reflected (at least as far as concerns legitimate marital sex relations) in the birth rate for the early months of 1965.

In January of 1965, the month that started a week more than nine months after the Coming, the birth rate in the United States dropped to 3 per cent of normal—and many of the births that did occur were early in the month and were probably due to longer-than-normal pregnancies, conception having taken place before the night of March 26, 1964. In most other countries the drop in the birth rate was almost as great; in England it was greater. Even in France the birth rate dropped to 18 per cent of normal.

In February, the tenth month (plus a week) after the Coming, the birth rate started to climb again. It was 30 per cent of normal in the United States, 22 per cent of normal in England and 49 per cent in France.

By March it was within 80 per cent of normal in all countries. And 137 per cent of normal in France; obviously the French were making up for lost time even while other countries still felt some degree of inhibition.

People were human, even if Martians weren't.

Several Kinsey-type surveys taken in April indicated that almost all married couples were again having at least occasional sex relationships. And since most of the interviews upon which these surveys were based were gleefully kibitzed by Martians who knew the facts, there is no doubt that they were much more nearly accurate in their conclusions than the original Kinsey reports of almost two decades before.

Almost universally, the sex act was practiced only at night, in complete darkness. Matins and matinees, even among newlyweds, were a thing of the past. And ear stopples were almost equally universal; even savages who had no access to drugstores selling stopples discovered the efficacy of kneaded mud for this purpose. So equipped and in complete darkness one (or, more properly, two) could ignore the presence of Martians and fail to hear their running commentaries, usually ribald.

But even under these circumstances, premarital and extra-marital sex relationships were pretty much out of the question because of the danger of being tattled on. Only the completely shameless could risk them.

And even in marriage sex relations were less frequent and, because there was always some degree of self-consciousness, not to mention the futility of whispering endearments to a stoppled ear, less enjoyable.

No, sex was not what it had been in the good old days, but at least there *was* sex, in marriage, enough of it to keep the race going.

CHAPTER THIRTEEN

The door of Dr. Snyder's office was open, but Margie Devereaux paused in the doorway until the doctor looked up and told her to come in. Then he saw that she carried two copies of a bound manuscript and his eyes brightened. "He finished?"

Margie nodded.

"And the last chapter? It's as good as the rest?"

"*I* think so, Doctor. You have time to read it now?"

"Of course. I'll take time. I was only making some notes for a paper."

"All right. If you've got paper and string, I'll get the package ready to mail while you're reading the carbon copy."

"Fine. You'll find everything you need in the cabinet there."

They were separately busied for a while. Margie finished first by a few minutes and waited till the doctor finished reading and looked up.

"It's excellent," he said. "And not only good writing, but commercially good. It will sell. And—let's see, you've been here a month now?"

"A month tomorrow."

"Then it took him only five weeks altogether. Your being here with him didn't slow him down much."

Margie smiled. "I've been careful to keep away from him during his working hours. Which hasn't been too difficult, since they're my working hours too. Well, I'll take this to the post office as soon as I'm off duty."

"Don't wait; take it now. And send it airmail. Bernstein will want to rush it into print. And we'll get by without you for that long. I hope not for longer."

"What do you mean, Doctor?"

"Do you intend to stay, to keep on working for me?"

"Of course. Why shouldn't I? Isn't my work satisfactory?"

"You know perfectly well that it is. And that I want you to stay. But Margie, why should you? Your husband has earned enough in the past five weeks for the two of you to live on for at least two years. With what the Depression has done to living expenses, the two of you can live almost royally on about five thousand a year."

"But—"

"I know the money isn't all in yet, but you've got plenty to start on. Luke's fourteen hundred is safely in hand. And since your earnings here have covered my charges for Luke, whatever savings you yourself had are intact. I'll predict Bernstein will send further advances any time you ask for them, even before the book is in print."

"Are you trying to get rid of me, Doctor Snyder?"

"You know better than that, Margie. It's just that I can't see why a person should want to work when he doesn't have to. I wouldn't."

"Are you sure? While the human race, with the Martians on their necks, needs psychiatric help more than it ever has, you'd retire *now* if you happened to be able to afford to?"

Dr. Snyder sighed. "I see your point, Margie. As a matter of fact, I *could* retire, I suppose, if I sold this place. But I didn't realize a nurse would feel that way."

"This one does," Margie said. "Besides, what about Luke? I wouldn't leave here if he didn't. And do you think he should?"

Dr. Snyder's sigh was a really deep one this time. "Margie," he said, "I believe that's what's been worrying me more than anything else—except the Martians. We seem to be remarkably free of them at the moment, by the way."

"There were six of them in Luke's room when I got this manuscript."

"Doing what?"

"Dancing on him. He's lying on the bed thinking out an idea for his next book."

"Doesn't he plan to take a rest first? I wouldn't want him—" Dr. Snyder smiled wryly. "I wouldn't want him to overwork. What if he cracked up?"

"He plans to take a week off, starting tomorrow. But he says he wants to get at least a rough plot and maybe a title for his next book first. He says if he does that his subconscious will be playing around with the idea while he's resting and when he is ready to start working again it'll be easy for him to get going again."

"Which doesn't give his subconscious a rest. Or do many writers work that way?"

"I know some of them do. But I was intending to talk to you about that vacation, Doctor. After I was off duty. Shall I, now?"

"You're off duty now. And a few minutes isn't going to matter on getting that manuscript into the mail, so go ahead."

"Luke and I talked it over last night, after he told me he'd definitely finish the novel today. He says he's perfectly willing to stay here on two conditions. One, that I take off work for that week too. And the other, that the lock be taken off his door so he can have the run of the grounds. He says he'd as soon rest here as anywhere else provided he didn't feel shut in and he said we could consider it a second honeymoon if I didn't have to work either."

"Done. There's been no reason for a lock on that door anyway. I'm sometimes not certain that he's not the only sane person here, Margie. Certainly he's the best adjusted one. Not to mention the one who's earning money the fastest. Know anything at all about his next book?"

"He said he was going to place it in Taos, New Mexico, in—I think it was eighteen forty-seven. He said he'd have to do a little research on this one."

"The assassination of Governor Bent. Very interesting period. I'll be able to help him with the research. I have several books that will help him."

"Good. That may save me a trip to the library or a book store. Well—"

Margie Devereaux stood and reached for the ready-to-mail manuscript, and then paused a second and sat down again.

"Doctor," she said, "there's something else I want to talk to you about. And a few minutes won't matter on mailing this. Unless you're—"

"Go right ahead. I'm as free now as I ever am. And there's not even a Martian around."

He looked to make sure. There wasn't.

"Doctor, what does Luke really *think?* I've managed to avoid talking to him about it, but I may not always be able to. And if Martians ever *do* come up in conversation—well, I want to know how to handle it. He knows that I see and hear Martians. I can't help being startled at one once in a while. And he knows I insist on darkness and wearing ear stopples when—uh—"

"When darkness and stopped ears are indicated," Dr. Snyder prompted.

"Yes. But he knows I see and hear them and he doesn't. Does he think *I'm* insane? That everyone is crazy except Luke Devereaux? Or what?"

Dr. Snyder took off his glasses to polish them. "That's a very difficult question to answer, Margie."

"Because you don't know the answer or because it's hard to explain?"

"A little of both. The first few days Luke was here I did quite a bit of talking with him. He was a bit mixed up himself—or more than a bit, I should soy. There weren't any Martians; he was sure of that. He himself had either been insane or suffering delusions while he'd been seeing them. But he couldn't account for why—if they are a mass hallucination for the rest of us—he recovered and the rest of us haven't."

"But—then he *must* think the rest of us are crazy."

"Do you believe in ghosts, Margie?"

"Of course not."

"A lot of people do—millions of people. And thousands of people have seen them, heard them, talked to them—or think they have. Now if you think you're sane, does that mean you think everyone who believes in ghosts is insane?"

"Of course not. But that's different. They're just imaginative people who *think* they've seen ghosts."

"And we're just imaginative people who think there are Martians around."

"But—but *everyone* sees Martians. Except Luke."

Dr. Snyder shrugged. "Nevertheless that's his reasoning, if you can call it that. The analogy with ghosts is his, not mine—although it's a good analogy, up to a point. Certain friends of mine, as it happens, are certain that they've seen ghosts; I don't think that means they're insane—nor that I'm insane because I haven't, or can't, or don't."

"But—you can't photograph ghosts or make recordings of their voices."

"People claim to have done both. Apparently you haven't read many books on psychic research. Not that I'm suggesting that you should—I'm just pointing out that Luke's analogy isn't completely without justification."

"Then you mean you don't think Luke is insane?"

"Of course he's insane. Either that or everyone else is insane, including you and me. And that I find impossible to believe."

Margie sighed. "I'm afraid that isn't going to help me much if he ever wants to talk about it."

"He may never want to. He talked to me rather reluctantly, I'm afraid. If he does, let him do the talking and just listen. Don't try to argue with him. Or, for that matter, to humor him. But if he starts changing in any way or acting different, let me know."

"All right. But why? If you're not trying to cure him, I mean."

"Why?" Dr. Snyder frowned. "My dear Margie, your husband is insane. Right now it is a very advantageous form of insanity—he's probably the luckiest man on Earth—but what if the form of his insanity should change?"

"*Can* paranoia change to another form?"

Dr. Snyder made an apologetic gesture. "I keep forgetting that I don't have to talk to you as a layman. What I should have said is that his systematized delusion might change to another and less happy one."

"Like believing again in Martians, but not believing in human beings?"

Dr. Snyder smiled. "Hardly so complete a switch as that, my dear. But it's quite possible—" His smile vanished. "—that he might come to believe in neither."

"You're surely joking."

"No, I'm not. It's really quite a common form of paranoia. And, for that matter, a form of belief held by a great many sane people. Haven't you heard of solipsism?"

"The word sounds familiar."

"Latin, from *solus* meaning alone and *ipse* meaning self. Self alone. The philosophical belief that the self is the only existent thing. Logical result of starting reasoning with *'Cogito, ergo sum'*—I think, therefore I am—and finding oneself unable to accept any secondary step as logical. The belief that the world around you and all the people in it, except yourself, are simply something you imagine."

Margie smiled. "I remember now. It came up in a class in college. And I remember wondering, why not?"

"Most people wonder that at some time or other, even if not very seriously. It's such a tempting thing to believe, and it's so completely impossible to disprove. For a paranoiac, though, it's a ready-made delusion that doesn't even have to be systematized or even rationalized. And since Luke already disbelieves in Martians, it's only another step."

"You think it's a possibility that he might take that step?"

"Anything's a possibility, my dear. But all we can do is to watch carefully and be prepared for any impending change by getting some intimation of it in advance. And you're the one best situated for getting an advance warning."

"I understand, Doctor. I'll watch carefully. And thank you, for everything."

Margie stood again. This time she picked up the package and went out with it.

Dr. Snyder watched her go and then sat for a while staring at the doorway through which she had disappeared. He sighed more deeply than before.

Damn Devereaux, he thought. Impervious to Martians and married to a girl like that.

No one man should be so lucky; it wasn't fair.

His own wife— But he didn't want to think about his own wife.

Not after he'd just been looking at Margie Devereaux.

He picked up his pencil and pulled back in front of him the pad on which he had been making notes for the paper he intended to present that evening at the meeting of his cell of the P.F.A.M.

CHAPTER FOURTEEN

Yes, there was the P.F.A.M. The Psychological Front Against Martians. Going strong if still—in mid-July now, almost four months after the Coming—apparently going nowhere.

Almost every psychologist and psychiatrist in the United States. In every country in the world almost every psychologist and psychiatrist belonged to an equivalent organization. All of these organizations reported their findings and theories (there were, unfortunately, more theories than findings) to a special branch of the United Nations which had quickly been set up for the purpose and which was called the O.C.P.E.—Office for the Coordination of Psychological Effort—the main job of which was to translate and distribute reports.

The Translation Department alone filled three large office buildings and provided employment for thousands of multilingual people. If nothing else.

Membership in the P.F.A.M. and in the similar organizations in other countries was voluntary and unpaid. But almost everyone qualified belonged and the lack of pay didn't matter since every psychologist and psychiatrist who could remain sane himself was earning plenty.

There were, of course, no conventions; large groups of psychologists were as impractical as large groups for any other purpose. Large groups of people meant large groups of Martians and the sheer volume of interference made speaking impractical. Most P.F.A.M. members worked alone and reported by correspondence, received reams of reports of others and tried out on their patients whatever ideas seemed worth trying.

Perhaps there was progress of a sort. Fewer people were going insane, at any rate. This may or may not have been, as some claimed, that most people insufficiently stable to stand up to the Martians had already found escape from reality in insanity.

Others credited the increasingly sensible advice that the psychologists were able to give to those still sane. Incidence of insanity had dropped, they claimed, when it was fully realized that it was safe, mentally, to ignore Martians only up to a point. You had to swear back at them and lose your temper at them once in a while. Otherwise the pressure of irritation built up in you as steam builds up pressure in a boiler without a safety valve, and pretty soon you blew your top.

And the equivalently sensible advice not to try to make friends with them. People did try, at first, and the highest percentage of mental casualties is believed to have been among this group. A great many people, men and women of good will, tried that first night; some of them kept on trying for quite a while. A few—saints they must have been, and wonderfully stable people to boot—never did quit trying.

The thing that made it impossible was that the Martians moved *around* so. No single Martian ever stayed long in one place or in contact with one person, one family or one group. It just might have been possible, unlikely as it seems, for an extremely patient human being to have achieved friendly footing with a Martian, to have gained a Martian's confidence, if that human being had had the opportunity of protracted contact with a given Martian.

But no Martian was *given,* in that sense. The next moment, the next hour— at most the next day—the man of good will would find himself starting from scratch with a different Martian. In fact, people who tried to be nice to them found themselves changing Martians oftener than those who swore back at them. Nice people bored them. Conflict was their element; they loved it.

But we digressed from the P.F.A.M.

Other members preferred to work in small groups, cells. Especially those who, as members of the Psychological Front, were studying, or attempting to study, the psychology of the Martians. It is an advantage, up to a point, to have Martians around when one is studying or discussing them.

It was to such a cell, a group of six members, that Dr. Ellicott H. Snyder belonged, and it was due to meet that evening. And now he was pulling paper into the roller of his typewriter; the notes for the paper are finished. He wishes he could simply talk from the notes themselves; he likes to talk and detests writing. But there is always the possibility that Martian interference will make coherent talking impossible at a cell meeting and necessitate papers being passed around to be read. Even more important, if the cell members approve the content of a paper it is passed up to a higher echelon and given wider consideration, possibly publication. And this particular paper should definitely merit publication.

CHAPTER FIFTEEN

Dr. Snyder's paper began:

> It is my belief, that the Martians' one psychological weakness, their Achilles' heel, is the fact that they are congenitally unable to lie.
> I am aware that this point has been stated and disputed, and I am aware that many—and particularly our Russian colleagues—firmly believe that the Martians can and do lie, that their reason for telling the truth about our own affairs, for never once having been caught in a provable lie about terrestrial matters, is twofold. First, because it makes their tattling more effective and more harassing, since we cannot doubt what they tell us. Second, because by never being provably untrue in small things, they prepare us to believe without doubt whatever Big Lie about their nature and their purpose here they are telling us. The thought that there must be a Big Lie is one that would

```
seem more natural to our Russian friends than to most people.
Having lived for so long with their own Big Lie...
```

Dr. Snyder stopped typing, reread the start of his last sentence and then went back and x'd it out. Since, he hoped, this particular paper would be distributed internationally, why prejudice some of his readers in advance against what he was going to say.

```
     I believe, however, that it can be clearly proved through
a single logical argument that the Martians not only do not
lie but cannot.
     It is obviously their purpose to harass us as much as
possible.
     Yet they have never made the one claim, the one state-
ment, that would increase our misery completely past bear-
ing; they have never once told us that they intend to stay
here permanently. Since Coming Night, their only answer,
when they deign to answer at all, to the question, however
worded, of when they intend to go home or how long they
intend to stay is that it is "none of our business" or words
to that effect.
     For most of us the only thing that makes survival desir-
able is hope, hope that someday, whether tomorrow or ten
years from now, the Martians will leave and we'll never see
them again. The very fact that their coming was so sudden
and unexpected makes it seem quite possible that they'll
leave the same way.
     If the Martians could lie, it is impossible to believe
that they would not tell us that they intend to be permanent
residents here. Therefore, they cannot lie.
     And a very welcome corollary of this simple step in logic
is that it becomes immediately obvious that they know their
stay here is not permanent. If it were, they would not have
to lie in order to increase our unhap—
```

A high-pitched chuckle sounded only an inch or two from Dr. Snyder's right ear. He jumped a few inches, but very carefully didn't turn, knowing it would put the Martian's face unbearably close to his own.

"*Ver-y* clever, Mack, *ver-y* clever. And screwy as a bedbug, screwy as a bedbug."

"It's perfectly logical," said Dr. Snyder. "It's absolutely proved. You can't lie."

"But I can," said the Martian. "Work on the logic of that a while, Mack."

Dr. Snyder worked on the logic of that, and groaned. If a Martian said he could lie, then either he was telling the truth and he could lie, or else he was lying and—

There was a sudden shrieking laugh in his ear.

And then silence in which Dr. Snyder took the paper from his typewriter, manfully resisted the impulse to fold it so he could tear it into paper dolls, and tore it into small pieces instead. He dropped them into the waste-basket and then dropped his head in his hands.

"Dr. Snyder, are you all right?" Margie's voice.

"Yes, Margie." He looked up and tried to compose his face; he must have succeeded for apparently she saw nothing wrong. "My eyes were tired," he explained. "I was just resting them for a moment."

"Oh. Well, I mailed the manuscript. And it's still only four o'clock. Are you sure there's nothing you want me to do before I take off?"

"No. Wait, yes. You might look up George and tell him to change the lock on Luke's door. Put on an ordinary one, I mean."

"All right. Finish your paper?"

"Yes," he said. "I finished my paper."

"Good. I'll find George." She went away and he heard the click of her heels on the stairs leading down toward the janitor's quarters in the basement.

He stood, almost without effort. He felt terribly tired, terribly discouraged, terribly futile. He needed a rest, a nap. If he slept, and overslept to miss dinner or the cell meeting, it wouldn't matter. He needed sleep more than he needed food or pointless argument with fellow psychiatrists.

He trudged wearily up the carpeted stairs to the second floor, started along the corridor.

Paused outside Luke's door and found himself glaring at it. The lucky bastard, he thought. In there thinking or reading. And, if there were Martians around, not even knowing it. Not able to see them or hear them.

Perfectly happy, perfectly adjusted. Who was crazy, Luke or everybody else?

And having Margie, too.

Damn him. He should throw him to the wolves, to the other psychiatrists, and let them experiment with him, probably make him as miserable as anybody else by curing him—or making him insane in some other and not so fortunate direction.

He should, but he wouldn't.

He went on to his own room, the one he used here when he didn't want to go home to Signal Hill, and shut the door. Picked up the telephone and called his wife.

"I don't think I'll be home tonight, dear," he said. "Thought I'd better tell you before you started dinner."

"Something wrong, Ellicott?"

"Just that I'm terribly tired. Going to take a nap and if I sleep through— well, I need the sleep."

"You have a meeting tonight."

"I may miss that, too. If I do go to it, though, I'll come home afterwards instead of back here."

"Very well, Ellicott. The Martians have been unusually bad here today. Do you know what two of them—"

"Please, dear. I don't want to hear about Martians. Tell me some other time, please. Good-bye, dear."

Putting down the phone, he found himself staring into a haunted face in the mirror, his own face. Yes, he needed sleep, badly. He picked up the phone again and called the receptionist, who also worked the switchboard and kept records. "Doris? I'm not to be disturbed under any circumstances. And if there are any callers, tell them I'm out."

"All right. Doctor. For how long?"

"Until I call back. And if that isn't before you go off duty and Estelle comes on, explain to her, will you? Thanks."

He saw his face in the mirror again. Saw that his eyes looked hollow and that there was at least twice as much gray in his hair as had been there four months ago.

So Martians can't lie, huh? he asked himself silently.

And then let him carry the thought to its horrible conclusion. If Martians could lie—and they could—then the fact that they did not claim they were staying here permanently wasn't proof that they weren't.

Perhaps they got more sadistic pleasure out of letting us hope so they could keep on enjoying our sufferings than by ending humanity by denying it hope. If everyone committed suicide or went insane, there'd be no sport for them; there'd be no one left to torment.

And the logic of that paper had been so simply beautiful and so beautifully simple...

His mind felt fogged now and for a moment he couldn't remember where the flaw in it had been. Oh, yes. If someone says he can lie, he can; otherwise he'd be lying in saying he could lie, and if he is already lying—

He pulled his mind out of the circle before it made him dizzier. He took off his coat and tie and hung them over the back of a chair, sat down on the edge of the bed and took off his shoes.

Lay back on the bed and closed his eyes.

Suddenly, a moment later, jumped almost three feet off the bed as two raucous and almost unbelievably loud Bronx cheers went off simultaneously, one in each ear. He'd forgotten his ear stopples.

He got up and put them in, lay down again. This time he slept.

And dreamed.

About Martians.

CHAPTER SIXTEEN

The scientific front against the Martians wasn't organized as was the psychological front, but it was even more active. Unlike the psych boys, who had their hands full with patients and could spare only stolen time for research and experimentation, the physical scientists were putting in full time and overtime studying the Martians.

Research in every other direction was at a standstill.

The active front was every big laboratory in the world. Brookhaven, Los Alamos, Harwich, Braunschweig, Sumigrad, Troitsk and Tokuyama, to mention only a few.

Not to mention the attic, cellar or garage of every citizen who had a smattering of knowledge in any field of science or pseudoscience. Electricity, electronics, chemistry, white and black magic, alchemy, dowsing, biotics, optics, sonics and supersonics, typology, toxicology and topology were used as means of study or means of attack.

The Martians *had* to have a weakness somewhere. There just *had* to be *something* that could make a Martian say "Ouch."

They were bombarded with alpha rays, with beta, gamma, delta, zeta, eta, theta and omega rays.

They were, when opportunity offered (and they neither avoided nor sought being experimented on), caught in multi-million-volt flashes of electricity, subjected to strong and weak magnetic fields and to microwaves and macrowaves.

They were subjected to cold near absolute zero and to heat as hot as we could get it, which is the heat of nuclear fission. No, the latter was not achieved in a laboratory. An H-bomb test that had been scheduled for April was, after some deliberation by authorities, ordered to proceed as planned despite the Martians. They knew all our secrets by then anyway so there was nothing to lose. And it was hoped that a Martian might be inspecting the H-bomb at close range when it was fired. One of them was sitting on it. After the explosion he kwimmed to the bridge of the admiral's flagship, looking disgusted. "Is *that* the best you can do for firecrackers, Mack?" he demanded.

They were photographed, for study, with every kind of light anybody could think of: infrared, ultraviolet, fluorescent, sodium, carbon arc, candlelight, phosphorescence, sunlight, moonlight and starlight.

They were sprayed with every known liquid, including prussic acid, heavy water, holy water and Flit.

Sounds they made, vocal or otherwise, were recorded by every known type of recording device. They were studied with microscopes, telescopes, spectroscopes and iconoscopes.

Practical results, zero; nothing any scientist did to any Martian made him even momentarily uncomfortable.

Theoretical results, negligible. Very little was learned about them that hadn't been known within a day or two of their arrival.

They reflected light rays only of wave lengths within the visible spectrum (.0004 mm. to .00076 mm.). Any radiation above or below this band passed through them without being affected or deflected. They could not be detected by X-rays, radio waves or radar.

They had no effect whatsoever on gravitational or magnetic fields. They were equally unaffected by every form of energy and every form of liquid, solid or gaseous matter we could try on them.

They neither absorbed nor reflected sound, but they could create sound. That perhaps was more puzzling to scientists than the fact that they reflected light rays. Sound is simpler than light, or at least is better understood. It is the vibration of a medium, usually air. And if the Martians weren't *there* in the sense of being real and tangible, how could they cause the vibration of air which we hear as sound? But they did cause it, and not as a subjective effect in the mind of the hearer for the sound could be recorded and reproduced. Just as the light waves they reflected could be recorded and studied on a photographic plate.

Of course no scientist, by definition, believed them to be devils or demons. But a great many scientists refused to believe that they came from Mars—or, for that matter, anywhere else in our universe. Obviously they were a different kind of matter—if matter at all, as we understand the nature of matter—and must come from some other universe where the laws of nature were completely different. Possibly from another dimension.

Or, still more likely, some thought, they themselves had fewer or more dimensions than we.

Could they not be two-dimensional beings whose appearance of having a third dimension was an illusory effect of their existence in a three-dimensional universe? Shadow figures on a movie screen appear to be three-dimensional until you try to grab one by the arm.

Or perhaps they were projections into a three-dimensional universe of four- or five-dimensional beings whose intangibility was due somehow to their having *more* dimensions than we could see and understand.

CHAPTER SEVENTEEN

Luke Devereaux awoke, stretched and yawned, feeling blissful and relaxed on this, the third morning of the week's vacation he was taking after having finished *Trail to Nowhere*. The best-earned vacation he'd ever had, after finishing a book in five weeks flat. A book that would probably make him more money than any book he'd written to date.

No worries about his next book, either. He had the main points of the plot well in mind already and if it weren't for Margie being so insistent that he take a vacation he'd probably be a chapter or so into it already. His fingers itched to get at the typewriter again.

Well, he'd made the bargain that he'd take a vacation only if Margie did too, and that made it a second honeymoon, practically, and just about perfect.

Just about perfect? he asked himself. And found his mind suddenly shying away from the question. If it wasn't perfect, he didn't *want* to know why it wasn't.

But why didn't he want to know? That was one step further removed from the question itself, but even so it was vaguely troubling.

I'm thinking, he thought. And he shouldn't be thinking, because thinking might spoil everything somehow. Maybe that was why he'd worked so hard at writing, to keep from thinking?

But to keep from thinking what? His mind shied again.

And then he was out of the half-sleep and was awake, and it came back to him. The Martians.

Face the fact you've been trying to duck, the fact that everybody else still sees them and you don't. That you're insane—and you know you aren't—or that everybody else is.

Neither makes sense and yet one or the other must be true and ever since you saw your last Martian over five weeks ago you've been ducking the issue and trying to avoid thinking about it—because thinking about such a horrible paradox might drive you nuts again like you were before and you'd start seeing—

Fearfully he opened his eyes and looked around the room. No Martians. Of course not; there *weren't* any Martians. He didn't know how he could be so utterly, completely certain of that fact, but he *was* utterly and completely certain.

Just as certain as he was that he was sane, now.

He turned to look at Margie. She still slept peacefully, her face as innocent as a child's, her honey hair spread about on the pillow beautiful even in disarray. The sheet had slipped down to expose the tender pink nipple of a softly rounded breast and Luke raised himself on one elbow and then leaned across to kiss it. But very gently so as not to waken her; the faint light coming in at the window told him it was still quite early, not much after dawn. And also so as not to wake himself, *that* way, because the last month had taught him that she'd have nothing to do with him that way by daylight, only at night and wearing those damned things in her ears so he couldn't talk to her. The damn Martians. Well, that part of it wasn't too bad; this was a second honeymoon, not a first, and he was thirty-seven and not too ambitious early in the morning.

He lay back and closed his eyes again, but already he knew he wasn't going back to sleep.

And he didn't. Maybe it was ten minutes later, maybe twenty, but he found himself getting wider awake every second, so he slid cautiously out of bed and into his clothes. It was still not quite half past six, but he could go out and take a walk around the grounds until it was late enough. And Margie might as well get as much sleep as she could.

He picked up his shoes and tiptoed out into the hall with them, closing the door quietly behind him and sitting down on the top step of the stairway to put on his shoes.

None of the outer doors of the sanitarium was ever locked; patients who were confined at all—fewer than half of them—were confined to private rooms except while under supervision. Luke let himself out the side door.

Outdoors was clear and bright, but almost too cool. Even in early August a dawn can be almost cold in Southern California; this one was, and Luke shivered a bit and wished he'd put on a pullover sweater under his sport jacket. But the sun was fairly well up and it wouldn't stay that cool long. If he walked fairly briskly he'd be all right.

He walked fairly briskly over to the fence and then along parallel to it. The fence was redwood and six feet high. There was no wire atop it and any reasonably agile person, Luke included, could have climbed it; the fence was for privacy rather than for a barrier.

For a moment he was tempted to climb it and walk in freedom for half an hour or so, and then decided against it. If he was seen, either going over or coming back, Dr. Snyder might worry about it and curtail his privileges. Dr. Snyder was very much of a worrier. Besides, the grounds were quite large; he could do plenty of walking right inside them.

He kept walking, along the inside of the fence. To the first corner, and turned.

And saw that he wasn't alone, wasn't the only early riser that morning. A small man with a large black spade beard was sitting on one of the green benches that were scattered around the grounds. He wore gold-rimmed glasses and was meticulously dressed down to highly polished black shoes topped by light gray spats. Luke looked curiously at the spats; he hadn't known anyone wore them any more. The spade-bearded one was looking curiously up over Luke's shoulder.

"Beautiful morning," Luke said. Since he'd already stopped, it would have been rude not to speak.

The bearded man didn't answer. Luke turned and looked over his own shoulder, found himself looking up into a tree. But he saw nothing there that one does not usually see looking up into a tree, leaves and branches. Not a bird's nest, not even a bird.

Luke turned back and the bearded man still stared up into the tree, still hadn't looked at Luke. Was the man deaf? Or—?

"I beg your pardon," Luke said. An awful suspicion came over him when there wasn't any answer to that. He stepped forward and touched the man lightly on the shoulder. The shoulder twitched slightly. The bearded man reached up a hand and rubbed it casually, but without turning his gaze.

What would he do if I hauled off and slugged him? Luke wondered. But instead he reached out a hand and moved it back and forth in front of the man's eyes. The man blinked, and then took off his glasses, rubbed first one eye and then the other, put the glasses back on and stared again into the tree.

Luke shivered, and walked on.

My God, he thought; he can't see me, can't hear me, doesn't believe I'm here. Just as *I* don't believe—

But, damn it, when I touched him he felt it, only—

Hysterical blindness, Doc Snyder explained it to me, when I asked him why, if Martians were *there,* I didn't see blank spots that I couldn't see through, even if I couldn't see *them.*

And he explained that I—

Just like that man—

There was another bench and Luke sat down on it, turned to stare back at the bearded one, still sitting on his own bench twenty yards back. Still sitting there, still looking up in the tree.

At something that isn't there? Luke wondered.

Or at something that isn't there for me but is there for him, and which of us is right?

And he thinks that *I* don't exist and I think I do, and which of us is right about that?

Well, *I* am, on that point if no other. I think, therefore I am.

But how do I know *he's* there?

Why couldn't *he* be a figment of *my* imagination?

Silly solipsism, the type of wondering just about everybody goes through sometime during adolescence, and then recovers from.

But it gives to wonder all over again when you and other people start seeing things differently or start seeing different things.

Not Spade-Beard; he was just another nut. No significance there. Just that maybe, just maybe, that little encounter with him had put Luke's mind to working on what could be the right track.

The night he'd got drunk with Gresham and just before he'd passed out there'd been that Martian, the one he'd cussed back at. "I 'nvented you," he remembered telling the Martian.

Well?

What if he really had? What if his mind, in drunkenness, had recognized something his sober mind hadn't known?

What if solipsism *wasn't* silly?

What if the universe and everything and everybody in it were simply figments of the imagination of Luke Devereaux?

What if I, Luke Devereaux, *did* invent the Martians that evening they came, when he was in Carter Benson's shack on the desert near Indio?

Luke got up and started walking again, faster, to speed up his mind. He thought back, hard, about that evening. Just before the knock had come on the door he'd had the start of an idea for a science-fiction novel he'd been trying to write. He'd been thinking, "What if the Martians..."

But he couldn't remember what the rest of that thought had been. The Martian's knock had interrupted it.

Or had it?

What if, even though his conscious mind had not formulated the thought clearly, it had already worked itself out in his subconscious mind: *What if the Martians are little green men, visible, audible, but not tangible, and what if, a second from now, one of them knocks on that door and says, "Hi, Mack. Is this Earth?"*

And went on from there.

Why not?

Well, for one reason, he'd worked out other plots—hundreds of them if you counted short stories—and none of them had happened the instant he'd thought of them.

But—what if, that night, something in the conditions had been a little different? Or, and this seemed more likely, there'd been a slip in his brain—from brain fatigue and from worry over his slump—and the part of his mind which separated "fact," the fictional universe which his mind ordinarily projected about him, from "fiction," the stuff he conceived and wrote *as* fiction and which would in that case really be fiction-within-fiction?

It made sense, however nonsensical it sounded.

But what had happened, then, a little over five weeks ago, when he'd quit believing in Martians? Why did other people—if other people were themselves products of his, Luke's, imagination—keep on believing in and seeing something Luke himself no longer believed in, and which therefore no longer existed?

He found another bench and sat down on it. That was a tough one to figure out.

Or was it? His mind had received a shock that night. He couldn't remember what it was except that it concerned a Martian, but from what it had done to him—knocked him temporarily into a catatonic state—it must have been a severe shock all right.

And just maybe it had knocked belief in Martians out of his conscious mind, the mind that was thinking right now, without having cleared from his subconscious the error between fact and fiction—between the projected "real" universe and the plot for a story—which had brought the fictional Martians into seemingly real existence in the first place.

He wasn't paranoiac at all. Simply schizophrenic.

Part of his mind—the conscious, thinking part—didn't believe in Martians, knew, in fact, that they didn't exist.

But the deeper part, the subconscious that was the creator and sustainer of illusions, hadn't got the message. *It* still accepted the Martians as real, as real as anything else, and so, of course, did those other beings of his imagination and its, human beings.

In excitement, he got up and started to walk again, rapidly this time.

That made it easy. All he had to do was get the message to his subconscious mind.

It made him feel silly to do it, but he subvocalized: *Hey, there aren't any Martians. Other people shouldn't be seeing them either.*

Had that done it? Why not, if he had the right overall answer and he was sure he had.

He found himself at a far corner of the grounds and turned to head back toward the kitchen. Breakfast should be ready by now and he should be able to tell by the actions of other people whether they still saw and heard Martians.

He glanced at his watch and saw that it was ten after seven, still twenty minutes before the first call for breakfast, but there was a table and chairs in the big kitchen and from seven o'clock on early risers were welcome to have coffee there ahead of the regular breakfast.

He let himself in the back door and looked around. The cook was busy at the stove; an attendant was readying a tray for one of the confined patients. The two nurses' aides who doubled as waitresses on the breakfast shift weren't around; they were probably setting tables in the dining room.

Two patients were having coffee at the table, both elderly women, one in a bathrobe and the other in a housecoat.

All looked calm and peaceful, no sign of a disturbance. Not that he'd see the Martian end of one if one did happen, but he should be able to tell by the reactions of the people he *could* see. He'd just have to watch for indirect evidence.

He poured himself a cup of coffee and took it to the table, sat down in a chair. Said, "Good morning, Mrs. Murcheson," to the one of the two women he knew; Margie had happened to introduce them yesterday.

"Good morning, Mr. Devereaux," Mrs. Murcheson said. "And your beautiful wife? Still sleeping?"

"Yes. I got up early for a walk. Beautiful morning."

"It seems to be. This is Mrs. Randall, Mr. Devereaux, if you two don't know each other."

Luke murmured politely.

"Pleased, I'm sure, Mr. Devereaux," said the other elderly lady. "If you've been out on the rounds perhaps you could tell me where my husband is, so I won't have to look *all* over for him?"

"I saw only one other person," Luke said. "A man with a spade beard?"

She nodded and Luke said, "Right near the northwest corner. Sitting on one of the benches, staring up into a tree."

Mrs. Randall sighed. "Probably thinking out his big speech. He thinks he's Ishurti this week, poor man." She pushed back her chair. "I'll go and tell him coffee is ready."

Luke started to push back his own chair and opened his mouth to say that he'd go for her. Then he remembered that Spade-Beard could neither see nor hear him, so the carrying of a message would be embarrassingly ineffective. He refrained from offering.

When the door had closed, Mrs. Murcheson laid a hand on his arm. "Such a *nice* couple," she said. "It's too bad."

"She seems nice," Luke said. "I—uh—didn't get to meet him. Are they both—uh—?"

"Yes, of course. But each thinks that only the other is. Each thinks he is here just to stay with and take care of the other." She leaned closer. "But I have my suspicions, Mr. Devereaux. I think they're both spies, just pretending to be insane. *Venusian spies!*" Both *s*'s hissed and Luke leaned back and under pretext of wiping coffee from his lips managed to wipe the spittle from his cheek as well.

To change the uncomfortable subject he asked, "What did she mean by saying he thought he was shirty this week?"

"Not shirty, Mr. Devereaux. Ishurti."

The word or name sounded familiar to him, now that he'd heard it repeated, but he couldn't place it.

But he realized suddenly that it might be embarrassing if Mrs. Randall brought her husband to the table while he was there, so instead of asking more questions he finished his coffee quickly and excused himself, saying he wanted to go upstairs to see if his wife was awake for breakfast yet.

He made his escape just in time; the Randalls were coming in the back way.

Outside their room he heard Margie moving around inside, knocked lightly so as not to startle her, and then went in.

"Luke!" She threw her arms around him and kissed him. "Have a walk around the grounds?" She was partly dressed—bra, panties and shoes, and the dress she'd dropped onto the bed to free her hands would complete the ensemble.

"That and one cup of coffee. Put that dress on and we'll be just in time for breakfast."

He dropped into a chair and watched as she lifted the dress overhead and started the usual series of contortions, ungraceful but fascinating to watch, that women always go through in pulling a dress over their heads.

"Margie, who or what is Ishurti?"

There was a muffled sound from inside the dress and then Margie's head came out of the collar of it, staring at him a bit incredulously as she smoothed the dress down her body. "Luke, haven't you been reading the newspa— That's right, you haven't been. But from back when you were reading them, you ought to remember Yato Ishurti!"

"Oh, sure," Luke said. The two names together reminded him now who the man was. "Has he been much in the news lately?"

"Much in the news? He's *been* the news, Luke, for the past three days. He's to make a speech tomorrow on the radio, to the whole world; they want *everybody* to listen in and the newspapers have been giving it top headlines ever since the announcement."

"A radio speech? But I thought that Martians were supposed to—I mean, I thought Martians interrupted them."

"They can't any more, Luke. That's *one* thing we've finally licked them on. Radio has developed a new type of throat mike, one that the Martians can't cut in on. That was the big story about a week ago, before Ishurti's announcement."

"How does it work? The mike, I mean."

"It doesn't pick up sound at all, as such. I'm no technician so I don't knew the details, but it picks up just the vibrations of the speaker's larynx direct and translates them into radio waves. He doesn't even have to speak out loud; he just— What's the word?"

"Subvocalizes," Luke said, remembering his experiment in trying to talk to his subconscious that way, only minutes ago. Had it worked? He'd seen no indication of a Martian around. "But what's the speech *about?*"

"Nobody knows, but everyone assumes it's about Martians, because what else, right now, would he want to talk to the whole world about? There are rumors—nobody knows whether they're true or not—that one of them has finally made a sensible contact with him, propositioned him by telling him on what terms the Martians will leave. And it seems possible, doesn't it? They must have a leader, whether it's a king or a dictator or a president or whatever else they might call him. And if he made contact, isn't Ishurti the man he'd go to?"

Luke managed not to smile, even to nod noncommittally. What a letdown Ishurti was going to have. By tomorrow...

"Margie, when did you last see a Martian?"

She looked at him a bit strangely. "Why, Luke?"

"I—just wondered."

"If you must know, there are two of them in the room right now."

"Oh," he said.

It hadn't worked.

"I'm ready," Margie said. "Shall we go down?"

Breakfast was being served. Luke ate moodily, not tasting the ham and eggs at all; they might as well have been sawdust. *Why* hadn't it worked?

Damn his subconscious; couldn't it hear him subvocalize?

Or didn't it believe him?

He knew suddenly that he'd have to get away, somewhere. Here, and he might as well face it that *here* was an insane asylum even if one called it a sanitarium, here was no place to work out a problem like that.

And wonderful as Margie's presence was, it was a distraction.

He'd been alone when he'd invented the Martians; he'd have to be alone again to exorcise them. Alone and away from everything and everybody.

Carter Benson's shack near Indio? Of course; *that's where it had all started!*

Of course it was August now and it would be hellish hot out there by day, but for that very reason he could be sure that Carter himself wouldn't be using it. So he wouldn't have to ask Carter's permission and not even Carter would know that he was there and be able to give him away if there was a search for him. Margie didn't know about the place; he'd never happened to mention it to her.

But he'd have to plan carefully. Too early to make his getaway now because the bank didn't open until nine and that would have to be his first stop. Thank God Margie had opened their account as a joint account and had brought out a signature card for him to sign. He'd have to cash a check for several hundred so he'd have enough to buy a used car; there wasn't any other way of getting out to Benson's shack. And he'd sold his own car before he'd left Hollywood.

Got only two hundred and fifty dollars for it, too, although a few months before—while there was still such a thing as pleasure driving—it would have brought him five hundred. Well, that meant he'd be able to buy one cheaply now; for less than a hundred he'd be able to pick up something good enough to get him there and let him run into Indio for shopping—if what he had to do took him that long.

"Anything wrong, Luke?"

"Nup," he said. "Not a thing." And realized he might as well start preparing the groundwork for his escape. "Except that I'm a little dopey. Couldn't sleep last night; doubt if I got more than a couple hours solid sleep all night."

"Maybe you should go up to the room and take a nap now, darling."

Luke pretended to hesitate. "Well—maybe later. If I get actually sleepy. Right now I feel sort of dull and logy but I doubt if I could sleep."

"Okay. Anything special you'd like to do?"

"How about a few games of badminton? That just might tire me out enough so I *could* sleep a few hours."

It was a little windy for badminton, but they played for half an hour—that made it half-past eight—and then Luke yawned and said that now he really *was* sleepy. "Maybe you'd better come up with me," he suggested. "If you want to get anything from the room, you can, and then you won't have to bother me until time for lunch, if I sleep that long."

"You go ahead; there's nothing I'll want. I promise not to bother you till twelve."

He kissed her briefly, wishing it could be a longer kiss since he might not see her again for a while, and went into the building and up to the room.

He sat down at the typewriter first and wrote a note to her, telling her he loved her but that there was something important he had to do, and not to worry because he'd be back soon.

Then be found Margie's purse and took enough money to pay cab fare into town in case he could catch a cab. It would save time if he could, but even if he had to walk all the way to the bank he could be there by eleven and that would be in plenty of time.

Then he looked out of the window to see if he could find Margie on the grounds, and couldn't. Tried the window at the end of the hall and couldn't see her from there either. But when he went quietly downstairs he heard her voice coming from the open doorway of Dr. Snyder's office. "...not really worried," he heard her saying, "but he did act just a bit strange. I don't think, though, that he..."

He let himself quietly out of the side door and strolled to the back corner of the grounds where a grove of trees hid the fence from the buildings.

His only danger now was that someone outside the fence might see him climb it, and phone the police or the sanitarium.

But no one did.

CHAPTER EIGHTEEN

It was the fifth day of August, 1964. A few minutes before 1 P.M. in New York City. Other time zones, other times, all over the world. This was to be the big moment, maybe.

Yato Ishurti, Secretary-General of the United Nations, sat alone in a small studio at Radio City. Ready and waiting.

Hopeful and frightened.

The throat mike was in place. There were stopples in his ears to prevent aural distraction once he had started to speak. And he would close his eyes, too, the instant the man behind the control room window nodded to indicate that he was on the air, so he could not be subject to visual distraction either.

Remembering that the mike was not yet activated, he cleared his throat as he watched the little glass window and the man behind it.

He was about to speak to the largest audience that had ever listened to the voice of one man, ever, anywhere. Barring a few savages and children too young to talk or to understand, just about every human being on earth would listen to him—either directly or through the voice of a translator.

Hurried as they had been, preparations had been exhaustive. Every government on Earth had cooperated fully, and every active radio station in the world would pick up and rebroadcast what he had to say. Every active radio station and many that had been abandoned but quickly reactivated for the purpose. And all the ships at sea.

He must remember to speak slowly and to pause at the end of each sentence or few sentences so the thousands of translators who would relay the broadcasts in non-English-speaking countries could keep up with him.

Even tribesmen in the most primitive countries would hear; arrangements had been made wherever possible to have natives come in and listen to on-the-spot translations at the nearest receiving sets. In civilized countries every factory and office not already closed by the Depression would be closed down while employees gather around radios and P.A. systems; people staying home who had no radios were requested to join neighbors who had.

As near as matters, three billion people would be hearing him. And, as near as matters, one billion Martians.

If he succeeded he would become the most famous— But Ishurti pulled his mind quickly away from that selfish thought. He must think of humanity, not of himself. And if he succeeded he must retire at once, not try to capitalize on success.

If he failed— But he must not think about that either.

No Martian seemed to be present in the studio, none in the part of the control room he could see through the little window.

He cleared his throat again, and just in time. He saw the man beyond the control room window flick a switch and then nod to him.

Yato Ishurti closed his eyes, and spoke.

He said: "People of the world, I speak to you and through you to our visitors from Mars. Mostly I speak to them. But it is necessary that you listen too, so that when I have spoken you can answer a question that I shall ask you."

He said: "Martians, you have not, for whatever reason of your own, taken us into your confidence as to why you are here among us.

"Possibly you are truly vicious and evil and our pain gives you pleasure.

"Possibly your psychology, your pattern of thinking, is so alien to ours that we could not understand even if you tried to explain to us.

"But I do not believe either of these things."

He said: "If you really are what you seem or pretend to be, quarrelsome and vindictive, we would find you, at least on rare occasion, arguing or fighting among yourselves.

"This we have never seen or heard.

"Martians, you are putting on an act, pretending to be something that you are not."

Across Earth, there was a stir as people moved.

Ishurti said: "Martians, you have an ulterior purpose in doing what you have been doing. Unless your reason is beyond my power to comprehend, unless your purpose is beyond the scope of human logic, it can and must be one of only two things.

"It can be that your purpose is good; that you came here for *our* good. You knew that we were divided, hating one another, warring and ever on the verge of final war. It can be that you reasoned that, being what we are, we could be united only by being given a common cause, and a common hatred that transcends our hatreds of one another and makes them now seem so ridiculous that they are difficult for us to remember.

"Or it is possible that your purpose is less benevolent, but still not inimical. It is possible that, learning we stand—or stood—on the verge of space travel, you do not want us on Mars.

"It could be that, on Mars, you are corporeal and vulnerable and that you are afraid of us; you fear that we might try to conquer you, either soon or centuries from now. Or perhaps we merely bore you—certainly our radio programs must have—and you simply do not want our company on your planet."

He said: "If either of those basic reasons is the real one, and I believe that one or the other of them is, you knew that merely *telling* us to behave ourselves or to stay away from Mars would antagonize us rather than accomplish your purpose.

"You wanted us to see for ourselves and to *volunteer* to do as you wish.

"Is it important that we know or guess correctly which of these two basic purposes is your true one?

"Whichever it is, I will prove to you that you have accomplished it."

He said: "I speak, and I shall now prove that I speak, for all the peoples of Earth."

He said: "We pledge that we are through fighting among ourselves.

"We pledge that we shall not, we shall never, send a single spaceship to your planet—unless someday you invite us to, and I think that we might need persuading, even then."

He said solemnly: "And now the proof. *People of Earth,* are you with me in both of those pledges? If you are, prove it now, wherever you are, with an affirmative in your loudest voice! But so that the translators may have caught up with me, please wait until I give the signal by saying...

"...Now!"

"YES!

    "SI!

        "OUI!

            "DAH!

                "HAY!

                    "JA!

                        "SIM!

                            "JES!

                                "NAM!

                                    "SHI!

                                        "LAH!

And thousands of other words that all mean the same thing, simultaneously from the throat and from the heart of every human being who had been listening.

Not a *no* or a *nyet* among them.

It was the damnedest sound ever made. Compared to it an H-bomb would have been the dropping of a pin, the eruption of Krakatao would have been the faintest of whispers.

There could be no doubt that every Martian on Earth must have heard it. Had there been an atmosphere between the planets to carry sound, the Martians on *Mars* would have heard it.

Through ear stopples and inside a closed soundproofed broadcasting studio, Yato Ishurti heard it. And felt the building vibrate with it.

He spoke no further word to anticlimax that magnificent sound. He opened his eyes and nodded to the man in the control room to take him off the air. Sighed deeply after he had seen the switch move and reached up and took the stopples from his ears.

Stood, spent emotionally, walked slowly and let himself into the little anteroom between the studio and the hallway, paused there a moment to regain his composure.

Turned by chance and saw himself in a mirror on the wall.

Saw the Martian seated cross-legged atop his head, caught its eye in the mirror, and its grin, heard it tell him, "—you, Mack."

Knew that he must do what he had come prepared to do in case of failure.

Took from his pocket the ceremonial knife and removed it from its sheath.

Sat himself upon the floor in the manner required by tradition. Spoke briefly to his ancestors, performed the brief preliminary ritual, and then with the knife—

Resigned as Secretary-General of the United Nations.

CHAPTER NINETEEN

The stock market had closed at noon the day of Ishurti's speech.

It closed at noon again on August 6th, the following day, but for a different reason; it closed for an indefinite period as a result of an emergency order issued by the President. Stocks that morning had opened at a fraction of their previous day prices (which were a fraction of their pre-Martian prices), were finding no takers and declining rapidly. The emergency order stopped trading while at least some stocks were still worth the paper they were printed on.

In an even more sweeping emergency measure that afternoon, the government decided upon and announced a ninety per cent reduction in the armed forces. In a press conference, the President admitted the desperation behind this decision; it would greatly swell the ranks of the unemployed, nevertheless the measure was necessary as the government was for all practical purposes bankrupt and it was cheaper to maintain men on relief than in uniform. And all other nations were making similar cuts.

And similarly, despite all cuts, tottering upon the verge of bankruptcy. Almost any of the established orders would have been a pushover for a revolution—except for the fact that not even the most fanatical of revolutionaries *wanted* to take over under such circumstances.

Harassed, heckled, hounded, helpless, hamstrung, harried and harrowed, the average citizen of the average country looked with heartfelt horror to a hideous future and hankered hungrily for a return to the good old days when his only worries were death, taxes and the hydrogen bomb.

Part Three — The Going of the Martians

CHAPTER ONE

In August of the year 1964 a man with the mildly improbable name of Hiram Pedro Oberdorffer, of Chicago, Illinois, invented a contraption which he called an anti-extraterrestrial subatomic supervibrator.

Mr. Oberdorffer had been educated in Heidelberg, Wisconsin. His formal education had ended at the eighth grade, but in the fifty-odd years that followed he had become an inveterate reader of popular science magazines and of science articles in Sunday supplements and elsewhere. He was an ardent theorist and, in his own words (and who are we to gainsay them), he "knew more science than most of them laboratory guys."

He was employed, and had been for many years, as janitor of an apartment building on Dearborn Street near Grand Avenue, and lived in a basement apartment of two rooms in the same building. In one of the two rooms he cooked, ate and slept. In the other room he lived the part of his life that mattered; it was his workroom.

Besides a work bench and some power tools the workroom contained several cabinets, and in and on the cabinets and piled on the floor or in boxes were old automobile parts, old radio parts, old sewing machine parts and old vacuum cleaner parts. Not to mention parts from washing machines, typewriters, bicycles, lawn mowers, outboard motors, television sets, clocks, telephones, tinkertoys, electric motors, cameras, phonographs, electric fans, shotguns and Geiger counters. Infinite treasures in a little room.

His janitorial duties, especially in summer, were not too onerous; they left him ample time for inventing and for his only other pleasure, which was, in good weather, to sit and relax and think in Bughouse Square, which was only a ten minute walk from where he lived and worked.

Bughouse Square is a city park one block square and it has another name but no one ever uses the other name. It is inhabited largely by bums, winos and crackpots. Let us have it clearly understood, however, that Mr. Oberdorffer was none of these. He worked for a living and he drank only beer and that in moderate quantity. Against accusations of being a crackpot, he could have *proved* that he was sane. He had papers to show it, given him upon his release from a mental institution where once, some years before, he had been briefly incarcerated.

Martians bothered Mr. Oberdorffer much less than they bothered most people; he had the very excellent good fortune to be completely deaf.

Oh, they bothered him some. Although he couldn't listen, he loved to talk. You might even say that he thought out loud, since he habitually talked to himself all the while he was inventing. In which case, of course, Martian interference was no nuisance; although he couldn't hear his own voice he knew perfectly well what he was saying to himself whether or not he was being drowned out. But he had one friend besides himself to whom he liked to talk, a man named Pete, and he found that Martians did interfere occasionally in his one-sided conversations with Pete.

Every summer Pete lived in Bughouse Square, whenever possible on the fourth bench to the left along the walk that diagonalled from the inner square toward the southeast corner. In the fall Pete always disappeared; Mr. Oberdorffer assumed, not too incorrectly, that he flew south with the birds. But the following spring Pete would be there again and Mr. Oberdorffer would take up the conversation again.

It was a very one-sided conversation indeed, for Pete was a mute. But he loved to listen to Mr. Oberdorffer, believing him to be a great thinker and a great scientist, a view with which Mr. Oberdorffer himself was in complete accord, and a few simple signals sufficed for his end of the conversation—a nod or shake of the head to indicate yes or no, a raising of the eyebrows to request further explanation or elucidation. But even these signals were rarely necessary; a look of admiration and rapt attention usually sufficed. Even more rarely was recourse to the pencil and pad of paper which Mr. Oberdorffer always carried with him necessary.

Increasingly, though, this particular summer Pete had been using a new signal—cupping a hand behind his ear. It had puzzled Mr. Oberdorffer the first time Pete had used this signal, for he knew that he was talking as loudly as ever, so he had passed the pad and pencil to Pete with a request for explanation, and Pete had written: "Cant here. Marsheys too noysy."

So Mr. Oberdorffer had obliged by talking more loudly, but it annoyed him somewhat to have to do so. (Not as much, however, as his talking so loudly— even after the interference had ceased, since he had no way of knowing when the Martians stopped heckling—annoyed the occupants of adjacent benches.)

Even when, this particular summer, Pete did not signal for an increase in volume, the conversations were no longer quite as satisfactory as they had once been. All too frequently the expression on Pete's face showed all too clearly that he was listening to something else instead of or in addition to what Mr. Oberdorffer was telling him. And whenever at such times Mr. Oberdorffer looked about he'd see a Martian or Martians and know that he was being heckled, to Pete's distraction and therefore indirectly to his own.

Mr. Oberdorffer began to toy with the idea of doing something about the Martians.

But it wasn't until in mid-August that he definitely decided to do something about them. In mid-August Pete suddenly disappeared from Bughouse Square. For several days running, Mr. Oberdorffer failed to find him there and he started to ask the occupants of other benches—those whom he had seen often enough to recognize as regulars—what had happened to Pete. For a while he got nothing but head shakes or other obvious disclaimers such as shrugs; then a man with a gray beard started to explain something to him so Mr. Oberdorffer said that he was deaf and handed over the pad and pencil. A temporary difficulty arose when the bearded one turned out to be unable to read or write, but between them they found an intermediary who was barely sober enough to listen to gray beard's story and put it in writing for Mr. Oberdorffer to read. Pete was in jail.

Mr. Oberdorffer hastened to the precinct station and after some difficulty due to the fact that there are many Petes and he didn't know his best friend's last name finally learned where Pete was being held and hurried to see him to help if he could.

It turned out that Pete had already been tried and convicted and was past help for thirty days, although he gladly accepted a loan of ten dollars to enable him to buy cigarettes for that period.

However he managed to talk to Pete briefly and to learn, via the pad and pencil route, what had happened.

Shorn of misspellings, Pete's story was that he had done nothing at all, the police had framed him; besides, he'd been a little drunk or he'd never have tried to shoplift razor blades from a dime store in broad daylight with Martians around. The Martians had enticed him into the store and had promised to act as lookout for him and then had ratted on him and called copper the moment he had his pockets full. It was all the fault of the Martians.

This pathetic story so irked Mr. Oberdorffer that, as of that very moment, he decided definitely to *do* something about the Martians. That very evening. He was a patient man but he had reached the limit of his patience.

Enroute home, he decided to break a long standing habit and eat at a restaurant. If he didn't have to interrupt his thinking to cook a meal for himself, he'd be off to a quicker start.

In the restaurant he ordered pigs' knuckles and sauerkraut and, while waiting for it to be brought to him, he started his thinking. But very quietly so as not to disturb other people along the counter.

He marshaled before him everything he'd read about Martians in the popular science magazines, and everything he'd read about electricity, about electronics and about relativity.

The logical answer came to him at the same time as the pigs' knuckles and sauerkraut. "It's got," he told the waitress, "to be an anti-extraterrestrial subatomic supervibrator! That's the only thing that will get them." Her answer, if any, went unheard and is unrecorded.

He had to stop thinking while he ate, of course, but he thought loudly the rest of the way home. Once in his own place, he disconnected the signal (which was a flashing red light in lieu of a bell) so no tenant of the building could interrupt him to report a leaking faucet or a recalcitrant refrigerator, and then he started to build an anti-extraterrestrial subatomic supervibrator.

"We use this outboard motor for power," he thought, suiting action to word. "Only the propeller it comes off and gives a generator to make the D.C. at—how many volts?" And when he figured that out, he stepped up the voltage with a transformer and then stepped it sidewise into a spark coil, and went on from there.

Only once did he encounter a serious difficulty. That was when he realized that he would need a vibrating membrane about eight inches in diameter. There was nothing in his workroom that would serve the purpose and since it was then eight o'clock and all stores were closed he almost gave up for the evening.

But the Salvation Army saved him, when he remembered it. He went out and over to Clark Street, walked up and down until a Salvation Army lassie came along to make the rounds of the taverns. He had to get as high as an offer of thirty dollars to the cause before she would agree to part with her tambourine; it is well she succumbed at that figure for it was all the money he had with him. Besides, if she had not agreed he would have been strongly tempted to grab the tambourine and run with it, and that would in all probability have landed him in jail with Pete. He was a portly man, a slow runner, and short of wind.

But the tambourine, with the jangles removed, turned out to be exactly right for his purpose. Covered with a light sprinkling of magnetized iron filings and placed between the cathode tube and the aluminum saucepan which served as a grid, it would not only filter out the unwanted delta rays but the vibration of the filings (once the outboard motor was started) would provide the required fluctuation in the inductance.

Finally, a full hour after his usual bedtime, Mr. Oberdorffer soldered the last connection and stepped back to look at his masterpiece. He sighed with satisfaction. It was good. It should work.

He made sure that the airshaft window was open as high as it would raise. The subatomic vibrations had to have a way out or they would work only inside the room. But once free they would bounce back from the Heaviside layer and, like radio waves, travel all around the world in seconds.

He made sure there was gasoline in the tank of the outboard motor, wound the cord around the spinner, prepared to pull the cord—and then hesitated. There'd been Martians in the room off and on all evening but there was none present now. And he'd rather wait till one was present again before starting the machine, so he could tell right away whether or not it worked.

He went into the other room and got a bottle of beer from the refrigerator and opened it. Took it back with him into the workroom and sat sipping it and waiting.

Somewhere outside a clock struck, but Mr. Oberdorffer, being deaf, did not hear it.

There was a Martian, sitting right atop the anti-extraterrestrial subatomic supervibrator itself.

Mr. Oberdorffer put down his beer, reached over and pulled the cord. The motor spun and caught, the machine ran.

Nothing happened to the Martian.

"Take it a few minutes to build up potential," Mr. Oberdorffer explained, to himself rather than to the Martian.

He sat down again, picked up his beer. Sipped it and watched and waited for the few minutes to pass.

It was approximately five minutes after eleven o'clock, Chicago time, on the evening of August 19th, a Wednesday.

CHAPTER TWO

On the afternoon of August 19, 1964, in Long Beach, California, at four o'clock in the afternoon (which would have been six o'clock in the afternoon in Chicago, just about the time Mr. Oberdorffer reached home full of pigs' knuckles and sauerkraut, ready to start work on his anti-extraterrestrial et cetera), Margie Devereaux looked around the corner of the doorway into Dr. Snyder's office and asked, "Busy, Doctor?"

"Not at all, Margie. Come in," said Dr. Snyder, who was swamped with work. "Sit down."

She sat down. "Doctor," she said, a bit breathlessly. "I've an idea finally as to how we can find Luke."

"I certainly hope it's a good one, Margie. It's been two weeks now."

It had been a day longer than that. It had been fifteen days and four hours since Margie had gone up to their room to waken Luke from his nap and had found a note waiting for her instead of a husband.

She'd run with the note to Dr. Snyder and their first thought, since Luke had had no cash except a few dollars that had been in Margie's purse, had been the bank. But a call to the bank had brought them the information that he had drawn five hundred dollars from the joint account.

Only one further fact had come to light subsequently. Police, the following day, had learned that less than an hour after Luke's call at the bank a man answering his description but giving a different name had bought a used car from a lot and paid one hundred dollars cash for it.

Dr. Snyder was not without influence at the police department and the entire Southwest had been circularized with descriptions of Luke and of the car, which was an old 1957 Mercury, painted yellow. Dr. Snyder himself had similarly circularized all mental institutions in the area.

"We agreed," Margie was saying, "that the place he'd most likely go to would be that shack on the desert where he was the night the Martians came. You still think so?"

"Of course. He thinks he *invented* the Martians—says so in that note he left for you. So what's more natural than that he'd go back to the same place, try to reconstruct the same circumstances, to undo what he thinks he did. But I thought you said you didn't have the faintest idea where the shack is."

"I still haven't except that it's within driving distance of L.A. But I just remembered something, Doctor. I remember Luke telling me, several years ago, that Carter Benson had bought a shack somewhere—near Indio, I think. That could be the one. I'll bet it is."

"But you called this Benson, didn't you?"

"I called him, yes. But all I asked him was whether he'd seen or heard from Luke since Luke left here. And he said he hadn't but promised to let me know if he did hear anything. But I didn't ask him if Luke had used his shack last March! And he wouldn't have thought to volunteer the information, because I didn't tell him the whole story or that we thought Luke might be going back to wherever he was last March. Because—well, it just never occurred to me."

"Hmmm," said Dr. Snyder. "Well, it's a possibility. But would Luke use the shack without Benson's permission?"

"He probably had permission last March. This time he's hiding out, don't forget. He wouldn't want even Carter to know where he went. And he'd know Carter wouldn't be using it himself—not in August."

"Quite true. You want to phone Benson again, then? There's the phone."

"I'll use the one in the outer office, Doctor. It might take a while to reach him, and you *are* busy, even if you say you aren't."

But it didn't take long to reach Carter Benson after all. Margie was back within minutes, and her face was shining.

"Doctor, it *was* Carter's place Luke used last March. And I've got instructions how to get there!" She waved a slip of paper.

"Good girl! What do you think we should do? Phone the Indio police or—?"

"Police nothing. I'm going to him. As soon as I'm through with my shift."

"You needn't wait for that, my dear. But are you sure you should go alone? We don't know how much his illness has changed and progressed, and you might find him—disturbed."

"If he isn't I'll disturb him. Seriously, Doctor, don't worry. I can handle him, no matter what." She glanced at her wrist watch. "A quarter after four. If you really don't mind my leaving now, I can be there by nine or ten o'clock."

"You're sure you don't want to take one of the attendants with you?"

"Very sure."

"All right, my dear. Drive carefully."

CHAPTER THREE

On the evening of the third day of the third moon of the season of kudus (at, as near as matters, the same moment Mr. Oberdorffer, in Chicago, was making inquiries in Bughouse Square about his missing friend) a witch doctor named Bugassi, of the Moparobi tribe in equatorial Africa, was called before the chief of his tribe. The chief's name was M'Carthi, but he was no relative of a former United States senator of the same name.

"Make juju against Martians," M'Carthi ordered Bugassi.

Of course he did not really call them *Martians*. He used the word *gnajamkata*, the derivation of which is: *gna*, meaning "Pygmy," plus *jam*, meaning "green," plus *kat*, meaning "sky." The final vowel indicates a plural, and the whole translates as "green Pygmies from the sky."

Bugassi bowed. "Make big juju," he said.

It had damned well better be a big juju, Bugassi knew.

The position of a witch doctor among the Moparobi is a precarious one. Unless he is a very good witch doctor indeed, his life expectancy is short. It would be even shorter were it not quite rare for the chief to make an official demand upon one of his witch doctors, for tribal law decreed that one of them who failed must make a contribution of meat to the tribal larder. And the Moparobi are cannibals.

There had been six witch doctors among the Moparobi when the Martians came; now Bugassi was the last survivor. One moon apart (for taboo forbids the chief to order the making of a juju less than a full moon of twenty-eight days after the making of the last previous juju) the other five witch doctors had tried and failed and made their contributions.

Now it was the turn of Bugassi and from the hungry way M'Carthi and the rest of the tribe stared at him it appeared they would be almost as satisfied if he failed as if he succeeded. The Moparobi had not tasted meat for twenty-eight days and they were meat hungry.

All of Africa was meat hungry.

Some of the tribes, those who had lived exclusively or almost exclusively from hunting, were actually starving. Other tribes had been forced to migrate vast distances to areas where vegetable foods, such as fruits and berries, were available.

Hunting was simply no longer possible.

Almost all of the creatures man hunts for food are fleeter of foot or of wing than he. They must be approached upwind and by stealth until he is within killing distance.

With Martians around there was no longer any possibility of stealth. They loved to help the natives hunt. Their method of helping was to run—or to kwim—well ahead of the hunter, awakening and alerting his quarry with gladsome cries.

Which made the quarry scamper like hell.

And which made the hunter return empty-handed from the hunt, ninety-nine times out of a hundred without having had the opportunity to shoot an arrow or throw a spear, let alone having hit something with either one.

It was a Depression. Different in type but at least as punishing in effect as the more civilized types of Depression that were rampant in the more civilized countries.

The cattle-herding tribes were affected too. The Martians loved to jump onto the backs of cattle and stampede them. Of course, since a Martian had no substance or weight, a cow couldn't *feel* a Martian on its back, but when the Martian leaned forward and screamed "Iwrigo 'm N'gari" ("Hi-yo, Silver") in Masai at the top of his voice in the cow's ear while a dozen or more other Martians were screaming "Iwrigo 'm N'gari" into the ears of a dozen or more other cows and bulls, the stampede was on.

Africa just didn't seem to *like* the Martians.

But, back to Bugassi.

"Make big juju," he had told M'Carthi. And a big juju it was going to be, literally and figuratively. When, shortly after the green Pygmies had come from the sky, M'Carthi had called in his six witch doctors and had conferred long and seriously with them. He had tried his best to persuade or to order them to pool their knowledge so that one of them, using the knowledge of all six, could make the greatest juju that had ever been made.

They had refused and even threats of torture and death could not move them. Their secrets were sacred and more important to them than their lives.

But a compromise had been reached. They were to draw lots for their turns, a moon apart. And each agreed that if, and only if, he failed, he would confide all of his secrets, including and in particular the ingredients and incantations that went into his juju, before he made his contribution to the tribal stomach.

Bugassi had drawn the longest twig and now, five moons later, he had the combined knowledge of all of the others as well as his own—and the witch doctors of the Moparobi are famed as the greatest of all Africa. Furthermore, he had exact knowledge of every thing and every word that had gone into the making of the five jujus that had failed.

With this storehouse of knowledge at his fingertips, he had been planning his own juju for a full moon now, ever since Nariboto, the fifth of the witch doctors, had gone the way of all edible flesh. (Of which Bugassi's share, by request, had been the liver, of which he had saved a small piece; well putrefied by now, it was in prime condition to be included in his own juju.)

Bugassi knew that his own juju could not fail, not only because the results to his own person were unthinkable if it did fail, but because—well, the combined knowledge of *all* of the witch doctors of the Moparobi simply *could* not fail.

It was to be a juju to end all jujus, as well as all Martians.

It was to be a monster juju; it was to include every ingredient and every spell that had been used in the other five and in addition was to include eleven ingredients and nineteen spells (seven of which were dance steps) which had been his own very special secrets, completely unknown to the other five.

All the ingredients were at hand and when assembled, tiny as most of them were individually, they would fill the bladder of a bull elephant, which was to be their container. (The elephant, of course, had been killed six months before; no big game had been killed since the Martians came.)

But the assembling of the juju would take all night, since each ingredient must be added with its own spell or dance and other spells and dances interspersed with the adding of ingredients.

Throughout the night no Moparobi slept. Seated in a respectful circle around the big fire, which the women replenished from time to time, they watched while Bugassi labored, danced and cast spells. It was a strenuous performance; he lost weight, they noticed sadly.

Just before dawn, Bugassi fell supine before M'Carthi, the chief.

"Juju done," he said from the ground.

"Gnajamkata still here," said M'Carthi grimly. They were very much still there; they had been very active all night, watching the preparations and joyfully pretending to help them; several times they had made Bugassi stumble in his dancing and once fall flat on his face by darting unexpectedly between his legs while he had danced. But each time he had patiently repeated the sequence so no step would be lost.

Bugassi raised himself on one elbow in the dirt. With the other arm he pointed to the nearest large tree.

"Juju must hang clear of ground," he said.

M'Carthi gave an order, and three black bucks leaped to obey it. They tied a rope of woven vines around the juju and one of them shinned up the tree and passed the rope over a limb; the other two hoisted the juju and when it was ten feet off the ground Bugassi, who had meanwhile climbed painfully to his feet, called to them that it was high enough. They secured it there. The one in the tree came down and they rejoined the others.

Bugassi went over to the tree, walking as though his feet hurt (which they did), and stood under the juju. He faced the east, where the sky was gray now and the sun just under the horizon, and folded his arms.

"When sun strike juju," he said solemnly if a bit hoarsely, "gnajamkata go."

The red rim of the sun came into sight over the horizon; its first rays struck the top of the tree in which the juju hung, moved downward.

In a very few minutes now, the first rays of the sun would reach the juju.

By coincidence or otherwise it was the exact moment when, in Chicago, Illinois, United States of America, one Hiram Pedro Oberdorffer, janitor and inventor, sat sipping beer and waiting for his anti-extraterrestrial subatomic supervibrator to build up potential.

CHAPTER FOUR

And as near as matters to three quarters of an hour before that exact moment, at about 9:15 P.M. Pacific Time in a shack on the desert near Indio, California, Luke Devereaux was making his third drink of the evening.

It was his fourteenth thwarting evening at the shack.

It was the fifteenth evening since his escape, if one can call so simple a walk-away an escape, from the sanitarium. The first evening had been thwarting too, but for a different reason. His car, the old '57 Mercury he had bought for a hundred dollars, had broken down in Riverside, about half-way between Long Beach and Indio. He'd had it towed to a garage, where they'd told him it couldn't possibly be fixed until the next afternoon. He'd spent a dull evening and a bad night (it seemed so strange and so lonesome to be sleeping alone again) at a Riverside hotel.

He'd spent the following morning shopping and carrying his purchases to the garage to load them in the car while a mechanic was working on it. He'd bought a used portable typewriter, of course, and some stationery. (He'd been in the process of choosing the typewriter when, at 10 A.M. Pacific Time, Yato Ishurti's speech had come on the air, and business had been suspended while the proprietor turned on a radio and everyone in the store had gathered around it. Knowing Ishurti's fundamental premise—that there really *were* Martians— to be completely wrong, Luke had been mildly annoyed at the interruption to his shopping, but had found himself quite amused at Ishurti's ridiculous reasoning.)

He bought a suitcase and some extra clothing, razor, soap and comb, and enough food and liquor so he wouldn't have to make a shopping trip into Indio for at least a few days after he got to the shack. He hoped what he had to accomplish there wouldn't take any longer than that.

He got his car back—with a repair bill almost half as much as the original cost of it—in midafternoon and reached his destination just before dark. He found himself too tired to try very hard that evening, and, anyway, he realized that he had forgotten something: Alone, he had no way of telling whether or not he had succeeded.

The next morning he drove back to Indio and bought himself the best and most expensive table model radio he could find, a set that would bring in programs from all over the country, a set on which he could find newscasts emanating from somewhere or other almost any time of day or evening.

Any newscast would tell him.

The only trouble was that for two weeks, until tonight, the newscasts had consistently told him wrong. They'd told him that the Martians were still around. Not that the newscasts opened with the statement, "The Martians are still with us," but almost every story concerned them at least indirectly or concerned the Depression and the other troubles they were causing.

And Luke was trying everything he could think of, and almost going crazy trying.

He *knew* the Martians were imaginary, the product (like everything else) of his own imagination, that he had invented them that evening five months ago, in March, when he'd been trying to plot a science fiction novel. He'd *invented* them.

But he'd invented hundreds of other plots and none of them had really happened (or *seemed* really to happen) so there had been something different that evening, and he was trying everything to reconstruct the exact circumstances, the exact frame of mind, the exact everything.

Including, of course, the exact amount of drinking, the exact tinge of inebriety, since that might have been a factor. As he had done while he was here the period preceding that evening, he stayed strictly sober by day—no matter how badly hung over he might awaken—pacing the floor and getting desperate (then, for a plot; now, for an answer). Now, as then, he would let himself start drinking only after he'd made and fed himself a dinner and then he'd space his drinks and pace his drinking very carefully—at least until he'd given up in disgust for the evening.

What was wrong?

He'd invented Martians by imagining them, hadn't he? Why couldn't he *un*-invent them now that he'd ceased to imagine them, now that he'd learned the truth? He had, of course, as far as he himself was concerned. Why wouldn't other people stop seeing and hearing them?

It must be a psychic block, he told himself. But naming it didn't help.

He took a sip of his drink and stared at it. Trying, for the thousandth time since he'd been here, to remember *exactly* how many drinks he'd had that night in March. It wasn't many, he knew; he hadn't been feeling them, any more than he was feeling the two he'd already had tonight before this one.

Or didn't the drinking have anything to do with it after all?

He took a second sip of his drink, put it down and started pacing. *There aren't any Martians,* he thought. *There never were any; they existed—like everything and everybody else—only while I imagined them. And I no longer imagine them. Therefore—*

Maybe that had done it. He went over to the radio and turned it on, waited for it to warm up. Listened to several discouraging items, realizing that even if he had just succeeded, it would be at least minutes, since Martians weren't seen everywhere all the time, before anyone began to realize that they were gone. Until the newscaster happened to say, "At this very moment, right here in the studio, a Martian is trying to..."

Luke flicked off the radio and swore.

Took another sip of his drink and paced some more.

Sat down and finished his drink and made another one.

Had a sudden idea.

Maybe he could outwit that psychic block by going around it instead of through it. The block could only be because, even though he knew he was right, he lacked sufficient faith in himself. Maybe he should imagine something else, something completely different, and when his imagination brought it into being, even his damned subconscious couldn't deny it, and then in that moment of undeniability—

It was worth trying. There was nothing to lose.

But he'd imagine something that he really *wanted,* and what did he want—outside of getting rid of Martians—most right at this moment?

Margie, of course.

He was lonesome as hell after these two weeks of solitude. And if he could imagine Margie here, and by imagining bring her here, he *knew* he could break that psychic block. With one arm tied behind his back, or with both arms around Margie.

Let's see, he thought: *I'll imagine that she's driving here in her car, already through Indio and only half a mile away. Pretty soon I'll hear the car.*

Pretty soon he heard the car.

He made himself walk, not run, to the door and open it. He could see headlights coming. Should he—now—?

No, he'd wait till he was *sure.* Not even when the car came close enough that he thought he could recognize it as Margie's; a lot of cars look alike. He'd wait until the car had stopped and Margie got out of it and he *knew.* And then, in that golden moment, he'd think *There Aren't Any Martians.*

And there wouldn't be.

In a few minutes, the car would be here.

It was approximately five minutes after nine o'clock (P.M.), Pacific Time. In Chicago it was five minutes after eleven and Mr. Oberdorffer sipped beer and waited for his supervibrator to build up potential; in equatorial Africa it was dawn and a witch doctor named Bugassi stood with crossed arms under the greatest juju ever made, waiting for the sun's first rays to strike it.

Four minutes later, one hundred and forty-six days and fifty minutes after they appeared, the Martians disappeared. Simultaneously, from everywhere. Everywhere on Earth, that is.

Wherever they went, there is no authenticated instance of one having been seen since that moment. Seeing Martians in nightmares and in delirium tremens is still common, but such sightings can hardly be called authenticated.

To this day...

Postlogue

To this day, nobody knows why they came or why they left.

Not that a great many people do not *think* they know, or at least have very strong opinions on the subject.

Millions of people still believe, as they believed then, that they were not Martians but devils and that they went back to hell and not back to Mars. Because a God who sent them to punish us for our sins became again a merciful God as a result of our prayers to Him.

Even more millions accept that they came from Mars after all and returned there. Most, but not all, give credit to Yato Ishurti for their leaving; these point out that even if Ishurti's reasoning was right down the line and even though his proposition to the Martians was backed by that tremendous affirmative, the Martians could hardly have been expected to react instantaneously; somewhere a council of them would have had to meet and weigh their decision, make up their minds whether we were by now sufficiently sincere and sufficiently chastened. And that the Martians stayed only two weeks after Ishurti's speech, which is certainly not too long a time for such a decision to have been reached.

At any rate, no standing armies have been built up again and no country is planning sending any rockets to Mars, just on the *chance* that Ishurti was right, or partly right.

But not everybody, by any means, believes that either God or Ishurti had anything to do with the departure of the Martians.

One entire African tribe, for instance, knows that it was Bugassi's juju that sent the *gnajamkata* back to the *kat*.

One janitor in Chicago knows perfectly well that he drove away the Martians with his anti-extraterrestrial subatomic supervibrator.

And of course those last two are, and were given as, only random examples of the hundreds of thousands of *other* scientists and mystics who, each in his own way, had been trying his best to accomplish the same thing. And each naturally thought that he had finally succeeded.

And of course Luke knows that they're *all* wrong. But that it doesn't matter what they think since they all exist only in his mind anyway. And since he is now a very successful writer of Westerns, with four best sellers under his belt in four years and with a beautiful Beverly Hills mansion, two Cadillacs, a loved and loving wife and a pair of two-year-old twin sons, Luke is being very careful indeed how he lets his imagination work. He is very satisfied with the universe as he imagines it right now, and takes no chances.

And on one point concerning the Martians, Luke Devereaux agrees with everybody else, including Oberdorffer, Bugassi and the Scandinavian.

Nobody, but nobody, misses them or wants them back.

Author's Postscript

My publishers write me:

> Before sending the manuscript of MARTIANS, GO HOME to the printer, we would like to suggest that you supply the story with a postscript to tell us and your other readers the *truth* about those Martians.
>
> Since you wrote the book, you, if anyone, must know whether they were really from Mars or hell, or whether your character Luke Devereaux was right in believing that the Martians, along with everything else in the universe, existed only in his imagination.
>
> It is unfair to your readers not to tell them.

Many things are unfair, including and particularly that request of my publishers!

I had wanted to avoid being definitive here, for the truth can be a frightening thing, and in this case it *is* a frightening thing if you believe it. But here it is:

Luke is right; the universe and all therein exists only in his imagination. He invented it, and the Martians.

But then again, *I invented Luke.* So where does that leave him *or* the Martians? Or any of the rest of you?

FREDRIC BROWN
Tucson, Arizona, 1955

Rogue in Space

Rogue in Space

CHAPTER ONE

Call him by no name, for he had no name. He did not know the meaning of *name,* or of any other word. He had no language, for he had never come into contact with any other living being in the billions of light-years of space that he had traversed from the far rim of the galaxy, in the billions of years that it had taken him to make that journey. For all he knew or had ever known he was the only living being in the universe.

He had not been born, for there was no other like him. He was a piece of rock a little over a mile in diameter, floating free in space. There are myriads of such small worlds but they are dead rock, inanimate matter. He was *aware,* and an entity. An accidental combination of atoms into molecules had made him a living being. To our present knowledge such an accident has happened only twice in infinity and eternity; the other such event took place in the primeval ooze of Earth, where carbon atoms formed sentient life that multiplied and evolved.

Spores from Earth had drifted across space and had seeded the two planets nearest to it, Mars and Venus, and when a million years later man had landed on those planets he found vegetable life waiting for him there, but that vegetable life, although it had evolved quite differently from vegetable life as man knew it, had still originated on Earth. Nowhere but on Earth had life originated to evolve and multiply.

The entity from the far side of the galaxy did not multiply. He remained unique and alone. Nor did he evolve except in the sense that his awareness and his knowledge grew. Without sensory organs, he learned to perceive the universe about him. Without language, he learned to understand its principles and its mechanics and how to make use of them to move through space freely, and to do many other things.

Call him a thinking rock, a sentient planetoid.

Call him a rogue, in the biological sense of the word rogue: an accidental variation.

Call him a rogue in space.

He roamed space but he did not search for other life, other consciousness, for he had long since assumed that none existed.

He was not lonely, for he had no concept of loneliness. He had no concept of good and evil, for a lone being can know neither; morality arises only in our attitude toward others. He had no concept of emotion, unless a desire to increase awareness and knowledge (we call it curiosity) can be called an emotion.

Now, after billions of years—but neither young nor old—he found himself nearing a small yellow sun that had nine planets circling about it.

There are many such.

CHAPTER TWO

Call him Crag; it was the name he was using and it will serve as well as any name. He was a smuggler and a thief and a killer. He'd been a spaceman once and had a metal hand to show for it. That, and a taste for exotic liquors and a strong aversion for work. Work would have been futile for him in any case; he would have had to work a week, at anything but crime, to buy a single binge on even the cheapest of the nepenthes that alone made life worth living. He knew good from evil but cared not a grain of Martian sand for either of them. He was not lonely for he had made himself self-sufficient by hating everyone.

Especially now, because they had him. And of all places here in Albuquerque, the center of the Federation and the toughest spot on five planets to beat a rap. Albuquerque, where justice was more crooked than crime, where a criminal didn't have a chance unless he belonged to the machine. Independent operators were not wanted and did not last long. He should never have come here, but he'd been tipped to a sure thing and had taken a chance. He knew now that the tipster had been part of the machine and that the tip had been a trap to entice him here. He hadn't even had time to case the job he'd come here to do—if such a job had existed at all except in the tipster's imagination. He'd been picked up leaving the airport and searched. Almost an ounce of *nephthin* had been found in his pocket, and it had really been there, concealed in the false bottom of a pack of cigarettes. The cigarettes had been given him by the talkative cigarette salesman who had sat next to him on the plane, as a free sample of a new brand his company was introducing. *Nephthin* was bad stuff; possession of it, however acquired, was a psychable offense. It had been a perfect frame. They had him cold.

There was only one question left, and that was whether they'd give him twenty in the penal colony on bleak Callisto or whether they'd send him to the psycher.

He sat on the cot in his cell and wondered which would happen. It made a big difference. Life in the penal colony might turn out to be better than no life at all and there would always be the chance, however slender, of escape. But the thought of the psycher was intolerable. Before he'd let them send him to the psycher, he decided, he'd kill himself or get himself killed trying to escape.

Death was something you could look in the face and laugh at. But not the psycher. Not the way Crag looked at it. The electric chair of a few centuries before merely killed you; the psycher did something much worse than that. It *adjusted* you, unless it drove you crazy. Statistically, one time out of nine it drove you stark mad, and for this reason it was used only in extreme cases, for crimes that would have been punishable by death back in the days of capital punishment. And even for such crimes, including *nephthin* possession, it was not mandatory; the judge chose between it and the alternative maximum sentence of twenty years on Callisto. Crag shuddered at the thought that if the psycher ever *were* perfected, if that one chance out of nine of being lucky were eliminated, it would probably be made mandatory for much lesser crimes.

When the psycher worked, it made you normal. It made you normal by removing from your mind all the memories and experiences which had led you into aberration from the norm. *All* your memories and experiences, the good ones as well as the bad.

After the psycher, you started from scratch as far as personality was concerned. You remembered your skills; you knew how to talk and feed yourself, and if you'd known how to use a slide rule or play a flute you still knew how to use a slide rule or play a flute.

But you didn't remember your name unless they told you. And you didn't remember the time you were tortured for three days and two nights on Venus before the rest of the crew found you and took you away from the animated vegetables who didn't like meat in any form and particularly in human form. You didn't remember the time you were space-mad or the time you had to go nine days without water. You didn't remember anything that had ever happened to you.

You started from scratch, a different person.

And while Crag could face dying, he could not and would not face the thought of his body walking around afterwards, animated by a well-adjusted stranger whose very guts he would hate. If necessary he'd kill that well-adjusted stranger by killing, before the stranger could take it over, the body which the stranger would make do and think things that Crag would never do or think.

He knew that he could do it, but it would not be easy; the weapon he carried was better adapted to killing others than to suicide. It takes a lot of courage to kill oneself with a bludgeon.

Even so efficient a bludgeon as Crag's metal left hand. Looking at that hand, no one had ever guessed that it weighed twelve pounds instead of a few ounces. Since the metal was flesh colored, one had to look closely to see that it was an artificial hand at all. If one did notice, since all artificial members had for over a century been made of duralloy, one assumed that Crag's hand was similarly made. Duralloy is a fraction of the weight of magnesium, not much heavier than balsa wood. And Crag's hand *was* duralloy on the outside, but it was reinforced with steel and heavily weighted with lead. Not a hand you'd want to be slapped in the face with, even lightly. But long practice and considerable strength enabled Crag to carry and use it as though it weighed the three or four ounces you'd expect it to weigh.

Nor had anyone ever guessed that it was detachable, since all similar artificial hands—or feet or arms or legs—were surgically and permanently attached to their wearers. That was why they had not taken it away from him when he was arrested nor when he had been stripped and given prison garb here at the jail. A renegade surgeon hiding out in Rio had fixed that part of it for him (Crag had fabricated the hand himself) by grafting and manipulating muscle tissue at the stump of the wrist so that holding it on was automatic and involuntary. But by willing the muscles to relax, the heavy hand was instantly detachable, and became a missile that his right hand could throw, after long practice, with deadly accuracy. One might well say that Crag had a long reach, for one blow. And one blow was always sufficient, against a single antagonist.

It was the only weapon Crag ever carried.

A voice from a grill in the ceiling of the cell said, "Your trial has been called for fourteen hours. That is ten minutes from now. Be ready."

Crag glanced upward and made a rude noise at the grill. Since it was strictly a one-way communicator, the grill paid no attention.

Crag walked over to the window and stood looking down at the vast sprawling city of Albuquerque, third largest city in the solar system, second largest city on Earth. Running diagonally off to the southeast he could see the bright ribbon of the shuttlejet track that led to Earth's largest spaceport, forty miles away.

The window was not barred but the transparent plastic of the pane was tough stuff. He could probably batter it out with his left hand but would need wings to continue an escape in that direction. His cell was on the top floor of Fedjude, the Federation Judical Building, thirty stories high, the wall sheer and the windows flush. He could only commit suicide that way, and suicide could wait, as long as there was even a chance of getting the penal colony instead of the psycher.

He hated it, that corrupt city, worse in its way than Mars City, vice city of the solar system. Albuquerque was not a fleshpot, but it was the center of intrigue between the Guilds and the Gilded. Politics rampant upon a field of muck, and everybody, except the leaders, caught in the middle, no matter which side they supported or even if they tried to remain neutral.

The voice from the ceiling said, "Your door is now unlocked. You will proceed to the end of the corridor outside it, where you will meet the guards who will escort you to the proper room."

Through the windowpane Crag caught the faint silver flash of a spaceship coming in, heard dimly the distant thunder of its jets. He waited a few seconds until it was out of sight.

But no longer, for he knew that, in a small way, this order was a test. He could wait here and force the guards to come and get him, but if he did so, and particularly if he tried to resist when they did come, his recalcitrance would be reported, would be taken into consideration when sentence was pronounced. It could make the difference between Callisto and the psycher.

So he opened the now unlocked door and went out into the corridor and along it; there was only one way to go. A hundred yards along it two green-uniformed guards waited for him. They were armed with holstered heatguns; they stood before the first door that otherwise would have stopped his progress.

He didn't speak to them nor they to him. They stepped apart and he fell in between them. The door opened automatically as they approached it, but he knew that it would not have opened for him alone.

He knew too that he could have killed both quite easily, literally and figuratively offhand. A backhand blow to the face or forehead of the guard to his left and then a quick swing across to the other one; both would have died without a chance to draw their weapons, without knowing what had happened to them. But getting past all the other barriers and safeguards would be something else again. Too remote a chance to consider now, before he had heard the sentence. So he walked quietly between them down the ramp to the floor below and along other corridors to the room where he was to be tried. And through the door.

He was the last arrival, if you didn't count the two guards who came in behind him.

The room was moderately large, but there were only an even dozen people in it, counting Crag and his two guards. Trial procedure had been greatly simplified under the Federation, although, in theory at least, it was as fair and impartial as it had ever been.

A judge, wearing an ordinary business suit, sat behind an ordinary businessman's desk, his back against one wall. The two lawyers, one for the prosecution and one for the defense, had smaller desks, one on each side of the judge's. The five jurors sat in comfortable chairs along one wall. Against a third wall, the sound technician had his machines and his rack of tapes. The defendant's chair was placed diagonally so it faced halfway between the judge and the jury. There were no spectators present and no reporters, although the trial was not secret; the entire trial would be recorded on tape and after the trial copies of the tape would be immediately available to representatives of any authorized news disseminating medium applying in advance for them.

None of this was new to Crag for he had been tried once before—acquitted that time because four of the five jurors, the number necessary for either conviction or acquittal, had decided that the evidence was insufficient. But one thing did surprise him and that was the identity of the judge. The judge was Olliver.

The surprising thing about that was not the fact that Olliver had been the judge who had presided at Crag's previous trial six years ago—that could be coincidence or it could be because Olliver had applied, a judge's privilege, to sit at this trial because of his previous interest in Crag. The surprising thing was that Olliver would be sitting as judge, at present, in *any* ordinary criminal case. In the six years since Crag's first trial, Olliver had become a very important man.

Judge Olliver, although less rabidly conservative than most members of the Syndicate Party—popularly known as the Gilded—had risen high in that party and had been its candidate for Coordinator of North America, second most important political office in the solar system, at the election only six months ago. True, he had lost the election, but he had polled more votes than any Syndicate candidate had in North America for almost a century. Surely he would have gained an important enough position in the party to have lifted himself above the routine work of judging criminal cases.

In Crag's opinion, he certainly should have, for although Crag hated him as a man, he had reluctant admiration for Olliver. Politically cynical though Crag was, he thought Olliver came nearer to being a statesman than any other man in politics. It seemed to Crag that the Syndicate Party would now be grooming Olliver for a try at the really top job—System Coordinator—at the next election. In North America, as on Mars, the Guild Party had a strong majority, but throughout the system as a whole the two parties were fairly equally balanced and the System Coordinator's job and the majority of seats on the System Council were toss-ups in any election. Surely Olliver, by his showing in an election where the odds had been strongly against him, had earned himself a chance at running for the higher job, which he would be almost certain to win.

As to why Crag hated Olliver personally, the answer lay in the blistering tongue-lashing Olliver had administered to him after the previous trial in the private conversation between the judge and the accused that was customary at the end of a trial whether or not the accused was found guilty. Olliver had called him names that Crag had not forgotten.

Now Crag faced him again, knowing that this time the jury would certainly find him guilty and that the designation of the sentence lay completely with Olliver.

The trial went like clockwork.

The formalities over, the depositions of the witnesses were played from tapes, to the court and into the record. The first was that of a Captain of Police who was in charge of the police office at the airport. He testified that just before the arrival of the plane he had received a long distance telephone call from Chicago. The caller, a woman, had refused to give her name but had told him that a man named Crag, whom she described, would be a passenger on the plane and was carrying *nephthin*. He described detaining and searching Crag, and finding the drug. Then, on the tape, he was questioned by Crag's attorney. Yes, he had tried to trace the Chicago call. They had found that it came from a public booth but found no clue or lead to the identity of the anonymous informant. Yes, the search had been perfectly legal. For such emergencies the airport police office kept on hand a supply of John Doe and Jane Doe warrants for detention and search. They were used whenever, in his judgment, use was indicated. In the case of a tip, anonymous or otherwise, a passenger was always detained and searched. No harm was done if the passenger was found innocent of contraband.

Three other members of the airport police detail told similar stories; all had been present at the search and testified that the *nephthin* had been in his possession. Crag's attorney had not questioned them.

Crag's own story came next. He had been permitted to tell it first in his own words and he described boarding the plane and finding his seat to be next to that of a man whom he described as tall, slender, well-dressed. There had been no conversation between them until the plane had neared Albuquerque, when the man had introduced himself as Zacharias and had claimed to be a cigarette salesman for a company introducing a new brand of cigarettes. He had talked about the new brand and had pressed a package of them on Crag as a free sample. The man had left the plane hurriedly and was out of sight when the police had stopped Crag and had taken him to the airport police office to search him.

Following on the tape was Crag's questioning by the prosecuting attorney. He failed to change any detail of Crag's story, but Crag had been forced to hurt his own case by refusing to answer any questions whatever about himself aside from the brief episode he had just narrated.

Then, in refutation of Crag's story, the prosecution introduced the tape of one further witness, a man named Krable, who testified after being shown a picture of Crag, that he had sat next to him on the plane flight in question, that he had not introduced himself as Zacharias or under any other name, that there had been no conversation between them and that he had given Crag nothing. Questioning by the defense attorney only strengthened his story by bringing out the fact that he was a respectable businessman, owner of a men's haberdashery, that he had no criminal record and that his life was an open book.

There was further testimony from Crag after he had been confronted with Krable. He agreed that Krable was the man who had sat next to him, but stuck to his story that Krable had introduced himself as Zacharias and had given him the cigarette package.

That was all of the testimony. While Olliver was briefly charging the jury Crag smiled to himself at the simplicity and perfection of the frame-up. So few people need have been involved. No more than four. The tipster who had sent him to Albuquerque. A person in charge of seating arrangements to see that he sat where they wanted him to sit. A woman to make the anonymous phone call. And Krable, who was no doubt as respectable as he claimed to be and who had been chosen for that very reason, so that Crag's story would sound like a desperate invention—as it had sounded, even to Crag himself—in comparison to Krable's story. The only reason he hadn't pleaded guilty was that the plea would not have been accepted unless he'd followed through and told them where and how he'd obtained the *nephthin*—and the only way he could do that was the way he'd done.

The five members of the jury filed into the little jury room adjoining the court. They were back within minutes and their chairman reported a unanimous verdict—guilty.

Judge Olliver crisply ordered the courtroom cleared and the sound machines cut off. The trial itself was over. Sentence was always pronounced after the private conversation customary between judge and prisoner. The judge might announce his verdict immediately thereafter or take up to twenty-four hours to make his decision.

The trial, to Crag, had been a farce. This was it, and he found himself growing tense. The courtroom was clear now, except for the two guards, the judge and himself.

"The prisoner will advance."

Crag walked forward and stood stiffly before the judge's desk, his face impassive.

"Guards, you may leave. Remain outside the door, please."

That was a surprise. True, a judge had the option of sending the guards outside or of having them remain, but he always had them remain when he felt that he was dealing with a dangerous man. At Crag's previous trial, despite the fact that the verdict had been an acquittal, Olliver had had the guards remain. Undoubtedly, then, Olliver had felt or recognized the savagery in Crag, had feared to provoke him to violence by the things he intended to say. That was understandable; under circumstances much more dangerous to himself, would he dismiss the guards?

Crag shrugged off the question. It didn't matter, and if Olliver delivered his verdict now and it was the psycher, he'd start his break from here, by killing Olliver. Then the two guards outside the door, and toward freedom as far as he could go before they shot him down.

He heard the door close behind the guards, and stood waiting, his eyes fixed on a point on the wall just over and behind Olliver's head. He knew well enough what Olliver looked like without looking at him. A big man, broad shouldered, with iron gray hair and a florid face that could be stern, as it was now and as it had been throughout the trial, or could be pleasant and winning, as it was when he made campaign speeches on television.

There was no doubt in Crag's mind which expression Olliver's face would be wearing now. Until Olliver said, "Look at me, Crag," and Crag looked down and saw that Olliver was smiling.

Olliver said softly, "Crag, how would you like your freedom, and a million dollars?"

And then, "Don't look at me like that, Crag. I'm not joking. Pull up a chair, one of those comfortable jurors' chairs, not the one you've been sitting on, have a cigarette, and let's talk."

Crag got a chair and sat down in it, but warily. He accepted a cigarette gratefully; they weren't allowed in the cells. Then he said, "You talk. I'll listen."

Olliver said, "It's simple. I have a job I'd like you to do for me. I think you're one of the few men alive who might be able to do it. If you agree to try it, your freedom. If you succeed, the million, And maybe more if you want to keep on working with me after that.

"And it's not a racket, Crag. The opposite. A chance to help humanity, to help me help to lift it out of the bog of decadence into which it has fallen."

"Save that for your speeches, Judge. I'll settle for freedom and the million—if you're on the level. A question first. The charge against me was a frame-up. Yours? To put me in a spot where I'll have to work for you?"

Olliver shook his head. "No. But I'll admit that, when I saw on the docket that you were to be tried, I deliberately obtained permission to sit at the trial. Was it a frame-up?"

Crag nodded.

"I suspected so. The evidence against you was too pat, your story too thin. Any idea who *did* engineer it?"

Crag shrugged. "I have enemies. I'll find out."

"No," Olliver said sharply. "If you accept my proposition, you'll have to agree to let any private vengeance you have in mind go, until you've done my job first. Agreed?"

Crag nodded a bit sullenly, but he said, "Agreed. What's the job?"

"This isn't the time or place to tell you that. Since you've agreed in advance to do it, and since it will take some explaining, we'll talk about it after you're a free man."

"But if I decide it's too dangerous and turn it down?"

"I don't think you will. It's a difficult job, but I don't think you'll turn it down, for a million dollars. And there may be more for you in it than merely money. I'll take a chance that you won't turn it down. But let's get to brass tacks, about your escape."

"Escape? Can't you—" Crag stopped, realizing that the question he'd been about to ask was absurd.

"Escape, of course. You were judged guilty of a major crime and on strong evidence. If I were to free you, even to give you a light sentence, I'd be impeached. *I* have enemies too, Crag; any man in politics has."

"All right, how much can you help me toward an escape?"

"Arrangements are being made; when they are completed you'll be told what to do."

"Told how?"

"By the speaker in your cell. A—a friend of mine has access to the circuits. In fairness, I should tell you that we can't arrange any foolproof escape for you. We'll do what we can and you'll be on your own from there."

Crag grinned. "And if I'm not good enough to make it from there, I wouldn't be good enough to do the job you have for me outside. So you've nothing to lose if I'm killed escaping. All right. What sentence are you going to give me meanwhile?"

"It will be better if I announce that I'm taking the full twenty-four hours to decide. If, now, I sentence you to either Callisto or the psycher, preparations to send you to one or the other will start immediately. I don't know exactly how fast such preparations would proceed, so it's safer to keep the sentence in abeyance."

"Good. And after I escape?"

"Come to my house. Seven-nineteen Linden. Don't call. My phone is tapped, undoubtedly."

"The house is guarded?" Crag knew that the houses of most important political figures were.

"Yes, and I'm not going to tell the guards to let you in. They're members of my own party, but I wouldn't trust them that far. Getting past them is your problem. If you can't do that, without help or advice from me, you're not the man I think you are, or the man I want. But don't kill them unless you have to. I don't like violence." He frowned. "I don't like it, even when it's necessary and in a good cause."

Crag laughed. "I'll try not to kill your guards—even in a good cause."

Olliver's face flushed. He said, "It *is* a good cause, Crag—" He glanced quickly over his shoulder at the clock on the wall and then said, "All right, we've time left. I've often talked to a prisoner half an hour or longer before sentencing him."

"You talked to me that long last time before *freeing* me, after I was acquitted."

"And you know you had it coming. You *were* guilty—that time. But I started to tell you what the cause is, so you won't laugh at it. I'm starting a new political party, Crag, that's going to bring this world, the whole solar system, out of the degradation into which it has sunk.

"It's going to end bribery and corruption by taking us back to old-fashioned democracy. It's going to be a middle-of-the-road party that will end the deadlock between the Guilds and the Syndicates. Both of those parties—I'll face it; even the one I'm a member of—represent ridiculous extremes. The Guilds grew out of Communism and the Syndicates grew out of Fascism and between them something we once had and called Democracy got lost."

Crag said, "I see your point. Maybe I even agree. But are you going to get anywhere with it? Both the Guilds and Gildeds have made Democracy a swear word and a laughingstock. How can you get the public to accept it?"

Olliver smiled. "We won't call it that, of course. It's the *word* that's discredited, not the idea. We'll call ourselves the Cooperationists, represent ourselves as trying to steer a middle course between extremes. And half the members of each of the old parties, those who want honest government, are going to come over to us. Yes, we're operating undercover, now, but we'll come into the open before the next elections, and you'll see. Well, that's enough for now. Everything between us understood?"

Crag nodded.

"Good." Olliver pressed a button on the desk and the guards came in. As Crag left with them he heard Olliver, the sound machine turned on again, saying into it that he was postponing his decision on sentencing for twenty-four hours.

Back in his cell, he paced impatiently. Tried to think ahead. Did the plan for his escape—or chance at escape—include a change of clothes? He looked down at himself. The gray shirt might pass, if he opened it at the throat and rolled up the sleeves above his elbows. But the baggy gray trousers shrieked of prison. He'd have to take the trousers off a guard, and even they wouldn't be too good and he'd have to change them for shorts as soon as he had a chance. Almost all private citizens of Albuquerque wore shorts in summer.

He rolled up the sleeves and opened his collar, then stopped in front of the metal mirror set into the wall over the washstand and studied himself, Yes, from the waist up he'd do. Even the short haircut, since it was almost as common outside of prison as in.

And his face—he was lucky there, for it was a very ordinary face that looked neither vicious nor criminal, a face that didn't stand out in a crowd, a hard-to-remember face. He'd paid plenty for that face, to the same surgeon in Rio who'd taken care of the artificial hand for him. The face he'd been wearing before that had been becoming a bit too well known in the underworld, a more dangerous thing than being too well known to the police.

The body under that face was just as deceptive. Neither taller nor broader than average, it masked the wiry strength and endurance of an acrobat and it knew every clean and dirty trick of fighting. Crag could take an average man with one hand, his right, and often had, in fights before witnesses when he didn't want to give away the secret of his left hand. That was ace-in-the-hole, for emergencies. When he used it, he meant business.

He paced again, stopped to look out the window. Thirty flights down to freedom. But only the top three levels were jail floors; if he got below them he could take an elevator from the twenty-seventh down and be comparatively safe.

But what were his chances of making those first three floors? Better than even, he guessed, with whatever help Olliver was going to give him. A thousand to one against him otherwise; that was how he'd guessed his odds before the trial.

Olliver, of all people! Turning out to be as big a crook as all the rest of the politicians after all. Aiding a criminal to escape so the criminal could steal something for him. Or could there be some truth in the story Olliver had handed him? Could Olliver really be acting from altruistic motives? Crag shrugged mentally. It didn't matter.

But Olliver had really surprised him. He wondered how his, Crag's, face must have looked when Olliver, instead of sentencing him, had smiled and asked him if he wanted freedom and a million.

Crag chuckled, and then suddenly was laughing aloud.

A woman's voice, amused, asked, "As funny as that, Crag?"

He looked quickly up at the grill in the ceiling. The voice said, "Yes, it's two-way now; you can answer back. Few people know it but any of the cell communicators can be used two ways. Sometimes the police want to listen in when a lawyer talks to his client. Even the police are crooked, Crag. Or do you already know that?"

"Are you using the communicator just to tell me that?"

"Don't be impatient, Crag. You have time to kill, and so do I. I took over this control cubicle from the guard on duty here by sending him on an errand. He'll be gone at least fifteen minutes."

Crag said, "You must be high brass to be able to do that."

"What I am doesn't matter, except that I'm helping you. Not for your sake, Crag, but because you may be able to help—you know whom. When the guard returns, I'll come to you."

"You'll come here?"

"Yes, to bring you certain things you'll need for an escape. While I'm here I'm going to activate the lock on your door, so I can get in when I come. But do not leave the cell now. In fact, you will not leave it for half an hour after I have come and gone. Understood and agreed?"

"Understood and agreed," Crag said. He heard a click in the lock of his door.

"What things are you bringing?" Crag asked. But there was no answer and he realized that the connection had been broken.

He sat on the cot and waited. Why did it have to be a woman who'd been assigned to help him? He hated women, all women. And this one had dared to sound amused, and condescending.

Then the door opened and the woman came in quickly and closed it. High brass, all right; her severe uniform was that of Chief Psycher Technician. Psycher technicians were important people and there were only a few of them. To become one, you had to have doctorate degrees in both psychology and electronics, plus a lot of political pull. Well, if she was closely associated with Olliver, the political pull was explained.

But she didn't look like a woman who would hold two doctorates. She was beautiful. Not even the uniform could conceal the soft curves of her body, nor could the horn-rimmed glasses she wore or the fact that she was completely without make-up conceal the beauty of her face. Her eyes, even through faintly tinted glass, were the darkest, deepest blue Crag had ever seen, and her hair, what showed of it beneath the technician's beret, was burnished copper. Crag hated her for being a woman and for being beautiful, but mostly he hated her for that hair; it was exactly the color Lea's hair had been.

Deliberately, to be rude, he remained sitting on the cot. But if she noticed the rudeness she did not show it in any way as she stood in front of him and opened her handbag. But her voice, now, was curt and businesslike, with no trace of amusement or friendliness.

"The most important thing is this," she said. She tossed a little metal bar onto the cot beside him. "Carry it in a pocket. It's radioactive; without it or without a guard with you who has one, most of the portals here are death traps."

"I know," he said shortly.

A paper, folded small, was next. "A diagram showing a way out along which you're least likely to encounter guards. In case you do—"

A small heatgun was the next offering, but Crag shook his head at that. "Don't want it," he said. "Don't need it."

She put the gun back in her purse without protest, almost as though she had expected him to refuse it. Next, "A visitor's badge. It won't help you on the upper three levels—no visitors allowed here without a guard accompanying them—but once you're below that, it will keep the regular building guards from asking questions."

He took that. Next was a short paper-thin durium saw blade. "You'll use this to cut through the sliding bolt of your door. I'll lock it from the outside when I leave."

"Why?"

"Don't be stupid, Crag. That door can be locked from the outside, but it can be *un*locked only from the control cubicle. And I just relieved the guard there. If your door is found unlocked, it will be known that only he or I could have released you. He would be more suspect than I, but I do not wish to draw even that much attention to myself."

"If you're being so careful," Crag said, "how do you know he's not listening in on our conversation now?"

"I don't know," she said calmly. "That is a chance I could not avoid taking. Now about clothes. I brought you shorts." From her purse she tossed a tight roll of silk onto the bed. "Couldn't bring shoes." She glanced down at his. "And those look like prison so I suggest you leave them. Civilians here wear sandals or go barefoot, about half and half, so you'll be less conspicuous barefoot than in shoes. I see you've had a thought about the shirt yourself, but I can improve it. I can leave you scissors, needle and thread; cut off the sleeves instead of rolling them. You can sew enough to baste a hem?"

"Yes." Crag hesitated. "But it would take me twenty minutes or so. I'd rather get going."

"You'll have time for that, for sawing the bolt, and for memorizing—and destroying—the diagram. All those together shouldn't take over forty minutes and forty minutes from now, on the hour, when you hear the clocks strike, will be the best timing for you. Don't leave until then even if you find yourself ready sooner."

"How about some money?"

"All right, here's twenty. You won't need more than that because you're to come to—you know where—as soon as you safely can. And sober."

Crag didn't bother to answer that. He never drank when he was working, or in danger. A criminal didn't live long if he drank at the wrong times.

"One more thing, Crag. You can fold the collar of that shirt so it looks more nearly like a sport shirt collar. Here, I'll—"

She reached for it and Crag jerked aside and stood up. "I'll take care of it," he said.

She laughed. "Afraid of me, Crag?"

"I don't like to be touched. Especially by a woman. Now if that's all, get out."

"Such gratitude, Crag. And about women—did anyone ever tell you you ought to be psyched, a little anyway? Well, at least you stood up for me, finally."

Crag didn't answer, and she turned and left. He thought she was still smiling. The lock of the door clicked again.

He wasted no time glaring at the door. He went to it quickly and started sawing at the bolt, venting his anger on the inanimate. He finished it and the other things he had to do long before the time allotted for them. He almost decided to leave right away, but reconsidered and waited until he heard the clocks striking the hour.

He left quietly then and found the corridor empty. Followed it quickly and silently, left it when his mental picture of the diagram he had destroyed showed him where to turn. He went along a corridor and down a ramp. Just as he approached another corridor he heard the footsteps of two guards coming. He went back a few steps and stood in a recess in the wall, his left hand ready to strike if they came his way. But they went the other way at the turn and he went on. He came to the second ramp and made it safely. On this level be found more corridors, more portals, but no guards.

Then the final ramp, the one that took him to the twenty-seventh floor. Not far now—but surely there'd be a guard stationed at the final door or portal that led to the elevator hallway and relative safety.

CHAPTER THREE

There was a guard. A quick look around the final turn showed him a closed door with a guard sitting in front of it. And he was awake and alert, although fortunately he did not happen to be looking straight ahead.

But he was awake and alert and with a heatgun unholstered and ready, held in his hand in his lap.

And on the wall over his head—

Crag smiled grimly as, back out of sight, he detached his left hand and got it ready to throw with his right. Either Olliver or the woman, or both, must have known what was on the wall over the guard's head—a small hemispherical blister that could only be a thermocouple set to give off an alarm at any sudden increase in temperature. Yet the woman had offered Crag a heatgun. It would have been suicide to shoot the guard with it. And if the guard had time to fire his own gun, even though it would be aimed away from the thermocouple, no doubt the rise in heat would be sufficient to set off the alarm anyway, even if he missed Crag. Not that he would miss, at ten feet or a bit less.

Nor would, nor did, Crag at that range. When he stepped out into sight his right hand was already drawn back to throw the missile, and it was in the air before the guard had time to more than start to lift the heatgun from his lap. Crag's hand hit him full in the face long before he had time to pull the trigger. And he'd never pull one again.

Crag walked to him and got his hand back, putting it on quickly as soon as he'd wiped the blood off it on the guard's uniform. Then he picked up the guard's gun, deliberately handling it by the barrel to get his prints on it, and deliberately bloodied the butt. They'd know who killed the guard anyway, and he'd rather have them wonder how he'd managed to take the guard's own weapon away from him and kill him with it than have them wonder, or perhaps guess, how he *had* killed the guard. Whenever Crag killed with that left hand and had time afterward he tried to leave evidence that some other blunt weapon had been used.

Then, using the key that had hung from the guard's belt, he went through the door and closed it behind him, and no alarm operated. He could probably thank the woman for that, anyway; without the radioactive bar he'd have had a slim chance indeed. Yes, they'd given him a fair chance—despite the fact that he'd also been given a chance to spoil everything if he'd been stupid enough to take that heatgun, and despite the fact that she hadn't told him to get rid of that bar here and now even though he knew, and she must have known, that outside the sacred precincts of the jail those bars often worked in reverse and set off alarms instead of stilling them.

He got rid of his in a waste receptacle outside the elevator bank before he pushed the button to summon an elevator. A few minutes later he was safely on the street, lost in the crowd and reasonably safe from pursuit.

The sidewalk was crowded with scantily clad people. Save those in one or another kind of uniform, few if any wore more than shorts or trunks, a sport shirt or a T-shirt and sandals. Many men wore nothing above the waist. So did a few women, mostly ones who had outstandingly good reasons for the extreme style. All of the women who were barefoot, and some of the men, had gaudily painted toenails, usually gold or silver.

Vocoads blared in his ears. Eat at Stacey's, wear Trylon, visit the House of Strange Pleasures, use Cobb's dentifrice, visit Madam Blaine's, drink Hotsy, use Safe and be safe, travel Panam, buy, drink, visit, use, buy.

Crag ducked into a hotel and in the privacy of a men's room booth he took off the gray prison shirt and got rid of it down a waste disposal chute. Not because the shirt itself would have been too likely to draw attention, not because he enjoyed semi-nudity, but because being shirtless made him look like a different man. The hard, flat musculature of his torso and shoulders made him look much bigger and at least twenty pounds heavier.

He broke the twenty-dollar bill to buy sandals at a little haberdashery shop off the hotel lobby and at a drugstore on the next corner he made two purchases: a cheap wrist watch—his own had been taken from him with his other possessions at the jail—that probably wouldn't run more than a few days but the band of which would cover the line where flesh met metal at his wrist, and a pair of sunglasses, which at least a third of the people on the streets were wearing. That was all he could do at the moment in the way of disguise, but it was enough. He doubted that even the prison guards who had been seeing him every day would recognize him now, certainly not from a casual glance or from passing him on the street.

Now, the sooner he got himself inside Olliver's house the less danger there'd be at that end. By now the guard's body would have been found and a check of cells would have been made. His escape was known and they were looking for him. They might well throw a protective cordon around the home of the judge who had presided at his trial. Escaped prisoners often hated their judges enough to attempt murder. True, in his case Olliver had deferred sentence, but all he had postponed was a choice between the two forms of maximum punishment he could deal out, so the police would logically reason that his deferring of that choice would not affect Crag's wish for vengeance, if he had such a wish.

They might also put men to guard the witnesses who had taped the testimony against him and there, in one case at least, they'd be justified. Crag had nothing against the airport police who had searched him and testified to finding the *nephthin,* for their testimony had been honest. But the man who had actually given him the drug and then had denied doing so was on Crag's list, although he could wait—and sweat—for a while, knowing the police couldn't guard him forever. So was the tipster in Chicago who had sent him to Albuquerque on Crag's list. And before one of the two of them died, he'd tell Crag which one of his enemies had engineered the deal. But all that could wait and would have to wait. Men who are violent are seldom patient, but Crag was both.

But it was the other way around when it came to reaching Olliver; the sooner he made it the less danger there would be.

He took a cab and gave an address that would be two blocks away from the one Olliver had given him. Paid off the driver and pretended to push a doorbell and wait until the cab had turned a corner and was out of sight. Then slowly he strolled past Olliver's house, keeping to the opposite side of the street. There was a guard at the front door so there'd be one at the back, too; no use checking that. But as yet no extra guards were in sight, no cars parked nearby with men in them.

He strolled on past, considering what would be the best plan of action. Getting in by killing either guard would be simple. He need merely approach on the pretext of asking whether the judge was home, and then flick the man's chin with his left hand. It would be simple but useless if he wanted to be able to stay inside for what might be a long talk with Olliver. A dead guard, or even a missing one if he took the body inside with him, would be a dead giveaway. Armies of them would come in looking for him; they'd probably insist on searching, for Olliver's protection, even if Olliver tried to tell them that he wasn't there. They'd have warrants of course and he wouldn't be able to keep them out.

Getting down from the roof was a much better bet, if he could make the roof from the roof of the adjacent building, and he thought he could.

Olliver's home was three stories high and roughly cubical. It was sizeable enough, probably fifteen to twenty rooms, but quite plain and simple, externally at least. It was not the fashion for politicians who aspired to elective office to live ostentatiously, no matter how much money they had. If they loved luxury—and most of them did—they indulged that love in ways less publicly obvious than by living in mansions. The public believes what it thinks it sees.

The building next to Olliver's house was the same height and roughly the same shape, although it was an apartment building instead of a private home. Crag's casual look upward as he had passed had shown him that the roofs were level with one another and about fifteen feet apart. That building would be his best bet; the one on the other side of Olliver's home was also three stories, but it was too far away.

Out of sight from Olliver's house he crossed the street and strolled back toward it. He entered the adjacent building and looked over the inset mailboxes and buzzer buttons in the hallway. There were six apartments; obviously two on each floor, and numbers five and six would be on the top floor. The glass-fronted mailboxes for both of those apartments had names on them, but the box for apartment five, labeled Holzauer, was stuffed with what seemed like an undue quantity of mail for one day's delivery. Crag took from his pocket the visitor's badge he'd worn until he had left the Federation Building and used it to pick the lock of the mailbox. The Holzauers were away, all right; the letters in the box were postmarked various dates over a period of almost a week.

He closed and relocked the box and used the pin to let himself through the inner hallway door. He went up the stairs and used the same means to let himself into apartment five and to lock the door after him. Luckily, it was on the side of the building nearest the Olliver house.

He scouted the apartment first, and at leisure, since he'd already decided it would be better to wait until after dark to take his next step. Many people used the roofs by day for sunbathing and there was too much chance of someone on a nearby building seeing him if he tried the building-to-building jump in broad daylight.

He looked first for clothes, hoping to find a better-fitting pair of shorts—the ones that had been given him were a bit skimpy and tight-fitting—and a shirt to go with them. But he was not in luck there. Although he found clothing, he'd rather have gone naked than wear any of the garments he found. From the clothing, and from other evidence including a book shelf of very specialized pornography, it was obvious that Holzauer & Co. was a pair of homosexuals. Crag did not care for lace-trimmed panties or pink tulle jackets trimmed with leopard skin. But, with time to kill, he amused himself tearing them to shreds. And he began to hope, after glancing again at the pornography, that his unwitting hosts would return while he was there to greet them. But they didn't, and he contented himself with garnishing the pile of torn cloth with confetti from torn books. Crag did not like homosexuals.

No money, no jewelry. But that didn't matter, with a million-dollar job coming up. And Olliver would certainly advance him whatever money he'd need for expenses.

Time to start thinking, while it was still light, about what he'd be doing as soon as it was dark enough. He studied the Olliver house from one window, then another. There'd no doubt be a hatch door in the roof but if it was bolted from the inside, as most such doors were, there'd be no way he could open it from the outside, without special tools or without making noise. But on the third story one window was open at the top. Hanging from the edge of the roof, he'd be able to get in by way of that window.

While he was studying it out and measuring with his eye the distances involved, he heard cars stop out on the street and ran lightly to a window at the front corner of the apartment from which he could see what was going on.

There were two cars parked in front of the Olliver house. Five policemen got out of one car and four out of the other. They walked toward the house, two of them going around it to the back and the other seven going to the front door. A man had remained in one of the cars and as he put his head out of a window to call something after the policemen, Crag saw that the man was Olliver.

So that was why they hadn't immediately tripled or quadrupled the guard on the house. They'd left it relatively unguarded, since Olliver had not been home as yet. Now they'd escorted him home but were going to search the house before he himself entered it. The house would be a trap for Crag now, if he'd entered it right away, by whatever means.

Had Olliver crossed him? Crag wondered for a moment, and then discarded the idea. What would Olliver have had to gain by helping him escape if so soon afterward he had helped the police lay a trap to catch him? No, this must have been an idea of the police, and Olliver must have been unable to dissuade them from giving him what they considered maximum protection. Olliver had no authority whatsoever over the police. Olliver must be hoping right now that Crag had not yet entered, or all of Olliver's trouble thus far would have been for nothing.

Crag congratulated himself on not having made that mistake.

Standing back far enough from the window not to be observed, he waited and watched. After about twenty minutes, ample time for that many men to have made a thorough search of a building that size, the nine men came out. Crag counted carefully to make sure no extra guards had been left. There'd still be one man and only one man at each of the two entrances.

Olliver got out of the car, talked to one of the policemen briefly, and then went to the front door of the house—and inside, no doubt, although Crag couldn't see the doorway from his window. The policemen got into the cars and both cars started. One of the cars U-turned and parked across the street and a few buildings away. Suddenly there seemed to be no one in it; the driver had used the control that activated the windows into one-way glass. The car was unmarked as a police car and from now on, to anyone walking or driving past, it would seem to be merely an empty car parked at the curb. The other car went on and turned the corner. But Crag knew it wouldn't really be leaving and got to a back window in time to see it park in the alley opposite the point where the other car parked in the street.

And from overhead came the drone of a helicopter. Crag listened long enough to make sure that it was circling the neighborhood and not just passing over, and swore to himself. That helicopter, with a good view of all the roofs in the block, would be a real obstacle to his entering by the route he'd planned to use.

But there was no use worrying about it now, since he did not plan in any case to make his entry before darkness fell, and by that time the situation might have changed. And a look at his wrist watch showed him that darkness was at least two hours away, so he decided that he might as well sleep for those two hours; it had been a big day and might, for all he knew, be the prelude to a bigger night. Or to no night at all, if he were discovered, for he was still determined that he would not be taken alive.

Crag had trained himself to be able to sleep on a minute's notice, any time and anywhere. Almost anywhere, that is; with a disgusted look at the oversized ornate bed of his hosts and a disgusted thought about the things that must have happened on it, he made himself comfortable in an armchair. And within a minute he was asleep, soundly but so lightly that the scrape of a key in the lock or any other sound that could indicate danger would have awakened him instantly.

No sound woke him, but the passage of an almost exact two hours did. He woke completely and suddenly, as a cat wakes. Stood and stretched, hearing the helicopter still circling overhead.

Quick looks out of two windows showed him that both of the police cars were parked as he had last seen them. And that, although it was fully dark, there was a bright moon. From the angle of shadows he determined that the moon was about halfway between the zenith and the horizon, and he wondered if he should wait until it had set, for moonless darkness. But that might make things even more dangerous. Without moonlight, the helicopter would be almost useless—even with a searchlight it could observe too small an area at a time—and they'd probably dispense with it and post men on Olliver's roof or on other roofs nearby. Right now, with the moon as bright as it was, they were probably depending upon it completely for watching roofs. It would be easier to fool one heli load of cops than an unknown number of watchers on roof tops.

Every helicopter had a blind spot, directly beneath itself. If it ever went straight over, instead of circling—

Crag groped on the dresser top and found a hand mirror and a nail file. In the living room he climbed the ladder to the roof hatch and pushed it ajar, propping it with the file. Watchers in the heli would think nothing of it being that way, if they noticed, for many top-floor dwellers so propped their hatches for ventilation on a warm evening. And the air, so soon after darkness, was still quite warm; probably there were dozens of raised hatches in the block. On evenings as warm as this, too, many people sat, or even slept, on their roof tops, and Crag used the mirror, held it at various angles, to check the roof tops in all directions. He saw no one and decided that those in the immediate neighborhood who might otherwise be using their roofs this evening were no doubt discouraged from doing so by the annoyance of having a heli so low and so continually overhead. If that was true, having the heli there might be more of an advantage than a disadvantage, and besides its constant drone would help to hide any slight sound he himself might make.

He put the mirror down flat on the roof and in it followed the motions of the heli as well as he could, for a long time. As nearly as he could judge, it was flying ninety or a hundred feet above the roof tops and holding the same altitude. Most of the time it flew in a circle the center of which was the Olliver residence and the radius of which was about half a block. But once in a while, either because the pilot wanted to vary the monotony or wanted to change his angle of observation, it would make a figure eight instead, with the Olliver roof dead center at the crossing at the center of the eight. Once in a while? Crag watched a while longer and counted; there was a figure eight after every fourth circle, and that meant the heli was on autopilot and that the pattern had been set deliberately and he could count on it.

And if, at one of those crossings directly overhead, he started at the exactly right instant, he'd have several seconds during which they wouldn't be able to see him at all, and if, at the end of that period he was hanging from the eaves of the roof opposite, he'd have a slightly longer period to get himself inside the open window while they turned and came back. It would take fast work and split-second timing. With his eye he measured the number of steps, six, he could take between the hatch and the edge of the roof, and decided it would be enough of a start for him to jump the fifteen feet. If it wasn't—well, he'd taken chances before.

He watched and timed three more figure eights until he could tell from the sound of the heli, coming from behind him, the exact moment when it was safe for him to start, and on the fourth he started.

And kept going. Dropped the hatch shut behind him, ran the six paces and jumped. Landed lightly and caught his balance only inches past the edge of the Olliver roof, took a step backwards and let himself drop, catching the edge of the roof with his right hand and holding. Got his feet through the open top half of the window and hooked the inside of the top of the frame with his metal left hand, and a second later was inside the window, silently and safely. A maneuver that only an acrobat, or Crag, could have made. Stood quietly inside the window listening to the heli until he was sure that it was continuing the pattern as before, that the pilot hadn't taken over from the autopilot to drop lower and hover to investigate any movement he might have seen.

He didn't think there'd be any guards inside the house, but there might be servants, so he took no chances. He faced away from the moonlight and let his eyes become accustomed to the relative darkness of the room—a bedroom, but unoccupied—before he crossed it and found himself in a hallway that was even darker. He found the stairs and went down them silently. There were no lights on the second floor and he went down another flight. The first floor hallway was lighted dimly, but there was a crack of brighter light under a door across from the foot of the stairs.

He went to the door and stood in front of it, listening. Heard two voices, Olliver's and that of a woman, but the door was thick and he heard too faintly to make out what was being said.

The fact that there was a woman's voice, too, made him hesitate. But Olliver had told him to come and must be expecting him; if he had a woman with him now she must be someone in his confidence, as the Chief Psycher Technician had obviously been.

Crag opened the door and stepped boldly into the room.

Olliver was seated behind a massive mahogany desk. His eyes went wide and his jaw dropped when he saw Crag. He said, "My God, Crag, how did you make it? I never thought of them searching and then guarding this place, since I hadn't sentenced you. But they insisted on it. I thought you'd hide out and look me up a week or two from now."

But Crag's eyes, after a quick look at Olliver, had gone to the woman. She looked familiar but at first look he couldn't place her, might not have placed her at all if it had not been for the burnished copper hair, now no longer confined under a technician's beret, and for her voice: her eyes glinted with amusement as she looked at the man behind the desk and said, "I told you he'd come this evening, Olliver, and you laughed at me. Isn't it my turn to laugh now?" And she did laugh, a pleasing sound. "And, Olliver, don't ask the man how he did it. He won't tell you, and why should you care?"

She was unbelievably beautiful. The costume of a technician had not completely hidden the fact that she had a beautiful body, but the costume she wore now flaunted the fact. In the bare-midriffed evening style, there was only a wisp of almost transparent material above her waist. The skirt was long and opaque, but before it flared at the knees it molded her hips and thighs by fitting her as a sheath fits a sword. Her face, now with subtle make-up and unmasked by glasses, was worthy of the blazing glory of the copper hair that framed it. She smiled at Crag, and her eyes danced, then very deliberately and very slowly her eyes went down him to his sandals and back again. She said, "Who would have guessed, seeing you in those prison clothes?" It was so frankly and so semi-humorously done that no man could have resented it.

Except Crag. He glared at her and then turned to Olliver. "Does this woman have to be here while we talk?"

Olliver had recovered his poise, and smiled. "I'm afraid she must be here, Crag. She's very important to my plans, our plans. But I'd better introduce you. Crag, this is Judeth. My wife."

Crag growled. "If she's got to stay, give me something to put on. I won't be looked at that way."

Olliver's face stiffened a bit but he said, "There are robes in that closet. But you're being ridiculous, Crag. These are not Victorian times. This is the twenty-third century."

Wordlessly Crag stalked to the closet and opened it. Several houserobes hung there and Crag grabbed at random a maroon silk one. He put it on, realizing too late, after he'd closed the closet door, that the robe must be Judeth's, not Olliver's; the shoulders fitted snugly and the sleeves were a trifle short, whereas Olliver had massive shoulders and long arms. But he realized by now that he'd already been a bit ridiculous and it would have made him seem more so to go back to the closet now and change robes. After all, houserobes were worn by both men and women and this was a plain one, although of beautiful material. Still—

"It won't contaminate you, Crag," Judeth said.

But he could keep his dignity only by ignoring that. And by, henceforth, ignoring *her,* and everything she said and did, insofar as possible. Either that or, if Olliver insisted on keeping her around, walking out on Olliver and a chance to make a million dollars. And a million dollars was real moolah, nothing to be taken lightly.

"Sit down, Crag," Olliver said.

He saw that Olliver had already sat down behind his desk and that Judeth had perched herself on a corner of it and was now looking at him quite seriously, not at all mockingly.

Crag seated himself stiffly in a straight chair, turning to face Olliver and not his wife. "One question," he said. "You really meant it this afternoon? And you have the million?"

Olliver nodded. "I really meant it. And I have most of the million now and will have the rest before you finish the job; it's nothing you can do overnight, and it's on Mars. Not my own money, you understand; it's a fund being raised by—"

Crag waved that aside. "I don't care whose it is as long as it will be mine if I do the job for you. And the sooner I start, the better. I got in here tonight and I can get out tonight. Tell me what the job is, give me expense money. I'll be on my way."

Olliver shook his head slowly. "I'm afraid it's not that simple, Crag. You see, to do this job you'll have to go to the psycher first."

CHAPTER FOUR

If Crag's mental reflexes had not been fully at fast as his physical ones, Olliver would have died in the next second. As it was, he came within six inches of dying; that was how far from his head Crag's hand—his left hand—stopped. Had that blow been completed, the woman would have died a fraction of a second later. Crag had taken the three steps that took him to the desk so fast one might have thought he blurred.

Two things saved them. One was the fact that Olliver's hands were in plain sight on the desk, nowhere near a push button or an open drawer. The other, the fact that the thought had time to flash across Crag's mind that it did not make sense for Olliver to have meant what he said. Psyching would make Crag's talents and skills useless for Olliver's purpose, whatever it was.

Judeth's voice was tense. "Wait, Crag." Out of the corner of his eye, Crag could see that she had not moved, was not moving, a muscle. Even her eyes were looking, not at him but at where he had been sitting. "As you have already seen, or we'd be dead by now, he did not mean that."

Olliver's handsome face was no longer florid, and his voice was hoarse. "All I meant was that—"

The woman's voice cut across his, sharply. "Be quiet, Ollie, and let me explain. That was incredibly stupid. I told you that Crag—" She broke off and her voice changed, becoming carefully impersonal. "Crag, will you sit down and let me explain? I promise you neither of us will move. Ollie, keep your hands as they are, exactly. And your mouth shut. Agreed, Crag?"

Crag didn't answer, but he backed away to the chair, watching both of them carefully. He sat gingerly on the edge of it; he'd be even faster this time if Olliver moved.

Judeth said, "As you realized in time, Crag, you would be useless to us psyched. But you'd be almost equally useless to us as a hunted criminal. Do you see that?"

"I've been hunted before," Crag said. "And by people more dangerous than the police."

"True, but this is a very special and difficult job. And besides, Olliver promised you your freedom. That meant your full freedom, not as a hunted man."

"You mean a faked psycher certificate."

"Of course. A start from scratch, a clean slate. Without even your underworld enemies interested in you."

"It can't be done," Crag said. "It's been tried before."

"Because it was only a forged certificate, not a genuine one fully backed by all the facts and records. The difference is that you really will have gone to the psycher—but without being psyched. It's foolproof." She moved, for the first time, to turn her head and look at Olliver. Scorn came into her voice. "Even against a fool like my husband here, who so nearly got both of us killed a moment ago."

Crag's mind was working furiously. It seemed too simple, too perfect. He said—although he himself saw a simpler answer to the problem— "I'll have to let myself be recaptured. What if the police shoot first and capture afterwards?"

"Because you'll be captured here and now, when we've finished talking. Olliver can have a gun on you when we call the police in from outside. You'll already be captured, and they'll have no possible excuse for shooting."

Crag nodded. "And you would handle the—psyching?"

"Of course. No chance of a slip-up there. I'm the only technician there right now; my assistant is on vacation. The timing is perfect. Any more questions?"

"Yes." Crag looked at her, his eyes hard. "How do I know that I can trust you?"

Her eyes met his unwaveringly. "You can, Crag. I can see why you doubt, and—I'm sorry. I should have known better than to tease you, to make you self-conscious, a few minutes ago. I apologize."

"And you promise, under the psycher, to do nothing whatever to my mind?"

"I do. Think, and you'll know I wouldn't want to. It would make you useless to us. And if I even tried to change one little thing, you'd kill me afterwards. I know that."

"If you erased the memory that you'd changed it?"

"You know better than that, Crag. The process is not that selective. I'd have to erase all your memories or none. Otherwise we'd take away only a man's criminal experiences and the things that led to them, and leave him the rest of himself. Someday we may be able to do that, but not as yet."

Crag nodded again. And this time Olliver, his face no longer pale, said, "Well, Crag?"

"All right. Get your gun."

Olliver slid open a drawer. "Put that robe back where you got it. Might be a little hard to explain."

"Wait. Why did we have to go through all this? Why couldn't you have explained this to me at your private talk after the trial? You could have sentenced me to the psycher then. Why the escape and recapture?"

Judeth said, "You wouldn't have believed him, Crag. You might have thought it was something he told to all the boys, to get them to go to the psycher happily. Or whatever you thought, you wouldn't have trusted him. The fact that we *did* help you escape takes care of that. We could have no possible motive for doing that and then sending you back to the psycher."

It made sense. Crag wouldn't have believed Olliver, then, to the extent of going to the psycher willingly. He'd have tried to escape, without help, before he'd have trusted anyone that far.

He stood up, reached to take off the robe and hesitated.

Judeth didn't laugh or mock him this time. She slid down from the desk and went toward the door. "I'll go for the police," she said. "Be ready."

Crag quickly hung up the robe and backed against the wall. He was standing there with his hands raised, Olliver holding a gun on him across the desk, when the police came in.

Nothing untoward happened on the way to the jail, but something unpleasant happened after six guards took him over from the police and took him to a cell. They beat him into insensibility before they left him there. But common sense and self-preservation made him take it without fighting back. There were six of them and each was armed with a heatgun besides the rubber truncheon he was using. Crag might have killed three or four of them but the chances were a thousand to one against his getting them all before dying himself. Those odds weren't good enough now; he'd have taken them gladly if the alternative had been a real trip to the psycher.

Consciousness returned to him in the middle of the night and, every muscle in his body aching, he managed to get from the floor to his cot. After a while he slept.

In the morning the speaker in the ceiling of his cell woke him with the news that sentence had been pronounced on him and that guards would come to take him to the psycher in half an hour. He sat up on the edge of the cot painfully. He was naked; the guards had stripped him the night before. But they had left prison clothes in a corner of the cell and he put them on.

Six other guards came for him, ten minutes early so they'd have time to beat him again. Less severely than the previous beating because they didn't want him to lose consciousness, and mostly about the arms and shoulders because they wanted him to be able to walk. When a buzzer sounded they took him to the psycher room one floor down and strapped him into the chair. They slapped his face a bit and one of them gave him a farewell blow in the stomach that made him glad he'd been given no breakfast, and then they left.

A few minutes later Judeth came in. Again she was dressed in uniform, as he had seen her the first time. But now her beauty showed through even more for, after having seen her as she'd been the evening before, he knew every curve that the tailored uniform tried to hide. She wore the tinted horn-rimmed glasses as she came in, but took them off as soon as she was inside.

Crag said nothing when she stood in front of him, looking down into his face.

She smiled slightly. "Don't look so worried. Crag. I'm not going to psych you. I'm not going to touch your mind in any way. I'm not even going to connect the electrodes."

He said nothing.

Her smile faded. "You know, Crag, I'd hate to adjust you, even if this was a straight deal. You're such a magnificent brute that I like you better the way you are than if you were a mild-mannered clerk or elevator operator. And that's what I could make you into—but I won't."

"Unstrap me," Crag said.

"With the door locked, and with us alone?" At his answering growl she smiled. "Oh, I'm not being femininely coy, Crag. I know how you hate women. But I also know your temper and I know how you've probably been treated since last night. With you free I'd have to watch every word I said to keep you from slapping me down—left-handed."

"You know about that?"

"I know more about you than you think. But I'm going to have to know a lot more. You're going to have to tell me a number of things about yourself."

"Why?"

"Because I'm going to have to turn in a report, of course. Including a case history, and a list of all major crimes to which you're supposed to be confessing right now under the machine. And that reminds me, I'd better turn it on." She went around the chair out of Crag's sight and a moment later a humming sound filled the room. Her voice said, "That's audible in the corridor outside and I don't want anyone to pass and notice that it isn't on by now. Don't worry; it's not connected to you in any way."

When she came into his sight again she was carrying a pad of paper and a stylus; she pulled up a chair this time and sat down in front of him, poising the stylus. "When and where were you born, Crag?"

"Make up your own story."

"Crag, this report will be checked against whatever facts are already known and recorded about you. If it doesn't hold up in every way, it will be obvious that this little séance was faked. There'll be an investigation as to why the machine failed to work properly on you. You'll be rearrested and brought back here—and *I* won't be the one operating the machine. I'll be in jail—or possibly even be sent to the psycher myself. To my knowledge, the crime that I'm committing right now has never been committed before and I don't know what my penalty would be. But there's no doubt about yours.

"I can't take any more chances than I'm already taking, so you *must* cooperate, or else. Or else I connect these electrodes right now and do the job honestly. I have no other choice. Do you understand that?"

"All right," Crag said grimly. "Go ahead."

"When and where were you born?"

Crag told her. And answered other routine questions. Through his graduation from space school, his early years as a spaceman.

"And your career as a spaceman ended when you lost your hand. Tell me about that."

"I'd been a spaceman seven years, and I was a lieutenant on the Vega III. On Earth at the time; we were readying the ship for a Mars run. It was a pure accident—not my fault or anyone else's. Just one of those things that happen. Mechanical failure in a rocket tube set it off while I was cleaning it."

"But they blamed you?"

"Not exactly, but they sprang a technicality on me and used it to keep me from getting the compensation I was entitled to. Not only that, but took away my license and rank, turned me from a spaceman into a one-handed bum."

"What was the technicality?"

"Test for alcohol. It showed a minute quantity. I'd had a farewell drink—just one and a weak one—with a friend six hours before. But there happened to be witnesses and they were able to prove it *was* six hours before. The rule is, no drinks for eight hours before blast-off, and our schedule called for blast-off one hour after the accident happened. That put me technically in the wrong by exactly one hour. They used that fact to save themselves a lot of money. There was nothing I could do about it."

"And after that?"

"Oh, I got kicked around a while. Then I started kicking back. Is this going to take much longer?"

"Another hour, to make it take as much time as a real psyching would."

"These straps are getting to hurt. Will you let me out of this chair if I give you my parole?"

Judeth hesitated. Then she said, "In a minute, yes. But there's one thing that will have to go in my report that you might resent my questioning you about. I'd rather get it over first. Why do you hate women so much?"

"A pleasure to tell you. I'd been married about a month at the time of my accident, to a girl I was mad about. Do I have to tell you what she did when she learned I was short a hand and a job?"

"Divorced you?"

"She was remarried before I got out of the hospital."

"Did you ever—do anything about it?"

"You mean kill her? I hated her too much ever to want to see or touch her again—even to kill her."

"And you won't admit to yourself that you're still in love with her?"

Crag's face turned red and his veins swelled with sudden anger as he strained against the straps. "If I were free, I'd—"

"Of course you would. Anything more you want to tell me about her, Crag?"

"She had hair just the color of yours. And she was as beautiful as you." He paused a second. "No, you are more beautiful. And more evil."

"Not evil, Crag. Just ruthless. Like you. All right, that's enough about that, for my report. We won't mention her, or women, again. And all right, I'll release you now."

She unfastened the strap buckles and Crag stood up, first rubbing his forehead—the strap that had held his head back had been the most uncomfortable—and then his wrists. "What else?" he asked.

"List of crimes, for one thing. They want that particularly, so they can be written off as solved crimes instead of carried as unsolved ones. Might as well be honest about it. You've nothing to lose and it might as well sound good."

Crag laughed. "Get ready for a lot of writing."

"You can talk it into a sound recorder for the police to transcribe later. But before I turn it on—keep your voice flat and emotionless, talk as though you were in a trance. That's the way you'd sound if you were giving this information under the machine. And sit down again so you'll be the right distance from the pickup. Ready?"

Crag said he was ready. She clicked on the recorder.

Crag described briefly the major crimes he had committed, leaving out only two, jobs on which he had used accomplices who were still, as far as he knew, living. Then he looked at Judeth and gestured, and she shut off the machine.

"How about the crime I was convicted for, the *nephthin* job. Am I supposed to confess to that too?"

"I think you'd better, Crag. If I had to report that you didn't, it might stir up further investigation, and that's the last thing we want. Let's see, you were on Venus a year ago?"

"Yes."

"Say you bought the *nephthin* then, from a man whom you knew as—make up any name and a few details they can't check as to where and how you knew him. Say you'd held it until now, until you heard the price was high in Albuquerque, but that you had no special buyer in mind, you intended to look for one."

Crag nodded and added that to the list when she turned on the machine again. "Anything else?" he asked, when the recorder was off again.

"Yes, your escape yesterday. You'll have to tell how that was worked. I've worked out a story for you that can't be disproved."

"What is it?"

"The guard you killed on your way out was named Koster. Up to a year ago he was a bartender in Chicago. Say you got to know him there. Say he came to you day before yesterday in your cell and offered to help you escape for ten thousand dollars you could pay him after you were free. You accepted, and he gave you the things you needed for the escape."

"And why would I have killed him then?"

"To save ten thousand dollars."

"No, I wouldn't have had to pay it anyway if I hadn't wanted to. This is better. He gave me a route and a time which would take me through the portal he was guarding. He'd never intended really to help me escape; he intended to kill me and get credit for stopping an escape, and get promotion. But he was a little slow pulling his gun, as I was watching for just that particular double-cross, and I got the gun away from him and killed him with it."

"Much better. Tell it that way. You think fast, Crag."

She turned on the recorder again long enough for him to tell how he had escaped.

"All right," she said when she'd shut it off. "That finished things. The psycher, right now, is supposed to be expunging from your memory everything that, under its first cycle, you told me about yourself and your crimes." She looked at her watch. "We've got about another fifteen minutes. Better let me strap you in the chair again now."

"Why?"

"You're supposed still to be strapped in when I leave and the guards come for you. And when they loosen the straps there'd better be marks from them, especially the one across your forehead. Otherwise, they'll wonder."

He bent down and fastened the straps on his own ankles, then leaned back with his arms on the arms of the chair and let her adjust the others. The one on his left wrist reminded him. "You knew about my hand," he said. "How many others know? Does that go in the report? They might want to insist on my getting a regular one."

"Don't worry, Crag. No one else knows, unless it's Olliver. From the way you raised your left hand to strike him last night, I guessed that it was weighted. I didn't mention it even to him and I don't know if he made the same deduction or not."

"Good. Since we've time to kill, how about telling me what the job is that Olliver wants me to do?"

Judeth shook her head. "He wants to explain it to you himself. Besides, I've something more important to brief you on. I've got to tell you how to act after I leave you."

"I know. Meek like a rabbit."

"I don't mean that. First, you're supposed to be unconscious when I leave you here. The guards come here and unstrap you, and—"

"Give me another beating in the process?"

"No. You're no longer the person who killed one of them and they have nothing against you. You're starting fresh, Crag. They put you on a stretcher and take you by elevator to a hospital room on the twentieth level. They'll put you on a bed there and leave you to come out of it."

"How long am I supposed to be unconscious?"

"At least an hour. Some of them take longer."

"And then?"

"Pretend to wake up, and be confused. Remember, you don't know who you are or how you got there. Sit on the edge of the bed a while, as though you're trying to orient yourself."

"And then?"

"You'll get instructions. A nurse will be keeping an eye on you from time to time through the door. When she sees you're awake, she'll take you to see someone who'll explain things to you and tell you what to do."

"And what attitude do I take?"

"You're puzzled, and it's all right for you to ask questions. But be polite. Accept and follow whatever suggestions he makes. You'll be all right from there."

"But when and how shall I get in touch with Olliver?"

"Don't worry about it. That will be taken care of. The less you know what to expect afterward the more naturally you'll be able to act the role. Just remember to watch your tongue—and your temper—every minute. Every second.

"All right. Crag—be careful. Now pretend unconsciousness. Close your eyes and breathe deeply and slowly."

Distrustful of women as he was, Crag might have expected it, but he didn't. So the kiss on his lips jarred him when it happened.

But he sat rigidly, not moving and not speaking, hating her so greatly that he would not give her the satisfaction of being cursed at, as she no doubt expected. Sat rigidly while he heard her walk to the main switch of the psycher machine and shut it off. Heard her, in the deep silence left by the sudden stoppage of the humming of the machine, walk to the door, open and close it.

Only when, minutes later, he heard footsteps approaching the door did he remember to force himself to slump into relaxation and breathe slowly and deeply.

By their footsteps and by the way they handled him, he could tell that there were only two guards this time. They weren't afraid of him any more, and they didn't beat him. They lifted him out of the chair and onto a stretcher. He was carried for a while, felt the sensation of an elevator descent, was carried again and then rolled from the stretcher onto a bed.

"The one that killed Koster," he heard one of the guards say to the other. "Shall we give him something to remember us by?"

"Nah," the other voice said. "What's the use? He ain't the same guy now. Even if he felt it he wouldn't know what it was for."

"Yeah, but—"

"Come on, Remember what's on tonight. Save your strength."

He heard them leave.

Already the psyching he was supposed to have had was beginning to pay off. He wondered how he was going to judge time—they'd taken his wrist watch, of course, along with his other possessions—until he heard a clock strike. That made it simple; all he had to do was wait until he heard it strike the next hour and it would be time for him to come back to consciousness.

Because of the pain in his muscles from the two beatings he'd had, it was hard to lie motionless that long, but Crag forced himself to do it. He opened his eyes then and as soon as he was sure he was alone in the room sat up on the edge of the bed. He was rubbing his shoulders gently when suddenly there was a nurse standing in the doorway.

"Feeling better?" she asked brightly.

Crag stood up, and winced. "I'm sore all over," he said. "What happened? Was I in an accident? How'd I get here?"

She smiled. "Everything's all right—and it'll all be explained to you. Or would you rather lie down again and rest some more first?"

He made his voice hesitant. "I'm—okay, I guess." He looked down at himself and pretended to be surprised. "Aren't these—prison clothes? Am I—?"

"Everything's all right. You're ready to leave as soon as things have been explained to you. And as for clothes—" She came on into the room and opened the door of a small closet. A shirt and slacks hung on hangers and a pair of sandals was on the floor under them. "—these are what you're to wear. If you want any help changing—"

"No," Crag said firmly. "But if there's a shower I could use, it might help this soreness."

She nodded and pointed to another door. "Right in there. You're sure you don't want help, for anything?"

Crag told her that he was sure, and waited until she had left. Then he closed the door to the hallway and took a long shower, first as hot as he could stand it and then cold. Then he put on the clothes that had been provided for him, then opened the door to the hallway and looked out, pretending uncertainty.

The nurse was seated at a desk a dozen paces down the corridor. She had heard his door open and had looked up. She smiled again and beckoned and Crag walked over to the desk.

"Feeling better?" she asked. "You're looking *much* better."

"Feeling fine," Crag told her. "But I've been trying to remember things, and I can't even remember who I am or—anything."

"Don't worry. Everything is all right. I'll take you to Dr. Gray now."

She stood up and moved down the hall and Crag followed her. She showed him into a small waiting room and told him the doctor would see him in a few minutes. And in a few minutes a man with a round moon face opened an inner door and said, "Come in, Crag." Crag followed him into the office and took the offered chair.

He said, "You called me Crag. Is that my name, Doctor?"

"Yes. Will you have a cigarette, Crag?" Crag took one from the offered package, and the doctor leaned across the desk and held a lighter for him.

"Your name is Crag," he said, "unless you decide you want to change it. That will be your privilege if you so decide, after you've oriented yourself. You see, Crag, you were a criminal and—to make you able to fit into society—it was necessary that your memory of yourself and of your crimes be erased from your mind."

"What kind of a criminal was I? What did I do?".

"It's better that I don't answer that question for you, Crag. You should concentrate on the future and not on the past. Especially now, since the past no longer matters. Whatever crimes you committed are now off the books, forgotten. And you need feel no guilt for them because *you* are not the person who committed them, not any longer. You have a fresh start and you owe society nothing."

Crag nodded. "I see, Doctor."

The moonfaced man glanced at a card on the desk before him. "In one way you are fortunate. You have no living relatives, so there are no ties with the past whatsoever. In such cases, there are sometimes complications. But—" He cleared his throat and abandoned the sentence. "In another way, too, you are fortunate. You have a sponsor who offers you a much better and better paying job than most of our—ah—graduates start with. You will be a space pilot."

"Space pilot?" Crag didn't have to pretend surprise at that. Maybe there was a bit too much surprise in his reaction, for the doctor looked at him sharply.

"Yes," he said, "for a private craft. You're qualified; you had an A-rating license once. It was revoked, but reinstatement of any such license is automatic for any man who has gone through the psyching process. Unless the revocation was for incompetence, and yours wasn't. You'll take a short refresher course, naturally."

"What kind of a craft is it?"

"Four passenger, semi-atomic Class J-14. And your employer, Crag, is a great man, a great man indeed. His name is Olliver and he is possibly the greatest statesman in the system. At least in my opinion. But you may feel very fortunate that he took an interest in you and applied for your services. Otherwise you'd have had to start your new life as—well, in one of the menial categories. We always have more applications for such employees than we can fill. But of course if you don't want to go into space again, you're perfectly free to choose. You're a free man, Crag. You're being offered that job, not ordered to take it."

"I'll take it," Crag said. And remembered to add, "Thanks. Thanks very much."

The moon face smiled meaninglessly. "Don't thank me, thank Judge Olliver. You'll have a room and your meals at his house, incidentally, so you won't have to worry about looking for quarters. Here is his address, and ten dollars." He handed a slip of paper and a bill across the desk. "Cab fare, unless you'd rather walk. No hurry about when you get there."

Crag stood up, put both pieces of paper into his pocket, and thanked the doctor again.

Five minutes later, on the crowded sidewalk in front of the Judicial Building, he took a deep breath. He was *free.*

And hungry, damned hungry. It wasn't quite noon yet, but he'd already missed two meals in a row. Dinner last night because of his escape and recapture. Breakfast this morning, no doubt because for physiological reasons one was supposed to be psyched on an empty stomach. Either that or the guards had deliberately not fed him for the same reason they'd given him the beatings.

Also he wanted a drink, several drinks. But ten dollars wouldn't buy much of the kinds of liquor he wanted, whereas it would buy as big a lunch as he could eat, and one that would be a real contrast to the soggy synthetics that made up the bulk of prison fare. So lunch, at the best restaurant he could find, won.

Afterwards, replete, he wanted a drink worse than before, and sat for a while thinking of ways of raising a hundred or so for a binge before reporting to Olliver. But even the best of them involved a slight risk and was a risk worth taking now? He decided that it wasn't; he could wait, at least until he learned the score.

But still he was in no hurry to get to Olliver's, so he rang for his waitress and asked her to bring the latest newstab with a second coffee.

The newstab carried mention of his having been sentenced to the psycher but no details were given. They never were, on a psyching sentence; the legal theory was that a psyched man was entitled to a fresh start from scratch with everything against him, even fingerprint records, destroyed. Since he himself had forgotten his identity and his crime, society was required to do no less.

He leafed through the rest of the newstab. There was nothing in it of interest to him. The usual politics and other crap.

Suddenly he wanted to walk, to savor his freedom. And, as well, it would be good for his muscles sore from the beatings. He paid his bill and left.

He took a roundabout course to Olliver's, partly to make the walk longer and partly to avoid the Martian Quarter, the spacemen's vice district. Too easy to get into trouble there, and much as he enjoyed trouble, this wasn't the time for it.

He walked fast, but with the catlike grace and easy balance of one used to a dozen variations of gravity. He thought about a million dollars.

A cool million dollars for one job.

The doorman at Olliver's front door was an ugly, a surly sadist, as were most guards, but he nodded politely to Crag and opened the door for him, told him the judge was waiting for him in the study. Crag followed the hall and let himself into the room he'd been in the evening before. He was glad to see Olliver was alone, again seated behind the massive desk.

Olliver said, "Sit down, Crag. You took your time getting here."

Crag didn't answer. "You've eaten?" Olliver asked, and Crag nodded.

"Good. Then we can talk. You *do* talk, don't you?"

"When necessary," Crag said. "Right now, I'd rather listen."

"All right. They told you you were being offered a job as my private pilot, and I presume you accepted."

"Yes."

"You can operate a J-14?"

"With a day or so to study the manual on it and familiarize myself with the controls."

"Good. You'll have a week before we take off for Mars. It's in Berth Ninety-six at the Port, and you can take as much time as you need to check yourself out on it. I can pilot it myself, but I never go into space without someone who can relieve me."

"And after we get to Mars?"

"You'll quit your nominal job and start on your real one. I'll tell you about it enroute; we'll have plenty of time."

"For the details, if you want to wait till then. But you can give me a general idea now. Maybe it's something I don't want to do, or think I can't do. Even for the price you offer I'm not taking on any suicide job. If I'm going to turn it down, it might as well be now."

"It's dangerous, but not that dangerous. I think you'll try it. I'll gamble that you will; you can still turn it down after we reach Mars."

"I'll wait for the details, but I still want to know the general nature of the job. Maybe I'll be wanting to make preparations even this coming week. Maybe there'll be something I'll want to get for the job that I can get on Earth more easily than on Mars."

"All right, I see your point on that. I suppose it might save time later to let you start planning as soon as possible. In fact, if you'll agree definitely to accept or decline the job now, I'll tell you everything about it right now—except one thing, and you can decide without knowing that."

"All right, go ahead."

"I want you to steal a certain object from Menlo."

Crag whistled softly. "Practically a fortress," he said.

"Yes, but not impregnable to someone taking a job as a guard to get inside it. And that's where your psycher certificate is important. Men otherwise qualified and with recent psycher certificates are *known* to be honest, are much more readily hired as guards than anyone else, no matter what they were before. In fact, no one even cares what they were before, and some of them never ask so you can safely deny that you know your former identity."

Crag smiled grimly. "And if there aren't any openings, I can waylay a guard in town and make one."

"Won't be necessary. Menlo is isolated and Eisen doesn't allow any women there. For those two reasons Eisen has to pay a premium price to get employees, and even so has quite a turnover. You'll have no trouble getting a job."

"And this object I'm to steal—is it easily portable?"

"You can carry it in a pocket."

"Menlo's a big place. Will you be able to tell me where to look for this object?"

"Yes, but not how to get it."

"Has anyone else made a previous attempt to get it?"

"Yes. I—we had a spy in Menlo, Crag, six months ago. As a technician, not a guard. He helped Eisen work on this—object, and told me about it. I ordered him to try to get it, made him the same offer I'm making you. A few weeks later I read a report that he'd been killed accidentally. Whether that was true or whether he was caught and privately executed or not, I don't know."

"Probably sprang a deathtrap. I've heard Menlo is full of them."

Olliver shrugged. "He wasn't a professional criminal. Not in your league at all. I should have been satisfied with using him as a source of information and not have expected more of him. But ever since then I've been looking for the right man for the job—until I saw your name on the docket a week ago and applied for jurisdiction. Well, Crag?"

"That's all there is to it? I obtain this object and give it to you?"

"One other thing, if possible. You're good with tools, aren't you?"

"Yes. If a guard job won't get me close enough I can probably get myself into the machine shop."

"Might help. But it wasn't what I had in mind in asking you. If you can possibly fabricate a dummy duplicate of the object and leave it in place of the real one, it will help. The object will be worth much more to us if Eisen doesn't know it's missing. But I'll settle for your getting it, under any circumstances."

"How many people aside from yourself and Eisen know of the existence of this object, and its value?"

"No one, to my knowledge, outside Menlo. And probably not very many there. That's as to its existence, Crag. As to its value, I don't believe anyone—not even Eisen himself—knows that, besides me. It's an invention of his which he thinks is impractical and almost worthless. But *I* see in it a possibility for making billions of dollars—and billions of dollars is what the Cooperationist Party is going to need before it comes out into the open against the two established parties." Olliver paused and then asked again, "Well, Crag?"

"One more question. Have you got a million dollars, in cash? Or am I supposed to wait for a pay-off out of hypothetical billions?"

"The million is in cash. Not my own personal funds, but in the war chest of the party. My collaborators in the party know only that I know a way to invest that million—which would be a drop in the bucket for launching a new political party—in such a way as to bring in all the money we'll need. They have agreed to trust me to do so, without knowing how. As head of the party and its future candidate for system coordinator, they've given me carte blanche in the disbursement of party funds. If I could tell you who was associated with me in this, Crag, you'd realize what a big thing it is."

"I don't care about that," Crag said. "The million's in cash and in your hands. That's all I wanted to know, and the deal is on. But I'll need an advance for expenses. A thousand ought to do it."

Olliver frowned. "You won't need that much, Crag. You're going to be living here, as my employee, for the week before we take off. I have an extra car you can use for your few trips to the Port. What do you need money for?"

"A wardrobe, for one thing. A binge, for another."

"I recovered the suitcases you had when you were arrested. They're in your room. As is, you've got a better wardrobe than you should have, to be looking for a guard's job. As for the binge, that's out, Crag. You'll have to stay sober until you've seen this through."

"*Have* to? I don't take orders, Olliver. I have been in jail, haven't had a drink in a month. Once we get to Mars I won't take a drink till the job's done, however long it takes. But in between, I'm going to get drunk once, whether you like it or not. If you won't advance me the money, I can get it."

"What if you get in trouble?"

"I'm a solitary drinker. I'll lock myself in my room and you can lock it from the outside, if you're worried."

"A lock that you couldn't get through?"

"A lock I'll have no inclination to get through. You can even put a guard outside the door."

Olliver laughed. "And how explain it to the guard, when he thinks you've been psyched? Psyched men do only social drinking. Besides, you could take care of the guard as easily as the lock, and I haven't any guards to spare. But all right, I'll go along on your having one binge, provided you agree to stay in your room. And that you sober up in time to check yourself out on the J-14."

"Right. Five hundred will be enough, since I've got my clothes back. How about your servants?"

"We have only two inside servants. I'll send them away for a few days. Judeth and I can eat out. But how about your meals? Or will you be eating any?"

"I won't. Where's my room? I'd rather change into some of my own clothes."

"Second floor opposite the head of the stairs. And here's five hundred. The servants will be gone by the time you come back."

Crag took the money and found his room. He checked through his luggage and found that the police had stolen only a few small, if valuable items, nothing that he'd have to replace immediately. He was lucky; a criminal, even if acquitted, was lucky to get any of his belongings back, and he hadn't counted on it.

He changed clothes quickly and went out. The psychological need for a spree was becoming more and more pressing, now that drinks were in sight, and he was in a hurry to get started. He found a shopping district with a liquor store that sold what he wanted. The price was three times what it would have cost him on Mars and half again what it would have cost in the spacemen's district downtown, but it was still less than two hundred dollars and he paid it without argument.

In his room he drank himself into drugged insensibility and kept himself that way throughout that day and the next by drinking more every time he returned to consciousness. On the morning of the third day he decided he'd had enough and poured what little was left of the liquor down the drain of the sink in his bathroom. There had been no pleasure in the binge, but it had filled a psychic need, and now he could go without drinking until such time as he could do it safely in a more pleasant manner.

He was not quite steady on his feet and his eyes were bloodshot and bleary, but he was under control mentally. He was haunted by a half-memory of having, several times in a half-conscious state, seen Judeth standing beside his bed looking down at him. But he checked the bolt on the door and decided that it must have been hallucination, along with the other dreams and hallucinations he'd had.

In the downstairs hallway he passed Judeth, about to leave. Her look took in his condition and she passed him without speaking. Which was what he wanted.

Olliver wasn't in his study, but Crag wrote a brief note and left it on his desk: "All right, you can get your servants back." He found the kitchen and prepared and ate a sizeable meal, then went back to his room and slept. He woke the next morning feeling fit.

Most of the next few days he spent at the Port inside Olliver's J-14, studying its operation manual and the books on space navigation it contained.

He did his thinking there too, and his planning for the job to come insofar as it could be planned in advance. He also read there books he bought in a book and tape store about Eisen and Menlo.

He already knew, of course, considerable about Eisen. Eisen was a scientist and inventor who, early in his career, must have been struck by the similarities—even the slight similarity of names—between himself and Edison, an inventor of several centuries before, and for that reason had named his workshop Menlo after Edison's Menlo Park. Like Edison, Eisen was an empiric rather than a theoretical scientist; his quick mind saw practical possibilities in what to others were abstract facts and purely mathematical equations. Like Edison, he made things *work* and he himself was an indefatigable worker. But he had gone far beyond Edison in the number and scope of his inventions and had become incomparably richer, one of the richest men in the system. He could have bought and sold governments, but had no interest in politics. Nor in power or glory, solely in his work.

Menlo had grown into a rambling building combining sleeping quarters and workshops, isolated—the nearest Martian village was several miles away and very small—and surrounded by reputedly impregnable defenses. Eisen lived there with an all-male ménage of employees and guards, about thirty of each.

Olliver had been right, Crag knew, in saying that the only way to steal anything from Menlo would be to get employment there first. Even so, there'd be traps within traps, and it was going to be the hardest thing Crag had ever tried. But then, a million dollars was the biggest prize he'd ever tried for.

Meanwhile, Crag kept to himself and avoided contact with the Ollivers, especially Judeth, as much as possible. He paid the servants extra to bring breakfasts to his room on a tray, and his other meals he ate downtown or at the Port restaurant.

After a week he knocked on the door of Olliver's den and was bidden to enter. He asked Olliver if he'd decided on a departure time and Olliver nodded. "Day after tomorrow. Everything in order on the cruiser?"

"Yes," Crag said. "Ready to take off any minute. Want me to arrange clearance?"

"Yes. Make it for 10 A.M. Or as soon after as possible if anything else is clearing then. Need any more money?"

Crag shook his head. "I've got enough to last me till I get to Menlo. If I get the job there I'll be searched—Eisen's guards are thorough—and don't want to have much on me."

"Right. And they'll investigate whatever you tell them, Crag. Not back of your psycher certificate, although they'll verify that, but your subsequent actions. Have you got a good story as to why you're going to quit your pilot's job when we reach Mars, to take a job that'll pay a lot less?"

"Yes. Meant to check with you on it so your story will back mine if they investigate. Psyched men sometimes lose their space guts, and that's what will have happened to me. I'll have been scared stiff all the way to Mars and never want to go into space again, at any price."

"Good. I'll back you on that, and so will Judeth."

Crag frowned. "Is she going?"

"Yes. Don't worry, there's plenty of room. That's a four-man cruiser. You don't mind?"

"No, if she lets me alone. You may as well tell me now what the object is that you want from Menlo. Why not now? I'm as committed now as I'll ever be. I'm not going to back out no matter what you tell me it is."

"All right. It's a device that looks like a flat pocket flashlight. Blued steel case. Lens in the center of one end—but you can tell it from an ordinary flashlight because the lens is green and is opaque—opaque to light, that is. I could give you a more exact description, but not exact enough for you to fabricate a duplicate in advance."

"And I couldn't take it in with me if I did. Where is it?"

"In the vault off Eisen's private workshop. I don't know just where in the vault but there's a card index to the drawers in the vault and the index is on Eisen's desk. The object is filed under the code designation DIS-1."

"That's all you can give me?"

"Yes. But a few other instructions. Don't steal anything else. Maybe there are other valuable things but I don't want them, and we don't want Eisen to know anything was stolen. And if you get it—"

"After I get it."

"All right, after you get it, don't try monkeying with it or using it. Promise me that."

"It'll be easier for me to promise that if I know what it is. My curiosity might get the better of me."

"All right, it's a disintegrator. It's designed to negate the binding force—well, I'm not up on atomic theory so I can't give it to you technically. But it collapses matter into neutronium."

Crag whistled softly. "A disintegrator—and you say Eisen considers it worthless?"

"Yes, because its range is short. The size needed increases with the cube of the distance. The model you're after works up to a distance of only two feet. To make one that would work at twenty feet the apparatus would have to be as big as a house, and to make one that would work at a thousand feet—well, there aren't enough raw materials in the system to make one; it would have to be the size of a small planet.

"Besides, there's a time lag. The ray from the disintegrator sets up a chain reaction in any reasonably homogeneous object it's aimed at, within its range, but it takes seconds for it to get started. No, it's valueless as a weapon, Crag. Take my word for it."

Crag said, "Then the value—if it's worth a million to you—must be in the by-product, neutronium. But what can it be used for?" Crag was familiar with the concept of neutronium, of course; every spaceman was. Even school children knew that some of the stars were made of almost completely collapsed matter weighing dozens of tons to the cubic inch. There were dwarf stars smaller than Earth and weighing more than its sun. But no such collapsed matter existed in the solar system. Pure neutronium, *completely* collapsed matter, would be unbelievably heavy, heavier than the center of any known star. Certainly, if it could be *handled,* it would have more important uses than weighting chessmen. But when the atoms of an object collapsed wouldn't they simply fall through the interstices of the atoms of whatever you tried to keep it in and simply fall through to the center of the Earth—or of whatever other planet you were on?

Olliver was smiling. "That's not your department to worry about, Crag. I may tell you later, if it fits into my plans. I've given you everything I can that can possibly be helpful to you."

Crag nodded. But he kept on wondering what Olliver's angle was. What value could there be in a weapon that would work only at shorter range than his own left hand, and much less suddenly? Or was there a way of saving and using the neutronium? Well, he'd worry about the answer to those questions when he had the thing in his hands—but before he turned it over to Olliver, even for a million.

The trip to Mars was dull and boring, as are all space trips. Fortunately, the J-14 was relatively a luxury ship and he had a cabin of his own. He spent most of his time in it, except when he was at the controls. He slept as much as he could and spent the rest of his time reading and listening to tapes. He talked as little as possible to Olliver and not at all—except occasionally to answer a direct question—to Olliver's wife.

Crag took the controls for the landing and set the ship down perfectly. He turned to Olliver. "Where'll I get in touch with you?"

"We have reservations at the Phobos. But you're coming that far with us, Crag. I took a room for you too."

"Why? I might as well head right for Menlo."

"Because I've got connections through which I can get you dope on the current situation there. Give me this evening and you can take off tomorrow morning knowing more than you know now."

Crag nodded. At the Phobos Hotel, he went right to his room and stayed there. In the morning he was dressed and ready when his phone rang and Olliver said he was ready.

Olliver met him alone in the main room of the big suite he'd taken for himself and Judeth. He said, "The news is good. Crag. Eisen's on Earth, in the middle of a month's holiday. You'll have two weeks before he gets back. Maybe it'll be easier for you with the cat away."

"Who does the hiring while Eisen's gone?"

"Nobody hires technicians, but the head guard, man named Knutson, is authorized to hire guards. Wasn't able to find out how they're staffed at the moment but the chances are good; they're usually one or two guards under their quota."

Crag said, "I'd rather run into Knutson in the town. Can you tell me how I'll know him if I do?"

"Yes, I met him myself when I visited Menlo six months ago. He's a big man with red hair, diagonal scar on one cheek—forget which. Surly, struck me as being a bully. Need any more money, Crag?"

"I could use a couple of hundred. I've got enough to get there all right, but I might not be able to get a job right away."

Olliver counted out two hundred dollars for him.

Judeth, in a robe, came in as he was putting it into his wallet, about to leave. She put out her hand to him. "Good-by, Crag. Good luck."

Crag wondered why her hand seemed to burn his as he took it. He got out quickly.

The little town of Pranger, population twelve hundred, which was Menlo's only link with civilization (except that, in a sense, Menlo *was* civilization) was in a high valley in the Syrtis Mountains. There were no direct flights between it and Mars City, so Crag had to make his journey in stages and didn't get there until early afternoon. He registered at the inn and had lunch there, then wandered out to see the town.

Not that there was much town to see. Besides two rough-looking taverns and a few stores, it was all miners' cabins. It was a molybdenum mining town and everyone living in it, except those who ran the stores and taverns, worked at the nearby mine. A poor, squalid town. If it was the only place accessible to workers and guards at Menlo, it was no wonder that few cared to work there. But still he didn't want to go directly to the place and apply for a job; that way all his chances would be killed if he were turned down. He'd have no logical excuse to hang around and try again. It would be far better to meet Knutson accidentally and to lay himself open to an offer of a job without having to ask for one. Then his chances wouldn't be ended by a refusal, for he couldn't be refused something he hadn't asked for.

It was early evening when he saw a tall red-haired man passing the inn, and hurried out to follow. He hadn't been able to make out the scar at that distance but the man he was following was better dressed than the miners and he felt sure it would turn out to be Knutson. And when he followed the man into one of the two taverns and was able to see the scar, he knew he was right. And he knew, too, that the big redhead was even more of a bully than Olliver had taken him for, and that meant there was an easy way to make friends with him. If letting oneself get beaten up is easy.

Crag stepped in beside Knutson at the bar and managed to slip and fall against Knutson, spilling part of the drink the man was already holding. But Crag apologized quickly; he had to be careful because he would later have to reveal his psycher certificate to Knutson and meanwhile must do nothing that would make that certificate suspect. A recently psyched man can defend himself if attacked, or, if he is a guard, can attack others in line of duty, but he is not naturally aggressive or on the prod.

But a moment later, again seemingly inadvertently, he again jostled Knutson and made him spill more of the drink. And this time Crag didn't have to apologize because there was no time for it. He managed to ride with the punch in his face so as to let it carry him back away from the bar, but kept from falling. He caught his balance and came in swinging. But with his right hand; he only feinted with his left. He made it look like a good fight, although he could have ended it with a single blow, even of his right hand, almost any time he wanted to. But he made it a good fight and a long fight and let himself be defeated only slowly and far from ignominiously. But finally he was down.

And Knutson, grinning a bloody grin, was helping him up and saying, "Man, you put up a good scrap, for a guy your size. Damn near beat me. Let me buy you a drink."

So he grinned back and let Knutson lead him to a table and order drinks for both of them. And a few minutes later, after he'd answered Knutson's question as to what he was doing in Pranger, Knutson said, "Man, you don't want to work in a moly mine, a guy that can fight like you can. How'd you like to work at Menlo?"

And, it turned out, Crag would very much like to work at Menlo, for his new-found friend. Checking antecedents, Knutson whooped when Crag showed him the psycher certificate. "Man, that's really good. Only two weeks old. We can skip investigating anything about you before that and you can't have got in much trouble in two weeks. What you been doing?"

Crag explained that, and the head guard said he'd phone Olliver at the Phobos in Mars City early the next morning for a reference. And then, if Crag's prints matched those on the psycher certificate, he was in and could start work as soon as he wanted to. "Don't pay any more than a mine job," Knutson told him, "but it's clean, easy work. Mostly loafing, in fact, as long as you stay awake and alert while you loaf. You on?"

Crag was on.

CHAPTER FIVE

He could have got on simply by going and applying for the job, of course, but it was far better the way he'd done it; he was a friend of Knutson's. The quickest way to make friends with a bully is to get into a fight with him and let him beat you, but after such a tough fight and by so narrow a margin that he respects you. Beat him and he'll hate you; go down easily and he'll be contemptuous of you. And as a friend of Knutson's, Crag got the shift he wanted to start with, the roving night shift that patrolled the interior of Menlo, not the periphery. He got to know every room of the place, except Eisen's private office and laboratory, kept closed and locked while he was away. More than locked, he decided; it must have been well booby-trapped as well. Not even Knutson or Cambridge, the head technician and the man closest to Eisen, knew how to enter it. No one but Eisen ever did enter it, except at his invitation when he was present.

Crag spent three nights and days doing nothing but learning the ropes, the position of every guard at every time, the obvious checks and safeguards, the routine, the layout. A lucky find solved one major future problem for him in advance; on the third floor was a small museum of primitive weapons from Earth. One of them—he'd decide which when the time came—would be just what he needed when the time came for him to get the disintegrator out of Menlo.

The next evening at dinner in the dining room, Knutson asked Crag, "Like fights? Boxing, I mean."

"Sure," Crag said.

"Damn good one on tonight from Mars City, welters. Want to come to my room and watch it on tele?"

"Sure," Crag said.

"It's on at seven. Drop up to my room then and we'll watch it. If you get there before I do, make yourself at home."

Crag made a careful point of getting there early and making himself at home. He loosened a vacuum tube in the teleset. When Knutson came in a few minutes later and turned it on, nothing happened. Knutson fiddled with the dials and swore.

Crag said, "I'm pretty good at fixing one of those things. Nobody's working in the main lab now; let's run down there and I'll see if I can get this thing going."

In the lab, he got it out of the case and started fooling with it. But by a few minutes after seven Knutson got restless. "We're missing the fight, Crag. Let's go to the main lounge and catch it on the big set. You can fix that later."

"You go ahead, Knut. I'm so close to getting this fixed I'd really rather stay with it. I'll probably join you there before the fight's over."

He did join Knutson before the fight was over and he had Knutson's teleset working. Also he had several small items in his pockets; a tiny atomic flashlight and a circuit detector, both jury rigged but small and efficient, and a few other things that might be needful.

The next night he settled for going over the outer door of Eisen's office with the flash and the circuit detector and working out the circuits of three separate alarms—or death-traps; it didn't matter which—and that was all he did. He didn't enter the room; he wanted a full night ahead of him for doing that, a night when he didn't have to punch check buttons at various places in the buildings at various times. The next day he talked Knutson into putting him on a day shift.

And the night after that, as early as was safe, he canceled out the three circuits in the door and let himself into Eisen's office, with five hours ahead of him. He spent the first of those hours very carefully going over the office and the laboratory behind it for further alarms or traps. He found and disconnected three. Then he turned his attention to the blank durasteel door of the vault.

It was right beside Eisen's desk and an article lying on the latter gave him a hunch that saved him a lot of time and experimenting. It was a little horseshoe magnet, a toy, that was apparently used as a paperweight. But what if it was more than that? Why couldn't it be the key to a magnetic lock?

He examined the surface of the vault's door inch by careful inch. It being durasteel there were no accidental scratches on it to confuse him. There was only an almost imperceptible flyspeck about a foot to the right of the center door. But flyspecks scrape off and this mark didn't—and besides, there are no flies on Mars. He tried the magnet in various positions about the speck and when he tried holding it with both poles pointing upward and the speck exactly between them the door swung open. Inside were hundreds of drawers of various sizes, each numbered.

Crag turned back to Eisen's desk and in the little card file on a corner of it looked under the code designation Olliver had given him and found the drawer number. A moment later the disintegrator was in his hand. There was no mistaking it, from Olliver's description. It looked for all the world like a tiny pocket flashlight, even smaller than the standard atomic one Crag had stolen from the main laboratory. Except for the lens, which was emerald green and was not transparent. Crag closed the drawer and started to close the vault door and then stopped. He had time to fabricate a dummy duplicate and he might as well follow Olliver's suggestion that he leave a substitute. True, if Eisen ever tried to use the device he'd discover the substitution, but if he made periodic checkups just to make sure that nothing was missing, he'd simply look at the duplicate and not check its workings. And the longer before he might discover the theft, the better.

He carried the thing into the private laboratory and went to work there. Eisen couldn't possibly have provided better equipment for a burglar who wanted to leave a duplicate of whatever small object he stole. Given time, Crag could probably have taken the thing apart and made an actual working duplicate. But he settled for a really good outward duplicate and when he had finished it, he made sure there was not even the slightest sign left that he had used the workbench or moved a single tool. He placed the duplicate in the drawer and closed the vault, reconnected the alarms or traps except those at the door, and then waited quietly in darkness until he heard the guard pass on a round. Ten minutes later, the door again a deathtrap, he was safely back in his room. In office and workshop, there was no trace of his having visited there—unless Eisen tried to work the disintegrator or had a careful inventory of all the scrap metal in the workshop's junk bins.

The several other things he had to do could wait till tomorrow, and he got two hours of sleep.

Getting the disintegrator safely out of the place was the most important thing the next day, and the easiest. The third-floor primitive weapons museum room was on his rounds. He picked the stoutest bow, a relatively modern twentieth century hunting bow, and a heavy hunting arrow. He taped the little disintegrator on the arrow just behind the steel head. Shot through the window it carried far over the electrified fence and down into a gully out of sight from any point in Menlo. Unless it had broken in the arrow's landing—and he had wrapped it in cloth against that contingency—the disintegrator was now safe for him to recover at leisure. A quick stop in the main workshop while the technicians were at lunch enabled him to replace the atomic flashlight and to throw in the scrap bins the parts of the circuit detector, which he had already disassembled, and to get rid of the few other small things he had taken.

But he didn't want to arouse suspicion by quitting suddenly. Or, worse, getting himself fired, which he could do only by conduct that would be suspiciously out of character for a psyched man. He took the safe way. The following morning he reported himself as having a severe headache and feeling dizzy. Knutson took him to the dispensary and left him there to find the technician who ran it and who had a lay knowledge of medicine. Crag took advantage of the temporary solitude by making free use of two drugs, one of them belladonna and the other a quick-acting cathartic, he found in the supply cabinet.

"Looks like rill fever," said the technician, examining Crag's contracting pupils. "Ever had it before?"

Crag grinned wryly. "I wouldn't remember. It might be on my record."

The technician looked at Knutson. "If it is, he'll have diarrhea starting within a few hours. And if it is, he'd better get to Mars City for treatment. I can't take care of him here, or even make a biopsy to make sure that's what it is."

"Maybe we shouldn't wait," Knutson said. "I can run him into Mars City and make sure."

"He's better off if he doesn't travel till this first attack is over. If that's what it is, he'll be all right by tomorrow and it's always several days at least before there's a second attack. As long as he gets a checkup—and treatment if that's what it is—before a second attack, he'll be all right."

Crag got worse and the expected diarrhea lasted most of the afternoon, but in the morning he felt better, much better. Knutson got his pay for him and even offered to forgo searching Crag and his luggage to save time, but Crag insisted on the search, saying he didn't want to be suspected in case, at a later date, anything at Menlo turned out to be missing. He also turned down Knutson's offer of a lift into Pranger by heli, insisting that the walk would make him feel better. Well out of sight of Menlo, he hid his suitcases along the path and circled around to the gulley where the arrow had landed and recovered it. He pocketed the disintegrator and buried the arrow in the sand.

He didn't try out the disintegrator so near Menlo for Olliver had not happened to mention whether or not its operation was silent; quite possibly it wasn't. He waited until he was back near his luggage and then took it from his pocket, aimed it at a bush half a dozen feet away and pushed the thumb slide. Nothing happened until, gradually, he moved it nearer to the bush. When he was within a few inches of two feet away the outlines of the bush became misty and then it was no longer there, nor was there any trace of the bush left on the sand from which it had grown. Olliver had not lied about the nature of the device nor about the limitation of its range. It might be of value to a criminal in disposing of a dead body, but almost any other weapon, even a knife, was more efficient in killing. It didn't look worth a million dollars to Crag, but that was Olliver's business.

That afternoon in Mars City he made his first business following through on his alibi for quitting the job, just in case. He went to a clinic and waited while a biopsy was made and checked. He was told he did not have rill fever and that the symptoms must have been something else. He promised to return for a full-scale checkup if the symptoms returned.

And he called Knutson to give him the news, as he'd promised. If he didn't Knutson might wonder, and anyway there was no use closing that door. He didn't have the million yet and if he got it, it might not last forever. It would be handy to be able to go back to Menlo and work there again any time he might want to. Knutson tried to talk him into coming back then, but Crag said that even though it wasn't rill fever he'd had, it had been something and he'd rather, for a while, work in Mars City so he'd be near a clinic if there was a recurrence.

He called Olliver's hotel and got him on the phone.

"Crag speaking," he said. "I've got it."

"Wonderful, Crag! Can you come right around?"

"Have you got your end of it, there in the room?"

"Here? Of course not. It'll take me until tomorrow afternoon to—"

"I'll phone you tomorrow afternoon."

"Wait, Crag. Where are you—?"

Crag hung up.

It was late the following afternoon when he called. Olliver said, "Crag, don't hang up! Listen to me. That much money in cash is hard to raise. Most of my investments are on Earth, and I'm trying—"

"How much have you got, there in the hotel?"

"Half. And it'll take me at least a few days more to raise the rest."

"All right," Crag said. "If you've got half I'll trust you for the rest. Is anyone else there now?"

"Just Judeth. Can you come right away?"

Crag said that he would, and got there in five minutes.

Olliver, his face tense with eagerness, let him in. "You brought it?"

Crag nodded and looked around. Judeth, dressed even more revealingly than she had been the first time he had seen her at Olliver's house in Albuquerque on Earth, lounged on a brocaded sofa staring at him with an unreadable expression.

Olliver turned to her. "We'll take his word that he has it. Get him the money, dear."

Judeth went into an adjoining room of the suite and came back with an inch-thick sheaf of money. She held it out to Crag. "Five hundred thousand, all there. Count it."

Crag thrust it into a pocket. "If I'm trusting you for the second half of the million I might as well take your count on the first half. All right. Olliver, here's your toy."

Olliver's hand trembled slightly as he took it. "Good boy, Crag. And you don't think they'll miss anything from Menlo?"

"They'll never miss it, unless Eisen tries actually to use the duplicate I left in place of that one. Now about that second half million. When and where do I collect?"

Olliver said, "Sit down, Crag," and went over to sit on the sofa beside his wife. "Let me explain part of my plans, and make a suggestion. First, I can get you the rest of the money within twenty-four hours of the time we get back to Earth. I've got it there; it's just a matter of turning investments into cash."

"All right," Crag said. "And when do you plan to get back to Earth?"

"Leaving tomorrow. But with one other place to go before we go to Earth. Whole trip will take us a week. But here's the second part of the suggestion. Why not come with us?"

"What's your other stop?"

"The asteroid belt. Just the near edge of it. I want to land on one small asteroid."

"To test the disintegrator?"

Crag nodded slowly, wondering why he hadn't thought of so simple an answer to getting neutronium in handleable form. Disintegrate an entire tiny asteroid and its atoms would collapse inward on themselves, since the asteroid would be in no gravitational field except its own; it would collapse into a tiny ball that could be carried back in a spaceship—providing it was a small enough ball that its mass, which would become weight again when you brought it back with you to a planet, wasn't great enough to crash the ship in landing it. Simple, once you thought of it. How come Eisen hadn't? Or maybe Eisen had, but hadn't seen any value in or use for neutronium. Olliver had something up his sleeve there too.

"All right," Crag said. "What time tomorrow do you clear?"

"Does noon suit you?"

"Any time," Crag said. "I'll meet you at the ship. You haven't used it? It's still in the same berth?"

"Yes, and refueled and ready. Glad you're coming, Crag. I've got something really important to talk to you about, and that will give us plenty of chance. We'll see you at the ship then."

Crag still had time to go to two different banks and, at each, to stash a sizeable fraction of the half million. And then he spent a quiet and thoughtful evening wondering, among other things, why he'd bothered to do so. He didn't trust Olliver—for the simple reason that he didn't trust anyone—and it was quite possible Olliver might be inviting him on that trip with the idea of recovering one half million dollars and saving another. But if Olliver did succeed in killing him, what difference could it make to Crag whether the money was on his person or safe back in Mars City? Well, it might make a difference at that, if he let Olliver know that he'd stashed the bulk of the money. Yes, he'd take that precaution and every other one he could think of. But he'd still have to sleep and... He shrugged; when you shoot for big money you take big chances and you might as well not worry about them. Possibly Olliver would be afraid to try to kill him, knowing that if he failed he himself wouldn't have long to live. And possibly Olliver's plan in connection with the disintegrator really was one that made peanuts out of a million dollars.

He slept well.

He was checking over the J-14 when Olliver and Judeth arrived the next day. Judeth immediately went to her cabin to change from street clothes into coveralls for the trip. Olliver sank into the co-pilot seat next to Crag, and leaned back. "Lots of time yet. And course is plotted."

"Where?"

"Simply the nearest point in the asteroid belt. When we get there we simply look till we find one the right size."

Crag said, "One weighing less than half a ton. That is, if you intend to bring it back. That's about all the extra payload this ship can make a safe Earth-landing with. Or do you intend to jettison anything already aboard?"

Olliver smiled. "I'm not planning to jettison anything aboard. But I'm surprised, Crag—and pleased—that you had the nerve and judgment to come along. A lesser man might figure I might leave him out there, if I got the chance, to save myself a half million."

Crag grunted. "I'll take my chances."

"You won't be taking any. Crag, this thing is *big*, and if you want to ride with me on it, you can be big too. That lousy million won't mean a thing to you. You'll have something more important than money. Power."

"And you?"

"I'll have more power. More power than any man has ever had in the history of mankind. I'll—well, I'm not telling you the details now, Crag. After we've been to the belt, after I'm sure of two certain points. Crag, what do you think of Judeth?"

"What does it matter?"

"I want to know."

Crag said, "I hate all women."

"And perhaps Judeth more than any other?"

"No," Crag lied. "Why?"

Olliver shrugged. "Forget it. Well, since you're in the driver's seat, might as well take off. Cold on the stroke of noon, and here are the coordinates. I'll tell Judeth to strap in."

He headed for the double cabin, and a moment later came back and strapped himself in the co-pilot chair. "She's strapping down in there," he said. And then thoughtfully, "A beautiful woman, Crag, but also a brilliant one. Never trust brilliant women; that's something I'm learning. Well, Crag, what do you think about my proposition?"

"I'll wait till I hear it. All right, five seconds of twelve. Four. Three. Two..."

Crag found the trip dull. So apparently did Judeth; she spent most of the time in her cabin. Only Olliver seemed eager, operating under a barely suppressed excitement that made him so restless that he seemed unable to sit still or to concentrate. At times he seemed lost in a dream from which he had to shake himself with difficulty if asked a question.

Such as when they were nearing the belt. Crag, at the controls, was decelerating and, at the same time, turning to match speed and directions with the asteroids revolving in it. Some were already showing in the detectors. "How big a one shall I pick?" he asked.

"Huh? Oh. It doesn't matter much. Few hundred tons. Size of a house, maybe."

"We can't take it back with us, no matter how small it gets, if you pick one with that much mass."

"We're not going to. Just a test."

"Then why not pick a big one? I can find Ceres for you. Little under five hundred miles in diameter."

"Take too long, Crag. This isn't an instantaneous chain reaction; there's a time lag, remember. If my information is correct, it'll take at least an hour for one of a few hundred tons."

Crag remembered that it had taken several seconds for the bush he'd tried it on; it seemed reasonable. He'd never told Olliver that he himself had disobeyed instructions and had already tested it.

There were asteroids all around them now, showing in the detectors at distances as close as a mile or two. Crag studied them and picked out one approximately the size Olliver had asked for, began the delicate maneuvering that would put the ship alongside it, exactly matching its speed and direction.

Olliver watched breathlessly. "You've got it, Crag."

Crag nodded and shut off the power. The spaceship and the asteroid, held close together by the few pounds of gravitational pull between the masses, would continue through space side by side until power was again applied to the ship.

Olliver clapped him on the shoulder. "Nice work, Crag. All right, let's get our suits on. I'll tell Judeth."

There would have been no real need for all of them to have left the ship for the test, but in any case they all had to put on space suits. A ship as small as a J-14 has no airlock; it is more economical, on the few occasions when one leaves it in space or on an airless body, simply to exhaust the air from the entire ship and let the airmaker rebuild an atmosphere after one's return—and before removing the space suit.

Crag was adjusting the transparent helmet of his suit when Judeth came out of the cabin, already suited. Olliver asked, "We all ready? I'll start letting the air out." They heard his voice now, of course, in their helmet radios. "You're both coming out, aren't you?"

Judeth said, "I wouldn't miss it for a million." And Crag nodded.

Olliver stood watching the pressure indicator and in a minute or two he said, "All right," and pushed the lever that activated the door mechanism. Standing in the doorway, he adjusted the grapples on his space boots to enable him to stand on the asteroid and jumped lightly across to it, abruptly, once outside the artificial gravity field of the ship, seeming grotesquely to be standing at right angles to the floor of the ship.

Unspacewise, he had not carried the mooring line and grapple, and the backlash of his jump sent the spaceship drifting away from the asteroid; had he been alone he would have had to jump back quickly before it drifted out of jumping distance. Crag called out to him and threw him the grapple and, when Olliver had attached it, reeled in until the ship was again only a few feet away from the surface of the asteroid, and safely anchored. He jumped down then, and Judeth followed him.

Olliver was walking rapidly toward the opposite side of the asteroid. Before following, Crag looked about him. Time and its relation to distance were strange in so tiny a world as this. A walk of thirty yards could carry you from night to day and back to night again. The ship was moored at the sunset line; Olliver had stopped at the opposite sunrise line and called out, "Here we go," and Crag knew he was holding the distintegrator down to the surface of the asteroid and flicking the switch.

Would it really, Crag wondered, disintegrate an object the size of this as easily as, even if more slowly than, the bush he'd tried it on on Mars? Why not, if what it started was a chain reaction that would go through any reasonably homogeneous substance? It had disintegrated *all* of the bush, although all of it had not been within two feet of the disintegrator. Good God, Crag thought, what if he had held the disintegrator closer to the ground, within two feet of it! Would it have started a chain reaction that would, however long it took to do it, have destroyed the Planet Mars? Why not, if it was going to work on an asteroid like this? The difference was only a matter of size and size doesn't matter in a chain reaction. A chill went down his spine at the thought of the risk he had unwittingly taken—the risk of not only having destroyed himself but a whole planet and having caused the death of almost fifty million people.

Olliver was coming back now and Judeth moved to meet him, so Crag followed. They stopped in the middle of the day side. Olliver was bending down again and Crag looked to see if he was going to apply the disintegrator to another point. But Olliver was merely laying a six-inch pocket rule against the surface of the asteroid and with a piece of chalk was making marks opposite both ends of the rule. "So we can tell quicker when it starts to happen—if it does. If those chalk marks get less than six inches apart, then it's happening."

"And then what?" Crag asked. "We'd better run for the ship before the asteroid goes out from under us?"

"Yes, but there'll be no hurry; we'll have at least half an hour."

"And then what?" Crag asked again.

"And then—Wait, I *think* those marks are closer together, but wait till we're absolutely sure, and then I'll tell. Look—" He grabbed Judeth's space-suited arm. "Look, my dear, *aren't* they closer? Isn't it shrinking?"

"I—I think it is. And isn't the horizon closer?"

Olliver straightened and looked toward the horizon and Judeth's face turned toward Crag, her eyes staring strangely at him. He got the idea she wanted to ask him a question but didn't dare—and was trying to find the answer by staring into his eyes. He met her gaze squarely, defiantly, but it puzzled him.

Olliver said, "I think— Well, why think? Another minute at the outside and we'll be sure."

And then, his voice very calm, he said, "Yes, those marks are almost half an inch closer together. It works." He stepped back away from them and his eyes went to Crag. He said, "Crag, that million of yours is wastepaper now. But how would you like to be my hatchet man, second in command of the Solar System?"

Crag looked at him without answering, wondering if Olliver could be mad. The thought must have showed in his face, for Olliver shook his head. "I'm not crazy, Crag. Nor do I know any important commercial use for neutronium—that was camouflage. But Crag—think of this—

"*Just one of these little gadgets set up in a hidden place on each of the occupied planets, each with a separate radio control so it can be triggered off from wherever I may be.* That's all it will take. If it works on an asteroid—and it does—it'll work on an object of any size. A chain reaction doesn't differentiate between a peanut and a planet."

Crag stared, wondering how he had been so stupid not to have guessed.

Olliver said, "You might as well know all of it, Crag. There isn't any political party behind me. That was just talk. But from now on, once I get this set up, there aren't going to *be* any political parties. There'll just be—me. But I'll need help, of course, and you're the man I'd rather have for my *segundo,* in spite of—"

Suddenly he laughed and his voice changed. "Judeth, my dear, that's useless."

Crag looked quickly toward Judeth and saw that she'd pulled a heatgun from the pocket of her space suit and was pointing it at Olliver.

Olliver chuckled. "I thought it was about time for you to show your true colors, my dear. And I thought this might be the time for it. I found that little toy in your space suit some hours ago and I took the charge out of it. Go ahead and pull the trigger. Or are you pulling it already?"

She was pulling it; standing alongside of her Crag could see that the trigger was all the way back against the guard, and the muzzle was aimed right at Olliver. Crag saw too that her face was pale—but he thought it was pale from anger rather than from fear.

She said to Olliver, "All right, you beat me on that one. But someone will stop you, somehow. Don't you realize that you can't do what you plan without destroying at least one planet to show them you're not bluffing? Millions of lives—billions, if Earth has to be one of the planets you destroy! If you destroy Earth, you'll kill off three-fourths of the human race, just to rule the ones that are left. You must be mad."

Olliver laughed. There was a heatgun in his own hand now, held not too carelessly, so it covered both of them as he took a step backward.

"She's a spy, Crag. A spy for the Guilds. I've known it all along—and kept her on a string. She married me because they wanted her to watch me. Well—I let her, and let her help me, and now God help her. Take that gun away from her, Crag."

The gun was empty and the command meaningless; Crag knew Olliver was testing him. Olliver was making him line up, one way or the other.

Crag hesitated; was Olliver mad, or would he really run the system and would he really make Crag his second in command? And did Crag *want* that, at the price of destroying one or more worlds? Killing men was one thing; he'd killed plenty of them. But destroying worlds, killing entire populations—

Olliver said, "Your last chance, Crag, or I'll burn both of you instead of just Judeth. Don't think I've been blind to the fact that you two are crazy about each other, and have been pretending to hate one another so I wouldn't guess. Well, you can have her, Crag, but she'll be dead when you get her. Or would you rather have power worth more than billions?" He laughed. "And any woman, *all* the women, you want."

Definitely the asteroid was shrinking in size. Olliver was standing closer to them, though he had not moved. He said, "Well, Crag?" and stepped back to reach a safe distance again.

If the attached glove of Crag's space suit had not prevented, he could have thrown his metal hand and had at least an even chance of its striking before Olliver could trigger the heatgun. As it was, there was only one other chance, and whether they both survived it depended on whether the woman's reflexes would be as fast, or almost as fast, as Crag's own. He turned to her and reached out with his right hand, as though for the gun she still held, but instead his hand flashed up to her shoulder and he pushed hard and snapped "Night side!"

The push carried her off balance and two steps backward; only another step was needed to carry her below the dwindling horizon and out of range of Olliver's weapon. Crag himself took a diagonally different course. And, as he'd hoped, the heat beam lanced out between them, hitting neither. A fraction of a second later both were in darkness on the side of the asteroid away from the sun. Safe, for the moment.

In his helmet radio, Crag heard Olliver curse. And then laugh. Olliver said contemptuously, "You're a damned fool, Crag. Turning down an offer like I made you—for a woman and a chance to be a hero, for a few minutes." He laughed again and this time there seemed to be genuine amusement in his laughter. "It's a small world, Crag, and getting smaller. How long do you think it will be big enough to hide behind?"

There was no point in answering, and Crag didn't. He stood still for the moment letting his eyes get accustomed to the almost perfect darkness, a darkness ameliorated only by faint starlight and light reflected dimly from a few other small but distant asteroids in orbits paralleling their own. One, he noticed, quite small in apparent size because of either genuine smallness or distance, seemed to be coming closer, growing larger. His eyes dropped and swept about the lessening horizon as he turned. No sign of Olliver; there wouldn't be. Olliver would take no chances in coming around to the night side where, because for at least a moment he'd be completely blind, his weapon would be of no advantage to him.

He could, of course, simply go back to the spaceship and maroon them here, but Crag didn't think Olliver would. Olliver would want the satisfaction of killing them in person; he felt sure of that. And it would be safe and easy for him to get them when the asteroid had shrunk enough. You can't hide behind an object the size of a basketball.

But where was Judeth? He looked around again. Had she gone toward the spaceship in the hope that she might round the opposite side of the asteroid and get a chance to board it?

Crag turned to look that way, and swore. The sunward side of the spaceship glinted—far away. It was moving outward from the asteroid, getting smaller in the distance. Not under power; it was drifting, but drifting fast. Had he misjudged Olliver, after all? Was Olliver simply going away and leaving them to die as soon as the air supply of their suits was exhausted?

A sudden bellow of rage in his helmet radio answered the question for him. Olliver was still on the other side, the day side, of the asteroid and he had just seen the dwindling ship.

And at that moment a hand closed on Crag's arm, and Judeth's voice said, "Crag, I'm sorry. I *had* to push it off. There wasn't a chance for us to get into it; the hatch was way on his side, the day side, and he'd have—"

"Wait," Crag said.

He groped in the darkness until he found the switch of her helmet radio, turned it off, and then his own. He leaned forward so the front plate of his helmet touched hers and said, "While our helmets touch we can hear one another, and Olliver can't hear us. You *can* hear me?"

"Yes." her voice was flat, but not frightened. "But what does it matter about Olliver? We're all dead, all three of us. I'm sorry, Crag. I had to do it."

"What did you do with the heatgun?"

"My pocket. Here. But it's not loaded."

Crag took it and hefted it. It was a little lighter than the missile he would have preferred, but his spacesuit kept him from using that one. He thought he'd be able to throw the gun fairly straight.

He said, "Wait here," and squeezed Judeth's arm gently, then turned and started back for the day side. The asteroid was shrinking fast now, only about twenty feet in diameter. He had to crouch to keep his head from showing as he neared the borderline between light and darkness. Then, as he stood only a step away from the edge, he abruptly straightened, the gun held back ready to throw,

Olliver stood there, turning in a tight circle, trying to watch all sides at once. The gun left Crag's hand, and didn't miss; Olliver's helmet shattered.

He took a deep breath and walked the rest of the way. He turned on the radio switch of his helmet and called out, "Judeth. Is your radio on? Can you hear me?"

"Yes, Crag." She was coming. She looked down at Olliver's body and shuddered. "He was a mad dog, Crag. And yet—I wasn't sure, clear till the last minute, after we landed here. I suspected him, but I was never sure, until then. I thought maybe he really meant—"

"Was he right about you being a spy for the Guild Party?"

"No. Nor for anyone else. I fell in love with him and married him, three years ago. And I believed in his new party that was going to end corruption and bring back decent government."

"You were still in love with him?"

"No, not for months now. Almost a year. But by the time I'd fallen out of love, I'd begun to suspect him. And stuck with him in case I was right and in case I could stop him. And thank God I did. He'd have destroyed most of the human race just to have absolute rule over whatever was left of it. You consider yourself a criminal, Crag; you're not one at all, compared to him."

She turned to stare up at the dwindling spaceship. "There's no chance of your reaching it and bringing it back?"

"Not now. I could jump after it, but the chance of hitting it would be one in a million." He picked up Olliver's fallen heatgun. "If this was a reactor gun, so I could steer myself in space—but it isn't, and a heat beam doesn't help. Well—"

"Crag, we've got to destroy that disintegrator. There's only a chance in a billion that our bodies will ever be found here, but if they are, that'll be found too and—someone might discover what it is and get the same idea Olliver had."

"All right." Crag reached down and went through pockets of Olliver's space suit, came up with the disintegrator. "Guess this heatgun will melt it to a lump of— Wait, might as well use it first. This small world of ours is getting smaller. No use having it unnecessarily crowded."

He flipped the thumb switch of the disintegrator, held it a foot above Olliver's body, moved it slowly from the shattered helmet to the space-booted feet. "We don't need him for company, do we?"

"Crag, a wonderful idea. Will you use it on me—in a few minutes?"

"A few minutes? The air in these suits should be good for another half hour, Judeth. Why be in a hurry?"

"My air's giving out already, Crag. Olliver must have tampered with it as well as with the charge in the heatgun I had in my spacesuit pocket. He must have *known* I'd turn against him when he told us his plans. Even if he didn't really think I was a spy."

Her breath was coming hard now. "Crag, you *will* use the disintegrator on me, please? I just don't want to be found, ever, looking the way a woman looks when she asphyxiates."

"Sure," Crag said.

"And—I'm afraid, Crag. Will you put your arms around me?"

He did, and he didn't hate her at all.

She clung to him. She was panting now, fighting for every breath. She said, "Good-by, Crag, I won't make you listen to—" She shut off her helmet radio.

Less than a minute later she was limp in his arms. Crag put her down gently and, as she had requested him to do, used the disintegrator. This time he didn't watch.

Then he put the disintegrator down, used Olliver's heatgun on it for a full minute at only a few inches, until it was a shapeless bubbling blob of molten metal.

His little world was almost too small to stand on now, but for another few minutes he managed to stand, looking upward at the bright little stars in the big black sky. He was breathing hard now; the oxygen in his own suit was nearly exhausted now and he didn't have more than another ten minutes or so to live. Judeth must have been wrong in thinking that air had been taken from her supply deliberately; Olliver would have had no reason to short the supply in Crag's. Probably both or even all three suits had been short of oxygen through Olliver's negligence, which wouldn't have mattered had the spaceship remained for them to return to.

The asteroid was less than a yard in diameter now, and Crag gave up trying to stand on it and sat down.

And smaller, until he got off it and looked and laughed at the poor shrinking thing, the world that had been an asteroid as big as Olliver's house when they'd landed on it.

Fought for breath and got ready to die. Alone, but that didn't matter, so long had he lived alone.

Held the small world in his hand now, the size of an orange. Laughed a final time as he put it in the pocket of his space suit, wondering what they'd ever make of finding it there, a three-inch ball with hundreds of tons of mass, if they ever found him here.

Slid into blackness as dark as the sky but unrelieved by stars.

And died.

CHAPTER SIX

Entering his several millionth solar system, he had expected nothing unusual. Why should he have? It seemed like any other.

He passed two cold dead giant planets, one with a ring around it. He had seen many such, and knew how they had been formed. He passed the orbit of Jupiter, but Jupiter was on the other side of the sun; otherwise, on certain of Big Jupe's moons, he might have encountered sooner that for which he had long since ceased to search, life other than his own.

Next toward the still distant yellow sun, a belt of asteroids. Chunks of rock like him, but unlike him, only lifeless rock, unthinking, unsentient. Some many times larger than he, some much smaller. In such a belt of orbiting asteroids he himself had been one of thousands until had happened the molecular accident that, billions of years ago, had brought consciousness to him and had made him unlike the others.

This belt had been formed the same way and was no different, he thought at first. Then, suddenly:

From only light-seconds away, at a point along the inner edge of the asteroid belt, he perceived *something*. Something confused and muddled, but which was, which had to be consciousness. Alien consciousness. Another being besides himself. Or beings; there seemed to be several of them.

Quickly he dropped into subspace and almost instantaneously reappeared in normal space a dozen miles from the point from which he had detected these emanations of consciousness. It was an asteroid, a small one. He matched his speed to its and maintained his distance from it, to observe. His reason for not approaching closer was not caution; it was simply that at this convenient distance he could observe as well as from any nearer point; he could perceive, through a sense that was not sight for he had no seeing organs, not only the outward appearance but the very arrangement of the molecules of the asteroid and the things or beings upon it or attached to it.

He was aware that a change was taking place in the molecular arrangement of the asteroid itself, a simple chain reaction that was collapsing not only the molecules but the very atoms of which the molecules were made in upon themselves, a reaction that once started would now continue until the asteroid was reduced to a tiny chunk of collapsed matter a minute fraction of the original size of the original form of the asteroid. This did not hold his interest; he was familiar with such reactions and could himself instigate or reverse them.

Nor did his interest center upon the subject moored to the collapsing asteroid, although in the absence of the alien life forms, it would have interested him considerably in that, by the fact that it was an artificial construction, it would have been his first discovery of evidence that sentient beings other than himself existed anywhere in the universe. But here were the sentient beings themselves and he concentrated his scannings upon them. One of them was at that very moment detaching the mooring line of the artificial construction from the asteroid and giving it an impetus that sent it drifting out into space.

The being in question, and the other two like it, were, he perceived, themselves encased within smaller constructions. Most parts of these smaller constructions, he could tell from their molecular structure, were flexible. As were most parts of the bodies of the beings inside the constructions. Strange, complicated bodies they were. And fragile, so fragile; there was an arrangement to produce heat within the constructions that housed them, and they held a gas; apparently both the gas and heat were necessary to these beings. He analyzed the gas and found it to be mostly oxygen and carbon dioxide; there were traces of other elements. The beings drew this gas into their bodies and exhaled it less much of its oxygen content; a container of concentrated oxygen automatically replaced the oxygen absorbed by the bodies inside the constructions. It seemed a very strange and limiting arrangement. There were planets, many of them, with oxygen atmospheres and with the degree of heat the construction supplied and held in. On such planets these beings could live without the artificial casings that now held them and it came to him that they must be from such a planet—possibly inhabited by others like them—and that their presence here on an airless asteroid in the cold of space was temporary, their casings designed to permit survival in—

Survival? Whence had that concept come to him? Until now, death had been a meaningless concept, one that had never occurred to him, but now suddenly he knew what it meant and knew that these beings he was observing lived for a short time only and then ceased to be. And that he now knew this was only in part a deduction from the study of their physical bodies, so it meant that their thoughts—at first a meaningless jumble of utterly alien concepts—were beginning to be understandable to him.

And then, quite suddenly, there were only two beings, two focuses of consciousness. One of the three had quite suddenly—died. His body had suddenly become a piece of lifeless rather than living matter. Another of the three had propelled an object that had broken a rigid and shatterable part of the first one's protective casing, and this had been the result. Now a device was being used on the dead one and his casing that was setting up the chain reaction of molecular collapse. Apparently these people had only slight mental powers, to use a physical contraption for so simple a matter.

He concentrated his study on the two remaining. One of them seemed to be having—the concept *pain* came to him, although he did not yet understand it fully—and the pain seemed to be connected with the fact that the oxygen content of the gas within its casing was lessening. And since the reserve of oxygen seemed exhausted, this being, too, would soon die, and he concentrated his study upon it while it lasted, which wasn't long.

The remaining one again used the device and again there wasn't even a body left. Were these creatures all so ephemeral?

Now, with only one of them left, the thoughts were more nearly clear. Completely alien concepts, though. With another device, one for producing heat, this last one was destroying the thing that had produced molecular collapse in the bodies of the first two.

Why? Again, he tried to probe the surviving mind, and found the thoughts confusing. They were completely alien concepts, behind which he sensed something fierce and wild. And then something calm and waiting, and again the pain. And nothing. The third being had ceased to be.

It had all happened so incredibly quickly. After these eons to have found three living beings, three sentient entities, and then to have had them all three flicker out as quickly as meteorites entering an atmosphere! For a moment he considered going on, searching for the planet from which these beings, he had already deduced, must have come. But there was something else he could try first.

Carefully and leisurely he examined the structure of the body of the last of the three to die, and the only one of the three which had not been disintegrated. Closely studied, much became obvious. He found two spongy organs that held air and muscles that gave bellows action to draw in the air and push it out again. He synthesized oxygen and teleported it into the casing's oxygen container and then activated the muscles that controlled the spongy organs. The being breathed. Simultaneously he activated an organ of heavy muscle which served as a pump to circulate a stream of fluid throughout the body. After a while he found he could cease to activate those muscles and they continued of themselves.

The top or conscious level of the being's mind remained dormant, passive, but the creature lived. He probed into the lower, the memory level of the mind and found with satisfaction that now, without the conflict of emotion or surface thought, his task was much easier. In Crag's memories he found the answers to his questions about the puzzling series of events upon the asteroid. He learned who the other two beings had been and why the three of them had been there.

He learned everything Crag remembered of Crag's own history and everything Crag had ever read or heard of human and planetary history, even the things Crag's conscious mind had long since forgotten. He got to know Crag, in the process, better than one entity has ever known another.

And, in the process, he found that he was no longer alone.

CHAPTER SEVEN

Crag awoke as an animal wakes, suddenly and completely aware of himself. But things were wrong—rather, things were right that should have been wrong—and he neither opened his eyes nor moved a muscle. He was breathing air, and he shouldn't have been. He'd been dying for lack of it; he should be dead now instead of awakening.

Besides that, he was lying on hard rock, with enough of a gravitational pull to hold his space suit as firmly against it as though he was on Earth again. Not even the largest asteroid had that strong a gravity; could he be back on Earth? Another spaceship could conceivably have found him and picked him up before he died, the air in his suit could have been replenished, but...it didn't make sense. His space suit would have been taken off him long before making planetfall. Or—another possibility occurred to him; he could be lying on a pile of rock in the ore locker of one of the wildcat mining ships that worked the asteroid belt for uranium and—

"No, Crag," said a voice inside his mind. "You are safe, but you are neither on Earth nor on a ship."

Crag opened his eyes and looked up—into space. Into blackness lighted by untwinkling stars and a distant sun. He sat up and looked around him. Again he was on the surface of an asteroid, but this time a much larger one. From what he could see of it from a sitting position, it was possibly up to a mile in diameter—but still far too small to have a gravity field equal to, or anywhere near, the normal Earth-gravity he was feeling.

"The gravity is artificial, Crag," said the voice inside his mind. "About the strength of that of your native planet. Would you prefer a lesser one, like that of the fourth planet, the one you think of as Mars?"

"Who are you?" Crag asked aloud. He wondered for a brief moment if he was really dead, and if this was some mad, weird dream in an afterlife; then he discarded the idea. This was real, and he was not dead.

"I have no name," said the voice. "I am what you think of as an asteroid on which you are sitting. And, in a sense, I am an asteroid, but from another solar system very far from here. But I am a sentient being, as you are."

"Siliceous life?" Crag asked. "But why did you—?"

"Is life based on silica any stranger than life based on carbon? As to why I saved you—brought you back to life, really—call it curiosity, if nothing more. You are the first alien being I ever encountered."

"Then—you came along and found me after what happened on the—the other asteroid?"

"While it was happening. But it was only confusion to me, until it was all over; I did not know what was going on there. I know everything that happened, though, now, from your thoughts and memories while you slept after I brought you back to life. You're finding it difficult to believe all this, but it is true. And you are not dead nor are you now dreaming." There was a slight pause and then the voice said, "That space suit is hurting you; you've had it on too long. Shall I enclose an atmosphere inside a force field so you can take it off for a while?"

"I'm all right," Crag said. He started to get to his feet, but found himself pinned to the ground by one side of his space suit, the side which had the pocket into which he had put the collapsed smaller asteroid. He grinned and said, "Except that I'm stuck. I've got a few hundred tons in my pocket, in this gravity. Could you unstick me?"

There was no answer but he felt suddenly very light, almost completely weightless. He took the orange-sized sphere of neutronium out of his pocket and put it down. Then as he stood up, his weight returned to Earth-normal.

"Damn clever," Crag said. "Do you do that without machinery?"

"I never heard of machinery, Crag, until I learned about it from your mind and memory while you were asleep. From your mind I learned—"

"Damn you," said Crag viciously. "Get out of my mind."

There was abrupt silence, a sense of withdrawal. And, after a moment, the voice spoke again, but this time Crag heard it as a sound, not thought; a vibratory manipulation of the air inside his helmet. "I am sorry," it said. "I should have realized that you would resent my sharing your thoughts. But without reading your thoughts, when I first returned you to life and while you slept, I could not be communicating with you now. I shall not enter your mind again."

Crag frowned. "Why didn't you leave me dead? What do you want of me?"

"I did not know then; it was only curiosity, the wish to find out about you and your race, that caused me to do what I did. Now, it is more. I would like your companionship—a concept which I did not know existed. I learned a word from your mind, the word *friend.*"

"A word I thought I had forgotten," Crag said. "I want no friends. Let me alone."

"If you wish again to die—?"

Crag laughed. "Twice in one day? No, thank you. But how am I going to get back to Mars? You got me into this, damn you, by bringing me back to life. Now get me to Mars. Or get that spaceship back and I'll get there myself."

"I was afraid that would be your decision," said the voice. "The spaceship is already back, is orbiting about me right now. Shall I bring it down?"

"Yes," Crag said.

It bumped gently to the ground beside him and he stepped into the still open door, slammed it shut after him. He turned on the airmaker and, while giving it a chance to build up atmosphere so he could take off his space suit, sat down at the controls and started making the observations that would enable him to set a course back toward Mars. Without too much surprise he saw from the reflector for the down view port that the asteroid—or whatever it had been—was gone; he floated free in space.

Half an hour later, on course and with nothing to do until, two days later, he'd be nearing Mars, he relaxed and found himself wondering: Was he really sorry he'd been brought back to life? In a way, yes; he'd died once and that ought to be enough for any man, and dead men have no problems. On the other hand, he had half a million dollars, part of it on him in cash and the rest in banks back in Mars City, and it seemed a shame to die and leave it unspent. It was more money by far than he'd ever had at one time before; it would last him for years no matter how prodigally he spent it.

And why miss those years? Wasn't money what he wanted?

Or was it? He remembered those few minutes when he and Judeth had been alone, after Olliver's death and before hers—and then, with an oath, thrust the thought from his mind. He'd let himself get soft in those few minutes, but he didn't have to let himself stay that way.

"Good-by, Crag," said a voice in his ear, startling him.

He looked in all the viewports, saw nothing. "Where are you?" he asked.

"Where you left me. But in a few minutes you'll be out of my extreme range for doing this, so I thought I would tell you now what I have decided."

Crag said, "I don't care what you've decided. Let me alone; that's all I ask of you."

"I shall, but I want you to know my plans. I am going to make a world."

"All right, go ahead."

"Thank you." Crag thought the voice sounded amused. "I will. And you'll know about it when it happens. I think possibly you may decide to come to me. I'll wait and see."

"Don't hold your breath," Crag said. "All right, good-by." And then: "Wait, if you're still there. What the hell do you mean, you're going to make a world? You can't create matter, can you?"

"No need to. The matter is here—the millions of small and large asteroids in this belt between Mars and Jupiter. It *was* a planet once, a few million years ago, before it broke up. Some chunks of it have been lost, but there's still enough rock here to make a planet almost the size of Mars.

"All I have to do, Crag, is use myself as a nucleus for it and gather it together. And it will be a new world and a raw one; it'll need tough colonists. Crag, I hope you'll decide to gather some people like yourself, ones who are tough and not soft and weak like the others, to come to me. I want men who, like you, would not take orders even if I should give them. I do not want to be a god, Crag, even though I have some powers beyond mankind's; I would not let my new world be colonized by people who might even be tempted to obey me."

"Most people will—if you reward them. How are you going to keep them away?"

There was a sound that might have been laughter. "I'll take care of that, Crag. Whenever you're ready, come. And if you know any others besides yourself who are like you, bring them. I'll make them welcome."

Crag laughed. "I'll think it over—after I've spent that half million."

"That is all I ask. Good-by, Crag."

And suddenly there was a sense of emptiness in the spaceship and Crag knew that whatever projection of force and thought had been there was gone.

He was alone; suddenly it was a strange feeling, and it was strange that it should be strange for, in all the years he had been a criminal, he had been alone and had wanted to be alone. Was it because for those few minutes after Olliver's death and before Judeth's he had forgotten to hate her because they were both dying so hatred no longer helped or even mattered? Or was it because it was lonelier to have died and been brought back to life? Or was it because an alien mind had probed and shared his mind and now—*knew* him.

Another man, a character in mythology, had once died and been brought back to life, and had life ever again been the same for him? *Damn him,* he thought of the alien, the sentient rock; *why didn't he leave me alone? Isn't it enough for a man to die once?*

The two days it took him to get back to Mars seemed an interminable length of time. But he had to curb his impatience for at least a week longer than that if he wanted to be safe. It would have been very unwise to have landed Olliver's ship at Marsport or any other spaceport. The ship's papers, which would be checked, showed its last clearance had been from Mars City's Marsport with three aboard; it would have been impossible for him to have told any story to account for their disappearance that would not have led to an investigation, and an uncomfortable degree of official interest would have focused on Crag. Far better for the ship itself and all three of its occupants to be presumed never to have returned from space.

He landed the ship and lowered it to the horizontal position in the shadow of a high sand dune in the New Lybian desert; it might have been undiscovered there for years. But he took no chances; he walked—it took him four days—to the nearest town, a small mining community. There, claiming to be a prospector, he rented a sand-cat with a bulldozer attachment. It took him less than a day to drive back to the spaceship with it and another day to shift enough of the dune to cover the ship with sand. Another day to return to the mining town, return the sand-cat, and buy air passage to Mars City.

He was safe now. With his fingerprints and records destroyed, there was nothing left to connect him with the Crag who would be presumed dead along with Olliver and Judeth when, within another week, their spaceship would be reported missing and presumably lost, since a ship of its class carried supplies for two weeks at maximum loading—and that much only when there were two people aboard instead of three.

It was evening when he reached Mars City but all the shops were open, as were all the bars and everything else, twenty-four hours a day, so he was able to buy himself a complete new wardrobe and swanky luggage to put it in. He hadn't bothered to take his old luggage out of the spaceship; it wouldn't have fitted his new-found status of wealthy man.

Oddly, he was no longer in a hurry to begin his debauch. He was tired, for one thing; after his herculean labor in burying the spaceship, he needed a long sleep worse than he needed a drink. But he was in no hurry, even for that.

He asked the clerk from whom he had made his purchases, "What's the top luxury hotel now? Is it still the Luxor?"

"It's still the best one, I hear. There are a few newer ones in the last year, but none of them quite so expensive."

"Will you have the clothes packed in the luggage and sent there, right away?"

"Of course, Sir. But unless you have a reservation—?"

"Have them sent there," Crag said.

He went out of the shop. It was late evening by now, but the streets were as crowded as at noon. Mostly with expensively dressed men and women—and with people who didn't quite fit either category. Crag was expensively dressed himself now, in clothes he had changed into after he had bought them, although his costume was somber and modest compared to most of the others.

The Luxor was ten blocks away; the walk, he thought, might cure him of his restlessness and make him sleepy. But walking bored him; halfway there he decided to take a cab the rest of the way and then decided to stop in at a bar before he took the cab.

He put a bill on the bar and decided to start with a highball, an old-fashioned alcoholic drink that antedated by centuries the newer and more potent drug-based liquors. He sipped it slowly and wondered why he didn't feel exhilarated. He had what he'd always wanted—money, half a million dollars of it. And perfect safety; not only wasn't he wanted but his records and fingerprints had been expunged from criminal files everywhere.

He was simply tired, he thought. He'd feel better tomorrow.

And stared at himself in the backbar mirror; strange—or was it?—for how many centuries bars had had mirrors behind them so their patrons could stare at their own reflections—and reflect.

Crag stared at his own reflection, and reflected. I am Crag, he thought. But who was Crag, now? Crag had been someone, as a criminal. But now he was a rich man, one of millions of rich men, with no need to steal or kill, or to run or to hide. His only need was to enjoy himself, and he was making a bad start of it; the highball didn't taste right.

He puffed a cigarette into flame and inhaled deeply.

Someone was sitting beside him at the bar, a girl. She said, "May I have—?" and Crag handed her a cigarette. He didn't turn to face her, but in the mirror he could see that she had bronze hair the color of Judeth's and of his ex-wife's. But there was no further resemblance to either of them.

"Thanks, Mister," she said. "Would you buy me a drink, huh?"

He pushed a ten-dollar bill in front of her, from his change. "Buy one and keep the change. But please let me alone and don't talk."

It was cheap at the price. There were other prostitutes in the bar, a dozen or so of them, of both sexes. As long as she sat there, he'd be left alone; if she went away another would try, and another, and his thoughts would be interrupted each time. His thoughts? What had he been thinking about, anyway? Nothing.

He needed sleep; that was all that was wrong with him.

He looked down into his drink between sips because now if he looked into the mirror he'd see the girl sitting beside him, and the color of her hair would make him think about Judeth. But why shouldn't he think about Judeth if he wanted to? She was dead now, and he didn't need to be afraid of her any more. *Afraid?* How had that word come into his mind? He wasn't afraid of anything. What he had meant in his thoughts was that now he didn't need to hate her any longer.

Inadvertently he looked up and his eyes caught those of the girl, in the mirror. She said, " 'Scuse me for talking once, Mister. But you look lonesome. Aren't you? Or are you just mad at someone?"

Instead of answering Crag downed the rest of his drink and left. Outside, he started to hail a cab and then changed his mind and walked the rest of the way to the Luxor Hotel.

It was small compared to the buildings around it, only six stories high, but it was set back in the middle of a full city block of garden—all Earth trees, flowers and grass growing in soil brought from Earth, not the dull scrubby vegetation of Mars.

He walked back to it, and into the gilded and silvered lobby, across it to the polished marble desk.

"Got a suite open?" he asked. Nothing less than suites were available at the Luxor.

The desk clerk stared at him disdainfully through pince-nez glasses on a gray silk ribbon. His head was the shape of an egg, and as bald. "You have a reservation, Mr.—ah?"

"You have the name right," Crag said. "Mr. Ah. No, I haven't any reservation."

"Then there is nothing—"

"I'm a friend of the manager's," Crag said. "If you take my card in I'm sure something can be arranged." Crag put a hundred-dollar bill on the counter.

A corner of the man's mouth twitched, and his eyes warmed somewhat behind the pince-nez glasses; they became no colder than hailstones. He said, "*I* am the manager, Mr. Ah. My name is Carleton. But I could have erred; I'll check the register." He didn't touch the bill, but he brought up a crocodile-bound ledger from under the desk and covered the bill with it while he thumbed through pages.

After a moment he said, "Yes, there *is* a suite open, sir. Number Fourteen."

"Is it your best suite?"

"One of our best. Two hundred and thirty dollars a day."

"I'll take it," Crag said. He peeled bills off his roll and put them on the desk atop the open ledger. "You register for me, please. My luggage is being sent here but won't arrive until tomorrow. You can have it sent up when it arrives."

"Certainly, Mr. Ah." The manager touched a button and a bellboy sprang up as though by magic. "Suite Fourteen," he said, handing the boy a key.

In the thirty-by-forty-foot beautifully furnished living room of the suite, Crag tipped the bellboy and assured him that he wanted nothing at the moment. He stood looking about him. Doors indicated that he had at least five other rooms at his disposal but before entering any of them he walked out on the balcony and stood a moment in the cool Martian night air looking out over the fabulously lighted streets and buildings that surrounded him. Quite a bit different from the spacemen's quarter, north of the city proper. But he was much safer here; in the luxury places like this one, no one who spent money freely was ever asked questions and it was almost impossible to get into trouble that you couldn't buy your way out of. If you threw money around they figured you were an important politician or a labor leader and expected you to be incognito as a matter of course.

He went back inside and tried a door. It led to a small but well-stocked bar. He studied the array of bottles and finally poured himself a small drink of *woji;* it would be more likely than any of the others to make him sleepy, and sleep was what he needed. It might even make him more cheerful. But its immediate effect seemed to be neither and it tasted bitter.

He went out into the main room and tried another door. It led to a library that was well stocked with books, records and tapes. He glanced over the books on the shelves, noticing that except for a few standard reference works that a traveler might want to refer to they were all pornographic; that meant that the tapes and records would be pornographic too. He didn't try any of them.

A double door in front of a pneumatic divan turned out to open on a video screen eight feet wide and six feet high. Crag turned on the switch and sat down on the divan. Bright colors flashed on the screen and settled into a picture, a musical show originating in London on Earth. Before a three-dimensional chorus undulating in full color a pale and slender tenor was singing:

Jet up! Jet down! On a slow ship to Venus!
Honey-wunny-bunny, how'd you like my...

Crag got up and turned off the switch. He went back and had another drink at the bar. This time he tried *estaquil,* one of the strongest of the hemp-derived drinks, supposed to be soothing and soporific. It tasted sickeningly sweet and seemed to have no effect on him otherwise.

He tried another door. It led to a room well supplied with gambling equipment of all kinds, one wall lined solid with solitaire gambling machines. Crag knew that all the machines would be rigged with high percentages against him and didn't bother trying them. Besides, what would be the fun in gambling when he already had more money than he knew what to do with. But one of the solitaire machines was an antique fifty-cent-piece one-arm bandit and Crag, for the hell of it and knowing that it would probably be set to pay off the first time, found a half dollar in his pocket, dropped it in and pulled the lever. The cylinders spun, one by one came to rest; a cherry, a cherry, an orange. Four half dollars clinked into the pay-off receptacle. Crag wandered on without bothering to take them out. He wandered back to the main salon and opened another door.

It led to the master bedroom, which was even larger than the living room or salon, whichever it was. It was much more richly furnished. Especially more richly furnished was the eight-foot-wide ebony bed; a blonde, a brunette and a redhead, all naked, lay upon it. For a second Crag thought that the redhead looked a little like Judeth, but she didn't.

She was the one, though, that caught his eye. She sat up and raised her arms above her head, stretching like a kitten as she smiled at him. "Hello," she said. The other two sat up and smiled at him too.

Crag leaned against the jamb of the door. He said, "Pardon my ignorance, but I've never had a suite here before. Are you standard equipment?"

The redhead laughed. "Of course. But you needn't keep *all* of us, unless you wish." She looked demurely at her gilded toenails.

The blonde smiled at him and then rolled over on her back, obviously figuring she showed to better advantage that way. She did.

The brunette gave him a gamin grin. "We're more fun three at a time," she said. "We know tricks."

Crag said, "Get out, all of you."

They didn't argue; they didn't even seem offended or annoyed. They got up calmly and went past him through the doorway of the bedroom and through the salon, through the door to the hallway, still stark naked but obviously completely unconcerned about the fact.

Crag laughed. He went back to the bar and poured himself another drink. Plain whisky this time. Since none of the drinks tasted right to him just now, he might as well vary them.

He sat sipping it, trying not to think.

There was a soft knock at the door. Crag put down his glass and went to answer it. His luggage, probably, although he hadn't expected it so soon; he'd told the clerk at the store that there was nothing he'd need tonight and that delivery tomorrow would be satisfactory.

But the bellboy outside his door didn't have luggage. He was a very beautiful young man, rosy and handsome, with soft ringlets of curly hair.

He smiled at Crag. "The management sent me, Sir. Since you did not want women, they thought perhaps— Is there anything I can do for you?"

Crag looked him over carefully. He said, "Turn around."

The young man smiled knowingly and turned gracefully around. He had a pleasingly plump posterior; he wriggled it a trifle, provocatively.

Crag drew back his foot and kicked hard.

He closed the door gently.

He got the glass of whisky again and downed what was left of it instead of sipping. He started wandering again, wondering why he couldn't get sleepy. He found another and smaller bedroom, but this one was untenanted. And he found the bathroom, with a sunken tub that was almost large enough to swim in. The tub was filled with lukewarm water and Crag stripped and got in.

But he got out quickly when he discovered that the water was perfumed. He finished washing himself with cold but unperfumed water from the tap of the washbasin. And then washed himself all over again when he found that he still smelled faintly of violets.

He put his shorts back on to sleep in—if he could sleep—and went into the master bedroom. But a look at the monstrous ebony bed there changed his mind; he went into the smaller bedroom and lay down on the smaller and less ornate bed there. Probably unspeakable things had happened on it too, but fewer of them. He turned out the light and tried to sleep.

But couldn't. He wondered if there was a drug cabinet in the liquor room. He didn't use drugs as such ordinarily, but he had to sleep. If he didn't he'd start drinking seriously and a time when he was dead tired already was a bad time to start that.

He wondered if music would help. He'd noticed knobs and luminous dials of a radio built into the wall above the head of the bed and he reached up now and flicked the switch. The radio hummed and then blared; he got it turned down to a bearable volume just in time to catch the end of a news broadcast.

"...in the asteroid belt," said a smooth voice. "Scientists of both Mars and Earth are working on the problem, but have thus far failed to formulate an acceptable theory to account for the unprecedented and incredible phenomenon. This concludes the two o'clock newscast; the next one will be presented at 3:15 A.M. Mars City time."

Crag sat up and turned the light back on. He shut off the radio and reached for the phone beside the bed. An obsequious voice asked him to wait for a moment and then came the dry voice of the manager with the pince-nez glasses. "Carleton speaking. Yes, Mr. Ah?"

Crag said, "I just tuned in on the last few sentences of a newscast from the official Mars City station. About something happening in the asteroid belt. Could you arrange with the station to have that particular part of the newscast played back for me over my set here?"

"I'm afraid, Mr. Ah, that would require rewiring the set; it is automatically tuned to the main carrier wave of—"

"Over this phone, then," Crag said. "They tape all broadcasts; for a fee they ought to be willing to play that part of the tape back for me."

"I'll see if that can be arranged, Sir. If you'll please cradle your phone I'll call you back as soon as I've found out what arrangement can be made."

Crag cradled the phone and drew a cigarette into flame while he waited. In a few minutes the phone buzzed and he picked it up again.

"It can be done, Mr. Ah. There will be a fee of fifty dollars. Is that satisfactory?"

"Yes. Hurry it up or I might as well wait till the next newscast."

"Very well. If you'll please hang up again—"

Crag put down the phone again and watched it, wondering now why he was so interested and in such a hurry. Whatever was going on out in the asteroid belt didn't concern him. If the alien out there was doing what he'd said he'd do, that still meant nothing to Crag. A new world, hell. For as long as his money lasted—and half a million dollars takes a lot of spending—he was going to enjoy a soft life here on a soft world, not help start a colony of criminals on a new, raw planet.

But just the same he watched the phone with mounting impatience until it buzzed for a second time.

"The station is ready, Sir. The management of the Luxor is glad to have been able to arrange—"

"Get off the wire, then," Crag said.

There was another minute of waiting and then came the voice of the announcer of the newscast.

"According to many reliable reports, a strange and incredible thing is happening in the asteroid belt. The first report came eight hours ago from Bellini, an astronomer who was at that time using the big scope on Luna to observe Ceres—largest of the asteroids, with a diameter of four hundred and eighty miles—when suddenly it vanished from the field of the scope, which had been set to track it, to follow its course automatically. When Bellini found it again by using the manual controls, it had changed both speed and direction considerably. The directional change was quickly analyzed by the computing machine and it was found that Ceres had lost much of the eccentric and parabolic aspect of its orbit; it was following a new orbit, more nearly regular and more nearly in the plane of the ecliptic. Subsequent observations fed into the computer showed that the change is progressive, and still continues. Within another forty hours, Bellini believes, Ceres will be following a perfectly circular orbit about the sun instead of the irregular one it followed heretofore.

"Luna immediately notified other observatories on Earth and on Mars and those in a position to observe Ceres confirmed his observations within the hour. Also, observations were made, and are still being made, of other of the asteroids, those large enough to be observable in telescopes. Hidalgo, whose eccentricity is—or rather was—point six five, was found with difficulty, considerably out of its former orbit. Upon study and analysis with the computer, it too was found changing in the direction of a perfectly circular orbit similar to that of Ceres—but Hidalgo is traveling at a far greater speed; it will overtake and crash into Ceres within a few days.

"The most amazing thing is that the speed of the asteroid Hidalgo in its new orbit and in relation to its mass is impossible according to the laws of angular momentum.

"Luna Observatory is now on the wrong side of Earth to enable continued observation of the asteroid belt, but every telescope on the night sides of Earth and Mars is now being used to check one asteroid after another—and as yet no single one has been found which is in its former orbit! All are now in, or tending toward, the same identical circular orbit. And there is only one conclusion to be drawn—since they are moving at greatly different speeds, they will eventually all crash into one another *and form a new planet!*

"If it can be assumed that the smaller asteroids, those too tiny to be seen telescopically, are joining in this movement then the new planet about to be formed will be slightly larger than Mars.

"Spaceships are now leaving Mars and Earth to place themselves near enough to observe this incredible development at close hand. Whatever its cause, an event of cosmic importance is taking place in the asteroid belt. Scientists of both Mars and Earth are working on the problem, but have thus far failed to formulate an acceptable theory to account for..."

Crag put the phone back on its cradle; that was the point at which he'd tuned in on the original broadcast ten or fifteen minutes before.

He thought, *So the little devil is really doing it.*

He chuckled and went back to the bar where he poured himself another drink, *woji* again this time. With it in his hand he wandered out onto the dark balcony and stood staring up at the moon Phobos hurtling across the Martian sky.

Then he stared at the stars until he had located the plane of the ecliptic and knew that he was looking at the belt in which the asteroids—each too small to be seen by the naked eye at this distance—were gathering themselves, or being gathered, to form a new planet. He chuckled again, but there was no real mirth in it.

He raised his fist at the sky and thought, *Damn you, I died; why didn't you leave me dead? Once is enough.*

He drank his bitter drink and threw the glass out over the railing into the garden below.

And then staggered, not from intoxication but from exhaustion, back into the smaller bedroom, fell upon the bed, and slept.

CHAPTER EIGHT

Crag woke, as always, suddenly and completely, instantly oriented. He was in his own suite at the Luxor, in the smaller of two bedrooms, and the dimness of the light coming in from outside didn't confuse him; he knew that it was dusk, not dawn, and that he'd slept fourteen or fifteen hours.

He sat up on the edge of the bed and got a cigarette going, then he wandered out into the salon. His luggage, he saw, had arrived and had been brought to his suite, left just inside the door so its arrival would not disturb him. He carried it into the bedroom and opened it, chose garments and put them on.

He felt rested. Today was the day, or rather tonight was the night, when he was going to start a historic binge, the binge he'd worked for and waited for.

But he was hungry; he'd better eat first. Once he'd started drinking he wouldn't eat until after he'd sobered up again, however long that might be. He considered having food sent up and then decided to go downstairs for it. The dining room of the Luxor was always open and served any kind of meal at any hour of the day, with a floor show every hour on the hour, twenty-four times a day. He was curious what the floor show would be.

A voice called, "Mr. Ah," as he was passing the desk. Crag turned and saw it was Carleton, the manager. He stopped and rested an elbow on the desk.

"May I ask how long you are staying, Mr. Ah?"

"I don't know," Crag said. "A few more days at least. Maybe forever."

"I see. I'm afraid, then, that I must ask you to pay for a second day. And besides smaller items, there are already two fifty-dollar debits against your account—"

Crag put a thousand-dollar bill on the desk. "Let me know when that's used up. One fifty-dollar charge is for the newscast repeat. What's the other?"

"A fee to the bellboy we sent to your room last night. You—ah—used his services in an unusual way, but what you did incapacitated him for a day and we thought it only fair—"

"Only fair," said Crag solemnly. "And well worth it."

He turned away but the manager's "Mr.—ah—Ah," made him turn back.

"The Luxor regrets that you did not care for the girls. Or for the bellboy, in the ordinary way. But we deem it a privilege to serve guests with extraordinary tastes. We can supply children of either sex, elderly people... If, as your treatment of the boy might indicate, you prefer satisfaction through the infliction of pain, we have a choice selection of very special equipment. And people in all categories who are willing, at a price, to submit to—ah—whatever you prefer."

"*Any* category?" Crag asked.

"Any, Sir. The Luxor prides itself on being able to please."

Crag said, "I like hotel managers. You might drop up yourself sometimes. And bring a corkscrew."

He walked into the dining room. A girl in a costume so abbreviated as to be almost nonexistent met him smilingly, led him to a table and took his order for a drink. He looked around and saw that all the waitresses were similarly undressed, and wondered vaguely what the floor show could offer to distract attention from the waitresses. Then the floor show started, and he saw. After a while he got up in disgust and walked out of the dining room and out of the hotel. A few blocks away he found a restaurant that specialized in food instead of sex; he ordered a big meal and ate it.

Then, over a cigarette and a brandy, he wondered if he should go back to the Luxor only long enough to get the change from his thousand-dollar bill and pick up his luggage. But he decided not to; any hotel in Mars City would be almost as bad if it was big enough and luxurious enough to provide the kind of quarters he wanted. And by now he probably had enough of a reputation at the Luxor that he'd be left alone as long as he stayed in his own suite. The door had a good solid bolt that he could use and privacy was all he wanted for his binge. He could, of course, go to a cheap hotel like the one he'd stayed in the night before he'd taken off with Olliver for the asteroid belt, but a single cheap room would be depressing and since he had so much money he might as well have the best quarters he could buy, even if he wasn't interested in all the sex and other vice—except drinking—offered with it.

What good was money if he didn't spend it?

Or maybe that was what was wrong with him, the fact that he *had* money. A criminal with money is an unemployed man, with nothing in life to interest him—until he's spent it and again has incentive to start casing another job. Maybe he should throw or gamble the money away and start working again. But that was ridiculous; he'd have admitted to himself that the new money he'd be working for would be worthless to him too. He'd be admitting to himself that he not only had no reason for stealing, but none for living.

Well, *did* he have?

There was only one answer to that, and it was to get drunk, so what was he waiting for?

He went back to the Luxor and to his suite; he put out the "Do Not Disturb" sign and bolted the door.

He went to the bar and started getting drunk. Slowly—he didn't want to knock himself out right away; he wanted to enjoy the drinking—but very thoroughly. Dawn found him still at it, pacing like a caged tiger up and down the salon with a glass in his hand. But not staggering, never spilling a drop, except down his throat. Drunk but under control, not blind drunk or raging drunk.

Only once had he interrupted himself, an hour before when the bar's supply of *woji* had run out. He was on a *woji* binge and didn't want to switch drinks so phoned down to the desk and asked that a case of it be sent up to restock the bar. But he hadn't wanted to see anyone or have anyone see him, so he'd unlocked the door and taken down the sign and then had gone into the bathroom and taken a shower. When he'd dressed and come out again the liquor was there. He'd relocked the door, put back the sign and started drinking again.

It was noon when he reached the stage of violence. He smashed gambling equipment, broke bottles, kicked in the eight-foot-wide television screen.

After that, he slept a while, woke feeling horrible and started drinking again. He lost track of time. Whenever he slept he had no way of knowing whether it was for a few minutes or for many hours. Nor could he even guess—or care about—the lengths of the periods when he drank. Sometimes it was light and sometimes it was dark, and neither mattered.

Nothing mattered except staying drunk and not thinking.

But not thinking about what? His mind shied away from that. Besides, he still hated her; the fact that she was dead couldn't change that. She was, or had been, a woman.

Then came the time when he awakened feeling nauseated and weak, and he knew the binge was over. He sat up on the edge of the bed—the one in the smaller bedroom—and picked up the phone, asked the day and the hour. He'd been drunk four days; again it was early evening, as it had been when he'd started his drinking. He made it to the bathroom and was sick. After that he felt better; he showered, shaved and put on clean clothes.

He looked around the suite and guessed the damage he'd done at close to a thousand dollars, which probably meant they'd charge him twice that. Which didn't matter; maybe the sooner his half million was gone the better. He'd have to figure ways of spending money; thus far he'd hardly made a dent in it.

Maybe gambling would be the answer, if he could find an honest game so he could enjoy it. But finding an honest gambling game in Mars City—or in most other places in the system—was almost as hard as finding an honest woman. Maybe there wasn't any such thing. There was no honesty anywhere, not only not in gambling or women but not in politics, business or anything else.

He went downstairs, and stopped at the desk. Carleton, the manager, wasn't on duty, but Crag told the clerk that a hurricane had struck his suite and that the hotel should make repairs immediately and bill him for them. He'd be gone a few hours and wanted the suite ready for use again when he got back. The clerk told him, "Yes, Sir."

He walked to the restaurant where he'd last eaten four days ago. He wasn't hungry but he forced himself to eat a fair meal and felt better. Only his mind still felt dull.

Walking, and the cool Martian night air, would cure that. And perhaps, now that he'd eaten, one pick-up drink. Besides, he had to kill time before going back to the hotel unless he wanted to be there while they were repairing or replacing the things he'd smashed.

He walked. Across the night and across the city he walked, and felt his mind clearing and his strength returning. He hated weakness, in himself or anyone else but especially in himself.

He passed a good many bars before he chose one for his pick-up drink, a plain simple bar that might have come out of the old days of a few centuries before. And was pleased when he entered it to see that he'd guessed right; there were no women there, and no homosexuals. Besides a bartender there were only two customers in the place, seated together at a table sipping drinks and talking quietly together.

Crag crossed to the bar and took a stool. The big lantern-jawed bartender moved down the bar opposite him without speaking. Crag ordered his drink and got it, having momentary trouble finding a bill small enough for a small bar like this one to be able to cash. He remembered he was trying to spend money, not to save it, and told the bartender to have a drink with him.

The bartender thanked him and poured a second drink. He reached behind him and flicked the switch of a radio. "May be a newscast on," he said.

There was, but it was a political discussion; the announcer was discussing probabilities and possibilities in the coming elections—just as though he meant what he was saying, as though he didn't know that there weren't any possibilities or probabilities, that the results of elections had already by now been decided in closed conferences between the leaders of the two big parties and that the casting and counting of votes was only a formality.

Crag said a four-letter word and the lantern-jawed bartender nodded. "Yeah, it's hogwash," he said. "I was hoping there'd be something on the new planet, but that would have been at the start of the 'cast. Well, I heard the report on it a couple hours ago; guess there hasn't anything much happened since then." He reached back to turn off the radio and then stayed his hand.

The newscaster was saying: "From Earth. The great Judge Olliver is reported missing in space. Olliver's private spaceship, a J-14 class ship, cleared from Mars City two weeks ago, presumably to return to Earth. Olliver was accompanied by his wife and his personal pilot. The ship has not been reported as landing on Earth or elsewhere, and since it carried supplies for three people for a period not to exceed ten days, it can only be presumed that..."

"Hell," he said, "that's one guy in politics who *might* have been straight. Say, what's your idea on this new planet business?"

"I haven't any," Crag said. "What's yours?"

"Damn if I know. Why should I, when even the science boys ain't got an idea what's going on. Oh, they got theories; they always got theories. But none of them makes any sense. The one thing they can't admit is that something goes on they can't understand. 'Nother drink?"

Crag said, "Thanks, no. I'm leaving now."

He got down off the stool and started for the door. There was a click and Crag recognized the sound and its source and reacted instantaneously; he saved his life by dropping so fast that the shot missed him. The click had been the lock of the door he'd been walking toward and it had been electrically activated from behind the bar.

The place was a deadfall, as some small quiet bars were, especially ones near the outskirts of a big city, as this one was. In such a place, a solitary customer didn't leave alive if he was foolish enough to be well dressed and to flash a roll of big denomination bills, as Crag had. He saw now, even as he fell, that the two customers who'd been seated at the table when he'd entered were no longer there; they'd happened to leave quietly while he'd been listening to the newscast or to the bartender.

The second drink the bartender had just asked him if he'd wanted would, no doubt, have been a poisoned one. Since he'd turned it down and started for the door, the bartender had fallen back upon his second line of offense; he'd activated the lock of the outer door by remote control and had picked up and used a weapon he'd had ready behind the bar.

The weapon, Crag could see now, from the floor, was an antique sawed-off shotgun, still—if you didn't mind noise, and this bar like most was doubtless soundproofed—as dangerous a weapon as existed for close or medium range shooting. It was being lowered now, the bartender was trying to line it up on Crag again before he pulled the second trigger.

But Crag was rolling fast toward the bar and close enough to it now so the gun couldn't aim at him, unless the bartender climbed up on the bar. And running footsteps behind the bar told Crag that the bartender was coming around the end of the bar—and which end he was coming around. Crag sat up, facing that way, his metal left hand gripped in his good right one, and his right arm cocked to throw.

It scored a bull's-eye in the bartender's face as he came around the end and before he could even begin to aim the shotgun.

That was the end of the fight; it had lasted less than three seconds, and the bartender was dead.

Crag got back his hand and dusted himself off. He went back of the bar to the cash register and found a little more than a hundred dollars. But in the bartender's pocket he found proof that the man had made a good haul, and recently. There were eight thousand-dollar bills. Crag grimaced, and then laughed at himself for doing so. He was getting ahead of the game instead of behind; his total expenditures out of the half million, even counting the damage to his suite for which he'd not yet paid, would be less than the eight thousand he'd just found.

Rather than risk being seen leaving the place, he left by a back door into an alley.

Back at the hotel a clerk, not the manager, was on duty at the desk. But he told Crag that the damage in his suite was repaired and presented him a bill. The bill was only slightly higher than Crag had guessed it would be; he paid it, and another thousand in advance.

"Thank you, Mr. Ah," the clerk said. "If there is anything—?"

There wasn't anything else he wanted, Crag assured him.

In his suite, he wandered around for a while and then turned on the radio in the salon; it was a few minutes before the hour and there would be a newscast on the hour. He suffered through a commercial and then sat down as the newscaster started talking.

"First the latest reports on the new planet forming in the asteroid belt—or in what was the asteroid belt.

"The planet is forming with incredible rapidity. It is estimated that nine tenths of all the former asteroids are now a part of it. It is currently approximately the size and mass of Mars, and will be slightly larger when the remaining free asteroids have crashed into it—as, within another four to six hours, all of them will have done. Those behind it in its orbit are accelerating speed so they will crash into it; those ahead of it in its orbit are decelerating and it will overtake them.

"The planet is revolving, but the period of revolution, even if it has as yet stabilized, cannot be determined until the clouds of dust thrown up by the crashing of the arriving asteroids have settled sufficiently to make the surface visible. The fact that this dust stays suspended in clouds is proof that the new planet, incredible as this may seem, already has an atmosphere. Because of the thickness of the dust an accurate spectroscopic examination cannot be made as yet, but the atmosphere definitely contains oxygen and will probably be breathable.

"Observations, spectroscopic and otherwise, are now being made from spaceships only a few hundred thousand miles away. Landings and exploration will be made as soon as the solar council deems them to be safe.

"No decision has been made yet on a name for the new planet. Majority opinion favors giving the honor of naming it to Bellini, the astronomer who, through the big scope on Luna, first observed the perturbation of the orbit of the asteroid Ceres. His report focused attention upon the asteroid belt and led to the discovery of what was happening there."

The newscast switched to politics and Crag shut it off.

He wondered if there might be a picture of the new planet on video; surely they'd be scanning it from the ships out there observing from so relatively close. He opened the double doors behind which was the big video screen, flicked the switch and backed away from it while it warmed up.

The set hummed and brilliant colors flashed on the screen; then the hum turned into music—if one could call it that—and the colors became a larger-than-life closeup of a beautiful young man with blond ringlets of hair, plucked eyebrows and full sensuous lips that were crooning:

Jet up! Jet down! On a slow ship to Venus!
Honey-wunny-bunny...

Calmly and soberly, without anger, Crag walked to the screen and kicked it in.

He went to the bar and poured himself a short nightcap, found himself yawning before he finished drinking it, and went to bed as soon as he'd finished it.

And dreamed, but in the morning did not remember any of the things he had dreamed. Which was just as well, for being Crag he would have been disgusted with himself for having dreamed them.

The next day he spent walking, refamiliarizing himself with the downtown business section of Mars City. He went to the two banks at which he'd left part of his money before leaving Mars with Olliver a couple of weeks before. He'd left it there because he hadn't trusted Olliver. But he didn't trust the banks either and decided now that he'd rather have his money in cash. True, there was a chance of his being killed and robbed, as he had almost been last night, but if he was killed it might as well be for a large sum as a relatively small one; whatever was left wasn't going to do him any good.

But he found that he had failed to realize how bulky half a million would be. Even with most of it in ten-thousand-dollar bills, the largest denomination available except for banking transactions, it made a stack of bills an inch thick. Even divided among several pockets he found it awkward to carry. So that evening he hid most of it in his suite, a hundred thousand dollars in each of four caches. He used ingenuity and imagination in finding those caches in places where it was almost impossible for them to be found, even by a person deliberately searching.

It killed the evening for him.

CHAPTER NINE

He went out again the next day and found himself gravitating into the spacemen's quarter, which was just north of the main downtown district. Spacemen did hang out there—especially when they were broke or nearly broke—but they made up only a small fraction of the floating population. In character it was a tenderloin district, a Skid Row.

Crag had no business going there, he knew, for the quarter offered nothing that he couldn't have obtained elsewhere—and much more safely. In the quarter, murders, fights and robberies were everyday matters, and the police went in squads of six; they were hated so much that a lone policeman wouldn't have survived a day. Let alone a night.

Yes, it was a dangerous district for a man who was dressed expensively and was carrying almost a hundred thousand dollars in cash. Maybe that was why

Crag liked it. Danger stimulated him, made him alert and alive. Only in danger of death did he find joy in life.

Was it because, he sometimes wondered, subconsciously death was what he really wanted? Was his hatred of humanity so great, and his loneliness so great that he could find happiness only in oblivion?

Sometimes he thought so, and at least casually contemplated the simple and obvious answer. *Nephthin* would do it. *Nephthin* was difficult to obtain, but anything could be obtained if you knew the ropes and had plenty of money. Even *nephthin,* the one drug that drug peddlers hated as much as policemen did. There was no future in selling *nephthin* because it didn't build any repeat trade; you could sell only one dose to a customer because it killed him within twenty hours. It put him into a state of ecstasy for a while that was more intense by a hundred times than any other drug could achieve, and then put him in a berserker rage in which he went out and killed as many people as he could before being killed himself. If he wasn't killed, if he was caught and restrained instead, he died just the same—but still in ecstasy, no matter what was being done to him. It was a perfect finish for a man who wanted, for whatever reason, to go out in a blaze of ecstatic glory, especially if he hated people and liked the idea of taking a few, or a dozen, of them along with him, so it was understandable why the sale or even the possession of *nephthin* had been legislated to be a crime punishable by nothing less than twenty years' labor on Callisto, or the psycher. Even most hardened criminals and dope peddlers took a dim view of it—unless they themselves felt inclined to sample its pleasures, in which case of course they had nothing to lose.

But oddly, although he would be perfectly content to be dead (and can the dead be otherwise than content?), Crag had no active desire to die. Not, at least, by his own hand.

He remembered a book, a very old one that he had read once, about the hunting of tigers in a part of Earth once known as India; it had told of a killer tiger, a man-eater, which had terrorized an Indian province for years and killed hundreds of people. To the terrified natives it had been known as "The Moaner" because of the sound it made constantly when it prowled near a village at night. When a white hunter, the author of the book, finally killed it, he had examined the tiger and found a very old and deep-seated infection; the bone was decayed and the flesh around it rotten and pulpy. For years every step the tiger had taken had been excruciating agony, yet he had prowled and killed and eaten. Tigers don't commit suicide, not even with *nephthin.*

Crag tried gambling, but there wasn't much in it for him. The big games, like the ones in the gambling rooms of the Luxor, were so ridiculously crooked that there was no point, no enjoyment, in bucking them. He might as well have made a bonfire of the money and enjoyed its warmth. He went to the Luxor's main gambling salon once, but only once, the second day after he'd finished his drinking binge. For a while he drew cards in a *mara* game at a hundred dollars a card and managed to lose a few thousand dollars but the dealing was so obviously sleight of hand that finally, in utter disgust, he slapped his metal left hand down, not too hard, on the hand of the dealer who was passing him a card. The dealer screamed and dropped two cards where only one should have been, and then stepped back whimpering to nurse his broken hand. Crag walked out, wondering whether the hotel would bill him for *that*. But the hotel didn't; too many people had seen that extra card.

For a while he gambled in Spacetown dives. Honest games could be found there, if one looked hard enough. But spacemen and the hangers-on of Spacetown aren't rich enough to play for high stakes and, after a while, low-stake play bored Crag because it didn't matter whether he won or lost.

He drank a lot, but not too much at any one time or place, never letting himself get out of control. The go-for-drunk kind of drinking was something Crag did only rarely and after a long period of abstinence, enforced or otherwise. He never drank while he was working on a job, or in space, but if the job or the trip took a long time he made up for it afterwards. Ordinarily he drank steadily but never to excess.

He did most of his drinking in Spacetown and found himself using the bar in his Luxor suite only for a first drink each morning and a final one each night. He considered taking a room in Spacetown—which had no luxury hotels, but a few fairly nice ones—but decided against it. Knowing full well that it was ridiculous of him to keep so expensive a suite when he made so little use of it, he still kept it. It cost money and when he faced things frankly he admitted to himself that the sooner he got rid of his money the less unhappy he'd be. While it lasted he had no reason for stealing more, and he was out of work.

He was like a tiger shut in an abattoir, surrounded by meat he doesn't have to hunt for. He can sate himself and keep himself sated, but pretty soon he comes to wish he was back in the jungle where the hunt and the kill comes before the feast. A sated tiger is only part a tiger, but still it does not kill for wanton enjoyment. A criminal with all the money he needs is no longer a criminal, but unless he is psychopathic he does not plot to get more.

Nor, unless he is psychopathic, does he deliberately throw away the money he has simply to restore his incentive. Because by doing so he negates to himself the value of money so no future sum of it would be worth having either, and willy-nilly destroys his incentive, his raison d'être, just as effectively.

No, the only thing Crag could do with the money was to *spend* it, and continuing to live at the Luxor was a help in that direction.

Too bad he'd never been interested in wealth per se, or in power. But he'd never considered money as other than something to spend, and power meant politics and he'd always hated politics, even before he'd become a criminal.

There were newscasts, of course. He never used the set in his suite any more but from time to time he couldn't avoid hearing or seeing the latest news on a set operating in whatever bar he happened to be in at the time.

On one of his early trips into Spacetown he was sitting in a small bar, one that was a bit more crowded than he liked although he had plenty of elbow room as he sat on the bar and stared into his glass of *woji*.

Suddenly the bartender flicked a switch under the bar and a radio blared into music, if you could call it music.

Crag reached across the bar and touched the man's arm. "Shut it off," he said.

The bartender met his gaze. "Mister, you ain't the only one in here. Some of them like that stuff and want it."

"I don't," Crag said, and his touch on the man's arm turned into a grip. "Shut it off."

The bartender winced and his eyes, looking into Crag's, saw something there that changed his tone of voice. He said, "Mister, I'll turn it down, but that's the best I can do. Guy down at the other end of the bar told me to turn it on and *he'll* make trouble if I turn it off. I don't know how tough you are, but he's plenty tough, as tough as they come in Mars City or anywhere else. You might make trouble if I leave it on, but I know damn well he'll mop up the place with me if I turn it off."

The bartender gently massaged his arm where Crag's hand had held it. He said hopefully, "Unless you and him want to go outside and settle it. Then I can obey whichever of you comes back in."

Crag grinned. He'd have enjoyed nothing better but he remembered he was getting into as few fights as possible these days and that anyway in this case he didn't have sufficient cause to start one.

"All right," he said. "Turn it down."

If the tough guy objected to that, then—

The bartender cut the volume to about half of what it had been. Then he said, "There's only another minute or two of that crap and then a newscast comes on. I think it's the newscast Gardin wanted me to turn it on for anyway. So what the hell."

Crag agreed, so what the hell.

He glanced toward the other end of the bar and had no difficulty in picking out which of the several men there was the one the bartender had called Gardin. There was only one of them who looked hard enough to scare a bartender. The others were space kids, cadets barely in their twenties. Gardin was more nearly like Crag, medium in size but compact, almost stocky but with a subtle suggestion of grace as well as strength. He was a little younger than Crag but not much, and he had black hair as against Crag's blond. Like Crag, he was a criminal, but the stamp of criminality showed much more obviously on him than it ever had on Crag.

The newscast came on but Crag, thinking his own thoughts, didn't hear the first part of it. But then, whether he wanted to or not, he found himself unable not to listen when the words "the new planet" penetrated his consciousness.

"...still shrouded in clouds of dust, but they seem to be thinning. However, Admiral Yates has forbidden any attempt at landing until the surface is visible from space. The landing expedition is standing by, ready, but it may be weeks before...many mysterious features, not least of which is the fact that the amount of heat radiation is entirely too high for a planet so far out from the sun; the new planet will have approximately the same temperatures and seasons as Earth, despite the fact that it is more than twice Earth's mean distance from the sun. The difference, most scientists believe, is from internal heat generated by the impact of the asteroids when they came together... *All* asteroids have now crashed into and become part of this new body; there is no loose matter of any size revolving in what was once the orbit of the asteroids and is now the orbit of the new planet.

"Current estimate of its diameter is six thousand miles, about halfway between the diameter of Mars and that of Earth. Density about five times that of water, almost the same as the density of Earth. Its gravity will be a little less than Earth's...definitely revolving but exact rate of revolution cannot be determined until the dust clouds settle and observations can be made of a fixed point on its surface...

"Pardon me for a second. I am being handed a bulletin...

"Big news, friends. The new planet has been named. Bellini of Luna Observatory, who was by acclamation of his fellow astronomers given the privilege of naming the new planet, has just announced his choice. He explains that he did not adopt a name out of mythology, since just about every mythological name was used up in naming the thousands of asteroids large enough to have been named, and he does not believe it a good idea to name the new body as a whole after any one of the smaller bodies which came together to comprise it.

"He chose therefore an arbitrary but euphonious combination of syllables, and has named the new planet—here it comes folks—Cragon. Spelled C-r-a-g-o-n—Cragon..."

Crag was leaning backward, holding onto the edge of the bar, roaring with laughter. It was the loudest, most sincere laughter he'd ever had since—since he could remember. *The little devil,* he thought. *The little devil got into an astronomer's mind and named himself after me. He thinks he's going to get me that way!*

There was a light tap on his shoulder and he quit laughing and turned around.

Gardin stood there, his face impassive but managing to look like a tightly coiled spring. He said, "Were you laughing at me, friend?"

Crag's laughter subsided, but he still chuckled slightly. "No," he said, "I wasn't. But I'll be glad to if you want me to, if it can lead to fun and games."

Gardin gestured to the bartender. "Shut it off," he said. And the radio, which was now playing music, clicked into silence.

"What *were* you laughing at?" Gardin asked gently.

Crag's eyes cooled, but not too cold. He said, "Something that's my business and too complicated to explain. But—say something funny, will you?"

Suddenly Gardin laughed too. "There isn't anything funny, is there? All right, I was off base. Forget it."

Crag said, "Unless you want to go outside, for laughs—"

"You had your laugh, whatever it was. I'll get by without. How's about a drink instead?"

"Sure," Crag said.

And he'd made a friend, or as near to a friend as he'd ever allowed himself to have.

He never learned anything about Gardin's past, but of course Gardin didn't learn anything about Crag's either. They didn't trust one another that far. At first they didn't trust one another at all, but time took care of that. Time and the fact that mounting evidence convinced each that the other wasn't on the make, at the moment. If Gardin had been broke...

But Gardin obviously wasn't broke; there was plenty of evidence for that. He was holing up, enjoying and spending a big haul. And being restless about it, too. Wanting action.

He knew these things about Gardin, as he knew Gardin knew these things about him. Oh, there were differences too; they weren't peas from a pod. Crag thought he was stronger, physically and mentally. But they never tested, or thought of testing, their physical strength. And mental strength—or will power or guts or whatever you want to call it—is something that only unexpected emergency or danger tests.

And in another way Gardin was different. He had a woman. He never mentioned whether she was his wife or not—which wouldn't have mattered to Crag in any case—but from things said from time to time, Crag gathered that they'd been together for several years. Her name was Bea, and she was a big brassy blonde. Crag found himself able to get along with her because she was so definitely someone else's property and so definitely a one-man woman. She left Crag strictly alone, the times the three of them were together. Whether this was because she was afraid of Gardin Crag didn't know, and didn't care; he did take care not to find out by ever being with her when Gardin wasn't around.

When Bea was with the two of them, Crag could almost forget that she was a woman. She drank and swore with them on equal terms, dressed modestly— for Mars City—and never coquetted, even with Gardin, when Crag was around. What they did when he wasn't around he managed not to think about.

Mostly Crag and Gardin wandered alone, although occasionally Bea went with them. Neither of them asked the other where he lived, or cared. There were places where they came to frequent when they felt like seeing one another, and that was enough.

For a while they found enjoyment—or surcease—in gambling with one another, head-to-head poker, *maraja,* and other games that two can play with a borrowed deck of cards in a quiet back room of a bar with no kibitzers. For a while the games ran even, and got higher. But then, as they got higher, Crag found himself winning more and more often. He knew Gardin well enough by then to be able to read subtleties of expression and manner well enough to know when to be cautious and when to plunge.

And suddenly he had about eighty thousand dollars of Gardin's money in front of him and suddenly he knew by the tiny signs that showed through the calm outwardness of Gardin's face, that Gardin was hurting, was going broke. And that quite likely the stake Gardin and Bea were living on was more likely in the neighborhood of a hundred thousand than half a million. And Crag didn't want their money; he had enough troubles of his own. Carefully he started losing, not so suddenly as to be obvious and not all in one game. But when they were back about even, several games later, he lost interest in gambling. And so did Gardin. After that they played only occasionally and then for relatively small stakes at games in which the skill and fun of beating your opponent is more important than the amount you win.

And bets, of course. They were constantly killing time by making bets on ridiculous and irrelevant things, usually five or ten dollar bets, but once in a while going higher when the thing they were betting on wasn't pure luck but was something on which they held divergent opinions. If they were alone in a bar, for instance, they'd sit in the middle and bet ten dollars on whether the next customer to enter it would go to the bar at the right or the left side of them. Whether the next customer to enter would be barefoot or wearing sandals—arguing over odds according to the weather and the time of day. If it had ever rained on Mars they would have bet on which raindrop of two would first reach the bottom of a pane. Ridiculous things, but the betting gave them something to talk about, for neither ever talked about himself, and talking about irrelevant things helped kill time.

Time was the enemy, although that was something neither of them talked about.

Once Crag took Gardin to his suite at the Luxor. Gardin had looked about him and whistled. "Where's the button you push for the dancing girls?" he wanted to know, and when Crag didn't answer, he asked, "You're a woman-hater, aren't you?" And when Crag didn't answer that, he let the subject drop.

Gardin wandered around the suite, hands in his pockets until he discovered the pornography room. Then he took his hands out of his pockets to look at the books and run a few of the tapes. Crag heard him chuckling to himself and saw a look on his face that disgusted him. "Come on out," he said. "Take some of those damn things home with you if you want, keep 'em, but don't read 'em here."

Gardin came out. His face was ugly now. "Pretty bluenose, aren't you?" he asked.

Crag shrugged. "What do you want to drink?"

"*Woji.* Unless you've got some *nephthin* around—wouldn't mind trying that once. No, I'm kidding."

Crag opened two *woji* bottles and handed one to Gardin with a glass.

Gardin poured himself a drink and put the bottle down by the chair he was sitting in. In a changed voice he said, "I'm feeling lousy, Crag. What's wrong with me?"

"You're getting soft."

"Soft?" Gardin stood up quickly. "Bet you a grand I can take you, here and now."

Crag grinned and for a moment something leaped inside him. Then he said, "No bet, Gardin. Sit down and drink your drink. I don't play Queensberry rules and you don't either. Once we got started if I didn't kill you you'd kill me. Let's not get into that, for a lousy grand bet or any other bet."

Gardin sat down but his face turned sullen. "Quit needling me then."

"I'm not needling you, just told you the truth. Hell, it's true about me too. I'm getting soft." But Crag didn't really believe it about himself.

Gardin was pacing around the suite again. He opened the double door that hid the six-by-eight video screen and whistled at the sight of it. "Boy, a big one. And that reminds me. Know what today is?"

"What?"

"Day they're going to land on Cragon. Been following the newscasts?"

"Not since yesterday. What gives?"

"The dust is gone. Didn't seem to settle, just to vanish all at once. And— this is impossible, but they say it's true—it's a finished planet."

Crag puffed a cigarette into flame. "What do you mean, a finished planet?"

"Not a raw one. Vegetation—trees and everything. Pretty much like Earth except it's mostly land instead of mostly ocean. But there are lakes and riv- ers—fresh water, and that doesn't make sense."

"Why doesn't it?"

"Streams and rivers get that way after rains, making channels for themselves over thousands of years of runoff from higher ground. Damn it, the planet's only two weeks old. How could the planet have formed river beds already?"

"Maybe it's precocious," Crag said.

"Whatever it is, it's not natural. Kid about it if you like, Crag, but even the toughest of the scientists are beginning to admit that this is something that couldn't happen naturally. Some of them are frank about saying they're scared stiff."

"Of what?"

"They don't know, and that's what scares them." Gardin turned back to the video screen. "I'd forgotten till I saw this, but it's about time for them to make a 'cast on that landing. Let's watch it. Okay?"

"Okay," Crag said. Gardin turned the switch and the big screen leaped into color and sound, an almost naked Amazonian woman singing of the joys of a certain unmentionable perversion.

"Shut the damn thing off," Crag said.

"Okay, but it's only for a minute—" Gardin reached for the switch but before he could turn it the song ended and the picture faded.

And on the big screen flashed the distant picture of a planet seen from space. A planet that, except for the contour of the continents, could have been Earth. Blue oceans, continents mottled green and brown, white polar regions.

"We show you Cragon," said an unctuous voice, "newest planet of the sun. The view of it that you see is being 'cast from the flagship *Dorai*, and is from two hundred thousand miles out. We shall maintain this position until a re- port has been received from the scoutship *Andros*, which is even now proceeding down to make the first landing on the surface. In a few minutes—it will be at least another twenty before the *Andros* enters the atmosphere of Cragon—we will switch you to the scoutship so you can be *with* them at the very moment of landing. The scoutship is manned by Captain Burke and Lieutenant Laidlaw. We regret that the scoutship is too small to carry transspace video equipment so the view upon your screen will continue to be broadcast from here, from the flagship. But let us introduce you via tridi photos to the two men aboard the scoutship while we contact them for you by radio. Captain Burke."

A tridi still of a middle-aged man with hard eyes but a weak chin flashed on the screen. "Are you ready, Captain?" The lips of the photograph didn't move but a voice said, "Yes, Burke reporting, sir."

"Anything to report yet?"

"Only that we are descending slowly and cautiously, in accordance with instructions. We are a hundred miles up, still well above the outer reaches of the atmosphere."

"Good. Then there is time for you to introduce your companion. Please put Lieutenant Laidlaw on."

Another tridi still flashed on. A very handsome young man with curly black hair. You would have expected his voice to be effeminate, and it was. "Lieutenant Laidlaw, sir."

"You are the one assigned to do the reporting while your captain navigates, Lieutenant. Am I right?"

"Yes, sir."

"Good. Then please remain at the microphone." The tridi photograph changed again to the distant view of a world revolving in space. "Have you chosen a point for your landing, Lieutenant?"

"Yes, sir. Approximately in the center of the day side, which is at the moment approximately in the center of the largest continent. Near the shore of a large lake—I think I can tell you which one. We have a monitor set here and are receiving your picture. Do you see a lake, almost exactly in the middle of your picture, that is roughly triangular in shape?"

"Yes, Lieutenant."

"Well, we plan on landing near the bottom point—the southern point of that triangle. You'll notice that a stream, or what looks like one, enters the lake at that point. And the area around the stream is green, but only a short distance from it is the edge of a large brown area. We figure that should be a good central point of observation. We can check the water of the stream and the water of the lake. And we can see what kind of vegetation makes up the green area and whether the brown area is sand or rock or what. Also our thermocouple observations indicate a temperature of about seventy degrees Fahrenheit, a nearly optimum temperature. We've got to land somewhere, and that looks like as good an all-around spot as any."

"Thank you, Lieutenant. And your altitude now?"

"A little under eighty miles. We're settling slowly, under antigrav."

Crag chuckled.

The Lieutenant's voice said, "Of course we'll make final observations before we make actual planetfall. We're now descending on automatics set to stop us at five miles. From there our telescopes will give us a very close view of the terrain. And by that time, we'll be within the atmosphere and can make a thorough check that will tell us whether it's breathable or whether we'll have to wear our suits."

"Thank you, Lieutenant Laidlaw. And now we will have a word from Admiral of the Grand Fleet Johnson, who is right here beside me aboard..."

Crag was chuckling again and Gardin turned away from the screen to look at him. "What's funny?" he wanted to know.

"The whole thing," Crag said. "They aren't going to land—or if they do they'll never take off again."

"Why not?"

"Not invited. Just watch."

Gardin grinned. "There's an old phrase—put your money where your mouth is. How much you want to bet?"

Crag shrugged. "You name it. But you'll lose."

Gardin was fumbling through bills. "Getting a little short, but I'll take a thousand of that. Or were you kidding?"

For answer Crag took a thousand-dollar bill out of his pocket and dropped it on the floor between them. Gardin covered it with ten hundreds.

The bulldog face of the Admiral was on the screen. "...seems no danger whatsoever, but the fleet takes no chances. Before those men leave the scoutship, the area will have been surveyed for every possible danger. It seems impossible that a newly formed planet could possibly harbor life, inimical or otherwise, yet the possibility will not be overlooked. There are mysteries to which we do not have the answer—especially the mystery of how Cragon was formed and how it could so incredibly quickly have acquired atmosphere, a well-developed topography and, especially in so short a time, what is almost certainly vegetation. It is because of these mysteries that we shall not land a big ship and risk the lives of thousands.

"Captain Burke and Lieutenant Laidlaw have volunteered for this mission and know they are risking their lives, even though no risk *seems* apparent. But a new planet always is an unknown quantity and this applies doubly in the current case, when the details of its formation are so mysterious, so sudden that one might almost think it was the deliberate act of an intelligent entity.

"However, no difficulty is anticipated in making the landing. All factors are known there. The biggest question mark is the atmosphere. Will it be breathable as is, or will we have to set up atmosphere plants as we have on Mars and Venus and under the Callisto domes? Spectographic analysis—the only analysis we can make until we get there—is encouraging. Oxygen is present in approximately the same proportion as in the atmosphere of Earth; so is carbon dioxide. Atmospheric density is a little less than that of Earth, but only slightly so; Kaperhorn estimates that its density at sea level is approximately that of Earth's at an altitude of one mile, the altitude of, say, Albuquerque or Denver.

"The element of uncertainty lies in the fact that there are certain trace elements which we have been unable to analyze completely at a distance, and there is of course the possibility that one of these trace elements may be poisonous. The scoutship has no chemical laboratory aboard, but does have cages of canaries and other small experimental animals, the use of which will enable Captain Burke to decide whether, for a short period, it will be safe to leave the ship without suits.

"But with or without suits they will explore the area immediately around their landing point—"

Crag made a rude noise. "Another *woji*, Gardin?"

Gardin nodded and Crag went to the bar, opened and brought back two fresh bottles. The sphere of the new planet was still on the screen but the voice of the Admiral had been supplanted by soft music. "What gives?" Crag asked. "Did he run out of crap to talk about?"

"Guess so. They're filling in until a report comes from the scoutship. Just a few minutes; it's nearing the top of the atmosphere now." Gardin glanced down at the money on the floor between them. "Crag, what was the crazy idea of making that ridiculous bet? You're practically giving me a grand."

"Maybe," Crag said.

"Unless you've got inside dope, and I don't see how you could have, but...you suggested the bet. I'm a sucker to bet a man at his own game."

Crag grinned at him. "Want to call it off? I'll give you a chance now, before the scoutship comes on."

Gardin hesitated a moment, then shook his head. "No, leave it lay." He took a long pull from his bottle.

The music stopped and the video spoke again with a human voice. "Lieutenant Laidlaw speaking from the scoutship. Captain Burke is at the controls. We are descending slowly, just entering the upper atmosphere of Cragon. That is, our instruments show a detectable pressure, although still not much above a laboratory vacuum. We are approximately fifty miles high and at the moment we are descending at the rate of five miles a minute, although we shall slow that rate of descent within a few minutes to avoid overheating the hull from atmospheric friction.

"Forty-five miles. We can see from here—I think with certainty—that the dark green areas of land of the surface really are forests. At least they give very much the same appearance as a dense Earth forest gives from the same height.

"We're thirty miles high now, almost into the stratosphere. But—Captain Burke is stopping our descent; we are holding position at this height, motionless. What's wrong, Captain?"

In the moment of silence Crag asked, "Want to double that bet?"

Gardin shook his head. "But how the hell—?"

"Never mind how the hell. Maybe I do have inside information. If you don't want to double it, I'll give you one last chance to call it off."

Gardin didn't hesitate. He scooped up the handful of bills, handed Crag his thousand and stuffed the ten hundreds into his own pocket. Crag grinned. "Now we'll see how he's going to work it."

"How who's going to work what?"

"Shhh," said Crag, as a different voice sounded from the video.

"Captain Burke taking the mike. And apologizing for the fact that the Lieutenant and I have been talking off mike for a moment. This is not an emergency, but something that must be investigated before we descend any lower. Something seems to be wrong with our air-conditioning system.

"At the point at which I stopped our descent I happened to glance at the cage in which we have three canaries—the use of which the Lieutenant explained to you a few minutes ago. And noticed that one of them is lying on the bottom of the cage and the other two seemed to be—well, in trouble.

"Obviously something has gone wrong with our air-conditioning system and we should not complete the descent until we have fixed it. The Lieutenant, who is more familiar than I with that part of the mechanism of the ship, is now investigating. I'll have his report—or give him back the microphone—in just a moment."

Just a moment passed. The Captain's voice spoke again. "Something strange here. Lieutenant Laidlaw reports that he can find nothing wrong with the equipment, that the indicators show proper proportion of oxygen and fail to indicate the presence of any foreign gas, and yet two of the canaries are now dead and the other apparently dying. The hamsters and the white rats are huddling together and breathing hard, showing signs of discomfort.

"And he and I seem to *smell,* very faintly, a foreign odor. I haven't checked with the lieutenant on this but I would classify it as something vaguely like sulphuric acid—but *sweetish,* as well. If you can imagine a mixture of sulphuric acid and gardenias—well, that's the way I'd describe it.

"Yet this ship is airtight—we are bringing in, even for processing purposes, nothing of the atmosphere outside, tenuous as it is at a height of thirty miles. It must be something wrong right here in the ship itself. There is no way it can conceivably concern the planet we are near. There is no way—"

"Captain Burke!" It was the voice of the bulldog-faced Admiral aboard the flagship. "Raise ship at once. Completely outside that atmosphere."

"Yes, Admiral."

"Keep reporting."

"Yes, Admiral... We're rising now. Thirty-three miles now, thirty-five. Lieutenant Laidlaw is staggering across the cabin toward me but he seems to be all right, maybe just off balance. And my headache—I didn't have time to mention it—is going away. Forty miles. I think we're out of it now, sir. Or our air-conditioning system is functioning properly again. Shall we try again, sir?"

"Report back to the fleet at once. Before we make another attempt, with a live or a drone ship, we want to check yours thoroughly. As well as your air-conditioning system, we want to check you and the Lieutenant, and those canaries."

"Yes, sir."

Gardin looked at Crag, and Crag laughed. He had, Crag realized, laughed more in the last half hour than he had for a long time.

"Bet you the drone ship doesn't land there either," Crag said.

"No bet." Gardin went over and shut off the video. "No use keeping on watching now. It'll be at least another day before they get a drone rigged up. Crag, what's it all about?"

Crag shook his head slowly. "Sorry. To tell you that I'd have to tell you too much about other things."

"It isn't something we can cash in on?"

Crag shook his head again. "Game of gin, to kill some time?"

Gardin stood up. "Sorry, I've got business. You might not be seeing me so much for a while, Crag. That thousand of mine you almost took—and thanks for calling off the bet, since you must have known it was a sure thing—was getting near rock bottom. I'm going to have to scrape up some more."

"Good luck," Crag told him.

CHAPTER TEN

Crag didn't see Gardin for longer than a week, although he continued to frequent the same places where he and Gardin had gone together. He didn't go to Gardin's hotel for two reasons; one, he knew that if Gardin was still there and wanted to see him, Gardin would do the looking up, and two, that Gardin might have left the hotel but left his woman there to wait for him. And he didn't want to see Gardin's brassy blonde without Gardin around. Preferably not even then.

He found himself following the newscasts about the new planet. None of them, after the fiasco of the would-be first landing, were telecast; they were merely reports. The space fleet couldn't hold back the facts, but they could avoid making fools of themselves by letting the public *watch* the failures.

No alien gas had been found in the hull of the scoutship that had been recalled from the first attempt. The only concrete evidence found in it was the bodies of the two dead canaries and the fact that the third canary had been very ill. So had the hamsters, the mice and the two humans. The Captain and the Lieutenant had spent hours after their return recovering from nausea.

The air-conditioning equipment had been found to be functioning perfectly and autopsies on the dead canaries had given no indication whatsoever of the cause of death.

The only conclusion the investigating scientists could draw was that there must be a hitherto unknown ingredient in the atmosphere of Cragon, one so deadly that even in the rarefied atmosphere thirty miles above the surface it could penetrate the solid hull of a spaceship, possibly by some process akin to osmosis, and kill or injure the occupants. Space suits seemed to offer no answer; anything that can penetrate the foot-thick hull of a ship can certainly penetrate the airtight fabric of a space suit.

Two days after the initial failure at landing, a drone ship was sent down to land. Since the manned ship had brought back no sample of the deadly gas— only of its effects—it was assumed that it had leaked out again on the return trip across space and that the same thing would happen to any that the drone ship picked up, in whatever type container. So instead of containers, the drone was packed with chemical testing equipment, some of it automatic and some operable by remote control, that would make many and delicate tests *in situ,* while the drone rested on the surface of the planet, and record the results for later analysis.

The only trouble was that the drone ship never landed. Never, in fact, got into even the most tenuous upper reaches of the atmosphere. Cragon changed tactics. Well over two hundred miles above the surface of the planet the drone ship—*bounced.*

It had hit an impenetrable force field.

Not even unmanned rockets were welcome to land on Cragon.

Crag chuckled to himself.

That ended the official telecasts of the attempts to land on Cragon. The admiralty made a very carefully worded announcement to explain the news blackout that indicated that the admiralty was scared stiff.

"It now seems possible if not probable that the solar system has been invaded by a race of aliens. The formation of a new planet from the debris of the solar system was too strange and too sudden to be accounted for by any theory of astrophysics known to man; it is therefore considered possible that it was accomplished deliberately by an alien race from outside the system.

"That the intention of this race is not friendly is strongly indicated by the fact that they have refused peaceable contact, which could have been established had they let us land freely. A force field is not known in nature and must therefore be artificial. So must a poisonous gas which penetrates the solid hull of a ship, but which vanishes completely when that ship is outside the atmosphere.

"While the planet Cragon has, to our knowledge, committed no overt act against the rest of the solar system, and while therefore a state of war need not be assumed, a *state of emergency* must be declared. A state of *protective* emergency. Since it is possible that advance spies of the race of Cragonians are already among us, this will require henceforth a strict censorship of..."

The Solar Council immediately decreed a state of emergency, and doubled taxes on low incomes (and increased them slightly on high incomes) to finance whatever plans they were making. Which, of course, could not be made public because of the possibility of Cragonian spies.

But rumors were rife, especially in the spacemen's quarter, where rumors, especially concerning matters in space, were uncannily accurate. Although there was strict security on any reports from the asteroid belt that could have reached Marsfleet headquarters from the vicinity of Cragon, somehow the contents of those reports became known around the quarter almost within minutes of the time they could have been received. And known, Crag knew, correctly.

The second drone ship hadn't tried gentle descent on antigrav; it had blasted down at the surface with all rockets flaring; it had bounced off just the same— because of its tremendous speed crumpled into a single massive ingot of incandescent metal. Rockets with atomic warheads exploded on contact with the force field and subsequent telescopic-spectroscopic examination of the planet under the point of contact indicated that not even any of their radiation had penetrated that field to reach the atmosphere under it.

Cragon was off bounds.

And the spy scare grew. The military didn't know whether Cragon was populated or not or, if it was, what its inhabitants looked like—but the military was afraid and because it couldn't reach Cragon, it was looking for something it *could* reach, and that meant spies. Transients, other people who couldn't explain themselves readily, were picked up for questioning, and if their answers weren't ready and provable, they were questioned further, under drugs or otherwise.

The fact was something for Crag to think about; even though the rich who stayed at the luxury hotels were never bothered by the police—most of them, even if they were vacationing under aliases, were too powerful for the police to risk exposing—he realized that the military might overlook that obstacle. They might figure that a Cragonian spy would deliberately pose as a wealthy debauchee for that very reason. And the military were less susceptible to intimidation and bribery than the police, especially if they thought they might be dealing with an alien enemy spy.

So Crag took a precaution he hadn't bothered with before; he visited the best forger-printer in Mars and had papers made that gave him a complete false identity and history back to birth. They wouldn't stand up under a full-scale investigation, of course, but they'd cover him in case of any spot check or other casual inquiry.

Afterwards he wondered if he hadn't wasted the time and money, because they wouldn't protect him against any *serious* suspicion, and he'd already laid himself open to serious suspicion—if Gardin talked about him. He hadn't anticipated the spy-scare angle the day he and Gardin had watched the video of that first attempt at a landing on Cragon. He'd put himself in Gardin's hands by offering that bet of a thousand dollars at even odds that the scoutship wouldn't successfully land and take off again. How could he have known that, the military would want to know. Sure, he could tell them the truth—and admit to having killed Olliver, among other crimes.

Gardin himself might be suspicious, and if Gardin was, Crag couldn't blame him for reporting the incident. But Crag shrugged the thought off. After all, he had to take *some* chances. Did he want to live forever?

Which reminded him that he'd been taking too few chances to keep life interesting and that evening he let himself drink just a little more than usual in one of the toughest dives in the quarter and got into a fight. There's never difficulty in getting into a fight in the quarter,

He let himself be drawn into an argument, that was all, with four husky cargo handlers from the port. He didn't really know what he was arguing about but they didn't either. He let himself get argumentative about whatever it was and suddenly there was a fist coming at his face. He deflected it with his left hand and sank his right hand into the belly of the fist-thrower, who folded up like an accordion and started retching.

Crag stepped back from the bar and the other three of them came at him. He stepped under a haymaker and landed a light left to the solar plexus of the leading one, and then there were only two, but one of those two caught him a wallop on the side of the head that staggered him almost to the doorway. He came back, coming in low and using both fists like pistons and suddenly there was only one of them still interested. He was the biggest one, though, and Crag made him last a little longer by using only his right.

It had all happened so suddenly that Crag was scarcely breathing hard, although his ears rang from the one hard blow he'd taken. He walked back to the bar to pick up his drink again. The bartender, a sizable club clenched tightly in his hand and his face a bit pale, backed away.

Crag nodded at him reassuringly. "It's okay," he said. "Nobody hurt, no damage done. And you don't have to join the party unless you want to."

The bartender relaxed. Crag took the final gulp of his drink and put a bill on the bar. "Give 'em each a drink on me when they come around," he said. And left.

It had been fun while it lasted, but—

He wondered where Gardin was, what kind of a job he was casing or doing. He wondered whether if he, Crag, had been getting low on funds too, Gardin would have asked him in the deal. And whether he'd have accepted, if Gardin had. He *thought* he'd trust Gardin enough, but...

But he was a long way from being near enough broke to give him excuse to plan another job. He still had well over nine-tenths of that damned half million. Half a million dollars was a lot of money, too much money. Damn money.

Or, more accurately, he thought, damn a man who couldn't find pleasure in the spending of it.

Back in his suite, too early, he opened the doors of the big video screen and flicked it on. Not because, if there was any new news about the new planet, he'd get it here, but he was curious about what kind of a stall the government was giving the people; they'd *have* to allow the newscasters to feed the public something, whether true or not.

But the screen flashed into the picture of a handsome gray-haired commercial announcer. His smile was so disgustingly sincere that Crag waited to see what he was going to say. And stepped closer to the screen because he knew what was going to happen when he heard it.

"Are you a *necrophile?* All your problems are solved. General Plastics now brings on the market a *simulacrum* that is almost completely undetectable, except for the fact that it does not deteriorate, from a real dead body. Available in models of either sex, it sells for a low, low price. Or can be rented if, like most nonfetishist necrophiles, you prefer a change from time to time in the object of—"

Crag kicked in the screen.

Seven hundred dollars, he'd learned by now, was the cost of replacement of a screen on that video. And his suite cost two thirty and he'd managed to spend about a hundred otherwise. Another day, another thousand dollars. But even at that rate, half a million was going to last a long time. What was Gardin doing?

He went out on the balcony and stared up at the sky. The new planet wasn't in sight; it was still below the horizon. Anyway, to hell with it.

Earth was in the sky, though, and he stared at it for a while, wondering if he should go back there for a while. But why? Earth was just as corrupt, just as decadent as Mars. Neither had anything to offer that the other hadn't, except that Earth was more crowded. And just a bit better policed, which made it just a bit less dangerous than Mars.

He went back in and to the bar and got himself a drink. Was that the only answer, drink, escape? Hell, if he had nothing better to do than to escape, why didn't he kill himself and get it over with? Why, except that a tiger doesn't commit suicide, even with *nephthin,* which lets him take however-many along with him in the process.

He drank enough to make him slightly sleepy, although he didn't feel it otherwise, and went to bed.

And slept, and dreamed. About a bronze-haired beautiful woman who was his wife—and in the dream, he didn't know that she had betrayed and deserted him, because it hadn't happened yet, and he was crazy in love with her. Only gradually—and yet understandably, because in dreams things that don't make sense otherwise are understandable—she changed. Her hair stayed the same, but she became more beautiful, more and more loved—and farther and farther away from him at the same time, and across a void of space and time he was calling out to her "Judeth! Judeth!" And wasn't aware of the change, didn't know that that hadn't been his wife's name. Because in that dream all women were the woman; there was only one woman and had never been any others. And then she came to him and he put his arms around her and—in the sudden quick inconsequence of dreams he was holding in his arms a dead woman, a corpse, and then his arms were empty as the corpse disintegrated and—

The phone was buzzing.

He swung himself to the edge of the bed and picked it up. "Yes?"

"Ah—Mr. Ah. There is a telephone call for you. A woman who refuses to give her name. But she says it is very important, a matter of life and death. Shall I—?"

"Put her on." He didn't ask for privacy on the circuit, although he had a hunch who it might be and what it might be about; because asking for a closed circuit was sure to make the management curious enough to listen in, whereas otherwise they wouldn't bother. In Mars City, only one woman could be calling him here.

"Yes?" he said.

It was the voice he expected, Bea's. It said, "I don't want to give my name, but you'll know who I am when I tell you we met at—"

"I know who you are," he interrupted. "What's the matter?" Although he could guess that, too.

"Our—mutual friend. I won't mention his name, but if you recognize my voice, you know who I mean. He's in an awful jam; I don't think there's anything you can do, but—"

"Where are you? Try to tell me without naming it."

"At our apartment. But I don't think it's going to be safe here. I'd better get out right away. Can you meet me at—at the place where he and you once played *mara* with three spacemen just back from a Callisto run and they tried to work a squeeze play on you in the game and you—"

"I'll be there in ten minutes," Crag said, and put down the phone.

He threw on clothes and dashed cold water into his face. He felt—awake, with danger and action impending.

CHAPTER ELEVEN

It was a bar like any bar, except for the few swanky expensive ones in the quarter. Crag made it in ten minutes, but Bea was there before him. Had apparently just got there, for she was just sliding into a booth at the side. A big cargo walloper from the Port had seen her come in and was just swaggering over from the bar to open negotiations, whatever type of negotiations he had in mind. Crag would have liked a fight, but there wasn't the time for one, so he walked fast and got there ahead of the dock hand, spoke to Bea by name—not her right one of course—and slipped into the booth across from her. The dock hand stood a moment, irresolute, and then went back to where he'd been standing at the bar.

Crag's first question was, "Do minutes, or seconds matter?"

She leaned forward and he could see that she'd been crying, although she'd covered the signs with make-up and they wouldn't show at a distance of more than a couple of feet. "I don't think so," she said. "But I don't know what you can *do,* if anything, but he's—"

"Wait, then." Crag got out coins and pushed several into the slot of the musicon at the end of the booth, turned up the volume control. The place was too quiet, and their conversation might have carried. A voice blared at them. "I'd like to get you on a slow ship to Venus! Honey-wunny-bunny—"

Crag winced, but didn't turn down the volume. He leaned close and said, "All right, give it to me fast."

"It was a jewel job, wholesale place. Curme's, on the top floor of the Rasher building, about ten blocks north of—"

"I know where it is. Go on."

"He's caught in there, and they've got a cordon around the place, around the whole block, and helis over the roof. He must have tripped an alarm or—"

"Is he alone?"

"Yes, he was working solo. He's been casing the place for two weeks and—"

"No one knew about it—except you?"

"Right. It must have been an alarm circuit. There's *no* way they could have been tipped off. It's not a cross. It's—"

"How do you know about it? I mean, about the fact that he's trapped now?"

She opened her purse and took out what looked like a fairly large make-up compact. She said, "It's a two-way; he carries the other end of it, except his looks like a tobacco pouch, and—"

"I've seen it. He called you on it, from Curme's?"

"Yes. It makes a faint buzz when he calls. And when he's on a job, I keep it right close in case he calls and there's anything I can do or—"

"What did he ask you to do? Notify me?"

"No, this time he didn't want anything—except to say so-long to me. He said it was hopeless, that they had every exit blocked solid—there are dozens of cops, hundreds maybe—and all he wanted me to do was get out of the apartment quick, before they got there to get *me*. I stayed long enough to call you, and then I got."

"They know who he is?"

She nodded. "I don't know how—unless one of them got a look at him when he was firing out a window and recognized him, but the loud-speaker they set up is calling him by name to come out and give himself up. That's how he knew they'd find out where he lived and get there to the apartment and why he called me to warn me to—"

"Can you call him back on that thing now?"

"Yes, but—"

"Get him, fast. Tell him I want to talk to him, and then put me on."

She held up the compact and opened it; there was a mirror inside the top and she pretended to be looking into it, and, after pressing a button somewhere, pretended to be talking to Crag.

"Gardin? You know who this is. And a friend of yours is here and wants to talk to you—you'll know his voice."

Crag reached for the tiny two-way; he held it as though he was examining it. And he talked as though he was talking to the woman across from him. "Let's talk fast, Gardin, before they might get a tracer beam on this thing and get to us here. They know where and who you are, so don't be coy on that end. What's the score?"

"They've got me bottled." The tiny, tinny voice just reached his ear over the blare of the music. "Nothing you can do about it, but thanks. They've got over a hundred cops here."

"How long can you hold out?"

"As long as I want to. They're not coming in to shoot it out. They'll wait till I give up or get bored and go through the door to shoot it out with them."

"How long can you hold out, damn it? In days or hours."

"Hell, a week if I have to. There's no food here but I won't starve in less than that. And there's plenty of water."

"Ammunition?"

"Whole rack of guards' weapons besides the one I brought. They know I'm well heeled."

"Can they gas you out?"

"Not without firing gas shells through the windows, and they're not going to take a chance on that. Why should they? They've got me cold, and they *like* sieges."

"Okay, hold out, Gardin. I'll get you out of there. May be a few days, but I'll get you."

"You can't. Don't try. It's—"

"I'm not telling you how in case they're finding this beam. Or exactly when, even if I knew. But hold out, damn it, and I'll get you out of there."

Crag snapped shut the compact and stood up quickly. "Come on, we're getting out of here, in case the cops did get on that beam and are tracing it now."

There was a helicab waiting outside and he pushed Bea into it and followed her in, gave the address of another bar. Once Bea grabbed his arm. "Crag, it's suicide—you *can't*—"

He shook off her grip. "We can, if he can hold out two days. Maybe we can do it in less, if we can get some more manpower. Has Gardin any other friends you'd trust in this?"

"One, Crag. Hauser. But—the cops are looking for him already. He's in hiding and that's why you haven't met him And it's a rough rap; he's—"

"Good. That makes him just the one we want, he's got nothing to lose. You can reach him?"

"Of course, but—"

"Don't argue. We'll go in the bar I told this cabby to take us to, so it doesn't look funny to him; we're almost there anyway. One quick drink; then we split up and here's what you do. Stay away from Gardin's apartment—he's probably right that they're there by now. Get Hauser, come with him to the Luxor, if he'll come. Or—do you want to go through with this, Bea? I can get Gardin alone, but it'll take longer."

They were entering the bar and Crag ordered quickly, then turned to Bea. "Well," he said, "made your mind up?"

"It's been made up all along. You're going right to the Luxor?"

"I've got a few things to buy first. How long will it take you to get this Hauser, or find out that you can't get him?"

"At least two hours. Unless I risk phoning him, and since he's in hiding he asked me not to."

"Don't phone him then. But I'll get to the Luxor before you do, in that case. Good luck, Bea."

They downed their drinks and Crag left first. He headed straight for an aircar agency and bought himself a six-place Dragoon, paid cash, and a premium price, to get the demonstrator model that was already on the roof, gassed and ready to go. He landed it on the roof of the Luxor only minutes later.

The attendant ran to get it and to put it away. Crag asked him, "Is there a store near that sells tools, hardware?"

"Yes, sir, about three blocks north on—"

"Can you go there right away and buy me three shovels and put them in the car?"

"Right now, sir, I'm afraid I couldn't take off for that long. Perhaps one of the bellboys—"

Crag handed him a hundred-dollar bill. "I don't want to waste time. You send one of the bellboys, fast. Large sand shovels. And split the change out of this between you. Also don't bury that aircar behind any others. Keep it out where I can take off the second I come back on the roof."

"Yes, *Sir.*" Since the shovels wouldn't cost over ten dollars apiece, it was a generous enough tip to get fast service on both them and the aircar.

Crag took the elevator down to his suite and let himself in. He buzzed the desk. "Two people are coming to see me. Send them up without delay the minute they get here."

"Yes, Sir. Their names?"

"Never mind what names they give. Send up anyone who asks for me."

He tossed a few things into a small suitcase. To hell with the rest of it; he wouldn't need it where he was going.

He took a screwdriver and unscrewed the plate of the main fluorescent switch, the first of the four hiding places in each of which he had stashed a hundred thousand dollars.

The money wasn't there. Crag swore and was beginning to work on the second of the hiding places—whoever had searched his room couldn't possibly have found *all* of them—when the door buzzer sounded and he went to answer it.

Bea stood there, and there were two other people with her. A small man, shifty-eyed and bald, but tough-looking, and a small dark Gypsy-looking woman—beautiful except for her eyes; they were the small beady eyes of a rodent.

Crag let them in and locked the door behind them.

"Crag, this is Hauser, and Gert. He says he'll help us get Gardin, but his woman has to go along—especially if we're all heading anywhere afterward."

Crag nodded. "Okay. Go in the bar and make drinks. We're almost ready; I've got one thing to do."

There was no money in the second cache. Or in the third or the fourth.

He went into the bar. "Job for you," he said. "Put down the drinks. I had money, big money, hidden in four different places in this suite. It's gone, from all of them. That means somebody watched me doing the hiding. No kind of a search—not even a squad of cops spending weeks at it—would have found all four of those places. That means there are one-way observation panels looking into this suite. Help me find them."

Hauser said, "Probably the mirrors. You've got them all over and they're set into the wall, not hanging. I worked a luxury hotel once and that's the usual thing, the mirrors."

Crag nodded. There was a mirror in the wall beside where he was standing, a small one. He picked up a bottle and smashed at the mirror; it crashed through, showing space, a passageway, behind it. But the space was too small for him to get through and he picked up another bottle and went out into the living room, looking for a big mirror. He found one and smashed it out.

Hauser was behind him. "Going to get your money back? Want help? I've got a heater."

Crag stepped through the space where the mirror had been. "This is a private deal; I'll take care of it. Keep the women amused but see that nobody drinks too much. We're going to have work to do."

There was a maze of passageways; every room of his own suite and of all the other suites on the floor were under observation from at least one mirror. Especially the bedrooms. And the passageways were used; there wasn't a bit of dust on their floors. Probably, besides their uses for criminal purposes, these passageways were rented occasionally to favored patrons, voyeurs, those who would rather watch than do. Well, the voyeurs would have been disappointed in watching the doings in Crag's suite.

Not so the suite adjacent. As he passed its master bedroom he couldn't help seeing through a big mirror that the three women who had welcomed him on his own arrival, the blonde, the brunette and the redhead, had all three been kept by the renter of the adjacent suite. And were very busy, all three of them.

He had to pass a lot of mirrors, a lot of suites, before he found steps leading downward. And from what he couldn't help seeing, he decided that he liked the clientele of the Luxor even less than he liked its management. There may have been those among the clientele who went in for ordinary unperverted sexual amusements, but he didn't happen to see any of them.

However, he wasn't interested in censoring morals, but in getting his money back. And he had a strong hunch, almost a certainty, that the management was responsible for the theft. He remembered now the gleam behind Carleton's pince-nez glasses when he had pulled out a sheaf of big bills to make an advance payment on the suite. Probably the manager had from that moment posted a bellboy or other menial to watch and see whether Crag would cache money in his quarters. The bellboy would have been in on it, of course, but he'd have been lucky if the manager had given him a single thousand out of the four hundred thousand.

He didn't investigate what was going on in any of the other floors of suites—one had been more than enough. He counted flights of stairs down until he knew he was on the main floor. And there he started looking for, and found, a panel that was locked from the other side. That would be either the manager's private office or his personal quarters. There was no peephole or one-way mirror here, of course, so he didn't know what was on the other side and picked the lock as silently as he had ever picked one in his life.

He inched open the panel quietly. It opened into the manager's office, and he could see Carleton's back only a yard from him. The manager was seated at an ornate desk, leafing through a sheaf of papers.

Crag stepped through and closed the panel behind him. He reached his right hand around the scrawny neck of the manager, squeezing just hard enough to prevent any outcry and pulling back just far enough to keep Carleton's frantically groping hands from reaching any of the buttons on or under the desk.

He said quietly. "If you don't already guess, or recognize my voice, you'll know who this is when I tell you I want four hundred thousand dollars. Where is it?"

He relaxed pressure enough to permit a whisper, and when none came he tightened his fingers again.

A trembling hand came up and pointed to a metal door with a combination knob set in the wall directly across the office. Crag relaxed pressure enough to hear a croaking voice: "Left four, then six, one, eight."

Crag pulled him out of the chair, to his feet. "Come on. You're going with me while I open it. If there's an alarm and any help comes, you'll die the second it gets here." He walked the man across the room until they stood facing the safe, Carleton between Crag and the knob. He reached, with his free left hand, around Carleton's body.

Carleton squeaked, but it sounded like, "Don't!" and Crag grinned and relaxed pressure on his throat a little.

"Trap?"

"Yes. It's booby-trapped. We'll both die if we're standing here. I'll open it. Let me open it."

Crag let him open it. Besides ledgers and tapes there were two money boxes in the vault. "Which?" Crag asked. The strangling manager pointed weakly at one of them. "That one. It's mine. The other's hotel money."

Crag held onto the neck. "Pick them both up. Carry them to your desk and open them there."

He waited until the second box was opened and the lid thrown back. Then gently, very gently, he tapped the manager behind the ear with his metal left hand. It would have given Crag pleasure to strike harder, but it was not in his nature to kill unnecessarily. He lowered Carleton into his chair, ripped off part of his clothing and bound and gagged him securely with it.

He took the large denomination bills out of both boxes; he didn't count them but obviously there was considerably more than the four hundred thousand dollars which had been his. He went back through the panel, closing and locking it behind him, and back up the stairs, counting flights again.

The three people he'd left in his suite—Bea, Gert and Hauser—had followed him through the broken mirror and were standing watching events through one of the one-way panels, the one where the blonde-brunette-redhead trio were operating. "Come on," he told them. "We've got to get out of here fast."

They didn't argue. They followed him back into the suite, out into the corridor and up to the roof via the elevator.

"Shovels?" he asked the attendant.

"In the aircar, sir. And—"

"Thanks, I see where it is." He ran toward it, the others following. He got in and made a fast takeoff.

"What did you mean asking him about shovels?" Bea asked him. He saw she'd brought an open bottle with her, and took it firmly from her and threw it out the window of the aircar. He said, "No more drinking till we're through. We've got work to do—if you want me to get Gardin out of there."

"But—shovels! You can't *dig* him out of the top floor of a twenty-story building."

Crag didn't answer. He was getting every mile of speed possible out of the aircar, heading south of the city. He didn't speak again, even to answer questions, until they were an hour away. Then he told Bea, "Get Gardin on that two-way of yours. Tell him we can make it in a few hours, if he can hold out that long."

"But we're heading away from Mars City, Crag. How can—?"

"Never mind. Do what I told you."

Bea took out the box, talked into it briefly, and listened. "He's doing fine, says he can hold out as long as he has to. But he can't believe there's any way you can get him out of there. He says there are at least two hundred cops, and six helis overhead. They can shoot down anything—"

"Tell him not to worry, just to hold out."

She talked briefly again and then closed the box. She turned in the seat to face Crag. "All right," she said, "I told him. But why can't you tell us and him what you're going to try? We're all in this."

"All right," he said. "I've got a spaceship hidden. We're going to get it. We rescue him in it. I can put it so he can step right from the window into the port."

"My God, a *spaceship* right down in Mars City. That's—" She laughed suddenly. "I started to say that's illegal, but—" She hesitated. "It might work, Crag. But why can't I tell Gardin? It'll make him feel better if he knows you're going to try something that's got a chance of working?"

"It's got better than a chance of working. But the cops may have tapped that beam by now and be monitoring it. Then they'd be ready for us and it wouldn't work. Nothing those helis can throw can touch a spaceship, nor anything they've got there for the siege, on the ground or in the building. But if they knew in advance, they could have a bigger spaceship waiting for us. Or an atomic cannon or two ready to shoot us down."

"But they'll *get* ships from the spaceport, Crag."

"And we'll be to hell and gone off Mars by the time they get one off the ground. Now shut up. I'm hedge-hopping this aircar and that takes concentration at night."

Two hours later he put it down. He pointed in the dim light of Phobos and Deimos to a dune of sand ahead. "The ship's in that," he said. "Hauser, bring those shovels out of the back and—"

"Shovels?" There was horror in Hauser's voice. "It'll take us months to shovel all that sand. Why don't we go and get a sand-cat?"

"That's the way I buried it. But it'll take hours to get one and drive it here. And we don't have to uncover the ship, damn it; all we have to do is to get a trench through to the port, and it's dead center on this side. Once I get in the ship I can rock it on the antigravs and most of that sand will roll off by itself and we can lift out of what's left."

They started shoveling. Crag worked continuously and made Hauser do the same, although after a while Hauser had to stop and rest on his shovel once in a while. The two women took turns with the third shovel; Crag hadn't known when he'd bought only three that there'd be a fourth in the party.

Hauser was panting. "My God, Crag," he said. "This is still going to take hours. Didn't you bring any grub? I'm getting hungry."

"Dig faster then," Crag told him. "There's food in the ship. Can you pilot one of these things?"

Hauser wiped sweat from his forehead and then shook his head. "Gardin can, though. Where we going in it? Venus?"

"We'll decide that when we get Gardin."

Even with three of them shoveling at a time, it was a longer and harder job than Crag had estimated it to be. It was dawn when they finally uncovered the port of the spaceship and got it open. Bea had wanted several times to call Gardin on the two-way, but Crag had forbidden it, since if the police had found the beam and were monitoring it, they could trace it directionally and the spaceship would never get off the ground.

Once in the ship, it was a tougher job than Crag had realized to use the antigravs to get rid of the rest of the sand. At first it seemed too solidly embedded for him to rock even a fraction of an inch. But finally he could rock it an inch, and then inches, and at last it was free, and rose.

He hedge-hopped it back to Mars City and because he couldn't use full speed at so low an altitude, it took almost an hour. En route Hauser and the two women gorged themselves with food from the ship's food locker—but drank nothing because Crag had taken the key from the locker that contained bottled goods and told them that no one would have another drink until they were safely away with Gardin—and then, exhausted from the digging, they slept.

Crag called out from the control panel and woke them when he was only a few minutes away from Mars City. He told Bea to get Gardin on the two-way and tell him to be ready near the center on the north side of the building.

It went like clockwork. Due to Crag's skill in jockeying the ship into exact position, the actual rescue was so easy that after their long labor in getting and freeing the ship, it was almost anticlimactic. From the ground, from windows and roofs of other buildings and from helicopters hovering overhead the police poured fire at them from every available weapon. But the fire, which would have melted an air car within seconds, barely warmed the thick and insulated hull of a spaceship. And the instant Gardin was inside and the port had closed, Crag flashed the ship upward, set a course and locked the controls.

"Safe now," he said. "They'll have ships after us within minutes, but they won't catch us."

"Are you sure?"

"Yes. We can't fight back because this baby doesn't carry armaments, but because of that it's faster than anything that does."

"But where are we going?" Gardin asked. "They'll have tracers on us; we can't land on Mars without their knowing where. Venus?"

"Cragon," Crag said.

"Cragon! Nothing can land on Cragon. Not even the whole space fleet."

Crag grinned at him. "That's why we'll be safe there."

CHAPTER TWELVE

There was argument, even after he had explained. But all of them, and especially the two women, at first thought Venus was a better idea.

A new, raw planet, they argued, wasn't civilization. On Venus they'd all be rich. Gardin had brought a bag of fabulous jewels with him from the rescue; he'd had plenty of time while under siege to pick them out. Their value was anybody's guess, but it couldn't be less than a million dollars, even sold through a fence; and Gardin was willing to split with the rest of them for having rescued him.

Of course there'd be a risk to landing on Venus; they'd have to land in a remote spot and hide the spaceship, as Crag had done on Mars. But once they got into a city and cashed in some of the jewels, they'd be safe enough. Even if identified, they'd be rich enough to buy immunity from extradition and still have plenty left.

"What good will jewels be on Cragon?" Bea wanted to know.

"You can wear them," Crag told her. "You'll be the best dressed women on the whole planet."

But Crag won, gradually talked them over. Gardin came to his side first, then Hauser; finally the women assented.

Two days later they approached Cragon. Crag took over the controls. Because the others wanted him to, remembering what had happened to the atmosphere inside the scoutship which had made the first landing attempt, Crag lowered very slowly, ready to raise ship fast if any of them started to experience difficulty in breathing. But none of them had, so he set the ship down in a gentle, perfect landing.

Just as the ship touched surface a voice in Crag's mind said, "Welcome, Crag." He answered mentally, not aloud, and looked quickly at the others to see if they had received any equivalent message; obviously none of them had.

Crag opened the port without bothering to check the atmosphere outside. He knew it would be good Earth-type air, and it was. It had a clear, cool sweetness that made the breathing of it almost a caress for the lungs. The others stepped down after him.

"Well, we're here," Gardin said. "Now what?"

"A drink," Bea suggested. "A lot of drinks."

Crag hesitated, then handed her the key to the locker. "All right," he said. "Break it out and we'll celebrate."

Bea went inside the ship and came out again shortly with an open *woji* bottle. She looked disgusted. "Big deal, that liquor supply," she said. "Ten bottles, two apiece. What are we going to do when they're gone?"

"Do without," Crag said. "Or find some equivalent of wild grapes and learn how to make our own."

"Damn it, Crag," Bea said. "If you knew when we were leaving Mars, why didn't you stock up the ship? After we picked up Gardin we could have raided some outpost station and—well, at least have stocked up on *liquor*, enough to last us a while."

Crag shrugged. Actually he'd thought of doing just that and had decided not to; the ship couldn't have carried enough liquor to have lasted five of them for their lifetimes anyway and so the sooner they learned to do without or to make their own the better.

He took the bottle when it was passed to him but took only a sip from it. He was more interested right now in looking around him and planning. He'd brought the ship down near a clear, gently meandering stream. He had no doubt that it was clean sweet water. A grassy plain sloped down to it. Beyond the stream was forest; some of the trees looked familiar to him, others strange. But no doubt they'd find edible things, good things. Everything they needed. Meat? As though in answer to his unspoken question—although he knew the alien who had made all this wasn't invading his privacy by listening in his mind— he heard the far cry of an animal of some kind. And in the stream a fish leaped. Yes, everything they needed. And probably dangers, too. He'd bet odds that there were predators there, hunters as well as hunted. Well, that was to the good. Nothing that is easy is fun; he'd learned that lesson at the Luxor.

A bottle was being handed to him and he saw that it was a fresh one. Again he took a sip, but as he passed it on he held out his hand toward Bea. "The key," he said. "That'll be enough for now. We've got work to do."

"Work? Already? We just got here. You mean you're not going to let us hang one on, to celebrate?"

Crag hesitated, and then shrugged. Why not? He'd landed on the day side but near the twilight zone; it would soon be evening. Why not let them hang one on, and himself with them; in the morning would be time to start planning and working. Besides, the five of them, all heavy drinkers, would probably kill the ten bottles and that would end the problem of liquor rationing. Why not get rid of it all at once?

"All right," he said. "We'll have a party. But first let's gather a lot of wood for a fire. It's cramped for us in the spaceship; we've had enough of that for a while."

"But why a fire?" Hauser wanted to know. "It's not cool."

"Probably will be after dark and it'll be too late to get wood then. Besides—" Crag gestured toward the forest across the stream. "—we don't know what might come out of those woods after dark. If something does come out, we want to be able to see it."

Hauser frowned. "What makes you think there might be anything dangerous, Crag? According to you, this—alien made this world to please you. Why'd he put anything in it that could hurt you?"

Crag said grimly, "Because he knows me and *did* make it to be the way I'd want it to be. Which would not be all lambs and no lions. Would you want it that way, Gardin?"

Gardin grinned. "Maybe not, but neither would I want it all water and no *woji*. Well, we haven't looked very far yet. Maybe there are streams that run *woji*. All right, gang, let's gather sticks."

Sticks were easy to find, just across the stream. Crag stationed Hauser to mount guard with a heatgun while the other four did the gathering; within an hour, just about as the sun was going down, they had an ample supply to keep a fair-sized fire burning through the night, in case they spent the whole night in the open.

And within another hour they admitted it had been a wise precaution—at least as far as warmth was concerned; otherwise the cool evening would have forced them back into the crowded quarters of the ship. They drank a bit, then brought out food from the ship and ate, then started in on their celebration, heavy drinking.

All but Crag, that is. For a while he took drink for drink with the others and then found himself taking more and more time between drinks, and not minding it. He told himself that one of them—and it might as well be he—should stay nearly enough sober to be sure the fire was kept going, and to be able to guard the others. But there was also the fact that he found himself wanting each drink less than the preceding one.

He'd never especially liked the taste of liquor; he'd drunk for effect, escape. And here...

By midnight—and Cragon had a period of rotation, of night and day, almost exactly the same as Earth's—all the liquor was gone and the others were drunk. And it was getting quite cold by then and Crag helped them help one another back into the ship and into bunks.

Then he went back outside, replenished the fire and sat in front of it. Alone. He didn't dare sleep, so he didn't. He could have, of course, in the ship, with the port shut, but he didn't want to have to go back in there, even for a few hours. It was better to be out here, alone, even if he had to stay awake. He could stay awake for days on end if he had to; and he often had.

In the morning—after the most beautiful sunrise he had ever seen—he was a little tired. But felt better than the others looked as though they felt, when he'd routed them out. Gardin admitted to a bad hangover, but didn't show it. The others admitted to hangovers and showed them.

They were moody over breakfast.

"Well, *Boss,*" Bea asked, "what are our orders for today? Or are we going to vote on what to do? Is this a democracy, or are you running it?"

"We'll vote if you want," Crag said. "But vote or no vote, there are certain things we've got to do ahead of other things. We need living quarters. That ship's too crowded and has too little privacy for five people to live in long. It's crowded, even for four. We've got to start on some adobe huts—small ones will do at first; we can build decent ones later."

"What's adobe?" Hauser wanted to know.

"Clay shaped into bricks and left to dry in the sun. If we scout both ways along that creek we'll find some clay."

"Mud huts? We're going to live in *mud huts?*" Gert sounded horrified.

Crag looked at her. "If you've got any better ideas—outside of five people trying to live in that ship—let's have them. And there's the question of food. I'd guess there's enough in the ship for five of us for another few days, a week if we go on rations. But we've got to learn how to hunt and fish, and start that right away. Gardin, you're a good shot, aren't you?"

Gardin nodded.

"Then here's my suggestion for today. Try that forest and see what you can find. Go heavily armed and don't go in too deep, because we don't know what we'll run into there. We want to learn the dangers gradually, not by one of us getting killed the first day. If you want me to go with you I will, but—"

Gardin said, "I won't need help. But what do you have in mind for yourself?"

"To scout along the stream for some clay. I once knew a little geology, not much, but I can probably recognize the kind of stuff we need better than any of the rest of you. If I find a deposit near, okay. If I find one but too far to carry bricks, we'll move headquarters, move the spaceship nearer to it. Hauser, have you ever done any fishing?"

"No."

"Good, then you won't have any preconceptions about it, and it'll probably be different here from on Earth anyway. Find some wire and make hooks, try to find out what bait they'll take. Or figure a way of making nets. Or make yourself a fish spear and try it out; the water's clear and there are places where it's shallow enough. Or—hell, just figure us a way of getting some fish, that's all. Okay?"

Hauser nodded, not too happily.

"And us?" Bea asked. "I suppose you've got *our* day planned too."

"I'd suggest you gather firewood for a starter, plenty of it. After that, we'll see. If I find a clay deposit you can help me get a start on making adobe bricks. Or if Gardin gets game, you can try your hand at skinning it—if it's got fur— and cooking it. Or see what you can figure out in the way of net making to help Hauser." He grinned. "Don't worry; there'll be plenty for you to do."

"I'm not worrying," Bea said. "Not about *that*." She glared at him.

Crag said, "I'm not a boss here. Those weren't orders, but they're all things that have to be done if we're going to survive. Anybody want to trade assignments, or add any other suggestions?"

"Yes," Gert said. "This is a hell of a place to have brought us. We should have gone to Venus."

"Maybe we should have," Gardin said. "But it's too late now. There isn't enough fuel in the ship even to get us back to Mars. We made our choice when we took off from Mars—and you can blame Crag if you want for talking us into this, but that isn't going to change things. Let's get going."

They got going. Crag had first luck; he found an excellent clay deposit only fifty yards upstream. He made a few bricks and put them in the sun to see how long they'd take to dry, and then came back. Bea and Gert had gathered some firewood and were moodily watching—not helping—Hauser file a barb on wire he'd bent into the approximate shape of a fishhook.

Clay told them about the clay and suggested they come and help him make more bricks.

Bea glared at him defiantly. "We talked that over, Crag. *We* don't want other quarters—not mud huts, anyhow. We're willing to sleep in the ship. You're the one who wants a private house and why should we help you?"

Crag sighed but decided not to argue. If the women were going to be recalcitrant, it was up to their men to put them into line and he wasn't going to mix in their domestic problems. Sooner or later they'd get tired of the spaceship bunks and change their minds. And when the food supply of the ship ran out they'd be in much better mood to help with other tasks.

He went back to his clay deposit and his brick making.

Hauser caught no fish that day. Gardin came back in late afternoon carrying one small rabbit-like animal. He seemed discouraged. "Saw several of these but wasted most of my shots. My God, but the things are fast."

He said he'd seen one bigger animal but at too great a distance to make a good guess at what type it was, and he couldn't stalk it closely enough to get in a shot at it. "Guess I'm a better city hunter than a country one," he admitted. "I can follow a man across a city for days and never lose him, but wild animals—guess it's out of my line. How'd the rest of you do?"

Just looks answered him, from Hauser and the two women.

Crag shook his head slowly. "Gardin, I guess I made a mistake. If you don't like it here, if this isn't a life for you, I guessed wrong. Do you still want to go to Venus and take your chances there?"

"Want to? Crag—maybe I could adjust here if Bea could, but all I have to do is to look at her to get the answer to that. Yes, we want to go to Venus. I'll swap a million dollars worth of jewels for enough fuel to get us there."

"Keep the jewels," Crag said. "The tank isn't almost empty; there's enough in it to get you to Venus. I jimmied the gauge on the way here, once while the rest of you were sleeping. I wanted to give Cragon a chance; I wanted you to land here *thinking* you were here for keeps. Take the ship and get going."

Both the women had leaped to their feet. Hauser was grinning.

Crag nodded. "Take it. Just unload whatever supplies you won't need on the trip. And whatever tools, and all the weapons and ammunition except a sidearm apiece for you and Hauser. And take this." He handed Gardin a thick roll of bills, the money he'd taken from the two boxes that had been in the Luxor safe.

Gardin took it. "What's this?"

Crag said, "I never counted it. But it's something over half a million dollars—or wastepaper. Here it's wastepaper, so you might as well have it. Now get going on that unloading, all of you."

Gardin seemed puzzled, almost reluctant, but the others worked faster, probably, than they'd ever worked at anything before, probably afraid Crag would change his mind.

An hour later, standing beside a tarpaulin covered pile of supplies that represented everything the ship could spare, he watched it go.

He felt dull inside, neither happy nor unhappy. This was the way it was going to be. This was his world and here he was going to stay until he died or was killed. He'd be lonesome, sure, but he was used to that. And this was infinitely better than the cesspools of corruption that Earth, Mars and Venus had become. This was a tough world but an honest one. It was, and would be, *his* world. During the time the alien who had created this world had been in Crag's mind, he'd learned enough to make the world for which Crag was fitted.

It was getting dusk as he watched the speck out of sight, too late to do any more brick making tonight. Almost time to start a fire; he might as well get it laid and ready to light. He started toward the pile of wood the women had gathered.

But he'd taken only a step when the voice of the alien spoke in his mind.

"You did right, Crag. Like yourself, they were rebels against a bad society. But rebellion had made them decadent rather than tough. I knew when I first contacted their minds that they wouldn't stay."

"I should have guessed myself," Crag said. "Except Gardin—I thought he might make it."

"He came closest. He might have if he'd been alone, not weakened by having the wrong woman."

Crag laughed. "Is there any such thing as a *right* woman?"

"Your subconscious mind knows that there is, Crag. One and only one for you."

Anger flared in Crag. "You dared—"

"Don't forget, Crag, that happened when I'd just revived you from being dead, before I knew you resented invasion of privacy. I told you I'd never enter your mind again and I have not. I can put my voice, as it were, in your mind; but what my mind receives from yours is only what you speak aloud or what you deliberately project to me as a thought. So I know only what was in your mind then—but I doubt that it has changed."

Crag didn't answer, and the voice went on. "Do you remember what happened to Judeth, Crag? The disintegrator, yes. But before that happened I had studied her mind and her body; she was the first of the three of you on that asteroid that I studied. But I did study her and I have not forgotten the position of a single atom or molecule. And those atoms, even after disintegration of her body, were still there. It was easy to segregate and preserve them."

"For what?" Crag almost shouted. "She's dead!"

"So were you, Crag. What is death? You should know. But I saved her, for you. Until you were ready, until you came to me as I knew you would. It was a relatively easy thing to restore life to your body and a relatively difficult one to replace every atom in every molecule of—"

"*Can* you? Are you sure?"

"I already have. She's coming this way now; if you turn you'll see her."

Crag turned. And stood trembling, unable for the moment to think, let alone to move.

"You won't need to explain anything to her, Crag. I put knowledge in her mind of everything that has happened. And I can tell you that she is not only willing but able— But I withdraw from your mind now, from both your minds. I'll let you tell—"

But Judeth was in his arms by then and Crag had quit thinking or hearing thoughts in his mind.

The Mind Thing

The Mind Thing

CHAPTER ONE

The mind thing used his perceptor sense to test this strange and alien environment in which he found himself. He had no organs of vision or hearing, but his perceptor sense was something far better; he could "see" all around himself, very clearly for about twenty yards, tapering to dim vision for another twenty or so, but his seeing was unimpeded by intervening objects. He could see the bark on the far side of a tree as plainly as that on the near side. He could see down into the ground as far and as clearly as in any other direction. His ability to sense vibrations extended even farther and was extremely acute within its range.

He could not only see but "hear" worms burrowing in the ground under him; they were puzzling, for no such life form existed in any other world he knew of. But they seemed to offer no danger. Nor did a few small birds in the trees overhead. They were almost familiar; bird life tends to evolve along quite similar lines on all warm planets that have atmospheres dense enough to permit natural flight. (But what monstrous trees they perched in! They were several times as large as any he had ever known.) And there was a strange four-legged animal sleeping in a burrow, a tunnel in the ground which it seemed to have made for itself, only about ten yards away.

Since the four-legged one was sleeping, the mind thing knew that he could enter into its mind, make it his host. But there seemed nothing to gain. Where there were small creatures there were almost certainly larger ones, with more strength and brain capacity. Possibly even...

Yes! His second scanning of his surroundings showed him something he had not noticed on the first one. Lying in the grass a dozen yards away was a rusted broken-bladed jackknife that had been thrown away or lost there. He didn't recognize it for a jackknife, but whatever it was it was plainly an artifact. And an artifact meant intelligent life!

It meant danger, too. Intelligent life could be inimical, and he was small and vulnerable. He had to know more about the intelligent life form, prefer-

455

ably by catching its first specimen when it was sleeping, so he could enter its mind. He could learn more that way than by any amount of observation.

He was in an exposed position right beside what seemed to be a path. He had to get himself at least as far as the tall grass a yard away where he would be out of sight. Such concealment would be useless, of course, against his own kind or any other race that had perception instead of sight. But the chances were thousands to one that the intelligent creatures here, whatever they might be like otherwise, had only sight. He knew that on none of the thousands of known planets had both vision and the sense of perception developed side by side. One or the other, only. And here the birds and the small four-legged animal all had eyes.

He tried to levitate himself to move that yard, and found that he could not. He was not surprised. He had already suspected from several indications that this, compared to his own world, was a heavy-gravity planet. And his species, even on their own planet, had almost lost the power of levitation. Levitation was a strain, and since they all had hosts it was so much easier to have their hosts move them, when moving was necessary, than to levitate. An unused power diminishes as surely as an unused muscle atrophies.

So he was helpless, until and unless he could find a host strong enough to move him. And the only creature *sleeping* nearby, the only one he could take over and make a host, was definitely too small, probably weighed about half what he did. Of course he could reduce his weight somewhat by *trying* to levitate while the four-legged—

Suddenly, at extreme range he perceived something, and concentrated all his attention in that direction. If danger was coming there wasn't time now to experiment with using the small animal to move him into concealment.

At first it was only vibration, vibration that could have been footsteps, footsteps of something relatively large. And there was another type of vibration that came through the air and not through the ground, that was like the sounds certain types of creatures, usually intelligent ones, who communicated vocally, used for that purpose. There seemed to be two voices, one higher in the vibration range than the other, talking alternately. Of course the words meant nothing to the mind thing, nor could he probe their thoughts; his species could communicate telepathically but only among themselves.

Then they came within range of visual perception. There were two of them. One was slightly larger than the other, but they were both big. Obviously they were members of the intelligent race, or *an* intelligent race, for they both wore clothing—and only intelligent races wear clothing, during a certain period of their development. They stood erect, and had two legs and two arms apiece. Also hands—and that would make them excellent hosts, but there was no time to think of that now, His problem was survival, until he could catch such a creature sleeping.

They were of a two-sexed species, he saw—for though he perceived their clothing his perception was not limited thereby; he could have studied their internal organs as readily as their nude bodies—and they were one of each sex. They were mammalian.

But the important thing was that they were coming closer, they were walking along the path and they would pass within one or two feet of him; they could hardly miss seeing him.

Out of desperation he grabbed at the mind of the only host available, the small four-legged one. He took no time to probe or study it; he started it scurrying madly out of its burrow. He'd have it intercept the two aliens. What would happen then he didn't know, but he had nothing to lose. He was less helpless with a small, weak host than with none at all. Perhaps, although it was unlikely, the tiny life form might be dangerous to the large strong life forms. Perhaps it was venomous or equivalently deadly in some other way. All over the galaxy there were planets on which some small life form was able, in one way or another, to terrorize larger creatures. It was at least equally possible that the two-legged creatures would look upon the little four-legged one as food and try to catch it to eat. In that case, he hoped the little creature could run as fast as they; if it could, he could have it lead them off the path for a while until they were safely past him. Then it would be safe to have them catch it and kill it.

It would have to be killed, or kill itself, in any case. Just as the only way he could enter a host was while it slept, the only way he could leave one was at the moment of its death. And this host was too frail and tiny a thing for him to want to use any longer than he had to stay in it.

Charlotte Garner stopped walking suddenly, and because she had her right arm linked with Tommy Hoffman's left he stopped too, so unexpectedly in his case that he almost went off balance for a second. He looked at Charlotte and saw that she was looking down at the path in front of them.

"Look, Tommy," she said. "A field mouse. And look what it's doing!"

Tommy looked. "I'll be darned," he said.

The field mouse, right in the middle of the path and not much over a foot away from them, was sitting up like a prairie dog. But quite unlike a prairie dog, it was waving its little front feet frantically, as though trying to signal to them. And its sharp little eyes looked directly up into theirs.

"I never saw one act like that," Charlotte said. "It acts as if it's *friendly*, not afraid. Maybe someone made a pet out of it, and then it got away—but still likes people."

"Could be, I guess. I never saw one act like that either. Okay, Mousie, move along so we don't have to step over you."

"Wait a minute," Charlotte said. She'd already disentangled her arm from his. "It's so tame I bet I can pick it up."

Even before she'd finished saying that, Charlotte bent down, swept out a hand, and grabbed the field mouse gently but tightly. Charlotte was a very quick-moving girl, with fast reflexes. She had the field mouse before Tommy could protest (if he would have) or before the mouse could turn and run (if it would have).

"Oh, Tommy, he's cute."

"Okay, he's cute. But you're not going to take him along, are you, Charl? You can't hold him while we—"

"I'll put him down in a sec, Tommy. I just wanted to see if I could pick him up. And pet him a little. *Ouch!*" She dropped the field mouse. "Little devil *bit* me."

The field mouse scurried away from them and off one side of the path and then, only about six feet away, stopped and looked back to see if they were chasing it. They weren't; they weren't even looking at it, and they hadn't moved.

"Hurt you, honey?" Tommy asked.

"No, just a little nip. Startled me, that's all." She happened to look down again. "Tommy! Look!"

The field mouse was running back, this time toward Tommy. It started to run up the leg of his trousers. He knocked it off with a hand, sent it rolling four or five feet. It came back to attack again—if attack was its intention. This time Tommy had kept his eyes on it, and was ready. His foot lifted and came down; there was a faint crunching sound. With the side of his shoe he kicked what was left of the field mouse off the path.

"*Tommy!* Did you have to—?"

His face was dark as he turned to her. "Charl, that thing was crazy, attacking me twice. Listen, if it drew blood when it bit you we've got to get back to town fast. And take it with us, so they can check to see if it was rabid. Where'd it bite you, Charl?"

"On the b-breast, the left breast, when I held it close against me. But I don't think it drew blood—not through this sweater and a bra. It was more a pinch than a bite. It didn't hurt much, just scared me into letting go of it."

"We'll have to check. Take off your— No, we're almost *there*. One minute won't matter, and somebody might come along here."

He took her arm this time and strode ahead so fast that she almost had to run to keep up with him.

"Look, a turtle," she said, a dozen steps on.

He didn't slow down. "Haven't you played with enough animals this afternoon? Hurry, honey."

Another dozen paces and they turned off the path, went around behind trees and bushes to the spot that they had discovered together and had made peculiarly theirs. It was a soft grassy spot screened from all directions by bushes, a perfect hideaway just far enough from the path so they couldn't even be heard there if they talked in normal tones of voice. It had all the privacy of a desert island and none of the latter's disadvantages. It was as sylvanly beautiful as it was secluded. And easily accessible, for young and healthy people to whom a two-mile walk each way was a pleasure and not a tiring chore.

They were young and healthy, and deeply in love, Tommy Hoffman was seventeen and Charlotte Garner was sixteen. They had played together as children. They still went to school together and were now in the same grade, for Tommy, who didn't care much for schooling, had flunked a grade once, putting him back to Charlotte's level. They had each completed two years of high school.

They had fallen in love a year ago and six months ago had decided to get married. They'd talked to their families about it and had met no opposition except on the subject of when the marriage might take place. Tommy, who had just passed his seventeenth birthday, wanted them to quit school right away and get married. There would be no difficulties, he pointed out. Tommy's father was a widower and Tommy an only child; they lived in a quite large farmhouse (Mr. Hoffman had been thinking ahead to a large family when he had built it), so there'd be not only room for Charlotte but for their children, if and when they had any. And Tommy, who knew a lot about farming already and wanted to be a farmer in any case, could help his father full time instead of part time; Charlotte would take over the house and between them they'd more than earn their keep. And that was the arrangement that would no doubt be made two years from now if they finished high school first, so why wait? What did a farmer want with a high school diploma? Mr. Hoffman himself, Tommy pointed out, had had only a grade school education, and had done all right for himself. Besides, neither he nor Charlotte *wanted* to finish high school. They didn't hate school, exactly, but they didn't think they were getting anything out of it either. What good would history or algebra do a farmer or a farmer's wife?

As usual in such discussions, when they are amicable on all sides, a compromise was reached. They didn't have to finish high school and lose two years. If they waited one year, continuing school meanwhile, until Tommy was eighteen and Charlotte seventeen, Tommy's father and Charlotte's parents would give them consent to quit school and get married.

That had been six months ago and now they had only another six months to wait. In another sense they had quit waiting a month ago. They had held out (or Charlotte had) until the day a month ago when, walking through the woods, they had found this tiny, secluded paradise. And that day the weather had been too perfect, the place too beautiful, the kisses too wonderful, and the petting too passionate; biology had taken over. There had been no tears or regrets; for a first experience (for both of them) it had been unusually wonderful. Of course, having no standard of comparison, they didn't know it was unusually wonderful; just that it was very wonderful indeed. Nor had they any regrets, then or since, on moral grounds. They had been brought up to believe that sex outside of marriage was wrong, but *this* wasn't wrong. They were going to be married anyway, weren't they, as soon as they could? Meanwhile they could consider themselves already married in the eyes of God—and if there is a God who cares about such things, no doubt he did so consider them. They were very much in love.

This was the third time they'd been back here since. But this one didn't start like the others, because of the field mouse.

"Quick, Charl," Tommy said urgently. "Peel off that sweater. I'll unhook your bra while you're doing it. And if there's the slightest break in your skin where that—that thing bit you, we'll have to get back, *run* back."

Her sweater was off, then her bra. They both examined her left breast. It was a very nice, very shapely breast; so was her right one. And one was as clear and unmarked as the other.

"Thank God," Tommy said. He sighed deeply with relief. "Does it hurt at all?"

She pressed an experimental fingertip just above the nipple. "Just enough so I can tell where it was." She lowered her hand and smiled at him. "You might kiss it and make it well. If you need an excuse."

Tommy didn't need an excuse. And they both knew that what was going to happen would be at least as wonderful as the other times, and maybe a little more so because of reaction from the scare they'd had.

And wonderful it was; but this time, although they didn't know it, something was different.

This time something watched them, something whose equivalent of vision was not blocked by intervening trees and bushes. Something more horrible (although dispassionately so) than anything either of them had ever conceived in nightmare.

CHAPTER TWO

The mind thing watched avidly. Not because of prurience; he would not have understood the meaning of the word. He had no sex himself; the pronoun *he* being used only because *it* becomes very awkward when repeatedly used as a personal pronoun. His species reproduced by fission, by one creature dividing himself and becoming two, as do only lower life forms, such as bacteria, on Earth.

But he watched as eagerly as though his interest were prurient, because of a sudden hope, once he saw and understood what they were doing. Now he felt hopeful of acquiring a suitable host, and soon. He knew, from his knowledge (some first hand, some acquired) of a thousand worlds which held creatures that, like these, were of two sexes and performed the sex act in at least a somewhat similar manner, that they had a strong tendency to sleep after performing their sex act. Not because it physically exhausted them, but because the intelligent species so sexed found themselves emotionally exhausted, and contentedly replete.

If either of them slept, he had a host. If they both slept, he decided, he would choose the male since he was definitely the larger and stronger of the two. Quite probably the more intelligent as well.

After a while they relaxed and were motionless for a moment and he began to hope. Then they moved again, kissed a few times, murmured a few things. But then, relaxing in a somewhat different position, they were quiet again.

The female slept first, and he could have entered her, but the male had his eyes closed and his breathing was slow and regular; obviously he was on the verge of sleep, so the mind thing waited.

Then the male slept, and the mind thing entered his mind. There was a brief but terrible struggle as the ego, the essence, the part of the mind that was Tommy Hoffman, fought back. There was always such a struggle in taking over an intelligent creature. (It was negligible in the case of an animal; it had taken him only a micro-second to enter the small four-legged one less than an hour ago.) But the more intelligent the species, the harder the struggle was; it varied, too, with the degree of intelligence of the individual within the species.

In this case it took him about a second, average for a moderately intelligent creature. Then he had Tommy Hoffman's mind and, through it, control of Tommy's body. The whatever-you-want-to-call-it that was Tommy Hoffman was still there, but locked up and helpless, unable to use its own body or its own senses. The mind thing had it, and it could obtain release now only through death. Tommy's death, or the mind thing's.

The mind thing now had all of Tommy's memories and all, such as it was, of his knowledge. But he was going to take time to assimilate all of that, make sense of it, and make his plans from it. First things came first.

And the first thing was to get himself—his own body—into a safe place of concealment. Before some other man or men (he had Tommy's vocabulary now to think with) might come along and harm or destroy it.

He let everything else go and searched Tommy's thoughts and memories for a good hiding place, and found one. Half a mile deeper in the woods was a cave in a hillside. A small cave, but a secret one. Tommy had found it years ago, when he was a boy of nine, and had thought of it as *his* cave and had never shown it to anyone else; to his knowledge no one else knew of its existence. Besides, it had a sandy floor.

Very quietly so as not to awaken the girl (he could have strangled her, of course, but that would be an unnecessary complication; he had no empathy for lesser creatures but neither did he kill wantonly) he got up and started for the path. Since time might be important—someone else might come along that path at any time—he didn't have his host dress. Tommy wore only a pair of blue socks; his other garments—shoes, shorts, trousers, and a shirt—lay in a pile beside where he had been lying.

Just before he parted the bushes to leave the secluded spot he looked back to make sure the girl was still sleeping. She was, her young body completely nude. Not even socks in her case, since she'd been wearing barefoot sandals to begin with. He knew, from Tommy's mind, why they hadn't put their clothes on after the act. The sun had felt pleasantly warm on their naked bodies, and besides Tommy had hoped that after a short nap—they knew one or the other would waken within half an hour—he would be able to—"go another round" was the phrase that had been in Tommy's mind. Obviously these creatures got considerable pleasure out of copulation. And also, although they always wore clothing except in privacy, from the sight and touch of one another's naked bodies.

At the path he picked himself up and started off at a trot in the direction of the cave he had found in Tommy's mind, the cave that would be his hiding place, at least for a while.

Probing Tommy's mind, he learned the answer to something that had puzzled him—why Tommy and the girl had seen him but had not stopped to investigate. Superficially, seen from above, he somewhat resembled an Earth (he knew the name of the planet now) creature called a turtle. To a casual glance he was a turtle about five inches long, with its feet and head pulled into its shell. Turtles were slow-moving and unintelligent; they did not bother humans, and humans seldom bothered them. True, they were edible—the concept and taste of turtle soup came to him—but unless he was hunting turtles a human would be unlikely to pick up and take home a single one only his size; it would weigh about two pounds, about his own weight, but it would yield only a few ounces of edible meat; not enough, except to a starving man, to be worth the trouble of killing and dissecting it.

That accidental resemblance had saved him. That and the actions of the field mouse while it had been his host. What he had done with the field mouse had been the right thing, if for the wrong reasons; another lucky accident. They had not been afraid of it nor would they have chased it off the path. But by biting the girl when she had picked it up and then attacking the boy when the girl dropped it, it had aroused fear that it had had something called rabies and that it might have infected the girl by biting her. And that fear had caused Tommy to rush the girl to their trysting place so they could check to see whether she had really been bitten; otherwise they would have continued to stroll leisurely and might well have stopped when the girl had said "Look, a turtle" for a closer look. And a closer look would have shown them—well, from above they'd only have decided it was a species of turtle they hadn't seen before, but that might have led one of them to pick it up for a closer look. And that would have been bad, because they would then have seen that it wasn't a turtle at all. Instead of having a plastrum, or bottom shell, under the carapace, it was one continuous shell with no openings for head or feet. They, or someone they took it to, might all too well have decided to crack it open to see what was inside. And that would have been all for the mind thing; even if it had found itself a host meanwhile it would have died in its host as well as in its own body. The mental extension of itself that controlled a host could not have independent existence.

Now he made Tommy sprint until he was well out of sight from the path and then, having learned that he could not keep up that pace for the half mile to the cave, slowed him down to a jog trot.

The entrance to the cave was small; one had to get down on hands and knees to go through it and, the mind thing saw with satisfaction, it was well screened by bushes.

Inside it was dim but, even through Tommy's eyes, he could see. But through Tommy's memory as well as Tommy's eyes he had a full picture of the place. (His sense of perception, which was independent of light or dark, functioned only when he was, sans host, in his own body. When in a host he was dependent upon the host's sensory organs, whatever they might be.) The cave wasn't a large one; it went back about twenty feet, and at its widest place, near the center, it was about six feet wide, and only at that point was it high enough for a man to stand erect.

At about that point the mind thing had Tommy put him down and then scrabble with his hands a hole in the sand. About nine inches down his/Tommy's hands found rock. He had Tommy put him down in the hole and then cover him and smooth the ground carefully. Then, on hands and knees, back to the entrance Tommy went, smoothing away as he backed the marks he had made coming in. The sand was as smooth now as when he had entered.

And he had Tommy sit just outside the cave entrance—but screened and hidden by the same bushes that hid the entrance itself—and wait.

Now there was no hurry. He was safely hidden now and he could take his time to digest all the knowledge that was in Tommy's mind, to catalogue it and, using it as a basis, to lay his own long-range plans.

And to lay short-range plans for his host. Already he knew that Tommy's mind was not the one he needed, ultimately, to control. But Tommy would serve for a while. Tommy probably had an average—but no better than average—I.Q. for his race (at least that was the way Tommy thought of himself), but he was only partly educated and had no knowledge whatsoever of science beyond a very few and extremely elementary principles.

But Tommy could serve him—for a while.

CHAPTER THREE

Charlotte Garner awoke, as suddenly and completely as a kitten awakens, completely oriented even before she opened her eyes. Her naked body felt uncomfortably cool and she shivered a little and then, opening her eyes, saw why the coolness had wakened her. She'd gone to sleep in warm sunlight, now she was in shadow. That meant the sun was low in the west, down behind the thick bushes at that end of the open space. Startled, she held up her wrist watch to read it—and was even more startled. They'd slept three full hours. Even leaving this minute and walking fast, they'd be half an hour late at their respective homes for dinner. Probably their folks, or hers anyway, were beginning to worry a little already.

Quickly she turned over to waken Tommy. Tommy wasn't there. But his clothes were there, just past where he'd been lying. After a brief shock, she realized what had happened, the only thing that could have happened. Tommy must have wakened a minute or so before she had, and before dressing himself or wakening her, he had gone out of the clearing somewhere nearby to answer a call of nature. He wouldn't have, couldn't have, gone any farther than that, for that or for any other reason, without his clothes. He'd be back in a minute.

And since he didn't carry or wear a watch he probably didn't realize quite how late it was. But *she* did. She stood up and brushed off the little grass that stuck to her body and then dressed quickly; there were only four garments— panties, bra, skirt, and sweater—and it didn't take her long to get them on. Then she sat down and strapped on the barefoot sandals, and stood up again.

Still no sign of Tommy; and while she wasn't worried yet, she wanted him to hurry, so she called out his name, but there wasn't any answer. He'd hardly have gone out of hearing distance—but probably he was already on his way back and for that reason hadn't bothered to answer. She realized that there was likely some grass in her hair, so she went to Tommy's clothes and got out the little pocket comb he kept clipped in his shirt pocket, ran it a few times through her short bobbed hair, and put it back.

Still no Tommy, and now she was getting a little worried. Not that she could think of anything that could have happened to him. She called out his name again, much more loudly this time, and then, "Answer me. Where are you?"

She listened hard, but there was only the faint rustle of leaves in a breeze that had just sprung up. Could Tommy be trying to frighten her? No, he wouldn't do anything like that.

But what could have happened? He couldn't have *gone* anywhere, naked except for those bright blue short socks he hadn't taken off, Could he have fainted, or had an accident? Fainting seemed impossible; Tommy was in perfect health. And if an accident—well, it would have to be the kind of accident that would make him unconscious (she didn't dare think the word *dead)*. If he'd just turned an ankle or even broken a leg, he'd still have answered her. In fact, he'd have wakened her sooner by calling her. She was a light sleeper and would have heard him call her from any reasonable distance.

Really worried now, she went out of the clearing through the bushes and started to circle around it, looking everywhere, behind bushes and trees, even on the side toward the path, although he surely wouldn't have gone that way; not for the purpose she'd originally thought of as his only reason for leaving her at all—and she still couldn't think of any other.

From time to time she called his name, and she was shouting now. She spiraled out, and when she realized, half an hour later, that she was a hundred yards or so from her starting point and had thoroughly searched an area with a hundred-yard radius, she was really scared. He wouldn't possibly have come this far.

She needed help, she realized. She hurried back to the path and started home, half walking, half running, keeping the fastest pace she thought she might possibly maintain for three miles. She'd have to tell them the truth, she realized, no matter what they thought about, or did about, Tommy and her jumping the gun and having premarital relations. No holding that back, since Tommy's clothes would have to be the starting point of the search. But that didn't matter now. Only finding Tommy mattered.

She was a tired, panting, disheveled girl when she stumbled into her parents' living room. They were listening to the radio but her father turned it off quickly and glared at her. "Fine time! I was just about to—" Then he saw her face and said, "What's wrong, Charl?"

She blurted it out. She was interrupted only once, by her mother's shocked voice. "You mean you and Tommy have been—" But her father stopped that. "Worry about that later, Mom. Let her finish."

Jed Garner stood up. "I'll call Gus," he said. "We'll get out there right away. He can bring Buck."

He went to the phone and called Gus Hoffman, who lived on the next farm, and started talking.

On the other end of the line, Gus Hoffman listened grimly. All he said when Garner had finished was, "Be right there."

He hung up the phone and stood a moment thinking. Then he went to a hamper of dirty clothes and found a sock of Tommy's, put it in his pocket. He'd want it to get Buck started on Tommy's trail. Not that Buck didn't already know Tommy's scent, but he wouldn't know he was supposed to follow it unless there was something of Tommy's to hold in front of his nose while you said, "Find 'im, boy."

He got Buck's leash from its nail in the kitchen and put it in another pocket. Buck was a good dog on a trail but he had one fault. Once you started him tracking you had to put him on a leash and keep him on it. Otherwise, since at least part of the time he wouldn't call back, he could get so far ahead you could lose him. Even following a trail, if it's a fresh and hot one, a dog can sometimes go faster than a man can keep up with him.

He made sure that he had matches, got the lantern and checked that it was full, then went out the kitchen door.

Buck was sleeping not in but in front of the doghouse Tommy had built for him. Buck was a big liver-and-white-colored dog; he wasn't all one breed, but he was all hound. He was seven years old, past his prime but still with a few good years in him.

"Come on, Buck," Hoffman said, and the dog fell in behind him as he went around the house and cut across the fields to the Garner farmhouse. It was just dusk.

They'd seen him coming and came outside, the three of them. Jed Garner had a lantern too, and a shotgun under his other arm.

There weren't any greetings. Hoffman asked Charlotte, "This path, it's the one that turns off the road to the north just past the bridge?"

"Yes, Mr. Hoffman. But I'm going along. I'll have to go to show you the place where we—where we went. Where his clothes are."

"You're *not* going, Charl," her father said firmly. "If for no other reason than that you're already so pooped out from practically running back the three miles that you'd slow us down."

"Buck will take us to the clothes," Hoffman said. "Then we'll have him circle the spot and pick up the trail. You said three miles—and it's about one to where the path starts. That'd make it about two miles back into the woods. Right?"

Charlotte nodded.

"Let's get going then," Hoffman said to Garner.

"Wait, Gus. Why don't we take my car for the first mile, along the road? Save time."

"You forget about Buck," Hoffman said. "He ain't gun-shy, but he's car-shy. If we forced him into a car he'd keep trying to jump out, and anyway it'd make him so damn nervous he might not be any good to us. We'll have to walk. Come on."

The two men went out to the road and started along it. There was a bright moon; they weren't going to need the lanterns until they were in among trees. And it wasn't fully dark yet, anyway.

"Why the gun, Jed?" Hoffman asked. "Thinking of a shotgun wedding?"

"Hell, no. Just that in the woods at night I feel better with one. Even though I know nothing's likely to jump me." After a minute he added, "I was just thinking, though. If we find Tommy—"

"We'll find him."

"All right, *after* we find him. If he's all right, I don't think we ought to make those kids wait another six months. If they're playing house anyway, what the hell, let 'em make it legal. And you wouldn't want your first grandchild born too soon after the wedding, would you? *I* wouldn't."

"All right," Hoffman said.

They walked in silence for a while. Then they saw the headlights of a car coming toward them on the road and Hoffman turned quickly and got a grip on Buck's collar, and pulled him off the side of the road. "Wait till it's by," he said to Garner. "Don't want Buck to bolt, and he might."

After the car was past them, they started walking again.

By the time they reached the start of the path it was fully dark except for the moonlight and they stopped and lighted their lanterns. From here on, part of the time they'd be under trees and need light.

They walked on. Garner asked, "Where the hell *could* Tommy have headed for, taking off stark naked that way?"

Hoffman grunted. "Let's not wonder. Let's find out."

Again they walked in silence until Hoffman said, "I figger we've come about a mile since the road. How about you?"

"I guess about that," Garner said. "Maybe a mite over."

"Then we better let Buck take over. Your gal could be wrong about the distance, and we don't want to overshoot."

He put down his lantern and snapped the leash onto Buck's collar, then held Tommy's dirty sock to Buck's nose, "Find 'im, boy."

The dog sniffed the path and started off at once. They followed, Hoffman holding the leash in one hand and the lantern in the other, Garner bringing up the rear. Buck kept moving steadily but not too fast for them; there was no strain on the leash.

About a mile farther on (Charlotte's judgment of the distance had been just about right) Buck wandered slightly off the path and sniffed something.

Hoffman bent over to look. "Dead field mouse. Squashed. Come on, Buck, back to business." He pulled Buck back to the path.

Garner said, "Charl told me about that—while we were waiting for you to come over. Didn't seem important, so I didn't mention it. But it means we're right close to the place. I mean to the place where they—went to sleep."

"What did she tell you about a field mouse?"

Garner told him. And then said, "Damn funny thing, a field mouse acting like that. Say, what if the thing *was* rabid? It didn't bite Charl, didn't break her skin, I mean; but Tommy brushed it off his pants leg. What if his finger hit its teeth and one of 'em broke the skin a little without his realizing it. Would that account for—?"

"Hell, Jed, you know better than that about rabies. If Tommy was infected, it wouldn't affect him this soon, or that way. It takes days." Hoffman rubbed his chin. "Just the same, when we find Tommy I'm going to check his hands. If there's even a scratch, we'll pick up that mouse on our way back, and have it checked. Come on, Buck, get going again."

Only about thirty paces farther on Buck turned off the path again and this time he didn't stop to sniff anything. He kept going. He led them back to where some clumps of bushes made a solid wall and started to push his way through them. Hoffman parted the bushes and held his lantern forward.

"This is it," he said. "His clothes are still here." He stepped through and Garner followed. They stood looking down.

"God damn," Hoffman said. "I'd hoped—" He didn't finish the sentence. He'd hoped the clothes would be gone, that Tommy would have returned here after Charlotte had left. He didn't know what that would have meant—since Tommy hadn't come home—but it seemed less dangerous than the alternative, Tommy being out there somewhere and still naked, whatever else might have happened to him. At any rate, he was more frightened now than when he had first heard the girl's story. The clothes looked so—empty. Until now this had seemed like a bad dream; it was becoming nightmare.

Buck was sniffing eagerly at the clothes and then at the grass where Tommy had lain. Then, circling, he started for the bushes, at a different point this time.

Hoffman let him through and went through behind him. "Come on, Jed," he said. "He's got the trail again, the way Tommy left."

Garner said, "Shall I bring the clothes?"

Hoffman hesitated. "All right," he said. "When we find him, he'll need 'em and no use our having to come back."

He waited, holding Buck back, until Garner had made a bundle of the clothes and rejoined him with them.

Then he started following the pull of the leash. Back to the path first and then off it at a diagonal, toward the northwest.

Buck was straining hard at the leash now. Not only was the trail fresher, but a man wearing only socks leaves a stronger scent than one wearing shoes. Also, on the path, there had been other if fainter human scents. Now there were none.

"Easy, boy," Hoffman said, as he and Garner followed the straining dog.

CHAPTER FOUR

The mind thing rested now. He had neatly catalogued and indexed, mentally, everything in the mind of his present host.

He knew everything about this planet Earth that Tommy knew, which was enough to give him a rough overall picture. He knew its approximate size, although not in figures, and he knew that it was mostly salt water but had considerable land area too, in several continents. He knew roughly how the world was divided into countries and the names and approximate locations and sizes of the most important of those countries.

His knowledge of local terrain and geography was much better. He knew that he was in wild country, hunting country, but only about four miles north of the nearest town. Its name was Bartlesville, and it had about two thousand inhabitants. It was in a state called Wisconsin, which was a part of a country called the United States of America. The nearest large town, or small city, about forty-five miles to the southeast, was Green Bay. Something over a hundred miles south of Green Bay was Milwaukee, the nearest large city. And ninety miles or so south of Milwaukee was a much larger city, one of the largest, Chicago. He could visualize those places; Tommy had been to them. But no farther; Chicago was as far from home as Tommy had been. But Bartlesville and the country around it he knew very well. And that was good, for this area might have to be the mind thing's scene of operations for some time. In addition to its geography, he now knew its flora and fauna. The flora didn't interest him, but the fauna did. He had mental pictures now of all the creatures of the countryside, wild and domestic. And he knew their abilities and limitations. If he should have to use an animal host again he would know which to choose for the job at hand.

Most important, he knew that man was the only intelligent species on Earth, and that man had science, apparently a fairly advanced science. While Tommy's knowledge of science was almost nil (he knew a little about elementary electricity, enough to wire a doorbell), he knew that science and scientists existed, and that (this was of major importance) science included electronics. The meaning of the word electronics was vague to him, but he had seen (and owned) a radio set. He had seen television. And he knew what radar did, if not how it worked. Where these things existed there was knowledge of electronics.

And the mind thing's eventual goal was to obtain control of an electronicist, one who not only knew the subject but who had or could obtain access to equipment and components. It would probably take him several steps—several intervening hosts—to get there, but he knew now that it could be done if he planned properly. And he had to do it. He wanted to go home.

He came from a planet of a sun seventy-three light-years away, in the direction of the constellation Andromeda, a sun too faint from Earth ever to have been named, although it has a number in Earth's star catalogues.

He had not come voluntarily; he had been sent. Not as a scout or as the spearhead of an invasion (although it could turn out that way if he could get back), but as an exile. He was a criminal. To explain what his crime had been would require the explanation of a social system so utterly alien to ours as to be almost incomprehensible; suffice it to say that he had committed a crime and that his punishment was exile.

He had not come in a spaceship. He had been sent along a—call it a force beam; that's a poor description of it but is as nearly accurate as any other simple phrase, in our language, would be. Transmission had been instantaneous; one second he was in the projector back home, the next second he was lying beside a path in the woods north of Bartlesville, Wisconsin, having experienced no impact on arrival.

The planet of his exile had been chosen at random, and with no knowledge of whether it was inhabited or inhabitable, out of the billions of planets in the galaxy which his race had charted but had never got around to investigating; there were so many billion planets that they never would get around to investigating more than a small fraction of them. The reason why they were able to chart planets as readily as we chart stars was that their equivalent of a telescope, based on magnification of the sense of perception instead of the far inferior sense of sight, enabled them to "see" planets almost as far as we are able to see stars.

So now he was here, and now he wanted to go home. It was far from impossible, for two reasons.

First, he had been extremely lucky in having come to a planet that had not only reasonably intelligent beings, but a science and a technology, however inferior to his own. The chances had been, say, a hundred thousand to one against it. If he had been sent to an uninhabited planet, he would have been completely helpless. If to a planet that had life but had not yet developed intelligence (like Earth of a million years ago) he *might* have been able to construct a projector to send himself back but the odds were against it. (Can you imagine the difficulties of a dinosaur, even with intelligent direction, in finding and refining germanium and then using it to make a transistor?)

Second, he would be welcomed home and pardoned—even honored—if he could get there. The exiles always had that chance, and one out of hundreds of them made it.

A returned exile was honored very highly indeed, and became a hero, if he brought back with him news of a species better fitted for hosts than the ones in current use. And that the mind thing could do. In having Tommy carry him he had discovered the opposable thumb and it was, as far as he knew, unique in the galaxy. It made grasping and handling things so much easier. Quite possibly he could make his projector big enough to let him take a sample human host back with him. If he did that he would save them sending a scouting expedition; they could make their first slave raid in full force.

All that was within his grasp if he worked slowly and carefully and made no mistakes. He had made one already, he now realized. He had lessened his present host's value to him by making him act in a manner against human mores, thereby attracting attention to him. For a while at least Tommy Hoffman would be an object of curiosity and suspicion, which would somewhat limit his usefulness. People would be watching him to see if he did anything *else* that seemed strange to them.

What he should have done, and would have done if he had taken a few minutes to study Tommy's thoughts, was this: He should have had Tommy come to him and move him from his dangerously exposed position, but not all the way to the cave. Tommy could have moved him to a place of temporary concealment—the high grass only a few feet off the path would have been good enough—and then returned and lain down beside the sleeping girl and pretended to sleep himself. That would have given him time to learn enough about Tommy and the girl, about human actions and emotions, so that when they awakened, he could have appeared to her to be perfectly normal. Possibly he could even (again to use the euphemistic phrase from Tommy's mind) have "gone another round" with her. The mind thing wouldn't have enjoyed it, of course; when in a host he felt no pain when he had it killed, but neither did he share any of its pleasurable sensations. He would have had intercourse with the girl simply because it would have been the natural thing for Tommy to have done.

Then they would have dressed and returned home as they had intended to do. (Once inside a host, he could control it at any reasonable distance.) In the morning Tommy could have come back, alone, and moved him to this much better place of concealment in the cave, and then returned home without having aroused anyone's curiosity.

That's what he should have done, but it was too late by the time he realized it. His alternate plan would have to suffice. It was based on the concept of something called amnesia that he had found in Tommy's mind.

Tommy could stay here on guard in front of the cave entrance all night. Early in the morning he could go back and get his clothes (the girl would have left when she got worried enough, but she wouldn't have taken them) and walk home. His story would be simple. He and the girl had got tired and lain down to rest. He'd gone to sleep. And at dawn he'd waked up in a different place, over a mile away and with no recollection of how he got there. He could hardly have walked that far in his sleep—and besides Tommy had never sleep-walked—so he must have had some reason for going there, but he couldn't remember what it was. It must be amnesia. They'd have him talk to a doctor a time or two, but nothing would come of that. And henceforth Tommy would, at least in the sight of others, appear to act completely normal—until his usefulness as a host came to an end; then he would either kill himself or, if possible, arrange his own death in some manner that would make it seem accidental.

Besides its simplicity and incontrovertibility, Tommy's story had another advantage; it would not cross up the girl's story, whichever way she told it. She might have been frightened enough to tell her family the whole truth—that she and Tommy had slept naked and that he had gone off in that state, or she might well have left that part out, If his first story didn't mention clothes at all, and if she hadn't, then their stories would match. If taxed with the fact that she had told the story differently, he could sheepishly admit that, yes, he had been naked when he had gone to sleep and had awakened the same way in the morning. His original omission of that part of the story would be entirely understandable to everyone.

Short- and long-range planning were suddenly interrupted. Through Tommy's eyes peering through the bushes that masked the cave entrance, the mind

thing saw two bobbing lights coming; through Tommy's ears it heard the excited baying of a hound on a scent, and recognized the dog's voice as that of
Buck, Tommy's father's dog.

Immediately he realized what had happened. Tommy's father had been
much more worried than Tommy could have realized. (Probably Charlotte had
told the whole truth—Tommy's leaving her without his clothes would have
been more puzzling and frightening than if he had wandered off clothed.) And
Tommy had thought (or rather, Tommy's mind would have thought if Tommy
himself had been the one using it) that they might come to look for him tomorrow but not tonight, after dark. Tommy's mind simply hadn't thought at
all of the possibility of Buck's being used to track him down.

But now they were coming, two men and the dog. One of the men would
be Tommy's father, the other probably Charlotte's father.

And the dog would lead them straight to the cave!

He had to distract them, lead them away. Even if it cost him his present
host, he couldn't let attention be drawn to the cave. They were less than a hundred yards away and were heading straight for it, the dog following Tommy's
trail.

Tommy, or Tommy's body, jumped up and ran around the bushes and toward the approaching lanterns. He ran until he was within the circle of light
of the first one and then stopped. Buck barked joyously and strained at the
leash to run to him. Gus Hoffman shouted, "Tommy? What the hell—?"

Too near the cave. He turned and started to run again, diagonally away from
the cave. He heard them start after him, still calling, "Tommy! Tommy, stop!"
He heard Garner say, "Slip the dog's leash. Buck can catch him." And his father's
reply, "Sure, and run *with* him. We'd just lose both of them."

He couldn't run in a straight line because he had to keep to open areas where
the moonlight would let him see. Occasionally, while they were still close
enough to follow him by sight, they could take short cuts through shadow
because of their lanterns, but he could run much faster and was soon outdis-
tancing them. Then he was definitely out of their sight and knew they'd have
to let Buck do the trailing again and follow his roundabout course; that would
slow them down still more.

He was able to rest a moment then, to catch his breath, and when he started
again it was at a fast trot instead of a sprint. He knew where he was going now,
and he began to circle to take himself back to his starting point.

And from there to the place, only a very short distance away, where he had
perceived the artifact (he knew now what it was, a jackknife) before the two
humans had come along the path.

It was in deep grass, and in shadow. Tommy's sense of sight didn't help at
all now, and he had to have Tommy's hands grope and feel. It was awkward,
but he knew where it was, within inches, and finally Tommy's fingers closed
over it and picked it up.

He broke one of Tommy's thumbnails trying to open the half-length rusted
blade, but finally he got it open with the other nail.

Without hesitation Tommy slashed one of his wrists, changed the knife to his other hand, and slashed the other wrist. Both cuts were deep, almost to the bone, and blood spurted freely. He didn't lie down, but within a minute loss of blood blacked him out and he fell heavily.

He was dead when the two men and the dog reached him.

And the mind of the mind thing was safely back within itself, buried under nine inches of sand in the cave.

CHAPTER FIVE

It had been a bad night for Gus Hoffman.

He had waited with the body while Jed Garner had gone back for help. While he waited he dressed Tommy's body in the clothes Garner had been carrying. Not because he had any intention of lying to the sheriff about how they had found Tommy, but because it just didn't seem decent for the body to be taken in naked.

Garner went straight home. After reaching the road he passed three other farms before he came to his own, but he wanted Charlotte to be the first to know and didn't want to tell her over a phone. She took the news more quietly than he had dared to hope, mostly because she was ready for it; she had felt instinctively from the moment she'd had to start home alone that she'd never see Tommy alive again.

Then Garner phoned the sheriff at Wilcox, the county seat, twenty miles away. The sheriff came in an ambulance to carry the body into town and, so the body could be examined quickly, he brought the coroner with him. Garner took them to the spot, and the four men, taking turns, carried Tommy out of the woods on a stretcher. Buck stayed with the party until the engine of the ambulance started; then he bolted home across the fields.

At the mortuary in Bartlesville the coroner examined the body while the sheriff talked to Hoffman and Garner. The coroner joined them to report that there was no doubt about the cause of death—loss of blood from the slashed wrists—and that the only other marks on the body were briar scratches on the legs and cuts and bruises on the bottoms of the feet. He was willing to do an autopsy if the sheriff requested it but said he didn't see what an autopsy could possibly bring out that wasn't already obvious.

The sheriff had gone along with that, but he said he thought an inquest should be held. There'd be no doubt about the verdict, suicide while of unsound mind, but he hoped something might be brought out that would help clear up the mystery of the reason for sudden and violent insanity in a boy who had never shown the slightest symptom even of instability. Also there was a minor mystery in the suicide weapon, the rusty, broken pocketknife. Hoffman was positive that it had never been Tommy's. And both Hoffman and Garner swore that when they had seen Tommy briefly before he ran away from them he could not possibly have been carrying anything; his hands had been open at his sides. He must have picked up the knife where he had used it, but how could he have known it was there, or found it in the dark?

"All right," the sheriff said, "we'll set the inquest for two o'clock tomorrow afternoon. That okay with everybody?"

Hoffman and Garner nodded, but the coroner asked, "Why so soon, Hank?"

"Had this in mind, Doc. Something just might come out at the inquest that might change our minds about an autopsy. Of course if there is an autopsy, the sooner the better. We'll have the inquest right here at the mortuary, good a place as any here, and there's no use moving it over to Wilcox. And, Gus, right after the inquest you can go ahead and make funeral arrangements. As soon as convenient if there's not going to be an autopsy—and I doubt if there will be. Who was Tommy's doctor? Doc Gruen?"

"Yeah," Hoffman said. "Not that Tommy saw him often. He was pretty healthy."

"We'll put him on the stand anyway. And maybe some of Tommy's teachers—but I'll check with them first, see if they ever noticed anything unusual that ought to go in the record. No use calling them if they haven't."

He turned to Garner. "Uh—Jed. Charlotte'll have to testify. I'll go as easy on her as I can, but it'll have to be brought out that Tommy was naked when he went off. To show he was—uh—off his rocker even then and didn't leave her for any sane reason like being mad at her, and then go off his rocker after. But what I'm getting at is—I can clear the court, except for the coroner's jury, while we take her testimony. Want me to?"

Garner scratched his head and thought a minute. He said, "I guess not, Sheriff. I think I can answer for her that she'd just as soon testify in front of everybody. Hell, the whole story's going to get out anyway and maybe sound worse, and like we're ashamed of her. Damn it, what they did wasn't so bad—they were in love and engaged, just jumped the gun a little. Don't tell my wife I told you this, but she and I did the same thing, so how can we bawl out Charlotte? And if the town or the neighbors turn thumbs down on her for it, the hell with 'em. I'll sell the farm and move. Always kind of wanted to go to California anyway."

So things had been left. Gus Hoffman had got home by one o'clock, home to the loneliest, emptiest house he'd ever known. He'd thought he wouldn't be able to sleep, until he remembered that there was most of a pint of medicinal whisky in the cupboard. He got it, and a glass. He wasn't a drinking man; he took an occasional nip on special occasions to be sociable, but this was more whisky than he ordinarily drank in the course of a year. Tonight, though, if this was enough whisky to bring oblivion, he was willing to let it. Tonight was the worst night of his life, even worse than the night his wife had died. For one thing, he'd known for weeks that she was dying; he'd been prepared for it. For another, he'd still had Tommy. Tommy had been three then, but Gus had managed to keep him on the farm and raise him there, with the help, until Tommy was of school age, of a woman who came daily to take care of him while Gus worked the farm.

Now he was completely alone, permanently alone. He knew that he'd never marry again. Not because he was too old—he was still a year short of fifty—

but because never since his wife's death had he ever even thought about living with another woman, or wanting one. He didn't know why it was impossible for him, but it was. Something in him had died when his wife had died. It was something psychological, of course, but it was something more than psychological impotence. A man suffering from that can still *want* a woman, at least in the abstract, and freeze only when he tries to have one in the flesh. But Gus Hoffman couldn't even want one; nor could he entertain the thought of making a sexless marriage just to have a woman around the house for companionship and as a helpmate. He didn't want a woman around the house, even on that basis. (Having Charlotte around as Tommy's wife would have been different, of course; he'd looked forward to that.)

All his hopes had been in Tommy. He was not a demonstrative man and had never let Tommy know how important to him had been the boy's decision to stay on the farm with him, even after his marriage. He'd wanted grandchildren and now he'd never have them; he was now the last of his line, a dead end.

Unless— With his third drink a sudden blazing hope came to him. Unless he was already scheduled to have a grandson. Charlotte could be pregnant and not even know it yet. Or had Tommy taken precautions against that happening?

Suddenly he wanted to know right away. He got up from the kitchen table to go to the telephone. Then he sat down again, realizing he shouldn't call the Garners in the middle of the night to ask them that. In fact, he shouldn't ask them at all. He should wait and see, and keep his hope alive for as long as he could.

Meanwhile it would give him something to think about besides his grief and loneliness. He could even plan. If and when Garner learned that Charlotte was pregnant he'd surely sell out and move away; he'd said he'd do that anyway if he found Charlotte in disgrace in the town or neighborhood—and while an affair might be forgiven her, an illegitimate child certainly wouldn't. Well, Gus Hoffman would sell out too and go with them, wherever they went, California or the moon. If possible, he'd talk Garner into their buying a farm together so he could live with them—or make himself living quarters in the barn if they didn't want him underfoot in the house—and help raise his grandson. Or granddaughter; he'd even settle for that. If Jed wouldn't agree to buying a farm jointly, he'd buy his as near as possible. The next-door one if he could get it, even if he had to pay a premium price to talk someone into selling it. Price need be no object, thank God; he had twelve thousand dollars in the bank and in investments, besides what he'd get for his farm here. And he'd had some pretty good offers for that.

He finished the whisky and realized that for almost the first time in his life, certainly for the first time since his twenties, he was drunk. When he stood up he found he had to hold onto things to keep from falling. He didn't bother to go upstairs or to undress; he made his way as far as the living-room sofa. He managed to get his shoes off, and that was the last he remembered.

That had been last night.

And now it was morning. He'd wakened at dawn. He'd made coffee and forced himself to eat some oatmeal. He'd done his milking and put out the cans for the dairy's route man to pick up, and had done the few other things that had to be done. All that took two hours, and it was still early. There was still work—there's always work to do on a farm—but nothing that couldn't wait until late afternoon, after the inquest. And he'd thought of something more important than work that he wanted to do.

He felt to make sure that Buck's leash and Tommy's sock were still in his pocket from last night, and then called Buck and walked across the fields to Jed Garner's farm.

Garner was hoeing in a small garden patch behind the house. He stopped and leaned on his hoe as Hoffman came up.

"Morning," Hoffman said. "How's Charlotte?"

"Still asleep, I hope. Didn't get to sleep till God knows when last night. What's on your mind, Gus?"

"Just dropped by to tell you where I'm heading. Back to where—where we were last night."

"Why?"

"Just want a look around by daylight. The place where we found Tommy's clothes, the place where we found *him*. We might've missed something, just with lanterns. I don't know what, but if there's anything to find now's the time, before the inquest."

"Makes sense," Garner said.

"Another thing, why I'm taking Buck. I'm going to where we first saw Tommy, when he ran up to us. See if Buck can back-trail him from there, find out where he'd been, in that direction. Dunno it'll tell me anything, but I want to know."

"I'll go with you," Garner said. "Might as well. Don't feel like working and I guess you're the same way. Wait till I tell Maw."

Gus Hoffman waited for him, and the two men started off.

The mind thing wasn't worried, but he was annoyed with himself for having panicked and killed his first, and thus far only, human host. Subsequent and calmer thought showed him that it hadn't been necessary. He had to lead them away from the cave, yes, but after that there had been no need for him to make his host kill himself. After he'd led them a safe distance he could have fallen and pretended to be asleep or unconscious when they reached him. When they awakened him he could have been surprised to find himself there, especially to find himself naked, and he could have remembered nothing since going to sleep beside his girl at their trysting place. True, his case would not have been diagnosed as simple amnesia, not after running away from his father as he had, but it would still have been called only temporary insanity. They wouldn't have locked him up in an asylum for that, which had been the thought that had made him make Tommy destroy himself—incarcerated, he would have been completely valueless as a host; also, he knew from Tommy's mind that mental institutions take elaborate precautions to prevent their inmates from committing suicide, and he might have been stuck in Tommy's mind for quite a while. And an unsuccessful attempt at suicide might have got him into a padded cell, which would have made it impossible.

But he realized now that they would not have incarcerated Tommy, not for one brief period of temporary insanity, They'd have watched him for a while, but not too closely or for too long, if he seemed again perfectly normal. There'd have been a talk with the doctor, of course, and he would probably have recommended taking Tommy to a specialist, a psychiatrist. But that would be good because, since there were no psychiatrists in Bartlesville or even in Wilcox (that Tommy had known of), it would have meant a trip to Green Bay or possibly even to Milwaukee. Either of those places would have a public library large enough to be worth while for him, and if he could have had some free time—or even have made a getaway for a while, if accompanied—he could have made at least a good start on learning some of the things he would have to know.

Yes, as Tommy's mind would have expressed it, he had goofed. However, he couldn't blame himself too much. It is tremendously difficult to understand immediately all the ins and outs of a completely alien world, a completely alien culture. Especially since thus far his only concepts of that world, beyond his immediate range of perception, had come from the mind of a not too bright, not too well educated high school boy who had taken no interest in any serious subject except farming. Tommy would have made an excellent farmer.

The main disadvantage of his present position, safe though he thought it was, was the fact that from here it would be almost impossible to get another human host. Men came through these woods, usually to hunt, but the chances of one happening to go to sleep near enough, within the forty-yard extreme range of his perceptive sense, were remote.

To get his next human host he'd have to use an animal host first, to transport him near enough to a place where a human would be sleeping. There would be risk in that, during transport, but it was a risk he would have to take. And, although he had actually not encountered as yet any animals within his range, he'd learned from Tommy that there were such animals, several of them. A deer could carry him easily in its mouth; so could a bear. There might be air transport, too. A chicken hawk, since it could carry off a chicken heavier than he was, would be ideal. An owl might serve; Tommy had known that owls swoop down on mice and fly off with them, but he'd had no clear idea of how heavy an object an owl could fly with.

On the whole, he thought, a bird would be best. A deer or a bear might have trouble with fences, and if there was a dog in the farmyard it would bark and waken the household. But a dog would not notice a chicken hawk circling down in the middle of the night to leave something on the roof. Then, as soon as the hawk had flown away and killed itself or got itself killed, he would have his choice of hosts among however many people would be sleeping in the house. The first act of his new host would be to retrieve the mind thing's corporeal self from its exposed position on the roof and put it in a safe place of concealment.

There was no hurry; this time he would think every detail through and make no more mistakes. Besides, no owl or chicken hawk had as yet come within his perception range. Nor a deer nor a bear. Only field mice, rabbits, and other small creatures had as yet passed within range.

But he had studied them, each of them. One can never tell when a small animal might, for some special purpose—burrowing under a wall, for instance—make a better host, temporarily, than a larger one.

Once he had studied an animal inside and out—studied it himself, not just examined the concept of it in a host's mind—he could get himself a host of that species at any distance up to about ten miles, provided that one was sleeping within that range. Having studied a rabbit, for instance, he had only to concentrate on the concept of a rabbit, if one was sleeping within ten miles or so—the nearest one, if there were several. Once a hawk had flown past within his range—no mattter at how fast a speed—he'd be able to get himself a hawk for a host any time he wanted one, if it was during the night when hawks slept. Sooner or later hawk, owl, deer, bear would come within range; he'd have himself a wide variety of potential animal hosts.

Things would have been easy for him—there'd have been no problem at all to speak of—if the same thing could have been done to highly intelligent hosts—which in the case of this planet meant human beings. Such creatures automatically resisted being taken over, and there was always a mental struggle sometimes lasting for seconds. To win he had to use all his power and to have the creature, the individual creature, within the limit of his sense of perception. And, of course, asleep.

That had been found to be true on almost all the inhabited planets which his species had visited or occupied. But there were rare exceptions, and during the night he had experimented to make sure Earth was not one of them.

He tried a field mouse first, concentrating on one by using the one which had been his first terrestrial host as a prototype. Annoyingly, it took him almost an hour to kill it so he could get his mind back into himself. First he had tried running it head-on into a tree and then into a stone. But it was so light, had so little inertial mass, that even against the stone the impact had served only to stun it momentarily. It couldn't climb well enough, he discovered, to get sufficiently high into a tree for a fall to kill it. He had taken it into the open, into a patch of bright moonlight, and had run it in circles there, hoping that the movement would draw the attention of an owl or some other nocturnal predator. But no predator seemed to be around. Finally he did what he should have done in the first place: he examined its thoughts and memories, such as they were. And he learned that there was water nearby, a shallow brook. The field mouse had immediately run toward it and into the water, and drowned itself.

Then back in himself in the cave again, he made his second experiment. He knew that there would be men sleeping within a few miles, past the edge of the woods to the south. Within ten miles in that direction was the town of Bartlesville where hundreds of men would be asleep. Using Tommy as his prototype, he concentrated on *man,* any man asleep. Nothing happened.

He made one further experiment. With some intelligent species it was possible to take over one at a distance if, instead of concentrating on the species, one concentrated on an individual, one which had already been studied and memorized. After studying Tommy, but before entering him, he had studied the girl Charlotte, inside and out. He tried concentrating again. And again nothing happened.

Although he couldn't have known it, Charlotte wasn't asleep as yet; she had gone to bed but was still crying into her pillow. But that didn't matter because it wouldn't have worked if she had been sleeping; mankind was no exception to the general run of intelligent creatures in respect to the distance at which he could make one his host.

After that he had rested; not sleeping, for his species never slept, but postponing further active thinking and planning. In any case he would have to wait until he had had a chance to study more useful potential hosts than the rabbits, field mice, and other small creatures which were all that had thus far passed within his ken. No larger creature came that night.

But now he heard—felt the vibrations of—something large coming his way. Two somethings, he decided—then three. Two bipeds and a quadruped, but one much larger than a rabbit. He concentrated his perception to its utmost limit and within a minute or two they were within its range. It was the same trio that had come last night trailing Tommy—Tommy's father, Charlotte's father, and Buck, the dog, straining at the leash and heading straight for the cave. They were taking Tommy's back trail to see where he had been before he had run toward them.

But *why?* He had recognized the possibility of their doing so, but had discounted it, not seeing any reason why they would be interested in where Tommy had been, once he was dead. Besides, since Tommy he had had no host or potential host capable of defending him or moving him. Nothing bigger than a rabbit. The sudden thought came to him of finding a rabbit, if one was sleeping near enough, and having it run across the trail to distract the dog. But as quickly, he realized that it wouldn't work. The dog was on a leash and if he tried to run after a rabbit they'd hold him back and put him on the trail again.

He was completely helpless. If they found him there was nothing he could do about it, nothing at all. But he didn't panic because the chance that they would find him was slight. They'd have no reason for digging. They'd find the cave, of course, and enter it. They'd wonder why Tommy had come here—but they wouldn't dig, he felt almost sure.

Now Buck was leading them around the bushes into sight of the entrance. He paused briefly to sniff where Tommy had crouched behind the bushes, and then started into the cave. Hoffman pulled him back.

"Damn," Garner said. "A cave, he came to. Wish now we'd of brought a gun or two and a flashlight or two. Size of that entrance, it's just the kind of cave a bear might pick."

Hoffman said, "If Tommy was in there last night, there wasn't a bear there then. And a bear's more likely to be to home by night than by day."

The mind thing understood, for it now knew the language that was being spoken. Before it had had a human host, such words would have been only meaningless sounds—like the sounds Tommy and the girl had made to each other along the path and in their hiding place before they had gone to sleep.

"Just the same, I'm going in," Hoffman said.

"Just a minute, Gus. I'll go in with you. But we might as well be sensible. Take that leash off Buck's collar and let him go in first. If there is anything dangerous in there, he's got a hell of a lot better chance than either of us of getting out safe. He'll be on his feet and we'll be on hands and knees."

"Guess that's sensible." Hoffman unsnapped the leash from Buck's collar, and Buck darted into the cave. Halfway, as far as Tommy had gone, and that was the end of the trail. He lay down.

The men listened for a while. "Guess it's all right," Hoffman said. "Nothing could of hurt him so fast he couldn't of let out a yip. I'm going in."

He entered on his hands and knees, and Garner followed. When they reached the center of the cave where Buck lay, they found the ceiling high enough and stood up. It was dim, but they could see a little.

"Well, this is it," Garner said. "Reckon this is as far in as he came, since Buck stopped here. And there's nothing here, but it's nice and cool. Let's sit down and rest a minute before we go back."

They sat down. The mind thing studied the dog. It was his first chance to do so, and thus far this was the biggest potential animal host he had had a chance to study.

Henceforth, Buck might be his if he ever needed a dog. Or the nearest other dog that happened to be asleep.

And now Buck, relaxed from his tracking, went to sleep. The mind thing considered, but waited. In Buck, he would have only Buck's senses, not his own.

"I'm trying to figure why he came here," Hoffman said.

"Anybody's guess, Gus. He was out of his mind, that's all. Probably discovered this cave when he was a kid and remembered it, came here to hide from—from whatever. You can't figure what's going through a guy's mind when he's out of his mind."

"Could be, to hide. But what if he came here to hide *something?* Or dig up something he'd hid here before? Don't ask me what, but this is soft sand, easy digging even with your hands."

"What would he be hiding? Or going to dig up?"

"Dunno. But if we found anything here—"

The struggle was less negligible than that with the mind of a field mouse, but the mind thing was in Buck's mind almost instantly. Buck lifted his head.

He—the mind thing in Buck—considered. He probably couldn't kill both of these men, but he could manage with a sudden attack to get in bites on both of them before they could subdue or kill him. That would certainly distract them from digging, at least right away. Probably it would send them hurrying back to town and a doctor. If not because the bites themselves were bad enough, then because of the same fear of rabies that Tommy and the girl had felt.

Garner said, "Not now, Gus. Look, I don't think we'll find anything or learn anything, but I'll go along on coming back with you and trying, tomorrow. Too dark in here, for one thing, to do a good job without flashlights or a lantern, and if we do it at all we might as well do a good job and be sure, huh? And it'll go quicker if we have a spade and a rake. Besides, there isn't time now. We won't get home much before lunch as it is, and after lunch we got to get cleaned up and dressed, for the inquest."

"Guess you're right, Jed," Gus said. "Okay, we might as well take off now. Least, we learned one thing we can tell at the inquest. Where Tommy went. And where he must of stayed till he saw our lanterns coming. If he'd left the cave here when he saw our lanterns he'd of met us just about where he did."

Buck put his head down again. When the men left to crawl out of the cave, he followed them, trotted alongside Hoffman as the real Buck would have done, for the two miles back to the road.

There he bolted suddenly away from them—along the road, but east, in the opposite direction from the way they were headed. He did not go back into the woods toward the cave; he didn't want them remotely to suspect that he might be going back there. Hoffman called after him, but he paid no attention and kept running.

When he was out of sight around a bend, he dropped to a trot and cut into the woods. There was no path here but, without regard to Buck's senses or his knowledge of the terrain, the mind thing had perfect orientation; he went straight back to the cave.

Once inside, Buck dug through nine inches of sand and picked up the mind thing's shell in his mouth, carried it out of the cave, and put it down gently. Then he went back into the cave and filled in the hole he had dug. When it was filled he rolled over it several times to eliminate all signs that there had ever been a hole there. Then he went outside and picked up the mind thing again in his mouth. It was no heavier than a partridge, and he was as soft-mouthed as he would have been in carrying a wounded bird.

He trotted into the woods, avoiding paths or even game trails, looking for the wildest, most secluded spot. In thick, high grass, screened by bushes, he found a small hollow log. It would serve, at least for a while. With his mouth he placed the mind thing in one end of the hollow log and with a paw pushed it in farther, completely out of sight.

Then he trotted on in the same direction—so that if anyone with another dog should follow Buck's trail, he'd simply be led past the log—and a hundred yards away sat down while the mind thing considered.

He was safe now from being found when the men came back to the cave to dig. But did he want to keep Buck as a host for a while? He considered carefully and decided against it. Buck had served his purpose, and if he stayed in Buck he would have only Buck's senses; he could not study other potential hosts and ready himself for them. He wanted to be able to get, when he wanted one, a hawk, an owl, a deer, other animals. And while he was in Buck he could not so ready himself by studying other creatures as they passed near him.

Buck trotted ahead, veering slowly till he was heading back toward the road.

At the edge of the road he waited until a car came along. Then, at the last moment, and before the driver could have time even to touch the brakes, he dashed forward, right under its wheels.

Back in himself in the hollow log one minute later (it had taken Buck just that long to die), the mind thing thought back over everything he had just done and decided that he had made no mistake this time.

Nor had he, except for one he could not possibly have foreseen. He should have let Buck wait for another car. The driver of the car that had killed Buck was Ralph S. Staunton, Ph.D., Sc.D., professor of physics at Massachusetts Institute of Technology.

Doc Staunton did not look impressive. He was small, about five feet six, and weighed slightly under a hundred and twenty-five pounds. He was fifty, and his crew-cut hair was graying, but he had a wiry strength and an agile body and mind that made him seem younger. The first thing you'd have noticed about him was his eyes, because they were the youngest thing about him. When he was amused, which was often, they didn't just twinkle; they seemed to sparkle like gray diamonds.

Right now, on vacation, he was dressed comfortably and somewhat sloppily, and he was in need of a shave. You'd never have guessed him to be one of the most brilliant men in the country.

CHAPTER SIX

Swearing under his breath, Doc Staunton braked the car to a stop. It hadn't been his fault; there was no possible way he could have avoided running over that dog, but still it was an unpleasant thing to have happened. What had been wrong with the dog? Mad and running blindly? It had simply come from nowhere, out of the bushes along the side of the road, Even if it hadn't stopped to look for cars, it couldn't have failed to *hear* his—the only sound in a quiet countryside. The car was a station wagon, ancient and quite noisy, that he had bought two weeks before in Green Bay after having flown that far. He'd paid so little for it that if he sold it even for junk at the end of his Wisconsin vacation it would have cost him less to own it than to have rented a car for six weeks.

He turned off the ignition, got out of the car and walked back, hoping that the dog was dead. It couldn't possibly survive; both the left front and the left rear wheels had gone squarely over its body. Since it would die anyway he hated the thought that it might have to live and suffer a while first. It was about twenty paces back of the car; it had taken him that far to stop. It didn't seem to be moving, nor was it making any sound that he could hear, but when he was about halfway to it he saw that it was still alive; its side moved with convulsive breathing.

Doc swore again and went back to the car. He didn't have either of his guns in it, but a tire iron would be better than nothing. He got one and hurried back to the dog, but it was dead by then; its eyes were open and glazed. Blood had run out of its mouth and there was no sign of breathing.

"Sorry, old boy," Doc said softly. "Guess I'll have to find out who owned you, and tell him."

He bent down to lift the dog by its legs to move it off the edge of the road, but then he straightened up instead and stood thinking. The dog would have to be buried in any case, whether by him or by its owner, and it would be a much less pleasant job—because of ants and possibly buzzards—if he left it here while he did his errands in Bartlesville, which might take hours. He had no shovel in the station wagon but there was a tarpaulin which was old enough to be expendable. He got the tarpaulin and spread it out, folded once, on the road; then he lifted the dog onto it, rolled the tarpaulin around it a few times, and put it into the back of the station wagon.

In town a little later he made purchases at several different places, describing the dog—it had been a hound, male, liver and white—at each, and on the third try he found someone who said that it must be the dog that belonged to Gus Hoffman, and that Hoffman would be in town because he'd be attending the inquest on his son, who had committed suicide last night, that was being held at the local mortuary.

Doc Staunton had never attended an inquest and since he was mildly curious how one was run, he went to the mortuary and found it just starting. All the chairs were taken, but several other men were standing at the back of the room and Doc stood there too and listened.

Charlotte Garner was testifying, and Doc found himself increasingly fascinated. First by her calm and courageous frankness in telling the full truth about her relations with the boy Tommy Hoffman, and then by the story itself of how she had awakened to find Tommy's clothes, but not Tommy. When she'd finished describing searching and calling for him and then running home to tell her parents, the coroner tried to dismiss her, but there was, she said, one thing that she wanted to add; his questions had led her to skip the part about the field mouse and she wanted to put it in the testimony because she thought possibly it had bitten Tommy when it had tried to run up his leg and he had knocked it off with his hand. And that maybe he had been infected by some form of hydrophobia...

The coroner let her finish, but before calling his next witness he talked to the jury a moment, explaining the symptoms of hydrophobia and its relatively long incubation period; a bite from the mouse could not possibly have affected Tommy so suddenly nor, for that matter, in such a way. Besides, he said, while it was possible that the mouse had had hydrophobia, which would account for at least most of its actions, it had not bitten Tommy; the skin on his hands had been unbroken. There had been scratches on his legs, but these were caused by his running barelegged through bushes in the woods; none of the scratches could have been a bite.

Gus Hoffman testified next, then Jed Garner. Their stories were identical because they had been together all the time.

Doc Staunton listened carefully, especially when the dog Buck was mentioned—Buck following the boy last night, Buck leading them to the cave this morning. The sheriff testified last, about being called and going into the woods with Hoffman and Garner to bring out the body.

The coroner's jury went into another room but came back almost immediately with a verdict of suicide while temporarily insane. People began to wander off.

Doc started to make his way toward the man whom he now knew to be Gus Hoffman, owner of the dog, but Hoffman disappeared into an inner office of the mortuary, no doubt to discuss arrangements for the funeral, and Garner and Garner's daughter had gone with him.

Doc then cornered the big man who was the sheriff, introduced himself, and told about running over the dog.

"Maybe it's just as well, Sheriff," he said, "that I'm talking to you instead of Mr. Hoffman because—well, Mr. Hoffman had a nasty blow losing his son last night. Possibly it would be better if he doesn't learn right away that his dog is dead too. It might be kinder to let him think the dog has just run away or got lost, and to realize gradually that it won't be coming back. What do you think?"

The sheriff scratched his head. "Well—" He hesitated.

"May I make a suggestion?" Doc asked. "To give you a few minutes to think about that and also to let me ask a question or two about the suicide, which interests me, will you have a drink with me at the bar across the street?"

"Well—guess I'll have time for one. Couple little things I gotta do here first, though. If you want to go ahead I'll join you over there in ten minutes."

At the bar, which he had investigated and found not wanting on his first day in Bartlesville, Doc ordered himself a beer and then got his pipe loaded and going. The cold beer tasted good, and he was just finishing it when the sheriff slid into the booth across from him. He said, "Beer looks good," and turned toward the bar and called out, "Hey, Hank, bring us two beers. Big ones."

And then to Doc, "Been thinking while I crossed the street. Guess you're right about not hitting Gus with the news about the dog right now. He's pretty broke up. But—uh, did you leave the dog along the road where he might see it driving home, or where somebody else might see it and phone him?"

Doc shook his head. "It's rolled up in a tarp in the back of my car. I'll bury it when I get home." He relighted his pipe, which had gone out. "Damned sorry about the dog, but I couldn't help running over it. It dashed from nowhere right under my wheels. Didn't even have time to touch the brakes before I hit it."

"Funny," the sheriff said. "Buck was always afraid of cars, ran into the fields when he heard one coming. Car-shy, like some dogs are gun-shy."

Doc stared at the sheriff. "Good Lord, Sheriff. Then he must have been crazy, running blind and deaf. Have there been any cases of rabies around here?"

"Not in a couple of years. Longer'n that, I guess." He seemed uninterested.

Doc stared at the big moon face, wondering whether or not the sheriff was stupid. Probably not, he decided; probably of average intelligence, but unimaginative. He could dismiss the strangeness of the actions of the field mouse and those of the dog as irrelevant and think only about the actions of the boy Tommy. They'd been peculiar, yes, but after all the boy had gone suddenly insane, and insane people do insane things. That would be the reasoning of the sheriff, and no doubt of everyone else, concerned or not concerned, who had attended the inquest.

Let's see, what had he wanted to ask the sheriff about the inquest? Yes... "Uh—Sheriff. I got to the inquest a little late; didn't hear the medical report. Was there an autopsy?"

"Autopsy? No, what for? Wasn't any doubt he killed himself, slashing his wrists with a knife. No other marks, except scratches on his legs, from bushes, and the bottoms of his feet cut and bloody."

Doc opened his mouth and closed it again.

The sheriff said, "Say, I been trying to place where you'd be staying or living out that road. House at the very end of it, about ten miles out?"

"That's right," Doc said. "The old Burton place, they call it; used to be a farm but it's gone wild now. Friend of mine back in Boston bought it to use as a summer vacation place. This summer he couldn't get away and offered to let me use it."

"Yeah, guy named—uh—Hastings. Met him a few times, summers. Wife with you, or staying alone out there?"

"I'm staying alone. Not married. I like to get a little solitude once in a while. When you teach—"

"What do you teach, Mr. Staunton?"

"Call me Doc, Sheriff. I teach physics at M.I.T. Specialize in electronics. I've done some work on the satellite program, too. Spent the first half of my vacation working on that, but I've got the rest of it to myself."

"You mean you work on rockets?" There was respect in the sheriff's voice.

"Not rockets themselves. Mostly on the detectors and transmitting sets in the satellites that send back information on radiation, cosmic rays, things like that. I helped design the components for the paddlewheel satellite, for one thing. But right now I'm more interested in fishing. There's a creek about a mile east of where I live that's—"

"I know it; I've lived there. But you—and your friend that owns the house, Hastings—ought to come out here in the hunting season sometime. Plenty deer out that way, in the woods north of you."

"Afraid I'm not much of a hunter, Sheriff. Brought along a rifle and a pistol, but just for some target practice. And a shotgun because Hastings said there might be rattlers around the place, but I haven't seen any yet. Have another beer?"

"Okay," the sheriff said; he held up two fingers to the bartender.

"Had any other strange deaths here, Sheriff?" Doc asked.

The sheriff looked at him curiously. "Don't know what you mean by 'strange,'" he said. "Couple of unsolved killings in the last few years, but they were robbery kills, nothing strange about them."

"No other case of anyone going suddenly suicidally—or homicidally—insane?"

"Ummm—not since I've been in office, six years almost. But what's strange about it? People *do* go crazy, don't they?"

"Yes, except that insanity usually follows certain patterns, and Tommy Hoffman's—well—"

"You're not suggesting it *wasn't* suicide, are you?"

"Of course not. Just wondering what kind of a psychosis he had, and why it hit him so suddenly, and right then. While he was, or should have been, happy and relaxed, taking a nap after—after what should have been a pretty pleasant experience. It just doesn't make sense. Well, let's skip it. You say you've fished my creek, Sheriff, What kind of fly do you use for trout?"

After he finished his second beer the sheriff said he'd better get back to Wilcox, and left. Doc ordered himself a third, and over it, and over a pipe that kept going out because he couldn't remember to keep puffing on it, he lost himself in thought. Was he going overboard in thinking that the three deaths—the field mouse, the boy, the dog—formed an almost incredible sequence? The sheriff hadn't seemed to think so, but—

Or was he making much ado about nothing? A field mouse had acted strangely. First it had sat up and pawed at the boy and girl as though to warn them away. Then it had let the girl pick it up but had nipped her. When she dropped it it had started to run away and then had run back and attacked the boy, thereby in effect committing suicide.

Then the boy, Tommy Hoffman. Again, sudden insanity starting while he was asleep or just after he awakened beside the girl, and again ending in suicide. Doc admitted that people do go insane and do commit suicide while in that state. But he'd read quite a bit about abnormal psychology and had never yet heard of a case of a person going suddenly and completely insane without having shown any preliminary symptoms and without there being some inciting cause, some traumatic experience, at the time of the onset of insanity.

Then the dog, which was where Doc had come in. Of course the dog could have had rabies, could have been running blindly and deafly—but if it hadn't, if it had been normal, then it too had in effect committed suicide by running in front of his car, especially since it had been car-shy. That was the one bit of new information he'd picked up from the sheriff, and it certainly did not make Buck's death seem more natural.

But animals, except possibly lemmings, simply do not commit suicide.

Suddenly Doc downed what little was left of his beer and knocked the dottle out of his pipe as he stood up. There were laboratories in Green Bay which could tell him whether or not Buck had been rabid; Green Bay was only forty-five miles away and it was only three o'clock in the afternoon. He had the dog's body in the station wagon and could get it there in plenty of time. Besides, he hadn't been farther from the house than the ten miles to Bartlesville in a week, and an evening in Green Bay would be a pleasant change. He could eat in a good restaurant and take in a movie if anything worth while was playing.

He did all of those things and, between leaving the dog at the laboratory—he paid in advance so he could get the report by telephone from Bartlesville late the next day—and having dinner, he picked up a dozen or so paperbacks for light reading. Strictly mystery novels. He did his serious reading at times when he was working, and read only escape literature while he was on vacation. The dinner was good; it was a change from his own cooking and better than anything he could get in Bartlesville. The movie he saw was a French farce featuring Brigitte Bardot; he had trouble following the plot but after a while gave it up and just watched Brigitte; he enjoyed the rest of it very much.

He got back a little after ten o'clock to the house at the end of the road, the house he had borrowed from his friend Hastings. It was a fair-sized house that had been a farmhouse once. There were three bedrooms upstairs, although only two of them were furnished, and a bath; there were three rooms downstairs, a big kitchen, a big living room, and an extra room used only for storage, in which he kept his guns and fishing equipment. Electricity was provided by a generator in the basement, run by a small gasoline engine, and the same engine could be used periodically to pump water from a well to a tank on the roof. There was no telephone, but he didn't mind that; in fact, he preferred it. The area around the house and to the south of it had once been a farm, but for whatever reason it had been abandoned it had not been farmed for at least twenty years. All of it except a yard immediately around the house had gone back to brush and woods, distinguishable from the wild country north of the road only in that trees were fewer and not so tall.

It had seemed a friendly, comfortable place, until tonight.

Doc got himself a can of beer from the refrigerator and sat down to read one of the books he'd brought back, but he couldn't get interested in it. For some reason he felt uneasy. For the first time since he'd been here, he felt his isolation. He fought an impulse to pull down the shades so he couldn't be seen by anything or anybody watching from outside.

But why would *anybody* have any reason for coming way out here to the last house to look through his windows? And what did he mean by *anything? Anything* capable of looking through a window could only be an animal, and why should he care how many animals might be watching him? He charged himself with being ridiculous, found himself guilty as charged, and sentenced himself to opening another can of beer and trying harder to concentrate on the mystery novel.

Going back to it, he discovered that it was open at page twenty, but he couldn't remember a single thing about the previous pages he had presumably read. He started over again. It was, or should have been, an exciting mystery; there was a murder on the very first page, But he just couldn't get interested in it; between the book and his mind there interposed the story of Tommy Hoffman... Getting up naked, except for blue socks, from lying beside his sweetheart, and running off to a sand-floored cave; crouching in it until he saw the lanterns approaching carried by his father and his sweetheart's father, and hearing the barking of Buck, the hound. Running away from them again, circling back to a point near where he had started, picking up a rusty, broken-bladed knife and slashing his wrists, both of them.

The book was open to page fifteen now, but again he had no recollection of anything beyond the first page. He tossed it down in despair and let himself think.

He decided to try his best to put the Hoffman case out of his mind until late tomorrow afternoon when, from Bartlesville, he could phone the laboratory for the report on Buck. Then, if the dog had had rabies, which would explain *one* of the three deaths, he would put the whole thing out of his mind permanently—and enjoy the five weeks remaining of his vacation without letting himself try to solve something that was probably a coincidence instead of a mystery... But if Buck had *not* had rabies...

He had one more can of beer to make himself sleepy, and went to bed. After a while he slept.

CHAPTER SEVEN

The mind thing was still in the hollow log. He had not had himself moved since the dog had put him there the day before, and then had killed itself by running in front of the car.

Since then he had taken only one host, and that for purposes of reconnaissance. He had wanted a better picture of the surrounding country, a better one than he had gained from Tommy's mind. A bird's-eye view. So just before dawn on his first morning in his second hiding place he had entered a crow (he knew it as such from the picture of "crow" that Tommy had had) while it was sleeping in a tree directly over him. He had tried the crow's night vision but it had been poor, so he had waited until light and then had flown it far and wide, watching through its eyes. First to the road and along it, flying high, memorizing the exact location of every farmhouse he passed and, by correlating Tommy's memories, knowing the number of occupants of most of them and roughly what kind of people they were. He flew east until the road ended. Tommy had thought that the last house there was vacant, but he had been wrong; there was a station wagon parked in the cleared space in front of it.

Then the crow had circled and gone back, following the road in the other direction, all the way to Bartlesville, passing the Garner and Hoffman farms on the way. He let the crow rest a while in a tree near the edge of town, and then flew him in circles over Bartlesville, again correlating Tommy's memories with what he was seeing.

A radio and television repair shop interested him most. Surely the man who ran it would know at least something of elementary electronics and would therefore be a good host, at least for a while. But Tommy hadn't known the man's name nor where he lived, although he had known that he didn't sleep at the shop. A lot of scouting would be required to learn that; and besides, with anything less than a human host to carry him, it would be highly dangerous for him to he carried into town and hidden somewhere where the repairman would sleep within his perception range.

When he had finished with the crow he had it dive and crash into pavement; there was no use in flying it back to the woods. And his mind was immediately back in himself, in the hollow tree.

And there his mind had stayed, but it had not been idle. He had, he found, been quite fortunate in one way in his choice of this second hiding place. It was deeper in the woods and in wilder country than the cave had been. Many more creatures passed within his ken, close enough for him to study them closely. Deer had passed, and a bear. A wildcat and a skunk. Many birds, including the two he knew of, which were large enough to carry him—an owl and a chicken hawk. Air transport by day or by night, when needed. From now on any one of those creatures could be his host any time he wanted one, as long as there was one of the variety he chose asleep within ten miles or so.

There had been smaller creatures, too, and he had studied them as well, when there was no larger one available at the same time for study. Snakes too, though they interested him little. They traveled slowly—and they died slowly. A hard-to-kill host was awkward. To be sure of killing one, he'd have to waste time crawling it to the road and waiting for a car. And even after that, even with a broken back, a snake could live quite a while.

So had passed the time until this afternoon, when something had happened, or had started to happen, that showed him he would soon have to make his next move.

He was getting hungry. More exactly, since he did not eat in the sense in which we think of eating, he was beginning to feel the need for nourishment. Time must have passed so rapidly for him back home before and during the furor that had led to his exile that he had not realized how long it had been, before his being sent here, since he had taken nourishment. This was something that he had to do only once every few months, and he had assumed that he had plenty of time to get himself established on Earth (once he had learned that there were intelligent creatures here) before he need worry about hunger; he had been wrong.

His species had evolved in water and had lived by absorbing microorganisms from the water directly into themselves; a digestive system had never been developed. When evolution had given them shells for protection the shells had been, despite their increasing strength, sufficiently porous to let them continue to absorb nourishment as before. Before developing shells their only protection against their natural enemies had been speed. On a light-gravity planet and in the buoyant medium of water their ability to levitate, to move in any direction, had been amazingly effective as a means of escape. That, and the sense of perception, had been theirs for as far back as they had been able to trace their own evolution.

The ability to control other minds, to make other creatures their hosts, had developed later, as their intelligence had grown. It had led the more intelligent among them to quit the deeps and live close to the shore, for evolution had proceeded in a different direction on land, and there were land creatures, who sometimes slept near enough a shore to be captured as hosts, who were much more suitable as such than anything the water had produced. They had *hands*—in fact, they were not too dissimilar to our apes and monkeys—and they could, with intelligent direction, be made to do things and make things. As a man could direct an ape, if it could control the ape's mind, to do things and make things almost as efficiently as a man himself could.

With the use of suitable hosts, the mind thing's species had developed a civilization and a science. At first they themselves had had to stay in water most of the time and operate their hosts on land. Finally they had developed a technique that eliminated that difficulty. They discovered that an occasional immersion in a nutrient solution permitted them to absorb their needed nourishment a thousand times faster and more effectively than continuous immersion in water. Now, with the help of suitable hosts, they could live as far from water as they wished and satisfy their food needs by having their hosts immerse them for an hour or so in a nutrient solution once every several months, Some of them still lived in the sea but these were relatively primitive groups, as far removed in development from their more progressive contemporaries on land as an Australian aborigine or an African Pygmy is from an atomic scientist.

But the highly civilized groups of his species had been fed by occasional immersion in a solution for so many thousands of years that they had lost the ability to live solely on what nourishment they could absorb from water. Their situation was roughly analogous to that of a human being kept alive by intravenous feeding for so many years that his digestive organs have atrophied and he can no longer survive by taking food in the manner that was once normal to him.

The mind thing could have had himself fed in the woods, using animal hosts; it is what he would have had to do if he had found no intelligent species available. But doing so, he knew, would be a long and difficult operation, involving the use of a considerable succession of hosts, each best adapted—or least poorly adapted—for one particular part of the task.

A human host working in a normally stocked kitchen could prepare an adequate nutrient solution quickly. Its exact ingredients didn't matter as long as it was rich in protein; his body would absorb only the things it needed and taste was no factor since he had no equivalent of a sense of taste. Soup stock, meat soup, or gravy would serve admirably. Even milk would serve in a pinch, although he would have to be immersed in it much longer than in a meat-rich solution.

Once he realized that he would have to take nourishment soon in any case, he decided that doing so at once and getting it over with for several months would be worth the slight risk of taking a human host sooner than he had planned to do.

He considered the choice of a human host for his purpose. Best would be someone living alone, someone who would not have to justify or explain his actions to anyone else if caught doing mysterious things in his kitchen in the middle of the night. But the nearest person he knew of living alone was Gus Hoffman, Tommy's father, and his farm was at least twice as far as the nearest one. Every extra mile he had to have himself transported increased his risk. The nearest farmhouse was occupied by only two people, an elderly couple named Siegfried and Elsa Gross. Siegfried was the dominant member of the partnership, as most German husbands are; if his wife awoke and came downstairs to see what he was doing, she'd go back to the bedroom if he ordered her to.

Of course it would be better if she stayed asleep. If, while using Gross, he was forced to draw attention to him it would diminish his further usefulness— but there was always a simple answer to that.

Since the foray would be at night, an owl would be his best means of transport. He'd test one first, of course, to make sure that it could carry his weight safely. His second choice, if the owl failed him, would be a chicken hawk, but in that case he would have to test its night vision as well as its carrying ability; it would be bad for it to fly into a tree, carrying him. If that failed—but there was no point in planning now for *all* eventualities; he would need to make alternate plans only if he found that both birds were inadequate for his purpose.

Just before dark, while most nocturnal creatures would still be sleeping, he concentrated on an owl and found himself in control of one. He was sure of getting one then, although it probably would not have been necessary. He knew enough about terrestrial creatures by now to know that, whether nocturnal or diurnal, their sleeping habits were not completely rigid. Diurnal man did most of his sleeping at night, but occasionally took naps by day—as Tommy and the girl had done. Lesser animals, since they slept more readily and more lightly, were even more prone to sleep or doze at times other than their regular sleeping periods. The dog Buck had gone to sleep in the cave, less than a minute after he had lain down there. And one of the deer that had passed near the mind thing, after browsing a while, had slept lightly on its feet for a few minutes before a sudden sound (a woodpecker in a nearby tree) had wakened it and it had moved on. No doubt the same thing was true of nocturnal creatures; after making a kill (they all seemed to be predators) and eating, they too no doubt slept or dozed a while before carrying on. He had no serious doubt that he would be able to find any kind of diurnal host sleeping somewhere by day or any nocturnal one by night, although not quite as readily as during their normal sleeping periods.

Once in control of the owl, he let it go back to sleep; he wanted it to be fully rested for the task ahead. Not until dark, when it would have done so anyway, did he let it awaken. Then he made it fly, testing the beat and strength of its wings and learning how sharply it could turn and climb. This had not mattered with the crow he had used for reconnaissance; he had simply flown it high and straight. But since the owl would be carrying him, he wanted to keep it close to the ground, flying it around trees or under their branches instead of over them. Taking the gravity of this planet into consideration—he estimated it to be about four times that of his own—he calculated that a fall of six feet would not injure him. One of twice that distance would probably be safe if he landed in grass or on soft ground. Being dropped from treetop level would certainly be fatal unless he should be lucky enough to have a thick bush cushion his fall.

When he had satisfied himself as to the owl's maneuverability, which turned out to be excellent, he used its eyes to watch for a stone of suitable size, and found one. It would weigh at least as much as he, probably half again as much, and it was flattish, roughly his own shape. He had the owl alight on the stone and grip it with its talons. Take-off was difficult, but once in the air the owl flew easily with its burden, and its grip was secure. He flew it a while to make certain of that, and then let the owl drop the stone and fly to a tree near the hollow log.

He let it rest there until he judged that it was about ten o'clock—and his time sense was excellent, as was his sense of direction. He estimated that the journey, since it would have to be a roundabout and zigzag course to avoid flying high, would take about an hour, and surely by eleven o'clock an elderly farm couple would be asleep.

When he thought it was time he flew the owl down and had it take him out of the hollow log. That was difficult, and for a while he thought he might have to destroy the owl so he could get another host for that purpose—perhaps a rabbit to crawl through the log from the far end and push him out; and then take another owl host for the trip. But finally he managed to have the owl reach one of its short legs far enough into the log to get a claw grip on the very end of his shell and pull him out.

The trip took longer than he had anticipated; the owl, although it flew easily with him, turned out to be less capable of sustained flight than he had realized, especially carrying a burden, and whenever he felt its wing muscles tiring he let it put him down and rest a while. Not out of consideration for the owl—he was not deliberately cruel, but simply had no empathy at all except for others of his own kind—but out of consideration for his own safety and because it would waste even more time to have to kill his host partway there and take another. He reached the Gross farm just before midnight.

He had the owl put him down in grass between the road and the farmyard fence and then fly several times around the farmhouse to reconnoiter and to choose a hiding place for himself. The house was dark and still. There seemed to be no dog on the premises, which eliminated one possible problem. And the best hiding place seemed to be under the wooden steps that led to the back door. It would have the additional advantage of being quite near the barn—before he tied himself up again by taking a human host, he would have a chance to study whatever animals might be in the barn. Thus far, except for dogs, all of his potential animal or bird hosts were wild ones; it might help on some future occasion—who knows what situation might arise?—to be able to use a domesticated animal as a host for some special purpose. As he had used the dog. There was nothing to lose except a little time that he could well afford.

He had the owl come back for him, carry him over the fence, and put him down beside the back steps. Then it pushed him under them and as far back as it could, which was far enough to put him completely out of sight.

That ended the usefulness of the owl, and he had it circle high and then put it into a power dive to have it kill itself against the side of the house, which would be harder than the ground. He knew the thud would probably awaken the occupants, but that wouldn't matter; they'd go back to sleep sooner or later, and meanwhile he'd be able to use his sense of perception on the barn and whatever animals were inside it.

At the last second of the owl's dive, something went slightly wrong. Finding itself flying at a solid wall, the owl closed its eyes. It was an involuntary, muscular reaction, not a conscious one, and the mind thing didn't have time to correct it; he could have if he'd concentrated on keeping the eyes open. He should have anticipated it, for the same thing had happened when he had crash-dived the crow into a Bartlesville street. But that he had hardly noticed because it didn't matter. Now with the owl it mattered to the extent that, flying blind for the last second, it crashed through the pane of an upstairs window instead of hitting the outer wall of the house.

It lay inside the house, still alive but slightly stunned and with a broken wing. A light switch flicked in the next room and the door opened, letting light into the room that almost blinded the owl—but not quite; it could still see. Siegfried and Elsa Gross stood in the doorway staring, both wearing cotton flannel nightgowns.

"A damn owl," Gross said. "Flew right through the window. I'll get my gun and—"

"Siegfried, why kill it? I mean, they kill mice and—"

The owl gathered itself, managed to get to its feet ready to attack if it had to attack to get itself killed.

The woman had taken a step toward it, but Gross said, "Back to bed, Elsa." Quite firmly. And then, "It'll claw or bite you if you try to pick it up. Them things can be vicious. Besides, look, it's got a busted wing."

They both stepped back out of sight and a moment later the man was in the doorway again, this time with a twenty-two-caliber rifle in his hands. He aimed right between the owl's eyes.

The owl stood still for the shot.

And the mind thing was back in his shell, but still watching what was happening—this time through his perceptive sense, which was a thousand times more efficient, within its range, than sight.

Gross pushed the dead owl with the barrel of the rifle and then picked it up and dropped it outside through the broken window. He went back into their bedroom and put the rifle in a corner. His wife was already back in bed and he turned out the light and got in beside her.

"Goddamn owl," he said, "must of been crazy or something. Or else blind."

"But its eyes—"

"People or animals can go blind and have their eyes look okay. 'Member the horse we had to shoot five years ago because he went blind. His eyes looked okay. Why not an owl's?"

"I guess so. Did you leave it there?"

"Threw it out the window," Gross said. "I'll bury it in the morning. Damn," he grumbled again. "Have to go in town for a pane of glass too."

"No hurry in this weather, Siegfried," his wife said. "It can wait till we go in to shop next Saturday. I can tack some cheesecloth over it to keep out flies. If you had put a screen on it—"

"Why should I, when we don't use the room and the window can stay shut? Besides, the owl would've gone through the screen too and I'd've had that to fix besides. Happen to notice the time while we were up?"

"Yah. A few minutes after midnight."

"Okay, go to sleep."

There was only silence in the bedroom and the mind thing withdrew the focus of his attention. Even if the man went to sleep right away, he wanted the woman to be sound asleep too so that, he hoped, the man could go downstairs without wakening her. He concentrated his attention in the direction of the barn.

There was a pig pen along one side of the barn and a chicken house and runway on the other, but he ignored both. A pig, he knew, was unlikely to be of any value as a host and, besides, if he ever entered one it was almost certain to be penned and so completely useless to him. The same thing was true of chickens, and either type of creature, penned in, would have considerable difficulty committing suicide or getting itself killed. It was always annoying and sometimes dangerous to be in a host that was difficult to get rid of, once it had served its purpose.

In the barn itself, besides a few mice, there were three cows, a horse, and a cat. He didn't bother studying the mice; there was nothing an ordinary mouse could do that a field mouse couldn't, and there were field mice everywhere, on farms as well as in the woods.

The cows were a little better and he took time to study one. At least they had considerable physical strength. Intelligently directed, one should be able to get out of any barn, if not by using a horn to lift a door catch, then by butting a door down; if the door was too strong for that, it could kill itself in the process of trying, so there was nothing to lose. Also, if the occasion should arise, it would be a very efficient killing machine; intelligently guided, it would be more dangerous than a bull. And one would be even easier to use by day; it dozed often while grazing or slept soundly in the shadow of a tree. And few if any fences of the kind used on farms would withstand a determined charge by a cow.

He studied the horse. It, too, could be useful in certain ways. Possibly more so than a cow. It could run faster than a cow, much faster, and it could jump a low fence or use its forefeet to batter down a higher one. And its hoofs could be as lethal as a cow's horns.

Last, the cat. As he studied it and (as he had with other animals) correlated his study with the knowledge of its characteristics and capabilities that he had learned in Tommy's mind, he gradually realized that here, for one special and important purpose, was an almost perfect host.

It could spy for him. It could go almost anywhere and hardly be noticed. It was fast and it could move silently. Its night vision was almost as good as that of an owl and, unlike an owl, it could see even better by day. Its hearing was excellent. And since there were dozens of cats between here and town and dozens more in the town itself, and since cats slept almost as much by day as by night, one would be an easy host for him to enter at any time,

He decided that, since there was plenty of time, he would try one now to determine the real extent of its capabilities. He entered the mind of the cat sleeping in the barn.

He opened its eyes. Yes, though its night vision was less than an owl's, it could see fairly well even in the almost complete darkness of the barn, relieved only by faint moonlight coming in through one open window. He guided the cat to the window, jumped it up to the window ledge and then down outside. In the moonlight, faint though it was from the thin crescent of a new moon, it could see quite well.

He ran it several times around the house, noting the silence with which it could run—scarcely a sound even on the gravel of the driveway—and checking its speed. He found that it could run very fast for short distances; for a spurt it could outdistance a dog easily, although in a sustained chase a dog would probably catch it unless it found cover or climbed a tree.

There was a tree behind the barn and he tested its climbing ability and found it excellent.

From near the top of the tree, through a space between branches, he could see that there was a light in an upstairs window of the next farmhouse toward town. He hadn't intended to keep the cat that long or take it that far, but here was an excellent chance to test its capabilities as a spying tool.

He brought the cat down from the tree and trotted it across the fields to the other farmhouse. The cat moved like a shadow in the night.

When he reached the farmhouse he saw that there were two windows lighted, both obviously windows of the same room, an upstairs corner room at the front of the house. The window he had seen from the tree on the Gross farm was the side one; the other was just above a front porch roof. There was a tree near the porch and the cat climbed it and jumped lightly from a branch to the porch roof, up its slight slope to the window and then to the outside window sill.

Its eyes adjusted quickly to looking into the lighted room. A child was lying in bed, coughing hoarsely. A woman in a bathrobe and slippers was bending over the child and a gaunt man in rumpled pajamas stood in the doorway. From their conversation—audible to the cat even though the window was closed—the mind thing learned that the child had croup; the man was asking the woman whether she thought she could take care of it or whether he should phone for Doctor Gruen.

The scene itself was of no interest to the mind thing, but he now knew that he had been right in assessing the value of the cat as a host perfect for spying, for fact-finding.

Had it not been for his need to nourish himself he would have kept the cat as a host overnight and used it the next day to widen his knowledge of the other farmhouses, even sent it into the town, perhaps to follow the proprietor of the television repair shop home from work to find out where he slept. But feeding himself came first, and there was no dearth of other cats he could use later at leisure.

His problem now was to get rid of this one. He'd been in it an hour now, longer than he'd intended. He examined the cat's thoughts to find the quickest and surest way of getting it killed, and found a ready answer.

On this farm there was a vicious dog that was kept chained in a corner of the barn. (Why, he wondered, would anyone keep a dog that had to be kept chained, which made it valueless as a watchdog? But that didn't matter now.)

He took the cat down from the porch roof by way of the tree, and ran it around the back to the barn. Again there was an open window. The dog started barking fiercely the moment the cat jumped up to the sill of the window. The cat waited a moment until its eyes became accustomed to the greater darkness inside the barn, until it could see the dog clearly. Then it jumped down inside, ran to the dog, and jumped lightly into the dog's jaws.

CHAPTER EIGHT

The mind of the mind thing, back in his own body under the back steps of the Gross farmhouse, probed the house, this time carefully to make sure that there was no other living creature in the house besides Gross and his wife—such as a dog that might bark and wake the woman when Gross came downstairs. There was no dog; only a canary bird in a covered cage in the downstairs room that would be their living room or parlor. His host would not have to go into that room.

In their upstairs bedroom Siegfried and Elsa Gross were both sleeping deeply.

The mind thing entered Gross's mind and again there was that terrible but brief struggle that always happened when he took over an intelligent entity. Disappointingly, it was briefer than had been the struggle in the mind of the boy Tommy. Was his new host even less intelligent than the boy who had failed a year of high school and who knew nothing and cared less about science, unless farming could be called a science? He'd hoped for more, from an older man, but it seemed that he'd been wrong. Gross, he saw at once, knew and cared even less about such things than Tommy Hoffman had. His education had stopped at the sixth grade and he knew little of anything outside his own farm. He didn't even own a radio and his only reading was a weekly paper and one magazine on farming, both of which he read with some difficulty.

The mind thing didn't move his host right away; he had Gross lie still until he had oriented himself in Gross's mind and had learned a few things he wanted to know before moving.

He got the answers immediately to two important questions, and both were satisfactory. First, Elsa Gross was a sound sleeper; no noise less than the owl had made crashing through the window in the next room would be likely to waken her. In the kitchen, which was not under this room, he need use only normal precautions against making noise, and not drop anything. Second, there was a quart jar of soup stock in the refrigerator, also half a bowl of rich beef gravy. Mixed together and warmed slightly—which would dissolve the probably partly solidified gravy and also enable him to absorb nourishment more readily—they would make a perfect nutrient solution. If they had not been there, and if there were no reasonable equivalent in canned goods, he would have had to use meat of some kind and cook it an hour or two to obtain a broth that still would not have been as rich as the stock and gravy combination.

That was all he needed to know for now, he decided; the rest—whatever else of interest to him might be in Gross's knowledge—he could examine at leisure later. He'd still be in the old man's mind while his body absorbed nourishment for an hour or so from the nutrient solution.

Under the mind thing's direction, Siegfried Gross slid quietly out of bed and tiptoed barefoot to the door of the room. He opened it and closed it from the outside as quietly as he could, felt his way through darkness to the stairs, and went down them. He didn't turn on a light until he was in the kitchen.

Working as quietly as possible, he got the jar and the bowl from the refrigerator. He poured the soup stock from the jar into a pan, one large enough to hold the shell of the mind thing, scraped the gravy into it from the bowl, and stirred the two together. He used a match to light a burner of the butane gas stove and put the pan over a low flame. He stirred the mixture as it warmed, occasionally testing the temperature by taking a sip from the spoon.

When the gravy was all dissolved and the temperature was right—quite warm, for the mind thing, protected by his shell, could stand quite a range of temperature, from fifty or more degrees below zero almost to the boiling point of water—he turned off the flame under the pan.

He went outside, leaving the kitchen door open to give himself light, reached back under the steps and found the mind thing. He carried it inside and placed it carefully in the liquid in the pan.

Then, after taking a look at the kitchen clock so he could time the operation, Siegfried Gross sat down to wait. While he waited, in Gross's mind the mind thing sorted out his knowledge and his memories.

What he learned was far from encouraging when he considered keeping his present host for any purpose other than his current one.

Siegfried Gross, at sixty-five, was a bitter and lonely man. He was on civil terms with some of his neighbors and with some of the merchants in the town, but he had no friends. He loved no one and no one loved him, not even his wife; there had been no affection between them for many years. They had stayed together for the simple reason that they needed one another, for different reasons. Elsa had no relatives to whom she could go, no way of earning a living on her own; Siegfried needed her help to run the house and to do certain chores allotted to her around the barn. And they tolerated one another; there was no hatred.

They had two children, one son and one daughter, but Siegfried had quarreled with both of them when, during their respective late teens, they had decided to leave the farm and go to the city. Each had written a few letters to Elsa, but Siegfried had forbidden her to answer them, and they no longer even knew where their children lived.

His future looked black because for several years he had been slowly developing arthritis, and it was progressive. He had no faith in doctors, and they probably would not have been able to help him much anyway. Already it was painful for him to do his work, and he knew that after a few more years of increasing pain he would have to give up working and sell the small farm. He owned it clear and would perhaps get enough for it to buy his and Elsa's way into a home of some sort for the rest of their lives, but that was all he had to look forward to—that, and the slowly increasing pain which would eventually cripple him completely, if he lived that long.

Part of the bitterness that had been with him all his life lay in the fact that he hated his country and its government. It was, in fact, only technically his country; he thought of himself as a German rather than as an American. His parents had brought him from Germany when he was only four years old. They had become naturalized citizens, for practical reasons only, which had made him a citizen too. But their true loyalty remained toward the old country, and so did his. He had spoken no English until he started to school at seven. He had been in his early twenties when the United States had entered World War I. They had tried to draft him and he had spent a miserable year and a half interned as a conscientious objector; actually he had no objection, conscientious or otherwise, to war. He had given that as his reason; but he had simply not wanted to fight on what to him was the wrong side.

He had welcomed the renascence of Germany under Hitler and had become an ardent Nazi, although he had never joined a Bund or any other group. When the United States got into the second war his opinions and his expression of them became even more violent. By then he was in his middle forties and there was no question of his being drafted, but he was also by then more intransigent and less discreet than he had been in his younger days. There was talk of putting him in a concentration camp, but the authorities decided that, however verbally violent, he was harmless and was in no position to sabotage the war effort. Besides, if all Nazi sympathizers in Wisconsin had been put into a concentration camp it would have required one the size of a Wisconsin county to hold them.

Often, during the war and after it, he thought bitterly of his son, who had left home shortly before the war had started. His son and his daughter had considered themselves Americans; that had been one thing, besides their wanting to leave the farm, that his quarrels with them had been about. Had his son let himself be drafted—or even volunteered—to fight against the Fatherland? If so, he hoped that he had been killed.

During the war, to follow the news, he had subscribed to a daily newspaper and had bought a radio. After Hitler's defeat he canceled the former, and vented his anger on the latter with an axe.

Always he had wanted someday, even if he had to wait until he retired, to return to the Fatherland. But always, at times when it might have been possible financially for him to do so, there had been reasons why he could not. Now he knew that it was no longer possible. He was fated to die in this foreign land in which he had already lived over sixty years, among strangers. Completely among strangers since the first years of his married life and since his parents' deaths.

In one way, and only one, had he compromised with this alien land: he spoke English and had almost lost his German. At first he and Elsa had spoken German, but she, so obedient in every other way, had been adamant, after their children were born, that only English be spoken. If he spoke to her in their own tongue, she answered him in the foreign one. Since he was no teacher, the children had never learned more than a few phrases of German, and he himself had gradually acquiesced and come to use the language he knew almost as well as the one he considered his own.

These facts about his host the mind thing bothered to learn only because he had time to kill while his own body absorbed nourishment, and because anything, however trivial, that concerned the mores and thought processes of human beings that he could learn might someday serve him. He had no sympathy for a host's despair or his problems; he was concerned only with a host's usefulness. And he had already decided that Siegfried Gross would be useless to him after tonight.

Gross was a recluse; he had no real communication with anyone else, no way of gathering information that would not be completely out of character for him and which would not arouse comment and curiosity. He had no telephone, wrote no letters, and received no personal mail. He rode into Bartlesville—in a wagon behind a horse; he'd never owned or wanted an automobile—once a week on Saturday afternoon to do whatever buying was necessary. Never oftener than that except during certain seasons when he had produce to take in to sell, something that could not wait until his next Saturday trip. He went only to certain places, and even in them he never stopped to talk or to listen to gossip or news. He had not been farther from his farm than the five miles into Bartlesville in over fifteen years—since, in fact, Germany had gone down in defeat for the second time in his lifetime.

No, Siegfried Gross, kept in character and made to act naturally, would be the worst information-finding instrument he could possibly have chosen. He was serving his purpose now, and when that purpose was finished, he must go.

Besides, the mind thing had already discovered tonight his perfect host for the gathering of information—the cat. As long as he kept Gross, he could not use cats, but one of them would eventually lead him to the human being nearby, in or out of Bartlesville, best adapted to be his host, for whatever period of usefulness. There was no hurry, now that he was being fed.

But while Gross sat waiting, the mind thing knew that he might as well gain from Gross's mind what little it did know about his neighbors. He did learn a few facts, although none of them seemed of immediate importance. Gross knew much less about his neighbors in general than Tommy Hoffman had known. And he had not yet learned of Tommy's suicide and the inquest; he probably would not have learned of it until his next Saturday trip into town.

The mind thing did learn, though, the answer to a question that had mildly puzzled him earlier: why Gross's nearest neighbor would keep a dog so vicious that it had to be kept chained in the barn. His neighbors were the Loursats (a French name, but they were of Belgian extraction). The dog was a Labrador retriever bitch, a fairly valuable dog that John Loursat used for duck hunting. Before it had suddenly turned vicious—toward everyone but Loursat himself—he had had it bred to another good Labrador and it was due to have a litter within a few weeks. Since it had attacked Loursat's wife—fortunately it had not bitten her—it was under sentence of death, but Loursat was hoping that it would not turn on its puppies when it had them and that he could let it nurse them long enough to salvage the litter before he had to shoot the dog. He had chained it in an unused corner of the barn and had given strict orders that neither his wife nor daughter was to go near it. Gross had happened to know this because Loursat, one of the neighbors with whom he was still on civil terms, had asked him if he wanted one of the puppies and, even when Gross had refused, went on to explain about them and why he would want to find homes for them as quickly as he could. Gross did not like dogs any more than he liked people; he tolerated a cat, so long as it lived in the barn, because it killed mice there.

Through Gross's eyes the mind thing looked at the clock and decided that he had been in the solution long enough; he had to decide it on a basis of timing because while in a host's mind he had no sensation in his own body.

Gross stood up and took the shell out of the now cooled solution and started with it toward the outer door. Then the thing in his mind had an afterthought and he turned back to the sink. He rinsed the shell off very thoroughly and dried it. The mind thing's afterthought had been that the odor of the solution might attract some animal and cause it to crawl under the steps and draw attention to them, perhaps even drag the mind thing out from under them. He himself had no odor whatsoever. He knew that from having been in the mind of the dog Buck when the dog had dug him up in the cave and moved him to the hollow log.

Gross carried him outside, again leaving the door wide to give himself a little light. The mind thing made his hiding place even safer by having Gross scoop out some dirt under the steps and bury him an inch or so deep, smoothing the ground carefully. Then from the steps he reached down and smoothed out the marks of his bare feet on the ground beside the steps.

Then he went inside to die.

But first he cleaned up the evidence of what he had been doing; he poured the rest of the solution down the drain and washed the three things he had used. He put the pan and the gravy bowl back where they belonged, the empty glass jar with other empty jars. Of course Elsa might miss the stock and the gravy and wonder a little, but there was nothing he could do about that. Besides, she was getting absent-minded lately and knew it; she'd probably think she'd used the stock and the gravy and forgotten about it. Then, too, there'd be the shock of his death to distract her from trivia. Although she wouldn't grieve for him, any sudden event that changes one's life is a shock. Later she'd come to realize that she was better off for his having killed himself. What the sale of the farm would bring would be much better provision for the old age of one person than of two.

Should he mention that in his suicide note? For a suicide note there was going to be, this time. That lesson the mind thing had learned from Tommy's death; it had aroused too much curiosity, enough to send Hoffman and Garner to the cave, even to make them decide to dig there. He wanted Gross's suicide to appear to be perfectly normal, fully motivated, so it would arouse no curiosity at all.

He had Gross get a writing tablet and a pencil and sit down at the kitchen table with them. Then he gave thought to how Gross would word a suicide note if he genuinely decided to kill himself. He would not have and would not mention any such unselfish motive as leaving more money for Elsa's old age. And his note, if he wrote one at all, would be short and to the point, with no apologies and no goodbyes.

Gross wrote slowly and laboriously, in a handwriting that still looked more like German script than English, although the words were English, spelled as Gross would have spelled them.

"I cant stand pane from artherites anny more. I kill myself."

He signed his name in full and then, under it, a final defiance, in German, to the country he hated. His last word. "Deutschland Über Alles."

Then he got his shotgun from the kitchen closet, loaded it, and sat down at the table again. He put the muzzle in his mouth, pointing upward, and pulled the trigger. Blood and brain matter splattered the note on the top page of the writing tablet, but the words were still legible.

Back in his own body, well hidden under the steps, the mind thing, able again to use his perceptive sense, heard Elsa cry out her husband's name upstairs. He watched her turn on the bedroom light, then the hall light, and come down the stairs.

CHAPTER NINE

Doc Staunton awoke slowly, turned over, and raised his arm to look at his wrist watch. It was after ten, which was not surprising since he'd got to bed pretty late the night before. He'd gone into Bartlesville late the previous afternoon so the time would be right for him to phone the laboratory in Green Bay about the dog. He'd phoned them and had learned what, he realized now, he'd known all along he would learn.

The dog Buck had not had rabies. Nor had he had, aside from the injuries that had caused his death, anything organically wrong with him that could be determined by dissection. The dog's having run in front of the car couldn't be explained by anything ascertainably physically wrong with him.

Doc had sighed, and had phoned into Wilcox to try to reach the sheriff. The sheriff would be interested, or at least he should be interested. But the sheriff wasn't available and his office didn't know where he was. Doc had stayed in town for dinner at the better—such as it was—of the two local restaurants. Then he'd tried to reach the sheriff again, this time first at his office and then at his home number. He got no answer at the former and no satisfaction at the latter.

He'd killed a little time in the tavern and had been enlisted in a poker game starting in the back room. One of the local merchants, Hans Weiss, the grocer from whom he bought most of his supplies, had invited him and vouched for him. There were only four others, counting Hans, ready to start the game and they'd needed a fifth. The stakes were just enough to make the game interesting; nickel ante, fifty-cent limit. Doc lost twelve dollars in the first half hour without winning a hand, then a big hand put him ahead and he stayed that way. Twice, once around eight o'clock and once around nine, he tried to reach the sheriff and failed. The next time he happened to look at his watch it was almost midnight and he decided it was too late to try again that night. By that time there were seven in the game and he was the big winner, about seventy dollars ahead, so he didn't think he should quit until someone else suggested breaking up the game. That hadn't happened until one-thirty and he'd got home at two, still forty-some dollars to the good. And he'd become a friend of everyone in the game and had accepted an invitation to play again. After all, he had to give the boys a chance to win their money back. As a comparative stranger in their midst, that was the least he could do.

Now, Thursday morning, he yawned and got up. Might as well get into Bartlesville before noon and phone the sheriff; he could make an appointment, if the sheriff was free, to drive on into Wilcox to see him. Unless, of course, the sheriff was coming into Bartlesville anyway; then he could ask the sheriff to have lunch with him.

He made himself only coffee for breakfast and got into town by half-past eleven, where he phoned the sheriff from the drugstore. This time he connected.

"Doc Staunton, Sheriff," he said. "Something I wanted to talk to you about, if you can spare me a few minutes. You coming here anyway, or shall I drive in to Wilcox and come to your office?"

"You caught me just as I was leaving, Doc. For Bartlesville."

"Good. Can you have lunch with me, then?"

"Guess so. Sure, thanks. Which restaurant?"

Doc said, "Let's meet at the tavern first. One drink won't hurt us, if we're eating right afterward."

The sheriff agreed and said he'd be there within half an hour.

Doc walked from the wall phone to the drug counter to make a few purchases. The druggist was one of the men with whom he'd played poker last night and they greeted each other by name.

"Heard you call the guy you were talking to 'Sheriff,' Doc," the druggist said. "Nothing wrong, I hope."

"No. Just want to pass on some information to him."

"Not about our poker games, I hope. Say, Doc, you live out the Bascombe Road, don't you?"

Doc nodded. "I've wondered why they call it that, but I do. Last house. Why?"

"Another suicide out your way, last night. Or maybe you heard about it already?"

Something prickled at the back of Doc's neck. "No, I hadn't. Just got in town; this is my first stop. Who was it?"

"Old geezer by the name of Siegfried Gross. Not much loss; nobody liked him and he liked everybody even less than that. He lives—lived—about five miles out from town. That'd be about three miles from your place."

Doc probed but found out only two things more: that Gross had killed himself with a shotgun sometime in the middle of the night, and that he had left a suicide note saying he was killing himself because of the pain of his arthritis.

He put his drugstore purchases in his car and strolled thoughtfully to the tavern. Mike, the bartender, was talking with two customers about the suicide of Gross, but none of them knew any more than Doc had already learned from the druggist.

Doc nursed a beer until the sheriff came in, then he downed what was left of it and he and the sheriff took the booth they'd sat in after the inquest.

"No beer for me this time," the sheriff said wearily. "I can use a pickup, Mike. Double bourbon, water on the side." Doc said he'd settle for another beer and Mike went back to the bar.

The sheriff yawned. "Guess you heard about Siegfried Gross," he said. "I had to go out there in the middle of the night and ain't slept since. Gawd, but I'm tired. And soon as we eat I got to go out there again."

"Mind if I go with you?" Doc asked.

"If you want. Was it something about the Gross business you wanted to tell me, Doc?"

"No, I didn't even know of it when I phoned you. It's about the Hoffman dog. It did not have rabies."

The sheriff raised bushy eyebrows. "You mean you had it checked? What for, it didn't bite nobody. Or did it?"

"No, it bit no one. But I was curious, especially after you told me it was car-shy, why it ran blindly in front of my car. If it had been rabid, that would have explained it."

"Hell, Doc, dogs get run over every day. He was probably tracking a rabbit that crossed the road there, had his nose down and wasn't watching. You can't make a supreme court case out of a dog getting itself run over."

"I suppose not, but— Sheriff, was there anything unusual in connection with Gross's suicide?"

"It was plenty messy. Put the barrel of a shotgun in his mouth and pulled the trigger, blew his brains all over the place. Took our mortician friend over an hour to clean up that kitchen. Lord, what a mess."

"Will there be an inquest?"

"With a suicide note in his own writing, what for? Just a waste of taxpayers' money. Well, let's have one more quick one and then go and eat, huh?"

It wasn't until over dessert and coffee that Doc again asked if there had been any unusual circumstances, anything at all, in connection with the suicide.

"Funny thing or two happened the same night, but nothing to do with the suicide," the sheriff said. "An owl flew through the window, through the glass, I mean, around midnight, and Gross had to shoot it because it had a busted wing."

"With the same shotgun?"

"Hell, no. Used a twenty-two rifle for that. And it was maybe three hours after that he killed himself, but I figure he couldn't go back to sleep and laid there suffering and finally decided to put himself out of his misery like he'd done to the owl, and went down to the kitchen and did it."

Doc frowned. "Was there any physical contact between Gross and the owl?"

"Not till after it was dead. After he shot it Gross tossed it out through the busted window and told his wife he'd bury it in the morning." The sheriff stopped to take a swallow of his coffee. "Loursat, that's the guy next door, buried it. And the cat. Sometime in the night Gross's cat got in Loursat's barn and a vicious dog there killed it."

Doc Staunton look a deep breath. He said softly, so softly that the sheriff could barely hear it, " 'The Owl and the Pussycat went to sea, in a beautiful pea-green boat.' "

"Huh?"

"Line from a nonsense poem by Edward Lear. Sheriff, have you ever known an owl to fly through a pane of glass before?"

"Dunno about an owl especially, Doc, but birds fly into glass all the time. Got a picture window in my house that a bird flies into—oh, maybe once or twice a week. Mostly sparrows. Usually just stun themselves a minute, but once in a while one breaks its neck. Well, guess we're ready. You want to ride out with me, or go in separate cars so you can go on home after?"

CHAPTER TEN

The mind thing had learned much that surprised him.

Since the suicide of Siegfried Gross he had spent most of the time deliberately hostless so he could stay within himself under the steps and use his perceptive senses to see and hear all that went on inside the Gross farmhouse or near it.

He learned above all that he had been careless, and had aroused curiosity by the things he had made his hosts, human or animal, do, especially by the manner in which he had made them kill themselves.

He had had no idea of the fuss and bother caused by a human suicide, even when the suicide left a note saying that he was killing himself. What had happened in the Gross house since Siegfried's suicide in the kitchen had been a revelation to him in human mores.

It had started immediately after the shotgun blast. Elsa Gross had come running down the stairs, and had been a good deal more excited and disturbed than he had anticipated, having known from Gross's mind that there was no real love between them.

Her initial shock had been tremendous. After the worst of it had worn off she had put her shoes on and a coat over her nightgown and had run out of the house and started off in the direction of the nearest neighbors, the Loursats, through whose window he had earlier seen the man and woman in the bedroom of the sick child. It was their vicious dog that had obligingly freed him from his cat host by killing the cat.

Elsa Gross had come back about half an hour later and Loursat had been with her. From their conversation the mind thing had learned that Loursat had phoned the sheriff and that he would be there within an hour; Loursat had come back with her to await the sheriff's coming. His wife would have come too, except that she had to stay with the sick child, who was better, but still shouldn't be left alone.

Loursat suggested that Elsa Gross go upstairs and dress, and while she did this he examined the kitchen as thoroughly as he could without stepping into any of the blood splatters. He read the suicide note several times and shook his head. But he didn't touch it or anything else in the kitchen.

Then he went into the living room—still well within range of the mind thing's perception—and waited there until Elsa Gross came down. There in the living room, out of sight of the thing in the kitchen, they talked.

The mind thing learned that, despite the note, Elsa Gross was bewildered by her husband's sudden suicide. He had had arthritis, yes, but it just couldn't have been bad enough to make him want to kill himself because of it. Why, he'd been perfectly normal and not in pain at all around midnight when the owl had waked them up flying through the window. Loursat had asked her about that and she'd told him what had happened.

"Funny about the owl," Loursat said. "Never knew one to do that before. Wonder if there's some kind of craziness going around. Like—you've heard about Tommy Hoffman, haven't you?"

She hadn't, and he told her.

It was a little after three o'clock in the morning when the sheriff came in an ambulance and brought with him the coroner and the mortician.

From all the questions and the conversations, the mind thing was learning how seriously human beings took the suicide of one of themselves, even when the suicide left a note to explain his reasons.

The next day he learned even more. Neighbors dropped in to sympathize with Mrs. Gross and to offer their help. Loursat came again, this time with the bad news that the Gross cat had somehow got inside his barn and that his dog, despite being chained in a corner, had killed it. Then more neighbors called and *that* became a topic of conversation.

At noon Mrs. Gross had missed the gravy and the soup stock. The mind thing knew she had missed them, or at least one of them, because she searched the refrigerator thoroughly, moving everything in it behind which a bowl or jar could have been hidden.

Shortly after noon the sheriff had come back, this time bringing a different man with him. He told Mrs. Gross that there would have to be an inquest, although with the suicide note it would be just a formality and wouldn't take long. He suggested having it the next afternoon, at the mortuary, and told her he'd pick her up in his car to take her there and bring her home again afterwards. While she was there she could make arrangements with the mortician for the funeral.

Then he had introduced the man who had come with him as a Mr. Staunton. He said Mr. Staunton was a scientist who was vacationing near Bartlesville, and that he had become interested in the completely mysterious suicide of Tommy Hoffman and had been trying to find a satisfactory explanation for it. And now, because of the coincidence of another suicide happening so soon after and so near the first one, he was curious about that too, and would like to talk to her about it if she was willing.

Mrs. Gross had been willing to talk; she even insisted on making coffee for them, since she said she hadn't bothered making any just for herself to go with her lunch.

Mr. Staunton was a small wiry man, somewhere in his fifties, with iron gray hair in a short crew cut and with dancing, piercing bright blue eyes.

His curiosity was almost insatiable. He must have asked at least a hundred questions, and Elsa Gross answered all of them. A question about whether anything else unusual had happened brought out the death of the cat and the missing items from the refrigerator. And then he'd asked a lot of questions about each of those matters. He seemed both excited and puzzled.

The mind thing was learning most of all how greatly he had underestimated the curiosity of human beings. Of course his only direct knowledge of their attitudes had come from an immature and incurious mind—Tommy had never been interested in problems and had simply accepted the world as he saw it— and from the rigid and dogmatic mind, phlegmatic and intractable, of a man who had cared nothing about anything outside his own narrow world and opinions.

The mind of this little man Staunton, so far as the mind thing could judge it from the questions he asked and his manner in listening to their answers, was something else again, a revelation. And he was, the sheriff had mentioned, a scientist. What kind of scientist? Probably, from the questions he'd asked, not one of the physical sciences; but even so, might he not make a better next host than the television repairman in Bartlesville, who after all would be more of a mechanic than a scientist?

Too late, just as Staunton and the sheriff were leaving, it came to him that he should keep track of this possibly desirable host, learn where he lived, and investigate his possibilities. When he thought of it they were almost outside his range of perception, on the way toward the car or cars they had left on the road, and he quickly tried to think of a host he might find near enough to be able to follow the car the man Staunton would get into.

The horse in the barn was his first thought, but he rejected it instantly, even though the horse did happen to be dozing at the moment. As has been said, he was learning much. The horse might have broken out of the barn and been able to follow the car, but for it to do so would have been completely outside the pattern of a horse's normal actions, and he knew now that whenever he drew attention to one of his hosts by having it perform an uncharacteristic act, he thereby endangered his own project. Horses simply did not go breaking out of barns and chasing automobiles to their destinations.

He thought of a bird. First of a chicken hawk, because it was fast, but none was sleeping within his range. Then of an owl, because it would be sleeping by day—but he discarded the thought quickly when he realized that an owl was much too slow a flier to keep up with an automobile.

Then he thought of a sparrow; he didn't know a sparrow's flying speed, but sparrows were plentiful and even by day he'd surely find one asleep somewhere nearby.

The sparrow he chose had been sleeping in a tree about two hundred yards back from the house. As he circled up into the air he saw that he was too late; the two cars that had been parked on the road in front of the farm were driving off in opposite directions, each already almost a quarter of a mile away. Too far, even through a sparrow's eyes, to be able to identify either car if he should ever see it again. Besides, he could see now that a sparrow could not possibly have kept up with a car.

He was careful in getting rid of his host. He flew it across the road and deep into the woods before he flew it head-on into a tree; and he remembered the involuntary closing of the owl's eyes and concentrated on keeping the sparrow's open. Even so, the attempt to kill the bird was not immediately successful; a twig too small to be seen at the speed at which it was flying deflected it, and instead of breaking its neck it broke a wing and lay helpless under the tree,

Since there was no alternative to patience, he was patient. The sparrow would die of hunger or thirst, if one of its enemies did not find it. And he himself, his shell, was safe under the steps at the back door of the Gross farm. He perceived but did not feel his host's pain; pain was something he could feel and understand only in himself, in his own body. Such pain could come from extremes of heat or cold, but extremes far greater than occurred on this particular planet. Or it could come at the moment of death if his shell were ever broken, or even cracked.

There was no hurry about anything, now that he had taken nourishment and would not have to do so again for months. He expected confidently to have possession by then of a really suitable host who had the knowledge, the money, and the ability to build him the electronic machine that would get him home. No one of those things would be of much value without the others—unless he used a succession of hosts, and that would be awkward, and dangerous.

He thought of reproducing himself, a voluntary process with his species, but immediately discarded it as impractical. Once the process of fission was started it could not be stopped, and for a long while he would be helplessly schizophrenic, in partial control of each of the two parts into which his shell would be forming, in insufficient control of either part to be able to take or direct a host. It was a penalty his species had paid for their highly specialized evolution, this state of helplessness during reproduction; each part needed the help of another or others of his kind to direct a host or hosts to care for him during a period of almost a terrestrial year.

On only a very few planets could a member of his species propagate alone; there were a few, a very few, moderately intelligent races in the galaxy which accepted host status willingly and could be trained in advance to continue to care for a mind thing during the period when he was helpless to keep a host under control.

He was resigned to waiting out the death of the sparrow even if it took days, but shortly after full dark he heard the flutter of an owl's wings overhead. He fluttered his own good wing to attract its attention, and the owl saw and flew down. Less than a minute later its cruel beak had killed the crippled sparrow, and the mind thing was back in his shell, on the Gross farm.

He was just in time to hear knocking at the door and to see—with his perceptive sense that made things simultaneously visible and transparent—the sheriff standing outside the front door and Elsa Gross going to open it. She was taking off a white apron that she was wearing over a plain black dress. Mrs. Gross would not have to spend money for mourning clothes, the mind thing knew from the contents of her closet upstairs. Almost all of her "good" clothes were black already.

"Evening, ma'am," the sheriff said, when she had opened the door. "Came out to take you in to see the undertaker, if you're ready to go."

"Thanks, Sheriff, but Mr. Loursat next door was here. He's coming in half an hour to take me in. Didn't he phone you? He said he would."

"Probably tried but didn't reach me. Been lots of places, but not home or back to the office." He took off his hat and rubbed the top of his balding head. "Well, if you don't need me—"

"Won't you come in anyway, just for a minute? Maybe have a cup of coffee? It's still hot, I think."

"Well—guess I could use a cup. All right, thanks."

She stepped back and he followed her in and closed the door.

"You set there, Sheriff." Mrs. Gross indicated a comfortable chair. "I'll bring us each a cup. Cream and sugar?"

"Just a little sugar."

She came back a moment later, handed the sheriff a cup, and sat down with another one in her lap. "Is it still hot enough?"

The sheriff took a sip. "Just fine. I don't like it *too* hot. Ma'am, have you made any plans? I mean, you don't intend to try to run the farm yourself, do you? I guess you could, with a hired hand, but—"

"I'm getting a little old for that, I guess, Sheriff. No, if I can sell the farm, I will. And maybe it's sold already, kind of."

"Who to, if I may ask, ma'am?"

"Mr. Loursat's got a brother, working in Menominee. He's a machinist but he was raised on a farm and likes farming; he's been talking about getting himself a little one instead of working in a town. Mr. Loursat's going to write him about it. They're close to one another, and he thinks his brother will jump at a chance to get a farm next to his. He says, too, he can raise enough money to lend his brother for a down payment if he hasn't got that much saved."

"Sounds like a good idea, ma'am."

"Yes, it does. And if it takes a little while to work out, I've got enough help to get me by, at least till the end of school vacation. Mr. Kramer, who owns the farm on the other side, has a boy in high school, doing nothing this summer but helping his father. He dropped in to tell me the boy's a good worker and would work half days for me if I wanted, the rest of the summer."

"Sounds fine, ma'am. Looks like you'll make out, all right. Plan to live in town? Here, I mean, in Bartlesviile!"

"I—haven't decided yet."

"Don't I remember you got a son and a daughter?"

"I—had. But Siegfried quarreled with them both, and wouldn't let me write to either. And they gave up writing, it's been over ten years now."

"You don't know the last addresses?"

"Not street addresses. Bertha was in Cincinnati, Max was in Milwaukee. But that was ten years ago."

The sheriff smiled. "Knew if I kept asking questions I'd find something I could do for you. I'll write the chief of police in both places. They'll be able to find a lead to at least one of them, maybe as easy as looking in the phone book. And if you find one, you'll find both; they're probably in touch with one another."

"Thank you, Sheriff." Mrs. Gross smiled, but then suddenly there were tears running down her cheeks.

Another knock, Loursat's, sent her to the door, hastily wiping her eyes and her cheeks as she went.

Within ten minutes they had all gone; the sheriff first and, a few minutes later, Mrs. Gross and Loursat; he had waited to show her the letter he had just written to his brother in Menominee, Michigan, which he intended to mail while they were in town.

The mind thing considered.

He had plenty of time to consider, during the two hours she was away, and afterwards when she had gone to bed and to sleep.

He planned. Now that he knew *her* plans, Elsa Gross was a possible next host. He planned ahead, but tentatively, contingent upon two ifs. One, that she should be able, as she hoped, to sell the farm. Two, that by that time—which would no doubt be a few weeks hence—the sheriff would have been able to locate either her daughter or her son, in Cincinnati or in Milwaukee—or for that matter, elsewhere, if elsewhere turned out to be any relatively major city.

She was asleep now and he could have taken over, but he didn't; he could wait—she'd be sleeping here every night for at least a couple of weeks. And after all, there was the possibility things wouldn't work out as she had planned; maybe Loursat's brother wouldn't want the farm, and maybe the sheriff would be unable to locate either her son or her daughter. Also, it would be bad to have to make her kill herself here, even if he could arrange to make it look like an accident; two deaths by violence would draw altogether too much interest to the farm.

But he could wait, and plan while he waited, always taking a better chance in another direction if he could find one. The sheriff would be an excellent next host, better than Elsa Gross even if her plans worked out; the sheriff could find reason any time to take a trip to Milwaukee and would have complete freedom of movement there to investigate things and people the mind thing would want investigated. And the sheriff drove a car, so it would be easy to get him killed when he had served his purpose; he could simply have a head-on collision in such a way that it would be presumed that he had gone to sleep at the wheel, or blacked out. If the sheriff turned out to be a drinking man so that getting drunk wouldn't be too out of character for him, it could be worked that way.

But getting the sheriff for a host was an outside chance, in any case. He lived, and slept, in the county seat. In Wilcox, not in Bartlesville. That was too far for the mind thing to risk having himself transported there by an animal host.

Meanwhile, though, he could expand his knowledge of the countryside and the nearby town, and of the inhabitants of the town. The radio-television repairman had turned out to be a poor prospect, but there might be better ones. Even if not, one could not have too much knowledge.

So—the cats. The silent-footed, keen-eared cats that made such perfect spy-hosts.

The mind thing concentrated upon the concept *cat*.

CHAPTER ELEVEN

Friday morning was cloudy in Bartlesville, and just before noon a slight drizzle of rain starred to fall. Willie Chandler looked out of the window of his radio and television repair shop and was glad he'd brought a lunch and wouldn't have to walk to the restaurant.

It was about the only thing he was glad about.

Business was poor and he was head over heels in debt. He'd made a bad mistake, three years ago, in believing that Bartlesville was large enough to support a repair shop for radio and television sets. Every family, almost, had a radio—but it was very seldom that anything went wrong with one, And there were few television sets; it was possible to get reception from Green Bay, but it was not too satisfactory at that distance. Even the few people who owned sets used them very little.

Willie Chandler was thirty-two; he was tall and lanky and wore shell-rimmed glasses. He had a cheerful smile and people liked him and gave him what repair business they had, but it just wasn't enough to let him support himself and an invalid mother.

He had been born and raised in Bartlesville. His father had owned a not too prosperous feed business there and, after high school, he had worked in his father's store until his father's death.

But he had never liked the feed business, and had always been interested in radio; he had made his own sets as a boy and understood a little, at least, of how they worked. He had talked his mother into selling the feed store—the only valuable part of his father's estate—and using part of the proceeds to send him to Chicago for four months to attend a technical school that taught radio and television repairing. His mother had not been an invalid then, so it had been all right for him to leave her that long. At the end of the course, most of the rest of his father's money had gone into setting him up in business as a repairman.

The shop had never actually lost money, but it had earned pitifully little. A year later his mother had been partly paralyzed by a stroke, and doctor and hospital bills had taken the rest of her money. He had had to borrow several times from the bank and to stretch his credit to the breaking point with wholesalers to keep up his stock of tubes and other parts. Currently the shop brought him in barely enough to stave off foreclosure by paying interest on his loans, and to provide the absolute necessities of life for his mother and himself. At their home, a small rented cottage with the rent usually a month or two overdue, a neighbor came in to feed Mrs. Chandler at lunchtime; Willie did all the rest of the work himself.

Except for his mother, whom he could not leave and who was unable to travel, he knew he'd be much better off to let the bank and his creditors foreclose and take his stock and equipment. In a city such as Milwaukee or Minneapolis, he could get a job as assistant in a repair shop big enough to use more than one man and make more money than he was making now, a lot more. But unless her condition should improve, and that seemed unlikely, he was stuck with the status quo. He couldn't even call the deal off and take a job in some other store in town, selling groceries or hardware or whatever, since there weren't any such jobs open. He'd even talked to the man who'd bought the feed store and had learned that there was no chance of his getting back the job he'd had with his father. He knew nothing of farming, and even if he could get a job as a farmhand he wouldn't make enough to take care of his mother in town; a good part of a farmhand's wages were in the form of room and board.

He was stuck with doing the best he could with what he had, at least until someday his mother got well or— He loved his mother too much to think about the "or."

He left the bleak view from his front window and went back to his workbench. He cleared space on it and opened the lunch he'd put up for himself that morning. Wrapped with a small thermos jar of hot coffee, there were two sandwiches. One was peanut butter and the other jelly; he'd been having to watch pennies for so long that he was used to such fare. Only on special occasions did he splurge on buying sandwich meat for a lunch. At home they seldom had meat other than hamburger, the cheapest kind, or a soup bone. Rent, both for the house and for the store, came first, and while he and his mother got enough to eat in quantity, it was seldom they could afford really good eating. The last really good eating he could remember had been for a month about three months ago when Walter Schroeder had been short of cash to pay for repairs to his television set and had offered him a smoked ham instead. It had been a twenty-pound ham and a real bargain for him, because he'd only replaced a couple of small tubes in the set and wouldn't have charged Schroeder more than six dollars in cash. The ham had been worth twice that and they'd eaten well for almost a month.

He finished the peanut butter sandwich and most of the jelly one and was finishing the hot coffee when he heard a scratching sound and looked around to see where it came from.

A cat was sitting on the sill of the side window, scratching at the glass with one paw. It was a big black cat and it looked as wet and bedraggled as though it had been in swimming. He walked over to the window and looked at the cat at closer range. He didn't recognize it as any cat he'd seen before. "Well, what do you want, cat?" he asked it. He liked cats.

This one looked gaunt and almost starved—although he realized that part of the reason for its looking that way was that the rain had plastered down its fur. As though in answer to his question the cat opened its mouth and probably miaouwed, although he couldn't hear the miaouw through the glass, and then it pawed and scratched again at the pane.

"Want to come in out of the rain? Sensible cat!" Willie opened the window and the cat dropped down lightly on the floor.

He closed the window and looked down at the cat. "Hungry?" he asked. " 'Fraid all I can offer you is bread crusts with a little jelly, and that's not exactly cat food, but if you're really hungry—"

He sat down at the workbench again and broke a cat-sized piece off one of the crusts of the jelly sandwich. The cat sniffed at first, as though puzzled, and then ate the bit of crust. What was left of the crusts followed, in small pieces. Willie knew enough about cats to know that they would eat things handed to them in bite-sized pieces which they would ignore if offered in bulk.

"Thirsty too?" Willie asked. He rummaged about the junk on the workbench until he found a tin lid that would hold water. He took it to the sink at the back and filled it, and put it down. "Sorry it isn't milk," he said, "but if you're thirsty enough—"

The cat took a few laps of the water. Willie looked at the two towels hanging over the sink. One of them was dirty enough to take home and wash, the next time he did washing. He took it down. "Rubdown's the only other thing I can do for you, cat. I can't get you dry, but I can get you less wet than you are now."

The cat held still and seemed to enjoy the rubbing. Willie had barely finished when the phone rang. He answered it, "Willie Chandler, radio and T.V. repairs."

"This is Cap Hayden, Willie." Cap Hayden ran the general store and was postmaster on the side. "Asked me to call you when a package came from Chicago. It's here."

"Swell, Cap. I'll be right over."

"Just a second, Willie. Bring some money with you. It's C.O.D., six dollars and eighty cents. And I can't put that on your bill 'cause it's government money for the post office department and I got to keep those things straight, in cash."

"Damn it," Willie said. "Listen, the reason I'm in a hurry for that package is that one tube in it, a kind I didn't have in stock, is for Dolf Marsh's T.V. set. I've put a lot of work in it already but I can't finish it without that one tube. I'll get twenty bucks for the job—put in plenty of time on it—and he pays cash on the barrelhead, so I won't have to wait. But I've got only three dollars and some change in cash. If you can lend me the difference—out of your pocket, not putting it on the bill—I'll pay you the minute Dolf pays me."

"Well—this one time, Willie. But like you said, in cash and you pay me when Dolf pays you."

"Thanks a lot, Cap. Seeing you."

Willie took his coat and hat from a hook on the wall, went to the door and turned. "Cat," he said, "you keep shop while I'm gone. I won't bother locking up, nothing worth stealing. If anyone comes in—but nobody will—tell 'em to wait, that I'll be right back."

He opened the door and then turned back again. "Cat," he said, "let's get one thing straight. You're welcome to stay here till it's through raining and till you're fully dry. But I can't keep you. Ashamed as I am to admit it, I can't afford to keep a cat, here or at home. If you heard that phone conversation, you know how broke I am. I hope you got a home to go back to, because I wouldn't keep a cat unless I could feed it right—cat food and milk. And while that wouldn't run much, not much is too much in my case, right now and for maybe a long time to come."

The cat didn't answer and Willie went out and closed the door behind him. He ran to the general store and post office and, after getting his package, ran back again. He kept close to the buildings and didn't get wet enough for the rain to have soaked through his coat. He hung the coat and his hat up again and then went to his workbench to open the package.

The cat had been up on the bench and had jumped down when he opened the door. Now, in the thin film of dust which covered most of the bench he saw tracks which showed that it had wandered about quite a bit up there. It had apparently examined and sniffed at two television-set chassis—the one he was going to work on now that he had the needed vacuum tube; and another that needed a new picture tube for which he had also sent away. And the cat had apparently examined various odd parts and tools that had been lying loose.

Also there had been a loose-leaf handbook of circuits lying open at the back of the bench; and now it was open at a different page than the one he remembered. He said, "Cat, you studying electronics?" and grinned down at it, amused at the thought. He'd thought he'd left the book open at the circuit for Dolf Marsh's set, but he must have been wrong about that.

He opened the package, threw the cardboard away, and put the various small items of its contents where they belonged, keeping out the tube for Dolf's set and pulling its chassis along the bench in front of him.

He patted the edge of the bench invitingly and said, "Come on, jump up again and watch me work. I don't mind teaching you electronics, except I don't know too much about it myself. Not the theory of it, that is. I just had a four months course. I can follow a circuit all right, but I don't know why it works any more than you do. But come on up."

He patted the edge of the workbench again and this time the cat jumped up. It sat still, curled up and watching him with the intentness and alertness with which only a cat can watch something.

He was lonesome and he talked to it while he worked. He seemed to feel its sympathy, or thought he did, when, after he had replaced the faulty tube and plugged in the set, he found that it still didn't work properly. He told the cat what he was doing while he checked condensers and capacitances, and looked for loose connections.

And then, having found the perfect audience, he found himself telling it his personal problems, his worries about the shop and whether he could keep it going, his worries about his mother, about his doubtful future. He could relieve his mind, he found, by telling the cat things he couldn't possibly tell to any human being; not to his mother, because they would cause her more worry and grief than she already had; not to anyone else, because to no one else could he admit how hopeless his prospects looked to him—let alone how much he wanted to get married, but couldn't see even dating a girl, under the circumstances. Even taking one to a movie would have taken money he could not afford from his slim budget.

The cat was a good listener. When finally it jumped down from the bench and ran to the door, where it miaouwed and pawed at the glass, he walked to the door reluctantly to let it out.

"Cat," he said. "Come back any time. Same window, same signal. I'll share my lunch with you if I can't do anything more."

The rain had stopped. He watched the cat through the glass of the door as it ran across the street and disappeared into an areaway.

Obviously it had a home somewhere. But, he thought, someday he'd have to get a cat of his own. It couldn't cost him much to feed one, and it would be the first extravagance he'd allow himself, if and when the pressure on him ever eased off a little.

He never knew, never suspected, that he had just been judged and found wanting; that he had been spared an experience which would have led soon to an early death.

CHAPTER TWELVE

Doc Staunton had spent the morning making voluminous notes on the two human suicides and the phenomena which seemed to have accompanied them— at least in regard to time and place, if no other connection could be traced. But he wanted more than notes; while statements at the inquest and conversations, especially the ones at the Gross farm, were so fresh in his mind he wanted them down on paper, as nearly verbatim as he could get them down.

But getting *everything* down, he realized, was going to be one hell of a job, especially as he didn't have a typewriter with him and was only a mediocre typist in any case. He spent half an hour writing in longhand and had only three pages, giving a detailed description of the manner of death of the dog and just a start into the inquest testimony of Charlotte Garner, when he began to get writer's cramp. It was going to take him thirty to fifty pages, he realized, to get all the facts down in detail, let alone his deductions, his mental processes which refused to permit him to accept the allied phenomena—the apparently suicidal animal deaths and the missing soup stock and gravy from Mrs. Gross's kitchen—as simply isolated and coincidental happenings having nothing to do with the human deaths. It would be almost as bad as writing a book in longhand.

But it had to be put down, somehow, while it was fresh in his mind. He considered going into Green Bay to try to rent a tape recorder, or to buy one if he couldn't rent one. But he hated the things, mostly because he liked to be able to pace while he dictated. And in any case he'd have to hire someone to transcribe the tapes, so it would be better to find a stenographer who could take his dictation in shorthand and transcribe it.

Probably he'd have to find someone in Green Bay, but he'd try Bartlesville first on his way through it.

The editor of the *Clarion,* Bartlesville's weekly newspaper, would be his best source of information. And Doc knew him because by now he'd played in two poker games with him. Yes, Ed Hollis would be the best person to ask. He might even know someone in Wilcox, which was a little bigger than Bartlesville and only about half as far as Green Bay.

Hollis was pounding an ancient Underwood when Doc walked in just before noon. He said, "Just a second, Doc," and finished a sentence before he looked up. "What gives? And are you playing in the game tonight? Hans just phoned me that there's one on—and there's no way of reaching you by phone. Lucky you dropped in, if you want to take some more of our money."

"I'll try to make it, Ed. But I dropped in to ask you something. Is there anyone in town here who can take shorthand and do typing?"

"Sure. Miss Talley, Miss Amanda Talley."

"Is she working now? Would I have to use her evenings?"

"She isn't working now, except an occasional part-time job. She's an English teacher at the high school. Summers—except for a short vacation, and she's already taken one this year—she stays in town and takes any small jobs like that she can get. Bookkeeping too. When a merchant here gets his books in a mess she can straighten them out for him. Things like that."

"She fast at taking shorthand?"

"She is," Ed said. "I've used her a time or two myself when I've got behind on something. Used to teach shorthand, typing, bookkeeping at a business college before she got into high school teaching. That was a long time ago, but she's kept up on it. She's been trying to get the county board to let her teach commercial classes in the high school here, but she hasn't got anywhere with them yet. Me, I'm for it, and I've run editorials saying so. Why make the kids here go to Green Bay or Milwaukee after high school and pay for a commercial course, if one can be given free here? Do 'em more good than a lot of other subjects they have to study."

"Sounds ideal," Doc said, "If she teaches English, she can probably even spell. But do you know if she's free now?"

"I can find out." Ed Hollis reached for the phone, but stopped before he picked it up. "How much of a job will it be? An hour or a week or what?"

Doc said, "I'd guess about four hours' dictation, give or take an hour. And then a day or two to transcribe it on a typewriter."

Hollis nodded and picked up the phone. He asked for a number and got it. "Miss Talley? Friend of mine here's got a couple of days' work, typing and shorthand. Can you do it for him? ... Fine. Just a second."

He held his hand over the mouthpiece and looked up at Doc. "Says she can start whenever you want her. But it's practically noon now. Shall I tell her you'll see her around one o'clock? I can tell you how to get there; it's only a few blocks."

"Excellent."

Hollis spoke into the phone again. "Right, Miss Talley. He'll see you somewhere around one o'clock. His name's Doc Staunton... Okay. 'Bye now."

He looked up at Doc again. "She reminded me to tell you her rates." He grinned. "Guess she thought they might scare you. Ten bucks a day. Or buck and a half an hour for shorter jobs."

"Reasonable as hell. Have lunch with me, Ed, to help me kill time till one?"

"Wish I could, but I've got about an hour's work and then I'm knocking off for the day. Rather get it over with first, and then go home. Just phoned the missus I'd be home between one and half past and to hold lunch."

He gave Doc Miss Talley's address and then walked to the door with him and showed him how to get to the place.

When Doc got there at one o'clock, he found it a neat, well-kept little cottage. Matching it in size was a little Volkswagen in the driveway beside it.

Miss Talley, when she answered his knock at the door, proved not to be equivalently small, at least vertically. She was almost a head taller than Doc, albeit so slender that their weight was probably just about the same. She could have been anywhere from fifty-five to sixty-five, and probably, Doc decided, was just about half way between. She wore steel-rimmed spectacles and was dressed neatly and conservatively in gray that just matched her hair, which she wore in a tight bun at the back of her neck.

Add a frumpy hat and an umbrella, Doc thought, and she'd exactly fit his mental picture of Stuart Palmer's female detective character, Hildegarde Withers. But she looked competent and, after all, he wasn't hiring her as a party girl.

"Dr. Saunders?" And when he nodded, the stepped back. "Won't you come in?" Doc said, "Thank you, Miss Talley," and entered.

"If you'll be seated, Doctor, I'll get my notebook and—"

"Uh—Miss Talley. I suppose I *can* dictate here, but I think I'd be distracted and I could do a lot better at my own place. It's about eight miles out of town, last house on what they call the Bascombe Road. If you could possibly work out there—for taking the dictation, that is; it will be perfectly all right if you do the typing back here. The only thing is that I'm staying there alone and—" He floundered.

Miss Talley smiled slightly. "We're alone here, Doctor, so that shouldn't matter. I assure you that I don't feel the need of a chaperone. Or rather, I'm one myself. I chaperone most of the high school dances and socials. Of course the time involved in traveling—"

"Naturally," Doc said. "We're punching the time clock as of now, one p.m. If you'll get your notebook and pencils—"

Outside, Miss Talley insisted that she wanted to take her own car, the Volkswagen, and follow him out instead of riding with him. She took as a polite lie (which it was) his statement that he had to come back to town anyway at the end of the afternoon so it would be no inconvenience for him to take her out and bring her back, but he finally convinced her; she got into the station wagon with him.

The quiet, stealthy little cats. Such wonderful hosts, with their soft padded feet, their quickness, their keen hearing. Able to go almost anywhere and to be taken for granted, not noticed.

With several of them—one at a time, of course—the mind thing had visited every farm between the Gross farm and town, except two that had fierce dogs that stayed around the barnyard; one of them had killed the cat-host in use at the time.

But it didn't seem to matter that he'd had to skip two of the farms; he'd learned nothing of importance at the other ones. He had started to make a survey of the town itself next, starting with the person who logically should have been his best bet as an electronics expert, the local television repairman, but he had proved utterly hopeless as a host, if for no other reason than that he was too tied down for financial reasons.

The big black cat that had shared Willie Chandler's lunch and then had left him spent the remainder of the afternoon exploring the rest of the town and listening to conversations here and there without learning much worth knowing; it spent the evening similarly until the mind thing remembered the interesting little man called Staunton who had visited the Gross farm with the sheriff, and who had been so interested in the suicide of Siegfried Gross. He decided to let the rest of the town go until he had found and investigated the man called Staunton.

And he must live, the mind thing decided, out farther from town than the Grosses, and on the same road. In the body of a sparrow, the mind thing had flown to the road to try to follow Staunton and had seen two cars moving away, in opposite directions, both too distant for him to catch up with or follow. Since it would have been much more likely that the sheriff would have been driving into Bartlesville, and through it to his office in Wilcox, Staunton must have been going in the opposite direction, away from town.

There were only fifteen or sixteen more farmhouses in that direction before the road ended, and he decided to investigate them the first thing in the morning, before finishing his check of the town.

He started the black cat out of town, but when it was only about halfway along the road it fell; he realized that he had overworked it and made it travel too fast. Not only was it in a state of utter exhaustion, but its feet were bleeding, leaving a noticeable trail. Even a night's rest, the mind thing realized, wouldn't restore it enough to make it a good host for another day. He forced the cat to get to its feet and stay that way, to leave the road and run across fields till it dropped dead of exhaustion within less than half a mile.

Early the next morning he took another host, a small gray cat that lived, with several other cats, on the third farm east from the Gross farm, toward the end of the road. He checked its memories first; luckily, it was a cat that had done exploring and from its mental pictures of the occupants of nearby farmhouses the mind thing was able to eliminate five of them, besides the farm on which the gray cat lived, as places where Staunton might be. These five farms included the ones between the Gross farm and the cat's own home farm, so he was able to start it directly east and skip the next three farms.

From there he checked each house carefully, staying as near the road as he could so he would not miss Staunton if Staunton should drive into town and pass him.

That is just what happened a little after eleven o'clock, when he was moving across a field between two farms, but near the edge of the road. He heard a noisy car coming from the east and hurried to the open in time to see an old station wagon pass on the way into town. The man Staunton was driving it.

At the next farm the gray cat was treed atop a small shed for almost an hour by a dog until the woman of the house, annoyed by the barking, came out and called in the dog. By now the mind thing, correlating many things, including Tommy Hoffman's memories, was sure that Staunton had come from the last house. Staunton, from his appearance and from his way of talking at the time he had been at the Gross house, was almost certainly not a farmer, and only the last house on this road was not being farmed. Someone in the East, Tommy had known vaguely, had bought it and lived in it only a month or two each year, using it as a base for fishing and relative seclusion. Almost certainly, Staunton would be living there.

He inspected the next two farms only casually and came to the last house.

Yes, there were recent tire tracks in the yard—where Staunton apparently kept his car, since there was no garage—and other signs of recent occupancy. But had Staunton left permanently?

Luckily there seemed to be no dog on the premises, so the cat was able to examine the house closely and at leisure. There were several cellar windows at ground level and through them he was able to hear the throbbing of a gasoline generator and the hum of an electric motor. That meant Staunton had not left permanently, and would be back. But was he living here alone, or had he left someone behind him in the house?

The cat made a full circuit of the house, looking for a way in. There was none. Several of the downstairs windows were open, but only an inch or two. Only one upstairs window was open wide.

The mind thing realized he would have to wait till Staunton came back to investigate further. But that might not be until late afternoon or evening, so he looked over the surrounding area. Keeping out of sight most of the time, in case someone was in the house, he made several circuits of the yard. The only building aside from the house was a small wooden one that had probably served as a tool shed, but the door was gone and the shed was empty. There were signs of what had once been the foundation for a barn, but the barn was long gone; either it had burned or had been razed for its lumber.

He went close to the house again, this time pausing under each window to listen for the sound of voices or of someone moving inside, but he heard nothing.

He walked over to where the cleared area of the yard ended in clumps of weeds and lay down behind one of them to wait. He let his host sleep; there was, he'd realized after what he'd done to the black cat, no advantage in pushing a host beyond its capacity and having to get a new one for each operation. And he knew it would awaken instantly at the sound of an approaching car.

The wait wasn't as long as he'd feared it might be. The cat had been sleeping only half an hour when its sensitive ears told the mind thing that a car was turning into the yard. He opened his host's eyes and moved to peer through the weeds.

It was Staunton's station wagon, and Staunton was driving it, but there was a woman with him. A tall, thin, elderly woman.

The mind thing knew her—from Tommy Hoffman's memories, which he had made his own. She was Miss Talley, and she had been Tommy Hoffman's high school English teacher. (Tally Ho, the students used to call her, among themselves.) Was she a friend of Staunton's? Was he another teacher? Then he saw that she carried a shorthand notebook and remembered that she sometimes supplemented her income by doing stenographic or bookkeeping work outside of school hours or during school vacations. That, then, must be Staunton's reason for bringing her here. That was good; if he was going to dictate letters to her, the mind thing could learn plenty about Staunton by listening to those letters.

The moment they had gone inside, he ran to the house and around it, so close that he could not be seen from the inside, pausing briefly to listen under each window to find out what room they were in. He heard them—their voices, but not the words—from under a window at the back, probably a kitchen window. He crouched under it to leap up onto the window sill, as he had done at other houses. From there he'd be able to hear everything said. And if he was seen, nothing would be thought of it, as he now knew by experience. Possibly if they were people who liked cats, they might even open the window and ask him in, as Willie Chandler had done. That would be even better.

He tried the jump and found to his annoyance that he was short by a full eight inches even of getting his host's front paws on the window ledge. The damned cat was too small. Any one of the fully grown cats that had been former hosts could have reached that ledge easily. For a moment he considered getting rid of his current host as quickly as he could kill it and trying for another— but the new one might be miles away, too far to bring here before Staunton had finished his dictating. He must keep that as a last desperate resort if everything else failed.

Quickly he ran to the back door, which would also open into the kitchen, put the cat's ear against it; the door was too thick; again he could hear voices but not words.

Around the house. Still the one upstairs window was the only one open wider than an inch or two. But he saw something now that he had not noticed before. There was a tree, an elm, at that side of the house, and one of its branches dipped near the open window, the tip of the branch about four feet above the sill. The branch tapered considerably; possibly the cat's weight would bend it down to a point from which he could jump to the window sill.

Quickly the gray cat climbed the tree and worked its way warily along the branch. Yes, as it neared the end, the branch bent; his jump from the end of it wouldn't be too difficult. But first, he looked into the room—it was a bedroom—and made sure that the door to it was open. It would have done him no good at all to get in, only to find himself blocked by a closed bedroom door.

He jumped. Then from the window sill he looked back and saw that, as he had suspected, it would not also serve him as an exit. The branch had sprung back and it was too far away from him to jump to it from the window. But other ways out would no doubt present themselves; Staunton wouldn't keep all the downstairs windows closed or almost closed all of the time.

He ran out into the hallway and down the stairs, and then quietly padded along the hallway that led from the front doorway to the kitchen. He stopped just short of the turn in the passage; it was a perfect listening post.

There was the sound of a refrigerator door opening, and now he could hear the words that were spoken.

CHAPTER THIRTEEN

"Are you sure you won't have a beer with me, Miss Talley?" Doc asked. "Dictating is dry work, and taking it down must be even drier."

Miss Talley smiled slightly, the first time Doc had seen her do so. "If you insist, Doctor. But you must promise to keep it a deep secret. In towns as small as this one, teachers simply do not drink or smoke."

"I'll keep your secret," Doc said over his shoulder as he took a second can of beer from the refrigerator. "I wish I could tempt you to smoke too, but alas, I have only pipes to offer. Uh—it won't bother you if I smoke while I'm dictating, will it?"

"Not at all. I rather like the smell of pipe smoke, except possibly in very confined quarters. And this is a magnificently large kitchen you have."

"The better to pace in. I like it; I practically live in it. Except when I'm out fishing or in town." He came back with two glasses of beer, put one in front of Miss Talley and the other across the table from it. He sat down. "You can put down that pencil, Miss Talley," he said. "I'm too lazy to start dictating this minute. Unless you'd rather have me dictate than listen to me talk. Sometimes I think my students would rather have me hew to the line more than I do."

"Your students? Are you a teacher too, Doctor?"

"Yes, Miss Talley. Physics, at M.I.T. I specialize in electronics and, though to a lesser degree, in nuclear physics."

Miss Talley had put down her pencil; she stared at him. "Staunton—Dr. Ralph S. Staunton? Of course. And you've worked on all the big satellite projects."

Doc smiled. "Not quite all. But I'm really flattered, Miss Talley, that you've heard of me. Are you interested in science?"

"Of course I am. Who isn't? Especially when it comes to matters of reaching the moon and the planets. I've been an avid reader of science fiction for a great many years."

"*You,* Miss Talley?"

"Of course. Why not?"

Why not indeed, Doc thought, feeling himself backed into a corner. He could hardly tell her that she had looked to him to be just about the least likely person to be an avid reader of science fiction, so he decided he'd best treat the "Why not?" as a rhetorical question. He said, "I'm afraid I do my escape reading in the form of mystery novels. I know some scientists do read science fiction and enjoy it, but when I read for relaxation I like to get as far away from science as I can."

"I can understand that," Miss Talley said. "Is what you're going to dictate now scientific matter, or are you just catching up on correspondence?"

"Not either—and I'm afraid it's difficult to explain just what I am doing. But something strange has been going on near here. I've been—well, investigating a bit, and I want to put what I've learned thus far down in the form of a statement of my investigation to date, before I might forget a point or two."

Miss Talley stared at him. "You mean—the suicides?"

"Yes. Don't tell me they've aroused your curiosity too? I thought everyone around here, from the sheriff down, took them as perfectly ordinary events."

"Not quite, Doctor. Incidentally, I know now where I saw you before—at the inquest on Tommy Hoffman. You must have been at the back; I passed you on my way out."

Doc filled his pipe and started to tamp it down. "I was there. I didn't see you, that I recall, but that's because I was trying to keep my eye on Mr. Garner and reach him before he got away. I didn't succeed, but talked to the sheriff instead."

"You mean you had further information on something connected with— Oh, never mind answering that, Doctor. If it's anything connected with Tommy's suicide, I'll learn about it while you're dictating; there's no need for you to say it twice."

Doc waited till he finished lighting his pipe before answering. "That makes sense, Miss Talley. But you say you've been interested too, so I'm going to ask what you know first. If you have any relevant facts that I don't already have, I might as well learn them before I start so I can add them to what I do know. Now, on Tommy Hoffman, do you know anything at all that didn't come out at the inquest?"

"Not facts exactly, but I knew Tommy. Charlotte, too, for that matter. I taught them both freshman English and had them in a class of mine in great English literature again last year. And I know that Tommy was as sane a boy as I've ever known. Not bright and not much of a scholar, but sane, ordinary, and uncomplicated. And perfectly sound physically. I talked to Dr. Gruen—he delivered Tommy and was his doctor all of his life—and he tells me that Tommy was in perfect physical shape. Measles and whooping cough, both years ago, were the only illnesses he ever had."

"But that could mean the doctor hadn't seen him for quite a few years."

"It could, but as it happens it doesn't. Tommy was injured playing high school baseball last spring. No, not a head injury; it was a broken rib. Dr. Gruen treated it. And our school has a strict rule, a very good one I believe, requiring that when a student is injured in any athletic contest he must have a thorough physical examination before his readmittance to the team. Dr. Gruen told me, when I asked him last week, that when he examined Tommy only about two months ago he was absolutely sound and in perfect health. *Mens sana in corpore sano*. I can guarantee the mental part; literally or figuratively, he didn't know what a neurosis is."

"Nor apparently," said Doc dryly, "was he suffering from sexual repression. What do you know about Charlotte Garner?"

"A good girl—and I mean that; I'm not a prude, Doctor, despite my age and occupation. And a smart girl, a little smarter than Tommy was. Even smart enough never to have let him suspect she was the smarter of the two."

"Imaginative?"

"No, very literal, Doctor. If you're thinking about her story about the field mouse, it would have happened just as she described it, not exaggerated in the slightest. And I admire her courage for having managed to bring it out at the inquest, despite the coroner and the sheriff both pooh-poohing it as irrelevant when they talked to her before the inquest. I don't know how it might *not* be irrelevant, but it's too—too bizarre an episode to be brushed off when it occurred in connection with as bizarre a suicide as that of Tommy."

"I agree with you, Miss Talley. Anything else you can tell me? Aside from what was brought out at the inquest, of course."

"I'm afraid not. And I know very little about the suicide of Mr. Gross. I mentioned 'two suicides' simply because of the coincidence of two suicides so close together, in time and in location, when we hadn't had a suicide closer than Wilcox for years, and when there could be no possible connection between them. I mean, Tommy must have known Gross by sight and possibly vice versa, but they wouldn't really have known each other."

Doc smiled and tamped his pipe to relight it. "What would you say, Miss Talley, to *six* suicides, two human and four animal, starting with that of the field mouse, which apparently forced Tommy to kill it by attacking him? What would you say to the apparent suicides of the mouse and a dog—the Hoffman dog—in connection with that of Tommy Hoffman? And the apparent suicides of an owl and a cat—the Gross cat—in connection with that of Siegfried Gross? Not to mention the minor mystery—or is it minor?—of the disappearance from Mrs. Gross's refrigerator, on the night her husband killed himself, of a quart of soup stock and a bowl of gravy?"

Miss Talley's eyes were wide, her face pale with—with what? Doc studied it and decided that it was excitement, not fear.

She said very quietly, "Dr. Staunton, if you're not—if those things are true, you'd better start dictating before I explode with curiosity." She picked up her pencil, opened the shorthand notebook.

Doc lighted his pipe again and started pacing and dictating. Not steadily, of course; sometimes there were minutes between sentences, since he wanted everything in sequence and in detail, coldly factual and without sensationalism or exaggeration. It took him an hour and a half, making the time a few minutes after three o'clock, to finish his description of the first three deaths and the negative rabies report from the laboratory in Green Bay.

He sat down across from Miss Talley and knocked out his pipe, which he'd refilled twice and relighted at least a score of times during his pacing. "Think we'd better rest a few minutes before I tackle the Gross case," he said. "I must have walked a good two miles and you must be getting writer's cramp."

Miss Talley shook her head. "I'm not, but I suppose you do deserve a rest. We're just getting to the really new part, for me. I knew everything about Tommy, up to the point where you ran over the dog. Almost everything about Mr. Gross will be new to me."

"Give me ten minutes, Miss Talley. And meanwhile shall we have another glass of beer?"

Miss Talley demurred at first, but let him talk her into it.

After their first sips, she asked, "How many copies of this will you want?"

"Three," Doc said. "One for myself and two I'm going to send to friends of mine for their opinions. One is a top research physician; I'm going to ask him if there's any possibility of the existence of a rare disease communicable, as is rabies, from animal to man and vice versa, which could lead to insanity and suicidal behavior. The other friend is an excellent mathematician; his specialty is symbolic logic, but he knows actuarial math too, and has cracked some pretty tough problems in it. I want him to quote me the odds on this series of events being coincidental as against interconnected. Later, probably not today, I'll dictate a letter to each of them to go with his copy of the statement."

"Would you mind if I make an extra copy for myself, Doctor?"

"Not at all, Miss Talley."

She smiled. "Wonderful. I would have made myself a copy anyway, but it's nicer to be able to do it with permission."

Doc laughed. He was finding Miss Talley's wide-open mind and curiosity very stimulating, after his failure to be able to convince the sheriff that his investigation, if one could call it that, wasn't even scratching the surface of events. And he liked her honesty in admitting she'd have made herself a copy even without his permission. In fact, he liked Miss Talley.

He was even beginning to think of propositioning her. His department's budget at M.I.T. had been increased for next year to include provision, for the first time, for a full-time secretary and record clerk. If he could get her in on his recommendation she'd be ideal for the job. It would pay at least as much as she could be making here and she was certainly wasted in teaching high school English in a small town. But he'd wait a while and be sure before mentioning the possibility to her. There was no hurry.

When their beer was finished Doc started pacing and dictating again. He finished the job at half past four, said, "That's all, Miss Talley," and sank into the chair. "Give me a few minutes to rest and I'll drive you home."

"You mean that's all? Or that's all for today? I thought you were going to go into your deductions from the facts."

"I've changed my mind," Doc said. "For one thing, I don't know what my deductions are, not surely enough to put them down. Besides, for the purpose for which I intend this, it would be wrong for me to draw conclusions. The two friends I mentioned, the medico and the mathematician, should have just the facts and draw their own conclusions without being influenced by mine, such as they are. Miss Talley, I have only wild ideas—and I can't believe any of them."

"I see your point. But it shouldn't take you long to dictate the two covering letters, should it? Why not get them out of the way today, so when I turn over the statements to you the letters will be with them, and you can mail them right away?"

"It makes sense, but I'm afraid I'm just not up to giving any more dictation today. Tell you what—when I drop around to your place to pick up the statements I'll dictate the two letters. They won't be long and you can type them while I'm reading over what I've just dictated, for any corrections. And if you'll address envelopes too, I can mail them while I'm in town. Will that be all right?"

"That will be fine." Miss Talley leafed back quickly through her notebook to see how many pages she had filled. "I think this is just about two full days' typing. And today is Tuesday. I think I can promise to have this ready for you any time after noon on Thursday, if I work evenings too."

"Do you usually work evenings?"

"Ordinarily I don't. But this isn't *work*—and I'm not going to take any pay for it, so that makes it different. Doctor, having the opportunity to do this is the most exciting and fascinating thing that's ever happened to me. And I don't need the money. So if you're going to insist on paying me, you've wasted an afternoon. I'll type myself a copy from these notes, but you'll have to dictate them all over to someone else for your copies."

Doc sighed. He realized that she meant what she said and that there was no use in arguing. His only recourse would be to send her a present from Boston after he was back there so she couldn't refuse it. Unless, of course, she did want and could get the secretarial job he had in mind for her there; in that case he'd make it up to her some other way.

"Very well, Miss Talley. But that makes you my partner in this, and I may ask you to do even more."

"I'll be glad to. What did you have in mind?"

"You might keep your ear to the ground for a while, in town. I usually get in once a day—at least since I got interested the day of the Hoffman boy's inquest—so if anything important happens I'll hear about it without too much delay, as I heard about the Gross suicide a few days ago. But, short of another human death, something interesting might happen without my hearing of it, something not necessarily spectacular in itself but that just might fit in with whatever I—I mean we—are investigating. You know as much as I do now, so your judgment would be as good as mine as to what might be worth reporting."

"I'll be more than glad to do that. But how shall I get in touch with you if I learn anything? You don't have a telephone this far out, do you?"

"No, I haven't. And now I'm sorry for the first time. But the one place I invariably go in town is the post office, to pick up my mail, if any. If you leave a message with the postmaster for me to phone you I'll be sure to get it. Well, everything's settled then and I'll see you early Thursday afternoon at your place. I'm rested now. Are you ready?"

She put notebook and pencil in her handbag and they left by the front door and went to the station wagon. Doc started the engine and threw the car into gear; he was just about to release the clutch when Miss Talley said, "Oh, I was going to ask you to introduce me to your cat, but I forgot. It doesn't matter."

Doc kept his foot on the clutch pedal and turned to her. "Cat?" he said. "Miss Talley, I don't have a cat. Do you mean you saw one in the house?"

"I—why, I thought I did. I was sure at the time, but—"

Doc put the shift lever back in neutral and turned off the ignition. "Must be a stray cat that got in somehow," he said. "If you don't mind waiting, I'll check. Might as well let it out so it can go home, if it's got a home."

He got out of the car and let himself back into the house, closing the door behind him. He made a quick round of the lower floor, seeing no cat. Nor any open window through which a cat could have come and left. Several windows were open an inch or two, but none wide enough for a cat larger than a small kitten to get through—and besides, a kitten couldn't jump up to a window ledge. The cellar door was closed and had been that way all day. He went up-stairs. Again no cat was in sight, although he didn't look under beds or behind the bathtub or other possible hiding places. The only window open upstairs was in the bedroom he slept in.

He went to the open window and looked out speculatively at a tree branch that came close to it, but considerably above the level of the sill. He leaned out and tugged lightly at the end of the branch; it bent downward easily. Yes, even a small cat's weight could bend that branch down so it might be able to jump to the window sill. But it could never get out that way. Nor, he decided, after looking down, by jumping down. Onto soft grass, just possibly, but the ground under the window was hard-baked and stone-studded. A cat jumping that far to such a surface would be, if not killed, too seriously injured to be able to get away.

But it came to him suddenly that a cat, if there was one in the house, just might want to die; the Grosses' cat had seemed to want to be killed, and the other animals—

He closed the window, went downstairs and left the house. If there was a cat inside now, it would still be there when he got back and he'd worry about it then.

He got back in the car, started it, and backed it around. "I didn't see a cat, Miss Talley," he said. "Are you sure you saw one? And just when and where?"

"I thought I was sure at the time, but I suppose it could have been a momentary optical illusion. It was while you were dictating; or rather, while you were pausing between sentences. I looked up, and saw, or thought I saw, the head of a cat sticking around the corner of the hallway passage leading to the kitchen alongside the stairs. I didn't say anything or call to it because I didn't want to interrupt your train of thought. Then you started dictating again, and when I looked that way again, it was gone."

She paused a moment. "Now that I think back, though, I'm sure I must have imagined seeing it. It was just a quick momentary glance and then I looked back at my notebook as you started talking. It's very easy to imagine something under those circumstances."

"I suppose so," Doc said, making his voice easier than he felt. "Well, if I do find a cat there, I'll let you know."

For a few minutes they rode in silence and then Miss Talley said, "Doctor, you don't really believe there could be a—a disease, a contagious disease, that could pass from man to animal and vice versa and—make its victims insanely suicidal?"

"I'll admit I've never heard of one, so it would have to be pretty rare."

"Pretty rare—but pretty well known just *because* it would be so unusual. If it were known at all, one of us would certainly have heard or read of it somewhere, sometime."

"I'm afraid that's rather probable. But, Miss Talley, aside from that possibility—or sheer coincidence—can you think of any other explanation?"

"Certainly I can. Don't you remember about the Gadarene swine, Doctor?"

CHAPTER FOURTEEN

"Gadarene swine..." Doc said musingly. "They sound familiar, but I'm afraid I can't place them."

"In the Bible," Miss Talley said. "Book of Luke, I think. Christ came upon a man who was possessed by devils, and ordered them to leave him. There was a herd of swine nearby. Let's see; I think I can quote the crucial verse: 'Then went the devils out of the man, and entered into the swine: and the herd ran violently down a steep place into the lake, and were choked.' "

Doc groaned softly. "Miss Talley, don't tell me you believe in demoniac possession. Please."

"Of course I don't. That is, I don't believe in demons. But possession—"

"Possession by what, then? I'm a materialist, Miss Talley. I'll admit that the Rhine experiments and some other things have shaken me just a little bit, enough so I don't dogmatically deny the possibility of wild talents like telepathy and telekinesis. And of course hypnosis and post-hypnotic suggestion are fully accepted scientifically, But not even the wildest enthusiast for parapsychology has suggested that one mind can take over another and control it from inside."

"One *human* mind," said Miss Talley firmly. "There are billions of planets besides Earth in the universe, and millions of them must be inhabited. How do we know what capabilities and limitations a *non*-human mind might have? How do we know what an alien, an extra-terrestrial, might be able to do?"

"Hmmm," said Doc. Wondering for a moment if Miss Talley was joking, he moved his head far enough to be able to see her face in the rear vision mirror, Her eyes looked excited, the rest of her face was calm.

She said, "Aren't we working right now to get men onto other planets? What makes you think we're the most advanced race in the universe? How do you *know* there isn't an alien here?"

"Hmmm," said Doc. "I suppose I don't, but then again I don't know that there is. But why *an* alien, instead of aliens?"

"Because only one person or animal has been—I'll call it possessed, for lack of a better word—at a time. The field mouse, then Tommy after the field mouse was dead, the hound after Tommy was dead, the owl after the hound was dead, the cat— You see what I mean, Doctor. Never two at any one time. And that's why he makes his hosts commit suicide, so he can get his mind back out of them and be free to take a different host."

Something seemed to prickle between Doc's shoulder blades. But he said, "You certainly have an imagination, Miss Talley. Possibly I should read science fiction instead of mysteries."

"Possibly you should. But with what's happening, possibly you won't have to, to have your imagination stimulated. If there *is* a cat at your place, maybe it's host to an alien who was spying on us. You might ask him."

Doc laughed. "And then kill the cat so the alien can take *me* over, eh? If that happens, I'll let you know, Miss Talley."

But after he'd dropped her off at her little house, his expression was thoughtful and a little worried as he drove home. It was ridiculous, of course, but what if—?

He let himself in the door carefully, making sure nothing got out past him. He saw nothing, heard nothing, out of the ordinary.

He leaned against the inside of the door, filled his pipe with tobacco and lighted it.

He went into the living room and sat down in his favorite chair, a leather upholstered morris. Backed against the biggest window and with a lamp standing beside it, it afforded excellent light for reading either by day or by night. A paperback mystery novel lay open on one arm of the chair, but he didn't pick it up.

Should he search the house? It would be a long and tedious job to look everywhere a cat might hide. And besides, downstairs here an intelligent cat wouldn't even have to hide, since there was no door in the doorway between living room and kitchen, or in the doorway between the kitchen and the hallway that led to the front door and back to the living room again. It could simply move from room to room ahead of him and stay out of his sight that way. Right now it could be sitting in the kitchen. And if it heard him heading that way it could come back here by way of the hall—or through the kitchen–living room door if he went by the hallway. It could move more silently than he could and would have better hearing.

That is, if there *was* a cat.

And if there was, why shouldn't it be a perfectly ordinary cat, here for perfectly good catlike reasons? Well...certainly it wasn't very usual for a cat to enter a house, without good reason at least, by making what must have been a fairly dangerous jump from a tree branch to an upstairs window. And another thing, why would it keep itself so well and thoroughly hidden for so long, all the time he'd been dictating?

His pipe had burned out and he knocked the dottle out of It and wondered if he should get himself something to eat, or drive into town for something. Somehow he didn't feel like making dinner for himself.

But the cat...?

Suddenly he thought of a way of telling, on return, whether or not there was a cat here in the house—at least, if it moved around and didn't stay hidden in one place. Along with the pots and pans in one of the cupboards there was a flour sifter; he'd used it a few times to flour fish when he was going to fry them. He got it now and put a little flour in it. Then he went to the foot of the stairs and over the bottom few steps scattered a thin, almost invisible film of flour, not turning the handle of the sifter but merely tapping the side of it lightly with one finger as he moved it. He did the same thing in the middle of the hallway, and at the doorway between the living room and the kitchen.

Then, so he wouldn't have to walk through any of the cat-traps he had just set, he left by the back door and drove into town.

He ate at the place where he knew he'd be served by the most talkative waitress in town. She lived up to her billing—but there was no new suicide, nothing new in the form of strange actions of either wild or domestic animals. The most exciting thing that had happened in the past twenty-four hours had been a fire at Smalley's Feed Store; the damage had been slight and the cause had been traced to defective wiring.

No pigs had sprouted wings; no dogs had been seen climbing telephone poles. He'd asked about those points specifically, not so much to get a laugh—although he had—but because they'd make her remember if she had heard any stories about animals behaving unnaturally.

He was heading for his car when someone called out, "Hey, Staunton." It was Dr. Gruen, and he came closer so he wouldn't have to yell the rest of what he had to say. "Getting up a little poker game and we need one more sucker. How's about it?"

"Well," Doc said, "guess I can sit in an hour or two. Back room at the tavern?"

Gruen nodded. "I'm going over to get Lem. We'll be starting in about fifteen minutes."

"Good," Doc said. "Just time for me to get a spot of fortification at the bar. See you when you get there."

Time can be subjective; a few minutes in a dentist's chair can be longer than a few hours in a good poker game. Doc played what he thought was a short time and suddenly realized, when they quit playing, that it was almost midnight. And also that he was hungry again; but both of the Bartlesville restaurants would be closed by now; he would have to wait till he got home and then make himself a sandwich.

At the house he parked his car in the yard and was almost at the door before he remembered that, unless Miss Talley had had a momentary hallucination, there was a cat in his house.

He let himself in by way of the kitchen door, being careful that nothing got past him. The moonlight was so bright that, until he closed the kitchen door, he could not possibly have missed seeing anything as large as a mouse. He heard no sound.

He flicked on the kitchen light and looked around. He remembered the flour he had sprinkled on the floor and walked over to the doorway.

There were cat tracks in the flour.

He called out, "All right, Cat. Show yourself if you want anything to eat or drink. I'm not going to hunt for you, but you're not getting out of here till I've met you."

He went to the refrigerator and opened it. He got out the necessary ingredients and made himself a ham sandwich and took it and a bottle of beer over to the table and sat down.

He did a lot of thinking while he ate the sandwich slowly and sipped the beer. He didn't think he liked what he was thinking. He was frightened, without knowing what he was frightened about. He knew that he didn't want to turn out the kitchen lights and go upstairs to bed in the dark. Although he knew the house so well by now that he seldom used his flashlight, he got it from a cupboard drawer. He had it in his hand and turned on when he flicked off the kitchen light.

He played it ahead of him as he went through the hallway and up the steps. He felt foolish doing it (how could a *cat* harm him?) but he did it just the same.

He saw nothing in the hall or on the stairs. In his bedroom he closed the door before he turned on the light and then, using the flashlight to help him, he searched the room thoroughly. This time he looked under the bed.

Wherever the cat was, it wasn't in this room. And, harmless and ordinary though it might be, it wasn't going to get in while he was sleeping. Luckily it was not a warm night and he would do without ventilation for once by sleeping with both the door and the window closed. Not, in the case of the window, because the cat could get through it from wherever it now was; but the cat must have got into the house that way in the first place, and what *else* might decide to come that way?

For some strange reason he wished he'd brought one of his guns upstairs with him.

But eventually he slept, and slept soundly.

CHAPTER FIFTEEN

The mind thing had panicked when he had heard the man he now knew was Doc Staunton call out: "All right, Cat..."

It was the reaction, mostly, from learning that, in addition to being the optimum host he could possibly expect to find, the man suspected something close to the truth, and could be dangerous. He'd had only contempt for any human intellect he'd hitherto encountered.

But Staunton was the perfect host—a top electronicist, solvent and free to travel, single and without responsibilities. He'd listened with increasing fascination to the conversation between Staunton and Miss Talley, and to what Staunton had dictated to her.

And, although this was extrapolating, he felt sure that Staunton would have, or have access to, every item of equipment that he would need. With Staunton as a host, he could be back on his own planet as soon as within a few weeks—and a hero of his race for having discovered a planet definitely worthy of colonization.

But why had he made the initial mistake of drawing back and hiding when Miss Talley had looked up suddenly and had caught a glimpse of him in the hall? If only he'd remembered—which he hadn't because of his excitement over the things he was learning about Staunton—to act like an ordinary cat! Once glimpsed, he should have strolled on out in the kitchen, right into their sight. If he'd acted friendly they might have petted him, if they were people who liked cats; possibly given him a bowl of milk and then let him out when he miaouwed and scratched at the door. At worst, if they were people who didn't like cats, they'd have opened the door and shooed him out with a broom. And he'd have been free, those many hours ago, to make an inconspicuous death and be back in his own body, his shell, under the back steps of the Gross farmhouse.

Free to plan and then choose his next host, one who could move his shell from the Gross farm to the Staunton place here, near enough for Staunton's bed to be within his range of perception so he could take over Staunton's mind the first time Staunton slept.

That is what he should have done, certainly. But having once hidden, he'd decided that the safest thing to do was to stay hidden until, through the first door or window left open, he could escape and be free. But Staunton—damn him for being so clever!—had left nothing open. And now, because of the catprints in that scattered flour, Staunton knew for sure that he was here.

How much more did Staunton guess? He'd definitely suspected something, even before he'd left the house, to have set that telltale trap with the flour. Alone in the house and wandering around to explore, he'd not known that he was walking in the thin film of flour until the sensitive pads of his feet had told him he was walking in something, and he'd looked down, too late. How hard he'd tried to think of a way of obliterating those paw prints, or of cleaning up the flour and spreading fresh flour! It was simply impossible, in this tiny body he now occupied. Not the cleaning up of the flour; he could have licked it up, but the problem of spreading fresh flour and doing it evenly and neatly was insuperable. He might have been able to open the cupboard door to get at the flour sifter but, small as he was and without hands, there was no way at all of his using it as the man had done. No way at all.

His real panic had come when Staunton, returning, had called him, addressing him as one intelligent being speaking to another. Had Staunton determined by logic or by intuition that a cat trapped in his house wasn't really a cat at all? It seemed incredible that he had worked it out from such slender evidence.

But it could be. Staunton, he must remember, was a scientist. The mind thing's contact, from inside, with human minds had been with the mind of a boy not yet out of high school and the mind of a stupid and barely literate old man. Perhaps there were things, many things, on this world that neither Tommy nor Gross knew or even suspected, but that would be elementary to Staunton. Perhaps there were species here on Earth which *were* capable of taking over and using hosts, as his species did. Perhaps some human beings could, with special abilities or special training, take over lesser creatures. Well, he'd find the answer to that in Staunton's mind if and when he could take it over.

The immediate problem was escape, getting out of this house, Suicide was definitely out, even if he could find the means of accomplishing it here. It had been the unexplained series of suicides of men, animals, and birds that had roused Staunton's scientific curiosity in the first place. Having one happen right here in his own house, and under these circumstances, might be just the final evidence that would convince him completely of what he now—the mind thing hoped—only suspected.

There was, he realized now, only one thing he could possibly do, and that was to come out of hiding in the morning, let Staunton see him, and try to the utmost of his ability to act like a cat, an ordinary cat. It would be dangerous, but there was no alternative. The danger was not that for any reason Staunton might kill him; that would free him immediately—and if Staunton knew about hosts, killing him was the last thing he'd do. He'd know that killing the host would free the being controlling it. The danger was that Staunton, knowing this, would catch him and keep him caged for study. If nothing worse, that would waste time; maybe he wouldn't be able to escape until the cat died a natural death, and cats lived for years. The danger was even greater that Staunton would know the psychological tests that could distinguish a controlled creature from a free one.

And if Staunton could prove that—? There'd been some vague knowledge in Tommy Hoffman's mind that something called truth serum existed. If Staunton injected that and forced him to communicate under its influence, he was through. He'd be forced to communicate the location of his own body, helpless at the Gross farm, and they'd have him.

Even, he realized in sudden despair, Staunton's caging the cat for study and keeping it caged indefinitely would cause his death if the cat lived long enough. In less than the natural length of a cat's life his own body would perish for lack of nourishment. The immersion in nutrient solution he'd had Gross give it was enough to last for months, but not for as much as a year. Being imprisoned indefinitely in the body of any host unable to feed him would be fatal for his own body.

He spent the whole night thinking, weighing odds. He considered leaping against a window in the hope that the glass would break and let him through— but the objection to that was the same as that to an attempt at suicide. Even if successful, either would confirm his captor's suspicions.

He could only hope that they *were* only suspicions and not certainties, and that Staunton would let him go in the morning. He could only hope so, and do his best to make the man think that he was only an ordinary cat, after all.

Doc Staunton hadn't got to bed until one o'clock, and hadn't gone to sleep until a good hour after that, so he slept later than he usually did, even on vacation. A little after ten in the morning he woke from a confused dream in which he was trying to design a metering device for a satellite but couldn't remember, or find out from anyone, just what it was supposed to meter. He lay a moment trying to recapture the earlier part of the dream, which still evaded him, and then suddenly remembered the matter of the cat in this house; he forgot about the dream and lay thinking about the cat.

But the matter didn't seem nearly so sinister now, in the light of day, as it had last night. Hadn't he been exaggerating the possibility of any connection between having a stray cat in his house and the strange deaths that had happened during the previous ten days?

Well...probably. But still there was something that needed explanation. It wasn't strange that a cat might enter a house out of curiosity, or out of hunger, through a door or window that had been left open. He doubted that many cats did, at least ones that had homes; but it was not too odd that one should do so. The strange thing was its method of entry.

Yet even that could be explained—if the cat was a homeless one, and hungry. Perhaps it had climbed the tree because it had seen a bird sleeping there and thought it might catch the bird. And then, once out on that particular branch and losing its quarry, the sight of an open window just might tempt it. Any cat, even a stray one, would know that there was food in houses.

But then it had hidden in the hall, near the kitchen doorway, almost as though spying on them, listening to their conversation. And hiding ever since...

Still, if it was a cat that had never had a home and, possibly because boys or a farmer had once thrown stones at it, was afraid of human beings...

He got out of bed and started dressing, deciding that he'd find the cat first, no matter how much searching he'd have to do, and then make up his mind.

He remembered there was a pair of fairly heavy leather gloves in a drawer of the dresser; he got them and put them in a pocket. If he was forced to corner the cat and catch it, and if it was a cat that was wild and might fight against being picked up—and even domestic cats sometimes did that with strangers—those gloves would come in handy. With them on, he should be able to handle it. From the size of the paw prints it had left in the flour, it certainly wasn't very large. And wild though it might be, it definitely wasn't a wildcat; his brief study of the prints had convinced him of that. He'd seen prints of a wildcat and they were quite different.

When he left the room he'd slept in he closed the door behind him. Might as well be systematic about his hunting, take the upstairs rooms before he went downstairs, and close the door of each after he'd searched it. He took the bathroom first, since he had to go there anyway, and then the other two bedrooms.

The cat wasn't upstairs.

He saw it when he was halfway down the steps. It was sitting calmly at the front door, as a cat or dog does when it wants to be let out.

It didn't look dangerous in the slightest. It was a small gray cat, perfectly ordinary-looking. It didn't look at all starved and it didn't seem frightened of him. In fact, it looked up at him as though quite friendly. It miaouwed and scratched lightly against the door.

Just a cat, a very normal cat, asking to be let out of the house.

Almost too normal, Doc thought, for a cat that had hidden from him for so long yesterday. He sat down on the bottom step of the staircase and stared at it, still at the front door, still wanting out. "Miaouw," it said.

Doc shook his head. "Not just yet, Cat. I'll let you out later, I guess, but I want to have a little talk with you first. And how about breakfast? I'm going to have some myself."

He got up and went into the kitchen, not looking behind him until he was at the refrigerator.

The cat had followed him, but not closely at his heels. Now it was sitting staring at him. Then, as though it had a sudden idea, it went past him—but, he noticed, circling far enough to keep out of his reach—and to the kitchen door. It scratched at that, miaouwed again, and looked back at him. It was saying "Let me out, please" as clearly as a cat can say it. An ordinary cat, that is.

Doc shook his head firmly. "No, Cat. Later, but not now. I want to think it over first."

He got milk from the refrigerator and put a bowl of it down on the floor. The cat didn't approach it; it stayed at the door while he got his own breakfast, frying himself a couple of eggs and boiling water for instant coffee.

When he took his breakfast across the room and sat down at the big table with it, the cat left the door and went to the bowl of milk. It started lapping hungrily.

"Nice kitty," Doc said through a bite of egg. "How'd you like to stay around and visit me a while?"

The cat didn't answer, but, staring at it, Doc decided he hadn't really been kidding. It would be pleasant to have a cat around, something to talk to. And if there was really anything strange about the cat, it would give him a chance to watch it for a while.

Of course he couldn't keep it shut up indefinitely, not without suffocating himself on hot days. Or could he, by buying some half-screens, the kind you could fit into a window opened halfway? There seemed to be so few flies around that the owner of the house had never bothered to screen it. Yes, Doc thought, he could go even further than that and have a carpenter come out from town and fit him a full set of screens. He'd been wanting to add some small improvement to the house as a token of gratitude for being allowed to use it. And after all there were *some* flies, and moths at night unless you closed the windows when you put on the lights... A set of screens would be just about right as a contribution. Maybe he'd have them put on, cat or no cat.

Of course he didn't want to steal anyone's cat, if its owner really wanted it back. He could take care of that by asking around town. If he found an owner, the man would probably gladly sell it to him for a few dollars, unless it was a child's particular pet. Cats are plentiful and cheap around a farming community, and they breed so fast that the supply always exceeds the demand.

When he left to go back to M.I. . to resume his teaching, he'd have to find a home for it before leaving, but that shouldn't be too difficult if he was willing to subsidize the deal by offering a slight bonus along with the cat. Feeding one more cat wouldn't matter much to a farmer who already had several, and even the most domesticated cats largely earn their own living in this kind of country by keeping down the field mice.

"Cat," he said, "speaking seriously, how *would* you like to live here a while? Oh, and by the way what's your name?" The cat, still lapping milk, didn't answer.

"All right, you won't tell me," Doc said. "In that case you're all set with a brand new name, the one I've been calling you. *Cat*. It's appropriate...I hope."

The cat had drunk only about half of the milk, but that was all right; he'd probably given it much too much for a cat its size to drink, and it was back sitting at the door again.

"Miaouw," it said.

"I understand, Cat," Doc said. "A call of nature, and that's not surprising considering how long you've been here. But the very fact that you want out so badly proves that you're housebroken. I'll take care of things."

He'd finished eating by then and went across to the door that led to the basement stairs, went down them. Someone who had stayed here, luckily, had done a lot of sawing for something or other; there was a fairish pile of dry sawdust in one corner of the basement. He found a shallow carton of about the proper dimensions and filled it with sawdust, took it up to the kitchen and put it in a corner.

"You'll have to use that, Cat," he said. "I'm afraid you're not going out for a few days."

The cat looked at the box of sawdust but stayed at the door. "Miaouw," it said. Very plaintively.

"You're an outdoor cat, maybe, and never used a sawdust box?" Doc asked it. "Well, you'll learn, when the pressure gets high enough."

He took his breakfast dishes to the sink and started washing them.

"Tell you what, Cat," he said over his shoulder. "Let's give it a try together, for a few days. For that length of time, I'll clean up if you don't figure out how to use the sawdust.

"And if you turn out to like me and I turn out to like you, then I'll give you your choice—you can go out, and come back if you wish or never darken my doorway again. Fair enough?"

The cat didn't answer, except possibly by not answering; it stayed by the door.

Doc decided to go about the things he had to do and pay no more attention to it for a while, to see what it did.

The mind thing, helpless in the cat-body of which it could not rid itself without giving away more than it already had, stayed by the door. The bladder- and bowel-pressure were considerable by now. And Staunton obviously wasn't going to let him out of the house. He didn't feel, except in the objective sense of being aware of, the pain of the body he was in; but that was not the problem. Staunton expected to keep him shut up for several days. He had to let this body evacuate itself before then or the very fact that it had not would be an additional cause for suspicion. Staunton had more than enough already. The question then was whether to use the floor or the box. If he pretended to be strictly an outdoor cat, unused to using a sawdust box, and dirtied the floor now and as often as he could, would that disgust Staunton and cause his release earlier than if he pretended to be housebroken to the extent of using the box?

He watched Staunton emotionlessly—not hating him, because the emotion of hatred was as alien to him as the feeling of mercy—except, in both cases, toward his own kind.

Suddenly a thought came to him. Staunton, with his suspicions already aroused, might well make an attempt to find out where the cat he was using had come from, who had owned it, how and when it had disappeared. And other facts about it—including the degree of its being housebroken. Any discrepancy would make Staunton still more suspicious. The mind thing knew he should examine the mind of his current host and let his actions as a cat correspond with what that particular cat would do under given circumstances, and guide his actions accordingly.

It took him only a second to locate that particular memory in the cat's brain. He walked over to the sawdust box.

Staunton, at the sink, glanced down casually. "Attaboy," he said. "Nice kitty."

Yes, the mind thing knew that this was what he should have done all along, examined the mind of his particular host and acted as the host would have acted under the same circumstances, any time he was under observation. Had he only done that yesterday when the woman had first seen him in the hallway—walked out into the kitchen and looked at the two of them calmly, instead of hiding...

This chore taken care of, he thought what he should do next to play his part to the hilt. He'd lie down and sleep a while, probably. Find a soft comfortable place to rest in. There was a sofa in the living room. He padded through the doorway, jumped up onto the sofa, and curled himself up comfortably.

Staunton was standing there in the doorway. "Okay, Cat," he said. "Might as well make yourself at home. What made you hide yesterday and last night?" Then he went back into the kitchen.

The mind thing let his cat-body rest and sleep, but his own mind was thinking what a fool he'd been, letting himself panic, and hiding twice, once when the woman had seen him in the hallway, once when, after he'd walked through the flour, Staunton had come home after midnight.

He let himself explore his host's mind thoroughly now, at leisure. Losing a few days being shut up here would be an annoyance but still only a minor delay. Apparently Staunton wasn't going to try him out with specific psychological tests, but just keep him under general observation. It should be easy for the mind thing, now that he knew what he had to do.

It was beginning to get a little warm and Staunton was going around opening all of the downstairs windows—but each only a carefully calculated scant two inches, just enough so a medium-small cat couldn't get through.

A little later, Staunton was looking down at him. "Cat," he said, "I'm going downtown a while; you hold the fort. I'll pick up some cat food or liver or something. While you're here, I might as well be the perfect host."

The mind thing almost made his present host jump; then he realized Staunton was using the word "host" in a different sense. He blinked at him sleepily.

When Staunton walked to the front door he jumped off the sofa and ran after him, to stay in character. But Staunton reached down a hand and took him gently by the scruff of the neck—the first time there had been physical contact between them—and held him back until he was able to get the door closed from the outside, with the cat inside.

In Bartlesville Doc made his first stop at the office of the *Clarion*.

Hollis looked up from the typewriter he'd been hammering. "Hi," he said. "What's new?"

"Nothing startling, Ed. Just wanted to ask you a question. Know anybody looking for a missing cat?"

Hollis laughed. "A cat? Cats are a dime a dozen around here. If one wanders off, it wanders off. Why? You find one?"

"Yes. And thought I might keep it a while if it wants to stay with me. But I wouldn't if I knew whoever owned it really wanted it. It might be a child's pet, for instance."

"There's that. Well, I can run an ad in the lost and found column for you. Deadline for that is Friday noon; that's when we start closing the forms."

Staunton thought a moment. He might as well save stopping in again by giving Hollis the ad now. He said, "Okay, I'll give you the ad now, 'Found, small gray cat.' And give it a box number; I'll check with you next week to see if there's been an answer."

"Sure." Hollis jotted it down on a pad. "But hey, I know whose cat it might be. I was out at Kramer's last week and he had a small gray cat, among several others. That's out your way, so it might be his."

"Just where out my way?"

"Next door to the Gross farm. You know where that is; heard you were out there with the sheriff after the suicide. It's the farm east of theirs; Loursat has the one to the west."

"Thanks, Ed. I'll drop in on my way home to find out. You run that ad, though, unless I tell you not to. So long."

When he did his shopping, Doc bought two cans of cat food. One can was surely enough for a cat that size for two days so two cans would run him until he let the cat out to see if it would stay around and come back, or would run away.

From the drugstore he phoned Miss Talley to ask her whether she was still sure she'd be done by Thursday noon, and whether she'd learned anything new. Yes, she was sure she'd be finished by the time she'd predicted, and no, she'd learned nothing interesting; she wouldn't have much chance to put or keep her ear to the ground until she'd finished the typing.

And, she wanted to know, had he found a cat at his house? He told her about the cat and about his decision in connection with it.

On his way home he stopped at the farm east of the Gross farm. There were two cats on the front porch. Both were about the same size as the gray one and could easily be from the same litter.

A plump, friendly woman answered his knock on the door.

"I'm Ralph Staunton," he told her. "I live in the last house down the road. I—"

"Oh, yes," she said. "I've heard your name, and I've seen you drive past. Won't you step in?" She moved back to make way for him.

"I might as well, but just for a moment. It's nothing very important, Mrs. Kramer. I hear you have a gray cat. I've found one, about the size of those two cats on the porch and I wondered—"

"Oh, yes. I hadn't seen him for a day or two and wondered if anything had happened to him."

"Nothing has, except that he wandered into my house. Thought I might like to keep him. Would you consider selling him?"

She laughed. "Sell him? Oh, goodness no. But you can have him if you want him. We've got three other cats—our old cat had a litter of six last time and we were able to find homes for only three of them. And she's going to have another litter soon." She shook her head. "I'm afraid after that we're going to get rid of her or take her to the vet and have her spayed. Else we'll be drowning in cats."

"Thanks a lot," Doc said. "I'll be glad to take him, and I'll promise to find a home for him when I leave at the end of the summer—or take him back with me if I can't. That is, if he stays with me."

"But I thought you said—"

"I've got him shut in the house right now, to see if he'll get used to it and to me and want to stay. But I can't do that forever so in a few more days I'll have to let him out—and we'll have to see whether he'll want to stay with me or come back to you. I can't very well keep him against his will; cats are very independent people."

"Oh dear. I guess you're right, but I do hope he'll stay with you. His name is Jerry, by the way."

"Not any more, if he stays with me," Doc said. "I've given him a new name. I call him Cat."

Mrs. Kramer laughed.

The cat must have heard Doc Staunton coming because it was waiting inside the door and tried to get past him, but he managed to catch it. "No, Cat," he said, this time taking it up in his arms and kicking the door shut with his foot. "I explained that to you; you're in stir for a few days. Then you can make up your mind whether you want to keep on being Cat with me, or go back to being Jerry with the Kramers. I know who you are now, you see."

He put it down on the sofa and stood looking down at it. "Or do I?" he added softly.

It wasn't until he went to open a window wider and remembered in time not to, that it occurred to him that he'd forgotten to check on getting screens fitted while he was in town. Well, he'd be in town again tomorrow; one day wouldn't matter.

CHAPTER SIXTEEN

One day didn't make the slightest difference, it turned out, on his ordering the screens. He went into town again the next day, Thursday, and saw Hank Purdy, the town's only really good rough carpenter. He learned that Hank had more work than he could handle for at least a week. He promised to come out later the following week, take measurements and make an estimate. Doc might have found someone else who could do the job sooner, but he liked Hank, whom he knew from the poker games in the back room at the tavern, and decided he'd rather wait and have Hank do the job. After all, he wasn't going to keep the cat shut up more than another few days, and after that the house would be in no more immediate need of screens than it had been all along. Besides, the weather was mild and having the windows as they were now, each of them raised about two inches, provided plenty of ventilation.

He parked the station wagon in front of Miss Talley's little house. She must have seen him stopping there, because she had the door opened before he reached it.

"Come in, Doctor. All ready for you. Sit down, and I'll bring the manuscripts. And my notebook."

"Thanks, Miss Talley, but I don't think I'm going to dictate those two letters today. I've decided I want a few days to think things over before I send them. And I may as well wait to write until I'm ready to mail them; something else might happen and I can put any subsequent information in the letter."

"All right, if you think so." She picked up a large brown envelope and gave it to him. "Want to read this now anyway?"

He shook his head. "Might as well read it at home. I'd rather talk a few minutes, if you've time."

She had time, she told him. He told her about the cat. "I started out being scared of it, or about its being there." He laughed. "You and your talk about possession did that to me, I suppose. But now I feel just the opposite. I hope it sticks around; it keeps me from getting lonesome. I think it's a perfectly normal cat, Miss Talley."

"And Buck was a perfectly normal dog, until he ran under your car. In spite of what you say, Doctor, I'm a little worried about its living there with you. I suppose it's silly of me, but—I do worry."

"I'll be all right, Miss Talley. I'm afraid I'm beginning to think we both went a bit overboard on this."

"Possibly, Doctor... Will you promise me you'll send those letters, and the reports, to the two friends you mentioned?"

Doc sighed. "All right, I'll send them. Just want a couple of days to think it over first."

"All right. For the rest of this week I'll be staying home, that is, early afternoons; so any day you want to come and dictate them..."

That evening after he had finished washing the dishes he went into the living room and sat on the sofa; the cat was already there and he reached over and stroked its sleek fur. The cat purred.

"Well, Cat, getting to like it here? And to like me? Let's see; this is Thursday evening. Let's set a date for giving you your choice, a date and an hour. How does Monday strike you? Let's see; I've been feeding you about the middle of the afternoon. I'll let you go out—if you still want to go out—about the middle of the morning. That'll give you time to think it over before you get hungry again.

"If I go into town I won't stay long; I'll go when I let you out, and be back by noon. Waiting and ready to feed you if you come back, Fair enough?"

The cat didn't answer, but it still purred.

Doc said, "If it relieves a worry on your part, the Kramers gave you to me; they don't want you back. Oh, they'll take you if you want to go home to them. They'll feed you, and forgive you.

"Yes, I know who you are, and that your name was Jerry there. Might have kept that name if another male cat had come with you. I'd have called him Tom. Tom and Jerry. Ever tasted one? They're good. But that's irrelevant. Which are you going to prefer, the Kramers or me?"

He got up and took a comfortable chair facing the sofa. He stared at the cat from across the room.

"Cat, why *did* you hide? Why did you come in an upstairs window? Don't you know cats just don't do that? Damn it, why didn't you act all along as you're acting now?"

The cat stretched languorously and then curled up again and closed its eyes.

"Cat." Doc said it sharply and the cat opened its eyes again and stared at him.

"Cat, don't go to sleep on me. I'm talking to you, and sleeping isn't polite when you're being spoken to. Cat, you used to live on the farm next to the Grosses. Did you know *their* cat? The one that committed suicide the night Gross did? Don't tell me it wasn't suicide, that cat jumping right into the jaws of a vicious dog it must have known was there. If it was suicide, why? And if it wasn't, what was it?"

The cat's eyes had closed, but somehow Doc felt that it wasn't asleep.

"And an owl killed itself that same night. What do you know about that? And before that, along with Tommy Hoffman's death we had a field mouse that got itself killed, seemingly deliberately. And a dog. Do you know that I was the one who ran over the dog? And that it had been hiding beside the road until my car got just the right distance away—only a few yards—and then ran right under my wheels? I'll *swear* that one was deliberate—especially since they tell me that dog was car-shy.

"Two human beings, four animals—that we know of. Of course any other human suicides we'd know about, but how many more animals, especially ones out in the woods and not under observation, might have brought about their own deaths recently after—After what? After they'd served the purpose of who-ever, or *whatever*, was using them?"

Outside, crickets were chirping, thousands of crickets. Doc's mind wandered and he thought how strange it was that one could tell the temperature, almost exactly, by timing the interval between the chirps of a cricket. A cricket was a thermometer, and probably as accurate as the average household thermometer. There were many strange things in nature. Lemmings, with their periodical suicidal migrations to and into the sea. Group insanity? Or do the lemmings know something that we don't know?

He heard the crickets, watched the black night press against the window pane. He turned back to the cat.

"Cat," he said, "why did those other animals kill themselves? If you're like them, why don't you? Is the only reason you're alive the fact that there isn't any way of killing yourself shut up here? Wait a minute, I'll find out."

He left the living room and went across the hall and into the third downstairs room, a small room that was only partly furnished and used mostly for storage. Except for items that were already there, Doc used it only to store his fishing tackle and boots, his guns and ammunition. Although he knew there was open season on nothing worth hunting in Wisconsin in summer, he'd brought a pistol and a rifle for target practice and a shotgun mostly because it was a brand-new one and he wanted a chance to try it out. All these things he'd had shipped ahead of him before his flight to Green Bay; he'd picked them up there after he'd bought the used station wagon which he'd sell before flying back at the end of the summer.

He took the pistol, a .38-caliber S. & W. Special, and took a cardboard rifle target from a package of them. In the doorway between the hall and the living room he put the square of cardboard down on the floor and went back to the chair he'd been sitting in. He cocked the gun and saw the cat raise its head at the sudden click.

"Listen, Cat," he said, "let's try this for size. If you're only wanting out of here so you can find a way to kill yourself, I'll save you the trouble. If you understand what I'm saying and want me to shoot you, prove it by going to the doorway there. Sit down on that target, that's all you have to do."

For a moment the cat blinked at him sleepily and then it put its head down again and went back to sleep—or pretended to. If it understood his offer, it wasn't having any.

Doc sighed; he hadn't really expected the cat to go and sit on the target. If it was—well, if it *wasn't* altogether a cat, it would be giving itself away by doing that. And shooting it would have been the last thing he'd have done under those circumstances. Especially with a gun he hadn't bothered to load.

He put the pistol and the target back where he'd taken them from and went into the kitchen. He'd have a final can of beer and a snack, if something in the refrigerator looked good to him, and then go to bed.

The sound of the refrigerator door brought the cat from the sofa into the kitchen. It paid no attention to anything he said but it had come to recognize that sound—or more likely was familiar with it from having been in the Kramers' kitchen—and he couldn't get anything from the refrigerator without the cat being there watching him. It didn't beg, but it was on the spot and ready for any handouts he might give it.

He found a few slices of liverwurst, dropped one into the cat's dish, and made himself a sandwich with the rest of it. He opened a can of beer and went over to the table. The cat finished its share of the liverwurst and went back to the living room, presumably to lie on the sofa again. Doc had managed to convince it that once he'd taken his own food to the table, further begging was useless. Besides, the cat couldn't be really hungry. It came to him when he went to the refrigerator only because it wanted a snack of something different from its staple diet of cat food and milk.

Doc got the flashlight before he turned off the lights; he still used one to light himself up to the bedroom as he had the first night the cat had been in the house, but not for quite the same reason. Now he simply didn't want to step on or fall over the cat in darkness. Since it could see in the dark itself, it couldn't realize that he couldn't.

The next day, Friday, nothing special happened. He made his usual trip into town but found no mail waiting for him, and didn't have to do any shopping. He dropped in at the newspaper office on the excuse of canceling his ad about having found a cat, but mostly just to talk to Ed Hollis a while to make sure nothing unusual had happened since the day before. Nothing had, except that the Garners had found a buyer for their farm and were planning to move west, possibly to the Ozarks, possibly on to California, And Gus Hoffman, Tommy's father, was putting an ad in the Bartlesville paper offering his farm for sale, and was planning to run one in the Green Bay paper too.

"My guess," Hollis said, "is that that means Charlotte's pregnant. The Garners moving, I mean."

"You'd better not put a guess like that in your paper, Ed."

Hollis looked at Doc so resentfully that Doc apologized.

"But why," Hollis wondered aloud, "would that make Gus Hoffman decide to move too? I mean, with Tommy dead, a scandal—not that there'd be much of one anyway—wouldn't hurt Gus."

"You're a damn fool, Ed. Hoffman will stick close to the Garners from here on in. He hasn't a wife or a child—but he's got a grandson or granddaughter on the way. Illegitimate or not, he'll be crazy about that kid."

"Hell, yes. Why didn't I think of that? Probably, wherever they go, he'll talk the Garners into letting him come in with them on a farm big enough for him too. And Charlotte will be a very young widow named Mrs. Hoffman and Gus will be her father-in-law. So the kid will even have Gus's name, and Gus will again have something to live for."

Doc had so few errands to do in town that day that he got back quite early and decided he might as well spend the rest of the afternoon fishing. It would be his first time fishing since he'd run over the dog and had through that episode become interested in the strange details surrounding the death of Tommy Hoffman.

He was glad to notice that the cat had apparently reconciled itself to staying in his house; at least—although he took precautions both times—it made no effort to get past him when he let himself in to get his fishing equipment or let himself out after he had gathered what he needed. It was becoming acclimated.

Or was it because it understood everything he'd told it and knew that he'd promised it its freedom on Monday anyway? He put that thought out of his mind and decided to concentrate on the pleasure of his hike to the nearest trout stream and his fishing when he reached it.

The fishing was quite good, considering that it was the wrong time of day for it. Within an hour he had five medium-sized trout in his creel. Enjoyable as the fishing was in itself, that satisfied him. It was more than he could eat today, possibly even tomorrow, even with the help of a cat. And fresh trout were infinitely more tasty than ones that had been in the refrigerator for more than a day or so.

After his return he cleaned the fish and cooked three of them. He ate two and the cat had no trouble disposing of the third, so avidly that Doc was amused. He said, "All right, Cat, consider that a bribe if you want. But over all, if you decide to stay with me, I'll promise you a trout about every third day. Not every day, though."

At breakfast Monday morning he gave thought to his decision to release the cat about mid-morning, then see whether, after five or six hours of freedom, it would return at the usual feeding time he had established for it. Oh, he'd do it; he couldn't keep, didn't want to keep, a cat shut up any longer than the few days he'd decided to keep it. He'd let it out; it would be a free agent as to whether it returned to him or not. But there was one little thing he could do and might as well do. He had a pair of excellent binoculars with him. The moment he let the cat out of the door he'd take them upstairs. From the window of one or another of the rooms up there he'd be able to follow it quite a distance, no matter which direction it went. If it headed toward the Kramer farm, he'd probably never see it again; if it went any other direction he might. If it stayed around the immediate vicinity, just wandering in the yard, it would be almost certain to come back in if he called it at feeding time.

Looking out, he saw that a light drizzle had started and wondered if a real rain was coming. If so, the cat probably wouldn't go out at all; cats hate water. But the drizzle lasted only ten or fifteen minutes, just enough to lay the dust and moisten the ground a bit.

At ten o'clock exactly—might as well keep his promise on the dot, he thought; he'd said the middle of the morning—he went into the living room past the cat on the sofa and to the front door. He opened it wide and said, "Well, Cat, want out a while?"

The cat understood the action if not the words. It got down from the sofa, stretched itself leisurely and unhurriedly, and then padded past him through the open doorway.

Quickly he got the binoculars and went upstairs with them. He tried the window of the front bedroom first and it turned out to be the right one; the cat was about halfway across the front yard, heading for the place where the road dead-ended. It was neither hurrying nor dawdling, walking unconcernedly at the pace of a cat that knows where it's going but is in no hurry to get there.

Probably heading back to the Kramers', he thought. Well, if that's what it wanted that was all right, and maybe all to the good. The Kramer woman's attitude in giving it to him had shown him that it might not be as easy as he had assumed for him to find a home for it later. And, since he certainly wouldn't abandon an animal, he might have to take it back to Boston with him, and that would be a confounded nuisance.

But when it reached the dead end of the road, the cat stopped. It turned its head and stared back at the house it had just left. Doc stepped hastily back

from the window, but kept the cat in the field of the binoculars. Was it looking back in indecision as to whether it wanted to go home, after all? Or was it
watching to see if *he* was watching it? He didn't think it had seen him, or that
it could see him now that he'd stepped back from the window.

It stayed there half a minute, either making up its mind or making sure
that it wasn't being watched. Which?

Then it started again, going a little faster this time, and not down the road
that would take it to the Kramers'. It went right across the end of the road
instead, into the woods. He could follow it only a few yards after that.

Doc put down the binoculars and scratched his head. After all, its behavior
was probably perfectly normal, but—

Then he remembered the drizzle that had fallen a while half an hour ago.
Because of that, it would be leaving paw prints. And why shouldn't he follow
them a while, for as far as he could, and see if he could find out where it was
going? After all, he had nothing else to do right now that had to be done today, and a walk would be as pleasant a way of filling in the time as any other.

He started at once, delaying only to put on a hat and to hang a raincoat
over his arm, in case the rain might start again. The cat's pawprints were clear
across the yard and once he bent down and studied a few prints to memorize
their size and shape; he didn't want to end up tracking some other small animal instead.

It was harder going when he got to the woods, for the prints didn't show in
grassy areas, nor did they show at all clearly under trees; the rain hadn't been
hard enough to work its way through the leaves and under every tree was a
completely dry circle.

Then it got easier again when he realized that the cat, wherever it was going, had been traveling in an almost perfect straight line.

After that, Doc was able to make better time; he simply walked in a straight line
himself across any grassy or dry areas and didn't have to cast about on the other side
to pick up the trail; it would be right at the place he himself came out.

He was at least a mile and a half into the woods when the trail ended. Suddenly, at the edge of a small stream of water that wasn't over four feet wide at
this point. Had the cat jumped across it? He jumped across it himself and tried
to pick up the trail on the other side. It simply wasn't there. The ground for
several feet on either side of the stream was bare and moist; the cat's prints
leading down *to* the water were as clear as any he'd found. But the cat hadn't
jumped across or its prints would be just as clear as the ones leading to the
stream.

Not quite daring to allow himself to think as yet, Doc followed the stream
along the far side. Downstream, of course. The current was slow.

It took him only about twenty paces to see what he had been afraid he would
see, ever since he reached the stream.

In the water, drowned, one small gray cat.

It was even more obviously a suicide than the dog that had run in front of
his ear, the owl that had flown through a window, the field mouse that had

attacked Tommy Hoffman, or the other cat that had attacked a vicious dog ten times its size.

And it had lived with him for days. It had refused his gambit with the pistol, it had not tried to starve itself or to bring about its own death in any other way.

It had waited till it could commit the act unobserved, so deep in the woods that—if he had not still had a residue of suspicion and the advantage of that brief drizzle that had made it trackable—its body would probably never have been found.

Had it, after all, understood every word he'd said to it and intelligently decided, when he promised to let it go this morning, that it would stand less chance of giving itself away by waiting that long than by making any attempt to die sooner?

But—suicide is no end in itself. What was the purpose?

The cat *had been* an ordinary cat once; he'd traced its origin. The dog Buck *had been* an ordinary dog until it had run away from its master only a short time before it had found death under the wheels of a car.

Was *something* using animals, each for some mysterious purpose, and then getting free of them by causing them to kill themselves?

What had been in the mind of that cat, all the time it had been with him?

And what of the human beings, Tommy Hoffman and Siegfried Gross? Had something been using them, controlling their minds, causing them to commit some action too difficult for an animal host, and then causing them to kill themselves?

But *what?* And *why?*

He remembered stroking the cat and enjoying its purring under his hand. What had he really been stroking?

He shuddered. The slight scare he'd had the night the cat had hidden from him—had that been only Tuesday night?—was nothing now. It had been based on nothing more than hunch or intuition.

Then he'd been only guessing. Now he *knew.*

But *what* did he know? Only that he was frightened.

He found a stick and maneuvered the small body to the edge of the water where he could reach it. He picked it up gingerly and carried it back with him to the house. He wrapped it in an old blanket and put it in the back of the station wagon. To take it to the laboratory in Green Bay and have it autopsied? He hadn't decided yet, but the body was there now if he should decide to take it in. But what could he tell them to check for? There was certainly no remote suspicion of rabies this time; the cat had been—or seemed—completely normal when he had let it out less than an hour before.

He smoked a pipe and thought a while and then realized what was the first thing he must do. He got the envelope with the copies of the statement he had dictated to Miss Talley and drove to town with them. He should have mailed them sooner; now he'd get them in the mail as soon as he could add the story of the cat to what they already contained and dictate the covering letters.

Miss Talley was not at home. There was a note on her door, "Back about 3 p.m." It was time for lunch anyway, so he drove back to the downtown district and ate, then killed time at the tavern drinking a few beers. He had several chances to get into conversation, but he didn't feel like talking. He could hardly bring up suddenly now what he was thinking about; there was too much to tell all at once to anyone with whom he hadn't talked before. And that left only Miss Talley.

He watched the clock and reached her place a few minutes early, but she was there.

"Doctor!" she said, when she saw his face. "Come in. Has something new happened?"

He nodded, a little grimly. "It's about the cat. But I want to dictate it as an addendum to the statement I dictated to you last week. If you'll get your note-book—"

Miss Talley got it, and her eyes danced as excitedly as her pencil point as he talked and she wrote. He told the whole story of the cat, from her first glimpse of it during his previous dictation to his finding it drowned in the little creek. He went into detail and it took him over an hour.

Miss Talley looked up then. "Doctor! Besides mailing these to your two friends, you've got to go to the sheriff now. Or call in the F.B.I.—or *something*, if he won't take it seriously."

Doc nodded slowly. "I'm going to, Miss Talley. I'll tell you my plans before I leave, but first, while I'm dictating, let me give you the two covering letters that go with the statements that I'm going to mail out."

He dictated again, and the letters ran longer than he had anticipated; it was almost five o'clock when he had finished. "Miss Talley, about how long do you think it will take you to transcribe all that?"

"A few hours, possibly four, but I'll start it right away; I won't even eat until I've finished. While I'm doing it you can go see the sheriff and—"

"No, I want to wait till I have a copy of the full statement to have him read when I see him. It'll impress him more that way, I think. After all, outside of the gray cat episode, nothing in here will be new to him, and for me just to tell him over again—well, I'd rather have him read the statement.

"And I'm not going to let you work all evening without eating, or waste time cooking for yourself either. Put your coat on and we'll eat together in town. Then I'll drive you back here and leave you. You can do your typing, and in the morning I'll talk to the sheriff and get those letters in the mail—airmail special delivery. It'll be too late by the time you finish this evening, even if I'd let you work straight through."

"Well—I suppose it would, even if you went in to Green Bay to mail them. But—are you going to take the chance of staying out there tonight? Every-thing that's happened has been, or has started, along that road you live on. And the last thing, the cat, right where you live!"

Doc smiled. "I'll be all right tonight, Miss Talley," he told her.

And he was, because the mind thing was otherwise occupied.

CHAPTER SEVENTEEN

The mind thing, finally freed of his annoying imprisonment in a host that had become of no further use to him, was back in his own body, his own shell, under the back steps of the Gross farmhouse. He felt relieved and well satisfied with what he had just done. He had taken his cat-host so far into the woods before drowning it that its body would probably never be found. Staunton might wonder if he learned that the cat had not returned to its former home— but Staunton would never learn that because tonight, while he slept, he would cease to *be* Staunton; the mind thing would have him.

The mind thing's plans were simple, and he'd had plenty of time to think them out while, as a cat, he'd nothing to do but laze around Staunton's house and play the cat role to the hilt. He felt sure that he'd done just that; he'd managed not to do a single thing out of character for a cat. He'd been tempted, just for a second, when Staunton had offered to shoot him—but he'd seen through the trap easily. If he'd gone to sit on the target on the floor, Staunton's suspicions would have been verified and shooting him would have been the *last* thing Staunton would have done. Instead, Staunton would probably have caged him and kept him indefinitely for intensive study. Possibly he'd even have fed him intravenously by force to keep him from achieving death by starvation.

But all that was safely past now, and after tonight he'd be really safe. He'd be in control of the only human being who was a menace to him and who at the same time was his optimum host.

It was of such major importance that he take over Staunton at the earliest possible time that he wouldn't even take the risk of using an animal or bird host for the purpose. Mrs. Gross would be safer and surer. He'd take her over as soon as she went to sleep. He'd wait until, say, one o'clock, by which time everyone between here and Staunton's place would certainly be sound asleep; then he'd have her carry him that distance. If there was a light on in Staunton's place, she'd wait until a full hour after it had gone out, then hide him within range of the sleeping Staunton. Then she'd come back home and die. He'd make it look like an accident—a fall down the stairs, perhaps, in the middle of the night. True, her death, in any way except a natural one, would be a suspicious coincidence so shortly after her husband's death, but that wouldn't matter, because within a minute after her death he'd have Staunton, the one person who could otherwise be dangerous to him. Let others wonder; he'd he safe.

He threw out his preceptor sense to refamiliarize himself with what was currently happening—what changes, if any, might have occurred during the days while his mind had been away.

Mrs. Gross was alone in the house, in the kitchen, at the moment sterilizing some mason jars in preparation for preserving or canning something.

Nothing had changed in the barnyard or in the barn except that the three cows were no longer in the latter. No doubt they were out in pasture. All was well.

Mrs. Gross came out of the house—walking right over him as she came down the kitchen steps. With mild curiosity, and since he had nothing else to do, he followed her with his sense of perception. She went around behind the barn, stopping just about at the limit of his ability to follow her. "Jim!" she called out, "Yoo-hoo, Jim!" He heard a voice call back in answer, although it was too far for him to hear the words.

He remembered now. The Kramer boy, he'd learned from conversations in the Gross house, had been willing, at his father's suggestion, to come over and work for Mrs. Gross for the rest of the school vacation, or until she had sold the farm and turned it over to the new owner.

He knew and could picture Jim—with the memories of the cat Jerry, which had been a Kramer cat: a husky young boy about the age of Tommy Hoffman. He'd be a much better host than the aging and frail Mrs. Gross. But of course he wouldn't be sleeping here.

"Will you bring in a few ears of the corn, Jim?" Mrs. Gross was calling out. "I'll cook it for our lunch, huh? And maybe some cucumbers when you pass the patch."

She came around the barn and went back into the house.

Jim Kramer stopped what he was doing, picking beans, and mopped his forehead with a handkerchief as he headed for the edge of the cornfield. He was husky all right, and just Tommy's age, and had known Tommy, although they hadn't been really close friends. One way in which they had differed was that Tommy had been interested in farming, would have been content to have spent the rest of his life as a farmer. Jim had bigger ideas. When he'd be graduated in June of next year, he was going to go to college and study engineering. Just what kind he hadn't fully decided yet. Probably mechanical engineering; chemical engineering, his alternative, would perhaps take him further and lead to bigger money, but he was a natural-born mechanic and more interested in machinery than in chemicals, so it would make more sense for him to study something at which he already had a good start. He could take apart and put together any car or tractor he'd ever had a chance to fiddle with, and after college he'd be able to design cars and other machinery.

Meanwhile, he didn't mind farm work and was good at it. He was glad this deal with Mrs. Gross had come along to let him earn some money this summer to add to his college fund. The pay wasn't generous, but it was adequate. And it was a full-time job while it lasted. At first he'd tried—it had been his father's idea—to spend only half of each day here, the other half back on his own farm. But after only a day or two it became obvious that, unless the Gross farm was to deteriorate and lose crops, it was a full-time job. His father had seen the point, and agreed.

He picked half a dozen of the best ears of corn—and then, after considering, two more. He had a healthy appetite and doing outdoor work sharpened it. Mrs. Gross would probably eat only two ears, but he might want six himself. On his way to the farmhouse he also picked half a dozen big cucumbers—

more than she'd need, but the extra ones would keep—and came around the barn and into the house with them. He put them down on the kitchen table.

When he turned to leave, Mrs. Gross said, "Wait, Jim. It's almost lunchtime; it won't take me long to cook that corn and everything else's ready except for cutting up a couple cucumbers. Hardly pay you to go all the way out to those beans and back again. Sit down or lie down and rest a little; you've been working hard."

"Fine," he said. "But in that case let me shuck that corn for you first, though. Then maybe I'll take a short nap in the barn till you call me."

"Barn? Why the barn when there's a nice sofa in the next room? And it'll be easier for me to call you there than having to go out to the barn."

"Well, all right."

He shucked the corn for her and then went into the living room and lay down on the sofa, after taking his shoes off so he wouldn't get it dirty. He wasn't really tired this early in the day, but a fifteen- or twenty-minute nap would be welcome. He was one of those fortunate people who can go to sleep easily and quickly anywhere at any time and awake fully refreshed after even a ten-minute nap.

He closed his eyes and slept—and, in his mind, there was sudden pain and sudden but very brief struggle.

He continued to lie there—but in his brain the mind thing was taking advantage of the rest of the nap period to sort through his memories and readying himself to *be*, or seem to be, Jim Kramer. For the rest of today. He wouldn't have to use the frail German hausfrau after all.

"Ready, Jim," Mrs. Gross called from the kitchen. "You awake?"

"Sure," he called back. "Just a sec." He swung his feet off the sofa and bent over to put his shoes back on.

He stood and stretched himself in the doorway to the kitchen. "Mmmm, smells good," he said.

"Sit down, sit down. Help yourself while it's hot."

When he had eaten his fill he went back to work. Finishing picking the beans that were ready took most of the afternoon. Tomorrow they'd have to be taken into town to sell to the trucker who'd take them to the cannery. But, the mind thing knew, not by his present host; Jim Kramer would be dead by tomorrow.

When he had brought the cows in from pasture and milked them, he was through for the day. He went home.

The Jim Kramer who ate dinner with his parents that evening was perhaps a little quieter than usual, but otherwise he seemed perfectly normal. The only uncharacteristic thing about him was the way he spent the evening. After the table had been cleared he took all ten volumes of an encyclopedia from the bookcase and started looking through them, reading an article in one volume and then picking another, apparently from some reference or word in the preceding article. His father, walking past the table once, saw him reading under "Electron" and a second time under "Radar."

"Thinking about electrical engineering, Jim, instead of mechanical or chemical?" he asked.

"Just looking up a little on it, Dad," Jim said over his shoulder. "Electrical engineering or electronics. Electronics is getting more and more important. Just might be the best bet, if I find it makes sense to me."

"Could be. Well, you got a year to make up your mind."

"Yes, but it will make some difference in what subjects I take my last year in high. And school starts next month, so I better make up my mind before then."

Mr. Kramer turned away. "Okay, Jim. Your decision; you know more about it than I do."

"Wait a minute, Dad. Can I borrow the truck for a few hours tomorrow morning?"

"I guess so; I won't be using it early. But what about working for Mrs. Gross?"

"That's okay. With the truck I can work for her and still do an errand of my own at the same time. Got five bushels of beans I got to take in town and sell tomorrow for her. With the pickup I can make it to Green Bay and back in the same time it'd take me to hitch up her horse and wagon and go to Bartlesville. And I'll get her a better price for them in Green Bay and have a chance to do what I want there."

"And what's that?"

"Just a stop at the library to borrow some books. It's kind of—well, spotty, trying to dig information out of assorted parts of an encyclopedia. One good elementary text on electronics would be a lot better."

"I can see that. Jim, if you can't find what you want at the library, go to a bookstore. And it they haven't got it, have them order it. I'll pay for it. For several books, if you want."

"Thanks a million, Dad. I think the library will do it, but if it doesn't, I'll take you up on that."

He gathered up the volumes of the encyclopedia and put them back in the bookcase. The mind within the mind of Jim Kramer had instantly memorized every page which Jim had apparently only glanced at, in addition to those he had pretended to read. At leisure later, he could digest and evaluate what he had learned.

For the rest of the evening he stayed in character by turning on the radio and listening to it while he read, or appeared to read, the subscription copy of *Popular Mechanics* which had come in the mail that day. At ten o'clock when his parents went up to bed he tuned down the radio but kept on reading for a while. Jim had managed to convince his parents that he didn't need quite as much sleep as they did and, since he got up at the same time, it was all right for him to stay up half an hour or an hour longer than they did. At ten-thirty he raided the refrigerator for a snack, as usual, and then went upstairs to his own bedroom. But not to sleep; he took off only his shoes and lay quietly on top of his bed until the luminous dial of his wrist watch told him it was half-past two. Then he left very quietly, carrying his shoes till he was safe outside the house.

There was bright moonlight, both an advantage and a danger, since he could see easily himself, but he also could be seen. When he died tomorrow morning in an auto accident on the way to Green Bay—and the mind thing had decided to wait that long; there was no logical way for him to die accidentally tonight without causing speculation and investigation—the mind thing did not want anyone to report having seen him abroad tonight. Quickly and quietly he made his way to the Gross farm, reached under the kitchen steps and dug briefly, bringing out the shell that was the material body, now deserted, of the thing that now animated Jim Kramer. He smoothed back the dirt so there would be no indication that anything had been buried there.

With the shell inside his shirt, so that if he *were* seen it would not he reported that he had been carrying something, he started back past his own house and toward Staunton's. Twice he made detours off the road and into the woods; two of the intervening farms had watchdogs that would bark if he went by on the road, perhaps waking someone who might look out a window and see him.

The house at the end of the road was dark; Staunton was in bed and probably asleep. But in case he might he lying awake, Jim took off his shoes for the trip across the yard and around the house. There were steps leading up to the kitchen door here too, and it would be as good a hiding place as any. He buried the shell again, this time being even more careful than at the Gross place to smooth over the dirt and leave no indication of digging and burying.

Then he went back home by the same route, let himself in quietly and tiptoed upstairs to his bedroom. Mission accomplished. This time he undressed down to his shorts, because his mother would look in to waken him in the morning and that was the way he had been sleeping. Deliberately he tossed and turned enough to rumple the sheets thoroughly, and then lay quietly until his mother opened the door and called him. He answered sleepily and sat up on the edge of the bed yawning.

At breakfast he still acted sleepy and yawned a few times. When his mother asked if he'd stayed up later than usual last night he told her that he hadn't, but that for some reason he'd had trouble getting to sleep, hadn't really slept soundly until maybe an hour or so before she'd waked him.

"Probably worrying about this career decision you're considering," his father said. "But, Jim, if you got only an hour or two of sleep, I don't like the idea of your driving into Green Bay; you might go to sleep at the wheel. Why don't you go back to bed, and let me tell Mrs. Gross you'll be able to work only a half day today? She won't mind for once and you can make that trip this afternoon instead."

Jim yawned again. "Thanks, Dad, but no; I'll be all right as soon as I start working and get waked up. I'll just turn in earlier tonight to make up for it. I'm okay."

Half an hour later he was through Bartlesville and on the way to Green Bay. He had let Mrs. Gross catch him yawning too, while he loaded the beans into the pickup truck. With both his parents and Mrs. Gross able to testify to how sleepy he was, there wouldn't be any question, when he ran off the road into a tree or swerved into a head-on collision with another car, of suicide—of anything but his having gone to sleep at the wheel.

He decided finally on a concrete bridge abutment he knew he'd he reaching in another ten miles or so. A swerve head-on into another car would provide even more impact, but would involve someone else's death besides his own.

So that was discarded, not out of any feeling of mercy for the other victim or victims—human lives meant nothing at all to the mind thing—but simply because it would make the accident more spectacular, more talked about.

The bridge abutment came, and he hit it squarely, at a little over sixty miles an hour. The impact was sufficient.

Instantly the mind thing was back in his own body, now under the back steps of the house Staunton was living in.

It was five minutes after nine o'clock.

CHAPTER EIGHTEEN

Doc Staunton had slept fitfully, not over the equivalent of two or three hours during the night, and when he awakened at seven and saw that it was light, he gave up trying to sleep.

He made himself breakfast and then sat over coffee waiting till it got late enough to go to town. He and Miss Talley had talked quite a while over dinner and he doubted that she'd finished his typing before midnight, or even later; he knew he shouldn't call at her house before nine at the earliest, and ten would be better. He was restless, though, and at eight-thirty he got into the station wagon and drove into town.

There was nothing to do when he got there. He didn't want to go to the post office or call the sheriff before he'd got the statements from Miss Talley and, even if he'd felt like having a beer so early in the morning, the tavern didn't open until ten. He stopped in the restaurant for more coffee.

At a quarter after nine, he decided he'd still wait fifteen minutes to call Miss Talley and see if she was up and ready to see him. By now the sheriff should be in his office in Wilcox; he could call there now and try to make an appointment for later in the morning.

He got the sheriff on the wire and was just getting around to setting the time for an appointment when the sheriff said, "Just a second, Doc. Hold the line." And then, a minute later, "Doc, it can't be this morning; you'll have to call me later. Just got a flash from a state police radio car. There's been an accident between Bartlesville and Green Bay; got to get there quick. Sorry." The line went dead.

Doc replaced the receiver and stared for a moment at the phone, wondering whether the accident could possibly have happened to anyone he knew. Probably not, he thought, or the sheriff would have mentioned it—but then again the sheriff didn't know exactly who Doc knew, except for a few people; and besides, the sheriff had been in a hurry.

He dropped another coin and called the sheriff's office. When a deputy answered, Doc identified himself and explained that he'd been talking to the sheriff when an accident flash had caused the sheriff to excuse himself; could the deputy tell him who, if anyone, had been hurt in the accident?

The deputy was cooperative. A high school student named James Kramer, who lived somewhere outside Bartlesville, had been killed. He'd been alone in a truck he was driving to Green Bay and he'd probably gone to sleep at the wheel; he'd driven straight into a concrete bridge abutment and had died instantly.

Doc thanked him and had hung up again before the name Kramer began to register. It was a family named Kramer who lived next to Mrs. Gross, and he remembered now having heard that their son, a high school boy about Tommy Hoffman's age, had been working for Mrs. Gross until she could sell her farm. And the Kramers had owned the gray cat that had spent almost a week with him—until yesterday!

And now the Kramer boy was dead—under circumstances that could all too easily have been suicide. Human suicide number three, and again a connection between it and an animal suicide!

Suddenly, Doc Staunton wasn't scared any more. He felt coldly calm, knowing what he had to do—and quickly, since he'd wasted too much time already.

This—whatever *this* was—was nothing for a county sheriff. This was something for investigation by the F.B.I. and by top scientists. Not that he wouldn't talk to the sheriff too, but this was way over the heads of local law enforcement officers, even of the state police—although the F.B.I. would want to use them for routine parts of the investigation. Maybe he could even get the army interested. Fortunately he knew, from his work on satellite and moon-probe projects, several top army security officers and two F.B.I. men. More to the point, they knew *him* well enough not to dismiss him as a crackpot and to give serious consideration to anything, however seemingly wild and impossible, that he told them.

He'd start phoning people, and stirring things up, the moment he got those statements from Miss Talley. But one thing came ahead even of that, something he could do right now that would take him less than an hour: Move out of the danger zone.

He was already walking to his car as he decided that. He'd go out to the house, pack his belongings and put them in the station wagon. Then, when he picked up Miss Talley's typing, he'd head right for Green Bay, make his headquarters at a hotel there, and start making long-distance calls. If he had half as much influence as he thought he had, there'd be F.B.I. men and security agents in town before the day was over. And while he was waiting for them he could find out as much as possible about the death of Jim Kramer and add that to his statement. A Green Bay stenographer could take care of that, unless Miss Talley wanted to go to Green Bay with him and follow through with what she'd started. He rather thought that she would.

The mind thing's first sweep with his preceptor sense told him that Staunton was not at home. This was mildly surprising, at a few minutes after nine in the morning; Staunton seldom went into town that early. Nor had he gone fishing or for a walk, because the car was gone too. Still—

The mind thing checked. All of Staunton's personal possessions were still there, except the clothes he'd been wearing. Dishes in the sink and other evidence showed that he'd had breakfast. He must have awakened earlier than usual and decided, for whatever reason, to take an early trip into town instead of going at his usual time, which was late morning or early afternoon. Nothing to worry about; he'd be back. And unless by fortunate circumstance he should take a nap today, then tonight—

Although, as a cat, he had spent several days and nights in this house, he had—in that form—been deprived of his preceptor sense. He couldn't see into closed rooms or closets, couldn't read closed books or folded letters. Now, at leisure, he could remedy those omissions, and he did.

For future reference—since, once he'd taken over Staunton as a host, he'd no longer be free to use his preception, but would have to depend upon the human being's relatively limited sense organs—he memorized the house and everything that was in it. Even with Staunton as host, he'd be here at least another week or two. Just how long he wouldn't know until he discovered the factors he'd find in Staunton's thoughts and memories. But it would be too suspicious to have his host leave immediately and suddenly, since his plans were apparently to stay the rest of the summer.

He felt the vibrations of the car approaching before it came within range of his preception. It was Staunton's station wagon and Staunton was in it alone. It was ten by the kitchen clock.

As Staunton came to the front door and let himself in, the mind thing, just to complete his inventory, used his preceptive sense on the car Staunton had just left. Suddenly, for the first time, he realized that something must have gone wrong. Carefully rolled up in an old tarpaulin was the dead, drowned body of a small gray cat. His second-last host. How had Staunton discovered it, and why did he now have it in his car? Had he been trailed through the woods to the stream? He'd never thought of that possibility, but he *must* have been. He'd been satisfied to look back at the house and to see that he wasn't being followed by sight. But that brief sprinkle of rain—of course, he'd left paw prints that Staunton had managed to follow. Again he'd given himself away.

Well, Staunton was back home now, and sooner or later he'd sleep. And after that, whatever he'd suspected wouldn't matter.

But what was Staunton doing now? He was getting his two suitcases from the storage room and carrying them upstairs, putting his clothes in them, packing his razor and other things from the bathroom. *He was packing to leave, and permanently, since he was taking everything.*

But he couldn't; he had to be stopped, at any cost.

Doc Staunton carried the suitcases out to the station wagon and put them in the back, then returned to the house. He made one quick round of it, closing all the windows and making sure that the back door was locked. In the kitchen he hesitated whether to flick the switch that would shut off the gasoline engine and generator in the basement, and then decided not to. There was still food in the refrigerator and it wouldn't spoil for a few days. And he'd be back, although not alone and not to stay here; but he'd certainly be showing the place to whoever would be in charge of the investigation. He might as well leave the current on.

That took care of everything except his fishing equipment, guns, and ammunition in the storage room. Using the creel to carry the boxes of cartridges and shells, he carried it and the other fishing equipment, including his high boots, out to the station wagon and then came back for the three guns—the pistol, the rifle, and the over-and-under shotgun. That was all, and he pocketed the pistol and held the two guns under one arm to give him a free hand to lock the front door behind him and pocket the key. Then he started for the station wagon.

He was almost there, just reaching for the door handle, when he saw the deer, a six-point buck. It was standing, with no attempt at concealing itself, about fifty feet away, at the edge of the woods, just past the point where the road started outside his yard. It stared back at him, then lowered its head and pawed the earth, readying itself for a charge.

Quickly he got inside the car and started the engine. He had a sudden hunch as to what was coming, but there was only one way to find out. He put the car in gear and started it. He'd have to drive right past the buck, within a few yards of it, to get away—if the buck would let him.

The buck wasn't going to let him. It started its charge the moment the car started to move. He braked to a stop and even tried—but didn't have time— to reduce the impact by getting the car moving in reverse. Head down, the buck was a two-hundred-pound missile that hit the radiator dead center, between the headlights, and then the buck was two hundred pounds of dead deer with broken antlers, broken skull, broken neck. The car had moved backward almost two feet and only Doc's final split-second move of throwing himself down sidewise across the front seat saved him from having at least a sore neck from the whiplash effect he'd have experienced had he remained sitting upright.

He sat up slowly. The engine had died, or had been killed by the backward motion of the car while it was still in a forward gear. He turned off the ignition; he didn't try to restart the car. He knew it would never run again until it had been towed to a garage and equipped, at the very minimum, with a new radiator and a new fan. It wouldn't have surprised him if other damage had been done, possibly even a cracked block.

The rifle, being only a .22, would be useless, and even with a pistol and a shotgun he'd never make it afoot to town, or even to the nearest farmhouse that had a telephone, if a series of animal hosts was to be sent against him. Not past fields, on one side of the road, that contained cows and maybe even a few bulls drowsing in the shade of trees. And on the other side of the road, a long stretch of virgin woodland that certainly contained more deer, possibly even a bear or two, and wildcats. There was an even nastier possibility than any one of these: what if the enemy could find a human host taking a midday nap? What could he possibly do if Mrs. Kramer, say, or Mrs. Gross should come out to the road with a shotgun or rifle and start shooting at him? Shoot back? Of course it wouldn't really be a *sane* Mrs. Kramer or Mrs. Gross doing the shooting—but even so, he knew he wouldn't be able to shoot a woman, And no matter how many animals or humans he might succeed in killing on the way to get help, sooner or later someone or something would manage to kill him instead. He knew, or felt fairly sure, that there was only one *mind* against him— but it was a mind that could send a practically endless succession of attackers against him, more than he could hope to handle.

Well, he reflected, at least the cold war is over. The enemy—whatever it was—was no longer pretending. At least from him, Doc Staunton, it would make no further attempt to conceal its powers. It wanted to keep him here, and it could. He reached into the back seat for the creel and loaded the shotgun and the pistol, and stuffed all the extra cartridges for the former and shells for the latter into various pockets.

Strangely, he wasn't scared at all. He was even more coldly calm, calmly analytical. And he knew that he would have to be if he was to stand a chance to win this war. If he was to win it, his mind would have to be his major weapon; firearms might win a battle, but never the war.

First, immediate survival. Would he be safer here in the car than back in the house? He thought he would be just as safe and much more comfortable, especially for an extended siege, back in the house. The enemy had served notice that it would kill him to keep him from reaching help. But would the enemy try to kill him anyway, even if he accepted the state of siege and didn't try to leave?

He couldn't be sure, but one thing had been a strong indication that the enemy was not trying to kill him unless again he tried to leave. If the enemy wanted his immediate death, he'd probably be dead already. He hadn't noticed the deer standing there until he had almost reached the car, but it had been watching him. It could have charged sooner than it did—and at him instead of at the car. And none of the guns had been loaded then,

So, the house. He got out of the car cautiously, the pistol in a pocket and the shotgun at ready, and looked about him. Nothing alive was in sight. Unless—

He looked upward. About a hundred feet in the air a wild duck was wheeling in slow circles—as a buzzard circles. A duck does not fly that way. Air attack? He hadn't thought of that when he had been considering the dangers of trying to reach town afoot, but he saw now that a kamikaze attack from the air by any reasonably heavy bird would be fully as dangerous as, say, a charge by a maddened cow or horse. He kept a wary eye on the circling duck as he started for the house. Suddenly, when he was about halfway, it dived. He jerked up the gun ready to fire and then leap aside—but he didn't have to. The bird wasn't dive-bombing *him,* but a point in the yard a dozen or so yards away from him; it hit the ground with a sickening thud that raised a cloud of dust and probably made a dent in the hard-packed soil of the yard.

Thoughtfully, Doc let himself into the house and locked the door. No, the enemy was not trying to kill him, only to keep him penned here. The dive of the duck couldn't possibly have missed him that much if it had been aimed at him. The enemy had done it merely to give him a demonstration of the futility of his trying to escape afoot by showing him, in case he hadn't thought of it (as he hadn't at first) one more deadly means of preventing his escape. The wild duck could as easily have dived at him as not; it had nothing to lose since it was making a suicidal plunge in any case. Therefore: the enemy did not *want* him dead, as long as it could keep him here instead.

He reloaded the upper barrel of the shotgun and leaned it against the window beside the front door. He emptied his pockets of the extra shells and cartridges and put them on the end of the sofa, in easy reach. Then he sat down on the arm of the sofa, facing the window and looking out.

Nothing moved outside. Was he imagining things? Would it be safe for him to leave and walk to town? No, if the deer hadn't been proof enough, then the plummeting duck had been the convincer.

There was no attack now, and he didn't think there would be, as long as he stayed here and made no attempt to leave. But why?

He started for the refrigerator to get himself a bottle of beer, but changed his mind and came back. Beer, in moderation, wouldn't impair much his ability to think. Still, even a trifling impairment might make all the difference.

What was the nature of the enemy? Human, possibly mutant, with a hitherto undemonstrated psi ability of being able to take over other minds? Demon? Alien? Somehow, the last seemed least unlikely of the three; as Miss Talley had pointed out, there are billions of habitable worlds in the universe; why shouldn't life and intelligence have developed on some of them? Why should Earth be unique? And why couldn't some intelligent life form have developed some form of space travel? Why should human beings be the first to do so?

Yes, definitely it seemed more possible than the only alternatives he could think of—and more dangerous.

But why was he now being singled out for attack? Because he now knew and suspected enough to be dangerous to the enemy? Yes, he was; regardless of how the enemy (keep calling it that, he decided, regardless of what he or it really was) knew about it.

Of course, he realized: using the gray cat as host, it had spent over five days with him. It had heard what he'd dictated to Miss Talley and knew that he planned to mail the statements he'd dictated to important friends. And it had studied *him* all the time he'd kept it captive—to study *it*.

Yes, he was dangerous to the enemy, and the enemy knew it. But why, then, hadn't the enemy killed him? With the deer, it could have, easily, simply by charging before he got into the car instead of after. And, with the dive-bombing duck, it hadn't even tried; the dive into the ground hadn't been a serious attempt to hit him. The enemy wanted him alive, but here, not elsewhere. Why?

Because it wanted him for a host? It seemed a possible answer, but why didn't it take him as one, or try to?

Nothing was happening outside, and he went into the kitchen and put water on the stove to boil for coffee. Was some special circumstance necessary for the enemy to take over a host?

Suddenly he thought of a possible answer, and the more he thought about it the more possible it seemed. Tommy Hoffman had been taken over while he was sleeping. So had Siegfried Gross. It was less certain that Jim Kramer had been sleeping, but he could have been. And the animal hosts: almost all animals—and especially cats and dogs—sleep frequently, if briefly, by day as well as by night.

But if the enemy was keeping him here until he slept, so he could be taken over, then why hadn't he been taken over last night? He'd not slept well, but off and on he had slept a little. Then the answer, or at least *an* answer, came to him. For whatever reason, after the death of the gray cat, the enemy had taken the Kramer boy as his next host—and had, this time, waited until he could make the boy's death seem an accident rather than a suicide. Which was another proof, or at least an indication, that the enemy was singular, not plural, and could operate only one host at a time. If he could only be sure—

Making his mind up suddenly, Doc picked up the shotgun and went to the door and opened it, took a cautious step out onto the small unroofed porch and looked up.

Birds, big birds, were circling up in the sky, six or seven of them. Birds, plural. Had he been wrong?

Then relief came to him as he watched them for a moment and saw them more clearly. These birds were not hosts; they were buzzards circling over the dead deer, circling slowly down for a carrion feast. Ordinary birds. Never before had buzzards seemed beautiful to him; they did in that moment.

Then, from the direction of the woods, he saw another bird coming; it looked like another duck. As it came nearer it flew higher to gain altitude and then started a dive, straight toward him. He could probably have shot it by throwing up the shotgun, but there was no point in taking the risk. He stepped back inside quickly and closed the door. A second later there was the loud thud of its crash-landing onto the boards of the porch.

Doc smiled grimly; by taking the slight risk he had taken in stepping outside he thought that he had verified at least one of his deductions. If the enemy could take over a creature which was awake it could easily have taken over one of those big circling buzzards already in the sky, much closer. Or all of them, if it could manage more than one host at a time. Instead, it had had to lose time by finding a bird farther away, a bird that was sleeping, probably.

Dangerous as the enemy could be, it must have limitations.

There was hope, then. Miss Talley was expecting him; sooner or later she'd get worried enough to call the sheriff. If the sheriff started for his place and didn't get through alive, that would be tough on the sheriff; but other officers would follow to see what happened to him, and if they were attacked the state police would get on the job. A *group* of armed men could get through anything the enemy could throw against them, one animal at a time.

Yes, help would come, eventually. His main problem would be to stay awake till then.

CHAPTER NINETEEN

For what seemed an eternity, nothing happened. Night fell, the time for sleep. Doc went around the house, upstairs and down, turning on the lights, all of the lights.

And then the lights went out, all together.

The generator? Of course the generator. The gasoline motor that ran it was not out of fuel; there was enough in the tank to run it for several more days. But either the generator or the motor that ran it had stopped.

The enemy had taken another host. A mouse? Probably a mouse—a domestic mouse if there were any in the cellar; otherwise a field mouse that had been taken over and directed to find a way in somehow, had got through the housing of the gasoline engine or the motor that it ran, and that mouse would now be dead, smeared around a commutator perhaps... And there was no use trying to restart the engine or the generator—there were more mice wherever the first one had come from. Or perhaps it had not been a mouse at all, Even an insect, directed by an intelligent mind, can so place itself as to die in the process of shorting a motor or a generator.

Darkness.

Above all, he must fight getting sleepy. Sleep would be the end.

A moon came up. It was only a three-quarter moon but it was bright in a clear, starry sky. He could see outside the house now, in all directions. And enough moonlight came in the front windows so he could see fairly well in the living room—well enough to pace without risking falling over anything. He had a flashlight, but even with the one extra battery he had for it, it wasn't going to last the whole night; he would have to use it sparingly.

How long would he be able to stay awake? Another twenty-four hours, he thought, despite the fact that he'd slept so little the night before and already felt tired.

He was getting hungry, too, but he decided not to eat anything. Food can tend to make one sleepy, especially when one is already tired before eating. A hungry man can stay awake more easily than a full one—at least up to the point where starvation or malnutrition weakens him. That wouldn't happen here; he knew that he could go without food for a much longer period than he could go without sleep.

He paced, thought, tried to think harder. Somehow he had to counterattack. But how?

In what way was the enemy vulnerable? Was it incorporeal or did it have a body of its own—perhaps dormant while it was using a host? He thought it must have a body: first, because he found it almost impossible to think of an incorporeal entity; second, because he was remembering now one strange thing in connection with the suicide of Siegfried Gross, A jar of meat stock and a bowl of gravy had disappeared from Elsa Gross's refrigerator that night. Gross would hardly have eaten them in that form; and he would have had no reason to pour them down the sink. But they were prime ingredients for a nutrient solution that should feed anyone or anything with a bodily chemistry remotely similar to that of a terrestrial creature. Had Gross been taken as a host for the purpose of feeding the enemy before killing himself? It sounded grotesque, yes— but what, in everything that had been happening, did *not* sound grotesque? It seemed at least possible.

He went out to the kitchen and made as brief use as possible of the flashlight to make another pot of coffee. When it was ready he returned with a cup of it and again sat on the arm of the sofa staring out into the bright moonlight.

Where would the enemy's body be? Quite probably, since there must be some limit to the range at which it could operate, it was nearby; this house was the focus of the attack. Quite possibly within sight of the house; conceivably even inside it. He didn't think the enemy would have taken that chance, but the fact that it might have did open up one possible line of counteroffensive. Not tonight, but as soon as it was light tomorrow, he'd search the inside of the house thoroughly, ready to shoot anything alive that he found.

It was a long, long night, and the lonesomest night he'd ever spent. But it *did* end.

When it was light enough, he searched the house thoroughly, room by room, and then the basement. He didn't know, of course, what he was looking for, or how small or how large an object it might be, but unless the enemy had the ability to disguise itself as a small household object, or to become invisible, both of which he doubted, he convinced himself that it wasn't there. In the basement he found that his guess about the generator had been right. Something like a mouse had crawled into it through the housing and was now nothing more than a red smear. He could have cleaned it and started it again, but to what purpose? If the enemy didn't want him to have electricity, another small something would stop either the generator or the motor the moment he went back upstairs.

Only one other possibility had come to him during the endless night. Since the enemy was the helpless prisoner, in a sense, of any host he took, and could escape to take another host only with the death of the current one, then there was one way in which he, Doc, might have a chance to turn the tables. If he could slightly wound and capture, or capture without wounding, whatever host might be used against him next—and keep that host alive under circumstances in which it could not bring about its own death, then the enemy would be helpless for a while. And that might be perhaps long enough to let him get into town alive and safe.

But would he have such a chance?

He stared up at the ceiling and felt sudden hope when he saw a moth flying around up there. *Could* it be? A moth was not dangerous in any way, but maybe the enemy was controlling it—was using the moth as a spy to keep closer track of him than could be done otherwise.

Casually he got up and strolled into the storage room, closing the door behind him. He went to work quickly and made a very crude butterfly net. He bent a coathanger into an approximate circle. He ripped apart a sleeping bag to get the piece of cheesecloth that was a part of it, the part that could be propped up over the head to keep insects away, and fastened it around the wire loop made from the coathanger. He managed to tie this onto the end of a broom handle. It looked like a far cry from a real butterfly net, but it might serve the purpose of one.

The moth was still circling. It took several passes, but he got it. He took it out of the net very carefully so as not to injure even a wing. Then, in the kitchen, he found a box of kitchen matches and emptied it; he put the moth inside and closed the lid. The moth would live for a while, long enough for him to make his getaway. That is, if the moth was—

He might as well find out right away, he decided. Getting the shotgun, he opened the front door and stepped through it, looked around and saw nothing to be frightened of. Not even in the air above.

He took a deep breath and started walking. He got only about ten paces before something made him look upward again. A chicken hawk, a big one, had just taken off from the eaves of the house and was rising to circle. It dived at him, and it was aiming to kill, not just to frighten him back into the house.

He got the shotgun up just in time and pulled the trigger when the chicken hawk was only eight or ten feet over his head and coming like the guided missile it was. Blood and feathers flew, some right into his face. The rest of what was left of the bird, knocked out of its straight-line trajectory, hit the ground only two feet away from him.

He ran back for the house. He washed the blood and feathers off his face and brushed his clothes. Then he opened the kitchen matchbox and released the moth—the moth that was only a moth, and not a host of the enemy. His idea had been a good one, but the enemy hadn't intended to give him that simple a way of winning.

CHAPTER TWENTY

And then—nothing happened.

Minutes dragged by like hours. He had by now not slept for a little over twenty-four hours; and, because of his wakefulness, had slept not longer than three hours out of the preceding twenty-four.

Most of the time he walked from window to window, looking out at—nothing. His legs ached with weariness and he would have given a thousand dollars just to be able to lie down a few minutes to rest, but it was too dangerous. He didn't even dare to sit down comfortably and lean back. When he did sit, it was either on the arm of the sofa, looking out the front window, or on the edge of a chair in the kitchen. From time to time he drank a cup of coffee, but now he drank it cold; he had realized some time ago that the soporific effect of drinking a bulk of hot liquid at least partially counteracted the effect of the caffeine.

The morning crawled along. Surely the sheriff or the state police would come; surely Miss Talley, no later than this morning, would have notified one or the other, would have told someone that he had failed to keep an appointment with her yesterday and might be in trouble or in danger.

He couldn't stay awake much longer. Now it was getting dangerous even for him to sit; he'd find his eyes starting to go shut and would have to force them open again. And although ordinarily he was only a moderate smoker, he'd been smoking his pipe so much that his mouth felt raw. Benzedrine would have been worth its weight in diamonds to him, but he had brought none with him; one doesn't think of having to stay awake when on vacation.

It was almost noon, and he was standing at the front window, wishing, but not daring, at least to lean his forehead against the pane, when he heard the sound of an approaching car.

He picked up the shotgun and opened the front door, but stood just inside, ready to cover the sheriff, or whoever it was, against attack from whatever direction.

Then the car turned into the yard. A tiny car, a Volkswagen—and Miss Talley was in it, alone.

He made frantic motions waving her away, hoping that if she turned and left quickly—

But: she drove on in, not looking toward him because her attention was distracted by the sight of his station wagon and the dead deer—from which buzzards rose lazily and flapped away as the car came near them. She'd shut off her engine before she looked toward the door and saw him.

"Miss Talley!" he called to her. "Turn around and get back to town, fast. Get the state police and—"

It wasn't any use. He heard hoofbeats—a bull was charging down the road, only a hundred feet away. The Volkswagen was only a dozen feet from Doc, and suddenly he saw a chance, if a dangerous one, to win. If he could wound the bull without killing it, put it out of action with, say, a broken leg so it couldn't kill itself and free the enemy to take another host—

Calling to Miss Talley to stay in the car, he ran out alongside it and raised the shotgun; if he could judge the distance just right and shoot low, hoping to hit the front legs—

His aim was good, but excitement made him shoot a little too soon. The charge hurt the bull, but didn't stop it. It bellowed in rage and changed direction, coming straight for him instead of for the Volkswagen. By the time he shot the second barrel it was too close, only ten feet away; the shot had to be fatal, and it was. Because of its momentum it kept coming and he had to step aside; it fell dead just beyond him.

He opened the door of the Volkswagen. "Hurry into the house, Miss Talley. We've got a minute's grace before it can try again, but don't waste any time."

He hurried with her. The shotgun was empty, and the extra shells were inside. At the door he turned and looked back and upward. A big bird of some kind, not a buzzard, was circling—but if it was about to attack it was too late. He stepped inside and closed the door.

Quickly, while he was reloading the shotgun, he told her what had happened yesterday and thus far today.

"Oh, Doctor," she said, "if I'd only insisted that the sheriff— I called him yesterday afternoon and he didn't seem to believe you were in trouble but he said he'd come out. I couldn't reach him again until this morning, and then he told me several things had come up, that he hadn't been able to make it yesterday and wouldn't be able to until tomorrow. I guess he thought it was just my imagination that anything could be wrong, and he isn't in any hurry."

"Tomorrow..." Doc shook his head gloomily. "I'll never make it—stay awake that long, I mean. And if I'm right that as soon as I go to sleep— I wish you hadn't come yourself, Miss Talley; now you're in trouble too."

"Don't you think there's even a chance of our making it into town in my car? With me driving so you can use the gun?"

"A chance in a hundred, Miss Talley. Aside from the fact that there must be cows wherever that bull came from, not to mention more deer in the woods, I'll bet a really big bird could dive-bomb right through the roof of a light car like that. How soon will you be missed? Will neighbors notice that you don't get home tonight, if you don't?"

"Oh, dear, I'm afraid not. Every once in a while I go in to Green Bay to see a show and I have a sister-in-law there who goes with me and I usually stay with her afterwards. So no one will think anything of my not getting home tonight, because my neighbors know that, and won't worry. Oh, if I'd only thought of calling the state police instead of coming myself—I never thought of them at all."

Doc Staunton gestured wearily. "Don't blame yourself for anything, Miss Talley. *I* made the first mistake—the first *two* mistakes. I should never have stayed here night before last, after the gray cat killed itself; that made this house, or at least this area, a focus. And yesterday morning, after I learned about Jim Kramer's death, I should never have come back here just to pack up my possessions. That was the big mistake, the one that caught me." He sighed.

"Let's have some coffee. I've been drinking it cold, but now that I have someone to talk to, I think I'll risk a cup of it hot. I'll even risk sitting down and letting you make it—if you'll keep talking to me, or vice versa. Maybe we can come up with something. We've *got* to come up with something."

In the kitchen he compromised by leaning against the wall while she started water boiling for fresh coffee. He did most of the talking, since he had more to tell.

"The *alien*," Miss Talley said firmly, the first time he mentioned the enemy. "Doctor, why not admit we're fighting—or at any rate defending ourselves against—an extraterrestrial intelligence? What else *could* it be?"

"A mutant human being, one who was born with or has acquired what Charles Fort called a wild talent."

"Do you really believe that?"

"No," Doc said. "Nor the only other possibility I've been able to think of— a demon or devil. But I won't narrow it down. Until I know for sure, or until

I lose, I'm going to call him the enemy. Let's not worry about nomenclature, Miss Talley. There's too much else to worry about. First and foremost, what chance have we got, if any? Of course I can *hope* I'm wrong in thinking the enemy is keeping me—us, rather—boxed in here until I have to go to sleep."

"Have you had any ideas at all?"

He told her his thought that wounding an animal controlled by the enemy might give them time for a getaway. "But," he added, "it's hard to wound a large animal with a shotgun in such a way that it couldn't attack, or manage to kill itself. You'd have to break a leg to immobilize it."

"You don't have a rifle?"

"Only a twenty-two; it's still in the station wagon, and not worth the risk of trying to get it. It would be if I had long rifle cartridges for it, but I have only shorts; I intended to use it only for target practice. I have a pistol, but I'm not accurate enough with it to take the risk of trying to wound a charging animal without killing it."

He shook his head wearily. "I think it recognizes the risk of being wounded and that's why it prefers to use birds. Even if I could shoot one high enough in the air only to wound it with a few pellets, it would already be diving and the fall would kill it... Lord, but I'm sleepy."

"Is there anything I can do to help?"

"Just keep talking, or listening. By the way, I'm on a hunger strike to keep awake, but don't let that stop you from getting yourself something any time you want. The refrigerator's been off since yesterday evening, so don't take a chance on anything in it. But there's plenty of canned goods."

The coffee was finished and she poured two cups and brought them to the table. "Thanks, I'm not hungry yet. But perhaps I should make two or three extra pots of coffee."

"If you wish. But why?"

"Since he managed to shut off your electricity, he just might figure a way to shut off the gas too. And you don't want to be without coffee, even if both of us will have to drink it cold."

"I don't think he could, short of using a human host. It takes a wrench to turn the valve on the butane tank. There's nothing to lose, though, if you want to make a couple of extra pots."

She put more water on the stove to boil and then came to the table and sat across from him.

"How about the water supply? Any chance of his shutting that off? If so, I'd better fill a few buckets, to be safe."

"I don't think it's necessary." He explained how the water supply worked. "He could easily enough wreck the pump that brings water from the well to the tank on the roof, but the tank itself is heavy and solid and it must be at least half full; more water than we'll need. It holds two hundred gallons."

He took a sip of his coffee. "Talking about water reminds me of something I'll do when I've finished this. A cold bath and a change of clothes will help me; I should have thought of it this morning, but I didn't."

"It sounds like a good idea. And I'll get myself something to eat while you're upstairs. You must be pretty hungry, and that way you won't have to watch me eat."

"Fine. But make a circuit of the windows once in a while and call me if you see anything. I'll take a robe into the bathroom with me so I can come quickly. And that reminds me—"

He started to get up, but Miss Talley, in her best schoolteacher manner, ordered him to sit still and got up to make a circuit of the downstairs windows. She came back to report nothing new except that the buzzards were back at the dead deer. None as yet had gone to the dead bull; the deer was riper and more to their taste.

Doc nodded. "I don't expect anything to happen, It's a waiting game—unless one of us tries to leave. He's made no attempt to get inside the house, in any form, and if he wanted to he could have, long ago. Any big animal could break through either door, unless I shot it first."

"Or a human being. I wonder why he hasn't sent one against you."

"No reason to, unless he wanted to kill me, and apparently he doesn't, unless I try to leave. In a way, I wish he would send one. It's dangerous to try to shoot a leg of a charging bull without killing it. But with a man, it would be relatively easy."

"Doctor, when I came—how did you know I wasn't—the enemy? You could have shot me in the leg easily enough."

He laughed. "It never occurred to me. And if it had, the bull coming right after you would have been proof enough. The thing we're most certain of is that he can't control more than one host at a time." He stood up and stretched his arms, fighting back a yawn. "Well, to my cold tub. And I'll make circuits of the upstairs windows while the water's running. You won't have to, until after you hear it stop."

He went upstairs, and half an hour later he came back down, looking at least outwardly refreshed. Miss Talley had finished eating and they sat in the living room and took turns talking. Doc insisted on making periodic rounds of the windows himself instead of letting her do it. He explained that the danger of his going to sleep if she left him alone was a more important factor than his doing an occasional bit of walking.

The hours dragged. One or the other of them thought of a dozen things to try, but for one reason or another had to reject each as impractical or too dangerous. Once Doc verified that the siege was still on by stepping outside with the shotgun. When he saw a high-circling bird start a dive, he fired at it without waiting for it to get close. But if any of the pellets hit and wounded it, the wound was insufficient to deflect it and he had to use the second barrel when it was dangerously close. Even then he had to jump back the instant he fired or the bird would have hit him. It thudded against the doorsill. He reloaded the shotgun before using its muzzle to push the dead bird—it was, or had been, a chicken hawk—off the porch.

Blood had spattered on his shoes and the cuffs of his trousers. He went upstairs to change them and to take another cold bath; he'd left the water in the tub, since he'd realized while taking the first one that even the hundred gallons that he estimated had been in the tank wouldn't fill the tub too many times. The second bath didn't help much; in fact, he almost went to sleep in the tub and he realized that he was almost at the limit of his ability to stay awake.

When he came downstairs he told Miss Talley so, and asked her to bring in a pan of cold water and a glass, and to keep the glass filled, or half filled, from the pan. She should sit facing him, he told her, with the glass in her hand, and throw water in his face whenever she might see his eyes close longer than to blink. She brought the water, and also a towel for him to use in case she had to use the water.

Twice within the next hour she had to throw water in his face. Both times he'd been talking and had stopped in the middle of a sentence as his eyes went shut. It was six o'clock when it happened the second time; it would be dark within another hour or so. He doubted that he could possibly stay awake even that long, and certainly not much longer.

When he had dried his face with the towel, he stood up, swaying a bit. "Miss Talley," he said, "it's no use going on this way; even if I put carpet tacks on a chair and sit on them I'll lose consciousness eventually. We've got to do one of two things. There's danger in both of them, for you as well as for me, so I'm going to let you decide which we should do.

"One, I leave now while there's time for me to walk to town—or at least to the nearest farm that has a telephone. I'll take the shotgun and leave you the pistol. Maybe I'll make it; maybe we're overestimating the danger and overestimating the range at which the enemy can operate. Anyway, if I do make it I'll see that you're rescued. There'll be state police, several carloads of them with shotguns and tommy guns... If I don't get through—"

"No," Miss Talley said firmly. "If you go, we both go, and I do the driving. Or afoot, if you think there's any advantage to that. But why would there be?"

"It should keep me awake, for one thing. And for another, I can watch upward. As I said before, a heavy bird diving from a sufficient height would probably go right through the roof of a car as light as that, and kill whichever one of us it landed on. But your going with me wasn't the alternative to my first suggestion. I don't know whether the alternative is more dangerous, or less.

"It's simply that I go to sleep, here in this room on the sofa, but that we take the precaution of having you tie me up first. There's fifty feet of clothesline in the kitchen, so you can do a thorough job of it. First, our idea of what may happen to me if I sleep is only a deduction; we can be wrong. Second, if the enemy does take me over, I'll be tied up so he'll be helpless to make me do anything, such as injure you, and also unable to make me kill myself so he'll be free to take another host. And that would mean it would be safe for you to drive into town and bring help."

"But—what kind of help, if you're—"

"We can't figure that till we see what happens. But if you're the one who gets to town, there'll be no hurry. Get your story—and take my statements with you to supplement it—before the highest authority you can reach. It'll be out of our hands and somebody will have to take over from there. Preferably the F.B.I.— phone them first and try to get either Roger Price or Bill Kellerman on the line; they're both friends of mine and will be more likely to take you seriously. You can remember the names, or do you want me to write them down?"

"Roger Price or Bill Kellerman, I'll remember. But—how would I know it would be safe for me to drive to town? Unless—well, unless once you go to sleep you wake up and act crazy, try to get out of the ropes or—or something like that?"

"If I do that, you'll know, of course. If I don't, you'll have to take the risk of doing what I did a little while ago. Step out on the porch with the shotgun and—well, see if anything attacks you. If nothing does, you'll have to take the chance that nothing will. Or—wait, you don't even have to take the chance. Once I'm tied up, and whether or not I'm still—myself, you can just wait it out until the sheriff shows up sometime tomorrow. That's safer for you; I should have thought of it first. I'm so sleepy that I'm not thinking clearly any more."

"All right," Miss Talley said. "I like that better than letting you try to make it to town alone. Or, for that matter, even both of us trying together."

"I'll get the rope then."

She went out into the kitchen with him and while he got the length of rope, she got a knife to cut it with.

Back in the living room Doc took the pistol from his pocket and put it and the ammunition for it and the shotgun on the mantel. He leaned the shotgun against the wall beside the front door. "Keep all those things out of my reach," he told her. "The knife too, once you've finished using it on the rope. Tie my hands first, behind me, then I'll lie down for you to tie my ankles." He turned his back to her and held his hands behind him for her to work on. "Listen, if I do go crazy and try to get out of the ropes, don't take any chances on what I might do. Hit me on the head with the pistol butt and knock me out. But try not to kill me; if the enemy is in control of me—and he will be if I try to es- cape—killing me would free him to take other hosts again and you'd be back where you were before. He might even take you over if you shouldn't be able to stay awake until the sheriff gets here tomorrow."

Miss Talley was working on the knot. "Are you sure that this isn't even more dangerous than—than trying to get to town?"

"Of course I'm not sure, but I think so. I'm almost sure that it's safer for you, and not any more dangerous for me."

"If you think so, all right. Is that tight enough?"

"Perfect. And you've got the knot where I can't reach it with my fingers. All right, I'll lie down now. And I can still force myself to stay awake long enough for you to tie my ankles."

He did, barely. The moment he approved the job she did on his ankles he sighed and closed his eyes. Instantly he was sound asleep.

Miss Talley stood watching him for a few minutes. And then, because she wanted to know, if possible, whether or not the enemy was in Dr. Staunton's mind but was still letting him sleep or pretend to sleep, she picked up the shotgun and opened the door, looked upward. Something big and black was coming down, diving at her, but she saw that she had time and that stepping back into the house would be safer than raising the gun and taking a shot that could miss, or fail to deflect even if it killed. She stepped back and closed the door just as something heavy thudded to the porch outside the door.

The thing that thudded had been a buzzard, one of several that had gorged themselves on the dead deer and flapped away to sleep in nearby trees. It was the third of these that the mind thing had used.

The mind thing had been annoyed by the unexpected arrival of the schoolteacher, Miss Talley. He had been aloft at the time he saw the coming Volkswagen, but had quickly crash-landed and killed his host and taken over the nearest bull. He'd charged it through the fence just after the Volkswagen went by, and followed. His first thought had been to charge and wreck the car, but when Staunton had fired the first barrel of the shotgun at him and he realized that the man had aimed low with intent to cripple rather than to kill, he had changed direction and charged so that Staunton had to shoot to kill in order to save his own life.

Then, back in his own body, the tortoise-like shell hidden under the back steps of the house, he had watched and listened to the conversation between the man and the woman long enough to realize that they knew the futility of their trying to get back to town, or even to a phone, either afoot or in the small car. That, of course, made it unnecessary for him to destroy the car.

He relaxed then and studied them and listened to their conversation, surprised that they had been able to deduce so many things about him, but understanding, after hearing their explanations, how they had been able to do so. It didn't worry him; there was nothing that they could do about it. He didn't have to maintain a host in the air; he knew, of course, whenever one of them planned to attempt leaving, and was able to have a bird aloft, usually by the time the door opened.

But then he learned from their conversation that Miss Talley had asked the sheriff to come out. True, she said the sheriff had promised to come tomorrow, but the sheriff could change his mind and come sooner, or send a deputy sooner. And if another car should approach he wanted advance warning so he could deal with the situation. Perhaps it would be better to wreck the car, and kill the occupant if and when he left it, than to let him reach the house alive and reinforce the opposition.

After that, as Staunton or Miss Talley made periodic circuits of the windows of the house, so the mind thing periodically took a flying host aloft to circle high into the sky to scan the road from town and still keep the house under observation, as when out of his own body he could not use his perceptive sense to check on what was going on inside the house. After each flight he had killed the bird by crashing it, and had been instantly back in his shell.

He had been just starting such a flight when Staunton had said he could not possibly stay awake much longer; he knew then it would probably be the last such reconnaissance flight he'd have to make. But because it might be his last, he had circled high to check the road as far as possible. And thus he had not been aware of the final conversation between Staunton and the schoolteacher, or the tying up of Staunton.

So he was surprised, when he was just about ready to crash his buzzard host, to see *Miss Talley* step outside alone with the shotgun. Of course he had dived at her immediately, and his buzzard host had died with the impact.

But then he was back in his own shell, as Miss Talley was back in the house, and was even more surprised to discover that his potential host, Staunton, was asleep and tied up in rope. That he was asleep was no surprise, but that he was tied up!

It was devilishly clever, and thwarting. Neither of them had thought of, or at least neither of them had mentioned, that idea in any part of their conversation that he had overheard. One of them must have thought of it suddenly, and they had executed it quickly.

Now if he entered Staunton's mind he would be helpless until Staunton's body was untied, and he hesitated and considered. He decided finally that it was safe. The woman couldn't keep Staunton tied up forever. And if he entered Staunton's mind now but caused Staunton's body to continue to sleep he could make good use of the time. He could study Staunton's most intimate thoughts and memories and by the time—say, in the middle of the night—he let Staunton's body awaken, he would be able to act the part of Staunton so thoroughly that Miss Talley would suspect nothing and untie him. And then—but the rest of his plans could also be worked out in the long hours he would be immobile in Staunton's mind while the body slept.

He entered.

And now he encountered something new to him—not in kind, but in degree. Every mind he'd ever entered fought back for a fraction of a second at least. A minor struggle in the case of an animal mind, a severe but brief one in the case of the three human minds he had previously taken over—the two high school boys and the old German farmer.

This fight was no different, except in degree. The struggle lasted for seconds longer than any other he'd engaged in—and during it Staunton was still in partial control of his own body. He fought against what was happening and managed to jerk his body up almost to a sitting position and to gasp out: "Under steps. Thing like—"

But then it was over; the mind thing was in control.

Doc Staunton lay back and breathed deeply a time or two, and then opened his eyes. They met those of Miss Talley, who was standing by the couch staring down at him. He said, normally and casually, "Think I had a touch of nightmare, Miss Talley. Probably from being overtired. Did I make any noises?"

Miss Talley didn't answer for seconds. Then, very quietly: "You made noises, Doctor—if you *are* Dr. Staunton. You said, and I quote, 'Under steps. Thing like—' and that was all, What *was* your nightmare about?"

"Good Lord, Miss Talley. How can I remember, except vaguely that it was something about a charging bull and—oh, yes, in the nightmare I ran and I was trying to crawl under the front steps to hide from it—in the dream I didn't have a gun. I think I can go to sleep again now—and let's hope, no more nightmares." He closed his eyes.

"Dr. Staunton, you told me that you thought 'the enemy,' as you called it, was nearby and could be hiding inside the house. And that you searched the house for it—which would include any area under the staircase inside. Besides, you didn't say 'staircase'; you said 'under steps.' And there are three steps leading to the front porch and another three leading to the back door. I'm going to look. Now, while it's still light outside."

"Miss Talley, that's ridiculous. A nightmare—"

But he was talking to empty space. Miss Talley was already out the front door, taking the shotgun and the pistol with her. And a flashlight; it was still light outside, but might be dim under the steps.

Outside, after looking up and then around to see if anything was about to attack—she didn't really think anything would be, but she had to make sure—she looked under the front steps, using the flashlight. She found nothing, but decided she'd investigate more thoroughly, and maybe dig a bit, after she'd made a quick investigation of the steps at the back of the house. She walked around to the rear.

Nothing was under the back steps either, at first glance; then the flashlight found a spot where the dirt looked as though it might have been dug up and then replaced and patted down. *Yes,* there was the imprint of a hand there, a human hand!

Paying no attention to getting her clothes dirty, she lay flat and wriggled until her head and one arm were under the steps. She clawed and scraped at the area under the hand print. The earth was loose there and moved easily. She felt—*something.* It could have been the shell of a turtle—except that turtles do not burrow, especially in dry ground. She came up with something, whatever it was, and pulled it out as she backed away. It was *something* like a turtle except that there were no open places for legs and head and tail— And on second glance it looked—*alien.*

She dropped it in revulsion, put the muzzle of the pistol against the center of what would have been the carapace, and fired.

Inside the house, Dr. Staunton screamed, as though in agony. She ran around to the front—since the back door was bolted—and into the house. She'd forgotten the shotgun but still had the pistol in her hand.

Doc was on the floor instead of on the couch, but he was lying quietly, a peaceful smile—a beatific smile—on his face. He said, "You did it, Miss Talley. That was *he*—and won't the terrestrial doctors have fun dissecting him, the first extraterrestrial life form they ever have had a chance at. A brain in a shell, and not much more. Not even digestive organs; he absorbed food by osmosis.

"Don't untie me, Miss Talley. It would be all right to, but you can't know it yet. Just let me talk. Lord, do I have things to talk about! And such important things that I feel as though I'll never sleep again."

He sighed. "Poor little alien. All he wanted was to get home—but it wouldn't have been good for the human race if he had. You see, Miss Talley, he was in my mind, after that short struggle when I managed to hold him off long enough to get out a few important words—and thank you for interpreting them correctly"—he shivered at the recollection—"but I was in *his* mind too. I know everything that he knew, including, although that's a long story, why he chose each of the hosts, human and otherwise, that he used, and the purpose for which he used it, or tried to use it."

"Where was he from—another planet in the solar system?"

"No, a planet of a very far star. One we'll stay away from for a long, long time. Do you want to know what else I learned. Miss Talley?"

She didn't even have to nod; the expression on her face was answer enough.

Doc said quietly, reverently, "A science new to us, one we haven't even suspected. Space travel without tears. We can scratch rockets; they're obsolete. With what I know now, we'll be in space within a year. Colonizing anything colonizable within two years—and not only possibly colonizable places in the solar system—anywhere; distance doesn't matter. We can hit a planet of Alpha Centauri—or any other star—as easily as we can move to the moon.

"And, Miss Talley, *anyone* can go—once the bright and strong young spacemen we'll develop have established that a planet is habitable and safe, even for people our age. Miss Talley, will you come with me and be my secretary and good right hand while I work things out?

"And—oh, say three years from now would you like to do a bit of planet-hopping with me? Quick shots to Mars and Venus, say, for a starter—they'll have to be quickies because we'll have to wear space suits—and then—anywhere, anywhere in the universe, or maybe just in the local galaxy for a start, where there are approximately Earth-type planets, ones we can spend at least a few days on without having to live in an artificial environment... Where would you like to go first, Miss Talley?"

She believed him, but she'd probably have untied him even if she'd been in doubt. She untied his ankles first and then he rolled onto his side so she could get at the knots on his wrists. He sat up, then moved to the sofa.

He asked, since she hadn't answered his first question—she couldn't; she'd have choked trying—"Is it a deal, Miss Talley?"

A simple *yes* she could say, and did say, fervently. But Dr. Staunton couldn't have heard it; when he'd finished asking his question, and before her quick answer, there intervened—a gentle snore. Dr. Staunton was sound asleep.

Miss Talley stared at him for a long moment. Then she went to the door, opened it, and went out onto the porch carrying no weapon, knowing that she was safe.

She stared up at the sky; it was early dusk and a few stars, the brightest ones, were already visible. Soon there'd be the thousands of visible ones, out of the trillions—

Her life, except for reading, had been dull—but it had not been in vain. She'd still be alive when the human race would begin to become—what the human race *would* become, *must* become. And she'd never need the outlet of reading imaginative literature again; imagination was about to be replaced by here-and-now current reality!

There were more stars visible now, but one of the at-first-visible ones—it was Sirius, she knew—was brighter than any of the others, She stared at it until it blurred and then became invisible because her eyes had filled with tears, tears of a rapture so intense that it was akin to pain.

Gateway to Darkness
Gateway to Glory

These two stories were extensively rewritten to form the novel *Rogue in Space,* which appears earlier in this volume.

Gateway to Darkness

CHAPTER I

There was this Crag, and he was a thief and a smuggler and a murderer. He'd been a spaceman once and he had a metal hand and a permanent squint to show for it. Those, and a taste for exotic liquors and a strong disinclination for work. Especially as he would have had to work a week to buy one small jigger of even the cheapest of the fluids that were the only things that made life worthwhile to him. At anything he was qualified to do, that is, except stealing, smuggling and murder. These paid well.

He had no business in Albuquerque, but he got around. And that time they caught him. It was for something he hadn't done, but they had proof that he did it. Proof enough to send him to the penal colony of Callisto, which he wouldn't have minded too much, or to send him to the psycher, which he would have minded very much indeed.

He sat on the bed in his cell and worried about it, and about the fact that he needed a drink. The two worries went together, in a way. If they sent him to the psycher, he'd never want a drink again, and he wanted to want a drink.

The psycher was pretty bad. They used it only in extreme cases, partly because they hadn't perfected it yet. Sometimes—statistically about one time out of nine—it drove its subject crazy, stark raving crazy. The eight times out of nine that it worked, it was worse. It *adjusted* you; it made you normal. And in the process it killed your memories, the good ones as well as the bad ones, and you started from scratch.

You remembered how to talk and feed yourself and how to use a slipstick or play a flute—if, that is, you knew how to use a slipstick or play a flute before you went to the psycher. But you didn't remember your name unless they told you. And you didn't remember the time you were tortured for three days and two nights on Venus before the rest of the crew found you and took you away from the animated vegetables who didn't like meat in any form and especially in human form. You didn't remember the time you were spacemad, the time you went nine days without water, the time—well, you didn't remember anything that had ever happened to you.

Not even the good things.

You started from scratch, a different person. And Crag thought he wouldn't mind dying, particularly, but he didn't want his body to keep on walking around afterwards, animated by a well-adjusted stranger, who just wouldn't be *he*.

So he paced up and down his cell and made up his mind that he'd at least try to kill himself before he'd let them strap him into the psycher chair, if it came to that.

He hoped that he could do it. He had a lethal weapon with him, the only one he ever carried, but it would be difficult to use on himself. Oh, it could be done if he had the guts; but it takes plenty of guts to kill yourself with a bludgeon, even so efficient a one as his metal hand. Looking at that hand, though it was obviously of metal, no one ever guessed that it weighed twelve pounds instead of a few ounces. The outside layer was Alloy G, a fraction of the weight of magnesium, not much heavier, in fact, than balsa wood. And since you couldn't mistake the appearance of Alloy G, nobody ever suspected that under it was steel for strength and under the steel lead for weight. It wasn't a hand you'd want to be slapped in the face with. But long practice and the development of strength in his left arm enabled him to carry it as casually as though it weighed the three or four ounces you'd expect it to weigh.

He quit pacing and went to the window and stood looking down at the huge sprawling city of Albuquerque, capital of SW Sector of North America, third largest city in the world since it had become the number one spaceport of the Western Hemisphere.

The window wasn't barred but the transparent plastic of the pane was tough stuff. Still, he thought he could batter through it with one hand, if that hand were his left one. But he could only commit suicide that way. There was a sheer drop of thirty stories from this, the top floor of the SW Sector Capitol Building.

For a moment he considered it and then he remembered that it was only probable, not certain, that they'd send him to the psycher. The Callisto penal colony—well, that wasn't so good, either, but there was always at least a remote chance of escape from Callisto. Enough of a chance that he wouldn't jump out of any thirtieth-story windows to avoid going there. Maybe not even to avoid staying there.

But if he had a chance, after being ordered to the psycher, it would be an easier way of killing himself than the one he'd thought of first.

A voice behind him said, "Your trial has been called for fourteen-ten. That is ten minutes from now. Be ready."

He turned around and looked at the grille in the wall from which the mechanical voice had come. He made a raspberry sound at the grille—not that it did any good, for it was strictly a one-way communicator—and turned back to the window.

He hated it, that sprawling corrupt city out there, scene of intrigue—as were all other cities—between the Guilds and the Gilded. Politics rampant upon a field of muck, and everybody, except the leaders, caught in the middle. He hated Earth; he wondered why he'd come back to it this time.

After a while the voice behind him said, "Your door is now unlocked. You will proceed to the end of the corridor outside it, where you will meet the guards who will escort you to the proper room."

He caught the distant silver flash of a spaceship coming in; he waited a few seconds until it was out of sight behind the buildings. He didn't wait any longer than that because he knew this was a test. He'd heard of it from others who'd been here. You could sit and wait for the guards to come and get you, or you could obey the command of the speaker and go to meet them. If you ignored the order and made them come to you, it showed you were not adjusted; it was a point against you when the time came for your sentence.

So he went out into the corridor and along it; there was only one way to go. A hundred yards along the corridor two uniformed guards were waiting near an automatic door. They were armed with holstered heaters.

He didn't speak to them nor they to him. He fell in between them and the door opened by itself as they approached it. He knew it wouldn't have opened for him alone. He knew, too, that he could easily take both of them before either could draw a heater. A backhand blow to the guard on his left and then a quick swing across to the other one.

But getting down those thirty stories to the street would be something else again. A chance in a million, with all the safeguards between here and there.

So he walked between them down the ramp to the floor below and to the door of one of the rooms on that floor. And through the door.

He was the last arrival, if you didn't count the two guards who came in after him. The others were waiting. The six jurors in the box; of whom three would be Guilders and three Gilded. The two attorneys—one of whom had talked to him yesterday in his cell and had told him how hopeless things looked. The operator of the recording machine. And the judge.

He glanced at the judge and almost let an expression of surprise show on his face. The judge was Jon Olliver.

Crag quickly looked away. He wondered what the great Jon Olliver was doing here, judging an unimportant criminal case. Jon Olliver was a great man, one of the few statesmen, as against politicians, of the entire System. Six months ago Olliver had been the Guild candidate for Coordinator of North America. He'd lost the election, but surely he would have retained a more important niche for himself, in the party if not in the government, than an ordinary criminal judge's job.

True, Olliver had started his political career as a judge; four years ago he'd been on the bench the one previous time Crag had been arrested and tried. The evidence had, that time, been insufficient and the jury had freed him. But he still remembered the blistering jeremiad Olliver had delivered to him afterward, in the private conversation between judge and accused that was customary whether the latter was convicted or acquitted.

Ever since, Crag had hated Jon Olliver as a man, and had admired him as a judge and as a statesman, after Olliver had gone into politics and had so nearly been elected Coordinator.

But Coordinator was the highest position to which any man could aspire. The only authority higher was the Council of Coordinators, made up of seven Coordinators of Earth and four from the planets, one from each major planet inhabited by the human race. The Council of Coordinators was the ultimate authority in the solar system, which, since interstellar travel looked a long way off, meant the ultimate authority in the known-to-be-inhabited universe. So it seemed almost incredible to Crag that a man who'd almost been a Coordinator should now, in the six months since his candidacy, have dropped back down to the unimportant job he'd held five years ago. But that was politics for you, he thought, in this corrupt age; an honest man didn't have a chance.

No more of a chance than he was going to have against this frameup the police had rigged against him.

The trial started and he knew he'd been right. The evidence was there—on recording tapes; there were no witnesses—and it proved him completely guilty. It was false, but it sounded true. It took only ten minutes or so to run it off. The prosecuting attorney took no longer; he didn't have to. His own attorney made a weak and fumbling—but possibly sincere–effort to disprove the apparently obvious.

And that was that. The jury went out and stayed all of a minute, and came back. The defendant was found guilty as charged.

Judge Jon Olliver said briefly, "Indeterminate sentence on Callisto."

The technician shut off the recording machine; the trial was over.

Crag let nothing show on his face, although there was relief in his mind that it had not been the psycher. Not too much relief; he'd have killed himself if it had been, and death wasn't much worse than life on Callisto. And he knew that indeterminate sentence on Callisto meant life sentence—unless he volunteered to be psyched. That was what an indeterminate sentence really meant; it gave the convicted his choice between a life sentence and the psycher.

A signal from the judge and the others began to leave Crag did not move; he knew without being told that he was expected to wait for the customary private conversation with the judge. That always came after the sentencing and, in very rare cases, could make a change in the sentence. Sometimes, but not often, after private conversation with a prisoner a judge lessened or increased the sentence; he had power to do so up to twenty-four hours after his original pronouncement.

It was optional with the judge whether the guards remained; if he thought there was a possibility of the prisoner attempting physical violence, he could have them remain, with heaters ready, but back out of hearing range in a far corner of the room. That was what Olliver had done the last time Crag had appeared before him, after the acquittal. Undoubtedly it was because he had recognized the violence in Crag and had feared to provoke him by the things he was going to say.

But this time Olliver signaled to the guards to leave the room with the others.

Crag stepped forward. He thought, *I can reach across that bench and kill him easily.* He was tempted, simply by how easy it would be, even though he knew that it would mean the psycher—or his own private alternative.

Olliver said, "Don't do it, Crag."

Crag didn't answer. He didn't intend to, unless he found himself provoked beyond endurance by what he was going to have to hear. But he knew the best way to handle one of these interviews was to keep it strictly a one-way conversation by refusing to talk back. Silence might annoy Olliver, but it would not annoy him sufficiently to make him increase the sentence. And nothing he could say would make Olliver lessen it.

"You'd be sorry if you did, Crag. Because I'm not going to ride you this time. In fact, I'm going to make you a proposition."

What kind of a proposition, Crag wondered, could a judge want to make to a man he'd just sentenced to life on Callisto? But he didn't ask; he waited.

Olliver smiled. His face was handsome when he smiled.

He leaned forward across the bench. He said softly, "Crag, how would you like your freedom, and a million credits?"

CHAPTER II: Escape to Danger

Crag said hoarsely, "You're kidding. And if you are—"

He must have swayed forward or, without knowing it, started to lift his hand, for Olliver jerked back and his face was a bit white as he said "Don't" again, this time sharply.

And he went on, fast: "I'm not kidding, Crag. A million credits, enough to keep you drunk the rest of your life. Freedom. And a chance to help humanity, to pull the human race out of the bog into which it has sunk in this period of mankind's decadence. A rare chance, Crag."

Crag said, "Save that for your speeches, Judge. The hell with humanity. But I'll settle for my freedom and a million. One thing, though. This trial was a frameup. I didn't do it. Was it *your* frameup?"

Olliver shook his head slowly. He said, "No, not mine. But I rather suspected it was framed. The evidence was too good. You don't leave evidence like that, do you, Crag?"

Crag didn't bother to answer that. He asked, "Who did it, then?"

"The police, I imagine. There's an election coming up—and the Commissioner's office is elective. A few convictions like yours will look good on the records. You're pretty well known, Crag, in spite of the fact that there's never been a conviction against you. The newscasts from the stations on the Gilded side are going to give Commissioner Green plenty of credit for getting you."

It sounded logical. Crag said, "I know what I'm going to do with part of my freedom, then."

Olliver's voice was sharp again. "Not until after, Crag. I don't care what you do—after the job I want you to do for me. You agree to that?"

Crag shrugged. "Okay. What's the job?" He didn't really care what it was, or even how risky it was. For the difference between life on Callisto and freedom and a million, he couldn't think of anything he wouldn't do. He'd try it even if there was one chance in a thousand of his pulling it off and staying alive.

Olliver said, "This isn't the time or place to tell you about it; we shouldn't talk too long. You'll be a free man when we talk. That much comes first. The million comes afterwards, if you succeed."

"And if I turn down the job after you've let me go?"

"I don't think you will. It's not an easy one, but I don't think you'll turn it down for a million, even if you're already free. And there might be more for you in it than just money—but we won't talk about that unless you succeed. Fair enough?"

"Fair enough. But—I want to be sure about this framing business. Do you mean to tell me it was just coincidence that you wanted me to do something for you and that I got framed and you sat on the case?"

Olliver smiled again. "It's a small world, Crag. And it's partly a coincidence, but not as much of a one as you think. First, you're not the only man in the system that could—do what I want done. You're one of several I had in mind. Possibly the best, I'll give you that. I was wondering how to contact one of you. And I saw your name on the docket and requested to sit on the case. You should know enough about law to know that a judge can ask to sit on a case if he has had previous experience with the accused."

Crag nodded. That was true, and it made sense.

Olliver said, "But to brass tacks; we shouldn't be talking much longer than this. I don't want any suspicion to attach to me when you escape."

"Escape?"

"Of course. You were judged guilty, Crag, and on strong evidence. I couldn't possibly free you legally; I couldn't even have given you a lighter sentence than I did. If I freed you now, I'd be impeached. But I—or perhaps I should say *we*—can arrange for you to escape. Today, shortly after you're returned to your cell to await transportation to Callisto."

"Who's *we?*" Crag asked.

"A new political party, Crag, that's going to bring this world—the whole System—out of the degradation into which it has sunk. It's going to end the bribery and corruption. It's going to take us back to old-fashioned democracy by ending the deadlock between the Guilds and the Syndicates. It's going to be a middle-of-the-road party. We're going to bring honest government back and—" He stopped and grinned boyishly. "I didn't mean to start a lecture. In which I suppose you aren't interested anyway. We call ourselves the Co-operationists."

"You're working under cover?"

"For the present. Not much longer. In a few months we come into the open, in time to start gathering support—votes—for the next elections." He made a sudden impatient gesture. "But I'll tell you all this later, when we're at leisure. Right now the important thing is your escape.

"You'll be taken back to your cell when I give the signal that we're through talk-ing. I'll put on the record that you were intransigent and unrepentant and that I am making no modification of your sentence. Within an hour from your return, arrangements for your escape will be made and you'll be told what to do."

"Told how?"

"By the speaker in your cell. They're on private, tap-proof circuits. A member of the party has access to them. Simply follow instructions and you'll be free by seventeen hours."

"And then? If I still want to earn the million?"

"Come to my house. It's listed; you can get the address when you need it. Be there at twenty-two."

"It's guarded?" Crag asked. He knew that houses of most important political figures were.

"Yes. And I'm not going to tell the guards to let you in. They're not party members. I think they're in the pay of the opposition, but that's all right with me. I use them to allay suspicion."

"How do I get past them, then?"

Olliver said, "If you can't do that, without help or advice from me, then you're not the man I think you are, Crag—and you're not the man I want. But don't kill unless you have to. I don't like violence, unless it's absolutely necessary and in a good cause. I don't *like* it even then, but—"

He glanced at his wrist watch and then reached out and put his fingers on a button on one side of the bench. He asked, "Agreed?" and as Crag nodded, he pushed the button.

The two guards came back in. Olliver said, "Return the prisoner to his cell."

One on each side of him, they led him back up the ramp to the floor above and escorted him all the way to his cell.

The door clanged. Crag sat down on the bed and tried to puzzle things out He wasn't modest enough about his particular talents to wonder why Olliver had chosen him if he had a dirty job to be done. But he was curious what dirty job a man like Olliver would have to offer. If there was an honest and fair man in politics, Olliver was that man. It must be something of overwhelming importance if Olliver was sacrificing his principles to expediency.

Well, he, Crag, certainly had nothing to lose, whether he trusted Olliver's motives or not. And he thought he trusted them.

He went back to the window and stood there looking down at the teeming city, thinking with wonder how greatly his fortunes had changed in the brief space of an hour and a half. That long ago he'd stood here like this and wondered whether to batter through the plastic pane and throw himself from the window. Now he was not only to be free but to have a chance at more money than he'd ever hoped to see in one sum.

When an hour was nearly up, he went over and stood by the speaker grille so he would not miss anything that came over it. One cannot ask questions over a one-way communicator, and he'd have to get every word the first time.

It was well that he did. The voice, when it came, was soft—and it was a woman's voice. From the window he could have heard it, but might have missed part of the message. "I have just moved the switch that unlocks your cell door," the voice said. "Leave your cell and walk as you did on your way to the court-room. I will meet you at the portal, at the place where two guards met you before."

The cell door was unlocked, all right. He went through it and along the corridor.

A woman waited for him. She was beautiful; not even the severe costume of a technician could completely conceal the soft, lush curves of her body; not even the fact that she wore horn-rimmed spectacles and was completely without makeup could detract from the beauty of her face. Her eyes, even through glass, were the darkest, deepest blue he had ever seen, and her hair—what showed of it beneath the technician's beret—was burnished copper.

He stared at her as he came near. And hated her, partly because she was a woman and partly because she was so beautiful. But mostly because her hair was exactly the same color as Lea's had been.

She held out a little metal bar. "Take this," she told him. "Put it in your pocket. It's radioactive; without it or without a guard with you who has one, every portal here is a death-trap."

"I know," he said shortly.

A paper, folded small, was next. "A diagram," she said, "showing you a way out along which, if you're lucky, you'll encounter no guards. In case you do—"

A pocket-size heater was the next offering, but he shook his head at that. "Don't want it," he told her. "Don't need it."

She put the gun back into her own pocket without protest, almost as though she had expected him to refuse it.

"One more thing," she said. "A visitor's badge. It won't help you on the upper three levels, but below that, it will keep anyone from asking you questions."

He took that, and put it on right away.

"Anything else?"

"Only this. Ten yards ahead, to your right, is a lavatory. Go in there and lock the door. Memorize this diagram thoroughly and then destroy it. And remember that if you're caught, it will do no good to tell the truth; your word won't mean a thing against—you know whose."

He smiled grimly. "I won't be caught," he assured her. "I might be killed, but I won't be caught."

Their eyes locked for a second, and then she turned quickly without speaking again and went through a door behind her.

He went on along the corridor, through the portal. In the lavatory he memorized the diagram quickly but thoroughly and then destroyed it. He had nothing to lose by following orders implicitly.

There was another portal before he came to the ramp. The radioactive bar she'd given him prevented whatever death-trap it concealed from operating.

He made the twenty-ninth level and the twenty-eighth without having met anyone. The next one, the twenty-seventh, would be the crucial one; the first of the three floors of cells and courtrooms. Despite that diagram, he didn't believe that there wouldn't be at least one guard between that floor and the one below, the top floor to which elevators went and the public—with visitor's permits—was allowed.

The ramp ended at the twenty-seventh floor. He had to go out into the corridor there, and to another ramp that led to the floor below. He felt sure there would be a guard at the door that led from the end of that ramp to freedom. And there was. He walked very quietly down the ramp. There was a sharp turn at the bottom of it and he peered around the turn cautiously. A guard was sitting there at the door, all right.

He smiled grimly. Either Olliver or the woman technician must have known the guard was there. It was only common sense that there'd be a guard at that crucial point, in addition to any death-trap that might be in the door itself. Olliver didn't want him unless he was good enough to do at least part of his own jailbreaking.

And, of all things, to have offered him a heater-gun. That would really have been fatal. There, right over the guard's head, was a hemispherical blister on the wall that could only be a thermocouple, set to give off an alarm at any sharp increase in temperature. A heater ray, whether fired by or at a guard, would give an immediate alarm that would alert the whole building and stop the elevators in their shafts. A fat lot of good that heater would have done him, and the gorgeous technician who'd offered it to him must have known that.

Crag studied the guard. A big, brutish man, the kind who would fire first and ask questions afterward, despite the visitor's badge Crag wore. And there was a heater in the guard's hand, lying ready in his lap. With a different type of man, or even with a ready-to-shoot type with a holstered heater, Crag could have made the six paces. But, with this guard, he didn't dare risk it.

He stepped back and quickly unstrapped the twelve-pound hand from his wrist and held it in his right hand. He stepped into sight, pulling back his right arm as he did so.

The guard looked up—Crag hadn't even tried to be silent—and started to raise the heater. It was almost, but not quite, pointed at Crag when the heavy artificial hand struck him full in the face. He never pulled the trigger of the heater. He'd never pull a trigger again.

Crag walked to him and got his hand back, strapping it on again quickly. He picked up the guard's heater, deliberately handling it by the barrel to get his fingerprints on it. They'd know who killed the guard anyway—and he'd rather have them wonder how he'd taken the guard's own weapon away from him and bashed his face in with it than have them guess how he *had* killed the guard. That method of killing was part of his stock in trade. A trade secret. Whenever he killed with it and there was time afterwards, he left evidence in the form of some other heavy blunt instrument that the police would think had been used.

He went through the door, using the key that had hung from the guard's belt, and whatever death-trap had been in the portal of it didn't operate. He could thank the girl technician for that much, anyway. She—or Olliver—had given him a fair break, knowing that without that radioactive bar, it would have been almost impossible for him to escape. Yes, they'd given him a fair chance.

Even if she hadn't told him to get rid of the bar here and now. It would have been bad if he hadn't known that, outside of the sacred precincts, those bars sometimes worked in reverse and set off alarms in elevators or at the street entrance. The guards never carried theirs below the twenty-sixth level. So he got rid of the bar in a waste receptacle by the elevator shafts before he rang for an elevator. The waste receptacle might conceivably have been booby-trapped for radioactive bars. But he took a chance because he didn't want to put it down in plain sight. No alarm went off.

A few minutes later he was safely on the street, lost in the crowd and reasonably safe from pursuit.

A clock told him that it was now sixteen o'clock; he had six hours before his appointment with Olliver. But he wasn't going to wait until twenty-two; the police might expect him to go to Olliver's house—not for the real reason he was going there, but to avenge himself on the judge who had sentenced him. As soon as he was missed, that house would be watched more closely than it was now. That was only common sense.

He looked up the address and took an atocab to within two blocks of it. He scouted on foot and spotted two guards, one at the front and one at the back. It would have been easy to kill either of them, but that would have defeated his purpose. It would definitely have focused the search for him on Olliver's house.

Getting into the house to hide would be equally dangerous; before they posted additional guards they'd search thoroughly.

The house next door was the answer; it was the same height and the roofs were only ten feet apart. And it wasn't guarded. But he'd better get in now. Later there might be a cordon around the whole block.

He took a tiny picklock out of the strap of his artificial hand: a bent wire as large as a small hairpin but as strong as a steel rod; and let himself in the door as casually as a returning householder would use his key. There were sounds at the back of the house, hut he drew no attention as he went quietly up the stairs. He found the way out to the roof but didn't use it yet. Instead, he hid himself in the closet of what seemed to be an extra, unused bedroom.

He waited out five hours there, until it was almost twenty-two o'clock, and then let himself out on the roof. Being careful not to silhouette himself, he looked down and around. There were at least a dozen more vehicles parked on the street before Olliver's house and in the alley back of it than there should have been in a neighborhood like this one. The place was being watched, and closely.

The big danger was being seen during the jump from one roof to the next. But apparently no one saw him, and he landed lightly, as an acrobat lands. The sound he made might have been heard in the upstairs room immediately below him, but no farther. His picklock let him in the door from the roof to the stairs, and at the foot of them, the second floor, he waited for two or three minutes until utter silence convinced him there was no one on that floor.

He heard faint voices as he went down the next flight of steps to the first floor. One voice was Olliver's and the other that of a woman. He listened outside the door and when, after a while, he'd heard no other voices, he opened it and walked in.

Jon Olliver was seated behind a massive mahogany desk. For once, as he saw Crag, his poker face slipped. There was surprise in his eyes as well as in his voice as he said, "How in Heaven's name did you make it, Crag? I quit expecting you after I found the search was centering here. I thought you'd get in touch with me later, if at all."

Crag was looking at the woman. She was the technician who had given him his start toward freedom that afternoon. At least her features were the same. But she didn't wear the glasses now, and the technician's cap didn't hide the blazing glory of her hair. And, although the severe uniform she'd worn that afternoon hadn't hidden the voluptuousness of her figure, the gown she wore now accentuated every line of it. In the latest style, bare-midriffed, there was only a wisp of material above the waist. And the long skirt fitted her hips and thighs as a sheath fits a sword.

She was unbelievably beautiful.

She smiled at Crag, but spoke to Olliver. She said, "What does it matter *how* he got here, Jon? I told you he'd come."

Crag pulled his eyes away from her with an effort and looked at Olliver.

Olliver smiled too, now. He looked big and blond and handsome, like his campaign portraits.

He said, "I suppose that's right, Crag. It doesn't matter how you got here. And there's no use talking about the past. We'll get to brass tacks. But let's get one more thing straight, first—an introduction."

He inclined his head toward the woman standing beside the desk. "Crag, Evadne. My wife."

CHAPTER III: Evadne

Crag almost laughed. It was the first time Olliver had been stupid. To think— Well, it didn't matter. He ignored it.

"Are we through horsing around now?" he asked.

Apparently Olliver either didn't recognize the archaic expression or didn't know what Crag meant by it. He raised his eyebrows. "What do you mean, Crag?"

"Making me take unnecessary risks just to show you how good I am."

"Oh, that. Yes, we're through horsing around. Pull up a chair, Crag. You sit down too, Evadne."

When they were comfortable, Olliver said, "First the background, Crag. You know the general political situation, but from the outside you probably don't know how bad it is."

"I know enough," Crag said.

"A two-party system, but both crooked. The only fortunate thing is the reasonably close balance of power between them. The Guilds—powerful organizations that evolved out of the workmen's unions of half a dozen centuries ago, pitted against the Syndicates—the Gilded—ruthless groups of capitalists and their reactionary satellites. The Guilds using intimidation as their weapon and the Gilded using bribery. Each group honeycombed with spies of the other—"

"I know all that."

"Of course. A third party, a middle-of-the-road one, is now being organized, under cover. We must get a certain amount of capital and of power before we can come out into the open." He smiled. "Or they'll slap us down before we get really started."

"All I want to know," said Crag, "is what you want me to do. You can skip the build-up."

"All right. A certain man has a certain invention. He doesn't know it's valuable. I do. With that invention, our party could have unlimited funds. Billions. We've raised a war chest of several million among ourselves already. But it isn't enough. A party, these days, needs billions."

"Sounds simple," Crag said, "but have you offered the inventor the million you offered me?"

"He won't sell at any price. For one thing, he's immensely wealthy already, and a million wouldn't mean anything to him. For another, the thing is incidentally a weapon and it would be illegal for him to sell it."

"What do you mean, *incidentally* a weapon?" Crag looked at him narrowly.

"That's its primary purpose, what it was made to be. But it's not a very efficient weapon; it kills, but it takes too long. It takes seconds, and whoever you killed with it could get you before he died. And the range is very limited."

"Its real importance, which he does not realize, lies in a by-product of its action."

Crag said, "All right, that part's none of my business. But tell me who and where the guy lives and what I'm looking for."

Olliver said, "When the time comes, you'll get the details. Something comes first—for your protection and mine. You won't be able to do this job right if you're wanted by the police, being hunted. For one thing, it's not on Earth. And you know—or should—how tough it is to get off Earth if the police are looking for you."

"Tough, but it can be done."

"Still, an unnecessary risk. And anyway, I promised you your freedom as part of this deal. I meant your full freedom, not as a hunted man."

"And how do you expect to swing *that?*" Crag asked.

"With Evadne's help. She's a psycher technician."

Crag turned and looked at her again. It didn't make him like her any better, but it did surprise him. To be a psycher technician you had to have a degree in psychiatry and another in electronics. To look at Evadne you wouldn't think of degrees, unless they were degrees of your own temperature.

Olliver said, "Now don't get excited, Crag, when I tell you that I'm going to send you—with your consent—to the psycher. It'll be a short-circuited one, with Evadne running it; it won't have any effect on you at all. But Evadne will certify you as adjusted."

Crag frowned. "How do I know the machine will be shorted?"

"Why would we cross you up on it, Crag? It would defeat our own purpose. If you *were* adjusted, you wouldn't do this job for me—or want to."

Crag glanced at the woman. She said, "You can trust me, Crag, that far."

It was a funny way of putting it and, possibly for that reason, he believed her. It seemed worth the gamble. If they thought he'd been through the psycher, he really would be free. Free to go anywhere, do anything. And otherwise he'd be hunted the rest of his life; if he was ever picked up for the slightest slip he'd be identified at once and sent to the psycher as an escaped convict. And without a psycher technician to render it useless.

Olliver was saying, "It's the only way, Crag. By tomorrow noon you'll be a free man and can return here openly. I'll hire you—presumably to drive my atocar and my space cruiser—and keep you here until it's time to do the little job for me. Which will be in about a week."

Crag decided quickly. He said, "It's a deal. Do I go out and give myself up?"

Olliver opened a drawer of the big desk and took out a needle gun. He said, "There's a better way. Safer, that is. You killed a guard, you know, and they might shoot instead of capturing you if you went out of here. I'll bring them in instead, and I'll have you already captured. You came here to kill me, and I captured you: They won't dare to shoot you then."

Crag nodded, and backed up against the wall, his hands raised.

Olliver said, "Go and bring them in, my dear," to Evadne.

Crag's eyes followed her as she went to the door. Then they returned to Olliver's. Olliver had raised the needle gun and his eyes locked with Crag's. He said softly, "Remember, Crag, she's my wife."

Crag grinned insolently at him. He said, "You don't seem very sure of that."

For a moment he thought he'd gone too far, as Olliver's knuckles tightened on the handle of the gun. Then the men were coming in to get him, and they held the tableau and neither spoke again.

He was back in jail, in the same cell, within half an hour. One thing happened that he hadn't counted on—although he would have realized it was inevitable if he'd thought of it. They beat him into insensibility before they left him there. Common sense—or self-preservation—made him wise enough not to raise his hand, his left hand, against them. He might have killed two or even three of them, but there were six, and the others would have killed him if he'd killed even one.

He came back to consciousness about midnight. and pain kept him from sleeping the rest of the night. At ten in the morning, six guards came and took him back to the same room in which he had been tried the day before. This time there was no jury and no attorneys. Just Crag, six guards, and Judge Olliver.

Sentence to the psycher was a formality.

Six guards took him back to his cell. And, because it was the last chance they'd have, they beat him again. Not so badly this time; he'd have to be able to walk to the psycher.

At twelve they brought him lunch, but he wasn't able to eat it. At fourteen, they came and escorted him to the psycher room. They strapped him in the chair, slapped his face a bit and one of them gave him a farewell blow in the stomach that made him glad he hadn't eaten, and then they left.

A few minutes later, Evadne came in. Again she was dressed as she had been when he'd first seen her. But this time her beauty showed through even more for, after having seen her dressed as she'd been the evening before, he knew almost every curve that the tailored uniform tried to hide. She wore the horn-rimmed glasses when she came in, but took them off as soon as she had locked the door from inside. Probably, Crag thought, they were only protective coloration.

She stood in front of him, looking down at his face, a slight smile on her lips.

She said, "Quit looking so worried, Crag. I'm not going to psych you—and even your suspicious, unadjusted nature will admit I'd have no reason for lying about it now, if I intended to. I've got you where I'd want you, if I wanted you."

He said nothing.

Her smile faded. "You know, Crag, I'd hate to adjust you, even if this was a straight deal. You're a magnificent brute. I think I like you better the way you are, than if you were a mild-mannered clerk or elevator operator. That's what you'd be if I turned that thing on, you know."

"Why not unstrap me?"

"With the door locked, and with us alone? Oh, I'm not being femininely modest, Crag. I know you hate women. I also know your temper, and I know how you've probably been treated since last night. I'd have to watch every word I said to keep you from slapping me down—left-handed."

"You know about that?"

"Olliver—Jon—knows a lot about you."

"Then he must know I wouldn't hit a woman—unless she got in my way."

"But I might." She laughed. "And you'd have to let me strap you in again anyway. And that reminds me. You're supposed to be unconscious when I leave this room. You'll have to fake that. The guards come in and unstrap you. They take you to a hospital room until you come around."

"Helping me do so with rubber hose?"

"No, that's all over with. You'll be a new man—not the man who killed a guard yesterday. They won't have any resentment against you."

"How long am I supposed to be unconscious?"

"Half an hour to an hour. And you may leave as soon thereafter as you wish. Better stay an hour or two; most of them do. You're supposed to be a bit dazed when you come to, and to orient yourself gradually. And don't forget you're not supposed to remember your own name, or any crimes you've ever committed—or anything you've ever done, for that matter."

"Just like amnesia, huh?"

"Exactly like amnesia—and, besides that, all the causes of maladjustments are supposed to be removed. You're supposed to love everyone in particular and humanity in general."

Crag laughed. "And does a halo come with it?"

"I'm not joking, Crag. Take that idea seriously—at least until you're safely away from here. Don't act as though you still have a chip on your shoulder or they may suspect that something went wrong with the psycher—and send you back for another try. And I'll be off duty by then."

"If I don't remember who I am—I mean, if I'm supposed not to remember—isn't it going to be funny for me to walk out without being curious? Do they just let psyched guys walk out without a name?"

"Oh no. Each one has a sponsor, someone who volunteers to help orient them to a new life. Jon has volunteered to be your sponsor and to give you a job. You'll be told that and given his address and cab fare to get there. He's supposed to explain things to you when you see him, to orient you."

"What if a guy would lam instead of going to his sponsor?"

"After the psycher, they're adjusted. They wouldn't. Remember, Crag, you've got to play it to the hilt until you're safe at our house. If anyone steps on your toe, apologize."

Crag growled, and then laughed. It was the first time he'd laughed—with humor—in a long time. But the idea of him apologizing to anyone for anything was so ridiculous he couldn't help it.

Evadne reached across his shoulder and did something; he couldn't tell what because his head was strapped against the back of the chair.

"Disconnected a terminal," she said. "I'll have to run the machine for a while; someone might notice that it isn't drawing any current."

She went to one side of the room and threw a switch. A low humming sound filled the room, but nothing happened otherwise. Crag relaxed.

She was standing in front of him again. She said, "You know, Crag, I'm almost tempted to give you a partial psyching—just to find out what made you what you are."

"Don't start anything you don't finish," he said grimly. His right hand clenched.

"Oh, I know that. I know perfectly well that if I got any information from you under compulsion—as I could if I reconnected that terminal—I'd have to finish the job and adjust you or blank you out. Your ego wouldn't let me stay alive if I knew things about you that you'd told me involuntarily."

"You're smarter than I thought," he said.

"That isn't being smart, for a psychiatrist. Even a layman could guess that. But, Crag, you've got to tell me a few things."

"Why?"

"So I can turn in a report. I don't have to turn in a detailed one, but I must at least write up a summary. I could fake it easily, but it just might be checked and fail to tally with some things about you that are already known. You can see that."

"Well—yes."

"For instance, the loss of your hand. That was back before you turned criminal, so the facts about it will be on record somewhere. And I'd be supposed to ask you about that because it may have been a factor in your turning against society."

"I guess it was," Crag said. "And, as you say, it's on record so there's no reason I shouldn't tell you. It happened on the *Vega III*, when I'd been a spaceman eight years. It was a pure accident—not my fault or anyone else's. Just one of those things that happen. Mechanical failure in a rocket tube set it off while I was cleaning it.

"But they sprang a technicality on me and kept me from getting the fifty thousand credits compensation I was entitled to. Not only that, but took my license and rating away from me, turned me from a spaceman into a one-handed bum."

"What was the technicality?"

"Test for alcohol. I'd had exactly one drink—a stirrup cup, one small glass of wine—six hours before, which was two hours before we left Mars. Orders are no drinks eight hours before blast-off, and I hadn't drunk anything for longer than that, except that one drink. And it had nothing to do with the accident— nobody feels one glass of wine six hours after. But they used it to save themselves what I had coming."

"And after that?"

"After that I got kicked around a while until I started in to do my share of the kicking."

"That wouldn't have been very long," she said. It wasn't a question and he didn't answer it.

She said, "I know what crimes they know you committed—without having been able to prove it. I'll say you confessed to them."

Crag shrugged. "Tell them what you like."

"Why do you hate women so much?"

"Is that personal curiosity? Or does it have to go in your report?"

She smiled. "As a matter of fact, both."

"I was married at the time I lost my job and my hand and my license. To a girl with hair like yours. Married only a few months and mad about her. Do I have to draw a diagram of what she did to me?"

She said soberly, "I can guess."

"You should be able to. You're more beautiful than she. And more evil."

Her face flamed and for a moment he thought she was going to strike him. But training told, and in seconds she was smiling again.

She said, "Not evil, Crag. Just ruthless, like you. I try to get what I want. But we're not psyching me, and it's time to end this now. Close your eyes and pretend to be unconscious."

He did. He heard her walk to the wall and throw the switch that shut off the machine. She came back and reconnected the terminal behind his shoulder, and still he kept his eyes closed.

He'd half-expected it, but it jarred him when it came. It was a kiss that should have wakened a statue, but—outwardly—he took it with complete passiveness. He kept his own lips still.

And he hated her the more because the kiss brought to life in him things he'd thought were dead. And he knew that he'd hate her forever and probably kill her when he saw her again if, now, she laughed.

But she didn't laugh, or even speak. She left the room very quietly.

CHAPTER IV: New Life

A few minutes later the guards came. Only two of them this time; they weren't afraid of him now. They unstrapped him from the chair and carried him somewhere on a stretcher and rolled him off onto a bed.

When he was pretty sure that at least half an hour had gone by, he opened his eyes and looked around as though dazed. But the acting had been unnecessary; he was alone in a room. A few minutes later a nurse looked in and found him sitting up.

She came on into the room. "How are you feeling, sir?"

Crag shook his head. He said, "I *feel* all right, but I can't seem to remember anything. Who I am, or how I got here—wherever here is."

She smiled at him and sat down on the chair beside the bed. "You've just had—the equivalent of an attack of amnesia. That's all I'm supposed to tell you. But as soon as you feel equal to it, we'll send you to a man who will explain everything to you, and help you. Meanwhile, there's nothing for you to worry about. When you feel able to leave, come to the desk in the hall and I'll give you the address and money to get there."

Crag swung his feet off the bed. "I can go now," he said. But he made his voice sound uncertain.

"Please lie down and rest a while first. There's no hurry."

She went out, and Crag lay back down, obediently. He let another half hour pass and then went out into the corridor and to the desk. The nurse looked up at him and handed him a card and a ten-credit note. She said, "Please go to that address before you do anything else. Judge Olliver has a job for you and he will explain about your amnesia and tell you as much as it is necessary for you to know about your past."

He thanked her and went out, alert to watch his temper if any incident were staged to test him. But none was, although he was, he felt sure, watched to see whether he headed immediately for the atocab stand just outside the building and gave the address he'd been handed on the card—an address he already knew but pretended to read off the card to the cabby.

Twenty minutes later he walked up to the guard at Olliver's front door and asked if he might see the Judge.

"Your name Crag?"

He almost said yes before he thought. "Sounds silly," he said, "but I don't know my name. I was sent here to find out."

The guard nodded and let him in. "He's waiting for you," he said. "Second door down the hall."

Crag entered the small room in which he'd talked to Olliver and Evadne the evening before. Only Olliver was there now, at the desk.

"Everything go all right?" he asked.

Crag threw himself into a chair. "Perfect," he said, "except for two beatings up that weren't on the menu."

"You should feel it's worth that to be free, Crag. And now—you're still interested in earning that million?"

"Yes. But the price has gone up."

Olliver frowned at him. "What do you mean?"

"I mean besides that I want you to do a spot of research downtown and get me twelve names, and addresses for each. The six guards who put me in a cell last night and the six—they were different ones—who put me back in the cell after the trial this morning."

Olliver stared at him a moment and then laughed. He said, "All right, but not till after the job is over. Then if you're fool enough to want to look them up, it's your business, not mine."

"Which gets us to the job. Where is it, what is it, how long will it take?"

"It's on Mars. We're going there in four days; I can't get away any sooner than that. I told you what it is—a job of burglary, but not a simple one. How long it takes depends on you; I imagine you'll need some preparation, but if you can't do it in a few weeks, you can't do it at all."

"Fair enough," Crag said. "But if I've got that long to wait, how about an advance?"

"Again on a condition, Crag. I don't want you to get into any trouble before you've done the job. I want you to stay here. You can send out for anything you want."

Crag's short nod got him a thousand credits.

He needed sleep, having got none the night before because of pain from the first, and worst, beating. And every muscle in his body still ached.

But before he even tried to sleep he sent out for Martian *zot,* and drank himself into insensibility.

He slept, then, until late afternoon of the next day. When he woke, he drank the rest of the liquor and then went downstairs, not quite steady on his feet and with his eyes bloodshot and bleary. But under control, mentally.

And it was probably well that he was, for in the downstairs hallway, he encountered Evadne for the first time since his return to Olliver's. She glanced at him and took in his condition, then passed him without speaking and with a look of cold contempt that—well, if he *hadn't* been under control mentally—

The next day he was sober, and stayed that way. He told himself he hated Evadne too much to let her see him otherwise. And after that he spent most of his time reading. He had breakfast and lunch alone, but ate dinner with Olliver and Evadne, and spent part of the evening with them.

He didn't mention the job again; it was up to Olliver, he thought, to bring that up. And Olliver did, on the evening of the third day.

He said, "We're going to Mars tomorrow, Crag. Forgot to ask you one thing. Can you pilot a Class AB space cruiser, or do I hire us a pilot?"

"I can handle one."

"You're sure? It's space-warp drive, you know. As I understand it, the last ship you worked on was rocket."

Crag said, "The last ship I flew legally was rocket. But how about a license, unless you want to land in a back alley on Mars?"

"You're licensed. If a license is invalidated for any reason other than incompetency, it's automatically renewed if you've been readjusted through the psycher. And today I picked up a stat of your license and a copy of the psycher certificate. After I got them, though, I remembered I didn't know whether you could handle space-warp."

Evadne said, "It doesn't matter, Jon. I'm licensed; I can handle the cruiser."

"I know, my dear. But I've told you; I do not think it safe to travel in space with only one person who is qualified to pilot the ship. Perhaps I'm ultra-conservative, but why take unnecessary risks?"

Crag asked, "Ready now to tell me about the job?"

"Yes. When we reach Mars, we'll separate. Evadne and I will stay in Marsport until you have—accomplished your mission."

"Which is to be done where?"

"You've heard of Kurt Eisen?"

"The one who helped develop space-warp?"

"That's the one. He has his laboratory and home just outside Marsport. He's fabulously wealthy; it's a tremendous estate. About eighty employes, thirty of them armed guards. The place is like a fortress. It'll almost have to be an inside job—another good reason why you couldn't have handled it without a psycher certificate."

Crag nodded. "At least it will be easier if I can get in. And just what am I looking for after I get there?"

"A device that looks like a flat pocket flashlight. Blued steel case. Lens in the center of one end, just like an atomic flashlight, but the lens is green and opaque—opaque to light, that is."

"You've seen it?"

"No. The party's source of information is a technician who used to work for Eisen. He's now a member of the party. He worked with Eisen in developing it, but can't make one by himself; he wasn't fully in Eisen's confidence—just allowed to help with details of design. Oh, and if you can get the plans, it'll help. We can duplicate the original, but it'll be easier from the plans. And one other thing. Don't try it out."

"All right," Crag said, "I won't try it out—on one condition. That you tell me what it is and what it does. Otherwise, my curiosity might get the better of me."

Olliver frowned, but he answered. "It's a disintegrator. It's designed to negate the—well, I'm not up on atomic theory, so I can't give it to you technically.

But it negates the force that holds the electrons to the nucleus. In effect, it collapses matter into neutronium."

Crag whistled softly. "And you say it's an ineffective weapon?"

"Yes, because its range is so short. The size needed increases as the cube of the cube of the distance—or something astronomical like that. The one you're after works up to three feet. To make one that would work at a hundred feet it would have to be bigger than a house. And for a thousand feet—well, there aren't enough of the necessary raw materials in the Solar System to build one; it would have to be the size of a small planet. And besides, there's a time lag. The ray from the disintegrator sets up a chain reaction in any reasonably homogeneous object it's aimed at, but it takes seconds to get it started. So if you shoot at somebody—at a few feet distance—they're dead all right, but they've got time to kill you before they find it out." Olliver smiled. "Your left hand is much more effective, Crag, and has about the same range."

"Then why is it worth a million credits to you?"

"I told you, the by-product. Neutronium."

Crag had heard of neutronium; every spaceman knew that some of the stars were made of almost completely collapsed matter weighing a dozen tons to the cubic inch. Dwarf stars, the size of Earth and the weight of the sun. But no such collapsed matter existed in the Solar System. Not that there was any reason why it shouldn't—if a method had been found to make atoms pack themselves solidly together. Pure neutronium would be unbelievably heavy, heavier than the center of any known star.

"Neutronium," he said, thoughtfully. "But what would you use it for? How could you handle it? Wouldn't it sink through anything you tried to hold it in and come to rest at the center of the Earth—or whatever planet you made it on?"

"You're smart, Crag. It would. You couldn't use it for weighting chessmen. I know how to capitalize on it—but that's one thing I don't think you have to know. Although I may tell you later, after you've turned over the disintegrator."

Crag shrugged. It wasn't his business, after all. A million credits was enough for him, and let Olliver and his party capitalize on neutronium however they wished. He asked, "Did this technician who worked for Eisen give you a diagram of the place?"

Olliver opened a drawer of the desk and handed Crag an envelope.

Crag spent the rest of the evening studying its contents.

They took off from Albuquerque spaceport the following afternoon and landed on Mars a few hours later. As soon as the cruiser was hangared, they separated, Crag presumably quitting his job with Olliver. He promised to report in not more than two weeks.

A man named Lane Knutson was his first objective. He had full details about Knutson and an excellent description of him; that had been an important part of the contents of the envelope he had studied the final evening on Earth.

Knutson was the head guard at Eisen's place and did the hiring of the other guards. According to Crag's information, he hung out, in his off hours, in spacemen's dives in the tough section of Marsport.

Crag hung out there, too, but spent his time circulating from place to place instead of settling down in any one. He found Knutson on the third day. He couldn't have missed him, from the description. Knutson was six feet six and weighed two hundred ninety. He had arms like an ape and the strength and disposition of a Venusian *draatr*.

Crag might have made friends with him in the normal manner, but he took a short cut by picking a quarrel. With Knutson's temper, the distance between a quarrel and a fight was about the same as the distance between adjacent grapes under pressure in a wine press.

Crag let himself get the worst of it for a minute or two, so Knutson wouldn't feel too bad about it, and then used his left hand twice, very lightly, pulling his punches. Once in the guts to bend the big man over, and then a light flick to the side of the jaw, careful not to break bone. Knutson was out cold for five minutes.

After that, they had a drink together and got chummy. Within half an hour Crag had admitted that he was looking for a job—and was promptly offered one.

He reported for work the following day and, after Knutson had shown him around, he was glad he hadn't decided to try the outside. The place really was a fortress. A twenty-foot-high electronic barrier around the outside; inside that, worse things. But it didn't matter, since he was already inside. Even so, he had to undergo a strenuous physical and verbal examination and Olliver had been right about the psycher certificate; without it, he'd have been out on his ear within an hour.

He spent the next five days learning all the ropes. He knew where the big safe was—in the laboratory. But he wanted to learn the position of every guard and every alarm between the room in which he slept and the laboratory itself. Fortunately, he was given a day shift.

On the fifth night he made his way to the laboratory and found himself facing the blank sheet of durasteel that was the door of the safe. All his information about that safe was that the lock was magnetic and that there were two alarms.

He'd brought nothing with him—all employees were searched on their way in as well as on their way out—but all the materials he needed to make anything he wanted were there at hand in the laboratory. He made himself a detector and traced two pairs of wires through the walls from the safe into adjacent rooms and found the two alarms—both hidden inside air ducts—to which they were connected. He disconnected both alarms and then went back to the safe. On Eisen's desk near it, he'd noticed a little horseshoe magnet—a toy—that was apparently used as a paperweight. He got the hunch (which saved him much time) that, held in the proper position against that sheet of steel—six by six feet square—it would open the door.

And, unless it was exactly at one corner, there'd have to be a mark on the door to show where the magnet was to be held. The durasteel door made it easy for him; there weren't any accidental marks or scratches on it to confuse him. Only an almost imperceptible fly-speck about a foot to the right of the center. But fly-specks scrape off and this mark didn't—besides, there are no flies on Mars.

He tried the magnet in various positions about the speck and when he tried holding it with both poles pointing upward and the speck exactly between them, the door swung open.

The safe—it was a vault, really, almost six feet square and ten or twelve feet deep—contained so many things that it was almost harder to find what he was looking for than it had been to open the safe. But he found it. Luckily, there was a tag attached to it with a key number which made it easy to find the plans for the disintegrator in the file drawers at the back of the safe.

He took both disintegrator and plans to the workbenches of the laboratory. Elsen couldn't possibly have provided better equipment for a burglar who wished to leave a possible duplicate of whatever object he wanted to steal. And he'd even provided a perfectly sound-proofed laboratory so even the noisier of the power-tools could be used safely. Within an hour, Crag had made what, outwardly, was a reasonably exact duplicate of the flashlight-sized object he was stealing. It didn't have any insides in it, and it wouldn't have disintegrated anything except the temper of a man who tried to use it, but it looked good. He put the tag from the real one on it and replaced it in the proper drawer in the safe.

He spent a little longer than that forging a duplicate of the plans. Not *quite* a duplicate; he purposely varied a few things so that no one except Eisen himself could make a successful disintegrator from them.

He spent another hour removing every trace of his visit. He reconnected the alarms, removed every trace—except a minute shortage of stock—of his work in the laboratory, made sure that every tool was restored to place, and put back the toy magnet on the exact spot and at the exact angle on Eisen's desk that it had been before.

When he left the laboratory there was nothing to indicate that he had been there—unless Eisen should ever again decide to try out his disintegrator. And since he had tried it once and presumably discarded it as practically useless, that didn't seem likely.

There remained only the obstacle of getting it out of the grounds, and that was simple. One large upstairs room was a museum which held Eisen's collection of artifacts of the Martian aborigines. Crag had seen several primitive bows and quivers of arrows. He wrapped and fastened the plans around the shaft of a long, strong arrow and securely tied the disintegrator to its crude metal head. He went on up to the roof and shot the arrow high into the air over the electronic barrier and the strip of cleared ground outside it, into the thick jungle beyond.

It was almost dawn. He went back to his room and got two hours of needed sleep. The hard part was over. The little capsule he'd brought with him would take care of the rest of it.

CHAPTER V: The Glory Hunters

He took the capsule as soon as the alarm buzzer awakened him, half an hour before he was to report for duty. It was the one thing he'd smuggled in with him, perfectly hidden in a box of apparently identical capsules containing neobenzedrine, the standard preventive of Martian amoebic fever. All Earthmen on Mars took neobenzedrine.

One of the capsules in Crag's box, though, contained a powder of similar color but of almost opposite effect. It wouldn't give him amoebic fever, but it would produce perfectly counterfeited symptoms.

He could, of course, simply have quit, but that might just possibly have aroused suspicion; it might have led to a thorough check-up of the laboratory and the contents of the safe. And he couldn't suddenly become disobedient in order to get himself fired. Psyched men didn't act that way.

The capsule took care of it perfectly. He started to get sick at his stomach. Knutson came by and found Crag retching out a window. As soon as Crag pulled his head back in, Knutson took a look at Crag's eyes; the pupils were contracted almost to pinpoints. He touched Crag's forehead and found it hot. And Crag admitted, when asked, that he'd probably forgotten to take his neobenzedrine for a few days.

That was that. There's no known cure for Martian amoebic fever except to get away from Mars at the first opportunity. He neither quit nor was fired. Knutson took him to the office and got his pay for him and then asked him whether he could make it back to Marsport by himself or if he wanted help. Crag said he could make it.

The search of his person and effects was perfunctory; he could probably have smuggled the tiny gadget and the single piece of paper out in his luggage. But the arrow had been safer.

Outside, as soon as jungle screened him from view, he took another capsule, one that looked just like the first but that counteracted it. He waited until the worst of the nausea from the first capsule had passed and then hid his luggage while he hunted for the arrow and found it.

Olliver had told him not to try it, but he tried it anyway. It wasn't exactly that he didn't trust Olliver—after all, if he got paid off, and he'd make sure of that, nothing else mattered—it was just that he was curious whether Olliver had told him the truth about the disintegrator's limitations.

He waited until he'd put a little more distance between himself and Eisen's place and then aimed the gadget at a bush and tripped the thumb catch. He held it about four feet from the bush the first time and nothing happened. He moved it to about two feet from the bush and tripped the catch again. He thought for a while that nothing was going to happen, but after a few seconds the bush took on a misty look, and then, quite abruptly, it wasn't there any more.

Olliver had told the truth, then. The thing had an effective range of only about three feet, and there was a definite time lag.

The rest of the way into Marsport—afoot as far as the edge of town and by atocab the rest of the way—he tried to figure out what Olliver's use for neutronium might be. He couldn't. In the first place he couldn't see how Olliver could *get* the collapsed matter, the tons-to-a-square-inch stuff, once he'd disintegrated objects into it. The bush he'd tried it on hadn't seemed to collapse inward on itself; it had simply disintegrated all at once and the dead atoms of it had probably fallen through the crust of Mars as easily as rain falls through air.

He still hadn't figured an answer when he reached the swanky Marsport hotel where Olliver and Evadne were staying.

He had himself announced from the desk and then went up to Olliver's suite. Olliver, his face both eager and tense, let him in. He didn't ask the question, but Crag nodded.

Evadne, he saw as he walked past Olliver, was there. She was sitting on the sofa looking at him, her eyes enigmatic. Crag tried not to look at her. It was difficult. She was dressed even more revealingly than she had been dressed the first night he had seen her at Olliver's house in Albuquerque, back on Earth. And she looked even more beautiful.

Crag decided he wanted to get away from there, quick. He took the disintegrator and the folded plans from his pocket and put them on the table.

Olliver picked them up with unconcealed eagerness.

Crag said, "One million credits. Then we're through."

Olliver put gadget and paper in one pocket and took out a wallet from another. He said drily, "I don't carry a million in ready change, Crag. The bulk of it is back on Earth; I'll have to give it to you there. But so you won't worry or think I'm stalling, I did bring two hundred thousand credits with me. Eight hundred thousand's waiting for you back home."

Crag nodded curtly, and took the offered money. He counted it roughly and put it in his pocket. It was more money than he'd ever had or hoped to have in one chunk. He was set for life, even if he never got the rest.

He asked, "At your home? Shall I look you up there?"

Olliver looked surprised. "Why not come back with us? We're leaving at once, now that I have this. As soon as we can get clearance. We're making one brief stopover—going one other place first, that is—but we'll be home within hours. You may have to wait days to get public transport, and you know all the red tape you'll have to go through."

It made sense, but Crag hesitated.

Olliver laughed. "Afraid of me, Crag? Afraid I'm going to disintegrate you en route? To get my money back?" He laughed harder; there was almost hysterical amusement in the laughter. Obviously the gadget Crag had stolen for him excited him immensely. "You needn't worry, Crag. With this—" He slapped his pocket. "—a million credits is peanuts to me."

From the sofa, Evadne's voice said with languid amusement, "He isn't afraid of you, Jon. He's afraid of me."

Crag didn't look at her. He was watching Olliver's face and he saw amusement change to jealousy and anger.

Crag hadn't been afraid of Olliver. It had occurred to him only as a remote possibility that Olliver might try to kill him. Now, from the look on Olliver's face, his trying to kill Crag looked like a fair bet. Not, though, to get his money back.

Crag said, "All right, Olliver. I might as well go with you."

Deliberately he turned away from possible danger to lock glances with Evadne.

She was smiling at him.

They got to the spaceport within an hour and through the formalities of clearance before noon.

Crag didn't ask, "Well, where?" until he was in the pilot's seat of the little cruiser.

"Asteroid belt," Olliver told him.

"Where in the belt? What asteroid?"

"Doesn't matter. Any one big enough to land on."

Crag had lifted the computation shelf, ready to calculate distance and direction. He folded the shelf back; a jump of a hundred million miles, straight out from the sun, would put him in the middle of the belt. He set the controls, made the jump, and put the ship back on manual control. His detectors would show the presence of any of the asteroids within ten million miles. They showed the presence of several right now.

He turned to Olliver. He said, "We're near Ceres. Four hundred eighty mile diameter. That one do?"

"Too big, Crag. It'd take days. Pick the smallest one you can land on."

Crag nodded and studied the other asteroids showing on the detector and picked the smallest of them. It wasn't much bigger than a fair-sized house but he could land on it. He did. Rather, he killed the inertia of the spaceship after pulling alongside the tiny asteroid and matching his speed to its. Ship and asteroid bumped together, held by not much more than a pound of gravitational pull between them. Had the asteroid had an atmosphere, the ship would have floated in it, so slight was the attraction.

Olliver clapped him on the shoulder. "Nice work, Crag. Want to put on a spacesuit and come out to watch the fun?"

Crag locked the controls. "Why not?"

He saw now what Olliver intended to do—try out the disintegrator on the asteroid. And he saw now how Olliver could get neutronium. Disintegrating an asteroid was different from disintegrating an object on the crust of a planet. Instead of falling through the crust, the asteroid would collapse within itself, into a tiny, compact ball of neutronium. Maybe the size of an apple or an orange. It could be loaded—

He stopped suddenly, half in and half out of the spacesuit he had started to pull on. He said, "Olliver, you can't take it back with you. Sure, we can put it in the spaceship, but when we get back to Earth we can't land with it. Near Earth, it's going to weigh ten times—maybe twenty times—as much as the ship itself. It'll either tear a hole through the hull or crash us, one or the other."

Olliver laughed. He was picking up a thermoglass helmet but hadn't put it on yet. He said, "This is just a tryout, Crag. We're not taking any neutronium back with us."

Crag finished putting on the spacesuit. Olliver had his helmet on, and Evadne was adjusting hers. He couldn't talk to either of them, now, until he had his own helmet on. Then the suit-radios would take care of communication.

He saw now how neutronium could be obtained, all right. There were rocks a lot smaller than this one whizzing around the belt, ones that weighed only a few tons, that a spaceship could handle easily and transport back to Earth after they'd been converted into collapsed matter.

He didn't see, as yet, what practical use neutronium could have that would make it as immensely valuable as Olliver seemed to think it would be. But that wasn't his business.

He got his helmet on, and nodded that he was ready. Evadne was standing by the air controls and she pulled a switch when he nodded. A space cruiser as small as Olliver's never had an airlock; it was simpler, if one wished to leave it in space or on an airless body, to exhaust the air from the entire ship and let the airmaker rebuild an atmosphere after one returned to the ship—and before removing one's spacesuit.

Now, in the earphones of his helmet, he heard Olliver's voice say, "Come on. Hurry up." Olliver opened the door and the last of the air whished out. But then, before stepping out, Olliver went back past Crag to the controls. He turned the lock on them and put the small but quite complicated key into one of the capacious pockets of his spacesuit. The plans for the disintegrator, Crag knew, were in the innermost pocket of his jumper.

Crag wondered which one of them he distrusted, or if it was both. Not that it mattered.

Crag shrugged and stepped out onto the tiny asteroid. Evadne followed him, and then Olliver.

He heard Olliver take a deep breath and say, "Here goes."

Olliver was pointing the little disintegrator down at the rocky surface of the asteroid, bending over so it was only a foot from the rock. Crag couldn't hear the click, but he saw Olliver's thumb move the catch.

Crag asked, "How long will it take?"

"For something this size? I'd guess half an hour to an hour. But we won't have to wait till it's completely collapsed. When it's gone down enough that I'm sure—"

Crag looked about him, at the spaceship behind them, bumping gently against the surface of the asteroid, right at the shadow line that divided night and day. Strange that a world only twenty or thirty yards in diameter should have night and day—and yet darkness on the night side would be even denser than the darkness on the night side of Earth.

Time, Crag thought, *and its relation to distance are strange on a world like this.* If he walked twenty paces ahead and put himself right under distant, tiny Sol, it would be high noon. Thirty or forty more steps—held down to the light asteroid only by the gravplates on the shoes of the spacesuit—and he'd be in the middle of the night side; it would be midnight.

He chuckled at the fancy. "It's a small world," he said, remembering that Olliver had said that to him in the conversation between judge and prisoner at the end of the trial, the conversation that had led to all of this.

Olliver laughed excitedly, almost hysterically. "And it's getting smaller already—I think. Don't you, Crag, Evadne?"

Crag looked about him and tried to judge, but if there'd been any shrinkage as yet, he couldn't tell. He heard Evadne say, "I'm not sure yet, Jon."

Olliver said, "We can be sure in a few seconds. I've got a rule." He took a steel foot rule from one of the pockets of his spacesuit and laid it down on a flat expanse of rock. He picked up a loose bit of rock and made a scratch opposite each end of the rule.

Evadne walked over near Crag. Her eyes, through the plastic of the helmet, looked into his intensely, searchingly. He got the idea that she wanted to ask him a question and didn't dare—because Olliver would have heard it too—but was trying to find the answer by looking at him and reading his face. He met her gaze squarely, trying to guess what she was thinking or wondering. It hadn't anything to do, he felt sure just then, with the fact that he was a man and she a woman. It was something more important than that.

He heard Olliver's voice say, "*I think so. I think it's— Wait, let's be sure.*"

He turned away from Evadne and watched Olliver as Olliver watched the rule and the scratches on the rock. There was tension among them, but no one spoke. A minute or two went by, and then Olliver stood up and faced them.

His eyes were shining—almost as though with madness—but his voice was calm now. He said, "It works." He looked from one to the other of them and then his eyes stopped on Crag. He said, "Crag, your million credits is waste paper. How would you like to be second in command of the Solar System?"

For the first time, Crag wondered if Olliver were mad. The thought must have showed in his face, for Olliver shook his head. "I'm not crazy, Crag. Nor do I know any commercial use for neutronium. That was camouflage. Listen, Crag— *A few of these little gadgets set up in hidden places on each of the occupied planets, set up with radio controls so they can be triggered off from wherever I may be—that's all it will take.* If this works on an asteroid–and it has—it'll work on an object of any size. A chain reaction doesn't care whether it works in a peanut or a planet."

Crag said slowly, "You mean—"

"You might as well know all of it, Crag. There isn't any political party behind this. That was just talk. The only way peace can be kept in the system is by the rule of *one man*. But I'll need help, Crag, and you're the man I'd rather have, in spite of—" His voice changed. "Evadne, that's useless."

Crag looked quickly toward the woman and saw that she'd pulled a heater from the pocket of her spacesuit and was aiming it at Olliver. Olliver laughed. He said, "I thought it was about time for you to show your colors, my dear. I expected that, really. I took the charge out of that heater."

Evadne pulled the trigger and nothing happened. Crag saw her face go pale—but it seemed anger rather than fear.

She said, "All right, you beat me on that one, Jon. But someone will stop you, somehow. Do you realize that you couldn't do what you plan without destroying a planet or two—billions of lives, Jon—and that Earth itself would have to be one of the ones you destroyed? Because Earth is the—the fightingest one and wouldn't knuckle under to you, even on a threat like that? Jon, you'd kill off more than half of the human race, just to rule the ones who are left!"

She didn't drop the useless heater, but it hung at her side.

Olliver had one in his own hand now. He said, "Take it away from her, Crag."

Crag looked from one of them to the other. And he looked around him. The asteroid *was* shrinking. There was now a definite diminution in diameter, perhaps by a tenth.

Olliver spoke again and more sharply. "Take it away from her, Crag."

Olliver's blaster covered both of them. He could have killed Evadne where she stood; the command was meaningless, and Crag knew it was a test. Olliver was making him line up, one way or the other.

Crag thought of Earth, that he hated. And he thought of it as a dead little ball of heavy matter—and he didn't hate it that much. But to be second in command—not of a world, but of *worlds*—

Olliver said, "Your last chance, Crag. And listen—don't think I'm blind to you and Evadne. But I didn't care. She's been spying on me all along. I know the outfit she belongs to—a quixotic group that's trying to end system-wide corruption another way, a way that won't work. She's a spy, Crag, and I don't want her.

"Here are my final terms and you've got a few seconds to decide. Disarm her now, and I won't kill her. We'll take her back, and you can have her if you're silly enough to want her—out of billions of women who'll be yours for the taking."

Maybe that was all it took. Crag decided.

He reached for Evadne with his good hand, seeing the look of cold contempt in her eyes—and the puzzlement in her eyes as he swung her around instead of reaching for the useless gun she held. He said quickly, *"Night side!"* He propelled her forward ahead of him and then ran after her. He hoped Olliver's reflexes would be slow. They *had* to be.

On a tiny and shrinking asteroid, the horizon isn't far. It was a few steps on this one, and they were over it in less than a second. He heard Olliver curse and felt a wave of heat go past him, just too late. And then they were in the darkness.

He found Evadne by running into her and grabbed her and held on because there wasn't going to be much time. In seconds, Olliver would realize that he didn't have to come after them, that all he had to do was to get into the ship and warp off—or even just close the door and sit it out until they were dead. Even though Olliver wasn't a qualified pilot he could, with the help of the manual of instructions inside the ship, have a fair chance of getting it back to Earth or Mars.

So Crag said quickly, "I can stop him. But it's curtains for both of us, too. Shall I?"

She caught her breath, but there wasn't any hesitation in her answer. "Hurry, Crag. Hurry."

He ran on around the night side—ten steps—to the ship. He braced his feet as he lifted it and then threw it out into space—the whole pound weight of it. It seemed to go slowly, but it kept going. It would keep going for a long time, from that throw, It might come back, eventually, but not for hours—and the air in spacesuits of this type was good for only half an hour or so without processing or renewal.

Olliver would never rule a system now, only the tiniest world.

But all three of them were dead. He heard Olliver scream madly with rage and saw him come running over the horizon for a shot at him. Crag laughed and ducked back into blackness. He ran into Evadne, who had followed him. He caught her quickly as he crashed into her. He said, "Give me the heater, quick," and took it from her hand.

He could see Olliver standing there, heater in hand, just where the spaceship had been, peering into the darkness, trying to see where to shoot them. But he could see Olliver and Olliver, on the day side, couldn't see him.

He'd rather have had his metal hand to throw—he was used to using that and could hit a man's head at twenty or thirty feet. But the heater-gun would serve now; Olliver wasn't even ten feet away and he couldn't miss.

He didn't miss. The missile shattered Olliver's helmet,

Crag walked forward into the light, keeping between Evadne and Olliver so she wouldn't have to see. A man whose helmet has been shattered in space isn't a pleasant sight.

He reached down and got the disintegrator out of Olliver's pocket. He used it.

Evadne came up and took his arm as he stood there, looking upward, seeing a distant gleam of sunlight on an object that was still moving away from them. He wished now he hadn't thrown the spaceship so hard; had he tossed it lightly it might conceivably have returned before the air in his and Evadne's spacesuits ran out. But he couldn't have been sure he could get Olliver before Olliver, who had a loaded heater, could get him. And when the asteroid got small enough, the night side would no longer have been a protection. You can hide on the night side of a world—but not when it gets as small as a basketball.

Evadne said, "Thanks, Crag. You were— Is *wonderful* too hackneyed a word?"

Crag grinned at her. He said, "It's a wonderful word."

He put his arms around her,

And then laughed. Here he was with two hundred thousand credits—a fortune—in his pocket and the most beautiful woman he'd ever seen. And her arms were around him too and—you can't even kiss a woman in a spacesuit! Any more than you can spend a fortune on an asteroid without even a single tavern on it.

An asteroid that was now less than ten yards in diameter.

Evadne laughed too, and he was glad, very glad of that. It *was* funny—if you saw it that way—and it made things easier in this last moment that she could see it that way too,

He saw she was breathing with difficulty. She said, "Crag—my dear—this suit must not have had its tank fully charged with oxygen. I'm afraid I can't—stay with you much longer."

He held her tighter. He couldn't think of anything to say.

She said, "But we stopped him, Crag. Someday humanity will get itself out of the mess it's in now. And when it does, there'll still—be an Earth—for it to live on."

"Was he right, Evadne? I mean, about your being a member of some secret organization?"

"No. He either made that up or imagined it. I was—just his wife, Crag. But I'd stopped loving him months ago. I knew, though, he planned to buy or steal that gadget of Eisen's—he'd have got it somehow, even if we hadn't helped him, And I suspected, but didn't know, that he was planning something—bad. I stayed with him so I'd have a chance to try to stop him if—I was right."

She was breathing harder. Her arms tightened around him. She said, "Crag, I want that—gadget. I'll use it on myself; I won't ask you to. But it will be sudden and painless, not—like this." She was fighting for every breath now, but she laughed again. "Guess I'm lying, Crag. I'm not afraid to die either way. But I've—seen people who died—*this* way and they're—well—I don't want you to see me—like that. I'd—rather—"

He pressed it into her hand. He tightened his arms one last time and then stepped quickly back because he could hear and see how much pain she was in now, how every breath was becoming agony for her. He looked away, as he knew she wanted him to.

And when he looked back, after a little while, there was nothing there to see; nothing at all.

Except the disintegrator itself, lying there on a sphere now only six feet across. He picked it up. There was still one thing to do. Someone, sometime, might find this collapsed asteroid, attracted to it by the fact that his detector showed a mass greater than the bulk shown in a visiplate. If he found the gadget clinging there beside it—

He was tempted to use it instead, to take the quicker way instead of the slower, more painful one. But he took it apart, throwing each tiny piece as far out into space as he could. Maybe some of them would form orbits out there and maybe others would fall back. But no one would ever gather *all* the pieces and manage to put them together again.

He finished, and the world he lived on was less than a yard in diameter now and it was still shrinking. He disconnected his gravplates because there wasn't any use trying to stand on it. But it was as heavy as it had ever been; there was still enough gravitational pull to keep him bumping gently against it. Of course he could push himself away from it now and go sailing off into space. But he didn't. Somehow, it was companionship.

A small world, he thought, and getting smaller.

The size of an orange now. He laughed as he put it into his pocket.

Gateway to Glory

CHAPTER I

There was this Crag, and he was a criminal and a killer and just about the toughest guy in the solar system. But it wasn't doing him much good right then because he was dying.

He was dying on a world no bigger than an orange. It had been an asteroid a little bigger than a house when he'd landed on it—with Jon Olliver and Evadne—less than an hour before.

And when he, Crag, had learned about Olliver's plans, he'd made a damn fool hero of himself; he'd shoved the spaceship off into space so none of them could get away again, ever. Then he'd managed to kill Olliver before Olliver had killed him and the atoms that had made up Olliver's body were now one with the collapsed atoms of the asteroid that was now too small a world to live on, but not to die on.

Already the oxygen tank of his spacesuit was almost empty; he was breathing hard and painfully. Too bad, he thought, that he'd had to destroy the disintegrator instead of using it on himself to shorten the final agony—as Evadne, beautiful Evadne—had been able to do when the air in her spacesuit had run out.

And Crag was dying now; he'd be dead in ten minutes or maybe five. And it was funny; he wanted to laugh because he had two hundred thousand credits, a fortune, in his pocket. And ten minutes ago, for the first time, he'd had the most beautiful woman he'd ever known in his arms and she had loved him. But you can't spend a fortune on an asteroid, especially one that's been collapsed into neutronium, and you can't get much satisfaction out of loving a woman in a spacesuit in the void.

Crag laughed. This was a piece with everything that had happened to him since the day, years ago, that he'd lost his rating as a spaceman when he'd lost his left hand cleaning a tube that had accidentally fired. He had been cheated out of his compensation, on a technicality, by the corrupt officialdom of the spaceways. He'd turned criminal then, and had been as ruthless to society as it had been to him. And this wasn't bad, compared to some of the ways he'd almost died, or worse than died, a dozen times before. Dying from lack of oxygen isn't exactly painless, but he'd endured worse pain, and stoically, and in situations that lacked the anodyne of humor, however bitter humor, that this one had.

A world in his pocket! When the disintegrated asteroid had collapsed into a solid little ball of neutronium, that unbelievably heavy stuff from which some of the stars are made, he'd put it in his pocket. Of course, actually, because of their relative mass, he'd moved his own body in relation to it rather than the other way around, but that was a detail. He took it out of his pocket now and looked at it in the dim light of the distant sun. There on the surface of it were the collapsed atoms that had been Evadne, Evadne of the lushly beautiful body and the hair like burnished copper, the eyes that were a deeper blue than space seen through an atmosphere. No one could recognize her now.

He thought how wonderful it would have been if Evadne had lived and if he were going to live. Or would it? There would have been no place for them, anywhere in the system. Crag sighed and it was such a strange sound that he realized it was the first time he'd done so for years. He was getting soft. Well, it didn't matter now. And it had been a rasping sigh because his body was fighting for breath.

He wished that he had enough control over his body to tell it to stop fighting, but no man, not even one as tough as Crag, can force his lung muscles to quit a struggle for breath.

Suddenly a voice inside his mind said, "What is wrong?" Not the words, but the thought.

It startled him because he was alone, more alone than he'd ever been before. It was like the way the telepathic semi-savages of Venus spoke to one, yet clearer, even more sharp than that, more nearly like an actual voice. One you could almost hear.

He looked around him and there was nothing but the void, distant Sol, the stars, and closer but still many miles away, the pinpoint reflections of the asteroids. And out there somewhere, although he couldn't spot it at the moment, was the spaceship he'd pushed away from the asteroid. But nowhere life. Who or what had spoken inside his mind?

He concentrated on the thought: *Who are you?*

"I do not know. I thought to discover the answer from you, but 1 do not find it in your mind. I find many confused things, but not that. I find pain and the thought that you are going to cease to exist. Why? What is wrong?"

"Oxygen," Crag thought. "I am dying from lack of oxygen."

"Do not think of the word," came the thought in his mind. "Think of the thing itself. I perceive now from your mind that it is a gas, that it is an element. Think of its structure."

Crag was not a physicist, but the atomic structure of oxygen is a comparatively simple one. He thought of it, pictured it.

And suddenly he wasn't fighting for breath any longer; he was breathing normally.

"That is better," came the alien thought. "Now will you think thoughts that will tell me who and what you are, why you are here and what has happened? From that, I can possibly determine who and what *I* am, how I came to be. I think it will be best if you tell it as though you were talking, but try to think, too, of the meanings of the words as you use them."

Crag said, "All right. I am Crag. A man named Olliver hired me to steal a device from a scientist, one that—I realize now—the scientist had suppressed because it was too dangerous to use; it could have destroyed entire planets. It was a disintegrator; it collapsed atoms into neutronium, setting up a chain reaction in any reasonably homogeneous substance, so that, although tiny, it could have destroyed Earth or Mars or Venus.

"I gave it to Olliver. Three of us—Olliver, his wife Evadne, and I—came here in Olliver's spaceship to try out the device. We landed on an asteroid and used the disintegrator on it; it collapsed, gradually, into a tiny ball of almost infinitely heavy matter, hundreds of tons to the square inch.

"While it was doing so, Olliver told us his plans and we learned that he had lied about them. He intended taking over rule of the solar system through his threat to destroy any planet that opposed him. He would have had to destroy at least one planet to rule the others.

"I learned then that Evadne was against him. She had hated him but had stayed with him because she suspected what his plans were and hoped to stop them. In the showdown, I sided with Evadne."

"Why?" came the thought.

Crag grinned. "I guess I'm not as much of a crook as Olliver was. I've killed plenty of people, but they all needed killing. It's a pretty corrupt place, right now, the solar system. I wouldn't have minded Olliver ruling it; he couldn't have been any worse than those who run it now. But I found out I didn't hate it enough to let a planet or two—and several billion people—be destroyed in order to put him into power. And maybe, too, because I found out that I—" he hesitated at the thought "—loved Evadne.

"Anyway, Olliver tried to kill us and I killed him. Evadne's oxygen ran out first and she used the disintegrator on herself rather than die more slowly. I would have, too, but I had to destroy the disintegrator so it would never be found. That is all until you asked in my mind, 'What is wrong?' All right, now what's this business about you not knowing who you are? How *can* you not know who you are or even what you are?"

"I am beginning to understand," said the thought in Crag's mind. "Will you concentrate on all you know of—matter, energy and thought?"

It wasn't a lot, and didn't take long. Crag knew only the general outlines of current theories. He knew more about rocket motors, spacewarp, and picking locks.

The thought in his mind said, "I understand, now. I am a new entity, a new consciousness created in the collapse of the atoms of the asteroid upon which the disintegrator was used. Even as matter can be converted to energy through fission, so matter can be converted to consciousness through disintegration."

Crag thought. It seemed possible. He'd wondered what had happened to the energy that had kept the atoms and molecules apart, once they had collapsed into that tiny, incredibly heavy ball he held in his hand. Matter into energy; energy into consciousness. Why not? And why not the third step: could consciousness create matter?

He'd been thinking, but he might as well have spoken aloud. The voice in his mind answered him. "I do not know. Perhaps, a strong enough consciousness. Not mine, any more than yours. No, I did not create oxygen in the tank of your suit. I—think of the word, please. Yes, I transmuted matter that was already there into the form of matter on which you concentrated. 1 can change the form of matter, I can cause it to move; I cannot create it. Now, what shall I do for you?"

Crag laughed. An asteroid—yes, he supposed that the ball of collapsed matter in his hand was still an asteroid regardless of its form—was asking him what it could do for him.

"There is a spaceship nearby," he said, "Can you bring it back, or take me to it? It's the ship we came in. I shoved it and the asteroid—you—apart to prevent Olliver from getting away in it."

"Yes, I perceive it. I can move it from here. I am doing so. It is coming toward us."

Crag looked around and saw it: a gray spot in Orion, growing slowly larger. He laughed again; he was going to spend that two hundred thousand dollars after all! Incredibly, he was going to live and to return to civilization, such as it was.

The asteroid caught the thought in his mind. It said, "Think about your civilization, Crag. Concentrate on it, that I may learn about it. It seems a strange, corrupt thing. I do not like it."

Sudden fear hit Crag. He had stopped Olliver's plans to take over and rule the solar system by destroying one or more planets of it. But had something even more dangerous happened? Would—

"No," said the asteroid. "Do not fear that, Crag. I would neither destroy nor rule your race or any other. I am not a monster. I am neither good nor evil. I think that I know what I am going to do, to become. But it will not affect the race to which you belong."

Crag relaxed his mind. Somehow, he knew that that was true.

He thought, "Anyway, do not judge the human race by my opinion of it. I am a criminal, every hand against me and my hand against every man—especially the metal hand that is my best weapon. Men have treated me badly; I have repaid them in kind. But do not judge them by what I think of them. Perhaps I am more warped than they."

"I do not think so. Please concentrate on how the system is governed."

Crag let his mind think about the two parties—both equally crooked and corrupt—that ran the planets between them, mostly by cynical horse trading methods that betrayed the common people on both sides. The Guilds and the Syndicates—popularly known as the Guilds and the Gildeds—one purporting to represent capital and the other purporting to represent labor, but actually betraying it at every opportunity. Both parties getting together to rig elections so they might win alternately and preserve an outward appearance of a balance of power and a democratic government. Justice, if any, obtainable only by bribery. Objectors or would-be reformers—and there weren't many of either—eliminated by the hired thugs and assassins both parties used. Strict censorship of newspapers, radio and television, extending even to novels lest a writer attempt to slip in a phrase that might imply that the government under which he lived was less than perfect.

Crag thought of instance after instance until the voice in his mind said, "Enough. Your spaceship is here."

He looked around and saw it; the handle of the door was within reach. He opened it and climbed in; the sphere of neutronium that had been an asteroid and was now a sentient being floated gently beside him, obviously managing in some way to neutralize its own mass in relation to that of the spaceship.

Crag turned on the airmaker. The spaceship was too small to have an airlock; on ships of such size it is more economical to let the air escape when leaving and build up an atmosphere again after return and before removing spacesuits. He watched the gauge, and while he was waiting for the air pressure to build up, he asked, "What now? What do you wish me to do?"

"You are very tired; you have not slept for several days. I suggest that you sleep."

"And you?"

"I intend to visit the planets to see at first hand what you have told me. I shall return by the time you awaken."

"You mean you can—" Crag started to question, and then stopped. After the powers he had seen the newborn entity exhibit already, he didn't doubt that it could do anything it said it could, even to an investigation of all of the planets and a return within a few hours.

Then it occurred to him that if the sphere was going to leave the ship, he was wasting time building up air pressure; might as well get the opening and closing of the lock over with first. He turned, but the sphere didn't seem to be anywhere around. He thought, "Where are you?"

The answering thought inside his brain was very faint. "Three hundred thousand miles toward Mars. Await my return, Crag."

CHAPTER II

Three hundred thousand miles, Crag thought, and the sphere couldn't have been gone more than seconds; it must be able to move itself at almost the speed of light! Not by teleportation, either; that would have been instantaneous.

He turned back to the gauge and saw that the air pressure was sufficient; he took off his spacesuit and made sure that the two hundred thousand credits were still safe in his pocket. Then he sighed with weariness and lay down on one of the twin bunks on either side of the ship.

He was too tired to go directly to sleep, too stunned by all that had happened to wonder much at it. He knew that after he'd slept he'd doubt it all and find the existence of the sphere of neutronium as a living entity incredible. Now he accepted it calmly. He even missed it; it had been companionship out here in the void. Although as a criminal Crag always played a lone hand, he didn't like to be alone at other times, especially out here in the void, probably a million miles from the nearest other human. Not even that near unless the other human or humans were on a spaceship curving around the asteroid belt on a run between one of the inner planets and one of the three habitable moons of Jupiter, the only inhabited bodies outside of the inner planets.

He tried to keep from thinking of Evadne, of how beautiful she was the first time he had seen her, even in the severe costume of a technician, and how impossibly like a flame she had been when he had seen her next, dressed in an evening gown which was little more than a wisp of material above the waist and fitting her hips and thighs like a sheath. He tried not to think of the blue of her eyes or the soft copper of her hair, the creamy smoothness of her skin. And so, of course, he thought of all these things.

He tried not to think of the one time she had kissed him, and his lips burned and then felt cold.

And above all, he tried not to remember that, only hours ago, they had been in one another's arms—in spacesuits in the void. If only her suit had contained its full supply of oxygen so she could have lived a little longer, as long as he had, until the awakening intelligence of the newborn entity that had been an asteroid had made mental contact and learned enough of thought and of itself to ask that question, "What is wrong?" that had changed everything.

If only— But why think of futile ifs, now that Evadne was dead? So, of course, he thought of them.

When he got back to Earth—no, to Mars; it was nearer—he'd get himself drunk on some of the most expensive and fancy liquors of the solar system. Then maybe he could quit thinking about her. And you can stay drunk a long time on two hundred thousand credits. You could stay drunk a thousand years on that much money, if you could live that long.

But you can't live at all if you can't sleep, so after a while Crag got up and hunted through the medical compartment until he found some sleeping powders. He took two of them in spite of the "Danger. Take only one" warning on the box.

And after a while he slept.

He awoke finally with a dull, lost feeling that he'd seldom had before except in jail. The small narrow bunk, the close confines of the ship to which he opened his eyes seemed like a cell to him. He reached into his pocket to be sure the money was still there and it was,

He wanted a drink worse than he'd ever wanted one in his life. What was he doing on a spaceship drifting idly out here in the void? Why hadn't he taken it into Marsport before he'd slept? Then he could have slept comfortably, luxuriously, in the best suite of the best Marsport hotel with a bottle to help him to sleep and to reach for when he awakened.

He swung his feet off the bunk and sat up. There, floating in the middle of the cabin, was the sentient sphere that had been an asteroid.

"You were right, Crag," spoke the voice in his mind.

Crag wondered what he'd been right about.

"About the corruptness of the race to which you belong. It is even worse than you thought of it as being. I have been inside many minds. They are weak minds, almost without exception morally weak."

Crag grinned. He thought, "I'm no lily myself."

"You are not, but you are strong. You are a criminal because you are a rebel against a society that has no place for strong men. In a society that is good, the weak are criminals; in a society that is bad, there is no place for a strong man except as a criminal. You are better than they, Crag. You have killed men, but you have killed them fairly. Your society kills them corruptly, by inches. Worse, those who are being killed acquiesce, not only because they are weak, but because they, too, hope to get on the exploiting side."

"You make the human race sound pretty bad."

"It *is* bad. This is a period of decadence. It has been better and it will be better again. I have studied your history and find that there were similar periods before and humanity has struggled out of them. It will again, Crag."

Crag yawned. He said, "You turned carbon dioxide to oxygen in my spacesuit. You wouldn't, by any chance, care to turn the water in that cooler into something stronger, would you? I could use a drink."

He felt in his mind a sense of amusement that was not his own, as though the entity that spoke there was laughing. The thought in his mind said, "Buy yourself your own drinks, Crag. You can afford them, and you can wait till you get to Marsport. I have something more important to do than to be a bartender for you."

"Such as?" Crag asked.

"To create a world."

Crag sat up straight and quit feeling sleepy. He said, *"What?"* aloud.

"Or possibly re-create one. There seems to be a difference of opinion among your astronomers as to whether the asteroids once formed a planet which broke up into many small pieces—of which I was one—or whether the gasses which, in the case of other planets, solidified into spheres, in the case of the asteroids formed a ring of gasses instead and solidified into many small bodies, planetoids.

"In either case, the matter for another planet is there, revolving around the sun in orbits between the orbit of Mars and the orbit of Jupiter. It is merely necessary to gather and coalesce them and there will be a new planet—or a scattered one will be re-created."

Crag started to ask why and then, instead, began to wonder why not. Neither question was answered.

Instead, the voice in his mind went on, quite calmly, "It is merely necessary for me to gather the other asteroids about myself as a nucleus. When all have been gathered, the planet will be larger than Mars, perhaps almost as large as Earth.

"It will be a new planet, a raw planet. It will need tough colonists, Crag. I want you to gather a few—criminals like yourself, who do not acquiesce in the social system of the rest of your race. Ones who are tough, not soft and weak like the others. Colonize and people me, Crag, with strong men like yourself."

Crag stared at the sphere. He asked softly, "Is that an *order?*"

"Of course not. It is a request. I can see into your mind enough to realize that you would die rather than obey an order—even if it was an order to do something you *wanted* to do. And that is why I want you, and men like you, to colonize the planet I shall create. Men who will not take orders." There was a pause and then the voice in Crag's mind said, *"I do not want to be a god,* Crag. I would not be colonized by anyone who *would* obey me. And yet I want people to live upon me."

Crag said, "You won't lack for people. If a new planet forms in the solar system—"

"No one will colonize me if I do not wish them to live there. I shall have a poisonous atmosphere, Crag. Poisonous to anyone I do not want. Crag, can you find other men who are, mentally and physically, as hard and as strong as you?"

"Perhaps, but—"

"I see your hesitation. On Earth or Mars you will be rich, with the two hundred thousand credits you have. They would be worthless on a new planet. You are right, but I think and hope you will soon tire of whatever that money will bring you. You are too strong to like a soft life. I think you will come to me. And when you do, bring others if you can—but they must be strong, too."

Crag said slowly, "I'll see. I'll think it over."

"Good. That is all I ask. Goodbye, Crag."

"Goodbye," Crag thought. Belatedly he remembered that the sphere had saved his life ten hours before when he had been dying in the void, The sphere was no longer there, but he thought "—and thanks," anyway, hoping that, even at the incredible speed at which it could travel, it would still catch the thought.

He stood up and stretched to get the stiffness of his long sleep out of his muscles. Then lie picked the lock on the controls and set course for Mars. Not for Marsport, of course, or any other city. The spaceship was registered in Olliver's name, and if he landed it in any spaceport, he'd have to explain what had happened to Olliver, and that wouldn't be easy. And even if he himself got through the hands of the spaceport guards and the police, the two hundred thousand credits definitely would not.

He put the ship down in the Martian desert, carefully choosing a spot where red sand dunes screened it from sight and it could be seen only from above. A patrol craft would probably spot it sooner or later, but it *might* still be there if he ever wanted or needed it. Long experience had taught him that it was good to have a possible ace in the hole, even with a fortune in his pocket.

It was early morning when he landed and he left the ship at once so he could reach civilization before the extreme heat of midday. Aside from the money, he carried nothing with him except a compass and a small paragun in case he should encounter any of the monster lizards of the Martian desert.

He met none, however, and reached the settlement of New Boston before the sun was halfway to the zenith. He chartered a plane there and was in Marsport before noon.

He spent a hundred credits for a fine wardrobe and luggage to contain it, then took an aircab to the Luxor, finest and most expensive hotel in a city whose major industry was catering to wealthy visitors from Earth.

The desk clerk stared disdainfully at Crag through pince-nez glasses. His gaze went to the four porters who were carrying Crag's new and expensive luggage. But so little of it!

His voice was cold and distant. "You have a reservation, of course, Mr.—ah."

"That's right," Crag said. "Mr. Ah. George Ah, to be exact. And I have no reservation, but I want the finest suite you have available."

"I am afraid, Mr.—ah—Ah, that there is nothing available."

Crag grinned. "If you'll take in my card to the manager, I'm sure he'll be able to arrange something."

He put down a ten-credit bill—at least a week's pay for the desk clerk, even of as swanky a hotel as the Luxor—on the desk.

The clerk's eyes warmed somewhat behind the pince-nez; they became no colder than hailstones and somewhat more protuberant. He said, "Pardon me, sir. I'll check the register." He didn't touch the ten-credit bill, but he pulled a crocodile-bound ledger from under the desk and covered the bill with it while he thumbed through pages. After a moment, he said, "The Gubernatorial Suite is open, sir. Twenty credits a day."

"I'll take it," Crag said. He signed "George Ah" on the register.

In the twenty-by-twenty living room of the suite, he tipped the four porters generously and then, as they left, looked about him. Doors indicated that he must have several other rooms at his disposal, but he walked out first onto the balcony and stood looking over the fabulous city of Marsport that lay below him in the bright, hot afternoon sun.

He felt strange here; he wondered for the first time what he, Crag, was doing here. It was the first time in his life that he had ever registered in a luxury hotel. It was plenty expensive—twenty credits a day was a month's wages on an average skilled job—but he had plenty of money and he should be safer here than in any inexpensive lodging. In Marsport, the more money you spent the less likely you were to be asked questions. If you spent money like water they figured you were a capitalist, a politician or a labor leader.

After a few minutes he went back inside, closing the balcony door on the afternoon heat, and wondered what he should do. He was going to get drunk, of course, but why rush it? Plenty of time for that. The rest of his life, in fact.

He tried opening doors. The first led to a well-stocked liquor cabinet. He poured himself one drink of Martian woji, hoping it would make him feel a bit more cheerful, but it didn't. He tried the next door and it led to a library that was well stocked with books, records and tapes. He wandered about it briefly, noting that most of the books were pornographic; that meant that the tapes were probably pornographic also.

A double door in front of a pneumatic divan turned out to open on a television screen eight feet wide and six feet high. Crag turned on the switch and sat down on the divan. It was a musical show originating in New York on Earth. Before a three-dimensional chorus undulating in full color a pale tenor was singing:

Jet up! Jet down! On a slow ship to Pluto!
Honey-wunny-bunny, how'd you like my...

Crag got up and turned off the switch. He went back and had himself another drink at the liquor cabinet. It didn't taste particularly good to him.

He tried another door. It led to a smaller sitting room, well supplied with gambling equipment of all kinds, the walls lined with solitaire gambling machines. Crag knew that all the machines would be rigged with high percentages against him and didn't bother trying them. Besides, what's the fun in gambling when you've already got more money than you know what to do with?

Another door led to the master bedroom. It was even larger than the living room and more ornately furnished. The ebony bed was at least eight feet wide and was ornately furnished, indeed; a blonde, a brunette and a redhead, all naked, lay upon it. For just a second, Crag thought that the redhead looked like Evadne. But she didn't.

She was the one, though, that caught his eye. She sat up and raised her arms above her head, stretching like a kitten as she smiled at him. "Hello," she said.

Crag leaned against the jamb of the door. He asked, "Are you standard equipment? Pardon my ignorance, but I've never had a gubernatorial suite before."

The redhead laughed. "Of course. But you needn't keep *all* of us. Unless you wish." She looked demurely at her gilded toenails. The blonde smiled at him and then rolled over on her back, apparently figuring that she showed off to better advantage that way. She did. The brunette gave him a gamin grin. "We're more fun three at a time," she said. "We know tricks."

Crag said, "Get out. All of you."

They didn't argue; they didn't even seem offended or even annoyed. They got up calmly and went past him through the doorway of the bedroom and on out through the outer door into the hallway, still stark naked but apparently completely unaware of the fact.

Crag went over and made sure that the door was locked behind them. Then he went to the liquor closet and poured himself another drink. He noticed, for the first time, the pornographic murals above the bar of the liquor closet. He took the bottle of woji with him, and the glass. He slammed the door of the closet.

He drank that drink slowly, thinking and trying not to think.

There was a soft knock on the door. Crag put down his glass and went to answer it. A bellboy stood there just outside the door, smiling at him. A very beautiful young man, rosy and handsome, with soft ringlets of curly hair.

He said, "The management sent me, sir. Since you did not want— Is there anything I can do for you?"

Crag grinned and pretended to look him over carefully. He said, "Turn around."

The young man smiled knowingly and turned gracefully around. He had a pleasingly plump posterior; he wriggled it a trifle, provocatively.

Crag drew back his foot and kicked hard.

He closed the door gently.

CHAPTER III

He wandered about the suite, wondering idly if there wasn't a cabinet of narcotics anywhere; it was equipped for everything else. But the management would probably send up any kind of dope you wanted if you phoned for it.

He found the dials of a newsradio in the wall and turned it on. Just before the end of a broadcast. "...in the asteroid belt," said the radio. "Scientists of both Mars and Earth are working on the problem, but have failed thus far to advance an acceptable theory to account for the unprecedented and incredible phenomenon. This concludes the newscast that started at three o'clock; the next newscast will be presented at four, Marsport time."

Crag glanced at his wristchrono and saw that there would be three-quarters of an hour to wait. He went to the phone and asked for the manager. An obsequious voice told him to wait a moment and a moment later a smooth voice said, "Carleton, manager, speaking."

"George Ah, suite two hundred," Crag said. "I just tuned in on the tail end of a newscast—Marsport news station—concerning something happening in the asteroid belt. Could you arrange with the station to have that part of the newscast played back for me immediately from the recording that was made of it at the time?"

"I fear, Mr. Ah, that would involve rewiring of the newscast set in your room. It is automatically tuned to the main carrier wave of—"

"Over the phone," Crag said. "Just put a call through to the station and have them play back that part of the newscast over the phone for me."

"I'll see if that can be arranged, Mr. Ah. If you'll please cradle your phone, I'll call you back as soon as..."

Crag cradled the phone and sat down beside it until the buzzer buzzed. He picked it up again.

"It can be arranged," said the manager's voice. "There will be a charge of ten credits. Is that satisfactory?"

"Arrange it," Crag said. "Hurry."

As he put the phone down again and watched it, he wondered what the hurry was. What went on out in the asteroid belt didn't concern him. *He* wasn't going to be sap enough to give up the soft life he could have here for anything as ridiculous as starting a colony of criminals on a new and raw planet.

But just the same he watched the phone, his impatience mounting until it buzzed again.

"The station is ready, sir. The management of the Luxor is glad to have been able to arrange..."

"Get off the wire, then," Crag said.

There was a short wait and then came the voice of the announcer of the newscast: "According to many reliable reports, a strange and incredible phenomenon is taking place in the asteroid belt. First report came in eight hours ago from Marsport astronomers who were observing the asteroid Ceres—largest of the asteroids, with a diameter of four hundred and eighty miles—when it vanished from the telescope, which had been set to follow its course automatically. When found again, it had changed speed greatly and direction slightly. The directional change was quickly analyzed by the computing machine and it was found that Ceres had now lost the eccentric and parabolic aspects of its orbit; it was following a perfectly circular orbit about the sun, perfectly in the plane of the ecliptic.

"When Ceres was found to be steady in its new orbit, observation was made of other of the asteroids—those large enough to be observable. Hidalgo, whose eccentricity is point six five, was found with difficulty, considerably out of its former orbit; its new orbit, upon analysis, also proved to be a perfect circle in the plane of the ecliptic, an orbit coinciding with that of Ceres—and Hidalgo is traveling at a far greater speed. Hidalgo will overtake and crash into Ceres within hours.

"The most amazing thing is that the speed of the asteroid Hidalgo in its new orbit and in relation to its mass is impossible according to the laws of angular momentum. Marsport Observatory immediately communicated with the other observatories of Mars and of Earth and for six hours now all telescopes in the system have been trained on the asteroids.

"No single asteroid large enough to be observable in a telescope is in its former orbit! All are now in, or moving toward, the same identical orbit—a perfect circle which lies exactly halfway between the mean distance of Mars and the mean distance of Jupiter from the sun. And as they are moving at different speeds, they will all crash together and *form a new planet.*

"If it can be assumed that the smaller asteroids—those which cannot be seen telescopically—are joining in this movement, then the new planet being formed will be slightly larger than Mars.

"Spaceships are now converging upon the asteroid belt to watch the incredible development at close hand. An event of cosmic importance is taking place in the asteroid belt. Scientists of both Earth and Mars are working on the problem, but have failed thus far to advance an acceptable theory to account for..."

Crag put the phone back in its cradle; that was where he'd tuned in on the newscast a few minutes before.

He thought, *So the little devil is really doing it.* He grinned and poured himself a drink from the woji bottle.

The grin faded slowly as he drank.

The shadows lengthened and vanished and it grew dark, and after a while he went out on the balcony and stood staring up at the moon Phobos hurtling across the Martian sky and after a while longer Deimos, too, rose.

He wondered why he couldn't get drunk and why, with so much money, he wasn't happy.

He stared upward and located the plane of the ecliptic—the plane in which the planets revolve and which, to an observer on any planet, is an imaginary line. He followed it through the familiar constellations, brighter through the thinner air of Mars than they are from Earth, until he found an unfamiliar dot in the constellation Virgo. He watched it for half an hour until he was sure that it was moving in relation to the stars around it. No other planet was then in Virgo; it must be the new one.

But he wasn't going there. Nothing would be crazier than to give up his sudden wealth for the rough life of a new planet.

He went back inside the suite and turned on the radio. The announcer was talking about the elections on Earth, pretending that there was a doubt of their outcome, that they hadn't been decided and bargained for in advance between the two parties that were really one.

Crag listened without hearing until the announcer's voice changed to real interest. "Now for the latest reports on the new planet which is forming with incredible rapidity. Observations are being made from spaceships only a few thousand miles away. The new planet is now approximately the size of Mercury.

"It is revolving apparently at random so that each new asteroid to strike it and become part of it hits a different spot and a sphere is being formed. The asteroids, large and small, which are not already a part of it are moving toward it—some with retrograde motion—at many times their former speeds. It is estimated that the last of them will reach the new planet, completing it, within twelve hours or even less. As soon thereafter as the surface has stabilized, landings will be made.

"No decision has been made yet on a name for the new planet. Majority opinion favors giving the honor of naming it to Dr. Henry Wilkins of Marsport Observatory. It was Dr. Wilkins who first observed the perturbation of the orbit of the asteroid Ceres. His report focused attention upon the asteroid belt and led to the discovery that the new planet was being formed."

The newscaster went back to Terrestrial politics and Crag shut off the radio. He thumbed his nose at it and went to the liquor closet for another bottle of woji.

He got drunk. And, as is the way with woji, he sat there, dull physically, but with his mind seeming more clear and brilliant than it had ever seemed before. He remembered everything that had ever happened to him and none of it seemed quite as bad as it had at the time. Not even the time he'd been tortured on Venus; thinking back about it, he had to laugh at the ridiculous seriousness with which the semi-savage Venusians took themselves and everything else. Why be serious? Everything was funny, even the new planet that wanted him, Crag, to colonize it. And bring other criminals, the toughest ones he could find, with him.

Male and female ones both?—or hadn't that ridiculous little sphere which was gathering a new world about it thought of that? He roared with laughter at how stupid the sphere had been not to have thought of that. How long could an all-male colony last?

Still—he had a serious thought—with a planet completely new and raw, perhaps that would be best at the very start, until they had the planet licked. Once they had living quarters and living arrangements and knew what was deadly and what wasn't; that would be the time for a return trip somewhere to pick up women for themselves. Or the others could, anyway.

He, Crag, hated all women—except Evadne, and Evadne was dead. All other women were soft and corrupt, like the one he'd been engaged to so many years ago and who'd deserted him when he'd lost his hand and his spaceman's job. Well, she'd have had some tough times if she'd stuck with him; there wasn't any denying that. But he wondered if she was still alive and what she'd think if she knew where he was now and that he had a fortune in his pocket. Probably come running to see if she could get him back. Women were like that. *Women.*

He laughed harder. And drank more, and his mind became even clearer although some of the laughter went away.

He thought of Evadne, of her lush body and her copper hair and her clear blue eyes that were straight and honest in a world that was as crooked as a poker game in a Martian gambling joint and as ugly as Evadne was beautiful.

And he drank more and he didn't laugh at all; he seemed to see Evadne standing there before him in the dimly lighted room, and he rose to go to her, but when he reached her she wasn't there.

He drank more and became angry and amused himself for a while walking about the suite smashing things that were smashable and some things that— by an ordinary man—wouldn't have been smashable at all. But Crag's missing hand had been replaced by a heavily weighted metal one—although he managed to carry it so lightly that no one suspected what a deadly weapon it was— and he could deal a blow with it that was as quick as the dart of a tsetse fly and had the authority of a sledgehammer. It wasn't a hand you'd want to be slapped with.

He smashed furniture and gambling equipment and the huge television screen and the equipment behind it. The hotel wouldn't mind; they'd simply put it on his bill—as the women and the bellboy and the liquor and even every minute he used the radio would be on his bill. The twenty credits—two hundred dollars—a day that one paid for a suite like this was merely the starting point of all they billed you for.

But after a while he tired of smashing things and drank some more and then lay down on the divan and slept—not using or wanting to use the great seven by eight foot bed in the bedroom.

It was almost noon when he awakened. He felt terrible until he'd groped his way to the liquor cabinet and taken a shot of antihang and then a quick pick-up shot of the fiery Martian liquor.

After that he was able to look about at the shambles he'd made of the place; and to laugh. It looked better that way, he thought.

Just the same, he stopped at the desk on his way out. A tall man in archaic full dress was behind it. Crag said, "The manager, please."

"I am the manager, Mr. Carleton. You are Mr.—ah—Ah?"

"Yes. There was a hurricane in my room last night. You will please have it refurnished immediately. Except, perhaps, for the television set I think I will be happier without a television set. The refurnishing at my expense, of course."

"Of course, sir. We shall have it done at once. There will, also, be put on your bill a charge for temporary incapacitation of the—ah—bellboy."

"Well worth it," Crag said. He went into the restaurant of the hotel and ordered and ate a meal. It was a wonderful meal made up of the choicest viands of three planets and it cost him more than he had earned in a week back in the days when he'd been a spaceman. He wondered why he didn't enjoy it especially. Even the rare vintage wines served with it didn't taste right although he knew that they were the best money could buy.

He wandered into the main gambling saloon and managed to divest himself of forty credits in the *mara* game, but the dealing was so obviously crooked that he played along merely for the privilege of watching so crude an exhibition. Even with only one good hand, he could have done better himself.

Finally, in utter disgust, he slapped his metal left hand down—not too hard—on the hand of the dealer who was passing a card to him. The dealer screamed and dropped two cards, where only one should have been. Then he stepped back, moaning, to nurse his broken hand. Crag left his bet and walked out.

Probably, he thought with grim amusement, he'd be billed for that, too.

He went back up to his suite and found it refurnished and in perfect shape. Even the monster television screen had been replaced; probably they'd billed him for twice its value and hoped he'd break it again.

Again, and more strongly, the sheer magnificence and expensiveness of the suite struck him and he laughed and then wondered, *What am I doing here?*

He poured himself a drink and then wandered over to the wall-radio and turned it on. Politics again. He went to the pneumatic divan and sat down with the bottle in one hand and a glass in the other and managed not to listen to that part of the newscast. But then he found himself leaning slightly forward to listen as, again, the newscaster's voice changed from simulated to genuine interest.

"The new planet between Mars and Jupiter is now complete, a sphere larger than Mars, almost identical with Earth in size. Slightly larger, in fact. Apparently estimates of the total volume of mass of the asteroids erred on the short aide, due to the great number of asteroids too small to have been charted.

"Strangely, considering the suddenness of its formation, the surface seems to be quite stable, free from quakes and convulsions. Landing parties will be organized very soon from among the patrol ships which have been observing the planet's formation. Pardon me a second—

"I have just been handed a bulletin informing me that the new planet has been named. Dr. Wilkins of Marsport Observatory has, with the concurrence of his colleagues, chosen the name Cragon—C-r-a-g-o-n, Cragon."

Crag put back his head and laughed.

CHAPTER IV

He thought, *The little devil names himself after me.* For Crag knew it couldn't be a coincidence that Cragon had been chosen as a name, even though a man he'd never heard of and who had never heard of him had done the choosing. Cragon had named itself; it must have planted that thought in the minds of the astronomers at Marsport Observatory when it had been here on Mars studying conditions and deciding what it was to do.

The announcer was going on. "The name has no special mythological derivation, Dr. Wilkins explains. It was chosen arbitrarily as a euphonious combination of syllables. All other planets, as you know, were named after prominent characters in ancient mythology, but the practice was abandoned after the discovery of so many asteroids that all such names had been used.

"In a few hours we shall be able to give you reports from the first landing parties."

And back to politics and the elections.

Crag shut off the newsradio. He got himself another drink and sat down with it, still chuckling. *Thinks he's going to get me that way*, he thought.

He had a few more drinks and then looked around the suite and decided that he hated it worse than any place he'd ever been in. He wanted to smash things again, but he knew that would be purposeless and that he wouldn't get any real pleasure out of doing it a second time.

But he had to get away from it for a while. He remembered, though, how much money he had and decided it wouldn't be safe to carry all of it. No one would take it away from him while he was conscious, but if he ended up—as he probably would—in a spaceman's dive, he didn't want to have to watch how much he drank.

He thought of putting it in a bank, but that would be even more dangerous; you could trust banks with small amounts, but with a sum like that they'd finagle him out of it some way. Besides, such a deposit in cash might interest government investigators if they heard about it, and they'd investigate him and want to know where he got it. And they'd try to take it away from him if the bank didn't. The vault of the hotel would be even more risky.

He took the money out of his pocket and studied what to do with it. There were still nineteen ten-thousand-credit bills; he'd broken only one of them. He decided that hiding the nineteen bills in various places about the suite would be safest.

He did a good job of hiding them, and when he left he did a bit of work on the lock of the door with some tiny tools he carried; no one could open it but himself when he'd finished with it.

When he got to Spaceman's Row, he thought at first he was on the wrong street. It had changed tremendously, but he remembered now that the change had already started the last time he'd been there, four years before. Some of the dives had been cleaned up and prettied up then; now, they all were. The picturesqueness was gone and if there was any dirt you couldn't see it for neon.

He walked the length of it, looking for a familiar place and failing to find one, before he chose the least garish of the bars and went in.

A few spacemen, with girls, were at the bar drinking and watching a television screen. The spacemen looked young, callow and almost effeminate compared to the men who used to fly the spaceways.

Crag paid no attention to them after a first glance, taking a stool at the bar and facing away from the television screen.

The bartender, although he was dressed in a fancy monkey suit, looked almost human, although his eyes were a little too shifty for Crag's taste.

He grinned when Crag ordered a woji. "Guess you haven't been around Marsport recently. Illegal now."

"Had some this morning," Crag said.

"Must've been at a fancy hotel. The law doesn't bother them, but it's sure clamped down on Spaceman's Row. It ain't what it used to be."

"So I notice."

"Nothing stronger than kodore. No fights now, no nothing. Plenty of women, though. Dope, if you want it, except the kinds that might make you feel scrappy. Nope, it ain't what it used to be."

Crag took the well stuffed wallet from his pocket. He put a five-credit bill on the bar, a dozen times the price of a glass of woji. He looked at the bartender inquiringly.

The bartender looked at the bill and then slid it off the bar and into his pocket. "Just a minute," he said.

Crag nodded and the bartender went through a door at the back and, a moment later, came back through it and nodded at Crag, beckoning.

Crag followed him through the door and closed it behind him. There was a bottle of woji on the table, and a glass. Crag reached for the bottle and the bartender stuck a heat-gun in his side. "Up," he said.

Crag raised his hands—apparently quite casually, but as they reached shoulder level the left hand—the metal one—flicked just slightly against the bartender's chin. The bartender and the heat-gun fell, separately. Crag pocketed the heat-gun.

He sat down at the table and poured himself a drink. After a few minutes the bartender blinked his eyes and then sat up, touching his chin gingerly and wincing. He looked at Crag curiously and Crag grinned at him. "Have a drink," he said. "Get yourself a glass."

The bartender got up slowly and then got himself a glass and another chair. Crag poured him a drink.

The bartender sipped it, staring at Crag. He said slowly, "You hit me with your left hand, lightly. So it's a metal one and weighted. I've heard stories about a guy named Crag. They're almost legends. And he was in Marsport four years ago and so were you. My name's Gardin and I'm sorry I tried to take you."

"That's all right," Crag said. They shook hands.

Gardin said, "Listen, Crag, don't flash that much dough. Not because of criminals; there aren't many of them—of us—left. On account of the law. The bulls pick up anybody they don't know who flashes money and the judges fine him every cent he's got on him and split with the bulls. It's not like the old days when a man had a chance."

Gardin stared straight ahead for a moment. "I wanted to get out of this place; that's why I tried to take you. Only, Crag, where is there to go that's any better?"

"Nowhere," Crag told him. "Have another drink."

"I better get back to the bar. Come on, I'll bring the woji with us, only I'll pour it in a kodore bottle. Same color and nobody'll know the difference."

They went back to the bar and Crag poured them each a drink while Gardin poured refills for the spacemen and their women. He came back to Crag.

He said quietly, "Careful if any coppers come in. Down that stuff quick and I'll cap the bottle. You can smell woji yards away and them coppers have noses."

Crag glanced at the spacemen and Gardin said contemptuously, "Don't worry about them; they never even smelled woji. Just out of school and don't know which way is up."

Crag nodded and turned to glance at the big television screen which the other group was watching. On the screen an almost naked woman was singing a more than suggestive song of the delights of perversion. The spacemen and their women watched with rapt attention, but when the song ended, they finished their drinks and left.

Crag said, "Shut the thing off."

Gardin started for the switch, but before he reached it, the scene changed; on the screen was a planet floating in space, seen from a distance of about ten thousand miles. It wasn't a planet Crag had ever seen before. The telecaster's voice said, "We bring you a special broadcast of the first landing on the new planet Cragon, suddenly and miraculously formed of the scattered matter of the asteroid belt between—"

Gardin was reaching for the switch, but Crag said sharply, "Don't. Leave it on."

He was studying the new planet with amazement. There were seas on it and he thought he could make out rivers and different colored patches that could only be vegetation—probably huge forests. *Water,* he thought with sudden curiosity; *where could it have got water?* And then he remembered that the entity which had been an asteroid had transmuted carbon dioxide in his helmet into oxygen. So why couldn't it transmute any element into any other one? Even so, how could it have created vegetation upon itself so quickly?

"The view upon the screen," said the voice of the telecaster, "is from a port of the mother ship. We shall maintain this distance above the surface while a two-man scouter we have sent out makes the first actual landing. It is on its way now and should reach the upper atmosphere within less than a minute. When it does we shall switch you to the voice of Captain Burke who has command of the scouter; Lieutenant Laidlaw is with him. The scouter is too small to hold a telecaster, so the view upon the screen will continue to be from the mother ship. However, if the scouter makes a successful landing and gives us the come-on signal, this ship shall follow it to the surface and you will have a close view of whatever lies on Cragon.

"The landing will be made regardless of the nature of the atmosphere, which has thus far defied complete spectroscopic analysis from a distance. Oxygen is present in about the same proportion as in the atmosphere of Earth, but there are other gasses present, one of which has new and unknown Fraunhofer lines, undoubtedly the lines of a hitherto undiscovered element.

"If you have missed recent newscasts and telecasts, I might tell you that it has been determined that the density of Cragon is about that of Earth, as is its gravity. The proportion of land to water is much greater, about half—as against Earth's one-fifth. The land surface, therefore, is almost two and a half times that of Earth, truly a magnificent place for colonization—if the air is breathable.

"I have a signal from Captain Burke. He is ready to cut in. Go ahead, Captain."

A different voice spoke. "Captain Burke talking from the scouter ship. We are entering the upper atmosphere. We are above the largest continent of Cragon. We are fifty miles high and our instruments show a slight increase of atmospheric pressure, although still not much over a laboratory vacuum—about the same reading for an equivalent height above Earth. We are descending at the rate of five miles a minute, although we shall have to slow our descent soon.

"We can see from here—I think with certainty—that the dark areas of the land surface really are forests, incredible as that is. At least they look the same as Earth's forest areas look from an equivalent height—forty-five miles now."

Crag grinned at Gardin. "They'll never make it. Bet you."

"Huh? Why not?"

"Atmosphere poisonous."

"So what? They're in a spaceship. That won't stop them from landing. And they won't get out without suits until they've checked the air."

"Bet they don't land. A thousand credits to the five I just gave you for the woji."

Gardin laughed. "You're crazy, Crag, but that's sure a bet,"

They turned back to the screen.

"Thirty miles now, almost into the stratosphere. Something seems to be wrong with the air conditioner in this scouter. It's getting hard to breathe. Lieutenant Laidlaw is working with it. Getting it fixed, Lieutenant?"

"He says he can't find anything wrong with it, and our oxygen indicator shows normal quantity. Can't understand it. We're twenty-two miles now. But both of us breathing hard. I—can't figure what's—"

Crag looked at Gardin. "Double the bet?"

Gardin shook his head.

The voice was labored. "We're going—back up. Something's wrong and it's not—our air conditioner. Going—fast as we can—take it. Thirty miles again. Not—quite so bad. Almost breathe.

"Checking with Laidlaw. Says—our air normal, but an added ingredient. The unknown element. Came right through the hull—osmosis or somehing. Thirty-five miles.

"We're all right now. But returning to the mother ship for a conference."

Crag grinned at Gardin and then walked over and shut off the television set. Gardin took the five credit note out of his pocket and put it on the bar. But he said, "I don't get it. How'd you know before it happened?"

"Inside information. That's one planet they'll *never* land on. Not alive, anyway. If they ever lick that trick, my pal's got other ones up his sleeve."

"Your pal?"

"Cragon. Named himself after me." Crag took another sip of his drink. "The little—"

"*Who?*"

"Cragon. I just told you. Listen, Gardin, how'd you like to—no, skip it." Crag turned morosely back to his drink.

The door behind Crag opened suddenly. Crag turned and saw three uniformed policemen—tough-looking mugs all, with heat-guns in spring holsters ready for action—coming in the door. Crag turned back to the bar casually and downed the last of his drink, and Gardin, equally casually, picked up the bottle and was replacing the cap, turning toward the back bar as he did so.

But the closest copper was sniffing audibly. "Hey, you," he told Gardin, "let's see that bottle."

Crag turned his head and saw that all three of them had heat-guns in their hands, one of them aiming at him and two of them at Gardin. It was going to be a stick-up, a legal stick-up—and to make it legal probably both Gardin and he would get five-year sentences on the technicality of selling and buying, respectively, a forbidden beverage.

CHAPTER V

Crag glanced back over the bar and, before Gardin turned, he caught Gardin's eyes in the mirror, just for a fleeting instant, but enough. The eyes said, "We'll make a break if we can."

Crag turned back on the stool, very casually, raising his hands at the menace of the heat-gun pointing at him and only two feet from him. A quick flick of his eyes downward showed him that it was going to be almost too easy; the safety stud of the heater was still in safe position and it would take the copper almost a second to fire. Obviously he wasn't anticipating trouble, with three armed men against two unarmed ones. The copper guarding Crag was at the bar beside him; the other two were also at the bar, and beyond, Gardin was turning around with the bottle.

It was almost too easy. Crag practically fell forward off the stool, his right hand, from a raised position, pistoning out for the jaw of the copper and his metal left hand chopping down at the heater. And he kept on going forward, pushing the first copper back against the others. Number one's heater hit the floor as he went back, unconscious from the blow to his chin. Number two went down, too, and Crag, keeping going right across Number one, put his left hand in Number two's stomach, just above the belt buckle.

Number three, knocked off balance against the bar, had time to trigger his heater wildly and the backbar mirror shattered under sudden heat as Gardin, who'd taken a reversed grip on the bottle, leaned across the bar and broke it over Number three's head.

Crag gathered the three heaters and looked quickly toward the window. No one was passing by. Gardin quickly came around the bar and helped Crag drag them into the back room. None of them was dead. Gardin got a stack of bar towels and started tearing them into strips; within minutes all three of the coppers were bound and gagged so efficiently that they wouldn't get loose, by their own efforts, for hours.

Gardin mopped sweat off his forehead and looked at Crag. Crag grinned. "You ruined that bottle of woji," he said. "Got another?"

Gardin got another and they went back to the bar. While Gardin filled their glasses, Crag fiddled with the dials of the television set. A blonde tenor with marcelled hair was singing:

"Jet up! Jet down! On a slow ship to Pluto!"

Crag switched it off and went back to the bar.

Gardin said worriedly, "We had to do it; if we hadn't, it'd've been five or ten years for each of us. But now it's life if they get us. What do we do, Crag?"

Crag suddenly knew, and he knew now that he'd known all along, that it had been only a matter of time until he'd decided.

"We go to Cragon," he said.

"But—the poisonous atmosphere!"

"I've got an in. It won't be poisonous for me, or for anyone I take with me. Do you know any others that would like to go? I've got a ship that will carry half a dozen for that short a trip."

"You serious, Crag?"

Crag nodded.

"I've got a pal that'll go. And his woman and mine."

"How long have we got?"

Gardin looked up at the clock in the wall. "Seven hours. I'd just started my shift. If I lock the door when we go, nobody'll bother the place till the next bartender comes here; everybody'll just think the place is closed."

"Want to call your friends from here?"

Gardin mopped his forehead again. "Sooner I get out of here—with those cops tied up back there—the better I'll feel. Let's go."

They left the place and Gardin closed the blinds and locked it.

"My woman lives just around the corner," Gardin said, "and Pete Hauser and his woman live only a block away. Shall we get them first?"

Crag said, "I'm going to buy an aircar. We'll need one to get to the spaceship and it'll be easier to buy one than to take a chance of being checked on if we hire one."

"You got enough money you'd *buy* an aircar just for one trip and leave it?"

Crag laughed. "Sure. And what good's money where we're going? I've got a hundred and ninety thousand credits back at the hotel and no use for it at all. But we'll go back and get it anyway, just in case."

Gardin whistled. "Pal, with *that* much money, we can buy our way out of this rap. We wouldn't have to lam."

"Don't you want to go?"

"Sure, sure. Look, this is the house. Can you pick us up here in an hour?"

Crag caught an aircab and went to the biggest aircar agency in Marsport. He was whistling now and felt happier than he'd felt in years. He wondered why he'd taken so long to make up his mind.

It took him less than an hour to complete the purchase of a five-place aircar and get it serviced and fueled for a five-hundred-mile trip. It was just turning dusk when he returned to the doorway where he'd left Gardin.

Four people were waiting for him there. Gardin's woman, a big blonde named Stell. Pete Hauser, a little man—but tough-looking—with a rodent face and beady eyes. Gert, small and dark, Gypsy-looking, quick and graceful in her movements. And Gardin, who had switched from his monkey-suit into spaceman's gear. He'd guessed right, then, about Gardin's having been a spaceman once—in the days when the spaceways weren't a tea party.

Crag drove them to the Luxor and suggested a stirrup cup in his suite.

The lock of his door hadn't been disturbed. He let them in and enjoyed—but not too much—watching the eyes of the two women as they took in the luxury of the gubernatorial suite. He opened the liquor closet and told them to help themselves and pour one for him while he gathered the money and decided what part of his luggage he'd take along.

The first ten thousand credit bill wasn't where he'd hidden it. Nor the second. Nor any of them.

Crag sat down, frowning, to drink the woji Stell brought him, and to think. It couldn't have been an outside job. The suite was accessible only through the door he'd fixed so no one but himself could open the lock. There must be a secret entrance somewhere and the hotel itself must have done the job. Besides, it would have taken a more detailed search to have found *all* of those bills than any casual thief could have made or would have dared to make.

After buying the aircar he still had several thousand credits and money would be useless on Cragon, anyway, but—

He told the others what had happened and sent each to a different room of the suite to look for a secret entrance. Pete Hauser found it, cleverly concealed in the shelving of the pornographic library.

Crag turned down Gardin's offer of help and told them all to wait. The secret entrance was locked from the outside, but that gave him only a minute's pause. Then he was in a narrow passageway and going down several narrow flights of padded steps. He passed other secret doors of other suites, all locked from his side, and he could have burgled as many suites as he wished—but there wasn't any reason to. He'd never stolen for the fun of it, and he didn't need money now, whether he got his own back or not.

There were peepholes into all the suites, too, an intricate system of them. More than peepholes, really; they were fair sized portions of the walls that were transparent from one side and not from the other. He realized now that he must have been watched while he was hiding the bills; otherwise, in the few hours he'd been out, no search would have found every last one of them.

He decided that he didn't like the Luxor Hotel nor its management. Glancing casually through the transparent areas into some of the suites he passed, he decided he didn't like the clientele of the place, either. In fact, he didn't like Marsport; he didn't like civilization in general—as civilization was just then.

And he particularly decided that he didn't like the manager of the Luxor, who undoubtedly had sole access to this system of secret corridors, peepholes and entrances.

When he'd counted enough flights to know that he was on the main floor, he started looking for—and found—a panel that locked from the other side. That would be either the manager's office or his private quarters. There wasn't any peephole for him to scout through, so he picked the lock more quietly than he had ever picked one before.

He inched the panel open silently. It opened into the manager's office. He could see the manager's back, as the panel opened behind the desk. Mr. Carleton still wore the archaic full dress suit, almost the only one Crag had ever seen.

Crag stepped out of the panel, more quietly than any cat. He reached his right hand around the scrawny neck of the manager and pulled back, squeezing just hard enough to prevent any outcry and pulling back just far enough to keep Carleton's groping hands from reaching any of the buttons on or under his desk.

"Where is the money?" he asked quietly.

He relaxed pressure enough to permit a whisper, and when none came, he tightened his fingers again. A thin hand came up and pointed to a metal door with a combination knob set in the wall directly across the room from where he stood.

"Come on," Crag said. "You're going with me while I open it, and if any help comes—whether you manage to call for it or not—you die when it gets here."

He pulled the man up out of the chair and walked him across the room until they stood facing the safe, Carleton between Crag and the door of it.

Crag said, "I'm letting go your neck now. Yell as loud as you want, if you want to make it your last yell."

He put his left arm around the manager's body and held tight while he reached for the combination knob with his right.

The manager didn't yell, but he squeaked—and both of his hands grabbed for Crag's wrist. "Don't! It's booby-trapped, and I'll die too if I'm standing here. Let me open it,"

Crag grinned and let him open it. There was quite a bit of money in the safe, although Crag's were the only ten thousand credit bills. Crag took it all except the change and the one and five credit bills; there were so many of those that his pockets wouldn't have held all of them.

He took Carleton back with him through the secret panel and there bound and gagged him with strips torn from the manager's dress coat.

He felt good again, despite some of the things he'd seen through the passageway peepholes. And he felt a little reckless—or maybe it was the woji. He leaned forward and whispered to Carleton, "If you report this, tell them to look for Crag. On the planet Cragon." He laughed. "Crag of Cragon."

He went back up the secret stairs and passageways to his own suite. He found that he must have been gone a little longer than he thought, for both of the women were drunk and Pete was almost so. Even Gardin's eyes were a little glassy.

Crag made all of them take sober-up powders and, since he was going to pilot the aircar and the spaceship, he himself took a neobenzedrine. He settled for a very few items out of the many things he'd bought before coming to the Luxor—all things that he could carry in his pockets so they wouldn't attract attention crossing the lobby.

"Get the money?" Gardin had asked him and he'd nodded and said, "With interest. Compound."

Maybe, he thought, they'd use that money to light fires with when they got to Cragon. but at any rate he hadn't left it with the manager of the Luxor.

They made the aircar without being questioned and Crag piloted the aircar slowly and carefully, not to attract attention, until they were well out of Marsport before he put on speed.

The spaceship was still where he'd left it, and that was good; he could have bought another—dozens of them—with all the money he had, but the delay would have been a risk.

Twenty hours later they landed on Cragon. Because the others lacked his confidence, Crag put the ship down through the atmosphere very slowly, ready to jerk it up quickly if any of them had any difficulty in breathing, but none of them had.

Just before the ship touched the surface, a voice in Crag's mind said, "Welcome, Crag." He answered mentally, not aloud, and looked at the others quickly to see if they had received any equivalent message; obviously none of them had.

He put the ship down gently in a perfect landing and opened the door without bothering to test the atmosphere. He stepped out, the others following him. The air was like the air of Earth on a crisp autumn morning. They were on a plain that stretched down to a river. There was short grass where they stood, bushes between them and the river; behind them was what might easily have been a forest of Earth and beyond the forest rose tall rugged mountains.

Crag liked it. He felt content and at peace.

He wondered what to do first and flashed a mental question, but there wasn't any answer—and that was answer enough. They were on their own and Cragon wasn't going to advise them.

He took a deep breath and turned to face the others. "All right," he said. "We're here. We start to work."

"Work?" Pete Hauser's rodent face looked surprised.

"Work," said Crag. "We'll find food—there'll be game in that forest and fish in that river and we'll find some edible plants that we can domesticate and grow. But we'll have to work for all of it. All of us. And since we've got food for a few days in the ship, the first job's to build ourselves quarters. The ship's too small for five people to *live* in."

"Build out of what?" Gardin wanted to know.

Both Gert and Stell looked displeased and petulant. Crag stared at them and wondered what they'd expected to find on a new planet.

He answered Gardin's question within an hour. There was clay along the river bank that would dry into good adobe bricks. He vetoed Stell's suggestion that they all have a binge to celebrate—although from her face she didn't seem to think there was much *to* celebrate—and put all of them, including himself, to work shaping clay bricks and putting them in the sun to dry,

The others worked listlessly and none of them, even Gardin, who tried to pretend interest, got very many bricks formed. Gert cut a finger on a stone in the clay and rebelled, her dark face sullen. She sat and watched the others, angry because Crag had locked the door of the ship and had kept the key; he curtly refused to give it to her so she could get a bottle and drink.

He kept them, and himself, at work until sundown.

They slept in the ship that night, and Crag slept lightly, but nothing happened.

The next morning he put Hauser and the two women back at the brick-making and he and Gardin went into the forest and found that he'd been right in guessing that there was game, although it was small and wary and was going to take very skilled hunting to get.

That night he again refused to let them get drunk, and he could feel the resentment against him, palpable as a Venusian fog.

He slept even more lightly that night, but the break he'd been expecting didn't come until morning. It came in the form of a heat-gun being shoved into his back as he was leaving the ship. Pete Hauser's voice said, "And don't try to use that metal hand of yours. I know about it. I can pull the trigger first. Keep your hands down."

Crag kept his hands down and turned around. He looked at Gardin and Gardin couldn't quite meet his eyes. He didn't have to ask if they were all in it.

Crag reached out casually and slapped the heater out of Hauser's hand—not until after Hauser had pulled the trigger, though, and nothing had happened. Crag said, "I unloaded it, unloaded all of them. All right, Gardin, you do the talking. What do you want? To elect your own leader? Or what?"

Gardin cleared his throat uncomfortably. "We want to go back, Crag. None of us have ever lived—wild, like this. We find we don't like it. We'd rather take our chances on Earth or Mars. We don't care whether you come with us or not, just so we get back."

Gert said, "But if you don't, if you're staying here, you might as well give us some—or all—of that money you've got. It's no good to you here."

Stell's voice was plaintive. "Please let us go, Crag. Or if you want the ship, take us back and then come here yourself."

Crag said, "I'm going to think it over. I'll be back."

He walked toward the forest, thinking. It was going to be lonesome and yet—well, he *wasn't* going back, ever. And to have others here wasn't any good unless they wanted to be here.

He tried thinking messages to Cragon, to get Cragon's advice, but there wasn't any answering voice in his mind. He was being left strictly alone in his decision.

He walked back to the spaceship and the four people waiting for him there.

He said, "Okay, take the ship and get out. Unload everything in it I can use and then take it. And here—" He took off the money belt with almost three hundred thousand credits in it and tossed it to them. "Divide this on the way. I'll give you the key to the controls when you've unloaded the ship."

They worked fast, willingly this time, obviously afraid he might change his mind.

An hour later, standing beside a tarpaulin covered pile of supplies that represented everything movable that had been in the ship, he watched it go.

He felt dull inside, neither happy nor unhappy. This was the way it was going to be. This was his world, and here he was going to stay until he died. He'd be lonesome, sure, but he was used to that. And, even alone, this was better than the cesspools of Earth, Mars or Venus. He'd thought once that having a fortune might make those places worth living in; he'd found out that it had made them worse.

He watched the speck out of sight in the blue and then sighed and started for the river to carry on with his brick-making. That still came first—or he thought then that it did.

But he'd taken only a few steps when the voice that was Cragon spoke in his mind.

"They were too soft, Crag. They weren't tough, like you are, tough enough to lick a new planet. I knew when I first contacted their minds that they wouldn't stay."

"Yeah," said Crag listlessly.

"That is why I waited," said the voice in his mind. "I made sure *you* wanted to stay here, even if it was to be alone. But it won't be alone, Crag."

"Yeah," Crag said. He supposed it wouldn't be quite so lonely if Cragon talked to him once in a while.

There was something in his mind like laughter, not his own. The voice said, "No, not I, Crag. I have other things to do, and this may be the last time I ever communicate with you. I mean—Evadne."

Crag stopped walking as though he had run into a stone wall.

"Remember what happened to Evadne, Crag? The disintegrator, yes. But every atom of her body remained, on the surface of the tiny ball of neutronium that I became, before she was disintegrated. It was simple to segregate them and preserve them, Crag, against your return. And I was conscious, Crag, a conscious entity, even before she disintegrated. The structure of her body and her mind was the first thing I studied, before I entered *your* mind, out there when I first spoke to you."

Crag's mind reeled. *"But she's dead. You can't—"*

"What is death. Crag? Can you define it for me? Can you tell me why, if every atom is replaced into its position in every molecule, just as it was—"

"But can you? Are you sure?"

"I have. She's coming this way now, Crag, from the edge of the woods. If you'll only turn, you'll see her coming."

Crag turned and saw her. He started to run toward her and saw the gladness in her face when she saw him coming.

"You won't need to explain, Crag; I've told her everything that has happened. Goodbye, Crag; I'm leaving your mind now."

Crag may or may not have answered that thought in his mind. He had his arms around Evadne, her soft body pressed against his. And they had a world of their own, a new world to live in—and to populate.

Editor's Notes and Acknowledgements

This volume completes the NESFA Press project to bring the SF works of Fredric Brown back into print.

Scanning was provided by Rick Katze and Judy Bemis. Proofreading help was provided by Mark Olson, Vincent Docherty, Art and Becky Henderson, and Seth Breidbart. Final proofreading was by George Flynn.

Typesetting was done by Mark and Priscilla Olson, who made the book get out on time.

As with *From These Ashes,* the novels appear in order of first publication. The two novelettes incorporated and rewritten for *Rogue in Space* appear after the novels.

The cover painting was done by Bob Eggleton, who told me when I first started the Brown project what he wanted to do, and proceeded to pull it off. The book jacket was designed by Geri Sullivan.

Thanks to everybody who made this book, and the Fredric Brown project, possible.

The New England
Science Fiction Association (NESFA)
and NESFA Press

Books from NESFA Press:

- *From These Ashes* by Fredric Brown $29.00
- *Strange Days* by Gardner Dozois $30.00
- *Dimensions of Sheckley* by Robert Sheckley $29.00
- *Here Comes Civilization* by William Tenn $29.00
- *Immodest Proposals* by William Tenn $29.00
- *Entities* by Eric Frank Russell $29.00
- *Major Ingredients* by Eric Frank Russell............................... $29.00
- *Shards of Honor* by Lois McMaster Bujold $22.00
- *Warrior's Apprentice* by Lois McMaster Bujold $22.00
- *The Best SF: 1964* $25.00
- *Quartet* by George R. R. Martin $15.00
- *Norstrilia* by Cordwainer Smith $22.00
- *The Rediscovery of Man* by Cordwainer Smith $25.00
- *Ingathering: The Complete People Stories of Zenna
  Henderson* $25.00

Find details and many more books on our web page: www.nesfa.org/press

Books may be ordered by writing to:
NESFA Press
PO Box 809
Framingham, MA 01701

We accept checks, Visa, or MasterCard. Please add $3 postage and handling per order.

The New England Science Fiction Association:

NESFA is an all-volunteer, non-profit organization of science fiction and fantasy fans. Besides publishing, our activities include running Boskone (New England's oldest SF convention) in February each year, producing a semi-monthly newsletter, holding discussion groups relating to the field, and hosting a variety of social events. If you are interested in learning more about us, we'd like to hear from you. Write to our address above!